Alex KAVA

Collector

COLLECTOR © 2015 by Harlequin Books S.A.

First Published 2000
Sixth Australian Paperback Edition 2015
ISBN 9781743690550

First Published 2001
Fifth Australian Paperback Edition 2015
ISBN 9781743690550

A PERFECT EVIL
© 2000 by S.M. Kava.
Australian Copyright 2000
New Zealand Copyright 2000

SPLIT SECOND
© 2001 by S.M. Kava.
Australian Copyright 2001
New Zealand Copyright 2001

Except for use in any review, the reproduction or utilisation of this work in whole or in part in any form by any electronic, mechanical or other means, now known or hereafter invented, including xerography, photocopying and recording, or in any information storage or retrieval system, is forbidden without the permission of the publisher.

This book is sold subject to the condition that it shall not, by way of trade or otherwise, be lent, resold, hired out or otherwise circulated without the prior consent of the publisher in any form of binding or cover other than that in which it is published and without a similar condition including this condition being imposed on the subsequent purchaser.

All rights reserved including the right of reproduction in whole or in part in any form. This edition is published in arrangement with Harlequin Books S.A..

This is a work of fiction. Names, characters, places, and incidents are either the product of the author's imagination or are used fictitiously, and any resemblance to actual persons, living or dead, business establishments, events, or locales is entirely coincidental.

Published by
Harlequin Mira
An imprint of Harlequin Enterprises (Australia) Pty Ltd.
Level 13, 201 Elizabeth St,
SYDNEY NSW 2000
AUSTRALIA

® and TM are trademarks of Harlequin Enterprises Limited or its corporate affiliates. Trademarks indicated with ® are registered in Australia, New Zealand, the United States Patent & Trademark Office and in other countries.

Printed and bound in Australia by Griffin Press

CONTENTS

A PERFECT EVIL   5

SPLIT SECOND   361

A Perfect Evil

In loving memory of
Robert (Bob) Shoemaker
(1922–1998)
whose perfect good continues to inspire.

PROLOGUE

Nebraska State Penitentiary
Lincoln, Nebraska
Wednesday, July 17

"Bless me Father, for I have sinned." Ronald Jeffreys' raspy monotone made the phrase a challenge rather than a confession.

Father Stephen Francis stared at Jeffreys' hands, mesmerized by the large knuckles and stubby fingers, nails bitten to the quick. The fingers twisted—no, strangled—the corner of his blue government-issue shirt. The old priest imagined those same fingers twisting and choking the life out of little Bobby Wilson.

"Is that how we start?"

Jeffreys' voice startled the priest. "That's fine," he answered quickly.

His sweaty palms stuck to the leather Bible. His collar was suddenly too tight. The prison's deathwatch chamber didn't have enough air for both men. The gray concrete walls boxed them in with only one tiny window, black with night. The pungent smell of green pepper and onion nauseated the old priest. He glanced at the remnants of Jeffreys' last supper, scattered bits of pizza crust and puddles of sticky soda. A fly buzzed over crumbs that were once cheesecake.

"What's next?" Jeffreys asked, waiting for instructions.

Father Francis couldn't think, not with Jeffreys' unflinching stare. Not with the noise of the crowd outside the prison, down below in the parking lot. The chants grew louder with the approach of midnight and the full effect of alcohol. It was a raucous celebration, a morbid excuse for an outdoor frat party. "Fry, Jeffreys, fry," over and over again, like a childhood rhyme or a pep-rally song, melodic and contagious, sick and frightening.

Jeffreys, however, appeared immune to the sound. "I'm not sure I remember how this works. What's next?"

Yes, what came next? Father Francis' mind was completely blank. Fifty years of hearing confessions, and his mind was blank. "Your sins," he blurted out over the tightness in his throat. "Tell me your sins."

Now, Jeffreys hesitated. He unraveled the hem of his shirt, wrapping the thread around his index finger, pulling it so tight that the tip bulged red. The priest stole a long glance at the man slumped in the straight-backed chair. This wasn't the same man from the grainy newspaper photos or the quick television shots. With his head and beard shaved, Jeffreys looked exposed, almost impish and younger than his twenty-six years. He had gained bulk in his six years on death row, but he still possessed a boyishness. Suddenly, it struck Father Francis as sad that this boyish face would never wear wrinkles or laugh lines. Until Jeffreys looked up at him. Cold blue eyes held his. Ice-blue like glass—sharp glass—vacant and transparent. Yes, this was what evil looked like. The priest blinked and turned his head.

"Tell me your sins," Father Francis repeated, this time disappointed in the tremor in his voice. He couldn't breathe. Had Jeffreys sucked all the air out of the room on purpose? He cleared his throat, then said, "Those sins for which you are truly sorry."

Jeffreys stared at him. Then without warning, he barked out a laugh. Father Francis jumped, and Jeffreys laughed even louder. The priest gripped his Bible with unsteady fingers while watching Jeffreys' hands. Why had he insisted the guard remove the handcuffs? Even God couldn't rescue the stupid. Drops of perspiration slid down the priest's back. He thought about fleeing, escaping before Jeffreys realized one last murder would cost him nothing more. Then he remembered the door was locked from the outside.

The laughter stopped as suddenly as it had begun. Silence.

"You're just like the rest of them." The low guttural accusation came from somewhere deep and dead. Yet, Jeffreys smiled, revealing small, sharp teeth, the incisors longer than the rest. "You're waiting for me to confess to something I didn't do." His hands ripped the bottom of his shirt, thin strips, a slow grating sound.

"I don't understand what you mean." Father Francis reached to loosen his collar, dismayed to find the tremor now in his hands. "I was under the impression you had asked for a priest. That you wanted to offer up your confession."

"Yes...yes, I do." The monotone was back. Jeffreys hesitated but only for a moment. "I killed Bobby Wilson," he said as calmly as if ordering takeout. "I put my hands...my fingers around his throat. At first, he made a sputtering noise, a sort of gagging, and then there was no noise." His voice was hushed and restrained, almost clinical—a well-rehearsed speech.

"He kicked just a little. A jerk, really. I think he knew he was going to die. He didn't fight much. He didn't even fight when I was fucking him." He stopped, checking Father Francis' face, looking for shock and smiling when he found it.

"I waited until he was dead before I cut him. He didn't feel a thing. So I cut him again and again and again. Then, I fucked him one last time." He cocked his head to the side, suddenly distracted. Had he finally noticed the celebration outside?

Father Francis waited. Could it be the massive pounding of his heart that Jeffreys heard? Like something out of Poe, it banged against the old priest's chest, betraying him just like his hands.

"I've already confessed once before," Jeffreys continued. "Right after it happened, but the priest... Let's just say he was a little surprised. Now I'm confessing to God, you understand? I'm confessing that I killed Bobby Wilson." The ripping continued, now in quick, jerky motions. "But I didn't kill those other two boys. Do you hear me?" His voice rose above the monotone. "I didn't kill the Harper or the Paltrow kid."

Silence, then Jeffreys' lips slowly twisted into a smirk. "But then, God already knows that. Right, Father?"

"God does know the truth," Father Francis said, trying to stare into the cold blue eyes but flinching and quickly looking away again. What if his own guilt should somehow reveal itself?

"They want to execute me because they think I'm some serial killer who murders little boys," Jeffreys spat through clenched teeth. "I killed Bobby Wilson, and I enjoyed it. Maybe I even deserve to die for that. But God knows I didn't kill those other boys. Somewhere out there, Father, there's still a monster." Another twisted smile. "And he's even more hideous than me."

Metal clanked against metal down the hall. Father Francis jerked, sending the Bible crashing to the floor. This time Jeffreys didn't laugh. The old priest held Jeffreys' stare, but neither man made an attempt to pick up the holy book. Were they coming to take Jeffreys away? It seemed too soon, although no one expected a stay of execution.

"Are you sorry for your sins?" Father Francis whispered as if back at the confessional window in St. Margaret's.

Yes, there were footsteps coming down the hall, coming toward them. It was time. Jeffreys sat paralyzed, listening to the *click-clack* of heels marching, getting closer and closer.

"Are you sorry for your sins?" Father Francis repeated, this time more insistent, almost a command. Oh, dear God, it was hard to breathe. The chants from the parking lot grew louder and louder, squeezing through the tightly sealed window.

Jeffreys stood up. Again, his eyes held Father Francis'. The locks grunted open, echoing against the concrete walls. Jeffreys flinched at the sound, caught himself, then stood straight with shoulders back. Was he frightened? Father Francis searched Jeffreys' eyes, but couldn't see beyond the steel blue.

"Are you sorry for your sins?" He tried once more, unable to offer absolution without an answer.

The door opened, sucking the remaining air from the room. Square-shouldered guards clogged the doorway.

"It's time," one of the men said.

"It's show time, Father." Jeffreys' lips curled over gritted teeth. The blue eyes were sharp and clear, but vacant. Jeffreys turned to the three uniformed men and offered his wrists.

Father Francis winced as the shackles snapped. Then he listened to the boot heels clicking, accompanied by the pathetic *shuffle-clank, shuffle-clank* all the way down the long hall.

A stale breeze seeped in through the open door. It cooled his wet, clammy skin and sent a shiver down his back. He gulped greedily at the air, limited to short, asthmatic gasps. Finally, the thunder in his chest eased, leaving behind a tight-fisted ache.

"God help Ronald Jeffreys," Father Francis whispered to no one.

At least Jeffreys had told the truth. He had not killed all three boys. And Father Francis knew this, not because Jeffreys had said so. He knew, because three days ago the faceless monster who had murdered Aaron Harper and Eric Paltrow had confessed to him through the black, wire-mesh confessional at St. Margaret's. And because of his holy vows, he wasn't able to tell a single soul.

Not even Ronald Jeffreys.

CHAPTER 1

Five miles outside Platte City, Nebraska
Friday, October 24

Nick Morrelli wished the woman beneath him wore less makeup. He knew it was ridiculous. He listened to her soft moans—purrs really. Like a cat, she slithered against him, rubbing her silky thighs up and down the sides of his torso. She was more than ready for him. And yet, all he could think about was the blue powder smeared on her eyelids. Even with the lights out, it remained etched in his mind like fluorescent, glow-in-the-dark paint.

"Oh, baby, your body is so hard," she purred in his ear as she ran her long fingernails up his arms and over his back.

He slid off her before she discovered that not all of his body was hard. What was wrong with him? He needed to concentrate. He licked her earlobe and nuzzled her neck, then moved down to where he really wanted to be. Instinctively, his mouth found one of her breasts. He ravished it with soft, wet kisses. She moaned even before his tongue flicked at her nipple. He loved those sounds a woman made—the short little gasp, then the low moan. He waited for them, then wrapped his tongue around her nipple and sucked it into his mouth. Her back arched, and she quivered. He leaned into her, absorbing the shiver, her soft, smooth flesh trembling against him. Normally, that reaction alone would immediately give him an erection. Tonight, nothing.

Jesus, was he losing his touch? No, he was too young to be having this problem. After all, he was four years away from forty.

When in the world had he started keeping track of his age by its distance from forty?

"Oooh, lover, don't stop!"

He didn't even realize he *had* stopped. She groaned impatiently and began moving her hips up and down, slowly, with a sensuous rhythm. Yes, she was definitely ready for him. And he was definitely not ready. Just once he wished women would use his name instead of baby, lover, stud muffin, whatever. Did women worry about yelling out the wrong name, too?

Her fingers twisted into his short, thick hair. She yanked hard, the streak of pain surprising him. Then she pulled his face back to her breasts. In the dim light, he noticed that the triangle of tanned skin was crooked. The point overlapped onto the underside of her breast. What was wrong with him? A beautiful blonde wanted him. Why didn't her breathless anticipation arouse him? He needed to focus. It all felt too mechanical, too routine. Nevertheless, he would compensate again using his fingers and tongue. After all, he had a reputation to maintain.

He began the descent down her body, devouring her with kisses and nibbles. Her body squirmed beneath his touch. She was writhing and gasping for breath even before his teeth tugged at her lace panties. He kissed his way to the inside of her thighs. Suddenly, a sound stopped him. He strained to hear from under the bedcovers.

"No, please don't stop," she groaned, pulling him back into her.

There it was again. Pounding. Someone was at the front door.

"I'll be right back." Nick gently pushed her hands away and stumbled out of bed, disentangling himself from the sheets and almost tripping. He pulled on jeans as he checked the clock on the nightstand—10:36.

Even in the dark, he knew every creak in the staircase by heart. Out of habit, he found himself tiptoeing, though his parents hadn't slept in the old farmhouse for over five years.

The knock was louder and more insistent now.

"Hold on a minute," he called out impatiently, yet relieved by the interruption.

When he opened the door, Nick recognized Hank Ashford's son, though he couldn't recall his name. The boy was sixteen or seventeen, a linebacker on the football team and built like he could move two or three players at a time off the line of scrimmage. Yet, tonight, as he stood on Nick's front porch, the kid slouched with his hands stashed in his pockets, eyes wild and face pale. He shivered despite the sweaty forehead.

"Sheriff Morrelli, you have to come…on Old Church Road…please, you have to…"

"Is someone hurt?" The crisp night air stung Nick's bare skin. It felt good.

"No, it's not...he's not hurt...Oh, God, Sheriff, it's awful." The boy looked back toward his car. It was only then that Nick saw the girl in the front seat. Even looking into the headlights, he could see she was crying.

"What's going on?" he demanded, sending the boy into a speechless, arm-crossing dance, shifting his weight from one leg to the other.

What stupid game had they been playing this time? Last week, the night before homecoming, a group of boys had played chicken with a couple of Jake Turner's tractors. The loser had tipped over into a rain-filled ditch, pinning himself under the water. The boy was lucky he had escaped with only broken ribs and the flimsy punishment of sitting out two football games.

"What the hell happened this time?" Nick found himself yelling at the shivering linebacker.

"We found...down off Old Church Road...in the tall grass. Oh God, we found...we found a body."

"A body?" Nick wasn't sure he believed him. "You mean a dead body?" Was the boy drunk? Was he stoned?

The boy nodded, tears filling his eyes. He scraped the sleeve of his sweatshirt across his face and looked from Nick to his girlfriend, then back to Nick.

"Hang on a minute."

Nick stepped back inside, letting the screen door slam behind him. They had probably imagined it. Or maybe it was an early Halloween prank. They'd been out partying. Both of them were probably stoned. He pulled on his boots, bypassing socks, then grabbed his shirt from the sofa, where it had been taken off him earlier in the evening. He was annoyed to find his fingers shaking as he buttoned the front.

"Nick, what is it?"

The voice from the top of the stairs startled him. He had forgotten about Angie. Roused from bed, her long, blond hair was ruffled and floated around her shoulders. The blue eye makeup was hardly noticeable from this distance. She wore one of his T-shirts. It was transparent in the hallway's soft light. Now, looking up at her, he couldn't imagine why he had been relieved to leave her.

"I've got to check something out."

"Is someone hurt?"

She sounded more curious than concerned. Was she only looking for a bit of gossip? Something to share with the morning coffee drinkers at Wanda's Diner?

"I don't know."

"Did someone find the Alverez boy?"

Jesus, he hadn't even thought of that. The boy had been missing since Sunday, gone, taken before he began his newspaper route.

"No, I don't think so," Nick told her. Even the FBI was certain the boy had more than likely been taken by his father, who they were still trying to locate. It was a simple custody battle. And this was simply teenage kids playing tricks on each other.

"I might be a while, but you're welcome to stay."

He grabbed the keys to his Jeep and found Ashford sitting on the front steps, his face buried in his hands.

"Let's go." Nick gently yanked a handful of sweatshirt and pulled the boy to his feet. "Why don't the two of you get in with me."

Nick wished he had taken time to put on underwear. Now, in the cramped Jeep, the stiff denim scraped against him every time he put the clutch in and shifted. To make matters worse, Old Church Road was filled with ruts from the rains of the week before. The gravel popped against the Jeep as he weaved from side to side, avoiding the deep gashes in the road.

"What exactly were you two doing out on this washboard?" As soon as he said it, he realized the obvious. He didn't need to be seventeen to remember all the benefits of an old deserted gravel road. "Never mind," he added before either of them had time to answer. "Just tell me where I'm going."

"It's about another mile, just past the bridge. There's a pasture road that runs along the river."

"Sure, okay."

He noticed Ashford wasn't stuttering anymore. Perhaps he was sobering up. The girl, however, who sat between Nick and the boy, hadn't said a word.

Nick slowed down as the Jeep bumped across the wood-slatted bridge. He found the pasture road even before Ashford pointed it out. They bounced and slid over the dirt road that consisted of rutted tire tracks filled with muddy water.

"All the way down to the trees?" Nick glanced at Ashford, who only nodded and stared straight ahead. As they approached the shelter belt, the girl hid her face in the boy's sweatshirt.

Nick stopped, killed the engine, but left on the headlights. He reached across the two of them and pulled a flashlight from the glove compartment.

"That door sticks," he said to Ashford. He watched the two exchange a glance. Neither made any attempt to leave the Jeep.

"You never said we'd have to look at it again," the girl whispered to Ashford as she clung to his arm.

Nick slammed the car door. Its echo sliced through the silence. There was nothing around for miles. No traffic, no farm lights. Even the night animals seemed to be asleep. He stood outside the Jeep, waiting. The boy's eyes met his, but still he made no motion to leave the Jeep. Instead of insisting, Nick pointed the flashlight toward an area down by the riverbank. The stream of light shot through thick grass, catching just a glimpse of rolling water. Ashford's eyes followed. He hesitated, looked back at Nick and nodded.

The tall grass swished around Nick's knees, camouflaging the mud that sucked at his boots. Jesus, it was dark out. Even the orange moon hid behind a gauze of clouds. Leaves rustled behind him. He spun around and shot a stream of light from tree to tree. Was there movement? There, in the brush? He could have sworn a shadow ducked from the light. Or was it just his imagination?

Nick strained to see beyond the thick branches. He held his breath and listened. Nothing. Probably just the wind. He listened again and realized there was no wind. A shiver caught him off guard, and he wished he had brought a jacket. This was crazy. He refused to be suckered by some high-school prank. The sooner he checked it out, the sooner he could be back in his warm bed.

The squashing sound grew louder the closer he got to the river. It was an effort to walk, pulling each foot out and carefully placing it to avoid slipping. His new boots would be ruined. He could already feel his feet getting wet. No socks, no underwear, no jacket.

"Damn it," he muttered. "This better be good." He was going to be mad as hell if he found a group of teenagers playing hide-and-seek.

The flashlight caught something glittering in the mud, close to the water. He locked his eyes on the spot and quickened his pace. He was almost there, almost out of the tall grass. Suddenly, he tripped. He lost his balance and crashed down hard, with his elbows breaking his fall. The flashlight flew out of his hand and into the black water, a tunnel of light spiraling to the bottom.

He ignored the sting shooting up his arms. The sucking mud pulled at him as he pushed himself to his hands and knees. A rancid smell clung to him, more than just the stench of the river. The silvery object lay almost within reach, and now he could tell it was a cross-shaped medallion. The chain was broken and scattered in the mud.

He glanced back to see what had caused his fall. Something solid. He expected to see a fallen tree. But not more than a yard away was a small, white body nestled in the mud and leaves.

Nick scrambled to his feet, his knees weak, his stomach in his throat. The smell was more noticeable now, and it filled the air, stinging his nostrils. He approached the body slowly as if not wanting to wake the boy, who looked asleep despite those wide eyes staring up at the stars. Then he saw the boy's slashed throat and mangled chest, the skin ripped open and peeled back. That's when his stomach lurched and his knees caved in.

CHAPTER 2

"All it takes is one bad apple," Christine Hamilton pounded out on the keyboard. Then she hit the delete key and watched the words disappear. She'd never finish the article. She leaned back to steal a glance at the hall clock—the lighted beacon in the tunnel of darkness. Almost eleven o'clock. Thank God, Timmy had a sleepover.

Janitorial services had shut off the hall light again. Just another reminder of how important the "Living Today" section was. At the end of the dark hall, she saw the newsroom's light glowing under the door that segregated the departments. Even at this distance, she could hear the wire services and fax machines buzzing. On the other side of that door, a half-dozen reporters and editors guzzled coffee and churned out last-minute articles and revisions. Just on the other side of that door, news was being made while she fussed over apple pie.

She whipped open a file folder and flipped through the notes and recipes. Over a hundred ways to slice, dice, puree and bake apples, and she couldn't care less. Perhaps her clever wit had run dry, used up on last week's hot little tomato dishes and a dozen ways to sneak fresh vegetables into your family's diet. She knew her journalism degree was rusty, thanks to Bruce's pigheadedness and his insistence that he wear the pants in the family. Too bad the asshole couldn't keep his pants on.

She slammed the folder shut and tossed it across her desk, watching it slide off and scatter clippings all over the cracked linoleum floor. How long would she remain bitter? No, the real question was, how long would it hurt? Why did it still have to hurt like hell? After all, it had been over a year.

She shoved away from the computer terminal and raked her fingers through her thick mass of blond hair. It needed to be trimmed, and she tried to remember how much time she had before the roots would start darkening. The dye job was a new touch, a divorce present to herself. The initial results had been rewarding. Turning heads was a new experience. If only she could remember to schedule the hairstylist like everything else in her life.

She ignored the building's no smoking rule and slapped a cigarette out of the pack she kept in her handbag. Quickly, she lit it and sucked in, waiting for the nicotine to calm her. Before she exhaled, she heard a door slam. She smashed the cigarette into a dessert plate that bulged with too many lipstick-covered butts for a person trying to quit. The footsteps echoed down the hall in quick bursts. She grabbed the plate and searched for a hiding place while swatting away the smoke. In a mad panic, she dumped the plate into the trash can under her desk. The stoneware shattered against the metal side just as Pete Dunlap entered the room.

"Hamilton. Good, you're still here." He swiped a hand over his weathered face in an unsuccessful attempt to remove the exhaustion. Pete had been with the *Omaha Journal* for almost fifty years, starting as a carrier. Despite the white hair, bifocals and arthritic hands, he was one of the few who could single-handedly put out the paper, having worked in every department.

"Major writer's block." Christine smiled, trying to explain why anyone would be working late in the "Living Today" section. She was relieved to see Pete instead of Charles Schneider, the usual night editor, who commandeered the place like a Nazi storm trooper.

"Bailey called in sick. Russell's still finishing up on Congressman Neale's sex scandal, and I just sent Sanchez to cover a three-car smashup on Highway 50. There's some ruckus out by the river on Old Church Road in Sarpy County. Ernie can't make out too much from the radio dispatch, but a whole slew of patrol cars are on their way. Now, it could just be some drunk kids playing with their daddies' tractors again. I know you're not part of the news team, Hamilton, but would you mind checking it out?"

Christine tried to contain her excitement. She hid her grin by turning back to the half-baked article on her computer screen. Finally, a chance at real news, even if it was a bunch of drunk teenagers.

"I'll cover your ass with Whitman on whatever you're working on," Pete said, misreading her hesitation.

"Okay. I suppose I can check it out for you." She chose her words carefully to emphasize that she was doing him a favor. Although she had been on the staff for only a year, she knew that journalists were promoted more quickly due to favors than talent.

"Take the interstate since Highway 50's probably tied up with that accident. Take exit 372 to Highway 66. Old Church Road is about six miles south on 66."

She almost interrupted him. As a teenager she had made out on Old Church Road many times. However, one slip-up could dismantle all her work to shed her country roots. So, instead, she jotted down some directions.

"Get back here before one so we can get a couple paragraphs in the morning edition."

"Will do." She slung her handbag over her shoulder and tried not to skip down the hall.

"Now, if I could just get Russell to write half as fast as he talks, I'd be a happy man," she heard Pete grumble as the door closed behind her.

Safe in the dark parking lot, she twirled once and shouted, "Yes!" to the concrete wall. This was her chance to get on the other side of the door, to go from recipes and household anecdotes to real news. Whatever was happening out at the river, she planned to capture all the nitty-gritty drama. And if there was no story…well, surely a good reporter could dig something up.

CHAPTER 3

He smashed through the branches, the cracking wood exploding in the dark silence. Were they following? Were they close behind? He didn't dare look back. Suddenly, he skidded on the mud, lost his balance and slid down the riverbank. He crashed knee-deep into ice-cold water. His arms and legs flayed in a panic, splashing water like claps of thunder. He dropped to his knees, burying his sweat-drenched body, sinking into the silt until he was up to his chin in the rolling river. The current sloshed against him, jerking him, threatening to sweep him back to where he had just escaped.

The cold water numbed the convulsions. Now, if only he could breathe. The gasps racked his chest and stabbed at his side. Breathe, he commanded himself as his lungs strangled for air. He hiccuped and swallowed a stomachful of the river, choking and gagging most of it back up.

He couldn't see the spotlights anymore. Perhaps he had run far enough. He listened, straining over his own gasps.

There were no running footsteps, no yelping bloodhounds, no racing engines. It had been a close call—the guy with the flashlight. Was it possible the intruder hadn't seen him crouched in the grass? Yes, he was sure no one had followed him.

He shouldn't have come tonight. It had become a stupid habit, a dangerous risk, a wonderful addiction, a spiritual hard-on. The shame spread through him, liquid and hot despite the cold water. No, he shouldn't have come. But no one had seen him. No one had followed him. He was safe. And now, finally, the boy was safe, too.

CHAPTER 4

The rancid smell clung to Nick. He wanted to crawl out of his clothes, but the scent of river and blood was already soaked deep into his pores. He peeled off his shirt and thanked Bob Weston for the FBI windbreaker. The sleeves stopped six inches above his wrists, and the fabric stretched tight across his chest. The zipper stuck halfway up. He knew he must look and smell like a putz. His suspicions were confirmed when he saw Eddie Gillick, one of his deputies, elbow his way through the crowd of FBI agents, uniformed cops and other deputies just to hand Nick a damp towel.

The scene looked pre-Halloween. Blinding searchlights teetered from branches. Yellow tape flapped around trees. The sizzle and smoke of night flares mixed with that awful smell of death. And in the middle of the macabre scene lay the little, white ghost of a boy, asleep in the grass.

In his two years as sheriff, Nick Morrelli had pulled three victims from car crashes. The adrenaline had erased the sight of tangled metal and flesh. He had witnessed one gunshot wound—a minor scrape, someone cleaning his gun while drinking a pint of whiskey. He had broken up numerous fistfights, sustaining his own cuts and bruises. Nothing, however, had prepared him for this.

"Channel Nine is here." Gillick pointed at the new set of headlights bumping down the path. The bright orange nine emblazoned on the top of the van glowed in the dark.

"Shit. How did they find out?"

"Police scanner. Probably have no idea what's going on, just that something is."

"Get Lloyd and Adam to keep them as far from that line of trees as possible. No cameras, no interviews, no sneak peeks. That goes for the rest of the bloodsuckers when they get here." That was all he needed—a stint on the morning news in his clown jacket and muddy jeans revealing his incompetence to the entire state.

"Oh, good. Another fuckin' set of tire tracks," Weston said to the agents who were on their knees working in the mud, but looked at Nick to make sure he knew the comment was meant for him.

Nick's face grew hot, but he swallowed his response and walked away. Weston made it no secret he thought Nick was a small-town hick of a sheriff. They had been at each other's throats since Sunday when Danny Alverez had disappeared into thin air, leaving behind a brand-new bike and a bagful of undelivered newspapers. Nick had wanted to call in the masses to search fields and parks, while Weston had insisted they wait for a ransom note that never arrived. Nick had succumbed to Weston's twenty-five years of FBI experience instead of listening to his gut.

Why didn't he buy Weston's suspicions that the boy had simply been taken by his disgruntled father? A father who had been enraged with his ex-wife for keeping him away from his only child. Hell, the paper was full of similar cases. When they couldn't locate Major Alverez, it only made even more sense. So why wouldn't Nick listen to Special Agent Bob Weston, despite his irrational dislike of the man?

From the very beginning, Nick resented Weston's arrogance. At five feet six inches, he reminded Nick of a little Napoleon, always using his wiseass mouth to compensate for his small frame. Weston was a good six inches shorter than Nick and a skinny bit of a man compared to Nick's athletic build. Yet tonight, anything Weston said made Nick feel small. He knew he had screwed up, from contaminating a crime scene to not securing a large enough area to bringing in too goddamn many officers. So, he deserved Weston's put-downs. Now he wondered if Weston had even given him the too-small jacket on purpose.

Nick saw George Tillie making his way through the crowd, and he was relieved to see the familiar face. George looked as if he had come straight out of bed. His sport jacket was crumpled and misbuttoned over a pink nightshirt. His gray hair stuck up everywhere. His face sagged with deep lines and gray fuzz. He carried his little black bag, hugging it to his chest as he stepped carefully through the thick mud in fuzzy slippers. If Nick wasn't mistaken, the slippers had little ears and dog snouts. He smiled and wondered how George had ever made it past the FBI sentries.

"George," Nick called and almost laughed when George raised his eyebrows at Nick's shoddy appearance. "The boy's over here." He took George's elbow and let the old coroner lean on him as they plodded through the mud and the crowd.

An officer with a Polaroid camera flashed one last picture of the scene, then made room for them. One look at the boy, and George froze. His slumped shoulders straightened, and his face went white.

"Oh, dear God. Not again."

CHAPTER 5

From a mile away, the pasture was lit up like a football stadium on game night. Christine stomped on the accelerator, weaving her car through the gravel.

Something big was definitely happening. The excitement fluttered in her stomach. Her heart pounded rapidly. Even her palms were sweaty. This was better than sex, or what she could remember of sex.

The police dispatch gave little information. "Officer requests immediate assistance and backup."

It could mean anything. As she skidded into the pasture road, her excitement only grew. Rescue vehicles, two TV vans, five sheriff cruisers and a slew of other unmarked vehicles were scattered at haphazard angles in the mud. Three sheriff deputies guarded the scene, which was cordoned off with yellow crime-scene tape. Crime-scene tape—this was serious. Definitely not some drunk teenagers.

Then she remembered the kidnapping—the paperboy whose face had been plastered over every newscast and newspaper since the beginning of the week. Had a ransom drop been made? There were rescue units. Perhaps a rescue was in progress.

She jumped from the car, noticed it still sliding in the mud and hopped back in behind the wheel.

"Don't be stupid, Christine," she whispered and slammed the car into Park, shoving the emergency brake into place. "Be calm. Be cool," she lectured herself, grabbing her notepad.

Immediately the mud swallowed her leather pumps, refusing to surrender them. She kicked out of her shoes, threw them into the back of the car and padded her way in stockinged feet to the crowd of news media.

The deputies stood straight and unflinching despite the questions being hurled at them. Beyond the trees, searchlights illuminated an area close to the river. Tall grass and a mass of uniformed bodies blocked any view of what was going on.

Channel Five had sent one of their evening anchors. Darcy McManus looked impeccable and ready for the camera, her red suit well pressed, her silky black hair and makeup all in place. Yes, she even had on her shoes. It was, however, too late at night for a live report, and the camera remained off.

Christine recognized Deputy Eddie Gillick in the line. She approached slowly, making certain he saw her, knowing one wrong move could get her throttled.

"Deputy Gillick? Hi, it's Christine Hamilton. Remember me?"

He stared at her like a toy soldier unwilling to give in to any distraction. Then his eyes softened, and there was a hint of a smile before he controlled the impulse.

"Mrs. Hamilton. Sure, I remember. You're Tony's daughter. What brings you out here?"

"I work for the *Omaha Journal* now."

"Oh." The soldier face returned.

She needed to think fast or she'd lose him. She noticed Gillick's slicked-back hair, not a strand out of place, the overpowering smell of aftershave lotion. Even the pencil-thin mustache was meticulously trimmed. His uniform looked wrinkle-free. His tie was cinched tightly at his neck and tacked down with a gold tie tack. A quick glance showed no wedding band. She'd take a chance that he considered himself a bit of a lady's man.

"I can't believe how muddy it is out here. Silly me. I even lost my shoes." She pointed to her mud-caked feet and the red-painted toenails peeking through her stockings. Gillick checked out the feet, and she was pleased when his eyes ran the length of her long legs. The uncomfortably short skirt would finally pay for its discomfort.

"Yes, ma'am, it sure is a mess." He crossed his arms over his chest and shifted his weight, visibly uncomfortable. "You should be careful you don't catch cold." One more look, this time his eyes took in more than just her legs. She felt them stop at her breasts and found herself arching her back to split the blazer open just a little more to accommodate him.

"This whole situation is a mess, isn't it, Eddie? It is Eddie, isn't it?"

"Yes, ma'am." He looked pleased that she remembered. "Although I'm not allowed to discuss the situation at hand."

"Oh, sure. I understand." She leaned in close to him, despite the smell of Brylcream. Even without shoes she was almost his height. "I know you're not allowed to discuss anything about the Alverez boy," she whispered, her lips close to his ear.

His glance registered surprise. An eyebrow raised, and his eyes softened again. "How did you know?" He turned to see if anyone was listening.

Bingo. She'd hit the jackpot. Careful now. Cool and calm. Don't blow it.

"Oh, you know I can't say who my sources are, Eddie." Would he recognize the low hushed voice as seductive or as a line of bull? She had never been very good at seduction, or at least that was what Bruce had told her.

"Sure, of course." He nodded, taking the hook.

"You probably didn't even get a chance to look at the scene. You know, being stuck out here doing the real dirty work."

"Oh, no. I got more than an eyeful." He puffed out his chest as if he dealt with this sort of thing on a daily basis.

"The boy's in pretty bad shape, huh?"

"Yeah, looks like the son of a bitch gutted him," he whispered without a hint of emotion.

She felt the blood rush from her head. Her knees went weak. The boy was dead.

"Hey!" Gillick yelled, and she thought for a second he had discovered the deception. "Shut that camera off! Excuse me, Mrs. Hamilton."

As Gillick snatched at Channel Nine's camera, Christine retreated to her car. She sat with the door open, fanning herself with the empty notepad and taking in long breaths of the cool night air. Despite the chill, her blouse stuck to her.

Danny Alverez was dead, murdered. To quote Deputy Gillick, "gutted."

She had her first big story, yet in the pit of her stomach the butterflies had turned into cockroaches.

CHAPTER 6

Saturday, October 25

Nick gritted his teeth, then swallowed the mouthful of thick, cold coffee. Why was he surprised to find it tasted just as bitter cold as it did hot? It reminded him how much he hated the stuff, but he poured another cup, anyway.

Maybe it wasn't the taste he hated as much as the memories. Coffee reminded him of all-nighters studying for the LSAT. It reminded him of that excruciating road trip to watch his grandfather die. A trip made after his grandmother had pleaded, and necessary because Nick's father, Antonio, had refused to be at the old man's bedside. Even back then, Nick saw the trip as some kind of omen of his own relationship with his father. And he wondered if his father would see the irony if and when the great Antonio Morrelli's time came due, and his own son would refuse to be at his bedside?

Once in a while the association still disarmed Nick—how he could smell the stout aroma of coffee and automatically think of his grandfather's wrinkled gray flesh and those urine-stained sheets. But now, the scent of coffee would forever remind him of the sad, painful screams of a mother identifying her only son's mangled body. It certainly was not much of a replacement.

Nick remembered the first time he had met Laura Alverez last Sunday night—Jesus, less than a week ago. Danny had been missing for almost twelve hours when Nick cut short a weekend fishing trip to question her himself. At first he, too, had been convinced it was one of those custody fights. Another woman using her son to either punish or retrieve her husband. Then he met Laura Alverez.

She was a tall woman, a bit overweight but with a voluptuous figure. The long, dark hair and smoky eyes made her look younger than her forty-five years. There was something statuesque about her that brought to mind the term "tower of strength."

Graceful despite her size, Laura Alverez had glided that evening from her kitchen sink to the cupboard and back to the sink, over and over. She had answered his questions calmly and quietly. Much too calmly. In fact, it had taken him ten, maybe even fifteen minutes before he had realized that, for every cup or plate she had washed and stacked in the cupboard, she removed a clean one, taking it back to the sink with her. Then he noticed the tag sticking out of the collar of her inside-out sweater and the two mismatched shoes. She had been in a state of shock, disguised by a calm Nick found more spooky than reassuring.

Her calm remained throughout the week. She had portrayed an unflinching rock of strength, pouring coffee and baking rolls for the men who had filled her small house each day. Had she displayed some form of emotion, perhaps it wouldn't have been so difficult, moments ago, when he had watched this same stately woman bend in two and crumple to the cold, hard floor of the hospital morgue. Her cries had sliced through the sterilized halls. Nick recognized that sound. It was the low-pitched scream of a wounded animal. No woman should have to face what Laura Alverez faced alone. Now he wished they had located her ex-husband, just so he could beat the crap out of him.

"Morrelli." Bob Weston came into Nick's office without knocking or waiting for an invitation. He plopped down in the chair across from Nick. "You should go home. Shower, change clothes. You stink."

He watched Weston dig the exhaustion out of his eyes and decided he was only stating facts, instead of hurling more insults.

"What about the ex-husband?"

Weston looked up at him and shook his head. "I'm a father, Nick. I don't care how pissed off he might be with his wife—I just don't think a father could do that to his kid."

"So where do we begin?" He must be tired, Nick realized. He was actually asking for Weston's advice.

"I'd start with a list of known sex offenders, pedophiles and child pornographers."

"That could be a long list."

"Excuse me, Nick," Lucy Burton interrupted from the doorway. "Just wanted to let you know that all four Omaha TV stations and both Lincoln stations are downstairs with camera crews. There's also a hallful of newspaper and radio people. They're asking about a statement or press conference."

"Shit," Nick muttered. "Thanks, Lucy." He watched Weston twist in his chair to follow Lucy's long legs down the hall. Maybe he should talk to her about the short skirts and stiletto heels now that they would be making the news. What a shame. She had lovely legs and a walk trained to show them off.

"We've avoided the press all week," Nick said, returning his gaze to Weston. "We're gonna have to talk to them."

"I agree. You need to talk to them."

"Me? Why me? I thought you were the hotshot expert."

"That was when it was a kidnapping. Now it's a homicide, Morrelli. Sorry, this is your ball game."

Nick slumped back in his chair, leaning his head into the leather and swiveling from side to side. This couldn't be happening. Soon he'd wake up in bed with Angie Clark beside him. God, last night seemed like a lifetime ago.

"Look, Morrelli." Weston's voice was soft, sympathetic, and Nick eyed him suspiciously without lifting his head. "I've been thinking. This being a kid and all, maybe I could request someone to help you put together a profile."

"What do you mean?"

"It may be too early for people to start noticing the similarities to Jeffreys, but when they do, you're going to have a frenzy on your hands."

"A frenzy?" Frenzies weren't part of his training. Nick swallowed the sour taste in his mouth. Suddenly, he was nauseated again. He could still smell Danny Alverez's blood soaked into his jeans.

"We have experts who can put together a psychological profile of this guy. Narrow things down for you. Give you a fuckin' idea of who this asshole is."

"Yeah, that would help. That would be good." Nick kept the desperation out of his voice. Now was not the time to reveal his weakness, despite Weston's sudden compassion.

"I've been reading about this Special Agent O'Dell, an expert in profiling murderers practically right down to their shoe size. I could call Quantico."

"How soon do you think they could get someone here?"

"Don't let Tillie cut up the boy yet. I'll call right now and see if we can get someone here Monday morning. Maybe even O'Dell." Weston stood up suddenly with new energy.

Nick untangled his legs and stood, too, surprised that his knees were strong enough to hold him.

Deputy Hal Langston met Weston at the door. "Thought you guys might be interested in this morning's edition of the *Omaha Journal*." Hal unfolded the paper and held it up. The headline screamed in tall, bold letters, Boy's Murder Echoes Jeffreys' Style.

"What the fuck?" Weston ripped the paper from Hal and began reading out loud. "Last night, a boy's body was found along the Platte River, off Old Church Road. Early reports suggest the still-unidentified boy was stabbed to death. A deputy at the scene, who will remain anonymous, said, 'It looked like the bastard gutted him.' Gaping chest wounds were a trademark of serial killer Ronald Jeffreys, who was executed in July of this year. Police have yet to make a statement concerning the boy's identity and the cause of death."

"Jesus," Nick spat as the nausea infected his insides.

"Goddamn it, Morrelli. You're gonna need to put a gag order on your men."

"It gets worse," Hal said, looking at Nick. "The byline is Christine Hamilton."

"Who the fuck is Christine Hamilton?" Weston looked from Hal to Nick. "Oh, please don't tell me she's one of the little harem you're bopping?"

Nick slid back into his chair. How could she do this to him? Had she even tried to warn him, to contact him? Both men stared at him, Weston waiting for an explanation.

"No," Nick said slowly. "Christine Hamilton is my sister."

CHAPTER 7

Maggie O'Dell kicked off her muddy running shoes in the foyer before her husband, Greg, reminded her to do so. She missed their tiny, cluttered apartment in Richmond, despite surrendering to the much-needed convenience of living between Quantico and Washington. But ever since they had bought the pricey condo in the expensive Crest Ridge area, Greg had developed an absurd obsession with image. He liked their condo spotless, an easy task since both their jobs kept them away. Yet, she resented coming home to a place that swallowed her monthly paycheck but felt like one of the hotels to which she had grown accustomed.

She peeled off the damp sweatshirt and immediately felt a pleasant chill. Though it was a crisp fall day, she had managed to work up a sweat after another night of tossing and turning. She balled up the sweatshirt and shot it into the laundry room as she passed on her way to the kitchen. How careless of her to miss the laundry basket.

She stood in front of the open refrigerator. A look inside revealed a pathetic view of their lack of domestic talents—a box of leftover Chinese food, half a bagel twisted in plastic wrap, a foam take-out container with unidentified gooey stuff. She grabbed a bottle of water and slammed the door, now shivering in only running shorts, a sweat-drenched T-shirt and sports bra that stuck to her like an extra layer of skin.

The phone rang. She searched the spotless counters and grabbed it off the unused microwave before the fourth ring.

"Hello."

"O'Dell, it's Cunningham."

She ran her fingers through her wet mass of short, dark hair and stood up straight, his voice setting her at attention.

"Hi. What's up?"

"I just received a phone call from the Omaha field office. They have a murder victim, a little boy. Some of the wounds are characteristic of a serial killer in the same area about six years ago."

"He's on the prowl again?" She began pacing.

"No, the serial killer was Ronald Jeffreys. I don't know if you remember the case. He murdered three boys—"

"Yes, I remember," she interrupted him, knowing he hated long explanations. "Wasn't he executed in June or July?"

"Yes...yes, in July, I believe." His voice sounded tired.

Though it was Saturday afternoon, Maggie imagined him in his office behind the stacks on his desk. She could hear him rustling through papers. Knowing Director Kyle Cunningham, he already had Jeffreys' entire file spread out in front of him. Long before Maggie started working under him in the Behavioral Science Unit, he had been affectionately nicknamed the Hawk because nothing got past him. Lately, however, it looked as though the sharp vision came at the expense of puffy eyes, swollen from too little sleep.

"So this might be a copycat." She stopped and opened several drawers looking for a pen and paper to jot down notes, only to find carefully folded kitchen towels, sterile utensils lined up in annoyingly neat rows. Even the odd utensils, a corkscrew and can opener, lay flat in their respective corners, not touching or overlapping. She picked up a shiny serving spoon and turned it in the wrong direction, making sure it crossed over several others. Satisfied, she closed the drawer and began pacing again.

"It could be a copycat," Cunningham said in a distracted tone. She knew he was reading the file while he talked, that worried indent between his brows, his glasses low on his nose. "It could be a one-time thing. The point is, they requested a profiler. Matter of fact, Bob Weston requested you specifically."

"So I'm a celebrity even in Nebraska?" She ignored the annoyance in his voice. A month ago, it wouldn't have been there. A month ago, he would have been proud that a protégé of his had been requested. "When do I leave?"

"Not so fast, O'Dell." She clutched the phone and waited for the lecture. "I'm sure Weston's pile of glowing reports about you didn't include the last case file."

Maggie stopped and leaned against the counter. She pressed the palm of her hand against her stomach, waiting, preparing for the nausea. "I certainly hope you're not going to hold the Stucky case over my head every time I go out into the field." The quiver in her voice sounded angry. That was good—anger was good, better than weakness.

"You know that's not what I'm doing, Maggie."

Oh, God. He had used her first name. This would be a serious lecture. She stayed put and dug her nails into a nearby hand towel.

"I'm simply concerned," he continued. "You never took a break after Stucky. You didn't even see the bureau psychologist."

"Kyle, I'm okay," she lied, irritated with the sudden tremor invading her hand. "It's not like it was the first time. I've seen plenty of blood and guts in the past eight years. There's not much that shocks me anymore."

"That's exactly what I'm worried about. Maggie, you were in the middle of that bloodbath. It's a miracle you weren't killed. I don't care how tough you think you are, when the blood and guts get sprayed all over you, it's a little different than walking in on it."

She didn't need the reminder. Fact was, it didn't take much to conjure up the image of Albert Stucky hacking those women to death—his bloody death play performed just for Maggie. His voice still came to her in the middle of the night: "I want you to watch. If you close your eyes, I'll just kill another one and another and another."

She had a degree in psychology. She didn't need a psychologist to tell her why she couldn't sleep at night, why the images still haunted her. She hadn't even been able to tell Greg about that night; how could she tell a complete stranger?

Of course, Greg hadn't been around when she had staggered back to her hotel room. He'd been miles away when she tore pieces of Lydia Barnett's brain out of her hair and scrubbed Melissa Stonekey's blood and skin out of her pores. When she had dressed her own wound, an unsightly slit across her abdomen. And it wasn't the kind of thing you talked about over the phone.

"How was your day, dear? Mine? Oh, nothing too exciting. I just watched two women get gutted and bludgeoned to death."

No, the real reason she hadn't told Greg was that he would have gone nuts. He would have insisted she quit, or worse, promise to work only in the lab, examining the blood and guts safely under a microscope and not under her fingernails. He had ranted and raved once before when she had confided in him. It had been the last time she had talked about her work.

He didn't seem to mind the lack of communication. He didn't even notice her absence beside him in bed at night, when she paced the floor to avoid the images, to quiet the screams that still echoed in her head. The lack of intimacy with her husband allowed her to keep her scars—physical and mental—to herself.

"Maggie?"

"I need to keep working, Kyle. Please don't take that away from me." She kept her voice strong, grateful the tremor was confined to her hands and stomach. Would he detect the vulnerability, anyway? He tracked criminals by reading between the lines. How could she expect to fool him?

There was silence, and she covered the mouthpiece of the phone, so he couldn't hear her staggered breathing.

"I'll fax over the details," he finally said. "Your flight leaves in the morning at six o'clock. Call me after you get the fax if you have any questions."

She listened to the click and waited for the dial tone. With the phone still pressed against her ear, she sighed, then breathed deeply. The front door slammed and she jumped.

"Maggie?"

"I'm in the kitchen." She hung up the phone and gulped some water, hoping to shake the queasiness from the pit of her stomach. She needed this case. She needed to prove to Cunningham that, although Albert Stucky had assaulted and toyed with her mental state, he had not stolen her professional edge.

"Hey, babe." Greg came around the counter. He started to hug her, but stopped when he noticed the perspiration. He manufactured a smile to disguise his disgust. When had he started using his lawyer acting talents on her?

"We have reservations for six-thirty. Are you sure you have time to get ready?"

She glanced at the wall clock. It was only four. How bad did he think she looked?

"No problem," she said, guzzling more water and purposely letting it dribble down her chin.

She caught him wincing at her, his perfectly chiseled jaw taut with disapproval. He worked out at the law firm's gym, where he sweated, grunted and dribbled in the appropriate setting. Then he showered and changed, not a shiny golden hair out of place by the time he stepped out into public again. He expected the same from her, had even told her how much he hated her running in the neighborhood. At first, she had thought it was out of concern for her safety.

"I'm a black belt, Greg. I can handle myself," she had lovingly reassured him.

"I'm not talking about that. Christ, Maggie, you look like hell when you run. Don't you want to make a good impression on our neighbors?"

The phone rang, and Greg reached for it.

"Let it ring," she blurted with a mouthful of water. "It's a fax from Director Cunningham." Without looking at him she could feel his annoyance. She raced to the den, checked the caller ID, then flipped on the fax.

"Why is he faxing you on a Saturday?"

He startled her. She didn't realize he had followed. He stood in the doorway with hands on his hips, looking as stern as possible in khakis and a crew-neck sweater.

"He's faxing some details on a case I've been asked to profile." She avoided looking at him, dreading the pouty lip and brooding eyes. Usually, he was the one interrupting their Saturdays together, but she convinced herself it was childish to remind him. Instead, she ripped off the fax and began transferring details from paper to memory.

"Tonight was supposed to be a nice quiet dinner—just the two of us."

"And it will be," she said calmly, still not looking at him. "It may just need to be an early night. I have a six o'clock flight in the morning."

Silence. One, two, three...

"Damn it, Maggie. It's our anniversary. This was supposed to be our weekend together."

"No, that was last weekend, only you forgot and played in the golf tournament."

"Oh, I see," he snorted. "So this is payback."

"No, it's not payback." She maintained her calm though she was tired of these little tantrums. It was fine for him to ruin their plans with only half an apology and that charming, smug "I'll make it up to you, babe."

"If it's not payback, what do you call it?"

"Work."

"Work, right. That's convenient. Call it what you want. It's payback."

"A little boy has been murdered, and I might be able to help find the psycho who did it." The anger bubbled close to the surface, but her voice remained amazingly calm. "Sorry, I'll make it up to you." The sarcasm slipped out, but he didn't seem to notice. She took the fax and started past him to the door. He grabbed her wrist and spun her toward him.

"Tell them to send someone else, Maggie. We need this weekend together," he pleaded, his voice now soft.

She looked into his gray eyes and wondered when they had lost their color. She searched for a flicker of the intelligent, compassionate man she had married nine years ago when they were both college seniors ready to make their marks on the world. She would track down the criminals, and he would defend the helpless victims. Then he took the job in Washington at Brackman, Harvey and Lowe, and his helpless victims became billion-dollar corporations. Still, in just a moment of silence, she thought she recognized a flicker of sincerity. She was on the verge of giving in to him when his grip tightened and his teeth clenched.

"Tell them to send someone else, or we're finished."

She wrenched her wrist free. He grabbed for it again, and she slammed a fist into his chest. His eyes widened in surprise.

"Don't you ever grab me like that again. And if this one trip means we're finished, then maybe we've been finished for a long time."

She brushed past him and headed for the bedroom, hoping her knees would carry her and the sting behind her eyes would wait.

CHAPTER 8

Sunday, October 26

And so it begins, he thought as he sipped the scalding-hot tea.

The front-page headline belonged on the *National Enquirer* and not a newspaper as respectable as the *Omaha Journal*. From the Grave, Serial Killer Still Grips Community with Boy's Recent Murder. It was almost as hysterical as yesterday's headline, but, of course, today's large Sunday edition would attract more readers.

The byline was Christine Hamilton again. He recognized the name from the "Living Today" section. Why would they give the story to a newcomer, a rookie?

Quickly, he turned the pages, searching for the rest of the story which continued on page ten, column one. The entire page was filled with connecting articles. There was a school photo of the boy. Beside it ran an in-depth saga of the boy's sudden disappearance during his early-morning paper route just a week ago. The article told how the FBI and the boy's mother had waited for a ransom note that never came. Then, finally, Sheriff Morrelli had found the body in a pasture along the river.

He glanced back at the paragraph. Morrelli? No, this was Nicholas Morrelli, not Antonio. How nice, he thought, for father and son to share the same experience.

The article went on to point out the similarities to the murders of three boys in the same small community over six years ago. And how the bodies, strangled and stabbed to death, had each been discovered days later in different wooded, isolated areas.

The article, however, made no mention of details, no description of the elaborate chest carving. Did the police hope to withhold that evidence again? He shook his head and continued to read.

He used the fillet knife to scoop jelly and spread it on his burnt English muffin. The stupid toaster hadn't worked right for weeks, but it was better than going down to the kitchen and having breakfast with the others. At least here in his room he could have the solitude of breakfast and the morning paper without the burden of making polite conversation.

The room was very plain, white walls and hardwood floors. The small twin-size bed barely accommodated his six-foot frame. Some nights he found his feet dangling over the end. He had added the small Formica-topped table and two chairs, though he allowed no one to join him. The utility cart in the corner housed the secondhand toaster, a gift from one of the parishioners. There was also a hot plate and kettle that he used for his tea.

On the nightstand stood the most elaborate of his furnishings, an ornate lamp, the base a detailed relief of cherubs and nymphs tastefully arranged. It was one of the few things he had splurged on and purchased for himself with his meager paycheck. That and the three paintings. Of course, he could only afford framed reproductions. They hung on the wall opposite his bed so he could look at them while he drifted off to sleep, though sleep didn't come easy these days. It never did when the throbbing began, invading his otherwise quiet life, crashing in with all those foul memories. Even though his room was simple and plain, it brought short periods of comfort, control and solitude to a life that was no longer his own.

He checked his watch and ran his hand over his jaw. He wouldn't need to shave today, his boyish face still smooth from yesterday's shave. He had time to finish reading, though he refused to so much as look at the ridiculous articles about Ronald Jeffreys. Jeffreys had never deserved the attention he had garnered, and here he was, still in the limelight even after death.

He finished his breakfast and meticulously cleaned the table, no crumb escaping his quick swipes with the damp rag. From his small, brown-stained bathroom sink he removed the pair of Nikes, now scrubbed clean, not a hint of mud left. Still, he wished he had taken them off sooner. He patted them dry and set them aside to wash the one plate he called his own, a fragile, hand-painted Noritake he had borrowed long ago from the community china cabinet. His matching teacup and saucer, also borrowed, he filled to the brim with more scalding-hot water. Delicately, he dunked the once-used tea bag, waiting for the water to turn the appropriate amber color, then quickly removed and strangled the tea bag as if making it surrender every last drop.

His morning ritual complete, he got down on his hands and knees and pulled a wooden box from under the bed. He laid the box on the small table and ran his fingers over the lid's intricate carving. Carefully, he cut out the newspaper articles, bypassing those on Ronald Jeffreys. He opened the box and put the folded articles inside on top of the other newspaper clippings, some of which were just beginning to yellow. He checked the other contents: a bright white linen cloth, two candles and a small container of oil. Then he licked the remnants of jelly off the fillet knife and returned it to the box, laying it gently on the soft cotton of a pair of boy's underpants.

CHAPTER 9

Timmy Hamilton pushed his mom's fingers away from his face as the two of them hesitated on the steps of St. Margaret's. It was bad enough that he was late. He didn't need his mom fussing over him in front of his friends.

"Come on, Mom. Everybody can see."

"Is this a new bruise?" She held his chin and gently tilted his head.

"I ran into Chad at soccer practice. It's no big deal." He put his hand on his hip as if to conceal the even bigger bruise hidden there.

"You need to be more careful, Timmy. You bruise so easily. I must have been out of my mind when I agreed to let you play."

She opened her handbag and began digging.

"I'm gonna be late. Church starts in fifteen minutes."

"I thought I had your registration form and check for the camp out."

"Mom, I'm late already."

"Okay, okay." She snapped the bag shut. "Just tell Father Keller I'll put it in the mail tomorrow."

"Can I go now?"

"Yes."

"You sure you don't want to check the tags on my underwear or something?"

"Smart-ass." She laughed and swatted him on the butt.

He liked it when she laughed, something she didn't do much of since his dad had left. When she laughed, the lines in her face softened, denting her cheeks with dimples. She became the most beautiful woman he knew, especially now with her new silky, blond hair. She was almost prettier than Miss Roberts, his fourth-grade teacher. But Miss Roberts was last year. This year was Mr. Stedman and, though it was only October, Timmy hated the fifth grade. He lived for soccer practice—soccer practice and serving mass with Father Keller.

In July, when his mom had interrupted his summer and sent him to church camp, he had been furious with her. But Father Keller had made camp fun. It ended up being a great summer, and he'd hardly missed his dad. Then, to top it off, Father Keller had asked him to be one of his altar boys. Though he and his mom had been members of St. Margaret's since spring, Timmy knew Father Keller's altar boys were an elite group, handpicked and given special rewards. Rewards like the upcoming camping trip.

Timmy knocked on the ornate door to the church vestibule. When no one answered, he opened it slowly and peeked in before entering. He found a cassock in his size among those hanging in the closet, and he ripped it from the hanger, trying to make up for lost time. He threw his jacket to a chair across the room, then jumped, startled by the priest kneeling quietly next to the chair. His rod-straight back was to Timmy, but he recognized Father Keller's dark hair curling over his collar. His thin frame towered over the chair, though he was on his knees. Despite Timmy's jacket almost hitting him, the priest remained still and quiet.

Timmy stared, holding his breath, waiting for the priest to flinch, to move, to breathe. Finally, his elbow lifted to make the sign of the cross. He stood without effort and turned to Timmy, taking the jacket and draping it carefully over the chair's arm.

"Does your mom know you throw around your Sunday clothes?" He smiled with white, even teeth and bright blue eyes.

"Sorry, Father. I didn't see you when I came in. I was afraid I was late."

"No problem. We have plenty of time." He tousled Timmy's hair, his hand lingering on his head. It was something Timmy's dad used to do.

At first, Timmy had been uncomfortable when Father Keller touched him. Now, instead of tensing up, he found himself feeling safe. Though he couldn't admit it out loud, he liked Father Keller way better than he liked his dad. Father Keller never yelled; instead, his voice was soft and soothing, low and powerful. His large hands patted and caressed—never hit. When Father Keller talked to him, Timmy felt as if he was the most important person in Father Keller's life. He made Timmy feel special, and in return, Timmy wanted to please him, though he still messed up some of the mass stuff. Last Sunday, Timmy brought the water to the altar but forgot the wine. Father Keller had just smiled, whispered to him and waited patiently. No one else even suspected his mistake.

No, Father Keller was nothing like his dad, who had spent most of his time at work, even when the three of them had been a family. Father Keller seemed like a best friend instead of a priest. Sometimes on Saturdays, he played football with the boys down at the park, allowing himself to be tackled and getting just as muddy as the rest of them. At camp, he told gory ghost stories—the kind parents forbid. Sometimes after mass, Father Keller traded baseball cards. He had some of the best ones, really old ones like Jackie Robinson and Joe DiMaggio. No, Father Keller was too cool to be like his dad.

Timmy finished and waited for Father Keller to put on the last of his garments. The priest checked his image in the floor-length mirror, then turned to Timmy.

"Ready?"

"Yes, Father," he said and followed the priest through the small hallway to the altar.

Timmy couldn't help smiling at the bright white Nikes peeking out from under the priest's long, black cassock.

CHAPTER 10

Platte City reminded Maggie of the fictional Mayberry R.F.D. She'd never understood the appeal of small towns. Quaint and friendly usually meant boring and nosy. Assignments in small towns made her cranky and edgy. She hated the presumed intimacy that found its way into "how are you?" and "good morning." Immediately, she missed the irritating but familiar sounds of honking taxis and six-lane traffic. Worse yet was settling for Chinese takeout from places called Big Fred's and watered-down cappuccino from convenience-store vending machines.

She had to admit, though, the drive from Omaha had been a scenic one. The foliage along the Platte River put on a show of spectacular colors: bright oranges and flaming reds mixed with green and gold. The overpowering scent of evergreens and impending rain filled the air with an annoyingly pleasant aroma. She kept the car window cracked, despite the chill.

A jet thundered overhead, and Maggie skidded to a stop at the intersection. The sudden burst of sound shook the car and left an echo rumbling through the quiet streets. She remembered that Strategic Air Command was only ten, maybe fifteen miles away. Okay, so perhaps Platte City possessed some familiar sounds, after all.

She purposely took a wrong turn away from downtown. The detour would only take a few minutes and would hopefully give her some insight into the community. A Pizza Hut took up one corner. Across the street was the obligatory convenience store and a shiny new McDonald's. Its golden arches stood taller than anything else for miles, competing only with a grain elevator and a church steeple.

The church's spiky iron cross stabbed at the thick clouds that had begun rolling in only moments ago. Its parking lot was beginning to empty with a line of snail-crawling churchgoers, putting Maggie in the middle of the traffic jam. She sat patiently watching as each car allowed the one in front to back out and get in line. No, it was much too organized. They even ruined a good traffic jam.

Maggie waited for room in front, then flipped the rented Ford around in one quick squeal of tires. Heads turned, the line of snails stopped and watched as she spun out in the opposite direction. She checked the rearview mirror. No flashing lights followed, though she wouldn't have been surprised if they had.

The information she had accessed from the Nebraska Tourism Web site described Platte City (population 3,500) as a growing bedroom community for many who worked in Omaha (twenty miles to the northeast) and Lincoln (thirty miles to the southwest). That explained the beautiful, well-manicured homes and neighborhoods—many recently built—despite the nonexistence of any nearby industry.

Small shops lined the downtown square: a post office, Wanda's Diner, a movie theater, something called Paintin' Place, a small grocery store and, yes, even a drugstore/soda fountain. Bright red awnings hung over some of the shops. Others had window boxes with geraniums still in bloom. In the center of the square, the red brick courthouse towered over the other buildings. Built during an era when pride overrode expense, its facade included a detailed relief of Nebraska's past—covered wagons and plow horses separated by the scales of justice.

The entire block was ornately fenced in with freshly painted, black wrought iron. The courthouse took up only half the space. Cobblestone walkways, bronze statues, a marble fountain, benches and old-fashioned lampposts made the rest of the area a quiet garden-like retreat. What impressed Maggie most as she made her way over the twists of cobblestone was the absence of trash. Not one single hamburger wrapper or foam cup dared to litter the hallowed ground. Instead, huge maple and sycamore leaves decorated the path with gold and red.

Inside the lobby of the courthouse, Maggie's heels clicked on the marble floor, sending an echo all the way to the vaulted cathedral ceiling. There was no security guard, not even a desk clerk. She scanned the wall directory. The county sheriff's department, along with several courtrooms and the county jail, resided on the third floor.

She bypassed the elevator and took the stairs, an open spiral that allowed a bird's-eye view of the atrium. Lavish white and gray marble lined the stairwells and the floor. Solid oak and shiny brass trimmed the banisters and doorways. She found herself tiptoeing.

The sheriff's department appeared empty, though the smell of freshly brewed coffee and the hum of a copy machine seeped in from one of the back rooms. The wall clock showed eleven-thirty. Maggie checked her watch. She was still on eastern time. She reset it as she walked to the windows facing south. The thick, gray clouds now blocked any hint of sun or blue sky. Below, the streets remained quiet. A few customers, dressed in their Sunday best, left Wanda's Diner. Behind the theater a small, gray-haired man heaved trash into a huge Dumpster.

It wasn't noon, and she was already exhausted. She was drained from her battle with Greg and another sleepless night avoiding visions of Albert Stucky. Then, this morning, the turbulent flight had jerked and jolted her thousands of feet above control. She hated flying, and it never got any easier.

It was the control, her mother reminded her whenever possible.

"You need to let it go, Mag-pie. You can't expect to be in control twenty-four hours a day."

This from a woman who, after twenty years of therapy, still struggled with the meaning of self-control. A woman who buried her grief for her dead husband by drinking herself into a stupor every Friday night and bringing home whatever stranger had supplied her with the drinks. It wasn't until one of her men friends suggested a threesome—daughter, mother and himself—that she stopped bringing the men home and insisted on motel rooms. Her mother hadn't seemed disgusted by the idea of sharing her twelve-year-old daughter, as much as intimidated by it.

Maggie rubbed the back of her neck, the muscles tight with tension—tension easily brought on by thoughts of her mother. She wished she had checked into a hotel first and eaten some lunch instead of coming directly here. But she was ready to dig in, having spent the hours in the air preoccupying herself with details of Ronald Jeffreys. The recent murder resembled Jeffreys' style, right down to the jagged X carved into the boy's chest. Copycats were often meticulous, duplicating every last detail to amplify the thrill. Sometimes that made them even more dangerous than the original killer. It removed the passion and thus the tendency to make mistakes.

"Can I help you?"

The voice startled Maggie, and she spun around. The young woman who appeared out of nowhere was far from what Maggie had expected of someone working in a sheriff's office. Her long hair was too tall and stiff, her knit skirt too short and tight. She looked more like a teenager ready for a date.

"I'm here to see Sheriff Nicholas Morrelli."

The woman eyed Maggie suspiciously, keeping her post in the doorway as though guarding the back offices. Maggie knew her navy blazer and trousers made her look official, hiding the slender figure that sometimes betrayed her authority. Early in her career she had developed an abrupt and sometimes abrasive manner that demanded attention and compensated for her slight stature. At five foot five and a hundred and fifteen pounds, she had barely met the physical requirements of the agency.

"Nick's not here right now," the woman said in a voice that told Maggie she wasn't about to reveal any additional information. "Was he expecting you?" The woman crossed her arms and stood up straight in an attempt to emphasize her authority.

Maggie looked around the office again, ignoring the question and showing the woman she wasn't impressed. "Can he be reached?" She pretended to be interested in the bulletin board that contained a wanted poster from the early eighties, a flyer announcing a Halloween dance and a notice advertising a 1990 Ford pickup for sale.

"Look, lady. I don't mean to be rude," the young woman said, suddenly a bit unsure of herself. "What exactly is it that you need to talk to Nick… to Sheriff Morrelli about?"

Maggie glanced back at the woman, who looked older now, the lines evident around her mouth and eyes. She teetered on the two-inch spiked heels and was biting her lower lip.

Maggie reached into her jacket pocket, ready to flip out her badge when two men came noisily in the front door. The older man wore a brown deputy's uniform, the pants impeccably pressed, the tie cinched tight at his neck. His black hair was slicked back, tucked behind his ears and curled over his collar, not a strand out of place. In contrast, the younger man was wearing a gray T-shirt drenched in sweat, shorts and running shoes. His dark brown hair, though short, was tousled, strands wet against his forehead. Despite his disheveled look, he was handsome and definitely in good shape, with long muscular legs, slender waist and broad shoulders. Immediately, Maggie was annoyed with herself for noticing these details.

Both men stopped talking as soon as they saw Maggie. There was silence as they looked from Maggie to the frazzled young woman still at her post in the doorway.

"Hi, Lucy. Is everything okay?" the younger man said as his eyes scanned the length of Maggie's body. When his eyes finally met hers, he smiled as if she had met his approval.

"I was just trying to find out what this lady—"

"I'm here to see Sheriff Morrelli," Maggie interrupted. She was getting impatient with being treated like a tax auditor.

"What did you need to see him about?" It was the deputy's turn to interrogate her, his forehead creased with concern, his stance straightening as though on alert.

Maggie ran her fingers through her hair, waiting for the impatience to settle before it turned to anger. She brought out her badge and flipped it open to them. "I'm with the FBI."

"You're Special Agent O'Dell?" the younger man said, now looking more embarrassed than surprised.

"Yes, that's right."

"Sorry about the third degree." He wiped his hand on his T-shirt and extended it to her. "I'm Nick Morrelli."

She was sure the surprise registered on her face, because he smiled at her reaction. Maggie had worked with enough small-town sheriffs to know that they didn't look like Nick Morrelli. He looked more like a professional athlete, the kind whose good looks and charm forgave his arrogance. The eyes were sky blue and hard to ignore against the tanned skin and dark hair. His grip was firm, no gentle graze reserved for women; however, his eyes held hers, giving her all their attention as if she were the only one in the room. A look he reserved for women, no doubt.

"This is Deputy Eddie Gillick, and I guess you already met Lucy Burton. I am really sorry. We're all just a little on edge around here. We've had a couple of really long nights, and there's been a lot of reporters snooping around."

"Well, you've certainly come up with an interesting disguise." This time Maggie let her eyes slowly scan the length of Morrelli's body, just as he had done to her. When her eyes finally met his, a flicker of embarrassment had replaced his arrogance.

"Actually, I just got back from Omaha. I ran in the Corporate Cup Run." He seemed eager to explain, almost uncomfortable, as though he had been caught at something he shouldn't be doing. He shifted from one foot to another. "It's a fund-raiser for the American Lung Association...or maybe it's the American Heart Association. I can't remember. Anyway, it's for a good cause."

"You don't owe me an explanation, Sheriff Morrelli," she said, although she was pleased that her presence seemed to demand one.

There was an awkward silence. Finally Deputy Gillick cleared his throat. "I've got to get back on the road." This time he smiled at Maggie. "It was a pleasure meeting you, Miss O'Dell."

"Agent O'Dell," Morrelli corrected him.

"Right, sorry." Flustered by the correction, the deputy was now anxious to make his exit.

"I'm sure I'll be seeing you again," Maggie added to his misery.

"Lucy, do I smell fresh coffee?" Morrelli asked with a boyish smile.

"I just made a fresh pot. I'll get you some." Lucy's voice was now syrupy and a feminine octave higher.

Maggie smiled to herself as she watched the young woman's rigid, authoritarian stature give way to a soft sway as she started to fetch coffee for the handsome sheriff.

"Would you mind getting a cup for Agent O'Dell, too?" He smiled at Maggie while Lucy turned and shot her an irritated glare.

"Cream or sugar?"

"None for me, thank you."

"How about a Pepsi, instead?" he asked, eager to please her.

"Yes, that sounds good." Perhaps the sugar would help fill her empty stomach.

"Forget the coffee, Lucy. Two cans of Pepsi, please."

Lucy stared at Maggie, all the excitement drained from her face and replaced by contempt. She spun around and left, the clicking of her heels echoing all the way down the hallway.

It was just the two of them. Morrelli rubbed his arms as if to ward off a chill. He looked uncomfortable, and Maggie knew she was the cause of his discomfort. Perhaps she should have called. She wasn't good at that etiquette stuff, and it was probably expected in Platte City, Nebraska.

"After almost forty-eight straight hours, we decided to take a break today." Again, he seemed eager to explain away his appearance and the silent department. "I really didn't think you'd be here until tomorrow. You know, it being Sunday."

Maggie found herself wondering if he had been appointed or elected. In either case, his boyish charm had probably outweighed his competence.

"My superiors gave me the impression that time may be important in this case. You are still holding the body for my examination, aren't you?"

"Yes, of course. He's..." Morrelli rubbed a hand across his bristled face. Maggie noticed a small scar, a puckered white line that blemished his otherwise perfect jaw. "We're using the hospital morgue." He dug his fingers into his eyes. Maggie wondered if it was simple exhaustion or an attempt to block out the image that probably haunted his sleep. The report indicated that Morrelli was the one who had found the boy.

"If you'd like, I can take you there," he added.

"Thanks. Yes, I will need to do that. But first, there's someplace else I'd like you to take me."

"Sure. You probably want to unpack. Are you staying here in town?"

"Actually, that's not what I meant. I'd like to see the scene of the crime." She watched Morrelli's face grow pale. "I'd like you to show me where you found the body."

CHAPTER 11

The pasture road dissolved into torn grass and jagged ruts. Tire tracks crisscrossed each other, stamped into the mud. Nick shifted the Jeep into second gear and the vehicle strained forward, the tires cutting still more deeply into the mud.

"I don't suppose anyone realized all this traffic in and out of here may have destroyed evidence?"

Nick shot Agent O'Dell a frustrated look. He was getting tired of being reminded of his mistakes.

"By the time we discovered the body, at least two vehicles had been through here. Yeah, we realized we may have messed up the killer's tracks."

He glanced at her again as he tried to keep the Jeep from sliding into the worst parts of the mud. Though she acted older, he guessed she was only in her late twenties, maybe earlier thirties—much too young to be an expert. Her age wasn't the only thing that disarmed him. Despite her cool, abrupt manner she was very attractive. And even the conservative-style suit couldn't hide what he suspected was a knockout body. Under ordinary circumstances he'd be preparing a full-throttled charm assault. But, Jesus, there was something about her that sent him into a tailspin. She carried herself with such poise, such confidence and self-assurance. She acted as though she knew what she was doing, which only made him more aware of his own lack of expertise. It was annoying as hell.

The Jeep jerked to a stop in front of the shelterbelt of trees, and immediately the nausea of that night struck Nick. The light-headedness surprised him. It was getting to be embarrassing. He heard O'Dell struggle with the door handle, the familiar click of metal against metal.

"Wait, that door sticks. Here, let me." Without thinking he reached across the seat, leaning against her. His hand was on the door handle before he realized his body hovered over her, his face dangerously close to hers. She pressed herself into her seat to avoid touching him, and he immediately jerked his hand away, returning to his own side.

"I'll get it from the outside."

"Good idea."

Outside the Jeep, Nick berated himself. What a stupid thing to do. Not very professional. He was certainly living up to his reputation as the incompetent playboy sheriff.

He sloshed around to the other side of the Jeep. Back at the office he had taken a quick shower, put on jeans and traded the running shoes for the same boots he had worn that night. Dry mud still clung to the expensive leather. They were instantly devoured again by the sticky ooze. The gray clouds rolled in, threatening to burst at any moment and guaranteeing the ooze would stay for days ahead.

The Jeep's door opened easily from the outside. Would O'Dell think his stupid move in the car was a cheap excuse just to get close to her? It didn't matter. Something told Nick this woman was immune to his charm, what little he seemed to have left.

"Hold on." He stopped her again. "I think I have some boots back here." He climbed inside the doorway, stopping in midair as he realized the inappropriateness of his actions, again. He avoided her eyes and waited until she slid to the other side and was a safe distance away. Then he stretched over the seat. Thankfully, the rubber work boots were within arm's reach.

"Are you sure those are necessary?" She looked at the black boots as though they were shackles.

"You'll never get anywhere in this mud. It's worse by the riverbank."

He had already begun undoing the laces. He handed her a boot and began on the other, distracted when she slipped off her expensive leather flats. Clothed only in sheer socks, her feet were small, slender and delicate. He watched her slide her foot into the oversize boot. It swallowed her foot, and even her attempt at tucking in her pant leg wouldn't guarantee that the huge rubber boot would stay attached.

As they began their hike through the mud, he was impressed that she kept up with him despite her clumsy footwear and her shorter stride. The area was still cordoned off by yellow tape strung from trees. Sections were torn, flapping in the breeze, a breeze that grew stronger as the fast-moving clouds rolled overhead. Nick pulled up the collar of his jacket. His hair was still damp. A shiver slipped down his back. He glanced at O'Dell, who wore only a wool suit jacket and matching trousers. She buttoned the jacket but showed no other sign of feeling the cutting cold.

He watched her step carefully around the impression of the small body that still remained pressed into the grass. She crouched down, examined the blades of grass, scooped up a fingerful of mud and sniffed it. Nick winced, remembering the rancid smell. His skin still felt raw from scrubbing the stench from his body.

O'Dell stood and looked out at the river. The bank was only three or four feet away. The unusually high waters churned, slapping at the banks.

"Where did you find the medallion?" she asked, without looking at him.

He walked to the spot and found the white stake one of his deputies had placed there. "Here," he said, pointing to the plastic marker sunk into the mud, barely visible.

She looked at the spot, then back at the boy's resting place. It was only a couple feet away.

"It was the boy's. His mother identified it," Nick explained, still regretting that he couldn't give it back to Laura Alverez when she had pleaded. "The chain was broken. It must have gotten pulled off in the struggle."

"Except there was no struggle."

"Excuse me?" He looked back at her for an explanation, but she was on her knees again with a small tape measure stretched between the marker and the pressed grass.

"There wasn't a struggle," she repeated calmly, getting to her feet and wiping at the leaves and mud she had gotten on her trousers.

"What makes you say that?" He was annoyed by her matter-of-fact attitude. She had been here only minutes and seemed to have it all figured out.

"You fell here when you tripped, right?" she said, pointing to the torn grass and the indent in the mud.

Nick winced again. Even his report made him look like a putz. "That's right," he admitted.

"The trampling around the perimeter is obviously from your deputies."

"And the FBI," Nick added defensively, though he knew she wasn't concerned with those details. "They were in charge until we ruled out a kidnapping."

"Other than this spot and where the body lay, there is no torn grass or any beaten down. The victim's hands and feet were bound when you found him?"

"Yeah, back behind him."

"My guess is that he was like that when they arrived here. Does the coroner have an approximate time and place of death yet?" She brought out a small notebook and jotted down details.

"He was killed out here, probably less than twenty-four hours before I found him." The nausea was back. He wondered if he would ever be able to get the image of the dead boy out of his mind. Those wide, innocent eyes staring up at the sky.

"When did the victim disappear?"

"Early last Sunday morning. We found his bike and bag of newspapers against a fence. He hadn't even started his route yet."

"So the killer had him for at least three whole days."

"Jesus," Nick mumbled and shook his head. He hadn't thought about the time between the abduction and the murder. They had all been so sure the boy had been kidnapped by his father or someone who would demand a ransom. Nick had believed the boy was being well cared for.

"So how did the chain get broken?" Nick wanted to think of something other than the torture the boy may have endured.

"I don't know for sure. Maybe the killer pulled it off. It was a silver cross, right?" She looked to him for assurance. He only nodded, impressed that she had equipped herself with so many details from his report. She continued as if thinking out loud. "Maybe the killer didn't like staring at it. Maybe he wasn't able to do what he wanted to do as long as the victim was wearing it. Its religious significance is some sort of protection. Perhaps the killer is religious enough to have known that and have been uncomfortable."

"A religious killer? Great."

"What other trace do you have?"

"Trace?"

"Other evidence—other objects, torn pieces of fabric or rope? Was the FBI able to pull any tire tracks at all?"

The tire tracks again. How many times would he need to be reminded of his screwup.

"We did find a footprint."

She stared at him, and he saw a flicker of impatience.

"A footprint? Excuse me, Sheriff, I don't mean to sound skeptical, but how were you able to isolate a footprint? From what I can tell, there must have been over a dozen pairs of feet out here." She waved her hand at the shoe impressions trampled in the mud. "How do you know that the prints you found weren't one of your men or the FBI?"

"Because none of us were barefoot." He didn't wait for her reaction but moved closer to the river. He grabbed on to a tree branch just as his boots slid partway down the bank. When he looked up, O'Dell was standing over him.

"Right here." He pointed to the set of toes imprinted in the mud and highlighted with remnants of casting powder.

"There's no guarantee those are the killer's."

"Who else would be nuts enough to be out here without shoes?"

She grabbed the same branch and slid down next to him.

"You mind giving me a hand?" She extended a hand to him and he took it, allowing her to hang on while she bent down and stretched over the impression without sliding into the water.

Her hand was soft and small in his, but her grip was strong. Her jacket swung open, and he made himself look away. Jesus, she certainly didn't look like an FBI agent.

After a few seconds she pulled herself up and immediately released his hand. Back on solid ground, she started writing in the notebook. Nick stared up at the thick, gray clouds. Suddenly, he wished he was anywhere else. The last forty-eight hours had drained him. His calf muscles ached from the 10K race he had pushed himself to run that morning. And now, here he was feeling incompetent and nauseated again, remembering Danny Alverez's white body, those wide eyes staring up at the stars. A flock of snow geese honked as they passed overhead. Nick caught himself wondering what had been the last thing Danny had looked up at. He hoped it had been some geese, something tranquil and familiar.

"The puncture marks and the carving in the boy's chest were exactly like the Jeffreys murders," he said, forcing his attention back to O'Dell. "How could anyone have that information?"

"His execution was recent. July, wasn't it?"

"Yes."

"Oftentimes, local news media run stories about the murders when an execution occurs. A person could get plenty of information from those accounts."

"The good ole media," Nick said, remembering the sting from Christine's articles.

"Or someone could get detailed information from the court transcripts. They're usually public record after the trial is over."

"So you think this is a copycat killer?"

"Yes. It would be too much of a coincidence to duplicate this many details."

"Why would anyone copycat a murder like this? For kicks?"

"I'm afraid I can't tell you that," O'Dell told him, finally looking up from the notebook and meeting his eyes. "What I can tell you is this guy is going to do it again. And probably soon."

CHAPTER 12

The hospital's morgue was in the basement where every sound echoed off the white brick walls. Water pipes thumped and a fan wheezed in motion. Behind them, the elevator door squeezed shut. There was a whirl and a scrape as cables strained and pulled the car back up.

Sheriff Morrelli seemed to be walking on tiptoe to avoid the clicking of his freshly cleaned boot heels against the tile floor. Maggie glanced up at him as they walked side by side. He was pretending that all of this was routine for him, but it was easy to see through the disguise. Back by the river, she had caught him wincing once or twice, betraying his calm, cool exterior.

Still, he had insisted on accompanying her here after discovering that the coroner had gone hunting for the day and couldn't be reached. Even the idea seemed ironic to Maggie—a coroner spending the day hunting. After all the dead bodies she had examined, she couldn't imagine spending a relaxing Sunday afternoon participating in more death.

She stood back while Morrelli fumbled with a tangle of keys, then discovered the door to the morgue unlocked. He held it open for her, pressing his body against its weight and requiring her to squeeze past him. She wasn't sure whether it was intentional or not, but this was the second or third time he had arranged for their bodies to be within touching distance.

Usually her cool, authoritarian manner quickly put a stop to any unwanted advances. But Morrelli didn't seem to notice. Somehow, she imagined he treated every woman he met as a potential one-night stand. She knew his type and also knew that his flirting and flattery, along with the boyish charm and athletic good looks, probably got him as far as he wanted to go. It was annoying, but in Morrelli's case it seemed harmless.

She had dealt with much worse. She was used to lewd comments from men who were uncomfortable working with a woman. Her experiences included plenty of sexual harassment, from mild flirtation to violent gropes. If anything, at least, it had taught her to take care of herself, protect herself with a shield of indifference.

Morrelli found the light switch, and like dominoes falling, the rows of fluorescent lights blinked on, one after another. The room was larger than Maggie had expected. Immediately, the smell of ammonia hit her nostrils and burned her lungs. Everything was immaculately scrubbed. A stainless-steel table occupied the middle of the tiled floor. On one wall was a large double sink and a counter that held various tools, including a Stryker saw, several microscopes, vials and test tubes ready for use. The opposite wall contained five refrigerated vaults. Maggie couldn't help wondering if the small hospital had ever had use for all five at one time.

She took off her jacket, laid it carefully over a stool and started rolling up the sleeves of her blouse. She stopped and looked around for a lab gown or utility apron. She looked down at the expensive silk blouse, a gift from Greg, a gift he would certainly notice if she never wore again because of unremovable stains. He would accuse her of being thoughtless and irresponsible, just as she had been with her wedding ring, which now sat somewhere on the murky bottom of the Charles River. Oh, well. She rolled up the sleeves.

She had brought with her a small, black bag that contained everything she would need. She opened it and began laying its contents on the counter, first taking out the small jar of Vicks VapoRub and dabbing a bit around her nostrils. She had learned long ago that even refrigerated dead bodies gave off a smell that was worth avoiding. She started to close the lid, then stopped and turned to Morrelli, who watched from the door. She tossed him the jar.

"If you're going to stay, you might want to use some of this."

He stared at the jar, then reluctantly opened it, following her example.

Next, she took out plastic surgical gloves. She handed him a pair, but he shook his head.

"You really don't have to stay," she told him. He was beginning to look pale again, and they hadn't even rolled out the body.

"No, I'll stay. I'll just...I don't want to be in your way."

She wasn't sure if it was out of a sense of duty, or if he simply felt it was required for his macho reputation. She preferred to do the examination alone but reminded herself this was Morrelli's territory and his case. Whether he assumed the role or not, he would technically be the head of this investigation.

She continued as though he weren't there. She pulled out a recorder, checked the tape inside and set it for voice activation. She took out a Polaroid camera and made sure it was loaded with film.

"Which drawer?" she asked, turning to the vaults, ready to begin, her hands on her hips. She glanced back at Morrelli, who stared at the wall of drawers as if he hadn't realized they would actually have to take the body out.

He moved slowly, hesitantly, then unlatched the middle drawer and pulled. The metal rollers squealed then clicked as the drawer filled the room.

Maggie kicked the brake off the wheels of the steel table and rolled it under the drawer. It fit perfectly. Together they unhitched the drawer tray with the small body bag, so that it lay flat on the table. Then they pushed the table back to the middle of the room under the suspended lighting unit. Maggie kicked the brakes back into place, while Morrelli closed the drawer's door. As soon as she began unzipping the bag, Morrelli retreated to the corner.

The boy's body seemed so small and frail, which made the wounds even more pronounced. He had been a good-looking kid, Maggie found herself thinking. His reddish-blond hair was closely cropped. The freckles around his nose and cheeks stood out against the white, pasty skin. He was bruised badly under the neck, the strands of rope leaving indents just above the gaping slash.

She began by taking photos, close-ups of the puncture marks and the jagged X on the chest, then the blue and purple marks on the wrists and the slashed neck. She waited for each Polaroid to develop, making sure she had enough light and the right angle.

With the recorder close by, she began documenting what she saw.

"The victim has bruise marks under and around his neck made by what looks to be a rope. It may have been tied. There appears to be an abrasion just under the left ear, perhaps from the knot."

She gently lifted the boy's head to look at the back of his neck. He felt so light, so weightless. "Yes, the marks are all the way around the neck. This would indicate that the victim was strangled, then his throat slashed. The throat wound is deep and long, extending just below the ear to the other ear. Bruises on the wrists and ankles are similar to the neck. The same rope may have been used."

His hands were so small in hers. Maggie held them carefully, reverently, as she examined the palms. "There are deep fingernail marks on the inside of his palms. This would indicate that the victim was alive while some of the wounds were inflicted. The fingernails themselves appear to be clean… very clean."

She rested the small hands at the boy's sides and began examining the wounds. "The victim has eight—no, nine—puncture marks in the chest cavity." She carefully poked the wounds, watching her gloved index finger disappear into several. "They appear to have been made by a single-edged knife. Three are shallow. At least six are very deep, possibly hitting bone. One may have gone through the heart. Yet, there is very little…actually, there is no blood. Sheriff Morrelli, did it rain while the body was in the open?"

She looked up at him when he didn't answer. He was leaning against the wall, hypnotized by the small body on the table. "Sheriff Morrelli?"

This time he realized she was talking to him. He pushed off the wall and stood straight, almost at attention. "I'm sorry, what did you say?" His voice was hushed. He whispered as if not to wake the boy.

"Do you remember if it rained while the body was out in the open?"

"No, not at all. We had plenty of rain the week before."

"Did the coroner clean the body?"

"We asked George to hold off doing anything until you got here. Why?"

Maggie looked over the body again. She stripped off a glove and pushed her hair back out of her face, tucking it behind her ear. There was something very wrong. "Some of these wounds are deep. Even if they were made after the victim was dead, there would still be blood. If I remember correctly, there was plenty of blood at the crime scene in the grass and dirt."

"Lots of it. It took forever to get it off my clothes."

She lifted the small hand again. The nails were clean, no dirt, no blood or skin, even though he had dug them into the palm of his hand at one point. The feet, also, showed no sign of dirt, not a trace of the river mud. Though he couldn't have struggled much with his wrists and ankles bound, there still should have been enough movement to warrant some dirt.

"It's almost as if his body has been cleaned," she said to herself. When she looked up, Morrelli was standing beside her.

"Are you saying the killer washed the body after he was finished?"

"Look at the carving in the chest." She pulled the glove back on and gently poked her finger under the edge of the skin. "He used a different knife for this—one with a serrated edge. It ripped and tore the skin in some places. See here?" She ran her fingertip over the jagged skin.

"There would be blood. There *should* be blood, at least initially. And these puncture wounds are deep." She stuck her finger into one to show him. "When you make a hole this size, this deep, it's going to bleed profusely until you plug it up. This one, I'm almost certain, went into the heart. We're talking major artery, major gusher. And the throat...Sheriff Morrelli?"

Morrelli was leaning against the table, his weight jerking the stainless steel and sending out a high-pitched screech of metal against tile. Maggie looked up at him. His face was white. Before she realized it, he slumped against her. She caught him by the waist, but he was too heavy, and she slipped to the floor with him, her knees crumpling under her. The weight of him crushed against her chest.

"Morrelli, hey, are you okay?"

She squeezed out from under him and propped him against a table leg. He was conscious, but his eyes were glazed over. She climbed to her feet and looked for a towel to wet. Despite the well-equipped lab, there were no linens—no gowns or towels to be found. She remembered seeing a pop machine next to the elevators. Fumbling for the correct change, she was there and back before Morrelli moved.

His legs were twisted underneath him. His head rested against the table. Now, at least, his eyes were more focused when she knelt next to him with the Pepsi can.

"Here," she said, handing it to him.

"Thanks, but I'm not thirsty."

"No, for your neck. Here..." She reached over and put a hand at the back of his neck, gently pushing his head forward and down. Then she laid the cold Pepsi can against the back of his neck. He leaned into her. A few more inches, and his head would rest between her breasts. But now, dealing with his own vulnerability, he seemed completely unaware. Perhaps the macho ego did come with a sensitive side. She started to pull her hand away just as Morrelli reached up and caught it, gently encircling it with his large, strong fingers. He looked into her eyes, the crystal blue finally focused.

"Thanks." He sounded embarrassed, but his steady gaze held hers. A bit shook up and yet, if she wasn't mistaken, he was still flirting with her.

In response, she jerked her hand away, too quickly and much more abruptly than necessary. Just as abruptly, she handed him the Pepsi, then sat back on her knees, putting more distance between them.

"I can't believe I did that," he said. "I'm a little embarrassed."

"Don't be. I spent a lot of time on the floor before I got used to this stuff."

"How *do* you get used to it?" He looked back into her eyes, as if searching for the answer.

"I'm not sure. You just sort of disconnect, try not to think about it." She looked away and quickly got to her feet. She hated how his eyes seemed to look deep inside her. She realized it as a simple device, a cunning tool of his charm. Still, she was afraid he might actually see some weakness she had carefully hidden. Months ago there wouldn't have been anything to hide. Albert Stucky had supplied her with her own vulnerability, and she hated that it stayed so close to the surface where others might see it.

Before she could offer him a hand, Morrelli slowly stretched his long legs from the twisted knot and got to his feet without staggering or assistance. Other than his almost fainting, Maggie noticed that Sheriff Morrelli moved very smoothly, very confidently.

He smiled at her and rubbed the cold condensation of the can against his forehead, leaving a wet streak. Several strands of hair slipped across his forehead and stuck to the wetness. "Do you mind meeting me up in the cafeteria when you're finished?"

"No, of course not. I won't be much longer."

"I think I'll take a Pepsi break." He lifted the can to her as if in a toast. He started to leave, glanced back at the boy's body, then walked out.

Maggie's stomach churned, and she regretted not eating the breakfast offered during her roller-coaster flight. The room was cool, but her shuffle with Morrelli had left her hot and perspiring. She pulled off a glove and wiped her hand across her forehead, not surprised to find it damp. As she did so, she glanced at the boy's forehead. From this angle she could see something smeared on his brow.

She bent over the table, looking closely at the transparent smudge in the middle of his forehead. She wiped a finger across the area and rubbed her fingers together under her nose. If the body had been washed clean, that meant the oily liquid had been applied after. Instinctively, Maggie checked the boy's blue lips and found a smear of the oil. Before she even looked, she knew she'd find more of the oil on the boy's chest, just above his heart. Perhaps all those years of catechism had finally paid off. Otherwise, she may have never recognized that someone, perhaps the killer, had given this boy last rites.

CHAPTER 13

Christine Hamilton tried to edit the article she had scribbled in her notebook while pretending to know the score of the soccer game being played on the field down below her. The wooden bleachers were terribly uncomfortable no matter how she shifted her weight. She wanted a cigarette, but chewed the cap of her pen instead.

A sudden burst of applause, hoots and whistles made her look up just in time to see the team of red-clad, ten-year-old boys high-fiving each other. She had missed another point, but when the small, red-haired boy looked up from the huddle, she gave him a smile and thumbs-up as if she had seen the whole thing.

He was so much smaller than his teammates, yet to her he seemed to be growing too quickly. It didn't help matters that he was looking more and more like his father every day.

She pushed her sunglasses on top of her windblown hair. The sun was disappearing behind the line of trees that bordered the park. Thankfully, most of the clouds had passed over without dumping more rain. It was bad enough they were playing a make-up game on a Sunday evening.

She had isolated herself on the top bleacher away from the other soccer moms and dads. She didn't care to know these obsessive parents who wore team jerseys and screamed profanities at the coach. Later, they would slap the coach on the back and congratulate him on yet another win.

She flipped a page and was about to return to her editing when she noticed three of the other divorced soccer moms whispering to each other.

Instead of watching the game, they were pointing to the sidelines. Christine turned to follow their gaze and immediately saw what had distracted them. The man striding up the sidelines typified the cliché—"tall, dark and handsome." He wore tight jeans and a sweatshirt with Nebraska Cornhuskers emblazoned across the chest. He looked like an older version of the college quarterback he used to be. He watched the game as he walked—no, glided—up the sidelines. But Christine knew he was well aware of the attention he was drawing from the bleachers. When he finally looked over, she waved to him, enjoying the look of envy on the women's faces when he smiled at her and made his way up the bleachers to join her.

"What's the score?" Nick asked, sliding in beside her.

"I think it's five to three. You realize, don't you, that you just made me the envy of every drooling, divorced soccer mom here?"

"See, the things I do for you, and you repay me with such abuse."

"Abuse? I never hit you a day of your life," she told her younger brother. "Well, not hard."

"That's not what I meant, and you know it." He wasn't joking.

She sat up straight, preparing to defend herself despite the guilt gnawing at her stomach. Yes, she should have called him before she turned in the story. But what if he had asked her not to run it? That story had put her on the other side of the door. Rather than being stuck writing helpful household hints, she had two front-page articles in two days with her byline. And tomorrow she'd be sitting at her own desk in the city room.

"How about I make it up to you? Dinner tomorrow night? I'll fix spaghetti and meatballs with Mom's secret sauce."

He looked over at her, glanced at the notebook. "You just don't get it, do you?"

"Oh, come on, Nicky. You know how long I've been waiting to get out of the "Living Today" section? If I hadn't filed that story, someone else would have."

"Really? And would they have quoted an officer who told them something off the record?"

"He never once said it was off the record. If Gillick told you otherwise, he's lying."

"Actually, I didn't know it was Eddie. Gee, Christine, you just gave away an anonymous source."

Her face grew hot, and she knew the red was quickly replacing her fair complexion. "Damn you, Nicky. You know how hard I'm trying. I'm a little rusty, but I can be a damn good reporter."

"Really? So far I think your reporting has been irresponsible."

"Oh, for crying out loud, Nicky. Just because you didn't like what I wrote doesn't make it irresponsible journalism."

"What about the headlines?" Nick spoke through gritted teeth. She couldn't remember the last time he'd been this upset with her. He avoided looking at her and watched the boys running up the field. "Where do you get off comparing this murder to Jeffreys'?"

"There are basic similarities."

"Jeffreys is dead," he whispered, looking around to make sure no one was listening. He clasped his hands together over a knee and tapped his foot on the empty bench in front of them, a nervous habit Christine recognized from childhood.

"Grow up, Nicky. Anyone with half a brain is going to compare this murder to Jeffreys'. I just wrote what everyone else is thinking. Are you saying I'm off target?"

"I'm saying we don't need another panic in a community that just started to feel like maybe their kids were safe again." He crossed his arms, looking unsure of what to do with his clenched fists. "You made me look like a goddamn idiot, Christine."

"Oh, I see. That's what this is really about. You don't care about a panic in the community. You're just worried about how you look. Why am I not surprised?"

He glared at her. For a moment, he looked as though he would defend himself, but instead he looked back out at the field. She hated when he absorbed her cheap shots without fighting back. Even as a kid, he never knew how to combat the insults—her secret weapons. She must be getting old, because suddenly she regretted hurting his feelings.

At the same time, though, she grew impatient with the way her brother approached things. He constantly took the easy way out, but then, why not? Everything seemed to be handed to Nick, from job opportunities to women. And he floated from one to the next without much effort, remorse or thought. When their father retired and insisted that Nick run for sheriff, Nick had left his professorship at the university without any hesitation. At least, none Christine had witnessed, though she knew he loved being on campus, being a walking legend and having coeds drool over him. Without a hitch—and quite predictably, in fact—he had been elected to the post of county sheriff. Though Nick would be the first to admit it was only because of their father's name and reputation. But he didn't seem to mind. He just took things as they came.

Christine, on the other hand, had to scrape and claw for everything she wanted, especially since Bruce's departure. Well, this time she deserved the break she was getting. She refused to apologize for capitalizing on her sudden streak of good fortune.

"If it is a copycat, don't you think people deserve a warning?" She kept her voice sincere, though she didn't want or need to justify herself. This was news. She knew what she was doing. The public had a right to know all the grisly details.

Nick didn't answer. Instead, he brought his feet up on the bench in front so he could lean forward, elbows on his knees, chin resting on clenched fists. They sat silently in the middle of whoops and howls. There was something different, something unfamiliar about him, and the change was disconcerting.

After what seemed like a long time, Nick said quietly, calmly, "Danny Alverez was just a year older than Timmy." His eyes were focused straight ahead.

Christine looked out at Timmy bouncing down the field, weaving in between the boys that towered over him. He was fast and agile, using his smallness to his advantage. And, yes, she had noticed the resemblance. Timmy looked very much like the school photo they had used in the newspaper of Danny. They both had reddish-blond hair, blue eyes and a sprinkle of freckles. Like Timmy, Danny also was small for his age.

"I just spent the afternoon at the morgue." His voice startled her back to reality.

"Why?" she asked, pretending not to be interested. She stared at the game, but watched Nick out of the corner of her eye. She had never seen him so serious before.

"Bob Weston called in an expert to help us come up with a profile—Special Agent Maggie O'Dell from Quantico. She got in this morning and was raring to get to work." He glanced over at Christine, then did a double take when he noticed her scratching down something in her notebook. "Jesus, Christine!" he spat out so suddenly it made her jump. "Isn't anything off the record with you?"

"If you wanted it off the record, you should have said so." She watched him rub his hand across his jaw as if she had sucker punched him. "Besides, by tomorrow everyone will know about Agent O'Dell when she starts asking questions. What are you worried about, Nicky? Calling in an expert is a good thing."

"Is it? Or will it just make me look like I don't know what the hell I'm doing?" He shot her another look. "Don't you dare print that."

"Relax. I'm not the enemy, Nicky." She noticed the boys doing their victory dance between the required handshakes. The game was over, and it was beginning to get dark. The park lights slowly turned on one by one. "You know, Dad wasn't afraid to work with the news media."

"Yeah, well, I'm not Dad." Now she had made him angry. She knew to stay away from the comparison, but she hated him treating her like an ambulance chaser. Besides, if he didn't like the comparisons, perhaps he shouldn't have followed in their father's footsteps. As usual, she simply sidestepped the subject.

"I'm just saying that Dad knew how to use the media to help."

"To help?" Nick asked incredulously, his voice rising above the cheering in front of them. He quickly looked around, realizing he was too loud. He lowered his voice again and leaned toward her. "Dad used the news media because he loved being in the limelight. There were so many leaks, it's amazing they ever caught Jeffreys."

"What leaks? What are you talking about?"

"Never mind," he said, glancing at her notebook.

Christine rolled her eyes at him, wondering if he was just baiting her now.

"But they did catch Jeffreys, and Dad solved the case," she reminded him.

"Yeah, they did catch Jeffreys, and good ole Dad took all the credit."

"Nicky, no one's asking you to fill Dad's shoes. You always take that on yourself." Okay, there it was. A slip, an innocent slip. She watched his face, waiting.

Instead, he simply shook his head. A frustrated smile caught at the corner of his mouth as if he thought she couldn't possibly understand.

"Haven't you ever wondered..." He hesitated, looking out at the field, his thoughts far away. "Didn't you ever think it happened all too quickly... too neat and convenient?"

"What are you talking about?"

This wasn't the response she expected. The night air was chilly, and Christine felt a shiver down her back. She rubbed her arms and tried to look into her brother's eyes. He was starting to scare her with his anger and his hushed manner. Normally, he joked around and never took anything too seriously, even their sibling banter. Had the mention of their father brought all this on? No, it was something else. What did he know? What was it that had her arrogant, confident little brother so spooked?

"Nicky, what do you mean?" she tried again.

"Forget it," he said, standing up and stretching, closing the subject.

"Uncle Nick, Uncle Nick! Did you see me score?" Timmy yelled as he ran up the bleachers, carefully watching his small feet the whole way up.

"You bet I did," Nick lied.

She watched as Nick's entire face changed, relaxing into a smile as he snatched her small son up into his long arms, wrestling him in close for a hug.

Christine knew her brother was hiding something, and she was going to find out what it was.

CHAPTER 14

He drove around the park again, this time slowly. The game was finally over. He pulled into a parking space far from the other cars, alone in the corner of the lot. He turned off the headlights and sat watching, listening to the music and waiting for the jerky strings of Vivaldi to smooth out and silence the throbbing in his temples.

It was happening again and so soon. He couldn't stop it, couldn't control it. And worse, he didn't want to. He was so tired. He tried to remember when he had last slept through an entire night, instead of pacing or wandering the streets. He rubbed his eyes, wiping at the exhaustion, then stopped suddenly. His fingers were trembling beyond his control.

"Dear God, make it stop," he whispered as he tore at the hair at his temples. Why wouldn't it stop? The throbbing, the pounding made his head ache.

He watched the group of boys in grass-stained uniforms. They looked so happy, fresh from their victory, arms crossing around one another, hands patting each other on the back. They touched so carelessly, so casually. Their singsong voices grew loud as they approached, drowning out Vivaldi with lyrics of gibberish.

The memory came flooding back to him, paralyzing him and pinning him to the stiff leather of the car seat. He was eleven years old and his stepfather had made him join the Little League team, bargaining with the coach to get him out of the house on Saturday mornings. He knew it was only because his stepfather wanted to fuck his mother all morning.

He had accidentally walked in on them the Saturday before, only because they were out of milk. The memory washed over him—powerful despite the years. So clear, so vivid he grabbed the steering wheel to brace himself.

He stood in the doorway of his mother's bedroom, paralyzed by the sight of his mother's skin, white and naked with the silver cross swinging between her big breasts. Her breasts wagged back and forth. She held herself up on her hands and knees while his stepfather rode her like a dog in heat.

It was his stepfather who saw him first. He yelled at him, panting and jerking, while his mother's eyes grew wide in horror. She twisted out from under his stepfather, falling and tumbling off the bed, grabbing for the sheet. It was then that he turned to run. He stumbled down the hall, tripping and falling only once before he got to his room. Just as he began to slam the door, his stepfather crashed through it.

His stepfather was still naked. It was the first time he had seen a grown man's penis, and it was horrible: huge, stiff and erect, protruding through the thick black hair. His stepfather grabbed him by the neck and shoved his face to the wall.

"You interested in watching or maybe you want some of this." He could still hear the man's graveled voice, out of breath and panting in his ear.

He stood perfectly still. He couldn't breathe. His stepfather's fingers strangled his neck with one hand while he ripped his pajama pants with the other. His mother screamed and pounded her fists against his locked door. Then he felt it. The intense pressure, the pain so stifling he thought his insides would explode. He kept quiet and still, though he wanted to scream. His cheek scraped against the rough texture of the bedroom wall. All he could do was stare at the crucifix hanging next to his face, while he waited for his stepfather to stop slamming into his small body.

A car's horn blasted. He jumped and clutched the steering wheel even harder. His palms were sweaty, his fingers still trembling. He watched the boys getting into the cars and vans with their parents. How many of them were hiding secrets like his own? How many of them hid their bruises and scars? How many waited for some sort of relief, some sort of salvation from their misery? From their torture?

Then he saw the small boy waving to the others as he started up the sidewalk. He watched to see if anyone would join the boy tonight, or if he would walk home alone as he usually did.

It was starting to get dark. Several street lights blinked on. He listened to the gravel grind beneath the cars as they pulled out and drove off. Headlights flicked on and blinded him as they turned to leave. No one noticed him. No one took extra time to look his way. Those who recognized him smiled and waved, for there was nothing unusual about him taking in a neighborhood soccer game.

Half a block away, the boy still walked alone, tossing the soccer ball from one hand to the other. He looked thin and small in his baggy uniform, so very vulnerable. The boy practically skipped, regardless of no one showing up to watch him play. Perhaps he had grown accustomed to his loneliness.

The last car left the parking lot. He silenced Vivaldi in the middle of *The Four Seasons: Autumn*. Without looking, his fingers found the small, glass vial from inside the glove compartment. Expertly, he cracked the vial and let it dampen the brilliant white handkerchief. He wished the extra precautions were not necessary, but he had been reckless with Danny. He grabbed the black ski mask and got out of the car, gently closing the door. Immediately, he noticed that his hands were no longer trembling. Yes, he was finally feeling back in control. Then he followed quietly up the sidewalk.

CHAPTER 15

Monday, October 27

Maggie poured the rest of the Scotch from the small bottle to the plastic cup. The ice cubes cracked and tinkled against each other. She took a sip, closed her eyes and welcomed the lovely sting sliding down her throat. Lately, she worried that she had acquired her mother's taste for alcohol, or worse, her addiction to the pleasant numbness promised by the sacred liquid.

She rubbed her eyes and glanced at the cheap clock radio across the room on the nightstand. It was after two in the morning, and she couldn't sleep. The dim table lamp gave her a headache. It was probably the Scotch, but she made a note to ask the hotel clerk for a brighter light.

The small tabletop was covered with the Polaroid photos she had taken earlier. She attempted to put them in chronological order—hands tied, neck strangled then slashed, puncture wounds. This madman was methodical. He took his time. He cut, sliced and peeled back skin with frightening precision. Even the jagged X followed a specific diagonal from shoulder blade to belly button.

She scattered two file folders full of police reports and newspaper clippings. There were enough gory details to provide nightmares for a lifetime. Except it was impossible to have nightmares if you couldn't sleep.

She pulled her bare legs up, tucking her feet underneath her in an attempt to make herself comfortable in the hard chair. Her Green Bay Packers jersey had stretched and become misshapen from too many washes. It barely covered her thighs, yet it was still the softest nightshirt she owned.

It had become a sort of security blanket that made her feel at home no matter how many miles away. She refused to get rid of it despite Greg's constant complaints.

She looked at the clock again. She should have called Greg when she had gotten back to the hotel. Now it was too late. Perhaps it was just as well. They both needed some cooling-down time.

She sifted through the scattered papers and examined her notes, several pages of details, small observations, some that would probably seem insignificant to anyone else. Eventually, she would pull them all together and create a profile of the killer. She had done it many times before. Sometimes she could describe the killer right down to height, hair color and, in one case, even his aftershave lotion. This time, though, it was more difficult. Partly because the obvious suspect had already been executed. And partly because it was always difficult to crawl inside the sick, disgusting mind of a child killer.

She picked up the silver medallion and chain from the corner of the desk. It resembled the one Danny Alverez had worn. Though this one had been given to Maggie by her father for her first Holy Communion.

"As long as you wear this, God will protect you from any harm," her father had told her. Though his own, identical medallion had not saved him. She wondered if he had gone into the burning building that night believing it would.

Until a month ago she had worn the medallion faithfully, perhaps out of routine and remembrance of her father rather than out of any sense of spirituality. She had stopped praying the day she watched her father's casket lowered into the cold, hard earth. At twelve, none of her catechism teachings could explain why God had needed to take her father away.

In fact, she had put aside Catholicism until she joined the forensic lab at Quantico eight years ago. Suddenly, those crude drawings in her Baltimore Catechism of demons with horns and glowing red eyes had made sense. Evil did exist. She had seen it in the eyes of killers. She had seen it in the eyes of Albert Stucky. Ironically, it was that evil that had brought her closer to believing in God again. But it was Albert Stucky who made her wonder whether God simply didn't care anymore. The night she watched Stucky slaughter two women, Maggie had gone home and removed the medallion from around her neck. And although she couldn't bring herself to wear it anymore, she still carried it with her.

She ran her fingers over the smooth surface of the medal and wondered what Danny Alverez must have felt. What must he have thought when the madman ripped away what the small boy may have seen as his last protection? Like her father, had Danny Alverez put his final breath of faith in a silly metal object?

She clutched the medallion tightly in her fist, pulled back her arm and was ready to fling the worthless charm across the room when a soft tap on the door stopped her. The knock was barely audible. Instinctively, Maggie got to her feet and slipped out her Smith & Wesson .38 revolver from its holster. She padded quietly to the door in bare feet, feeling vulnerable in only the nightshirt and underpants. She gripped the revolver, waiting for its power to remove her sense of vulnerability. Through the peephole she could see Sheriff Morrelli, and the tension slid away from her shoulders. She opened the door, but just enough to look out at him.

"What's going on, Sheriff?"

"Sorry. I tried to call, but the night desk clerk has been on the phone for over an hour."

He looked exhausted, his blue eyes swollen and red, his short hair sticking up out of place and his face still unshaved. His shirt was untucked, the tails hanging out over his jeans and peeking out from under his denim jacket. She noticed that several of the top buttons were missing, and his twisted collar was open, exposing wisps of dark curly hair. Immediately, she looked away, annoyed with herself for noticing this last detail.

"Is something wrong?" she asked.

"Another boy's missing," he said, swallowing hard as if it was difficult to get the words out.

"That's impossible," she said, but knew, in fact, that it wasn't. Albert Stucky had taken his fourth victim less than an hour after his third victim was discovered. The beautiful, blond coed had been sliced in pieces, some of which were stuffed in takeout boxes and discarded in the Dumpster behind a restaurant Stucky had eaten at earlier that evening.

"I've got men going door-to-door in the neighborhood and searching alleys, parks, fields." He rubbed his hand over his exhausted face and scratched his bristled jaw. His eyes were a watery blue. "The kid was walking home from a soccer game. He only had five blocks to walk." His eyes darted down the hall, avoiding Maggie's gaze while pretending to make sure no one else was in the deserted hallway.

"Maybe you should come in."

Maggie held the door open for him. He hesitated, then walked in slowly, staying in the entrance as he glanced around the room. He turned back to Maggie, and his eyes dropped to her legs. She had forgotten about the short nightshirt. He looked up quickly, met her eyes and looked away. He was embarrassed. The charming, flirtatious Morrelli was embarrassed.

"Sorry. Did I wake you?" Another glance, and this time when his eyes found hers, she felt her face grow hot. As nonchalantly as possible, she squeezed past him and went to the dresser.

"No, I was still up."

She slid her gun back into its holster, opened one of the dresser drawers and started digging for a pair of jeans. Finally, she found a pair and pulled them on while she watched Morrelli pace the small space between the bed and table.

"Did I mention that I tried to call first?"

She looked up in the mirror and caught him watching her. Their eyes met again, this time in the mirror.

"Yes, you did. It's okay," she said, struggling with the zipper. "Actually, I was going over my notes."

"I was at that game," he said softly, quietly.

"What game?"

"The soccer game. The one the boy was walking home from. My nephew played. Jesus, Timmy probably knows this kid." He continued to pace the room, making the space seem even smaller with his long strides.

"Are you sure the boy didn't go home with a friend?"

"We called other parents. His friends remember seeing him start walking up the sidewalk toward home. And we found his soccer ball. It's autographed by some famous soccer player. His mom says it's one of his most prized possessions. She insists he wouldn't have just left it."

He scraped a sleeve across his face. Maggie recognized the panic in his eyes. He wasn't prepared to handle a situation like this. She wondered what experience he had in crisis management. She sighed and raked her fingers through her tangled hair. Already she regretted that it would be up to her to keep him focused.

"Sheriff, maybe you should sit down."

"Bob Weston suggested I compile a list of pedophiles and known sex offenders. Do I start hauling them in for questioning? Can you give me any idea who I should be looking for?" He glanced over the papers spread out on the table in one of his passes.

"Sheriff Morrelli, why don't you sit down?"

"No, I'm fine."

"No, I insist." She reached up and grabbed him by the shoulders, gently shoving him into a chair behind the table. He looked as though he'd stand up again, thought better of it, then stretched out his long legs.

"Did you have any suspects at all when the Alverez boy was taken?" Maggie asked.

"Just one. His father. His parents are divorced. The father was refused custody and visitation because of his drinking and abusiveness. We were never able to track him down. Hell, the air force can't even find him. He was a major at the base, but went AWOL two months ago. He ran off with a sixteen-year-old girl he met over the Internet."

She found herself pacing as she listened. Perhaps it had been a mistake to make him sit. Now that he gave her his full attention it dismantled her thought process. She rubbed her eyes, realizing how exhausted she was. How long could a person function without sufficient sleep?

"Have you made any progress in tracking him down?"

"We stopped."

"What do you mean you stopped?"

"After we found Danny's body, Weston said it couldn't be the father. That a father wouldn't be able to do that to his own son."

"I've seen what fathers can do to their sons. I remember a case three, no, four years ago where a father buried his six-year-old son in a box. He dug a hole in the backyard and left just a small airhole with a piece of rubber hose. It was punishment for something stupid. I can't even remember now what the kid had done. After several days of rain, he couldn't find the air hole. Instead of digging up his entire backyard, he tried to make it look like a kidnapping. The wife went along with his crazy scheme. She probably didn't want to end up in a box of her own. Maybe you should continue searching for Mr. Alverez. Didn't you say he was abusive?"

"Yeah, the guy's a real asshole. Beat up regularly on his wife and Danny, even after the divorce. She's had a half-dozen restraining orders out on him. But what possible connection could there be with this boy? I don't think Matthew Tanner even knew Danny Alverez."

"There may not be a connection. We don't know for sure that this boy was taken. He could still show up at a friend's house. Or he may have run away."

"Okay." He sighed, not looking convinced. He slid down farther in the chair to rest his head against the back. "But you don't really believe he ran away, do you?"

Her eyes searched his. Despite his confusion and panic, he wanted the truth. She decided to level with him.

"No. Probably not," she said. "I knew the killer would strike again. I just didn't think it would be *this* soon."

"So tell me where to begin. Have you had time to figure out anything about this guy?"

She came around the table and stared at the montage of photos, notes and reports.

"He's meticulous, in control. He takes his time, not only with the murder, but in cleaning up after himself. Though the cleaning isn't to hide evidence—it's part of his ritual. I think he may have done this before." She fingered through her notes. "He's definitely not young and immature," she continued. "There was no sign of struggle at the site, so the victim was tied beforehand. That means he has to be strong enough to carry a seventy-to-eighty-pound boy at least three hundred to five hundred yards. I'm guessing he's in his thirties, about six feet tall, two hundred pounds. He's white. He's educated and he's intelligent."

At some point during her description, Morrelli sat up, suddenly alert and interested in the mess she poked through.

"Remember at the hospital after I examined the Alverez boy, I told you he may have given the boy last rites? That would mean the killer's Catholic, maybe not practicing, but his Catholic guilt is still strong. Strong enough that he's bothered by a medallion in the shape of a cross, so he rips it off. He performs extreme unction, perhaps to atone for his sin. You might check to see whether this boy, Matthew Tanner," she said, looking at Nick to make certain she had the name right. When he nodded, she continued, "if he belonged to the same church as the Alverez boy."

"Right offhand, I'd say it's unlikely," Nick said. "Danny went to school and church out by the base. The Tanner house is only a few blocks from St. Margaret's, unless the Tanners aren't Catholic."

"Chances are, the killer doesn't even know the boys." Maggie started pacing again. "It could be he simply looks for easy targets, boys out alone, with no one else around. I do think he may still be connected somehow to a Catholic church, and quite possibly in this area. Odd as it might seem, these guys don't often stray too far from their own familiar territory."

"He sounds like a real sicko. You said he may have done this before. Is it possible he may have a record? Maybe child abuse or sexual molestation? Maybe even beating up a gay lover?"

"You're assuming he's gay or that he's a pedophile?"

"An adult male who does this to little boys—isn't that a safe assumption?"

"No, not at all. He may be worried that he is, or he may have homosexual tendencies, but no, I don't think he's gay, nor do I believe he's a pedophile."

"And you can tell all that just from the evidence we've found?"

"No. I'm guessing that from the evidence we haven't found. The victim didn't appear to be sexually abused. There were no traces of semen in the mouth or rectum, though he may have washed it off. There were no signs of any penetration, no indication of sexual stimulation. Even with Jeffreys' victims, only one—Bobby Wilson," she said, checking her notes. "Only the Wilson boy showed signs of sexual abuse and those seemed very obvious. Multiple penetration, lots of tearing and bruising."

"Wait a minute. If this guy is only copying Jeffreys, how can we be sure any of what he does is an indication of who he is?"

"Copycats choose murders that often play out their own fantasies. Sometimes they add their individual touches. I can't find any indications that Jeffreys gave his victims last rites, though it could easily have been overlooked."

"I do know he asked for a priest to hear his confession before he was executed."

"How do you know that?" She looked down at him, only then realizing she was half sitting on the chair's armrest. Her thigh rubbed against Morrelli's arm. She stood up. Perhaps a bit too suddenly. He didn't seem to notice.

"You probably know that my dad was the sheriff who brought in Jeffreys. Well, he had a front-row seat at the execution."

"Is it possible to ask him some questions?"

"He and my mom bought an RV a few years ago. They travel year-round. They check in from time to time, but I don't know how to get ahold of them. I'm sure once they hear about this, he'll be in touch, but it may take a while."

"I wonder if it's possible to track down the priest?"

"No problem. Father Francis is still here at St. Margaret's. Though I don't know what help he could be. It's not likely he'll share Jeffreys' confession."

"I'd still like to talk to him. Then we better talk to the Tanners. You've obviously met them already?"

"His mom. Matthew's parents are divorced."

Maggie stared at him, then began digging through her files.

"What is it?" Nick leaned forward, almost touching her side.

She found what she was looking for, flipped through the pages, then stopped. "All three of Jeffreys' victims came from single-parent households. Mothers raising their sons alone."

"What does that mean?"

"It means there may be nothing random about how he picks his victims. I was wrong about him waiting to simply find a boy alone. He chooses each one very carefully. You said the Alverez boy left his bike and newspapers against a fence somewhere?"

"Right. He hadn't even started his route yet."

"And there was no sign of a struggle?"

"None. It looked like he carefully parked his bike and got in with this guy. That's why we thought it might be someone he knew. These kids are small-town kids, but they still know the drill. I just don't think Danny would get into a stranger's vehicle."

"Unless he thought it was someone he could trust."

Maggie could see Morrelli growing more and more concerned. She recognized the panic, that look on people's faces when they realized the killer could be someone in their community.

"What do mean? Like someone who pretended to know him or his mom?"

"Perhaps. Or someone who looked official, maybe even wearing a uniform." Maggie had seen it dozens of times before. No one seemed to question whether a person in uniform actually belonged in the uniform.

"Maybe a military uniform like his dad's?" Nick asked.

"Or a white lab coat, or even a police officer's uniform."

CHAPTER 16

Timmy slid against the wall until he was sitting on the floor, watching the bathroom door. He had to pee but knew better than to interrupt his mom. If he knocked, she would insist he come in and take care of business while she finished her makeup. He was getting too old to pee with his mom in the same room.

He listened to her singing and decided to retie his tennis shoes. The crack in the sole had spread. Soon he'd need to ask for new ones, even though his mom couldn't afford them. He had overheard her on the phone with his dad and knew his dad hadn't sent them any of the money the court had said he was supposed to send each month.

It was something from *The Little Mermaid*—that's what his mom was singing. Her Jamaican accent needed help, even though she had watched that movie almost as many times as he had watched *Star Wars*. The phone started ringing. She would never be able to hear it down "under the sea." He scrambled to his feet to answer it.

"Hello?"

"Timmy? This is Mrs. Calloway—Chad's mom. Is your mom there?"

He almost blurted out that Chad had hit him first. If Chad said it was the other way around, he was lying. Instead, he said, "Just a minute. I'll get her."

Chad Calloway was a bully, but if Timmy had told his mom that Chad had purposely inflicted the bruises, she would have most definitely made him quit soccer. And now the bully had probably lied about his own bruises.

Timmy knocked softly on the bathroom door. If she didn't answer, he'd have to tell Mrs. Calloway that his mom couldn't come to the phone right now. The door, however, clicked and opened. His heart sank down to his cracked shoes.

"Was that the phone?" She came out smelling good and bringing a trail of perfume with her.

"It's Mrs. Calloway."

"Who?"

"Mrs. Calloway, Chad's mom."

She squinted at him, her eyebrows raised as she waited for more.

"I don't know what she wants." He shrugged and followed her to the phone even though he still had to pee, more than ever now.

"This is Christine Hamilton. Yes, of course." She spun around to Timmy and mouthed, "Calloway?"

"She's Chad's mom," he whispered. She never listened to him.

"Yes, you're Chad's mom."

He couldn't tell what Mrs. Calloway was telling his mom. She paced as she normally did while on the phone, nodding though the other person couldn't see her. Her answers were short. A couple of "uh-huhs" and one "oh, sure."

Then suddenly, she stopped and gripped the phone. Here it was. He needed to prepare his story. Wait a minute. He didn't need a story. The truth was, Chad had picked on him. No, beat the shit out of him was more accurate. And for no real reason, other than he liked it.

"Thank you for calling, Mrs. Calloway."

His mom hung up the phone and stared out the window. He couldn't tell whether she was angry. She couldn't make him quit soccer. He was ready to spit out his defense when she turned and beat him to it.

"Timmy, one of your teammates is missing."

"What?"

"Matthew Tanner never came home last night after the soccer game."

So it had nothing to do with Chad?

"Some of the other soccer parents are meeting at the Tanner house this morning to help out."

"Is Matthew in trouble? Why didn't he go home?" He hoped he didn't sound relieved, but in fact, he was.

"Now, I don't want you to worry, Timmy, but do you remember my articles about that boy, Danny Alverez?"

He nodded. How could he not remember? She had sent him out yesterday morning to buy five extra copies of the newspaper, even though she could have had as many copies as she wanted from work.

"Well, we don't know for sure yet, so I don't want you to get scared, but the man who took Danny may have taken Matthew."

His mom looked worried. Those lines around her mouth showed up every time she frowned.

"Go use the bathroom, and I'll take you to school. I don't want you walking today."

"Okay." He raced back to the bathroom. Poor Matthew, he found himself thinking. Too bad Chad couldn't have been the one taken, instead.

CHAPTER 17

Christine couldn't believe her luck, though she tried to contain her excitement. While Timmy had been in the bathroom, she had called Taylor Corby, the news editor, her new boss. They had talked several times over the weekend by phone, and, although they had never met, Christine knew exactly who he was. Her co-workers in the "Living Today" section called Corby a news nerd. He wore funky wire-rimmed glasses and seemed to own only black trousers and white oxford shirts, which he decorated with different Looney Tunes ties. To make matters worse, he rode a bicycle even in the winter—and not because he couldn't afford a car, but simply because he wanted to.

This morning when she told him about Matthew Tanner, Corby quietly listened.

"Christine, you know what that means?"

It was easy to understand why he had chosen print instead of broadcast journalism. His voice never changed, showed no emotion. And regardless of his choice of words, it was sometimes difficult to tell whether he was excited, bored or simply disinterested. "If you have copy for this evening's paper, we will have scooped the other media three days in a row."

"I still need to convince Mrs. Tanner to let me interview her."

"Interview or not, you already have enough for a great story. Just make sure you substantiate your facts."

"Of course."

Now, Christine looked over at her son, knowing he must be worried about his friend. He had made no fuss about her driving him to school and had sat most of the trip in silence. She turned the corner to the school and immediately slammed on the brakes. A line of cars extended to the corner as parents pulled in front of the school to drop off their children. On the sidewalks, parents walked alongside their kids. Every intersection in view had adult crossing guards accompanying their smaller charges.

A horn behind them blasted, making both Christine and Timmy jump. She inched the car forward, getting in line.

"What's going on, Mom?" Timmy snapped out of his seat belt so he could sit on his feet, allowing a view over the dash.

"Parents are just making sure their kids get to school okay." Some of the parents looked frantic, scurrying along with one hand on a shoulder, an arm, a back, as though the extra contact would add protection.

"Because of Matthew?"

"We don't know what's happened to Matthew yet. He may have just gotten upset and run away from home. You shouldn't say anything about Matthew." She shouldn't have told Timmy about Matthew. Though she had promised to be open and honest with her son after Bruce left, this was not something she should have shared with him. Besides, very few people even knew about Matthew. This panic was in response to her articles. Just the mention of Ronald Jeffreys invoked a protectiveness in parents. This was the same panic parents had displayed when Jeffreys had been on the prowl.

Christine recognized Richard Melzer from KRAP radio. He hurried up the sidewalk in his trench coat, carrying his briefcase and holding the hand of a small blond girl, his daughter no doubt. Christine needed to get to Michelle Tanner's as soon as possible. It wouldn't be long before others found out about Matthew.

The line moved along at a crawl, and she searched for an opening. Perhaps she could just let Timmy out here. She knew he wouldn't mind, except everyone would notice.

"Mom?"

"Timmy, we're moving as fast as possible."

"Mom, I'm pretty sure Matthew wouldn't just run away from home."

She glanced at her small son perched on his feet, watching the unusual parade outside his window. His hair stuck up where he had plastered down the cowlick. The sprinkle of freckles only made his skin more pale. When had this little boy grown so wise? She should have felt proud, yet this morning it made her a little sad that she could no longer preserve his innocence.

CHAPTER 18

Brightly colored stained-glass figures stared down from their heavenly perch. The scent of burning incense and candle wax filled Maggie's nostrils. Why was it that being inside of a Catholic church always made her feel as if she was twelve again? Immediately, she thought of the black bra and panties she wore—too much lace, an inappropriate color. The butt of her gun stabbed into her side. She reached inside her jacket and readjusted the shoulder strap. Should she even be carrying a gun inside a church? Of course, she was being ridiculous.

She glanced over her shoulder as if expecting to see a casket being rolled up the aisle behind them. She could still hear the *click-clack* of rollers, the soft tap of a dozen leather shoes marching in unison along with her father's casket. When she looked up, Morrelli was watching her, waiting for her at the altar.

"Everything okay?"

He had left her hotel room at five o'clock to go home, shower, shave and change clothes. When he arrived two hours later to pick her up, she hardly recognized him. His short hair was neatly combed back. His face was clean-shaven, and the white scar on his chin—even more pronounced—added a rugged edge to his good looks. Underneath his denim jacket he wore a white shirt and black tie with crisp blue jeans and shiny black cowboy boots. It was a stretch from the customary brown uniforms the rest of his department wore, but he still looked official. Perhaps it was simply the way he carried himself, straight and tall, self-assured with long, confident strides.

"O'Dell, are you okay?" he asked again.

She looked around the church. It seemed large for a town of Platte City's size, with rows and rows of wooden pews. She couldn't imagine all of them being filled.

"I'm fine," she finally answered, then regretted taking so long because he truly did look concerned. His eyes betrayed his fresh appearance, still puffy from too little sleep. She had tried to hide her own signs of fatigue with a bit of makeup.

"It seems so big," she said, trying to explain her distraction.

"It's relatively new. The old church was a small country parish about five miles south of town," he told her. "Platte City's grown, practically doubled in the last ten years. Mostly people tired of living in the city. They still commute to work either in Omaha or Lincoln. Kind of ironic, huh? People moving out here to get away from big-city crime, thinking they'll raise their kids someplace quiet and safe." He shoved his hands into his pockets and stared off over her head.

"You folks need some help?" A man appeared from a curtain behind the altar.

"We're looking for Father Francis," Morrelli said without offering any more explanation.

The man eyed them suspiciously. Though he carried a broom, he was dressed in dress slacks, a crisply pressed shirt, tie and long, brown cardigan. He looked young despite his dark hair peppered with gray. When he approached them, Maggie noticed he had a slight limp and wore bright white tennis shoes.

"What do you want with Father Francis?"

Morrelli glanced at Maggie as if asking how much to reveal. Before he had a chance to say anything, the man seemed to recognize Morrelli.

"Wait a minute. I know who you are." He said it as if it were an accusation. "Didn't you play quarterback for the Nebraska Cornhuskers? You're Morrelli, Nick Morrelli, 1982 to 1983."

"You're a Cornhuskers fan?" Morrelli grinned, obviously pleased by the recognition. Maggie noticed dimples. A quarterback—why wasn't she surprised?

"Big-time fan. My name's Ray...Ray Howard. I just moved back here last spring. They didn't televise very many games back East. It was horrible, just horrible. Actually, I played a bit." His excitement rambled on in quick bursts. "In high school. At Omaha Central. Even had Dr. Tom come check me out. Then I boogered up my knee. Our final game. Against Creighton Prep, of all the sissy teams. I twisted it up pretty good. Never played again."

"Sorry to hear that," Nick said.

"Yeah, the Lord moves in mysterious ways. So, is this here your wife?" He finally acknowledged Maggie. She felt his eyes slide over her body, and she resisted the urge to button her jacket.

"No, we're not married." Morrelli seemed embarrassed.

"Your fiancée then. That's probably what you want to see Father Francis about, huh? He's married hundreds."

"No, we're not—"

"It's an official matter," Maggie interrupted, relieving Morrelli. The man stared at her, waiting for an explanation. Now she crossed her arms over her chest, emphasizing her authority and stifling his wandering eyes. "Is Father Francis here?"

Howard looked at Morrelli, then back at Maggie when he realized neither was willing to say more.

"I think he's in back changing. He said mass this morning." He made no effort to leave.

"Would you mind getting him for us, Ray?" Morrelli asked much more politely than Maggie would have.

"Oh, sure." He turned to leave, then stopped. "Who should I say wants to see him?" He looked at Maggie, waiting for an introduction.

Maggie sighed and shifted her weight impatiently. Morrelli shot her a look, then said, "Just tell him Nick Morrelli, okay?"

"Oh, sure."

Howard disappeared behind the curtain. This time Maggie rolled her eyes at Morrelli, and he smiled. "A quarterback, huh?" she said.

"That was a long time ago. Actually, it seems like a lifetime ago."

"Were you any good?"

"I had a chance to go on and play for the Dolphins, but my dad insisted on law school."

"Do you always do everything your dad tells you to do?"

She meant it as a joke, but he bristled, and his eyes told her it was a touchy subject. Then he smiled, and said, "Apparently, I do."

"Nicholas." A small gray-haired priest glided onto the altar in his black, floor-length cassock. "Mr. Howard said you had official business to talk to me about."

"Hello, Father Francis. Sorry I didn't call before we dropped in on you."

"That's perfectly all right. You're always welcome here."

"Father, this is Special Agent Maggie O'Dell. She's with the FBI and is here to help me on the Alverez case."

Maggie offered her hand. The old priest took it in both of his and held it tightly. Thick blue veins protruded from the thin, brown-spotted skin. A slight tremor jiggled her hand. He looked deep into her eyes, and suddenly she felt exposed, as though he could see clear into her soul. A slight shiver slid down her back as she held his gaze.

"It's a pleasure to meet you." When he let go, he grasped the nearby podium, depending on it for strength. "Christine's son, Timmy, reminds me of you, Nicholas. He's one of Father Keller's altar boys." Then to Maggie, he said, "Nicholas was an altar boy for me years ago at the old St. Margaret's."

"Really?" Maggie glanced at Morrelli, anxious to witness his discomfort. Something behind him caught her eye. The altar curtain moved. There was no breeze, no draft. Then she saw the toes of two white tennis shoes poking out from underneath. Instead of drawing attention to the intruder, she smiled at Morrelli, who now seemed flustered by the priest's attention.

"Father Francis." He was anxious to change the subject. "We wondered if you could answer a few questions."

"Certainly. What can I do to help?" He looked at Maggie.

"I understand you heard Ronald Jeffreys' last confession," Nick continued.

"Yes, but I cannot share any of that with you. I hope you understand." His voice was suddenly frail, as though the subject drained the energy from him.

Maggie wondered whether he was sick, something terminal that would explain the gray pallor to his skin. Even his breathing came in thick, short gasps when he talked. When he was silent, a soft wheeze lifted his bony shoulders in an odd rhythm.

"Of course, we understand," she lied. The fact was, she didn't understand, but she prevented the impatience from creeping into her tone. "However, if there is anything that would shed light on the Alverez case, I would hope you'd share it with us."

"O'Dell, that's Irish Catholic, yes?"

Maggie was startled and annoyed by his distraction. "Yes, it is." Now she allowed a bit of the impatience to slip out. He didn't seem to notice.

"And Maggie, named for our very own St. Margaret."

"Yes, I suppose so. Father Francis, you do understand that if Ronald Jeffreys confessed anything that would lead us to Danny Alverez's murderer, you must tell us?"

"The sanctity of confession is to be preserved even for condemned murderers, Agent O'Dell."

Maggie sighed and glanced back at Morrelli, who also looked as though he was becoming impatient with the old priest.

"Father," Morrelli said. "There's something else you might be able to help us with. Who, other than a priest, can or is allowed to administer last rites?"

Father Francis looked confused by the change of subject. "The sacrament of extreme unction should be administered by a priest, but in extreme circumstances, it's not necessary."

"Who else would know how?"

"Before Vatican II, it was taught in the Baltimore Catechism. The two of you may be too young to remember. Today, I believe, it is taught only in the seminary, although it may still be a part of some deacon training."

"And what are the requirements for becoming a deacon?" Maggie asked, frustrated that this might add to their list of suspects.

"There are rigorous standards. Of course, one must be in good standing with the church. And unfortunately, only men can be deacons. I'm not sure I understand what any of this has to do with Ronald Jeffreys."

"I'm afraid we can't share that with you, Father." Morrelli smiled. "No disrespect intended." Morrelli glanced at Maggie, waiting to see if she had anything more. Then he said, "Thanks for your help, Father Francis."

He motioned to her for them to leave, but she stared at Father Francis, hoping to see something in the hooded eyes that held hers. It was almost as though they were waiting for her to see what they revealed. Yet, the priest only nodded at her and smiled.

Morrelli touched her shoulder. She turned on her heels and marched out alongside him. Outside on the church steps she stopped suddenly. Morrelli was down on the sidewalk before he realized she wasn't beside him. He looked up at her and shrugged.

"What's wrong?"

"He knows something. There's something about Jeffreys that he's not telling us."

"That he *can't* tell us."

She spun around and ran back up the steps.

"O'Dell, what are you doing?"

She heard Morrelli behind her as she threw open the heavy front door and walked quickly up the aisle. Father Francis was just leaving the altar, disappearing behind the thick curtains.

"Father Francis," Maggie yelled to him. The echo instantly made her feel as though she had broken some rule, committed some sin. It did, however, stop Father Francis. He came back to the middle of the altar where he watched her hurry up the aisle. Morrelli was close behind.

"If you know something... If Jeffreys told you something that could prevent another murder... Father, isn't saving the life of an innocent little boy worth breaking the confidence of a confessed serial killer?"

She didn't realize until now that she was breathless. She waited, staring into those eyes that knew so much more than they were willing or able to reveal.

"What I can tell you is that Ronald Jeffreys told nothing but the truth."

"Excuse me?" Her impatience was rapidly changing to anger.

"From the day he confessed to the crime to the day he was executed, Ronald Jeffreys told only the truth." His eyes lingered on Maggie's. But if there was something more they were saying, she couldn't see it. "Now, if you'll excuse me."

Morrelli was at her side. They stood quietly, watching the priest disappear behind the flowing fabric of the curtains.

"Jesus," Morrelli finally whispered. "What the hell does that mean?"

"It means we need to take a look at Jeffreys' original confession," she said, pretending to know what she was talking about. Then she turned and walked out, this time carefully keeping her heels from clicking noisily on the marble floor.

CHAPTER 19

He skidded out of the church parking lot. The bag of groceries tumbled across the seat and spilled onto the floor. Oranges rolled underneath his feet as he pressed down on the accelerator.

He needed to calm down. He searched the rearview mirror. No one followed. They had come to the church asking questions. Questions about Jeffreys. He was safe. They knew nothing. Even that newspaper reporter had insinuated that Danny's murder was a copycat. Someone copycatting Jeffreys. Why hadn't it occurred to any of them that Jeffreys was the copycat? The fact that Jeffreys had also been a cold-blooded murderer had simply made him the perfect patsy.

Within blocks of the school, parents scurried like frightened rats leading their children, huddling at intersections. They carted them to the curb. They watched them skip up the steps of the school until they were safely inside. Until now, they hardly noticed their children, left them alone for hours, pretending that "latchkey" was a term of endearment. Leaving them with bruises and scars that, if not stopped, would last a lifetime. And now those same parents were learning. He was actually doing them a favor, providing a precious service.

The wind hinted at snow, biting and whipping at jackets and skirts that would be quickly out of season. It reminded him of the blanket in the trunk. Did it still have blood on it? He tried to remember, tried to think while he watched the rats cover the sidewalks and clog the intersections. He stopped at a stop sign. Waited for the crossing guards. A stream of rats crossed. One recognized him and waved. He smiled and waved back.

No, he had washed the blanket. There was no blood. The bleach had worked miracles. And it would be warm, should the weather turn cold.

As he drove out of town, he noticed a flock of geese overhead getting into formation like fighter pilots from the base. He rolled down his window and listened. The squawks and honks cut through the crisp morning air. Yes, this time the thick, bulging clouds would bring snow, not rain. He could feel it in his bones.

He hated the cold, hated snow. It reminded him of too many Christmases, quietly unwrapping the few presents his mother had secretly put under the tree for him. Following his mother's instructions, he would get up early Christmas morning and unwrap his gifts by himself. Quiet enough to hear his mother keeping his stepfather preoccupied in their bedroom, just several feet away.

His stepfather never suspected a thing, grateful for his own early-morning present. Had he found out, he and his mother would have both received beatings for their frivolous waste of his stepfather's hard-earned money. For it was that first Christmas beating that had initiated their secret tradition.

He turned onto Old Church Road and drove along the river. The riverbank was on fire with brilliant reds, oranges and yellows. Thousands of cattails waved at him, poking up out of the tall, honey-colored grass. The snow would ruin all of this. It would cover the vivid colors of life and leave its shroud of white death.

It wasn't much farther. Suddenly, he remembered the baseball cards. In a mad panic, he patted himself down, checking all his jacket pockets while he steered with one hand. The car veered sharply to the right. The tire slammed into a deep rut before he twisted the steering wheel and gained control. Finally, he felt the bulge in the back pocket of his jeans.

He pulled off the road into a grove of plum trees. The canopy of branches and leaves hid the car. He stuffed the spilled groceries back into the sack and shoved it under his arm. He popped the trunk. The thick wool blanket was rolled neatly and tied with rope. He grabbed it and slung it over his shoulder. He slammed the trunk, its echo bouncing off the trees and water. It was quiet and peaceful despite the wind whispering through the branches, threatening to bring cold. It swept up the smell of river water, a wonderful musty mixture of silt, fish and decay. He stopped to watch the water rolling in ripples and waves, moving quickly and carrying with it driftwood and other debris. It was alive and dangerous with powers of destruction. It was alive and redemptive with powers of healing and cleansing.

The muddy leaves hid the wooden door so well that even he had to search for its exact location. He cleared it of all debris, then, with both hands, yanked and pulled until it creaked open. A haze of light dimly lit the steps as he descended into the earth. Immediately, the smell of wet dirt, moist with mold, filled his lungs. As soon as he reached the bottom, he put down the sack and blanket.

From his jacket pocket he pulled the rubber mask. It was better than the ski mask, less frightening and more appropriate for this time of year. Although he hated the damn thing. But even more, he hated remembering the look in Danny's eyes, recognizing him, trusting him and then looking at him as though betrayed. If only Danny had understood. But that look and that damn cross around the boy's neck had almost unraveled him. No, he couldn't take any more chances. He yanked on the mask. In seconds, his face began to perspire.

Like a zombie, with hands and arms outstretched, he took small steps until he bumped into the wooden shelf. His fingers found the lantern and matches. Fur brushed against his skin. He jerked his hand away, hitting the lantern and catching it without seeing it before it slid off the shelf.

"Damn rats," he muttered.

His fingers lifted the rusty metal. He struck the match and lit the wick on the first try. The dark came to life in the yellow glow. Pieces of dirt wall crumbled and filtered down on him. He avoided looking up at the scratchy skitters of night creatures escaping. He waited. In a few seconds they would find new darkness and all would be safe and quiet again.

He shoved his weight against the thick wooden shelf, using his shoulder to push. The heavy structure groaned, wobbled and began to move. It scraped against the floor, taking clumps of dirt with it. Sweat rolled down his back. The mask was excruciatingly hot—his face crushed by a vapor lock. Finally, the secret passage revealed itself. He crawled through the small hole, reaching back to grab the sack and drag the blanket.

He hoped Matthew enjoyed the baseball cards.

CHAPTER 20

The Tanner house sat on the corner of its block at the edge of town. Behind it stretched an open field where huge, yellow construction equipment chomped at the landscape like hungry monsters removing trees in one gulp. It was one of the sights Nick hated most about Platte City's rapid growth. Countryside covered with pink wild roses, blazing goldenrod and waving prairie grass suddenly turned into perfect sections of bluegrass and gray pavement sprinkled with plastic swing sets and Big Wheels.

"Jesus," he muttered at the line of vehicles parked in front of the Tanner house.

"You have someone here to contain things?" O'Dell asked.

Nick glanced at her next to him in his Jeep.

"I'm only asking, Morrelli. There's no need to get defensive."

She was right. There was no accusation in her tone. He needed to remember that she was on his side. So he filled her in on what he had done so far, details they hadn't had time to discuss in the early hours of the morning.

Last night, almost near panic, he and Hal Langston had set up a mini-command post in Michelle Tanner's living room. Grudgingly, he had relied on lessons Bob Weston had taught him during the Alverez case. Within minutes of Michelle Tanner's desperate phone call, Nick had sent Phillip Van Dorn to tap her phones and set up a surveillance around her house. Before midnight Lucy Burton had begun converting the sheriff's office conference room into a strategy briefing room with maps and enlarged photos of Matthew tacked up and a hot line ready.

This time Nick had immediately called in the county police chiefs from neighboring Richfield, Staton and Bennet for extra feet to scour the alleys, surrounding fields and even the riverbank. His own men had gone door-to-door, instructed to politely ask questions without stirring panic. If that was possible. In fact, he wondered if it may already be too late. Especially after this morning's drive and witnessing the panic of parents accompanying their children to school. The frenzy had already begun, thanks to his sister. He hated to think what would happen when everyone found out about Matthew. Nick knew he was fooling himself if he thought he could stop the frenzy or even contain it.

The front door of the Tanner house was open. The chatter of voices drifted into the yard. O'Dell knocked on the screen door and waited. Nick would have knocked and entered. Standing so close behind her he noticed she was about six inches shorter than he was. He leaned closer to smell her hair just as a breeze whipped several strands against his chin in a soft caress.

Her fingers brushed her hair back into place, almost grazing his skin. He stepped back and watched her tuck the unruly strand behind her ear, revealing soft, white skin. This morning she wore a dark burgundy suit jacket and matching trousers. The color made her skin seem softer, smoother.

The screen door screeched on old hinges as a man Nick didn't recognize opened it just enough to examine the two of them.

"Who are you?" the man asked suspiciously, wasting no time on good manners as his eyes darted over them.

"It's okay." Hal Langston came up behind him and gently nudged the man to the side. Hal grabbed the screen door and opened it. The man shot Hal a look, but walked away. Hal could be as imposing as hell when he wanted. He and Nick had played football together in high school, and although Hal had added some softness to his bulk, he was still in good shape.

"Married life," he explained when Nick teased him about the extra weight. "You should try it, buddy," he would always add. And to his credit, Hal had snagged one of the best catches in town.

Tess Langston had moved to Platte City ten years before to teach high-school history. As beautiful as she was smart, she had intimidated all the bachelors who drooled in her presence. All but Hal. For almost three weeks, he had called Nick, who'd been tucked away out East in law school, every night, racking up his long-distance bill. Between torts and breaches of contract, Nick had helped plot Hal's next move.

Nick wrote snippets of poetry, recommended what flowers—daisies, not roses—and even advised when and where to touch—gentle flicks to the earlobe when cuddling, no breast groping. He had felt as though he was wooing Tess himself, so much so that, when the calls stopped, Nick had felt a loss. It wasn't until later he realized the loss wasn't of his buddy, but of a woman he had met only once and had come to know so intimately through his friend that he, himself, had fallen in love.

Hal and Tess had married after six short months, and even today Nick felt a closeness to Tess that he could never explain. Didn't want to explain, really. He had no idea whether Hal had shared with her the secrets of their courtship, yet sometimes Tess looked at Nick in a way that told him she knew, and that she was grateful.

The Tanner living room was filled with his deputies and with police officers he didn't recognize. Some were drinking coffee, while others huddled over notes and maps. Nick looked for Michelle Tanner and wondered whether he would recognize her. Last night in her pink chenille robe and red eyes and blotchy face, she had looked drunk and disoriented. Her red hair had fallen partially out of its bun and flew around her head like wild snakes. Her entire small body had seemed to convulse with arms swinging and legs pacing.

The kitchen was clogged with more bodies.

"Who the fuck are all these people, Hal?" He turned and bumped into Hal, who was close behind. O'Dell had wandered over to Phillip Van Dorn, and without any introduction seemed to have Phil revealing all his secrets of the technology he strung around the house.

"It was her idea," Hal whispered in his defense. "She called a few neighbors, her mother, the parents of her kid's soccer team."

"Jesus, Hal. We've got the whole fucking soccer team here!"

"Just a few parents."

Nick elbowed his way through the crowd. Then he began shoving when he recognized the woman sitting at the table, sipping coffee with Michelle Tanner.

"What the hell are you doing here?" he bellowed, and the entire room went silent.

CHAPTER 21

Before Christine could answer, her brother charged through the group, spilling Emily Fulton's coffee and almost knocking Paul Calloway to the floor. Everyone stared as Nick pointed his finger at her and said to Michelle Tanner, "Mrs. Tanner, do you realize this woman is a reporter?"

Michelle Tanner was a petite woman, slender to the point of being frail and, from what Christine had already learned, easily intimidated. Michelle's small face went pale, the large hazel eyes widened. She looked at Christine, fumbled with her coffee cup, then stared at it as though surprised by its *click-clack* rattle amplified in the silence. Finally, she looked up at Nick.

"Yes, Sheriff Morrelli. I'm well aware that Christine is a reporter." She folded her hands together, apparently noticed a slight tremor and tucked them under the table, safely into her lap. With her eyes now on her coffee, she continued, "We think it would be beneficial to have something in tonight's paper...about Matthew." The tremor was now in her voice.

Christine saw Nick softening. If there was one thing her macho brother couldn't handle, it was a tearful woman. She had used them herself, though there was nothing manipulative about Michelle Tanner's tears.

"Mrs. Tanner, I'm sorry, but I don't think that's a good idea."

"Actually, it's a very good idea."

Christine shifted in her chair, so she could see the woman who appeared from behind Nick. She could have been a model, with flawless skin, lovely high cheekbones, full pouty lips and silky, short dark hair. Her suit draped over a slender, athletic figure with enough curves to hold every man's attention in the room. However, her voice and stance showed she was unaware of the effect of her femininity. She carried herself confidently and with an air of authority. This woman was not easily intimidated by anything or anyone, let alone a roomful of people who had no idea who she was. Already, Christine liked her.

"Excuse me?" Nick seemed irritated with the woman.

"I think it would be a good idea to involve the media right away."

Nick glanced around the room. He looked uncomfortable and flustered.

"Can I talk to you a minute? Alone." He took the woman's arm, but she immediately jerked it away. Still, she turned to leave the room with him. The crowd opened for her exit. Nick followed.

"Excuse me." Christine patted Michelle's hand. She grabbed her notebook. Despite Nick's fury, she wanted to meet the woman who had just put him in his place. This had to be the FBI expert from Quantico, Special Agent Maggie O'Dell. She wondered what information Agent O'Dell might be willing to supply. Information Nick would keep in a vise grip if it meant protecting his precious reputation.

Nick and Agent O'Dell huddled in a corner of the living room next to the bay window that overlooked the front yard. Several of the police officers stared. Nick's men knew better and pretended to be occupied with their work.

"I told you he wouldn't like you being here," said a voice behind her.

Christine glanced over her shoulder at Hal. "Well, it looks like someone might be changing his mind."

"Yeah, he's definitely met his match with that one. I'm going outside for a smoke. Why don't you join me?"

"Thanks, no. I'm trying to quit."

"Suit yourself."

He headed out the front door. The screen whined, then slammed. Nick and Agent O'Dell didn't even notice. Nick spoke in a hushed tone, confining his anger with clenched teeth. Agent O'Dell looked unscathed by any of it, her voice calm and even.

"Excuse me for interrupting." As she approached Christine felt Nick's glare like a slap in the face. She avoided his eyes. "You must be Special Agent O'Dell. I'm Christine Hamilton." She offered her hand, and O'Dell took it without hesitation.

"Ms. Hamilton."

The grip was strong and steady.

"In his fury I'm sure Nicky failed to tell you that I'm his sister."

O'Dell glanced up at Nick, and Christine thought she saw a hint of a smile on the otherwise stoic face.

"I wondered if there was a personal connection."

"He's obviously pissed at me, so it's hard for him to see that I'm really here to help."

"I'm sure you are."

"So, you won't mind answering some questions?"

"I'm sorry, Ms. Hamilton..."

"Christine."

"Of course, Christine. Despite my opinions, this isn't my investigation. I'm here strictly to profile this case."

Christine knew without looking at him that Nick was smiling now. It only made her angry. "So what does that mean? Another press blackout like in the Alverez case? Nicky, that's only going to make matters worse."

"Actually, Christine, I think Sheriff Morrelli has changed his mind," O'Dell said, watching Nick, whose smile transformed into a grimace.

He pushed his hair from his forehead. O'Dell folded her arms over her chest and waited. Christine looked from one to the other. The tension filled the corner, and she found herself taking a step backward.

Finally, Nick cleared his throat as though his discomfort was lodged somewhere between his larynx and tongue. "There'll be a press conference in the courthouse lobby tomorrow morning at eight-thirty."

"Can I print that in tonight's article?" She looked from Nick to O'Dell and back to Nick.

"Sure," he grudgingly answered.

"Anything else I can use in tonight's article?"

"No."

"Sheriff Morrelli, didn't you say you already have copies of the boy's photo?" Again, O'Dell said this very matter-of-factly, no underlying edge. "It may jog some memories if Christine included one with her piece."

He shoved his hands into his pockets, and Christine wondered whether it was so he wouldn't strangle both her and O'Dell.

"Stop by the courthouse and pick one up. I'll instruct Lucy to leave it at the front desk. The front desk, Christine. I don't want you in my office snooping around."

"Relax, Nicky. I keep telling you I'm not the enemy." She started to leave, but turned back at the door. "You're still coming over for dinner tonight, aren't you?"

"I may be too busy."

"Agent O'Dell, would you like to join us? Nothing fancy. I'm fixing spaghetti. There'll be plenty of Chianti."

"Thanks, that sounds nice."

Christine almost burst out laughing at the surprise on Nick's face.

"I'll see the two of you about seven. Nicky knows the address."

CHAPTER 22

The sheriff's department bristled with nervous energy. Nick could feel it as soon as he and O'Dell walked in the door. Here he was, worried about a frenzy taking over the community, and he had one in his own department.

Phones rang incessantly. Machines beeped. Keyboards clicked. Faxes hummed. Radios squawked. Voices yelled out to each other from room to room. Bodies dashed and scurried, amazingly not bumping into one another.

Again, there were police officers he didn't recognize and equipment he couldn't identify. He was depending on people he barely knew to handle things he hardly understood. It made him as uncomfortable as hell.

Lucy looked relieved to see him. She smiled and waved from across the room. There was a quick glance of contempt in O'Dell's direction. O'Dell didn't seem to notice.

"Nick, we've checked every inch of this city," Lloyd Benjamin's voice rasped with exhaustion. He removed his glasses and wiped his eyes. The deep worry lines in his forehead were pronounced, like permanent indents. The oldest member of Nick's team, Lloyd was also the most reliable next to Hal. "Richfield's men are still checking the river where we found the Alverez kid. I've got Staton's men on the north side of town. They're going to check that gravel pit and Northton Lake."

"Good. That's good, Lloyd." Nick patted him on the back. There was something else. Lloyd rubbed his jaw, glanced at O'Dell.

"Some of us were talking," Lloyd continued in a low voice, almost a whisper. "Stan Lubrick thought he remembered Jeffreys having a partner...you know...sort of a...well, a lover, at the time he was arrested. I do kind of remember us bringing a guy in for questioning, but I don't think he ever testified. A Mark Rydell," he said, scanning a notepad with illegible scratches. "We were wondering if we should try and check the guy out. See if he's anywhere around."

They both looked at O'Dell, who was distracted by the chaos. Nick wasn't even sure she had heard Lloyd. Her hands were shoved deep into her jacket pockets. Her eyes darted back and forth, watching the commotion. Then suddenly, she seemed flustered when she realized they were waiting for her to answer.

"I didn't realize Jeffreys was gay. How do know this guy was his lover?" Again, her tone was matter-of-fact. No hint of condescension, though Nick knew she was capable of turning stubborn speculation into ridiculous trivia.

Lloyd loosened his tie and collar. The subject obviously made him uncomfortable.

"Well, they were living together at the time."

"Wouldn't that make them roommates?"

O'Dell was as tough and unflinching as she was beautiful. Nick found himself relieved that this time he wasn't on the other side of her questions. Lloyd looked to him for help. Nick only shrugged.

"Is it possible to check if Rydell kept in touch with Jeffreys after he was sentenced?" O'Dell asked Lloyd, instead of dismissing his hunch.

"They may have some information at the penitentiary."

"You might check out what other visitors Jeffreys had or who else he may have kept in touch with. See if there were any prisoners or even guards he befriended. On death row they don't have much contact with other prisoners, but there may have been someone."

Nick liked the way her mind processed information quickly, refusing to disregard even the slightest details. A lead that Nick had believed far-fetched materialized into something substantial. Even Lloyd, who proudly came from a generation of keeping women in their place, seemed satisfied. He had added more scratches to his notes while O'Dell had been talking. Now he nodded at both of them and wandered off to find a phone.

Nick was impressed once again. O'Dell caught him watching her, and he simply smiled.

"Hey, Nick. That woman called again," Eddie Gillick called out from behind his desk, a phone cradled under his chin.

"Agent O'Dell, here's a fax from Quantico for you." Adam Preston handed her a roll of paper.

"What woman?" Nick asked Eddie.

"Sophie Krichek. Remember, she was the one who said she saw an old blue pickup in the area when the Alverez kid was snatched."

"Let me guess. She saw the pickup again. This time with another little boy who happens to look like Matthew Tanner."

"Wait a minute," O'Dell interrupted, looking up from the trail of fax paper that stretched to the floor. "What makes you think she's not serious?"

"She calls all the time," Nick explained.

"Nick, here's your messages." Lucy handed over a stack of pink "while you were out" slips and waited in front of him. She was dressed in the usual tight sweater and tight skirt. It would be so much easier to stop her if she didn't have such a voluptuous figure.

"Let me get this straight. You're not going to check out this lead because this woman has surpassed her quota of phone calls?" O'Dell had that look in her eyes that told Nick she thought he was bordering on incompetent. He wondered whether it had anything to do with his slight distraction over Lucy's stretched blue-and-green-knit stripes.

"Three weeks ago she called to tell us she saw Jesus in her backyard pushing a little girl on a swing set. She doesn't even have a backyard. She lives in an apartment complex with a concrete parking lot. Lucy, are the transcripts from Jeffreys' confession and trial here yet?"

"Max said she'd bring them over herself as soon as possible." Lucy swayed on the spike heels, and he knew it was strictly for his benefit. "They need to make copies of everything. Max won't let the originals out of the clerk's office. Oh, Agent O'Dell, a Gregory Stewart called for you like three or four times. He said it was important and that you have his number."

"Your boss checking up on you?" Nick smiled at O'Dell, who suddenly looked distraught.

"No, my husband. Is there a phone I can use?"

Nick's smile disappeared. He glanced at her hand. No wedding ring. Yes, he was sure he had checked before, simply out of habit. She was waiting for an answer.

"You can use my office," he said, trying to sound disinterested and shuffling through the stack of messages. "Down the hall, last door on the right."

"Thanks."

As soon as she disappeared around the corner, Eddie Gillick stopped beside Nick on his way to the fax machine. "Why do you look so surprised, Nick? She's quite a catch. Why wouldn't she be married?"

It was ridiculous. This morning at Michelle Tanner's he had been ready to strangle her. But now he suddenly felt as if someone had punched him in the stomach.

CHAPTER 23

The office was simple and small with a gray metal desk and matching credenza. Shelves displayed a variety of trophies—all football championships of some sort. Several pictures hung on the wall behind the desk. Maggie sank into the soft leather chair, the only extravagance in the otherwise plain office. She picked up the phone while she got a better look at the wall of honor.

There were several photos of young men clad in red and white football jerseys. One photo was obviously a young Morrelli under the sweat and dirt. He stood proudly next to an older gentleman, who, from the scratched autograph, was a Coach Osborne.

In the corner, almost hidden behind a file cabinet, hung two framed degrees collecting dust. One was from the University of Nebraska. The other was a law degree from... Maggie almost dropped the phone. The other was a law degree from Harvard University. She stood up to examine it more closely, then sat back down, embarrassed that she even, for one fleeting moment, thought it a fake, a practical joke. It was, in fact, very real.

She looked back at the football photo. Sheriff Nicholas Morrelli was certainly full of surprises. The more she learned, the more curious she became. It didn't help matters that they seemed to spark off each other with an unhealthy amount of electricity. It was a part of Nick Morrelli's personality. It was not, however, a part of her own, and she found it annoying.

She and Greg had always had a comfortable relationship. Even in the beginning it wasn't so much heat or chemistry that had brought them together, but friendship and common goals. Goals that had changed over the years.

And a friendship that had turned to complacency. They didn't even extend each other the common courtesies of friendship anymore. Lately, she wondered if they had drifted apart, or if they had ever been close.

It didn't matter. Marriage was something a person worked at, despite the changes. She believed that. She wouldn't have made it this far if she didn't. Now, at least, Greg had called her, made the first move toward reconciliation. That had to be a good sign.

She dialed his office and waited patiently through four, five, six rings.

"Brackman, Harvey and Lowe. How may I help you?"

"Greg Stewart, please."

"Mr. Stewart is in a meeting, may I take a message?"

"Could you please see if you can interrupt him. This is his wife. He's been trying to reach me all morning."

There was a pause while the receptionist decided how unreasonable a request it was. "One moment, please."

One moment turned into two, then three. Finally, after five minutes, Greg's voice said, "Maggie, thank God, I got ahold of you." His voice sounded urgent, but not remorseful. She was immediately disappointed instead of alarmed. "Why isn't your cellular phone turned on?" Even in his urgency he had to get in a scolding.

"I forgot to recharge it. I'll have it by this evening."

"Well, never mind." He sounded irritated, as if she were the one who had brought it up. "It's your mother." His tone automatically changed to that sympathetic one he used with clients who had just lost their case. She dug her fingernails into the leather armrest and waited for him to continue. "She's in the hospital."

Maggie leaned her head back, closed her eyes and swallowed hard. "What was it this time?"

"I think she might be getting serious, Maggie. She used a razor blade this time."

CHAPTER 24

Maggie hung up the phone and massaged her temples. A throbbing invaded her head, reaching down into her neck and shoulder blades. She had spent the last twenty minutes arguing with the doctor assigned to her mother's case. He had graduated at the top of his class, the arrogant, little bastard had reassured her. Fresh out of medical school and he thought he knew it all. Well, he didn't know her mother. He hadn't even looked at her history yet. When Maggie recommended he call her mother's therapist, he sounded relieved, even grateful when she gave him the name and phone number. She wondered how many people kept the name and phone number of their mother's therapist in their memory bank.

They *did* agree that Maggie shouldn't hop on the next plane to Richmond. Her mother was screaming for attention, but Maggie dropping everything and rushing to her side only seemed to reinforce the behavior. Or at least it had the last five times. Dear God, Maggie thought, one of these times her mother would succeed, if only by sheer accident. And although she agreed with Greg that razor blades were a serious advancement, the cuts—according to Dr. Boy Wonder—were horizontal, not vertical.

Maggie sank her throbbing head into the soft leather back of the chair and closed her eyes. She had been taking care of her mother since she was twelve. And what did a twelve-year-old girl, who had just lost her father, know about taking care of anyone? Sometimes she felt as though she had let her mother down, until she remembered that it was her mother who had abandoned her with her drunken stupors.

There was a soft tap on the frosted glass of the office door. Without prompting, the door eased open just enough for Morrelli to peek in.

"O'Dell, you okay in here?"

She remained paralyzed, her body scrunched down in the chair. Suddenly, legs, arms, everything seemed too heavy to move. "I'm fine," she managed to say, but knew immediately that she didn't sound or look very convincing.

His brow furrowed, and soft blue eyes showed concern. He hesitated, then came into the office slowly, cautiously. He set a can of Diet Pepsi in front of her. The cold condensation dripped down the side, and she wondered how long he had stood outside his own office before getting the nerve to come in.

"Thanks." She still made no effort to move, and it obviously made Morrelli uncomfortable. He stood with arms crossed, then shoved his hands into his pockets.

"You look like hell," he finally said.

"Thanks a lot, Morrelli." But she smiled.

"Listen, could you do me a favor? Call me Nick. Every time you call me Morrelli or Sheriff Morrelli, I start looking around for my dad."

"Okay, I'll try." Even her eyelids felt heavy. If she closed her eyes right this minute, would she finally sleep?

"Lucy is ordering lunch up from Wanda's. What can I get for you? Blue plate special on Monday is meat loaf, but I'd recommend the chicken-fried steak sandwich."

"I'm really not very hungry."

"I've been with you since two this morning, and you haven't eaten a thing. You need to eat, O'Dell. I'm not going to be responsible for you whittling away that cute little..." He caught himself, but it was too late. The embarrassment washed over his face. He wiped a hand across his jaw as if to erase it. "I'm ordering a ham and cheese sandwich for you." He turned to leave.

"On rye?"

He glanced at her over his shoulder. "Okay."

"And with hot mustard?"

Now he smiled, and there were definitely dimples. "You're a pain in the ass, you know that, O'Dell?"

"Hey, Nick." She stopped him again.

"What now?"

"Call me Maggie."

CHAPTER 25

"Do you like the baseball cards?" The mask muffled his voice. He sounded as though he were underwater. With all the dripping perspiration, he felt like it, too.

Matthew stared at him from the small bed in the corner. He sat on top of tangled bedcovers and hugged a pillow to his chest. His eyes were red and puffy. His hair stuck up in places. His soccer uniform was wrinkled. He hadn't even taken off his shoes to sleep last night.

Light filtered in through cracks in the boarded-up window. Pieces of broken glass rattled as the wind crept in through the rotted slats. It whistled and howled, creating a ghostly moan and licking at the corners of the posters hiding the cracked walls. It was the only sound in the room. The boy hadn't said a word all morning.

"Are you comfortable?" he asked.

When he approached, the boy skittered into the corner, smashing his small body against the crumbling plaster. The chain that connected his ankle to the steel bedpost clanked. There was enough length for the boy to reach the middle of the room. Yet, the cheeseburger and fries he had left last night sat untouched on the metal tray table. Even the triple-chocolate shake was still filled to the brim.

"Didn't you like your dinner, or do you prefer hot dogs? Maybe even chili dogs? You can have anything you want."

"I wanna go home," Matthew whispered, squeezing the pillow, one hand twisted so he could bite his fingernails. Several were chewed down to the quick and had bled during the night. Dried blood spotted the white cotton pillowcase. It would be hell to wash out.

"Maybe you'd enjoy comic books more than baseball cards. I have some old Flash Gordons I bet you'd like. I'll bring them with me next time."

He finished unpacking the contents of the grocery sack: three oranges, a bag of Cheetos, two Snickers bars, a six-pack of Hires root beer, two cans of SpaghettiOs and a snack pack of Jell-O chocolate pudding. He laid each item on the old wine crate he had found in what must have been a supply room. He had gone to great lengths to get all of Matthew's favorites.

"It may get chilly tonight," he said as he unrolled the thick wool blanket and draped it over the bed. "I'm sorry I can't leave a light. Is there anything else I can get for you?"

"I wanna go home," the boy whispered again.

"Your mom doesn't have the time to take care of you, Matthew."

"I want my mom."

"She's never home. And I bet she brings strange men home at night, doesn't she? Ever since she threw your dad out." He kept his voice calm and soothing.

"Please let me go home."

"She leaves you alone all the time. She works late. She even works on weekends."

"I just wanna go home." The boy began to cry, quiet sniffles he muffled with the pillow.

"And you can't stay with your dad." Calm and cool. He must remain calm, though already he could feel the anger starting in his gut. "Your dad beats you, doesn't he, Matthew?"

"I just wanna go home," the boy whined, no longer keeping quiet.

"I'm going to help you, Matthew. I'm going to save you. But you must be patient. Look, I brought all your favorite things."

But still, the boy cried, a high-pitched whine that made him grimace. He felt the explosion racing up from his stomach. He must control it. Calm, why couldn't he just remain calm? Yes, cool and calm.

"I wanna go home." The wail grated.

"Goddamn it! Shut up, you fucking crybaby."

CHAPTER 26

Christine's article in the evening edition hit downtown Omaha's newsstands at three-thirty. By four o'clock, newspaper carriers tossed the rolled-up *Omaha Journal* onto porches and lawns in Platte City. By four-ten, phones started ringing nonstop in the sheriff's department.

Nick assigned Phillip Van Dorn the task of adding more phones and phone lines, even suggesting to go as far as commandeering the county clerk's office down the hall. This was exactly what he had hoped to avoid. The frenzy had officially begun, and already Nick could feel it churning up his insides.

Angry citizens demanded to know what was being done. City Hall wanted to know how much the extra personnel and equipment would cost the city. Reporters badgered for an interview of their own, not wanting to wait for the morning press conference. Some were already camped out in the courthouse lobby, restrained by manpower better used on the street.

Of course, there were also leads. Maggie was right. Matthew's photo jogged plenty of memories. The problem was sorting the real leads from the crackpot ones—although Maggie insisted the crackpot leads could not be thrown out entirely. Tomorrow Nick would even send someone to check on Sophie Krichek's story about an old blue pickup. He still believed it would be a waste of time. Krichek was just some lonely old woman looking for attention. But he didn't want anyone thinking he hadn't checked every lead, especially Maggie.

"Nick, Angie Clark has called for you four times." Lucy caught up with him in the hallway, obviously irritated with being the messenger for his love life.

"Next time tell her I'm sorry, but I just don't have time to talk."

She seemed pleased and started to walk away, but spun back. "Oh, I almost forgot. Max is on her way down the hall with those transcripts from Jeffreys' confession and trial."

"Great. Tell Agent O'Dell, would you please?"

"Where do you want me to put them?" She skipped alongside him as he made his way to his office.

"Can't you just give them to Agent O'Dell?"

"All five boxes?"

He stopped so suddenly she bumped into him. He grabbed her by the elbows as she teetered on her two-inch spiked heels.

"There's five boxes?"

"You know Max. She's pretty thorough, so everything's labeled and cataloged. She said to tell you she also included copies of all the evidence that was entered and logged, as well as affidavits from witnesses who didn't testify."

"Five boxes?" He shook his head. "Put them in my office."

"Okay." She turned to leave, then stopped again. "Do you still want me to tell Agent O'Dell?"

"Yes, please." Her distrust, contempt—whatever it was—for Maggie was beginning to wear thin.

"Oh, and the mayor's holding on line three for you."

"Lucy, we can't afford to hold up any of those lines."

"I know, but he insisted. I couldn't just hang up on him."

Yes, he was sure Brian Rutledge would have insisted. He was a royal pain in the ass.

Nick retreated to his office. Behind closed doors he plopped into his leather chair and uncinched his tie. He wrestled with the collar button, almost ripping it off. He dug a thumb and forefinger into his eyes, trying to remember how much sleep he had gotten since Friday. Finally, he grabbed the phone and punched line three.

"Hi, Brian. It's Nick."

"Nick, what the hell's going on over there? I've been on hold for goddamn near twenty minutes."

"Don't mean to inconvenience you, Brian. We're a little busy."

"I've got a crisis of my own, Nick. City council thinks I should cancel

Halloween. Goddamn it, Nick, I cancel Halloween and I look like the goddamn Grinch."

"I think the Grinch is Christmas, Brian."

"Goddamn it, Nick. This isn't funny."

"I'm not laughing, Brian. But you know what? I have a few more serious things to worry about than Halloween."

Lucy peeked in from behind his door. He waved her in. She opened the door and motioned for the four men following her to set the boxes in the corner under the window.

"Halloween is serious, Nick. What if this nut ends up pulling something when all those kids are out running around in the dark?"

Rutledge's whiny, tin voice grated on Nick's nerves. He smiled and mouthed "thank you," to Maxine Cramer, who had hauled in the final box. Even at the end of the day and after hauling a box halfway down the hall, her royal-blue suit held its sharply pressed seams. Her blue-gray, salon-permed hair matched her suit, not a strand out of place. She smiled back at Nick and nodded, then made her way out the door.

"Brian, what do you want from me?"

"I want to know how goddamn serious this thing is. Do you have any suspects? Are you making any arrests in the near future? What the hell are you doing over there?"

"One boy is dead and another is missing. How goddamn serious do you think this is, Brian? As far as how I handle the investigation, it's none of your fucking business. We need this phone line open for more useful things than reassuring your sorry ass, so don't call again." He slammed the phone down and noticed O'Dell standing in the doorway, watching him.

"Sorry." She seemed embarrassed to have witnessed his fury. Twice in one day. She must think he was a madman, a raving lunatic, or worse, simply incompetent. "Lucy told me the transcripts were in here."

"They are. Come on in. Close the door behind you."

She hesitated as though assessing whether it was safe to be behind closed doors with him.

"That was the mayor," Nick explained. "He wanted to know if I'm going to have an arrest made by Friday, so he won't have to cancel Halloween."

"What did you tell him?"

"Pretty much what you just heard. The boxes are here under the window." He rolled his chair around to point to them, then kept it there to stare out the window. He was tired of cloudy weather. Sick of rain. He couldn't remember the last time there'd been a full day of sunshine. It was as though all of Sarpy County were trapped under one of those glass globes. The kind you shake and it snows. Only here, you shake it and the clouds rolled in, over and over again—the same clouds, rounding the globe and passing over again.

O'Dell was on her knees. She had several box lids off and files scattered on the floor around her.

"Can I get you a chair?" he offered, but made no motion to leave his own.

"No, thanks. It'll be easier this way."

She looked as though she had found what she was looking for. She opened the file and began scanning the contents, flipping pages, then settling on one. Suddenly, her entire face went serious. Her eyes darted over the page. She sat back on her feet.

"What is it?" Nick leaned forward, trying to see what had grabbed hold of her so intensely.

"It's Jeffreys' original confession, right after his arrest. It's very detailed, from the kind of tape he used to bind the hands and feet to the carvings on the hunting knife he used." She spoke slowly, continuing to scan the document.

"Okay, and Father Francis said Jeffreys hadn't lied. That means the details are true. So what?"

"Did you realize that Jeffreys confessed to murdering only Bobby Wilson? In fact," she said, flipping through several more pages, "in fact, he was adamant about having nothing to do with the other two boys' murders."

"I don't remember hearing any of that. They probably thought he was lying."

"But if he wasn't?" She looked up at him, her brown eyes haunted by something more than the file she held.

"Okay, if he wasn't lying, and he did kill only Bobby Wilson…" Nick didn't finish. Suddenly, he felt sick to his stomach, even before Maggie finished his sentence.

"Then the real serial killer got away, and he's back."

CHAPTER 27

Christine hoped Nick didn't detect the relief in her voice when he called to cancel dinner. If this new lead panned out, she'd be working late to claim yet another front page on tomorrow morning's paper.

"Can we do it tomorrow night?" he asked, almost apologetic.

"Sure, no problem. Is something big going down tonight?" she added, just to push his buttons.

"This newfound success of yours is ugly on you, Christine." He sounded tired, drained of energy.

"Ugly or not, it feels wonderful."

"So this number the paper gave me, it sounds like a cellular?"

"Yep, just one of the perks of my new, ugly success. Look, Nick." She needed to change the subject before he asked where she was or where she was headed. "Can you please bring your sleeping bag tomorrow night when you come over? Remember, Timmy asked if he could borrow it for his camping trip?"

"They're going camping on Halloween?"

"They'll be back Friday night. Father Keller has mass. Remember, for All Saints' Day? Will you remember the sleeping bag?"

"Yes, I will."

"And don't forget Agent O'Dell."

"Right."

She turned the corner into the parking lot as she flipped her cellular phone closed and shoved it into her purse. Nick would be furious if he knew where she was.

The four-story apartment building looked run-down. The bricks were weathered and chipped. Rusted air conditioners hung out windows, clinging to rickety brackets. The building looked out of place in an old neighborhood of small, wooden-framed houses. Despite being old, the houses were well kept. Their backyards were filled with sandboxes, swing sets and huge old maples perfect for tree houses and hammocks.

The air filled with the smell of burning wood from someone's fireplace. A dog barked down the street, and she heard the tinkling of a wind chime. This was Danny Alverez's neighborhood. Danny's shiny, red bike had been found leaning against the chain-link fence that separated the apartment's parking lot from the rest of the neighborhood. It was right here that the horrors of his last days began. Here in a place he had come to take for granted as safe.

Inside the main entrance a heavy metal trash can held open the security door. It overflowed with cigarette butts falling onto the floor. Christine stepped carefully.

The elevator smelled of stale cigarettes and dog urine, and she eyed the stained carpet. She pushed the button for the fourth floor, stabbing it two, then three times before it lit up and the doors whined shut. The elevator rattled, shook and wheezed. She started to push the open-door button when the elevator finally started up slowly. Pulleys ground and whined.

She hated elevators. Hated small places. She should have taken the stairs. Her eyes searched for the emergency phone. There wasn't one. Seconds flew by and the light above showed only that she had reached the second floor. She punched three, hoping to cut short her trip, but the button crumbled into pieces. Frantically, she picked up the bigger pieces and began replacing them into the frame like a puzzle. Two stayed, one fell down into the hole, the others fell back to the floor. The elevator jolted to a stop, and finally its doors screeched open. Christine squeezed through before they were completely open.

She stopped in the hallway, leaning against the dirty wall, waiting to catch her breath. The light was dim, the carpeting filled with more stains. Again, the smell of dog urine mixed with the scent of old, musty newspapers and someone's burnt dinner. How could anyone live in a hole like this?

Apartment 410 was at the end of the hallway. A hand-braided welcome mat lay outside the scratched and battered door. The mat was clean, spotless.

Christine knocked and held her breath to avoid the hallway's suffocating odors. Several locks clicked inside, then the door opened just a crack. A pair of hooded and wrinkled blue eyes peered at her through thick glasses.

"Mrs. Krichek?" she asked as politely as possible while holding her breath.

"Are you that reporter?"

"Yes. Yes, I am. My name is Christine Hamilton."

The door opened, and she waited for the woman to back out of the way with her walker.

"Any relation to Ned Hamilton, owns the Quick Mart on the corner?"

"No, I don't think so. Hamilton is my ex-husband's name, and he isn't from around here."

"I see." The woman shuffled away.

Once inside, Christine was accosted by three large yellow and gray cats rubbing against her legs.

"I just fixed a pot of hot chocolate. Would you like some?"

She almost said yes, then saw the steaming pot on the coffee table where another large cat helped itself to several licks off the top.

"No, thank you." She hoped her voice disguised her disgust.

Other than the cats, the apartment smelled much cleaner than the hallway. The ammonia of a hidden litter box was obvious but bearable. Colorful afghans and quilts were draped over the couch and a rocker. Green plants hung above the windows, and crocheted doilies dotted an antique buffet and secretary's desk. Both tops were filled with black-and-white photos of servicemen, a young couple in front of an old Buick and three colored photos of a little girl at various stages of her life.

"Sit," the old woman instructed, backing herself into the rocker. "Oh, the pain in this shoulder," she said, rubbing the bony knob sticking up through her sweater. "Such pain I wouldn't wish on my worst enemy."

"I'm sorry to hear that."

Her bones did look brittle. Knobby knees stuck out from under her plain cotton housedress. Her round face twisted into a permanent scowl. Her brilliant blue eyes were magnified and distorted by the thick wire-rimmed glasses. Her white hair was twisted neatly into a bun, clasped by beautiful turquoise hair combs.

"It's hell getting old. If it wasn't for my cats, I think I'd call it quits."

Christine sat and watched her navy skirt fill with cat hair. Two of the cats still circled her legs while one jumped onto the back of the couch to take a closer look.

"Rummy, get down from there," the woman scolded, waving a bony finger at the cat. He ignored her.

"It's okay, Mrs. Krichek. I don't mind," she lied. "I'd like to get right to what you saw the morning Danny Alverez disappeared. You don't mind, do you?"

"No. Not at all. I'm glad somebody's finally interested."

"The sheriff's office has never come here to question you?"

"I called them twice. In fact, just this morning before I seen your article. They hemmed and hawed like they think I'm making it up or something. So, then I called you. I don't care what anybody says, I seen what I seen."

"And just what did you see, Mrs. Krichek?"

"I seen that boy park his bike and get in an old blue pickup."

"Are you sure it was the Alverez boy?"

"Seen him dozens of times. He was a good little paperboy. Brought my newspaper all the way to my door and laid it on my mat. Not like the kid we have now. He steps off the elevator and tosses it down here. Sometimes it makes it. Sometimes it doesn't. It's not easy getting this walker through that doorway. I think your paper should make sure those kids do a better job."

"I'll let them know. Mrs. Krichek, tell me about the pickup. Could you see the driver?"

"No. It was still dark out. I stood right at that there window. Sun was barely coming up. He pulled into the parking lot so that the passenger's side was all I could see. He must've said something to the boy, 'cause Danny leaned his bike against the fence, came around and got up into the pickup."

"Danny got into the pickup? Are you sure the man didn't grab him and pull him in?"

"No, no. It was all quite friendly—otherwise, I would have called the sheriff sooner. It wasn't until I heard Danny was missing that I put two and two together and called."

Christine couldn't believe no one had checked out this woman's story. Was she missing something? The woman was old, but her story seemed believable. She stood and went to the window the woman had pointed to. Below was a perfect view of the parking lot and the chain-link fence. Even someone with poor vision could make out the events Mrs. Krichek had described.

"What kind of pickup?"

"I know little about cars and trucks." The woman hoisted herself back into the walker and shuffled her way over to join Christine. "It was old, royal blue with paint chipped and some rust. You know, on the bottom part. It had running boards. I remember 'cause Danny stepped up on it to climb in. And it had wooden stockracks, homemade ones on the back. The kind farmers put on when they're hauling something. Oh, and one of the headlights wasn't working."

If the woman was senile, she had a creative imagination. Christine jotted down the details. "Were you able to see any of the license plate?"

"No, my eyes aren't that good."

A screen door slammed below, and a little girl raced out into a backyard on the other side of the fence. She jumped onto a swing and called out to the man who followed. He had long hair and a beard and wore blue jeans with a long tunic-like shirt.

"They just moved in last month." Mrs. Krichek nodded down at the pair as the man pushed the little girl, and she squealed with delight. "The first day I saw him, I tell you I thought I was looking down at the Lord himself. Don't you think he looks like Jesus?"

Christine smiled and nodded.

CHAPTER 28

Maggie watched Nick step carefully around the piles she had scattered all over the floor of his office. He cleared a spot and set down the steaming pizza and cold Pepsis. Then he joined her on the floor, his long legs stretching out next to her. A foot almost brushed her thigh. All day she had found herself acutely aware of his presence. She thought she was too tired to feel, but then her body surprised her every time his elbow accidentally brushed her arm or his hand grazed her thigh while he shifted the Jeep into gear.

She had removed her shoes hours ago and had sat on her feet until they fell asleep. Now she massaged them one at a time while she read the coroner's reports on Aaron Harper and Eric Paltrow, the two dead, little boys whom Jeffreys may have erroneously been convicted of killing.

The pizza smelled good despite the gruesome details she read. She glanced up to find Nick watching her rub her feet. Immediately, he looked away as though she had caught him at something. He popped open a can of Pepsi and handed it to her.

"Thanks." This time she was actually hungry. The ham and cheese sandwich from Wanda's had sat on a plate with only two bites removed when young Deputy Preston had finally volunteered to take it off her hands. That was hours ago. Now it was black outside the window. Phones down the hall had quieted. Staff had thinned out. Some had been sent home to rest while others were sent back out to search for a little boy who seemed to have disappeared off the face of the earth.

Nick lifted a thick slice of pizza, pulling it expertly away so he didn't lose the cheese. He plopped it down onto a paper plate and handed it to Maggie. She could smell green peppers, Italian sausage and Romano cheese. He had done good. She bit off more than she should have, dripping cheese and sauce down her chin.

"Jesus, O'Dell. You've got sauce all over your face."

She licked the side of her mouth while he watched.

"Other side." He pointed. "And on your chin."

Her hands were full of pizza and coroner reports. She licked at the other side while she fumbled for a safe spot to set something down.

"No, higher," he still instructed. "Here, let me."

As soon as his thumb touched the corner of her mouth, her eyes met his. His fingers wiped at her chin. His thumb rolled over her lower lip where she was certain there was no sauce or cheese. In his eyes she saw that he felt the unexpected surge of electricity, too. His fingertips lingered longer than necessary on her chin, moved up, caressed her cheek. His thumb took its time to leave her lip and wipe the corner of her mouth. Completely surprised by her body's reaction, she shifted away, just out of his reach.

"Thanks," she managed to say, now avoiding his eyes. She practically flung the plate with pizza to the side, grabbed a napkin and finished the job, rubbing harder than necessary in an attempt to wipe away the electrical current.

"I think we might need more napkins and Pepsis." Nick scrambled to his feet.

Maggie looked up at him, and he seemed flustered. From the small refrigerator in the corner of his office, he pulled two more cans and added napkins to the pile already on the floor. This time when he sat down, he kept more distance between them. She noticed his charm had been put on hold, his flirting almost nonexistent since he had discovered she had a husband. So the touch, the caress had caught him off guard, too.

"There are so many discrepancies," she said, trying to get her mind back on the coroner's reports. "I don't know why anyone believed Jeffreys killed all three boys."

"But don't serial killers change the way they do things?"

"They may add things. They may experiment. Jeffrey Dahmer experimented with different ways to keep his victims alive. He'd drill holes in their skulls that would incapacitate them but keep them alive."

"So maybe Jeffreys liked to experiment, too."

"What's unusual here is that the Harper and Paltrow murders were almost identical. Both were bound, hands behind their backs, with rope. They were strangled and their throats slashed. The chest wounds resembled each other almost exactly down to the number of puncture wounds. The same knife was used to carve the X's. Neither boy appeared to have been sexually molested. Their bodies were found in different remote areas near the river."

She referred to several documents laid out in front of her, leaning carefully so she wouldn't soil them. In the last hour she had started to feel the full impact of her exhaustion. Her eyes blurred as she looked over the coroner's scratchy notes. George Tillie had not been as precise as he should have been. The Paltrow report was the only one to mention the body being clean with little residue found. None of the reports indicated a smudge of oil on the forehead or anywhere else on the body.

Maggie glanced at Nick, who slumped against the hard credenza and rubbed at his eyes. His hair was tousled from too many reckless run-throughs with his fingers. His sleeves were rolled up to the elbows, revealing muscular forearms. He had gotten rid of the tie and had undone several buttons on his wrinkled shirt, exposing enough of his chest to distract her. She shook her head, grabbed a report off the floor and tried to stay focused.

"The Wilson boy, on the other hand—"

"I know," Nick interrupted, sitting forward. "His hands were bound in front with duct tape, no rope. He was stabbed to death—no signs of strangulation. His throat wasn't slashed. A hunting knife was used. Though there were plenty of puncture wounds..."

"Twenty-two."

"Twenty-two puncture wounds, but no carving."

"The Wilson boy was also sodomized, repeatedly."

"And his body was found in a park Dumpster, instead of by the river. Jesus, this stuff makes me sick to my stomach." He shoved the pizza aside, grabbed his Pepsi and emptied the can, wiping his mouth with the back of his hand. "Okay, there's a lot of differences, but couldn't Jeffreys have changed things? Even the sodomy, couldn't that be seen as...I don't know...an escalation?"

"Yes, it could. But remember the sequence was Harper, Wilson, Paltrow. It would be very unusual for a killer to change, to experiment, to escalate and then go back to the exact format. He uses one knife—something with a small blade—perhaps a fillet knife. Then he changes to a hunting knife, then back to the other knife. Even the styles are very different. The Harper and Paltrow murders are meticulous in detail. Both boys were murdered by someone taking his time—someone who enjoys inflicting pain. Very much like Danny Alverez's murder. Bobby Wilson's murder, however, looks like it was done in the heat of the moment with too much emotion and passion to pay any attention to detail."

"You know, I always thought it seemed too easy," Nick said wearily. "I've been wondering if my dad wasn't so caught up in the media circus that he may have overlooked something."

"What do you mean?"

"Well, you know how you hear about things getting missed in the excitement, the so-called rush to judgment? My dad's always enjoyed being the center of attention. The year I started as quarterback for UNL, he'd meet me at the locker room, insisted on it, in fact—every single game. My mom said it was because he was so proud of me. Except there were too many times when he greeted the TV cameras before he even acknowledged me."

Maggie listened patiently, then waited out his silence. Nick and his father obviously had a complex relationship. And though he was uncomfortable discussing it, she knew he was trying to tell her something important, something pertinent to the Jeffreys investigation. Did Nick really believe his father may have mishandled the case?

Finally, he glanced at her as though he'd read her thoughts.

"Don't get me wrong. I'm not saying my dad would purposely jeopardize any case. He's very well respected and has been for years. In fact, I know I would never have been elected if I wasn't Antonio Morrelli's son. I'm just saying that it all seemed a bit too easy—the way my dad caught Jeffreys. One day there was an anonymous tip, and the next day they had Jeffreys babbling out a confession."

"What kind of anonymous tip?"

"It was a phone call, I think. I don't know for sure. I wasn't living here at the time. I was teaching down at UNL, so I got most of this stuff secondhand. Isn't there anything in the reports?"

Maggie searched through several file folders. She had read most of them and couldn't remember any phone calls being mentioned. But she also had seen no phone logs of any kind, even for a hot line.

"I haven't seen anything at all about an anonymous tip," she said, handing him the file labeled Jeffreys' Arrest. "What do you remember?"

He seemed flustered, and she wasn't sure if it was his memory he questioned or his father. She watched him look over the reports filed and signed by Antonio Morrelli.

"Your father's reports are very detailed, including a blow-by-blow of the actual arrest. He even includes the evidence they found in the trunk of

Jeffreys' Chevy Impala." She checked her own notes and read the list. "They found a roll of duct tape, a hunting knife, some rope…wait a minute."

She stopped to check that she had copied the list correctly. "A pair of boy's underpants, which were later identified as belonging to…" She looked up at Nick, who had found the list in the report and was reading the same items she had in front of her. His eyes met hers, revealing he was thinking precisely what she was.

She continued, "A pair of underpants later identified as Eric Paltrow's."

Maggie rifled through the coroner's report to double-check her memory, though she already knew what she would find.

"Eric Paltrow's body was found with his underpants on."

Nick shook his head in disbelief.

"I bet even Jeffreys was surprised to find all that stuff in his trunk."

They stared at each other, neither wanting to acknowledge out loud what they had stumbled upon. Ronald Jeffreys had been framed for two murders he hadn't committed, and there was a good chance the frame-up had been done by someone in the sheriff's department.

CHAPTER 29

Tuesday, October 28

The day had not gone well, and Nick blamed the two hours of sleep in his office chair. Maggie had gone back to her hotel room at three in the morning to rest, shower and change. Instead of driving the five miles to his house in the country, Nick had fallen asleep at his desk. All day his neck and back had reminded him again that he was only four years away from forty.

His body certainly wasn't what it used to be, although his concerns about sexual performance may have diminished thanks to Agent O'Dell. Last night, the touch of her lips against his fingers, the look in her eyes, the electricity. Jesus, he was grateful the county jail's shower blasted only cold water. Even he had rules about married women. Now if only his body didn't talk him into changing the rules.

Unfortunately, his stash of clean clothes at the office had been used up in the last few days. He had resorted to the uniform browns, a more appropriate choice for the morning press conference. Not that it had made a difference. The press conference had quickly turned into a lynch mob within minutes, especially after Christine's morning headline: Sheriff's Department Ignores Leads in Alverez Case.

He thought for sure Eddie had checked out where old lady Krichek lived, a long time ago, after her first call. Why the hell wouldn't he have realized Krichek had a perfect view of the parking lot where Danny had been abducted? Jesus, he wanted to strangle Eddie or worse, offer him up to the media as a scapegoat. Instead, he let him off with a simple and private verbal lashing and a warning.

Hell, right now he needed every officer he had. It was no time to be losing his cool, which he almost did at the press conference when the questions got ugly. But O'Dell, in her calm and authoritative manner, had rapidly put things back in perspective. She had challenged the media to help find the mysterious blue pickup, making them a part of the hunt for the killer instead of hunting for faults in the sheriff's department. He began wondering what he'd do without her and hoped he wouldn't have to find out any time soon.

He turned the Jeep onto Christine's street just as the sun made a rare appearance from a hole in the clouds, then sank slowly and gently behind a line of trees. It had gotten colder with a biting wind promising the temperature would drop even more.

Maggie had spent the entire trip next to him quietly buried in the Alverez file. Photos from the crime scene and her own Polaroids were scattered across her lap. She was obsessed with completing her profile as though it could somehow save Matthew Tanner. After an afternoon of contradictory leads and a string of unimpressive witnesses, Nick worried that it was too late. Since Matthew's disappearance, a hundred and seventy-five deputies, police officers and independent investigators had been searching almost nonstop. Not one shred of evidence brought them closer to finding the boy. It really did seem as though someone had pulled up alongside Matthew and had him willingly get into his vehicle, just as Sophie Krichek had described.

If that was true, then there was a good chance the killer was someone the boys knew and trusted. Jesus, Nick would rather believe the boys were disappearing into thin air than being killed and mutilated by someone they knew. Someone who lived in the community. Maybe someone *he* knew.

Nick absently pulled into the driveway and hit the brakes, sending photos across the seat and onto the floor.

"Sorry." He shoved the Jeep into park, his hand sliding along Maggie's thigh. He jerked his hand away and reached to pick up the photos. Their arms crisscrossed each other. Their foreheads brushed. He handed her the photos he had retrieved, and she thanked him without looking at him. They had been tiptoeing around each other all day. He wasn't sure if it was to avoid talking about their discovery in the Jeffreys case or to avoid touching one another.

At Christine's door, Maggie's cellular phone began ringing.

"Agent Maggie O'Dell."

Christine motioned for them to come in. "I thought for sure you'd cancel," she whispered to Nick and led him to the living room, leaving Maggie to the privacy of the foyer.

"Because of the article?"

She looked surprised, as though she hadn't even thought of the article. "No, because you're swamped. You're not mad about the article, are you?"

"Krichek is nutty as a fruitcake. I doubt she saw anything."

"She's convincing, Nicky. There's nothing wrong with the lady. You should be looking for an old blue pickup."

Nick eyed Maggie. He could see her pacing. He wished he could hear her conversation. Then, suddenly, he got his wish as her angry voice carried into the living room.

"Go to hell, Greg!" She snapped the phone shut and shoved it into her pocket. It began ringing again.

Christine looked at Nick, eyebrows raised.

"Who's Greg?" she whispered.

"Her husband."

"I didn't know she was married."

"Why wouldn't she be?" he snapped, then regretted his abruptness as soon as he saw his sister's smile.

"No wonder you've been on your best behavior with her."

"What the hell is that supposed to mean?"

"In case you haven't noticed, little brother, she's gorgeous."

"She's also an FBI agent. This is strictly professional, Christine."

"Since when has that stopped you? Remember that cute little attorney from the state attorney's office? Wasn't that supposed to be only professional?"

"She wasn't married." Or if he remembered correctly, at least, she was getting a divorce.

Maggie came in, that distraught look invading her face again.

"Sorry about that," she said as she leaned against the doorjamb. "Lately, my husband has had the annoying tendency of pissing me off."

"That's why I got rid of mine," Christine said with a smile. "Nicky, get Maggie some wine. I need to check up on dinner." She patted Maggie on the shoulder on her way out.

The wine and glasses were on the coffee table in front of him. He poured, watching Maggie out of the corner of his eye. She paced, pretending to be interested in Christine's decorating talents, but obviously distracted. She stopped at the window and stared out into the backyard. He picked up the glasses of wine and came alongside her, startling her.

"You okay?" He handed her the wine, hoping for a glimpse of her eyes.

"Have you ever been married, Nick?" She took the glass without looking at him, suddenly interested in the shadows swallowing Christine's garden.

"No, I've done a pretty good job avoiding it."

They stood quietly, side by side. Her elbow brushed his arm when she took a sip. He stood perfectly still, enjoying the surprising rise in his temperature the slight contact generated, and hoping for more. He waited for her to continue, wanting to hear how her marriage was falling apart. Then immediately, the guilt hit him. Perhaps to justify his thoughts, he said, "I couldn't help noticing you don't wear a wedding ring."

She held up her hand as if to remind herself, then tucked it into her jacket pocket. "It's at the bottom of the Charles River."

"Excuse me?" Without seeing her eyes, he wasn't sure if it was a joke or not.

"About a year ago, we were dragging a floater from the river."

"A floater?"

"A body that's been in the water a while. The water was very cold. My ring must have slipped off."

She kept her eyes ahead, and he followed her lead. As twilight set in, he could see her reflection in the glass. She was still thinking about the conversation with her husband. He wondered what he was like—the man who had, at one time, captured the heart of Maggie O'Dell. He wondered if Greg was some intellectual snob. He bet the guy didn't even watch football, let alone like the Packers.

"You never replaced it?"

"No. I think maybe subconsciously I realized all those things it was supposed to symbolize were gone long before it fell to the bottom of the river."

"Uncle Nick," Timmy interrupted, running into the room and jumping up into Nick's arms, giving Nick little time to even turn around. Immediately, he felt the results of his chair nap. His back screamed at him to put the boy down, but he spiraled Timmy around, hugging him close while his little legs threatened to knock down the knickknacks scattered about.

"You guys!" Christine yelled from the doorway. Then to Maggie, "It's like having two kids in the house."

Nick set Timmy down and gritted his teeth into a smile as he straightened out and absorbed the pain that trailed all the way down his spine. Jesus, he hated these physical reminders that he was getting older.

"Maggie, this is my son, Timmy. Timmy, this is Special Agent Maggie O'Dell."

"So you're an FBI agent just like Agent Mulder and Agent Scully on *The X-Files*?"

"Except I don't track aliens. Although some of the people I track down are pretty scary."

Nick was always amazed at the effect children had on women. He wished he could bottle it. Maggie tucked her hair behind her ear, and she was smiling. Her eyes sparkled. Her entire face seemed to relax.

"I have some *X-Files* posters in my bedroom. Would you like to see them?"

"Timmy, we're going to eat soon."

"Do we have time?" Maggie asked Christine.

Timmy waited for his mom's "sure." Then he grabbed Maggie's hand and led her down the hall.

Nick didn't say anything until they were out of earshot. "It's nice to see he's learning from the master. Although I've never thought of using the old line, 'would you like to see my *X-Files* posters.'"

Christine rolled her eyes and threw a dish towel at him. "Come help. Oh, and bring me a glass of wine, too."

CHAPTER 30

Maggie hated to admit that she had never watched *The X-Files*. Her lifestyle allowed little time for television or movies. Timmy, however, seemed unconcerned. Once in his room, he anxiously showed off everything, from models of the *Starship Enterprise* to his collection of fossils. One, he said with certainty, was a dinosaur tooth.

The small room was wonderfully cluttered. A baseball mitt hung on the bedpost. A *Jurassic Park* bedspread covered lumps she guessed were matching pajamas. On a corner bookshelf, an old microscope propped up copies of *King Arthur, Galaxy of the Stars* and *The Collector's Encyclopedia of Baseball Cards.* The walls were hidden, plastered with an odd assortment of posters including *The X-Files,* the Nebraska Cornhuskers, *Star Trek, Jurassic Park* and *Batman.* She took it all in, not as an observant FBI agent, but as a twelve year old robbed of this part of her childhood.

Then she remembered her conversation with Greg. The tension was hard to shrug off. He had now accused her of ignoring her own mother. She reminded him that she was the one with the degree in psychology. It didn't matter. He was still angry with her for ruining their anniversary and carried that anger like some trophy he had won that he deserved. How did they ever get to this point?

Timmy grabbed her hand again and led her to the dresser. He pointed to the empty hull of a horseshoe crab.

"My grandpa brought this home for me from Florida. He and Grandma travel a lot. You can touch it if you want."

She ran her finger over the smooth shell. She noticed a photo behind the crab. About two dozen boys in matching T-shirts and shorts lined the inside of a canoe and the dock behind it. She recognized the boy at the front of the canoe and leaned in for a closer view. Her pulse quickened. She lifted the photo, careful not to disturb the crab. The boy was Danny Alverez.

"What's this photo, Timmy?"

"Oh, that's church camp. My mom made me go. I thought it'd ruin my summer, but it was fun."

"Isn't this boy Danny Alverez?" She pointed, and Timmy took a closer look.

"Yeah, that's him."

"So you knew him?"

"Not really. He was down in the Red Robin cabins. I was in the Goldenrod."

"Didn't he go to your church?" She examined the other faces.

"No, I think he went to school and church out by the air force base. Do you want to see my baseball card collection?" He was already digging through the drawers of his nightstand.

Maggie wanted to know more about church camp. "How many boys were there at camp?"

"I don't know. Lots." He set a wooden box on the bed and began taking out cards. "They come from all over, different churches around the county."

"Is it just for boys?"

"No, there's girls, too, but their camp's on the other side of the lake. Somewhere in here I've got a rookie Darryl Strawberry." He sorted through piles he had scattered on the bed.

There were two adults in the photo. One was Ray Howard, the janitor from St. Margaret's. The other was a tall, handsome man with dark curly hair and a boyish face. Both he and Howard wore gray T-shirts with St. Margaret's written across the front.

"Timmy, who's this guy in the photo?"

"Oh, that's Father Keller. He's really cool. I'm one of his altar boys this year. Not many boys get to be his altar boy. He's really choosy."

"How is he choosy?" She made sure that she sounded only interested, not alarmed.

"I don't know. Just by making sure they're reliable and stuff. He treats us special, sort of like our reward for being good altar boys."

"How does he treat you special?"

"He's taking us camping this Thursday and Friday. And sometimes he plays football with us. Oh, and he trades baseball cards. Once I traded him a Bob Gibson for a Joe DiMaggio."

She started to put the photo back. Another face caught her eye. This time she almost dropped the frame. Her heart began to pound. Up on the dock, partially hidden behind a bigger boy, peered the small, freckled face of Matthew Tanner.

"Timmy, do you mind if I borrow this photo for a few days? I promise I'll get it back to you."

"Okay. Do you carry a gun?"

"Yes, I do." She kept the frantic tone from her voice. Carefully, she tugged the photo out of its frame, noticing a slight tremor in her fingers from the sudden rush of adrenaline.

"Are you wearing one now?"

"Yes, I am."

"Can I see it?"

"Timmy," Christine interrupted them. "It's time for dinner. You need to wash up." She held the door open and swatted him with a kitchen towel on his way out.

Maggie slipped the photo into her jacket pocket without Christine noticing.

CHAPTER 31

After dinner Nick insisted he and Timmy do the dishes. Christine knew it was all for Maggie's benefit, but she decided to take advantage of her little brother's temporary generosity.

The two women retreated to the living room where they heard only the muffled discussion of Nebraska football. Christine set the coffee cups and saucers on the glass tabletop and wished Maggie would sit down and relax. Stop being Agent O'Dell for a few minutes. She'd seemed restless throughout dinner and was now pacing. Her body seemed wired with energy, though she looked exhausted. The puffy eyes were poorly concealed with makeup. She was easily distracted.

"Come, sit," Christine finally said, patting the spot on the sofa next to her. "I thought I couldn't keep still, but I think you've got me beaten."

"Sorry. Maybe I've been spending too much time with killers and dead bodies. My manners seem to have disappeared."

"Nonsense. You've just been spending too much time with Nicky."

Maggie smiled. "Dinner was delicious. It's been a long time since I've had a home-cooked meal."

"Thanks, but I've had lots of practice. I was a stay-at-home mom until my husband decided he liked twenty-three-year-old receptionists." Immediately, Christine realized she had revealed too much and made Maggie uncomfortable. She certainly hadn't intended for this to be some sort of tit-for-tat girl talk.

When Maggie crossed the room to sit down, she chose the recliner instead of sitting next to her. Christine wanted to tell Maggie she knew it wasn't a lack of manners as much as an avoidance of intimacy on any level. It was easy to recognize. Christine did it herself. Since Bruce's departure, she had kept plenty of distance from everyone, with the exception of her son.

"How long will you stay in Platte City?"

"For as long as necessary."

No wonder her marriage was in trouble. As if reading Christine's mind, Maggie explained, "Developing a killer's profile, unfortunately, is something that takes time. It helps to be in his surroundings, his environment."

"I did some research on you. I hope you don't mind. You have an impressive background—a B.S. in criminal psychology and premed, with a master's in behavioral psychology, a forensic fellowship at Quantico. Eight short years with the FBI and already you're one of their top profilers of serial killers. If I calculated right, you're only thirty-two. That's got to feel good—to have accomplished so much."

She expected Maggie might be a bit flustered with the attention. Instead, her vacant stare seemed haunted. From her research, Christine also knew about some of the psychos Maggie had helped put away. Perhaps her success had come with a hefty price tag.

"I suppose it should feel good," Maggie finally said.

Christine waited for more, then realized there would be no more. "Nicky will never admit it, but I know he's grateful to have you here. This is all pretty new to him. I'm certain he didn't expect something like this when my dad talked him into running for sheriff."

"Your father talked him into it?"

"Dad was getting ready to retire. He'd been sheriff for so long, I think he couldn't stand to not have a Morrelli take his place."

"But what about Nick?"

"Oh, he was teaching in the law school down at the university. I think he actually liked it." Christine stopped herself. She wasn't quite sure she understood the complexities of her father and Nick's relationship, let alone explain them to an outsider.

"Your father must be a remarkable man," Maggie said quite simply, without surprise or accusation.

"Why do you say that?" Christine eyed her suspiciously, wondering what Nick may have told her.

"For one thing, he practically captured Ronald Jeffreys single-handedly."

"Yes, he was quite a hero."

"Also, he seems to have a lot of influence over Nick's decisions."

She did know something more. Now Christine was uncomfortable. She poured herself more coffee, taking time with the cream.

"I think our dad just wants Nicky to have all the opportunities he never had. You know, do the things he didn't have a chance to do."

"What about you?"

"What do you mean?"

"Doesn't he want those same opportunities, those same things for you?"

Christine had to admit, the woman was good. Maggie O'Dell sat in Christine's recliner, sipping coffee and very coolly and calmly probing her.

"I love my dad, knowing full well that he's a bit of a male chauvinist. No, whatever I did was fine with him. I was a girl. Anything out of the ordinary that I did impressed him. Nicky, on the other hand, had it tougher. It's a little more...complex. Nick's constantly had to prove himself, whether he wanted to or not. I suppose that's one of the reasons why he gets so pissed at me."

"No, usually it's because of your big mouth." Nick startled them from the doorway. Timmy stood beside his uncle, smiling as though he was about to get in on something Christine would normally censor.

The phone rang, saving her from a lecture. Christine jumped up, almost knocking her coffee cup off its saucer. She crossed the room and picked up the phone before its third ring.

"Hello?"

"Christine, it's Hal. Sorry to bother you. Is Nick still there?" His voice crackled. She heard humming, an engine. He was in his car.

"Yes. As a matter of fact, you may have just saved my day." She glanced back at Nick and stuck out her tongue, making Timmy giggle and Nick fume.

"That would be nice—to save someone's day." The crackle couldn't hide the distress in his voice.

"Hal, are you okay? What's going on?"

"Could I just talk to Nick, please?"

Before she could say anything more, Nick was at her side, reaching for the phone. She surrendered it and loitered by the desk until Nick shot her a look.

"Hal, what is it?" He turned his back to them and listened. "Don't let anyone touch anything." The panic in his voice exploded, laced with urgency.

Maggie responded, immediately getting to her feet. Christine gently grabbed Timmy by the shoulders.

"Timmy, go get ready for bed."

"Ah, Mom, it's early."

"Timmy, now." Her brother's panic was contagious. The boy grudgingly headed upstairs.

"I mean it, Hal." Now there was anger to camouflage the panic. It didn't fool her. Christine knew her brother all too well. "Secure the area, but don't let anyone touch a thing. O'Dell's here with me. We'll be there in about fifteen to twenty minutes." When he turned, his eyes immediately sought out Maggie's as he hung up the phone.

"My God. They found Matthew's body, didn't they?" Christine said what only seemed obvious.

"Christine, I swear, if you print a word." The angry panic threatened to turn into fury.

"People have the right to know."

"Not before his mother. Will you, at least, please have the decency to wait—for her sake?"

"On one condition…"

"Jesus, Christine, listen to yourself!" he spat out in such anger it forced her to take a step backward.

"Just promise you'll call me when it's okay to go ahead. Is that too much to ask?"

He shook his head in disgust. She looked to Maggie, who waited by the door, no longer willing to come between brother and sister. Then, she looked back at Nick. "Come on, Nicky. You don't want me camped out on Michelle Tanner's front porch, do you?" She smiled, just enough to let him know she wasn't serious.

"Don't you dare talk to anyone or print a damn thing until you hear from me. And stay the hell away from Michelle Tanner." He wagged an angry finger in her face, then stomped out.

Christine waited until the Jeep's taillights turned the corner at the end of the street. She grabbed the phone and punched *69. It rang only once.

"Deputy Langston."

"Hal, hi, it's Christine." Before he could ask any questions she hurried on. "Nicky and Maggie just left. Nicky asked me to keep trying George Tillie. You know, ol' George, he could sleep through World War III."

"Yeah?" The one word was filled with suspicion.

"I can't remember the exact location, you know to tell George."

Silence. Damn, he was onto her.

She took a stab. "It's off Old Church Road…"

"Right." He sounded relieved. "Tell George to go a mile past the state-park marker. He can leave his car in Ron Woodson's pasture, up on top of the hill. He'll see the spotlights down in the woods. We'll be close to the river."

"Thanks, Hal. I know it probably sounds insensitive and unlikely, but I keep hoping it's some runaway and not Matthew, for Michelle's sake."

"I know what you mean. But there's no doubt. It's Matthew. I gotta go. Tell George to be careful walking down here."

She waited for the click, then dialed Taylor Corby's home number.

CHAPTER 32

Light snow glittered in the Jeep's headlights. They parked on an incline that overlooked the river. Bright spotlights illuminated the grove of trees below, creating eerie shadows, ghosts with spindly arms that waved in the breeze.

It reminded Maggie of a similar night, years ago, searching for a killer in the dark woods of Vermont. She wondered how much of her memory bank was filled with horror stories where other normal people stored things like Christmas traditions and family events.

The temperature had plunged in the last two hours. The cold cut through her wool jacket, sharp slashes like tiny knives. She hadn't thought to pack a coat. Even Morrelli shivered in his denim jacket. Within seconds, snowflakes clung to her eyelashes, her hair and her clothes, adding wetness to the biting cold. To make matters worse, they had over a quarter of a mile to walk. After contaminating the last crime scene, Morrelli was now overcompensating, instructing his officers and deputies to create a wide perimeter. A perimeter they guarded like military sentries.

The underbrush was thick—like walking through knee-deep water. What was once mud had begun to freeze, leaving a crunchy film. A narrow path twisted through the trees. Nick led the way, snapping branches and twigs. Those that escaped his grasp whipped Maggie's face. She could no longer feel the sting of some where the cold had left her skin numb.

Tree roots jutted up out of the earth, tripping her once. The final descent to the riverbank was steep, forcing them to hang on to branches, tree roots, vines, anything strong enough. The snow had accumulated just enough to add a slick finish to the rugged terrain. Nick lost his footing, slipped and slammed down hard on his butt. He scrambled back to his feet more embarrassed than hurt, waving off her help.

The path ended at the river's bank, where a line of cattails and tall grass separated the woods from the water. Hal met them. Maggie noticed that a pasty white had replaced his normal ruddy complexion. His eyes were watery, his demeanor quiet. She had witnessed it before—the murder of a child momentarily reducing men to speechless shells. He led the way while Nick threw questions at him, receiving only nods as answers.

"Bob Weston is sending an FBI forensic team to collect evidence. Nobody else gets through. Nobody. You got that, Hal?"

Suddenly, Hal stopped and pointed. At first, Maggie saw nothing. It was peaceful and quiet despite the presence of over two dozen officers scattered throughout the woods. In the distance, a train whistle cut through the thick silence. Snowflakes danced like fireflies in the harsh light of the massive spotlights. Then she saw him, the little, white body with a necklace of blood, naked in the snow-laced grass. His chest was so small, the jagged X slashed from his neck to his waist. His arms lay by his sides, his fists clenched. There had been no need to tie this boy who was much too small to present any threat to his killer.

She left both men and approached slowly, reverently. Yes, the body had been washed clean. Of that, she was already certain. She knelt beside him and carefully brushed the snow from his forehead. Without leaning forward, she saw the smudge of oily liquid. It smeared his blue lips and left another smudge between the X over his heart.

He seemed so fragile, so vulnerable, she wanted to cover him, protect him from the snow that glittered on his gray skin, covering the nasty red-raw slashes and gaping wounds.

He had been out here for a while. Even the sudden cold couldn't disguise the smell. She noticed small puncture marks on the inside of his left thigh, deep but leaving no trace of blood. They had been made after the boy was dead. Perhaps an animal, she thought as she dug out a small flashlight. The punctures were definitely teeth, but human teeth, she realized, overlapping several times as though bitten in a madness or purposely to disguise the imprint. They were close to the groin, but she couldn't see any marks on the penis. He hadn't done this before. The killer was adding to his routine, getting reckless and accelerating. He had only taken the boy two days ago. Something had changed. Maybe the news reports were making him nervous. Something was different. Something was wrong.

She sat back on her feet, suddenly dizzy and a bit nauseated. She never got sick at crime scenes anymore. In fact, years ago when she stopped vomiting at the sight and smell of dead bodies, she had seen it as an initiation passage. Had Albert Stucky dismantled her defense system, punctured her armor? Or had his evil simply made her human again? Retaught her to feel?

She started to crawl back to her feet when she noticed it. A torn piece of paper peeked from between the tiny fingers. Matthew Tanner had something clutched tightly in his fist. She glanced over her shoulder. Nick and Hal stood where she had left them. Their backs were turned to her as they watched five men in FBI windbreakers descend the wooded ridge.

As gently as possible, she twisted the fingers, now stiff and unbending in the advance stages of rigor mortis. She dislodged the crumpled piece of paper. It was thicker than paper and no more than a torn corner. Without even examining it closely, she recognized what it was. Just hours ago she had seen dozens spread out on Timmy Hamilton's bed. Twisted tightly in Matthew Tanner's fist was the corner of a baseball card, and Maggie was pretty sure she knew whom it belonged to.

CHAPTER 33

The forensic team worked quickly, now threatened by a new enemy. Snow fell more heavily and in large, wet flakes, covering leaves and branches, sticking to grass and burying valuable evidence.

Maggie and Nick were huddled near the tree line, out of the wind's merciless path. Maggie couldn't believe how cold it had become. She dug her hands deep into her jacket pockets, trying not to wrinkle the photo she had borrowed from Timmy. She and Nick watched in silence as they waited for Hal to bring a blanket, extra jackets, anything to warm them. They stood so close Nick's shoulder brushed against her. She felt his breath against her neck, reassuring her that she could still feel despite the numbness.

"Maybe we should just head back." It was cold enough to see his breath. "There's nothing more we can do here." Nick rubbed his arms, shifted his weight from one foot to the other. She could hear the soft chatter of his teeth.

"Do you want me to go with you to Michelle Tanner's?" She pulled her jacket collar up. It didn't help. The cold had invaded every inch of her body.

"Tell me if you think this is a cop-out." He hesitated, gathering his thoughts. "I'd like to wait until morning, not just because I'd be waking her up in the middle of the night. She probably hasn't slept since Sunday. But it might be a while before they get him to the morgue. And no matter how painful it is, she'll want to see him. Laura Alverez insisted on identifying Danny. She wouldn't believe me until she saw him herself." His eyes were watery blue from the wind and the memory. He wiped a sleeve across his face.

"It's not a cop-out. It certainly makes sense. In the morning she may have more people there to lean on. And you're right. By the time they get finished here, it will be morning."

"I'll let these guys know we're leaving."

He started for the forensic team when Maggie saw something and grabbed his arm. Not more than fifteen feet behind Nick was a set of footprints—bare footprints, freshly stamped in the snow.

"Nick, wait," she whispered. "He's here." Her heart started pounding in her ears. Why hadn't she thought of it before? Of course, it made perfect sense.

"What are you talking about?"

"The killer. He's here." She held his arm, digging her nails into the denim jacket to immobilize him and to steady her nerves. Her eyes surveyed the area while she tried to keep her body from twisting and turning, from tipping off the killer who she knew was watching them.

"Do you see him?"

"No, but he's here," she said, carefully glancing around now, making sure he wasn't within earshot. "Try to stay calm and keep your voice down. He could be watching us."

"O'Dell, I think the cold has frozen your brain." Nick looked at her as though he thought she was nuts, but he obeyed her instructions and spoke softly. "There's over two dozen deputies and police officers surrounding this area."

"Directly behind you, next to that tree with the huge knot. There's a set of footprints, bare footprints made in the snow."

She loosened her grip, allowing him to look.

"Jesus." His eyes darted around before they made their way back to hers. "With the snow falling as heavy as it is, those were made recently, very recently. Like, say, minutes ago. The son of a bitch may have been right behind us. What the hell do we do?"

"You stay here. Wait for Hal. I'll head up the path like I'm going back to the cars. He must still be inside the perimeter of your people. He shouldn't be able to get out without going past one of them. From up above I might be able to see him."

"I'll come with you."

"No, he'll notice if he's watching. Wait for Hal. I'll need the two of you as backup. Stay calm and try not to look around."

"How will we know where you are?"

"I'll let you know somehow." She kept her voice calm and even, while the adrenaline began to surge. "I'll fire my gun into the air. Just don't let any of your men shoot me."

"Like I can control that."

"I'm not joking, Morrelli."

"Neither am I."

She glanced up at him. He wasn't joking, and for a moment she realized how stupid it might be to sneak around in a woods filled with armed police. But if the killer was still here, she couldn't hesitate. And he *was* here. He was watching. She could feel it. This was part of his ritual.

She started up the path. Her leather flats were caked with snow, making the climb even more slippery. She grabbed at branches, tree roots and vines. Within minutes she was out of breath. The adrenaline pumped through her veins, propelling her numb body.

A branch snapped off in her hands, sending her skidding. She slammed to a stop, ramming her hip into a tree. Her hands were raw with cold, but she crawled back to her feet, digging her fingers into the bark. She was almost to the perimeter. She could hear the crime-scene tape flapping in the wind. Just above her, she heard voices.

The ground finally leveled enough for her to stand without assistance. She veered off the path and headed into the thick brush. From above she could see Nick at the bottom of the tree line. Hal was just joining him. Between the trees and the river, the forensic team worked quickly, hunching over the small body and filling little plastic bags of evidence. They were bringing out special equipment from their backpacks to deal with the accumulating snow. Behind them, beyond the cattails and tall grass, she could see the black waters of the river churning with motion.

Down below something moved in the trees. Maggie froze. She listened, trying to hear over the pounding in her ears and her rapid breathing. It was hard to breathe in the cold air. Had she imagined seeing movement?

A twig snapped not more than a hundred feet below her. Then she saw him. He was pressed against a tree. In the shadows of the spotlights he looked like an extension of the bark. He blended in, tall, thin and black from head to bare feet. She had been right. He was watching, twisting and leaning to see the forensic team below. He started moving from tree to tree, a low crouched-over motion, smooth and sleek like an animal sneaking up on its prey. He slithered his way down the ridge and around the murder site. He was leaving.

Maggie crept through the thicket. In her urgency, snow and leaves crunched beneath her. Branches snapped and creaked in what seemed like explosions of sounds. But no one heard, including the shadow who was quickly and silently moving toward the riverbank.

Her heart pounded against her rib cage, and her hand shook when she pulled out her gun. It was only the cold, she convinced herself. She was in control. She could do this.

She followed, never letting him out of her sight. Twigs scratched her face and grabbed her hair. Branches stabbed at her legs. She fell and smashed her thigh against a rock. Each time he stopped, she skidded to a halt and slammed her body against a tree, hoping to be hidden in the shadows.

They were on level ground, just on the edge of the woods. The forensic team was behind them. She heard them call to each other. Their equipment whined in the wind. He was making his way to the perimeter, using the trees to camouflage himself. Suddenly, he stopped again and looked back in her direction. She scrambled behind a tree, pressing herself into the cold, rough bark. She held her breath. Had he seen her? She hoped the pounding of her heart didn't betray her. The wind whirled around her, a ghostly moan. The river was close enough for her to hear its rolling water and smell the musty decay it carried with it.

She peered out from behind the tree. She couldn't see him. He was gone. She listened but only heard voices behind her. There was only silence ahead. Silence and darkness, well beyond the spotlight's reach now.

It had only been seconds. He couldn't be gone. She slid around the tree and strained to see into the darkness. There was movement in the dark, and she aimed her gun, arms stretched out in front of her. It was only a branch, swaying in the wind. But was something, or someone, hiding behind it? Despite the cold, her palms were sweaty. She walked slowly and carefully, keeping close to the trees. The river ran close to the tree line. As she walked into the darkness, she noticed that even the cattails and grass disappeared. There was nothing separating the woods from the steep riverbank, a ridge of three to four feet that the water had carved. Below, the water was black and fast-moving, dotted with eerie shapes and shadows that rode the waves.

Suddenly, she heard a twig snap. She heard him running—legs swishing through grass—before she could see him. She spun to her right where branches cracked. An explosion of sound came at her. She turned and fired a warning shot into the air just as he emerged from the thicket, a huge, black shadow, charging straight for her. She aimed, but before she had time to squeeze the trigger, he knocked into her, sending her backward, flying through the air and plunging the two of them into the river.

The cold water stung her body like thousands of snakebites. She clung to her gun and raised her arm to fire at the floating black mass only feet away from her. Pain shot through her shoulder. She twisted and tried again. This time she felt metal stabbing into her flesh. It was only then she realized she had crashed into a pile of debris. It held her from being washed away by the current. And something was ripping into her shoulder. She tried to break free, but it only stabbed deeper and tore into her flesh. Then she noticed blood dripping out the bottom of her sleeve, covering her hand and gun.

She heard the voices above yelling to each other. The stampede of footsteps ground to a halt, and a half-dozen flashlights came over the edge, blinding her. In the new light she twisted again, despite the pain, just enough to find the floating shadow. But there was nothing on the river's surface for as far as she could see.

He was gone.

CHAPTER 34

The frigid water paralyzed his body. His skin burned. His muscles screamed with pain. His lungs threatened to burst. He held his breath and kept his body submerged just under the surface. The river carried him in a violent rocking motion. He didn't fight its power, its rapid force. Instead, he allowed it to cradle him, to accept him as its own. To rescue him once again.

They were close. So close he could see the flitters of flashlights dance across the surface. To his right. To his left. Just above his head. Voices yelled to each other. Voices filled with panic and confusion.

No one dived in after him. No one attempted the black water. No one except for Special Agent O'Dell, who wasn't going anywhere. She had entangled herself neatly into the little present he had found for her. It served her right for thinking she could outsmart him, sneak up on him and trap him. The bitch had gotten what she deserved.

The flashlights found her. And soon the people on the riverbank would no longer search for him. He sneaked to the surface for air. The wet ski mask clung to his face like a spiderweb. But he didn't dare remove it.

The river carried him downstream. He watched men scramble down the riverbank, silly, slip-sliding shadows dancing in the light. He smiled, pleased with himself. Special Agent O'Dell would hate being rescued. First being incapacitated and helpless and now being rescued. Would it shock her to discover how much he knew about her? This she-devil who claimed to be his nemesis. Did she really expect to dig inside his mind and not have him return the gesture? Finally, a worthy adversary to keep him on his toes, unlike these other small-town hicks.

Something floated next to him, small and black. A trace of panic fluttered inside his gut until he realized it wasn't alive. He grabbed the hard plastic. It flipped open and a light flashed on, startling him. It was a cellular phone. What a shame to see it go to waste. He stuffed it deep into the pocket of his pants.

He maneuvered himself closer to the riverbank. In seconds, he found his marker. He grabbed the crooked branch that hung over the water. It creaked under his weight, but didn't break.

The current pushed and slapped against his body. The water possessed a strength, a power that demanded respect. He understood that, welcomed it and used it to his advantage.

His fingers stung with cold as he clawed at the branch. Bark flaked off and threatened to send him downstream. His arms ached. Only another foot, a few more inches. His feet struck land, ice-cold, snow-covered land, but his feet were already numb. The soles, heavily callused, expert navigators. He ran through the ice-coated sea of grass. It clinked and tinkled like breaking glass as hundreds of clinging icicles shattered. He gasped for breath but didn't slow his pace. The silvery snow floated through the pitch-black night—small angels dancing alongside him, running with him.

He found his hiding spot. The grove of plum trees sagged with snow-covered branches, adding a cavelike effect to the already thick canopy. Just then, a sudden ringing sent him into another frenzy. Quickly, he realized it was the phone vibrating inside his pants. He dug it out, held it for two, three rings, staring at it. Finally, he flipped it open. It lit up again. The ringing stopped. Someone was yelling,

"Hello!"

"Hello?"

"Is this Maggie O'Dell's phone?" the voice demanded. The man sounded angry, and for a second he thought about hanging up.

"Yes, it is. She dropped it."

"Can I talk to her?"

"She's kind of tied up right now," he said, almost laughing out loud.

"Well, tell her that her husband, Greg, called, and that her mother is in serious shape. She needs to call the hospital. You got that?"

"Sure."

"Don't forget," the man snapped at him and hung up.

He smiled, still holding the phone to his ear and listening to the dial tone. But it was too cold to take much pleasure in his new toy. Instead, he peeled off the black sweat pants, sweatshirt and ski mask. He threw them into the plastic garbage bag without even wringing them dry. The wet hairs on his arms and legs developed ice crystals before he wiped himself down and pulled on dry jeans and a thick wool sweater.

He sat on the running board to tie his tennis shoes. If it continued to snow, he might have to resort to wearing shoes. No, shoes would make it impossible to maneuver the river. They only acted as anchors. Besides, he hated getting them dirty.

If only he could be crawling into the nice, warm Lexus, but someone would have noticed it missing tonight. So, he climbed up into the old pickup, instead. The engine sputtered to life, and he drove home, shivering and squinting as the one headlight cut through the black night and white snow.

CHAPTER 35

It had seemed like a good idea at the time. His house was less than a mile away. She had been soaked to the bone and bleeding. Now Nick wasn't so sure he should have brought her here. As he strung up Maggie's clothes to dry in the utility room, he fingered the soft lace of her bra, and he couldn't help imagining what it would look like filled. It was ridiculous, especially after all that had happened in the last several hours. Yet, the soft scent of her perfume calmed him, soothed him, not to mention turned him on.

He had left her in the master bathroom upstairs. He had taken a shower downstairs, lit a fire in the fireplace and hung her clothes to dry. From the sound of running water in the pipes above him, he knew she was still in the shower. He wondered whether he should check on her. Despite that irritating calm, she had been shaken up, even if she wouldn't admit it. And in pain. The bastard had managed to shove her into a tangle of old splintered fence posts and rusted barbed wire.

The water shut off above him. He grabbed a fresh shirt from the dryer and fumbled with the buttons. He felt like a high-school kid unable to control his body's responses. It was crazy. After all, it wasn't as though a naked woman had never been in his house before. Fact was, there had been plenty—more than plenty.

The medicine cabinet was well stocked, remnants of his mother's paranoia. He filled his arms with cotton balls, rubbing alcohol, gauze, washcloths, hydrogen peroxide and a tin of salve probably as old as his mother. He set up his nursing station by the fire, adding pillows and blankets. The furnace was making that thumping sound again. He should have had it checked. He stuffed huge logs on the fire, filling the fireplace and warming the room with a glowing yellow heat. Of course, it couldn't possibly match the one already roaring inside him. For once he'd ignore his raging hormones and do the right thing. It was as simple as that.

He turned to find her coming down the long, open staircase. She wore his old terry-cloth robe. It parted with every step, just enough to reveal well-shaped calves, sometimes a glimpse of a firm, smooth thigh. No, there would be absolutely nothing simple about this.

Her wet hair glistened. Her cheeks were ruddy from too much hot water. Her pace was slow, almost hesitant. The water had washed away her defenses. A hidden vulnerability exposed itself in those luscious, brown eyes.

As soon as she saw his arsenal of healing tools, she shook her head and dismissed them with a wave of her hand.

"I think I washed everything out. None of that is necessary."

"It's either this or I take you to the hospital."

She frowned at him.

"Humor me, okay? That wire was full of rust. When was your last tetanus shot?"

"I'm sure it's up-to-date. The Bureau hauls us in every three years, whether we need it or not. Look, Morrelli, I appreciate the gesture, but I really am fine."

He uncapped the alcohol and peroxide, lined up cotton balls and pointed to the ottoman in front of him. "Sit."

He thought she would refuse again, but perhaps she was too tired to argue. She sat down, loosened the robe's cinch, hesitated, then let the robe drop off her shoulder while she held it tightly at her breasts.

Immediately, he found himself distracted by her smooth, creamy skin, the beginning swell of her breasts, the curve of her neck, the fresh scent of her hair and skin. He felt light-headed, and already he was hard. How could he touch her and not want to do more? It was stupid. He needed to concentrate and ignore his erection for once in his life.

About a half-dozen bloody, triangular marks marred her beautiful skin, starting on top of her shoulder and trailing down her shoulder blade and arm. Several were deep and bleeding. In one place, the skin had ripped open, leaving a gash of torn skin.

He dabbed an alcohol-soaked cotton ball against the first puncture, and she jerked from the sting. However, she made no sound.

"Are you okay?"

"Fine. Let's just get this over with."

He tried to be gentle with dabs and soft wipes. Still, she winced and grimaced beneath his touch. He cleaned each wound, hoping the alcohol would sterilize as much as it stung. Then he applied gauze and tape to those that kept bleeding.

Finally finished, he ran his open palm over the top of her shoulder and continued the slow caress down her arm, letting his hand make the journey he wished his mouth could. He felt her tremble, just slightly. Her back straightened, alerting her body to danger or responding to the electricity. His hand lingered, enjoying the sensation of silky skin. Then gently, reluctantly, he lifted the robe up over her shoulder, covering the beautiful and battered skin. She hesitated, as if surprised, as if expecting something more. Then she gathered the robe together and tightened the cinch.

"Thanks," she said without looking back at him.

"We have several hours before morning. I thought we could rest here, by the fire. Can I get you anything...hot chocolate, brandy?"

"Brandy would be nice." She left the ottoman and sat on the rug in front of the fireplace, leaning against a pile of pillows and tucking the robe in around her shapely legs.

"Can I get you anything to eat?"

"No, thanks."

"You sure? I could fix some soup, maybe a sandwich."

She smiled up at him. "Why is it that you're always trying to feed me, Morrelli?"

"Probably because I'm not allowed to do the things I'd really like to do with you."

Her smile disappeared while he looked into her eyes and held her gaze. The color rose in her cheeks. He was bordering on totally inappropriate behavior. Yet, all he could think about was whether she felt as hot as he did. Finally, she looked away, and he retreated to the kitchen while he was still able to move.

CHAPTER 36

The photo Maggie had retrieved from her jacket pocket was creased and wrinkled. The corners curled as it dried. Lint from the robe's pocket stuck to the glossy finish. She owed Timmy a replacement, though she didn't know how she'd accomplish that. At least the photo hadn't disappeared into the dark water like her cell phone. She seemed destined to lose things at the bottoms of rivers and lakes.

Nick was taking a long time in the kitchen. She wondered whether he had decided on a sandwich, after all. His last remark left her with an unsettled feeling, nothing she could even describe without using an annoying reference to butterflies. He was being a perfect gentleman. She had absolutely no reason to be concerned, even though she leaned against pillows scented with just a hint of his aftershave lotion. Even though she sat in front of his fireplace wearing nothing but his robe.

The entire time he dressed her wounds, she welcomed the sting of pain. It was the only thing that kept her mind from relishing his touch. When he finished by running his hand over her shoulder and down her arm, she was shocked to find herself waiting breathlessly, hoping for the caress to continue. Now, she wondered what it would feel like to have his big, steady hands caressing her neck, sliding gently over her shoulders and slowly down to her breasts.

She heard Nick come into the room and her hand flew to her face. Her skin was flushed again, but the fire would account for that. It would not, however, account for her shortness of breath. She steadied herself and avoided looking up at him as he approached.

He handed her a glass of brandy, then sat next to her. He pulled his long, bare feet up underneath himself, leaning so close he brushed her shoulder.

"So, that's the photo you told me about?" He nodded in its direction as he grabbed a handmade quilt off the sofa. He began wrapping it around their legs. He did this as though it was natural for the two of them to be curling up next to each other. The intimacy of the act immediately sent the heat from her face down to other parts of her body.

Perhaps he recognized it. Maybe he felt it. Suddenly, he looked embarrassed as he explained, "The furnace isn't working quite right. I need to have it checked. I just didn't expect it to get this cold in October."

She handed him the photo. With both hands now cupped around the globe of brandy, she swirled the liquid in the glass, breathed in its sweet, stout aroma, then took a sip. She closed her eyes, tilted her head back against the soft pillows and enjoyed the lovely sting sliding down her throat. Several more sips would release her from that unsettled feeling. It was during these initial light-headed moments that she understood her mother's escape. Alcohol possessed the power to level tension and dissolve unwanted feelings. There was no pain if she couldn't feel it. Grief didn't exist if she was too numb to recognize it.

"I agree," Nick said, interrupting her pleasant descent into numbness. "It is too much of a coincidence. But I can't just haul Ray Howard in for questioning, can I?"

Her eyes flew open, and she sat up. "Not Howard. Father Keller."

"What? Are you nuts? I can't haul in a priest. You really can't believe a Catholic priest could kill little boys."

"He fits the profile. I need to find out more about his background, but yes, I do think a priest is capable."

"I don't. It's crazy." He avoided her eyes and gulped his brandy. "The community would hang me by my thumbs if I hauled in a priest for questioning. Especially this Father Keller. He's like Superman with a collar. Jesus, O'Dell, you're way off target."

"Just listen to me for a minute. You said yourself it looked like Danny Alverez didn't put up a fight. Keller was someone he knew and trusted. Father Francis told us it was unlikely for a layperson post-Vatican II—which would be anyone under the age of thirty-five—to know how to administer last rites, unless that person had some training."

"But this guy is a hero with kids. How could he do something like this and not slip up?"

"People who knew Ted Bundy never suspected anything. Look, I also found a torn piece of a baseball card in Matthew's hand. Timmy told me earlier tonight that Father Keller trades baseball cards with them."

Nick wiped at the wet strands on his forehead, and she could smell the same shampoo she had used upstairs. He leaned back against the pillows, set his glass on his chest and watched the last bit swirl around.

"Okay," he said finally, "you check him out. But I need something more than a photo and a piece of baseball card before I haul him in for questioning. In the meantime, I want to do some checking on Howard. You have to admit he's a weird character. What kind of guy dresses in a shirt and tie to clean a church?"

"It's not a crime to dress inappropriately for your job. If it were, you would have been arrested long ago."

He shot her a look, but couldn't hide the smile caught at the corner of his mouth.

"Look, it's late. We're both wiped out. How 'bout we try to get some sleep?" he said, then emptied his glass and set it aside on the floor. He stretched his legs under the quilt. He grabbed a remote from an end table, pressed a few buttons and the lights dimmed. She smiled at his handy little toy for his romantic romps in front of the fire. Why did she find herself almost disappointed that she didn't need to worry about this being one of them?

"Maybe I should go back to the hotel."

"Come on, O'Dell. Your clothes are still wet. All your stuff's labeled dry-clean. I couldn't just stick them in the dryer. Look, I'm too tired to make a pass, if that's what you're worried about." He made himself comfortable against the pillows, his body close to her.

"No, it's not that," she said and wondered why her own body wasn't too tired. Instead, every muscle, every nerve ending seemed attuned to the proximity of his body. Would she even resist if he did make a pass? Did she have no feelings left for Greg? What exactly was going on with her? This was beyond annoying. "I don't usually sleep much. I might just keep you awake," she offered in place of the real reason.

"What do you mean you don't sleep?" He slumped down next to her, his head almost touching her arm. He closed his eyes, and she noticed how long his eyelashes were.

"I haven't been able to sleep for over a month now. If I do, I usually have nightmares."

He looked up at her but kept his head on the pillow. "I imagine with the stuff you see, it's hard not to have nightmares. You probably noticed I didn't spend a lot of time looking at Matthew's body. Did something in particular happen?"

She looked down at him. His body curled under the quilt. Despite the dark bristle on his face, there was something boyish about him. Then he pulled himself up on one elbow, twisting open his half-buttoned shirt in the process and exposing his muscular chest and the curly wisps of dark hair. The boyish image disappeared quickly, and she imagined slipping her hand into his shirt and letting her fingers explore. She needed to stop. This was absolutely ridiculous. Suddenly, she realized he was waiting for an answer, his eyes filled with concern.

"Did something happen?" he asked again.

"Not anything I care to discuss."

He stared at her as though trying to look deep inside her. Then, he sat up.

"Actually, I think I have a remedy for nightmares. It works with Timmy when he sleeps over."

"Well, then, it can't be more brandy."

"No." He smiled. "You hang on to someone else real tight while you fall asleep."

Her eyes met his. "Nick, I don't think that's a good idea."

His face was serious again. "Maggie, this isn't some cheap trick to get close to you. I just want to help. Will you let me do that? What do you have to lose?"

When she didn't answer, he slid closer. Slowly, hesitantly, he put his arm around her as though waiting, giving her plenty of opportunity to protest. When she didn't, he put his hand on her shoulder and gently pulled her into him so that her face rested hot against his chest. She heard his heart pound in her ear. Her own heart beat so noisily it was difficult to distinguish between the two. Her cheek brushed against the opening in his shirt, the coarse, wiry hair wonderfully scratchy and soft against her skin. She resisted the temptation of allowing her fingers access. He rested his chin on the top of her head. His voice vibrated against her.

"Now relax," he said. "Imagine that nothing can get to you without going through me first. Even if you can't sleep, just close your eyes and rest."

How could she possibly sleep with her entire body alive, alert and on fire everywhere it touched his?

CHAPTER 37

Maggie awoke groggy, her arms and legs heavy. She was cold. The fire had gone out. Nick was no longer beside her. She looked around the dark room and saw the back of his head, asleep on the sofa.

A flicker of light outside the window caught her eye. She sat up. There it was again. A dark shadow with a flashlight passed the window. Her heart began to pound. He had followed them from the river.

"Nick," she whispered, but there was no movement. Her mind raced. Where had she left her gun? "Nick," she tried again. No response.

The shadow disappeared. She crawled to the bottom of the staircase, watching the window. The room was lit only by the ghostly glow of the moon. She had taken off her gun when they first came in, on her way upstairs. She had laid it on a stand near the staircase. The stand was gone, moved, but where? Her eyes darted around the room. The pounding of her heart made her chest ache. It was cold without the fire, so cold her hands shook.

Then she heard the twist and click of the doorknob. She searched for a weapon, anything sharp, anything heavy. The metal clicked again and held. The door was locked. She grabbed a small lamp with a heavy metal base and ripped off the shade. She listened. Her breathing came in gasps and gulps. She tried to hold it as she listened again.

She crawled back to the sofa, clutching the lamp close to her.

"Nick," she whispered and reached up to poke him. "Nick, wake up." She shoved his shoulder, and his body rolled toward her, tumbling onto the floor. Her hand was smeared with blood. She looked down at him. Oh God, oh, dear God. She stuffed her bloody hand into her mouth to prevent the scream, to stop the terror. Nick's blue eyes stared up at her, cold and vacant. Blood covered his shirtfront. His throat was slashed, the gaping wound still bleeding.

Then she saw the flicker of light again. The shadow was at the window, looking in, watching her, smiling. It was a face she recognized. It was Albert Stucky.

This time she awoke with a violent flaying of arms, beating and thrashing at anything nearby. Nick grabbed her wrists, preventing her from pummeling his chest. She tried to breathe, but it only came in rapid gasps. Her body shook, wild convulsions beyond her control.

"Maggie, it's okay." His voice was soft and soothing but alarmed and urgent. "Maggie, you're safe."

She stopped suddenly, though her body still shook. She stared into Nick's eyes. They were warm blue filled with concern, and they were alive. Her eyes darted around the room. A fire raged, licking at the huge logs Nick had fed it earlier. The room was lit by the fire's warm yellow glow. Outside the window, snow glittered against the glass. There was no flicker of a flashlight. No Albert Stucky.

"Maggie, are you okay?" He held her fisted hands against his chest, caressing her wrists.

She looked into his eyes again. Her own were suddenly very tired. "It didn't work," she whispered. "You lied to me."

"I'm sorry. You were sleeping peacefully for a while. Maybe I wasn't holding you tight enough." He smiled.

She relaxed her fists against his chest while his hands continued to caress her arms, moving up over her elbows, up inside the wide sleeves of the robe. They made it all the way to her shoulders before they began their slow descent. Inch by inch, they warmed her. But the chill was deeper, crawling beneath her skin like ice in her veins.

She leaned against him. He radiated heat. Her cheek brushed against his shirt, the warm cotton fibers. It wasn't enough. She lifted herself away, just enough to give her fingers room while she unbuttoned the rest of his shirt. She avoided his eyes, and felt his body stiffen. His own hands stopped. Perhaps his breathing had, also. She opened the shirt, resisted the urge to run her hands over the bulging muscles, her fingers through the coarse hair.

Instead, she leaned her face against him, listening to the thunder of his heart and allowing his heat to warm her. She only hoped he understood.

    He trembled, though she knew he wasn't cold. Then, finally, she felt his body relax. His breathing began again, a little rapid at first, though it was clear he was trying to steady it. His arms wrapped around her waist, but he allowed them no exploration, no caresses. He simply held her body close to his, and this time, he held her tightly.

CHAPTER 38

Christine held her breath and double-clicked on Send. In minutes her article would spit out from the newsroom's printer, then roll on the presses—presses that were actually stopped and waiting. Never in her wildest dreams had she imagined being in this position.

Despite her exhaustion, the adrenaline had kept her mind racing and her fingers flying over the keyboard. Her palms were still sweaty. She wiped them on her jeans before she shut off the laptop computer, folded it shut and unplugged it from the phone jack. Modern technology—she didn't understand how it worked, but she was grateful. It had allowed her son to sleep soundly down the hall while she pounded out her fifth consecutive front-page article. She wondered what the record was at the *Omaha Journal*.

She glanced at her watch. The newspaper would be an hour late hitting the streets, but Corby seemed content. She gulped down the last of her coffee, avoiding the glob of cream and sugar congealed at the bottom. She couldn't believe she had gotten through it without a cigarette.

She slid the laptop off the desk, knocking a pile of envelopes to the floor. Picking them up put an immediate end to her elation. Several were late notices for bills she couldn't pay. One, from the State Department of Nebraska, remained unopened. It contained more forms in triplicate with old-fashioned blue carbon paper between each copy. How could she trust and believe in a state that still used carbon paper? This was the system that was going to track down her ex-husband and make him pay child support? It was bad enough that Bruce had screwed her. But how could he screw his son? She hated that Timmy couldn't see his own father, that she didn't even have a way to contact Bruce. And all because he didn't want to pay her any child support.

She stuffed the pile of envelopes behind a lamp on the desk, hidden for the time being. Her newfound success had only brought a small raise in pay, and it would be weeks, months, before it made a difference.

She could sell the house. She plopped onto the sofa and looked around the room she had spent hours wallpapering. She had pulled up musty carpeting and sanded the wood floor herself until she saw her reflection in its varnished surface. Outside the window—now black with night—she knew every inch of her backyard. She had replaced scraggly bushes with beautiful pink roses. A brick walkway—bricks she had laid herself—had transformed her garden into a retreat. How could she be asked to give this up? Outside of Timmy, this house was all she had.

Nick didn't understand, *couldn't* understand. Her journalistic success wasn't about hurting him. It was about saving herself. For once, she was doing something all on her own—not as Tony Morrelli's daughter or Bruce Hamilton's wife or Timmy's mom, but as Christine Hamilton. It felt good.

She regretted all those years she had put on a show for her family and friends. She had played the role of supportive wife and good mother. All those years she had obsessed in making Bruce happy. For over a year she had known about the affair. It was hard to miss the credit card bills for hotels she had never stepped foot into and flowers she had never received. It had only made her more obsessed. If her husband was having an affair, it had to be her fault—something she lacked, something she wasn't able to give him.

Now, it embarrassed her to remember the expensive Victoria's Secret teddies she had bought to lure him back to her. Their lovemaking, which had never been fantastic, had become quick, sultry one-act plays. He had slammed into her as if punishing her for his own sins, then rolled over and slept. Too many nights she had snuck out of bed after waiting for his snores. She'd peeled off the sometimes torn and soiled teddies, and then cried in the shower. Even the pulsating, scalding water couldn't make her whole again. And that the love had disappeared from their marriage was surely her fault, as well.

Christine curled up on the sofa and pulled an afghan over her shivering body. She was no longer that weak, obsessive wife. She was a successful journalist. She closed her eyes. That's what she would concentrate on—success. Finally, after so many failures.

CHAPTER 39

Wednesday, October 29

Maggie had offered to go to Michelle Tanner's with Nick, but he insisted on going alone. Instead, he dropped her off at the hotel. Despite their intimacy—or perhaps because of it—she found herself relieved to be away from him. It had been a mistake getting so close. She was angry and disappointed in herself, and this morning during the drive into town, she punished Nick with her silence.

She had to maintain her focus, and in order to do that, she needed to maintain her distance. As an agent, it was stupid to get personally involved, not just with one individual, but with a community. An agent could quickly lose his or her edge and objectivity. She had seen it happen to other agents. And, as a woman, it was dangerous to get involved with Nick Morrelli, a man who rigged his house with romantic booby traps for his one-night stands. Besides, she was married—degrees of happiness didn't count. She told herself all this to justify her sudden aloofness and to absolve herself of her guilt.

Her damp clothes still reeked of muddy river and dried blood. The ripped sleeves of her jacket and blouse exposed her wounded shoulder. As she entered the hotel, the pimple-faced desk clerk looked up, and his expression immediately changed from a "good morning" nod to an "oh, my God" stare.

"Wow, Agent O'Dell, are you okay?"

"I'm fine. Do I have any messages?"

He turned with the gawkiness of a teenager—all arms and legs—almost spilling his cappuccino. The sweet aroma drifted in the steam, and despite being a fast-food imitation of the real thing, it smelled wonderful.

The snow—almost six inches and still falling—clung to her pant legs and dripped inside her shoes. She was cold and tired and sore.

He handed her a half-dozen pink message slips and a small sealed envelope with SPECIAL AGENT O'DELL carefully printed in blue ink.

"What's this?" She held up the envelope.

"I dunno. It came in the mail slot sometime during the night. I found it on the floor with the morning mail."

She pretended it didn't matter. "Is there someplace here in town I can buy a coat and boots?"

"Not really. There's a John Deere implement store about a mile north of town, but they just have men's stuff."

"Would you mind doing me a favor?" She peeled a damp five-dollar bill from the folded emergency bills she kept stuffed in the slot behind her badge. The kid seemed more interested in the badge than the five. "Would you call the store and ask them to deliver a jacket? I don't care what it looks like, as long as it's warm and a size small."

"What about boots?" He jotted down instructions on a desk pad already filled with doodles and notes.

"Yes, see if they have something close to a woman's size six. Again, I don't care about style. I just need to get around in the snow."

"Got it. They probably don't open until eight or nine."

"That's fine. I'll be in my room all morning. Call me when they're here, and I'll take care of the bill."

"Anything else?" Suddenly, he seemed eager to earn his five dollars.

"Do you have room service?"

"No, but I can get you just about anything from Wanda's. They deliver for free, and we can put it on your hotel tab."

"Great. I'd like a real breakfast—scrambled eggs, sausage, toast, orange juice. Oh, and see if they have cappuccino."

"You got it." He was pleased, taking his tasks all very seriously as if she had given him an official FBI assignment.

She started sloshing down the hall, but something made her stop. "Hey, what's your name?"

He looked up, surprised, a bit worried. "Calvin. Calvin Tate."

"Thanks, Calvin."

Back in her room, she kicked off the snow-caked shoes and wrestled out of her trousers. She turned up the thermostat to seventy-five, then peeled off her jacket and blouse. This morning her muscles ached from her neck to her calves. She tried rolling the wounded shoulder, stopped, waited for the streak of pain to pass, then continued.

In the bathroom, she turned on the shower and sat on the edge of the bathtub in her underwear while she waited for hot water. She flipped through the messages recorded in two different handwritings. One was from Director Cunningham at eleven o'clock, no a.m. or p.m., no message. Why hadn't he called her cellular? Damn, she had forgotten. She needed to report it missing and get a replacement.

Three messages were from Darcy McManus at Channel Five. The desk clerk, obviously impressed, had recorded the exact times on all three. Each message had a new set of detailed instructions telling when and where to call McManus back. They included her work, cellular and home numbers and an e-mail address. Two messages were from Dr. Avery, her mother's therapist, both late last night with instructions to call when possible.

She was guessing the sealed envelope was from the persistent Ms. McManus. Steam rolled in over the shower curtain. Usually, hotel showers barely reached lukewarm. She got up to adjust the water, then stopped at her reflection in the mirror. It was quickly disappearing behind the gauze of steam. She wiped an open palm across the surface until she could examine her shoulder. The triangular punctures looked red and raw against her white skin. She yanked off Nick's homemade bandage, revealing a two-to-three-inch gash, puckered and smeared with blood. It would leave a scar. Wonderful. It would match her others.

She turned and twisted, lifting the lower section of her bra. Under her left breast was the beginning of another puckered red scar, recently healed. It trailed four inches down and across her abdomen—a present from Albert Stucky.

"You're lucky I don't gut you," she remembered him telling her as the knife blade sliced through her skin, carefully cutting just the top layer of skin, ensuring a scar. At the time, she hadn't felt anything, too numb and drained. Perhaps she had already resigned herself to die.

"You'll still be alive," he had promised, "when I start eating your intestines."

By then, nothing could shock her. She had just watched him slice and dice two women, cutting off nipples and clitorises despite the women's horrible, ear-piercing screams. Then came the gutting, followed by the smashing of skulls. No, there was nothing more he could have done to shock her. So, instead, he left her with a constant reminder of himself.

She hated that her body was becoming a scrapbook. It was bad enough that her mind had been stamped and tattooed with the images.

She rubbed her hands over her face and up through her hair, watching her reflection. It startled her how small and vulnerable she looked. Yet, nothing had changed. She was still the same determined, gutsy woman she had been when she had entered the Academy eight years ago. Maybe a little battle-fatigued and scarred, but that same restless determination existed in her eyes. She could still see it behind the steam, behind the horrors she had witnessed. Albert Stucky was a temporary setback—a roadblock she needed to plow through or go around, but never retreat from.

She unhooked her bra and let it fall to the floor. She started slipping out of her underpants when she remembered the unopened envelope on top of the other messages spread across the sink's counter. She ripped it open and pulled out the three-by-five index card. It took only one glance at the boxy lettering, and her heart began racing. Her pulse quickened. She grabbed the countertop to steady herself, gave up and slid to the damp, tiled floor. Not again. It couldn't happen again. She wouldn't allow it. She hugged her knees to her chest, trying to silence the panic rising inside her.

Then she read the card again:

WILL YOUR MOTHER BE NEEDING HER LAST RITES SOON?

CHAPTER 40

It was too early for any traffic, so Nick let the Jeep slide and cut through the drifts on its own. Street lamps continued to glow as the thick mass of snow clouds kept the sun from appearing. The windshield iced up again, and he blasted it with hot air, even though he was sweating. He turned up the radio and punched several buttons before leaving it on KRAP—"News every day, all day."

He dreaded telling Michelle Tanner about her son. He wanted those images—no, he *needed* those images of Matthew and Danny out of his mind or he'd be of no use to Mrs. Tanner. So he kept his mind on Maggie. He had never felt so pleasantly uncomfortable in all his vast experiences with women. The woman had managed to turn him inside out. Something he didn't think was possible for any one woman to do. What was worse, Maggie hadn't intended for any of it to be sensual, making him even more hot and bothered. He couldn't erase the image of her cheek pressed against his chest, the feel of her breath on his skin. He didn't want to erase it, so he played it, over and over again, until he could conjure it all up on demand—the smell of her hair, the feel of her skin, the sound of her heart. It seemed ironic—criminal—that the one woman who had revived him was the one woman he couldn't have.

He skidded onto Michelle Tanner's street just as the radio announcer was explaining that Mayor Rutledge was canceling Halloween because of the snow, which was expected to keep falling throughout the day.

"Lucky bastard." Nick smiled and shook his head.

He pulled into the Tanner driveway, almost sliding into the back of a van. It wasn't until he was at the front door that he noticed the KRAP News Radio sign, partially hidden by plastered snow. Panic chewed at his insides. It was awfully early for a simple "how are things going?" interview. He knocked on the screen door. When no one came, he opened it and pounded on the inside door.

Almost immediately it opened. A small, gray-haired woman motioned for him to come into the living room. Then she scurried back into the room and took her seat beside Michelle Tanner on the sofa. A tall, balding man with a tape recorder sat across from them. In the doorway to the kitchen towered a barrel-chested man with a crew cut and thick forearms. He looked familiar, and with a quick glance around the house, Nick realized he must be the ex-husband, Matthew's father. There were still several framed photos with the three of them—taken in happier times.

Nick heard voices and the banging of pots and pans coming from the kitchen. The smell of fresh-brewed coffee mixed with the scent of melting wax. A row of candles burned on the fireplace mantel next to a large photo of Matthew and a small crucifix.

"Is it true?" Michelle Tanner looked up at Nick with red, puffy eyes. "Did you find a body last night?"

All eyes stared at him, waiting. Jesus, it was hot in the house. He reached up and loosened his tie.

"Where did you hear that?"

"Does it fucking matter?" Matthew's father wanted to know.

"Douglas, please," the old woman reprimanded him. "Mr. Melzer, here, from the radio said it was in the *Omaha Journal* this morning."

Melzer held up the paper. Second Body Found was emblazoned across the front. Nick didn't need to see the byline. There was no time for anger. The panic backed up into his throat, leaving an acidy taste in his mouth and a lump obstructing his air. Christine had done it to him again.

"Yes, it's true," he managed to say. "I'm sorry I didn't get here sooner."

"You're always just a few steps behind, aren't you, Sheriff?"

"Douglas," the old woman repeated.

"Is it him?" Michelle looked up at Nick, pleading, hoping.

He thought it had been obvious. But she needed the words. He hated this. He shoved his hands into his jean pockets and forced himself to look into her eyes.

"Yes. It's Matthew."

He expected the wail and yet wasn't prepared for it. Michelle fell into the old woman's arms, and they rocked back and forth. Two women appeared from the kitchen. When they saw Michelle, they broke down into tears and hugged each other. Melzer watched, glanced at Nick, then gathered up his equipment and quietly left. Nick wanted to follow him out. He wasn't sure what to do. Douglas Tanner stared at him, leaning against the wall, his anger red on his face and clenched in his fists.

Then suddenly, in three steps, the man came at him. Nick didn't see the left hook until it slammed into his jaw, knocking him backward into a bookcase. Books flew from the shelves, crashing into him and onto the floor. Before he regained his balance, Douglas Tanner came at him again, pounding a fist into his stomach. Nick gasped for breath and stumbled, slipping to his knees. The old woman was yelling at Douglas. The commotion silenced the painful cries, while the women watched, wide-eyed.

Nick shook his head and started to crawl back to his feet when he saw the blur of another fist coming at him. He grabbed Tanner's arm, but instead of swinging back, Nick simply shoved the man away. He probably deserved this beating.

Then he caught a glimpse of the shiny metal. In one quick burst, Tanner came at him again, and this time stabbed at his side. Nick jumped out of the way, grabbing for his gun and ripping it from its holster. Tanner froze, a hunting knife gripped expertly in his left hand, and a look in his eyes that said he had every intention of using it.

The old woman got up from the sofa and quietly walked over to Douglas Tanner. She pulled the knife out of his fist. Then she surprised all of them and slapped him across the face.

"Damn it, Mom. What the fuck?" But Tanner now stood perfectly still, red-faced and hands silent at his side.

"I'm sick and tired of you beating on people. I've sat back and watched for too long. You just can't treat people like this—not your family or strangers. Now, apologize to Sheriff Morrelli, Douglas."

"No fucking way. If he had done his job maybe Matthew would still be alive."

Nick rubbed his eyes, but the blur stayed. He realized his lip was bleeding, and he wiped it with the back of his hand. He put his gun away but leaned against the bookcase, hoping the ringing in his head would stop.

"Douglas, apologize. Do you want to get arrested for assaulting a law officer?"

"He doesn't need to apologize," Nick interrupted. He waited for the room to stop spinning and for his feet to hold him up. "Mrs. Tanner," he said, leaving the safety of the bookcase and finding Michelle's eyes, grateful for finding only one pair in the blur. "I'm very sorry for your loss. And I apologize for waiting until this morning to tell you. I really didn't mean any disrespect. I just thought it would be better to tell you when you were surrounded by family and friends than pounding on your door in the middle of the night. I promise you, we'll find the man who did this to Matthew."

"I'm sure you will, Sheriff," Douglas Tanner said from behind him. "But how many more boys will he murder before you get a clue?"

CHAPTER 41

No one had to tell him. Timmy just knew. Matthew was dead, just like Danny Alverez. That's why Uncle Nick and Agent O'Dell left all of a sudden last night. Why his mom sent him to bed early. Why she stayed up almost all night writing for the newspaper on her new laptop computer.

He climbed out of bed early to listen to the school closings on the radio. There had to be at least a half foot of snow, and it was still coming down. It would be excellent tubing snow, though his mom forbade him to use anything but his boring plastic sled. It was bright orange and stuck out like some kind of emergency vehicle in the snow.

He found her asleep on the sofa, curled up in a tight ball and tangled in Grandma Morrelli's afghan. Her hands were balled up in fists and tucked under her chin. She looked totally wiped, and he tiptoed into the kitchen, leaving her to sleep.

He tuned the radio to the news station, away from the sappy elevator music his mom listened to. She called it "soft rock." Sometimes she acted so old. The announcer was already in the middle of the school announcements, and he turned the radio up loud enough to hear over his breakfast fumblings.

Instead of dragging a chair to the counter, he used the bottom two drawers to reach a bowl from the cupboard. He was tired of being short. He was smaller than all the boys in his class and even some of the girls. Uncle Nick told him he'd probably have a growth spurt and pass them all up, but Timmy didn't see it coming anytime soon.

He was surprised to find an unopened box of Cap'n Crunch between the

Cheerios and the Grape-Nuts. Either it had been on sale, or his mom hadn't realized what she had bought. She never let him have the good stuff. He grabbed it and opened it before she discovered her mistake, pouring until the bowl overflowed. He munched the excess, making room for milk. As he poured, the radio announcer said, "Platte City Elementary and High School will be closed today."

"Yes," he whispered, containing his excitement so he didn't spill any milk. And since tomorrow and Friday were teachers' convention, that meant they had five days off. Wow, five whole days! Then he remembered the camping trip, and his excitement was short-lived. Would Father Keller call off the trip because of the snow? He hoped not.

"Timmy?" Wrapped in Grandma's afghan, his mom padded into the kitchen. She looked funny with her hair all tangled and sleep crusted in the corners of her eyes. "Did they close school?"

"Yeah. Five days off." He sat down and scooped up a spoonful of cereal before she noticed the Cap'n Crunch. "Do you think we'll still go camping?" he asked over a mouthful, taking advantage of her being too tired to correct his manners.

She filled the coffee machine, shuffling back and forth. She almost tripped on the drawers he had left out and kicked them back in without yelling at him.

"I don't know, Timmy. It's only October. Tomorrow it could be forty degrees and the snow will all be gone. What are they saying about the weather on the radio?"

"So far it's just been school closings. It'd be really cool to camp out in the snow."

"It'd be really cold and stupid to camp out in the snow."

"Ah, Mom, don't you have any sense of adventure?"

"Not when it means you coming down with pneumonia. You get sick and hurt enough without any outside help."

He wanted to remind her that he hadn't been sick since last winter, but then she might bring up the soccer bruises again.

"Is it okay if I go sledding today with some of the guys?"

"You have to dress warm, and you can only use your sled. No inner tubes."

The school closings were finally finished and the news came on. His mom turned up the volume just as the announcer said, "According to this morning's *Omaha Journal,* another boy's body was found along the Platte River last night. It has now been confirmed by the sheriff's department that the boy is Matthew Tanner, who has been…"

His mom snapped the radio off, filling the room with silence. She stood with her back to him, pretending to be interested in something out the window. The coffee machine hummed, then started its ritual gurgling. Timmy's spoon clicked against the bowl. The coffee smelled good, reminding him that it didn't seem like morning until the kitchen was filled with that smell.

"Timmy." His mom came around to the table and sat across from him. "The man on the radio is right. They did find Matthew last night."

"I know," he said and kept eating, though the cereal didn't taste as good all of a sudden.

"You know? How do you know?"

"I figured that's why Uncle Nick and Agent O'Dell left in such a hurry last night. And why you were up all night working."

She reached across the table and brushed his hair off his forehead. "God, you're growing up fast."

She caressed his cheek. In public he'd have batted her hand away, but it was okay here. He actually kind of liked it.

"Where did you get Cap'n Crunch cereal?"

"You bought it. It was down with the other cereals." He filled his bowl again though it wasn't quite empty, just in case she took the box away.

"I must have grabbed it by mistake."

The coffee was ready. She got up, leaving the afghan draped over the back of the chair and the box of cereal on the table.

"Mom, what does dead feel like?"

She spilled coffee all over the counter and snatched a towel to stop the puddle from running over the edge.

"Sorry," he said, realizing it had been his question that had caused her clumsiness. Adults got so bent out of shape about stuff.

"I really don't know, Timmy. That's probably a good question for Father Keller."

CHAPTER 42

The breakfast Maggie had ordered from Wanda's sat untouched on the small table. It had come bundled in an insulated pack, served on stoneware and encased in stainless-steel covers. Steam had risen from the plate when the desk clerk had proudly unveiled it as though he had prepared it himself.

She was becoming a regular of Wanda's cuisine without ever stepping foot in the diner. And although the golden eggs, butter-slathered toast and glistening sausage links smelled and looked delicious, she had lost her appetite. She had left it somewhere on the bathroom floor while she fought to gain control over her panic. The only thing she touched was the frothy cappuccino. One sip, and she thanked Wanda for having the good sense to invest in a cappuccino maker.

Her laptop occupied the other side of the table, close to the wall where a recently installed phone jack allowed the hotel to advertise itself to business travelers. She paced while her computer slowly connected her to Quantico's general database. She wasn't able to access any classified information. The FBI remained skeptical about the confidentiality of modems, and rightly so. They were constantly a target for hackers.

She had already put in several calls to Dr. Avery. The old-fashioned desktop phone confined her to the bed, so she couldn't do her usual pacing. She stretched out on the hard mattress. After her shower, she had put on jeans and her Packers jersey. The exhaustion was overwhelming. It had taken every last bit of her strength to pull herself together, and that frightened her. How could one simple note provoke such terror? She had received notes from killers before. They were harmless. It was only a part of the sick game. It came with the territory. If she were going to dig into a killer's psyche, she had to be prepared for the killer to dig back.

Albert Stucky's notes had not been harmless. God, she needed to get past Stucky. He was behind bars and would be there until they executed him. She was safe. At least this note hadn't been accompanied by a severed finger or nipple. Besides, the note was now carefully packaged and on its way Express Mail to a lab at Quantico. Maybe the idiot had sent her his own arrest warrant by leaving his fingerprints or his saliva on the envelope's seal.

By this evening, she would be on a plane home, and this bastard wouldn't be able to play his sick, little game. She had done her job, more than what was asked. So why did it feel as if she was running away? Because that's exactly what she was doing. She needed to leave Platte City, Nebraska, before this killer unraveled any more of her already frazzled psyche. She could feel the vulnerable fray already, starting when she had cowered on the cold bathroom floor.

Yes, she needed to leave, and she needed to do it quickly—today—while she still felt in control. She would tie up a few loose ends and then get the hell out. Get out while she was still in one piece. Get out before she started coming apart at the seams.

She decided to make a quick phone call while she waited for her computer to connect on the other line. She found the number in the thin directory and dialed. After several rings, a deep male voice answered, "St. Margaret's rectory."

"Father Francis, please."

"May I tell him who's calling?"

She couldn't tell whether or not the voice belonged to Howard.

"This is Special Agent Maggie O'Dell. Is this Mr. Howard?"

There was a brief pause. Instead of answering her question, he said, "One moment, please."

It took several moments. She turned to see the computer screen. Finally, the connection was completed. Quantico's royal-blue logo blinked across the screen.

"Maggie O'Dell, what a pleasure to talk with you again." Father Francis' high-pitched voice was almost singsong.

"Father Francis, I wonder if I might ask you a few more questions."

"Why, certainly." There was a faint *click-click*.

"Father Francis?"

"I'm still here."

And so was someone else. She'd ask the questions, anyway. Make the intruder sweat.

"What can you tell me about the church's summer camp?"

"Summer camp? That's really Father Keller's project. You might speak to him about it."

"Yes, of course. I will. Did he start the project, or was it something St. Margaret's has been doing for years?"

"Father Keller started it when he first came. I believe that was the summer of 1990. It was an instant success. Of course, he had a track record. He had been running one at his previous parish."

"Really? Where was that?"

"Up in Maine. Let's see, I usually have a very good memory. Wood something. Wood River. Yes, Wood River, Maine. We were quite lucky to get him."

"Yes, I'm sure you were. I look forward to talking to him. Thanks for your help, Father."

"Agent O'Dell," he stopped her. "Is that all you needed to ask me?"

"Yes, but you've been very helpful."

"Actually, I was wondering if you found the answers to your other questions. Your inquiries about Ronald Jeffreys?"

She hesitated. She didn't want to sound abrupt, but she didn't want to discuss what she knew with someone listening. "Yes, I think we did find the answers. Thanks again for your help."

"Agent O'Dell." He sounded concerned, the lilt no longer present in his voice. If she wasn't mistaken, he suddenly sounded distressed. "I may have some additional information, though I'm not certain of its importance."

"Father Francis, I can't talk right now. I'm expecting an important phone call," she interrupted before he revealed anything more. "Could I meet you perhaps later?"

"Yes, that would be nice. I have morning confessions and then rounds at the hospital this afternoon, so I won't be free until after four o'clock."

"As a matter of fact, I'll be at the hospital this afternoon. Why don't I meet you in the cafeteria about four-fifteen?"

"I look forward to it. Goodbye, Maggie O'Dell."

She waited for him to hang up, then heard the second set of clicks. There was no mistake. Someone had been listening.

CHAPTER 43

Nick stormed into the sheriff's department, slamming the door so hard the glass rattled. Everyone came to a halt in midsentence and midstride. They stared at him as though he had gone mad. He felt as if perhaps he had.

"Listen up, everybody!" He yelled over the ringing in his ear. He waited for those sauntering in from the conference room with their mugs of coffee and glazed doughnuts. "If we have another breach of confidence from this department, I personally will kick the ass of whoever is responsible and see to it that that person never works in law enforcement ever again."

His jaw hurt like hell, especially when he clenched his teeth. The tip of his tongue found a sharp edge where a tooth had chipped. The corner of his mouth bled again, and he wiped at it with the sleeve of his shirt.

"Lloyd, I want you to get some men together and check every abandoned shack within a ten-mile radius of Old Church Road. He's keeping these boys somewhere. Maybe it's not here in town. Hal, find out everything you can about a Ray Howard. He's a janitor at the church. Not just where he's from and details about his unpleasant childhood. I want to know this guy's shoe size and whether or not he collects baseball cards. Eddie, get over to Sophie Krichek's."

"Nick, you can't be serious. The lady's loony."

"I'm dead serious."

Eddie shrugged, and there was a smirk under the pencil-thin mustache that Nick wanted to knock off.

"Do it this morning, Eddie, and treat it like your job depends on getting the details right."

He waited for any other grumbling, then continued, "Adam, call George Tillie and tell him Agent O'Dell will be assisting him this afternoon with Matthew's autopsy. Then call Agent Weston and get the evidence his forensic team found. I want photos and reports on my desk by one this afternoon.

"Lucy, find out anything you can about a summer church camp that St. Margaret's sponsors. Get together with Max and see if you can connect Aaron Harper and Eric Paltrow to that camp."

"What about Bobby Wilson?" She looked up from her notes.

He paused while he watched their faces, wondering whether he'd be able to pick out the Judas—that is if he was still a part of the department. Six years ago, someone had gone to the trouble of making it look as though Ronald Jeffreys had killed all three boys. Someone had taken Eric Paltrow's underpants from the morgue and planted them in Jeffreys' trunk with other incriminating evidence connecting Jeffreys to all three murders. It could easily have been someone in the sheriff's department, someone who was still here. And if he was, why not make the bastard sweat?

"If I read any of this in tomorrow's paper, I swear I'll fire the whole lot of you. Ronald Jeffreys may have only murdered Bobby Wilson. There's a good chance that the guy who killed Danny and Matthew also killed Eric and Aaron." He watched their faces as it sank in, especially the group that had worked with his father and had celebrated the capture of Jeffreys.

"What are you saying, Nick?" Lloyd Benjamin had been one of them, and now his wrinkled forehead looked angry. "You saying we messed up the first time?"

"No, Lloyd, you didn't mess up. You caught Jeffreys. You caught a murderer. But it looks like Jeffreys may not have murdered all three boys."

"Is that what you think, Nick, or is it Agent O'Dell maybe influencing your way of thinking?" Eddie said, again with the smirk.

Nick felt the anger rising and knew he had to contain it. Now was not the time to defend his relationship with Maggie. He wasn't even sure he could without getting tangled in his own personal feelings. And he certainly didn't want to share any details about Jeffreys, especially since he was beginning to question the loyalty of his own department.

"I'm saying there's a good chance. Whether it's true or not, let's make sure this bastard doesn't get away with it, maybe for a second time." He shoved past Eddie, knocking against his shoulder and dismissing the group. Lloyd caught up with him down the hall at his office door.

"Nick, wait up." Lloyd's short, stubby legs jogged to keep up with Nick. He was breathing hard and loosened his tie. "I didn't mean anything back there. I'm sure Eddie didn't, either. This thing is just taking a toll on all of us. Just like before."

"Don't worry about it, Lloyd."

"About checking old shacks. Nick, there's not much out there that we didn't check the first time. There's an old barn about ready to fall down on Woodson's property. Other than a deserted lean-to or grain bin, there isn't anything else. Except for the old church, but it's boarded up tighter than a virgin on Sunday."

Nick frowned at the reference.

"Sorry," Benjamin apologized though he didn't look sorry. "You're getting awfully touchy, Nick. O'Dell isn't even here."

"Check the church again, Lloyd. Look for broken windows, footprints, any sign of entry in the last several days."

"Hell, we're not gonna find any footprints with this snow coming down."

"Just check, Lloyd."

Nick retreated to his office, already exhausted, and the morning had just begun. Within seconds there was a knock on the door. He slumped into his chair and yelled to come in.

Lucy peeked around the door, assessing his mood. He waved her in. She carried an ice pack and cup of coffee.

"What in the world happened to you, Nick?"

"Don't even ask."

She put aside her initial hesitation and came around the desk. She leaned against the corner and her skirt hiked up over her thighs. She saw him notice and made no effort to pull it down. Instead, she reached for his chin, cupping it in her hand and laying the ice pack against his swollen jaw. He jerked away, using the pain as an excuse to wheel out of her reach.

"Oh, poor Nick. I know it hurts," she said, making baby talk sound sensual.

This morning she wore a rose-colored sweater pulled so tight across her breasts the knitted loops hinted at a black bra underneath. She scooted across the desk toward him, and he jumped out of his chair.

"Look, I don't have time for ice packs. I'll be fine. Thanks for thinking of it."

She looked disappointed. "I'll leave it in your little refrigerator, in case you want it later."

She crossed the room to the small cube on the floor. She bent at the waist, purposely giving him a view of what he was missing, and put the ice pack in the small freezer space. She glanced back at him as if checking to see if he had changed his mind, smiled, then swayed out the door.

"Jesus," he muttered, plopping down into the chair again. What kind of a department had he created? Michelle Tanner's raging ex-husband was right. No wonder he was no closer to finding the killer.

CHAPTER 44

Father Francis gathered the newspaper clippings and slid them into his leather portfolio. He stopped, held up his hands and stared at the brown spots, the bulging blue veins and the trembling that had become commonplace.

It had only been three months since Ronald Jeffreys' execution. Three months since he had listened to the confession of the real killer. He could no longer keep silent. He could no longer preserve the sanctity of a killer's confession. Maybe it wouldn't make a difference, but he had convinced himself that it was the right thing to do.

He shuffled down the hall to the church. His footsteps were the only sound echoing off the majestic walls. No one waited for confession. It would be a quiet morning. Still, he entered the small confessional.

Despite his having seen no one in the church, the door in the black cubicle next to him opened within minutes. Father Francis sat up and laid his elbow on the shelf, allowing himself to lean closer to the wire-mesh window between the two small rooms.

"Bless me, Father, for I have killed again."

Oh, dear God. The panic came crashing against the old priest's chest. It was difficult to breathe. Suddenly, the small, wooden box had only hot and stale air. The throbbing began in his ears. Father Francis strained to see beyond the thick wire mesh that separated them. All he could see, though, was a huddled black shadow.

"I killed Danny Alverez and Matthew Tanner. For these sins, I am truly sorry and ask forgiveness."

The voice was disguised, barely audible, as if forced through a mask. Was there anything, anything at all, that he could recognize?

"What is my penance?" the voice wanted to know.

Could he speak if he could not breathe?

"How can..." It was difficult. His chest ached. "How can I absolve you of your sins...heinous, horrible sins...if you only intend to do them again?"

"No, y-you don't understand. I only bring them peace," the voice sputtered. He obviously hadn't come prepared for a confrontation, Father Francis realized with some degree of satisfaction. He had come only for absolution and to do his penance.

"I cannot absolve you of your sins if you intend to only go out and do it again." Father Francis' strong, unflinching voice surprised him.

"You must...you have to."

"I absolved you once before, and you've made a mockery of the sacrament by committing the sin again, not once but twice."

"I am truly sorry for my sins and ask forgiveness from God," he tried again, mechanically saying the phrase like a child memorizing it for the first time.

"You must prove your remorse," Father Francis said, suddenly feeling powerful. Perhaps he could influence this black shadow, make him face his demons, stop him once and for all. "You must show your repentance."

"Yes. Yes, I will. Just tell me what my penance is."

"Go prove your repentance and come back in a month."

There was a pause.

"You aren't absolving me?"

"If you can prove your worthiness by not killing, I will consider absolving you then."

"You will not give me absolution?"

"Come back in a month."

There was silence, but the shadow made no motion to leave. Father Francis leaned closer to the wire mesh, again straining to see into the pitch-black cube. There was a soft smack, then a hiss as a spray of saliva flew through the wire mesh, hitting him in the face.

"I'll see you in hell, Father." The low guttural tone sent shivers down Father Francis' spine. He clung to the small shelf, gripping the Bible. And though the sticky saliva dripped down his chin, he couldn't move even to wipe at it. When he heard the door open and the shadow exit, his paralyzed body made no attempt to follow or look out after him.

He sat for what seemed like hours. Thankfully, no one else came in. Perhaps the snow had kept other sinners home, he thought absently. Which meant no one had seen the shadowy figure enter or exit the confessional.

Finally, his heart resumed its normal beating. He could breathe again. He fumbled for a handkerchief and wiped his face with hands trembling more violently than usual. He held on to the walls of the small confessional as he eased himself out of the hard chair and onto wobbly knees. He gathered his leather portfolio and Bible and peered out. The church was empty and silent. Outside, he heard the laughter of children, probably crossing the parking lot to go sledding on Cutty's Hill. At least they traveled in groups.

He shuffled to the front of the church, hanging on to the backs of pews as he made his way down the aisle. The panic and terror had exhausted him, drained him of energy. He would share this morning's visit with Maggie O'Dell. The decision to do so made him feel stronger. Already the guilt lifted from his soul. Yes, it was the right thing to do. He started down the hallway from the church to the rectory, and even his feet seemed lighter. The ache in his chest eased to a mere annoyance.

On the way to his office he noticed that someone had left the door to the wine cellar open. He stopped in the doorway and peered down the dark steps. He could smell the musty dampness. A draft made him shiver. Was there a shadow? Down in the far corner, was someone huddled in the darkness?

He stepped onto the first step, clinging with a shaky hand to the railing. Was it his imagination, or was someone huddled between the stacked wine crates and the concrete wall?

He leaned forward on weak knees. He never saw the figure behind him. He only felt the violent shove that sent him sailing down the steps headfirst. His frail body crashed against the wall, and he tumbled the rest of the way. He was still conscious when he heard the steps creak, one by one by one. The sound of the slow descent sent terror through his aching body. He opened his mouth to scream but only a moan erupted. He couldn't move, couldn't run. His right leg was on fire and twisted beneath him at an abnormal angle.

The last step creaked just above him. He lifted his head in time to see a blaze of white canvas smash into his face. Then darkness.

CHAPTER 45

Christine treated herself to Wanda's homemade chicken noodle soup and buttercrust rolls. Corby had given her the morning off, but she had brought her notepad and jotted down ideas for tomorrow's article. It was early, and the lunch crowd filtered in slowly, so she had a booth to herself in the far corner of the small diner. She sat next to the window and watched the few pedestrians shuffling through the snow.

Timmy had called and asked whether he and his friends could have lunch at the rectory with Father Keller. The priest had joined them sledding on Cutty's Hill and, to make up for the inevitably canceled camping trip, he had invited the boys for roasted hot dogs and marshmallows by the huge fireplace in the church's rectory.

"Great series of articles, Christine," Angie Clark said as she refilled Christine's cup with more steaming coffee.

Caught off guard, Christine swallowed the bite of warm bread. "Thanks." She smiled and wiped a napkin across her mouth. "Your mom's rolls are still the best around."

"I keep telling her we should package and sell some of her baked goods, but she thinks if people can take home a batch, they won't stay here for lunch or dinner."

Christine knew that Angie was the financial mind behind her mother's business. Not able to build on to the small diner, it was Angie's advice to start a delivery service. After only six short months, they had added an extra cook and were keeping two vans and drivers busy, without jeopardizing their normal crowded breakfast, lunch and dinner rushes.

Sometimes Christine wondered why Angie had stayed in Platte City. She obviously had a mind for business and a body that drew plenty of attention. But after only two years at the university and a rumored affair with a married state senator, she had returned home to her widowed mother.

"How's Nick?" Angie asked while pretending to rearrange the silverware on a nearby table.

"Right now he's probably pissed at me again. He hasn't appreciated my articles." She knew that wasn't what Angie had wanted to hear, but Christine had learned long ago to keep out of her brother's love life.

"Next time you see him, tell him I said hi."

Poor Angie. Nick probably hadn't called her since any of this mess started. And though he denied it, Christine knew his mind was filled with the lovely and unavailable Maggie O'Dell. Perhaps his heart would finally get broken, and he'd get a taste of his own medicine.

She watched Angie greet two burly construction workers who came in and began peeling off their layers of jackets, hats and overalls. Why did women knock themselves out over Nick? It was something Christine had never understood as she had watched him go from one woman to another without any explanation or hesitation. He was a handsome, charming jerk, and even after days—maybe even weeks—of not calling, she knew Angie Clark would still welcome him back with open arms.

She sipped the steaming coffee and jotted down "coroner's report." George Tillie was an old family friend. He and her dad had been hunting buddies for years. Maybe George could supply her with some new information. As far as she could tell, the investigation was at a standstill.

Suddenly, the volume on the corner television blasted the room. She looked up just as Wanda Clark waved at her.

"Christine, listen to this."

Bernard Shaw on CNN had just mentioned Platte City, Nebraska. A graphic behind him showed its location while Shaw talked about the bizarre series of murders. They flashed Christine's Sunday headline, From the Grave, Serial Killer Still Grips Community With Boy's Recent Murder, as Bernard described the murders and Jeffreys' killing spree six years before.

"A source close to the investigation says the sheriff's department still has no clues, and that the only suspect on their list is one who was executed three months ago."

Christine cringed at Shaw's hint of sarcasm, and for the first time she sympathized with Nick. The rest of the diner broke into applause and waved thumbs-up gestures at her. They'd simply heard that their town had made the national news. The sarcasm and befuddled-country-folk references fell on deaf ears.

The volume went down, and she went back to her notes. Soon her cellular phone began ringing, screaming at her from the bottom of her purse. She dug for it, removing wallet, hairbrush and lipstick and scattering them on the table. She looked up to find all eyes on her again. Finally, she ripped the contraption from the bag and waved it at her audience, who smiled and went back to their meals. The phone rang two more times before she found the On switch.

"Christine Hamilton."

"Ms. Hamilton, hello. This is William Ramsey at KLTV Channel Five. I hope I'm not interrupting anything. Your office gave me this number."

"I am having lunch, Mr. Ramsey. How can I help you?"

The last several nights the television station had depended on her newspaper articles for information on the murders. Other than a few fluff pieces interviewing relatives and neighbors, their newscasts had lacked the hype they counted on for ratings.

"I wonder if we might get together for breakfast or lunch tomorrow?"

"My schedule is very full, Mr. Ramsey."

"Yes, of course it is. Then I guess I'll have to get to the point."

"That would be nice."

"I'd like you to come work for Channel Five as a reporter and weekend co-anchor."

"Excuse me?" She almost choked on her roll.

"Your gutsy reporting on these murders is just the kind of thing we need here at Channel Five."

"Mr. Ramsey, I'm a newspaper reporter. I don't—"

"Your style of writing would lend itself very well to broadcast news. We'd be willing to coach you for the anchor position. And I happen to know you're quite easy on the eyes."

She wasn't above flattery. Fact was, she craved it, having had so little in the past. But Corby and the *Omaha Journal* had given her a big break. No, she couldn't even entertain the idea.

"I'm flattered, Mr. Ramsey, but I just can't—"

"I'm prepared to offer you sixty thousand dollars a year if you start right away."

Christine dropped her spoon. It catapulted off her bowl, splattering soup onto her lap. She made no motion to wipe it up.

"Excuse me?"

Her surprise must have sounded like another decline, because Ramsey hurriedly said, "Okay, I can go to sixty-five thousand. In fact, I'll throw in a two-thousand-dollar bonus if you start this weekend."

Sixty-five thousand dollars was more than twice the amount Christine made even with her meager pay increase. She could pay off her bills and not worry about hunting down Bruce for child support.

"Can I get back to you, Mr. Ramsey, after I've had some time to think about it?"

"Sure, of course you should think about it. Why don't you sleep on it and give me a call in the morning."

"Thank you. I will." She slapped the phone shut and was still in a daze when Eddie Gillick slid into the booth next to her, shoving her up against the window. "What do you think you're doing?" she demanded.

"It was bad enough when you tricked me into giving you a quote for your newspaper article, but now your little brother is giving me chicken-shit assignments, so I figure you also told him I was your anonymous source."

"Look, Deputy Gillick..."

"No, hey, it's Eddie, remember?"

He helped himself to her coffee, adding a heap of sugar and gulping it without scalding himself. The smell of his aftershave lotion was overpowering.

"I didn't exactly tell Nick. He—"

"No, that's okay, because the way I figure it, now you owe me one."

She felt his hand on her knee, and the look of contempt in his eyes immobilized her. His hand moved up her thigh and under her skirt before she wrestled it away. The corner of his mustache twitched into a smile as she felt the color rise into her face.

"Can I get you anything, Eddie?" Angie Clark stood over the table, obviously well aware that she was interrupting and not about to leave until she had succeeded.

"No, Angie dear," Eddie said, still smiling at Christine. "Unfortunately, I can't stay. I'll just have to catch up with you later, Christine."

He slid out of the booth, ran a hand over his slicked-down black hair and replaced his hat. Then he sauntered back down the aisle and out the door.

"You okay?"

"Of course," Christine answered. She kept her trembling hands out of sight under the table.

CHAPTER 46

The door flung open just in time for Nick to see Maggie race back across the room.

"Come on in," she yelled to him as she poked at the keyboard of her laptop computer. Then, she stood back and watched the screen. "I'm accessing some information from Quantico's database. It's proving to be very interesting."

He came into the small hotel room slowly, passing the bathroom, and was immediately accosted by the scent of her shampoo and perfume. She wore jeans and the same sexy Packers jersey from the other night. Its color was faded. The neckline was stretched and misshapen so that it draped down and exposed a bare shoulder. Knowing she had nothing underneath made him hot, and he tried to divert his attention to something, anything else.

She glanced up at him, then did a double take. "What happened to your face?"

"Christine didn't wait. There was an article in this morning's paper."

"And Michelle Tanner saw it before you got there?"

"Sort of. Someone told her about it."

"She hit you?"

"No," he snapped, then realized there was no need to be so defensive. "Her ex-husband, Matthew's dad, sort of let me have it."

"Jesus, Morrelli, don't you know how to duck?"

The anger must have still been in his eyes, because she quickly added, "Sorry. You should put some ice on it."

Unlike Lucy, Maggie went back to the computer screen, offering no nursing services.

"How's the shoulder?"

She looked up again. Her eyes met his. For a brief moment they softened, remembering. Then she quickly looked away. "It's okay." She rolled it as if to check. "It's still pretty sore."

The Packers jersey slipped further down her shoulder, revealing creamy, soft skin. It easily distracted him. God, he wanted to touch her so bad it hurt. It didn't help matters that her rumpled bed was just feet away.

"So, you're a Packers fan." He filled the silence while she clicked through information on the computer screen.

"Actually, my dad grew up in Green Bay," she said without looking up. The computer screen changed quickly as she scanned its contents. "My husband keeps trying to get me to throw this old thing away. But it's one of the few things I have that reminds me of my dad. It was his. He used to wear it when we watched the games together."

"Used to?"

There was a pause, and he knew it had nothing to do with the information on the screen. He watched her tuck her hair behind her ears and recognized it as a nervous habit.

"He was killed when I was twelve."

"I'm sorry. Was he an FBI agent, too?"

She stopped and stood up straight, pretending to stretch, only he knew it was to buy time. It was easy to see the subject of her father brought back memories.

"No, a firefighter. He died a hero. I guess you and I have that in common." She smiled up at him. "Except your father managed to stay alive."

"Just remember, my father had a lot of help."

She searched his eyes, and this time he quickly looked away before she saw something he wasn't ready to reveal.

"You don't think he had something to do with Jeffreys being framed, do you?"

He felt her watching him. He purposely came up beside her to view the computer screen, making it impossible for her to examine his eyes.

"He gained the most from Jeffreys' capture. I don't know what I believe."

"Here it is," she said, watching the screen fill with what looked like newspaper articles.

"What is this?" He leaned forward. "The *Wood River Gazette,* November 1989. Where is Wood River?"

"Maine." She poked at the scroll button, scanning the headlines. Then she stopped and pointed to one.

"'Boy's Mutilated Body Found Near River.' This sounds familiar." He started reading the article that stretched over three columns of the front page.

"Guess who was a junior pastor at Wood River's St. Mary's Catholic Church?"

He stopped, looked back at her and rubbed his jaw. "You still don't have any evidence. It's all circumstantial. Why didn't this case come up during Jeffreys' trial?"

"There was no need. From what I've been able to find, a transient working at St. Mary's Church took the blame."

"Or maybe he did it." He hated where this was leading. "How did you find out about it?"

"Just a hunch. When I talked to Father Francis this morning, he told me Father Keller had started a similar summer camp at his previous parish in Wood River, Maine."

"So you looked for murdered boys in the area at the time he was there."

"I didn't have to look very hard. This murder matches right down to the X. Circumstantial or not, Father Keller needs to be considered a suspect." She closed down the program and shut off the computer.

"I've got to meet George in about an hour," Maggie said, "then I'm meeting with Father Francis." She started taking clothes out of the closet and laying them on the bed. "I need to leave for Richmond tonight. My mother's in the hospital." She avoided looking at him while she pulled more of her things from drawers.

"Jesus, Maggie, is she okay?"

"Sort of...I guess she will be. I'll have some information for you on disk. Can you access Microsoft Word?"

"Sure...yeah, I think so." Her matter-of-fact attitude flustered him. Was something wrong, or was she simply concerned about her mother?

"I'll leave my notes from this afternoon's autopsy with George. If I find out anything from Father Francis, I'll call you."

"You're not coming back, are you?" The realization struck him like another fist to the jaw. It also stopped her. She turned to face him, though her eyes darted from his to the blank computer screen to his to the mess on the bed. She had never had a tough time meeting his eyes before.

"Technically, I finished what I was asked to do. You have a profile and maybe even a suspect. I'm not even sure that I need to be involved with this second autopsy."

"So that's it?" He shoved his hands into his pockets. Suddenly, he felt nauseated at the thought of never seeing her again.

"I'm sure the Bureau will send someone else to help you."

"But not you?" He caught something in her eyes. Was it a flicker of regret, sadness? Whatever it was, she didn't let him see it. She started filling her suitcase. "Does this have anything to do with what happened this morning?"

"Nothing happened this morning," she snapped, and stopped shoving things into her bag. She kept her back to him. "I'm sorry if I gave you the wrong impression." Then she glanced over her shoulder at him. "Look, Nick, I don't mean to sound ungrateful." She kept her hands busy folding, tucking and shuffling items into her bag.

Of course, she hadn't given him the wrong impression. He had done that all on his own. But what about the heat, the electricity? He certainly hadn't imagined that.

"I'm gonna miss you." The words surprised him. He hadn't meant to say them out loud.

She stopped, straightened and turned slowly, this time meeting his eyes. Those luscious brown eyes made him weak in the knees, like a high-school kid admitting to his first girlfriend that he liked her. Jesus, what was wrong with him?

"You've been a pain in the ass, O'Dell, but I'm going to miss you giving me a hard time." There. He corrected his slip.

She smiled. There was the hair-tuck behind the ears. At least she wasn't totally in control.

"Do you need a lift to the airport?"

"No, I have a rental I need to turn in."

"Well, have a good flight." It sounded cold and pathetic when what he really wanted to do was wrap his arms around her and convince her to stay. He crossed the room to leave in three long strides, hoping his knees didn't buckle.

"Nick."

He stopped at the door, his hand on the handle, and glanced back at her.

She paused, and in a brief moment he saw her change her mind from whatever she was going to say.

"Good luck," she said simply.

He nodded and left, feeling lead in his shoes and an ache in his chest that made it hard to breathe.

CHAPTER 47

Maggie watched the door close as her hands strangled and twisted a silk blouse.

Why didn't she just tell Nick about the note, about Albert Stucky? He had understood about the nightmares. Maybe he'd understand about this. Maybe he'd understand that she just couldn't allow herself to be psychologically poked and probed by another madman. Not now. Not when she felt so vulnerable, so damn fragile, like she could shatter into a million tiny pieces, just as she had earlier on the bathroom floor. She couldn't risk it. It would cloud her judgment.

Perhaps it already had. Last night in the woods she hadn't even seen the killer coming at her until it was too late. He could easily have killed her. But like Albert Stucky, this killer wanted her alive, and oddly enough, that terrified her even more. Somehow she knew sharing all that with anyone would make her feel more vulnerable. No, it was best this way—to leave Nick and everyone else thinking her departure was only because of her mother.

She stuffed the garment bag, crushing and wrinkling her dry-cleanables. Director Cunningham had been right. She needed to take some time off. Maybe she and Greg could take a trip. Someplace warm and sunny, where it didn't get dark at six in the evening.

The phone rang, and she jumped as if it were a gunshot. She had already talked to Dr. Avery. Her mother had survived the seventy-two-hour suicide watch and was doing quite well. But this was the part her mother was good at—playing the model patient and devouring all the special attention.

Maggie grabbed the phone. "Special Agent O'Dell."

"Maggie, why are you still there? I thought you were coming home."

She lowered herself to the bed, suddenly exhausted. "Hi, Greg." She waited for a real greeting, heard papers shuffling and knew she had only half his attention. "I'm catching a flight tonight."

"Good, so that dunce actually gave you my message last night?"

"What dunce?"

"The one I talked to last night who picked up your cellular. He said you must have dropped it and couldn't come to the phone."

Her grip tightened. Her pulse raced.

"What time was that?"

"I don't know...late. About midnight here. Why?"

"What did you tell him?"

"Oh, for cryin' out loud. That asshole didn't give you the message, did he?"

"Greg, what did you tell him?" Her heart thumped against her rib cage.

"What kind of incompetent hicks are you working with, Maggie?"

"Greg." She tried to stay calm, to keep the scream from clawing its way out of her throat. "I lost my cellular phone last night when I was chasing the killer. There's a good chance he was the one you talked to."

Silence. Even the paper shuffling had come to a stop.

"For God's sake, Maggie. How was I supposed to know?" His tone was subdued.

"There's no way you could have known. I'm not blaming you, Greg. Just please, try to remember what you told him."

"Nothing really...just to call me and that your mother wasn't doing too well."

She leaned back on the bed, sinking her head into the pillows and closing her eyes.

"Maggie, when you get home we need to talk."

Yes, they would talk on a beach somewhere, sipping fruity drinks, the ones with little umbrellas stuffed in them. They'd talk about what was really important, rekindle their lost love, rediscover the mutual respect and goals that had brought them together in the first place.

"I want you to quit the Bureau," he said, and then she knew there would never be a sunny beach for them.

CHAPTER 48

The snow exploded into flying white powder as his feet came down with heavy thuds, smashing through drifts. Snow clung to his pant legs and leaked inside his shoes, turning his feet to ice. His body wasn't his own, propelling him through branches and down the side of the hill at a speed that would surely send him tumbling headfirst at any moment.

Then he heard them, squealing and giggling. He slid to a halt, crashing into shrubs and snow-laced prairie grass that prevented him from rolling into the sledders' path. He lay there, pressed into the snow, the white death sucking the heat from his body. He hid, trying to control his rapid breathing, inhaling through his mouth and creating a vapor each time he exhaled.

They should have gone home while the throbbing in his head was silent. Why hadn't they gone home? It would be getting dark soon. Would there be plates set on a dinner table waiting for them or only a note and a microwave dinner? Would their parents be there to make sure they took off their wet clothing? Would anyone be there to tuck them into bed?

He couldn't stop the memories, and he no longer tried. He laid his face into the snow hoping it would stop the pounding. He could see himself at twelve, wearing a green army jacket with little lining to keep out the cold. His patched jeans allowed drafts to assault his body. He hadn't owned a pair of boots. The snowfall had been over ten inches and the entire town ground to a stop, leaving his stepfather with nowhere to go except his mother's bedroom. He had been told to leave the house, to "go play in the snow with his friends." Only he had no friends. The kids had only paid attention to him to make fun of his shabby clothes and his scrawny build.

After hours of sitting in the cold backyard watching the other kids sledding, he had gone back to the house only to find the door locked. Through the thin wood and fragile glass, he had listened to his mother's screams and moans—pain and pleasure indistinguishable. Did sex have to hurt? He couldn't imagine growing to enjoy such pain. And he remembered feeling ashamed because he had been relieved. He knew as long as his stepfather slammed into his mother, he wouldn't slam into his small body.

It was while he sat in the bitter white cold that day that he had plotted, a plot so simple it required only a ball of string. The next morning when his stepfather retreated to his basement workshop, he would come back up on a stretcher. He and his mother would never feel ashamed or scared again. How could he have known that his mother would go down to the basement first that morning? That morning when his life had ended; when that horrible wicked, little boy had ended his mother's life.

Suddenly, he felt someone above him, breathing and sniffing. He slowly looked up to find a black dog within inches of his face. The dog bared his teeth, emitting a low growl. Without warning, his hands shot out at the dog's throat and the growl became a quiet whine, a stifled gurgle, then silence.

He watched the boys dressed in thick parkas running and jumping with stiff legs and arms. Finally, they gathered up their sledding contraptions and said their goodbyes. One boy called for the dog several times but gave up easily to catch up with his friends. They separated and headed in different directions, three one way, two another while one crossed the church's parking lot alone.

The sky changed from light gray to slate. Streetlights blinked on one at a time. A jet thundered overhead, the sound amplified by the white, silent town. There wasn't a single vehicle or pedestrian when he climbed into his own car. He pulled the ski mask back on despite the perspiration gathering on his forehead and upper lip. On the seat next to him, he laid out a fresh handkerchief, carefully and meticulously as though it were already a part of the ceremony. He brought a vial out of his coat pocket, cracked it and anointed the white linen. Then he kept the headlights off and the engine soft as he slowly followed the boy who dragged his bright orange plastic sled behind him.

CHAPTER 49

The sheriff's department could afford only five fully equipped squad cars, and four were parked outside the courthouse when Nick returned. Immediately, the fury burned in his stomach. What would it take to get these people to listen to him, to take his orders seriously? Yet, he knew it was his own fault.

He had treated his position as sheriff with the same reckless disregard that had ruled the rest of his life—to simply kick back and take nothing too seriously. That was before. Before he had fallen into Danny Alverez's blood. Now he couldn't help wondering whether a real sheriff could have saved Matthew Tanner. But Platte City had a skirt-chasing college quarterback with a law degree, absolutely no experience and only his father's name and reputation to win him the right to call himself sheriff and to carry a badge and a gun. A gun, by the way, that he hadn't fired since target practice to get the job nearly two years ago.

Michelle Tanner's ex-husband had knocked more than just his jaw out of whack. Too bad it had taken a fist to knock some sense of responsibility into him. And now that Maggie was leaving, it was up to him to take control. He just wished he knew how the hell to do that.

He entered the courthouse and immediately wanted to flee in the other direction. The huge marble lobby echoed with the chatter of reporters. Cords and cables snaked over the floor. Bright lights blinded him and a dozen microphones were shoved into his face while reporters assaulted him with questions.

Darcy McManus—an ex-beauty queen turned TV anchor—barricaded the staircase with her tall, lean body. It was hard to ignore the long legs she showed off in the short skirts she pretended were part of a suit. She offered him a spot beside her in front of Channel Five's camera. He shoved his way to the staircase but purposely kept his distance. In the past, he would have flirted with her and taken advantage of the attention. Maybe he would have even gotten her phone number. Now he just wanted to get past her and escape to his office.

"Sheriff, do you have any suspects yet?" She looked older than she did on TV. Up close he saw the caked makeup concealing the lines at the corners of her mouth and eyes.

"I have no comment at this time."

"Is it true Matthew Tanner's body was decapitated?" a man in an expensive double-breasted suit wanted to know.

"Jesus. Where the hell did you hear that?"

"Then it's true?"

"No. Absolutely not."

Others joined in, pressing against Nick. He tried to elbow his way through.

"Sheriff, what about the rumor that you've ordered the exhumation of Ronald Jeffreys' grave? Do you believe Jeffreys wasn't the one executed?"

"Was the boy sexually assaulted?"

"Have you found the blue pickup yet?"

"Sheriff Morrelli, can you at least tell us whether this boy was murdered in the same manner? Are we dealing with a serial killer?"

"What shape was Matthew's body in?"

"Stop! Hold it," Nick yelled, raising his hands to ward off any more questions. The shuffle halted. The shoving came to a standstill, and there was silence as the vultures waited. The sudden quiet disarmed him. He glanced around and backed his way to the first step of the open staircase. A trickle of sweat rolled down his back. He raked his fingers through his hair and noticed his fingers trembling. He was used to being confronted with accolades, not criticism and skepticism.

What the hell was he supposed to tell them? Last time, Maggie had bailed him out. Now, in her absence, he felt exposed and vulnerable, and he hated it. He grabbed the handrail to steady himself and pulled himself up beside McManus. She looked pleased and began smoothing her hair and clothing, preparing for the camera. He ignored her and looked out over the crowd, eyes staring back at him, pens, cameras and recording devices ready. His gut told him to turn around and leave them in silence. He could take the stairs three at a time and be in his office before they could follow. After all, he didn't owe them an explanation. None of this would help him catch the murderer. Or would it?

"You all know I can't reveal specific details about the victims' bodies. But for God's sake, for Mrs. Tanner's sake, Matthew's body was not—I repeat—not decapitated. That's not to say that this guy isn't one sick son of a bitch."

"Is this a serial killing, Sheriff? The people deserve to know if they should lock up their children."

"Early indications do show that Matthew was killed by the same person who killed Danny Alverez."

"Any suspects?"

"Is it true you have absolutely no leads?"

Nick backed up another step. He had nothing to satisfy them. The crowd and bright lights made him hot and nauseated. He pulled at his jacket's zipper and tugged at his tie, loosening its strangling hold.

"We do have a couple of suspects. I'm not at liberty to say who they are. Not yet." He turned and a flood of questions assaulted his back as he started up the steps.

"When will you be able to tell us?"

"Are they local men?"

"Will your father be heading the investigation now?"

"Have you tracked down a blue pickup?"

Nick spun around, almost losing his balance. "What about my father?"

Everyone stared at the man in the double-breasted suit. Nick noted the man's shiny, dark hair. It looked professionally manufactured, and his goatee was perfectly trimmed with just a hint of gray. His expensive leather shoes labeled him an outsider—his shoes and the way he cocked his head to one side with the impatience of a man who had better things to do than repeat himself to a small-town sheriff. Nick wanted to grab him by the collar of his monogrammed shirt. Instead, he waited, teetering in snow-caked cowboy boots that were creating puddles and threatening to send him sliding down the smooth, marble steps.

"Why in the world would my father head this investigation?"

"He *did* catch Ronald Jeffreys," Darcy McManus said into her channel's camera, and only then did Nick realize they had been filming this whole fiasco. He avoided looking into the camera and stared at the man, waiting and ignoring his expression of boredom.

"When your father talked to us earlier, he made it sound—"

"He's here?" Nick blurted, and immediately regretted it. His incompetence was showing once more.

"Yes, and he made it sound as though he had returned to help with the investigation. I believe his exact words were..." The man slowly and deliberately flipped through his notes. "'I've done this before. I know what to look for. You can bet this guy's not getting by this old bloodhound.' I'm not familiar with bloodhounds, but I did interpret it to mean he was here in a professional capacity."

Other reporters nodded in agreement. Nick looked from one to another while his insides churned. His collar strangled him, the jacket made him sweat. Another trickle slid down his back. They waited. Every word would be weighed, every gesture measured. He imagined tonight someone would rewind their videotaped version of the news just to see him run down the steps backward. He didn't care. He turned and ran up the staircase, taking two and three steps at a time, silently praying he didn't trip and end up back at the bottom.

He crashed through the sheriff's department doors, smacking the glass against a metal trash can and a wall. A spider crack raced through the bottom of one of the doors, but no one seemed to notice. Instead, all eyes stared at Nick, their heads turned, their attention diverted from the tall gray-haired man in the center of them.

The same group Nick couldn't get to check a lead without a groan or a question was gathered around the distinguished-looking gentleman, an aging prophet with the beginning of a paunch over his belt and the bushy eyebrows that were now raised in indignation.

"Slow down, son. You just damaged government property," Antonio Morrelli said, pointing to the crack in the glass.

Despite the rage and frustration, Nick shoved his hands into his pockets, felt his shoulders slump as his eyes found his boots. Suddenly, he found himself wondering how much it would cost to replace the glass.

CHAPTER 50

Maggie sipped her Scotch and watched from a corner table as she tried to determine which of the airport-lounge customers were business travelers and which were vacationers. The storm had delayed flights, hers included, and had packed the small, poorly lit lounge, which consisted of an L-shaped bar, several small tables and chairs, dozens of model airplanes suspended from the ceiling and an old jukebox filled with songs like "Leaving on a Jet Plane" and "Outbound Plane."

Her green and black John Deere jacket was stretched across the chair opposite her to prevent any unwanted company. She had already checked her luggage, everything except her laptop computer, which was secure underneath the John Deere green. She thought about calling St. Margaret's again. She was beginning to think something dreadful may have happened. Otherwise, why would Father Francis have stood her up at the hospital? And why was there no one at the church rectory to answer the phone?

She wanted to call Nick, had in fact dialed the number but then hung up. He had enough things to handle without checking on her hunches. Besides, she was running out of change for the pay phone and had spent her last ten-dollar bill on this and the two previous Scotches. Not much of a dinner, but after spending the afternoon slicing Matthew Tanner's small body, weighing pieces of him and poking through his tiny organs, she had decided she deserved a dinner of Scotch.

The mark on Matthew's inside thigh had indeed been human bite marks. Poor George Tillie had tried to come up with several other theories before giving in to the realization that the killer had bitten Matthew over and over again in the same spot, making it impossible to register a set of dental prints. What made matters worse and more bizarre—the bites had occurred hours after Matthew was dead.

The killer didn't return to the scene of the crime only to watch the police. He continued his absurd fascination with the victim's body. He was slipping from his carefully planned ritual. Something was causing him to degenerate, to lose control. In his recklessness, he could soon leave incriminating evidence.

Maggie had told George they should look for smudges of semen; that the killer may have masturbated this time, while biting the dead boy, and may have smeared some on the victim. The old coroner's face had turned scarlet as he mumbled something about doing his job in private.

She didn't blame George. It had been obvious her presence made him uncomfortable. His manner and method resembled the reverence of a priest, with his careful and deliberate touches and his hushed speech. It was almost as though he hadn't wanted to disturb the boy's soul.

Maggie, on the other hand, had cut with clinical precision and had spoken loud and clear for her voice-activated recorder. It was a dead body, void of life and warmth. Whatever had resided within the bone-and-flesh cavity had escaped hours ago. Yet, she had to admit there was something wrong, something almost sacrilegious about slicing apart a child's body. The soft, smooth and hairless skin hadn't seen nearly enough scrapes and bruises, nor the bones enough chips and breaks to have really lived. It seemed such a waste, such an injustice. But that was what the Scotch was for—to make sense of it all or, at least, to take her to a place where she wouldn't care, even if only temporarily.

"Excuse me, ma'am." The young bartender stood over her table. "The gentleman at the end of the bar bought you another Scotch." He set the glass in front of her. "And he asked me to give you this."

Maggie recognized the envelope and the boxy handwriting before he handed it to her. Her stomach lurched, her pulse quickened. She stood up so abruptly, her chair teetered on two legs.

"Which man?" She stretched to see over the crowd. The bartender did the same, then shrugged his shoulders.

"He must have left."

"What did he look like?" She patted her side through her blazer, reassured by the feel of the butt on her gun pressing against her just under her breast.

"I don't know...tall, dark hair, maybe twenty-eight, maybe thirty. Look, I didn't pay a whole lot of attention. Is there a problem with—"

She shoved past him and pushed through the crowd, racing out into the bright airport walkway. Frantically, she searched and scanned the passengers coming and going. Her heart pounded against her chest. Her head throbbed, and her vision was a bit blurred from the Scotch.

The long walkway stretched straight in both directions. There was a family with three children, several businessmen carrying laptops and briefcases, an airport employee pushing a handcart, two gray-haired women and a group of black men and women in colorful robes and headdresses. But there was no tall, dark-haired man without luggage.

He couldn't possibly have gotten beyond the walkway. She ran toward the escalator at the far end, bumping into passengers and almost tripping over a deserted luggage gurney. The escalator went up and down. She chose up and twisted over the handrail to see down. Again, the array of passengers didn't include a tall, dark-haired man. He was gone. He had slipped by her again.

She made her way back to the lounge, only now realizing she had left her jacket and laptop along with the envelope. Though the lounge was packed, no one had attempted to take over her small table. Even the envelope leaned against the fresh drink where the bartender had left it.

She eased into the hard chair and stared at the small envelope. She gulped the remainder of Scotch in her glass and set it aside. She started on the fresh drink despite the swirling inside her head. She wanted to be numb.

She took the envelope carefully by a corner. The seal broke easily, and she slipped the index card out onto the table without touching it. Even the Scotch couldn't prevent the nausea and the stab of terror the words inflicted.

In the same boxy lettering, the note said:

SORRY TO SEE YOU LEAVE SO SOON. PERHAPS I CAN STOP BY YOUR CONDO THE NEXT TIME I'M IN THE CREST RIDGE AREA. SAY HI TO GREG FOR ME.

CHAPTER 51

From down on the sidewalk, he could see Maggie O'Dell inside, scrambling up the escalator. He did have to admit she moved quite nicely—definitely a runner. He imagined those strong, athletic legs looked good in a pair of tight shorts, though the image didn't much interest him.

He pushed the handcart aside and removed the cap and jacket he had borrowed from the sleeping airport employee. He rolled them into a ball and shoved them into a trash can.

He had left the Lexus with the radio blaring in the loading zone. With the radio and the jets overhead, no one would ever hear Timmy, should he wake up sooner than expected. Besides, the trunk was tight, almost soundproof, meaning there was also very little air.

He got into the car just as a security guard with a pad of tickets started in his direction. He squealed away from the curb and zipped around the unloading vehicles. It would be pitch-black by the time he got Timmy settled in, but the detour had been worth seeing the look on Special Agent O'Dell's face.

The wind had picked up, creating swirls of snow and promising drifts by morning. The kerosene heater, lantern and sleeping bag in the back seat, originally packed for the camping trip, would come in handy, after all. Perhaps he would drive through McDonald's on the way. Timmy loved Big Macs, and he found himself getting hungry.

He eased into traffic, waving a thank-you to the red-haired lady in the

Mazda who let him in front of her. The day had not been a waste. He gunned the engine, ignoring the slip and slide of the tires on icy pavement. He was in control again.

CHAPTER 52

"This guy's making a fuckin' spectacle out of you," Antonio Morrelli lectured Nick while looking quite comfortable behind Nick's desk, twirling back and forth in the leather chair that was once his. It was the only piece of the elaborate furnishings Nick had kept when replacing his father as sheriff.

"You need to spend some time with those TV people," his father continued, "reassure them you know what you're doing. Last night Peter Jennings made you sound like some country hick who couldn't find his own ass with a flashlight. Goddamn it, Nick, Peter fucking Jennings!"

Nick stared out the window, past the snow-covered streets and toward the dark horizon beyond the streetlights. A hint of an orange moon peeked from behind a veil of clouds.

"Did Mom come with you?" he asked from his window perch without looking at his father, ignoring his insults. It was the same old game they played. His father hurled insults and instructions, and Nick kept quiet and pretended to listen. Most of the time he followed the instructions. It was easier. It had come to be expected.

"She stayed with your aunt Minnie and the RV down in Houston," his father answered, but his look told Nick he wouldn't be sidetracked from the real subject. "You need to start hauling in suspects off the street. You know, the usual scumbags. Bring 'em in for questioning. Make it look like you're on top of things."

"I do have a couple of suspects," Nick said suddenly, remembering that he did, indeed.

"Great, let's haul them in. Judge Murphy could probably get a search warrant by morning. Who are your suspects?"

Nick wondered whether it had been that easy with Jeffreys: a late-night search warrant used only after the evidence had been carefully planted.

"Who are your suspects, son?" he repeated.

Perhaps he just wanted to shock his father. Common sense should have kept his mouth shut. Instead, he turned from the window and said, "One of them is Father Michael Keller."

He watched his father stop rocking in the chair. The older man's face registered surprise, then he shook his head and frustration creased the leather-like forehead.

"What the fuck are you trying to pull, Nick? A fucking priest—the media will crucify you. Is this your idea, or that pretty, little FBI agent the guys told me about?"

The guys. His guys. His department. Nick could imagine them laughing and making jokes about Maggie and him.

"Father Keller fits Agent O'Dell's profile."

"Nick, how many times do I have to tell you. You can't go letting your Mr. Johnson make your decisions for you."

"I'm not." Nick's face grew hot. He turned back toward the window, pretending to stare down at the streets, but his vision was blurred by his anger.

"O'Dell makes a good point. And I'm sure she makes a good omelet for breakfast after a night of fucking. Doesn't mean you should listen to her."

Nick rubbed a hand across his jaw and mouth to prevent the rage that formed its own words. He swallowed hard, waited, then turned to face his father again.

"This is my investigation, my decision, and I'm bringing in Father Keller for questioning."

"Fine." His father held up his hands in surrender. "Make a fucking asshole of yourself." He got up and started for the door. "In the meantime, I'll see if Gillick and Benjamin can round up some real suspects."

He waited until his father was out the door and down the hall. Then Nick turned and slammed his fist into the wall. The rough texture ripped open his knuckles and pain shot up his arm. He tried to control his breathing, waiting for the rage to settle, for the frustration and humiliation to be overwhelmed by the pain. Then, without thinking, he wiped at the blood running down the wall using his white shirtsleeve. He already had to pay for a broken glass door; he couldn't afford to have his office repainted, too.

CHAPTER 53

The house was dark when Christine pulled into the driveway. She loaded the warm pizza box on top of her laptop computer and realized she'd probably be eating the pizza herself if Timmy was still at one of his friends' houses. He'd come home with storybook descriptions of something they called meatloaf and mashed potatoes—food that didn't come from a can, a box or a carton. Surely he remembered the days when she had actually fixed real dinners and had them on the table at the same time every night. She wondered if he missed their life as a family. What had she cost him for the price of her own self-respect?

She fumbled through the dark foyer until she found the light switch. For some reason the quiet sent a chill down her spine. Perhaps it was only the wind. She kicked the front door closed and made her way to the kitchen, stopping by the answering machine. No blinking red light, no messages. How many times did she have to tell Timmy to call and leave a message? There was no excuse, especially now that she had a cellular phone, although even she hadn't memorized that number yet.

She threw her coat over a kitchen chair and piled her computer and handbag onto its seat. The pizza's aroma reminded her how hungry she was. After Eddie Gillick's visit at Wanda's, she had lost her appetite and left most of her lunch unfinished.

She poured herself a glass of wine, tucked a folded newspaper under her arm and scooped up a piece of pizza, using only a napkin as a plate. Hands filled, she kicked off her shoes and padded into the living room, finding refuge on the soft sofa. No food was allowed in the living room, especially on the sofa. She expected Timmy to come in at any moment and catch her in the act.

She set her dinner on the glass coffee table and unfolded the newspaper. This evening's paper carried the same headline from the morning: Second Body Found. Only underneath, she had now confirmed that the body was Matthew Tanner's. Tonight's article also included a quote from George Tillie. She found the paragraph and reread her handiwork, letting George confirm that the murders were the work of a serial killer, since Nick wouldn't.

She had closed the article with a quote she had gotten from Michelle Tanner on Monday, a melodramatic plea for her son's return. Christine followed the quote with, "A mother's desperate plea has, once again, fallen on deaf ears." Now, seeing it in print, it seemed a tad too much; however, Corby had loved it.

She flipped through the rest of the paper and scanned the readers'-comment column to see whether her name was mentioned. Suddenly, she remembered the time, frantically searched for the remote and turned on the TV, flipping to Channel Five.

As usual, Darcy McManus looked impeccable in a deep purple suit and crimson red blouse. Christine examined McManus's silky black hair, large brown eyes, darkened even more by the eyeliner and smudge of highlight on the eyelids. The lipstick was bold, a red to match her blouse. Christine couldn't imagine herself in McManus's place. She'd need a whole new wardrobe, but then she'd be able to afford one with what Ramsey was offering to pay her.

She had to admit the idea of being on TV did excite her. The Omaha ABC affiliate claimed a viewership of almost a million people throughout eastern Nebraska. She'd be a celebrity and maybe even cover national events. Though she had told Ramsey she needed time to decide, she knew her mind was already made up. She couldn't justify turning down the money. Not with bills stacking up and the remote possibility of losing their home. No, she had no room for principles. She would accept the position in the morning, but only after talking to Corby.

She finished her wine. Another piece of pizza sounded good, but suddenly she was too exhausted to move. She decided to lay her head down for just ten or fifteen minutes. She closed her eyes and thought of all the things she and Timmy would spend her new salary on. In minutes, she was fast asleep.

CHAPTER 54

"Why don't you eat some of your Big Mac?" the man in the dead president's mask was saying.

Timmy curled into the corner. The bedsprings squeaked each time he moved. His eyes darted around the small room lit only by a lantern on an old crate. The light created its own creepy shadows on the walls with spiderweb cracks. He was shaking, and he couldn't control it, just like last winter when he got so sick his mom had had to take him to the emergency room. And he did feel sick to his stomach, but it wasn't the same. He was shaking because he was scared, because he didn't know where he was or how he had gotten here.

The tall man in the mask had been nice so far. When he had stopped Timmy by the church to ask for directions, he had been wearing a black ski mask, the kind robbers wore in the movies. But it was cold out, and the man seemed lost and confused but not scary. Even when the man had gotten out of his car to show Timmy a map, Timmy hadn't felt scared. There was something familiar about him. That was when the man had grabbed him and shoved a white cloth against his face. Timmy couldn't remember anything else, except waking up here.

The wind howled through the rotted boards that covered the windows, but the room was warm. Timmy noticed a kerosene heater in the corner, the kind his dad had used when they had gone camping. Only that was ages ago, when his dad still cared about him.

"You really should eat. I know you haven't had anything since lunch."

Timmy stared at the man, who looked more ridiculous than scary dressed in a sweater, jeans and bright white Nikes that looked new except that one shoestring was knotted together. A pair of huge, black, dripping rubber boots sat by the door on a paper sack. It struck Timmy as odd that such new Nikes could already have a broken and knotted shoestring. If *he* had new Nikes, he'd take better care of them than that.

There was something about the muffled voice that Timmy recognized, but he wasn't sure what it was. He tried to think of the president's name—the one the mask resembled. It was the guy with the big nose who had to resign. Why couldn't he think of his name? They had just memorized the presidents last year.

He wished he could stop shivering, but it hurt to try to stop, so he let his teeth chatter.

"Are you cold? Is there anything else I can get you?" the man asked, and Timmy shook his head. "Tomorrow I'll bring you some baseball cards and comic books." The man got up, took the lantern from the crate and started to leave.

"Can I keep the lantern?" Timmy's voice surprised him. It was clear and calm, despite his body shaking beyond his control.

The man looked back at him, and Timmy could see the eyes through the mask's eyeholes. In the light of the lantern, they were sparkling as if the man were smiling.

"Sure, Timmy. I'll leave the lantern."

Timmy didn't remember telling the man his name. Did he know him?

The man set the lantern back down on the crate, pulled on his thick rubber boots and left, locking the door with several clicks and clacks from the outside. Timmy waited, listening over the thumping of his heart. He counted out two minutes, and when he was sure the man wouldn't return, he looked around the room again. The rotted slats over the window were his best bet.

He crawled off the bed and tripped over his sled on the floor. He started for the window when something caught his leg. He looked down to find a silver handcuff around his ankle with a thick metal chain padlocked to the bedpost. He yanked at the chain, but even the metal-framed bed wouldn't budge. He dropped to his knees and tore at the handcuff, pulling and tugging until his fingers were red and his ankle sore. Suddenly, he stopped struggling.

He looked around the room again, and then he knew. This was where Danny and Matthew had been taken. He crawled into his plastic sled and curled up into a tight ball.

"Oh, God," he prayed out loud, the tremble in his voice scaring him even more. "Please don't let me get dead like Danny and Matthew."

Then he tried to think of something, anything else, and he began naming the presidents out loud, starting with, "Washington, Adams, Jefferson…"

CHAPTER 55

After making several phone calls and getting no response, Nick decided to drive over to the rectory. He couldn't go home. Eventually, that would be where his father would go. That was the one disadvantage of living in the family home—the family moved back whenever they wanted. And although the old farmhouse was certainly large enough, Nick didn't want to see or talk to his father for the rest of the evening.

The rectory was actually a ranch-style house connected to the church by an enclosed brick walkway. The church's stain glass hinted at just a flicker of candlelight, but the rectory was lit up inside and outside as if for a party. Yet, Nick waited a long time before anyone answered his knock.

Father Keller opened the door, dressed in a long black robe.

"Sheriff Morrelli, sorry for the delay. I was taking a shower," he said without surprise, as if he had been expecting him.

"I did try calling first."

"Really? I've been here all evening, except I'm afraid I can't hear the phone from my bathroom. Come in."

A freshly fed fire roared in the huge fireplace that was the room's center of attraction. A colorful Oriental rug and several easy chairs sat in front. Books were piled up next to one of the chairs, and at a glance Nick noticed they were art books—Degas, Monet, Renaissance painting. He felt silly expecting them to be on religious and philosophical topics. After all, priests were people. Of course, they had other interests, hobbies, passions, addictions.

"Please sit down." Father Keller pointed to one of the chairs.

Though he knew Father Keller only from the few times he'd attended Sunday mass, it was hard not to like the guy. Besides being tall, athletic and handsome, with boyish good looks, Father Keller possessed an ease, a calm that immediately made Nick feel comfortable. He glanced at the young priest's hands. The long fingers were clean and smooth with fingernails well manicured—not a cuticle in sight. They certainly didn't look like the hands of a man who strangled children. Maggie was way off base. There was no way this guy killed little boys. Nick should be questioning Ray Howard, instead.

"Can I get you some coffee?" Father Keller asked, sounding as if he genuinely wanted to please his guest.

"No, thanks. This won't take long." Nick unzipped his jacket and pulled out a notepad and pen. His hand ached. The knuckles bled through his homemade bandage. He tucked it up into the sleeve of his jacket to avoid attention.

"I'm afraid there's not much I can tell you, Sheriff. I think he simply had a heart attack."

"Excuse me?"

"Father Francis. That is why you're here, isn't it?"

"What about Father Francis?"

"Oh dear, God. I'm sorry. I thought that was why you were here. We think he had a heart attack and fell down the basement steps sometime this morning."

"Is he okay?"

"I'm afraid he's dead, God rest his soul." Father Keller picked at a thread on his robe and avoided Nick's eyes.

"Jesus, I'm sorry. I didn't know."

"I'm sure it's a shock. It certainly was for all of us. You served mass for Father Francis, didn't you? At the old St. Margaret's?"

"Seems like ages ago." Nick stared into the fire, remembering how fragile the old priest had looked when he and Maggie questioned him.

"Excuse me, Sheriff, but if you're not here about Father Francis, what is it I can help you with?"

For a moment the reason escaped him. Then Nick remembered Maggie's profile. Father Keller matched the physical characteristics. His bare feet even looked about a size twelve. But like his hands, his feet looked too clean, too smooth to have been out in the cold, trampling through rocks and branches.

"Sheriff Morrelli? Are you okay?"

"I'm fine. Actually, I just had a few questions for you about...about the summer church camp you sponsor."

"The church camp?" Was the look one of confusion or alarm? Nick couldn't be sure.

"Both Danny Alverez and Matthew Tanner were in your church camp this past summer."

"Really?"

"You didn't know?"

"We had over two hundred boys last summer. I wish I could get to know them all, but there just isn't time."

"Do you have pictures taken with all of them?"

"Excuse me?"

"My nephew, Timmy Hamilton, has a photo of about fifteen to twenty boys with you and Mr. Howard."

"Oh, yes." Father Keller raked his fingers through his thick hair, and only then did Nick realize it wasn't wet. "The canoe photos. Not all the boys qualified for the races, but, yes, we did take pictures with the ones who qualified. Mr. Howard is a volunteer counselor. I've tried to include Ray in as many church activities as possible ever since he left the seminary last year and came to work for us."

Howard had been in a seminary. Nick waited for more.

"So Timmy Hamilton is your nephew? He's a great kid."

"Yes, yes, he is." Did he dare ask more questions about Howard or was the distraction exactly what Father Keller wanted? There was no need to have mentioned Howard leaving the seminary.

"You started a similar church camp for boys at your previous parish, didn't you, Father Keller? In Maine." Nick pretended to look at his notepad, though it was blank. "Wood River, I believe it was." He watched for a reaction, but there was none.

"That's right."

"Why did you leave Wood River?"

"I was offered an associate pastor position here. You might say it was a promotion."

"Were you aware of a murder of a little boy in the Wood River area just before you left?"

"Vaguely. I'm not sure I understand your line of questioning, Sheriff. Are you accusing me of having some knowledge about these murders?"

Still, there was no alarm in his voice, no defensiveness, only concern.

"I'm just checking as many leads as possible." Suddenly, Nick felt ridiculous. How could Maggie ever have led him to believe that a Catholic priest was capable of murder? Then it hit him. "Father Keller, how did you know I served mass for Father Francis at the old St. Margaret's?"

"I'm not sure. Father Francis must have mentioned it to me." Again the priest avoided Nick's eyes. A sudden knock at the door interrupted them, and Father Keller quickly got up, almost too quickly, as if anxious to escape. "I'm certainly not dressed for company." He smiled at Nick as he tucked in the lapels of his robe and tightened its cinch.

Nick took the opportunity to escape the fire's heat. He got up and paced the large room. Huge built-in bookcases made up one wall, on the opposite were a bay window and window bench used for green plants. There were few decorations—a highly-polished, dark wooden crucifix with an unusual pointed end. It almost looked like a dagger. There were also several original paintings by an obscure artist. Quite nice, though Nick knew little about art. The swishes of bright color were hypnotic, swirling yellows and reds in a field of vibrant purple.

Then Nick saw them. Tucked away around the side of the brick fireplace that jutted out into the room was a pair of black rubber boots, still plastered with snow and sitting on an old welcome mat. Had Father Keller lied about being out this evening? Or perhaps the boots belonged to Ray Howard.

From the foyer Nick heard voices raised, a hint of frustration in Father Keller's and accusations from a woman's voice. Nick hurried to the entrance, where he saw Father Keller trying to remain calm and cool while Maggie O'Dell assaulted him with questions.

CHAPTER 56

At first Nick didn't recognize Maggie's voice. It was loud, shrill and belligerent—this from a woman who appeared to be the essence of control.

"I want to see Father Francis now," she said and pushed past Father Keller before he could explain. She almost ran into Nick. She backed away, startled. Her eyes met his. There was something wild and dark in hers—something a bit out of control to match her voice.

"Nick, what are you doing here?"

"I could ask you the same thing. Don't you have a flight to catch?"

She looked small in the oversize green jacket and blue jeans. Without makeup and with her windblown hair, she could have passed for a college coed.

"Flights are delayed."

"Excuse me," Father Keller interrupted.

"Maggie, you haven't met Father Michael Keller. Father Keller, this is Special Agent Maggie O'Dell."

"So you're Keller?" There was accusation in her voice. "What have you done with Father Francis?"

Again, the belligerence. Nick couldn't figure out this new approach. What happened to the cool, calm woman who usually made him look like the hothead?

"I tried to explain..." Father Keller tried again.

"Yes, you do have some explaining to do. Father Francis was supposed to meet me at the hospital this afternoon. He never showed up." She looked to Nick. "I've been calling here all afternoon and evening."

"Maggie, why don't you come in and calm down?"

"I don't want to calm down. I want some answers. I want to know what the hell's going on here."

"There was an accident this morning," Nick explained, since she wouldn't allow Father Keller to speak. "Father Francis fell down some basement steps. I'm afraid he's dead."

She was quiet, her entire body suddenly still. "An accident?" Then she looked up at Father Keller. "Nick, are you sure it was an accident?"

"Maggie."

"How can you be sure he wasn't pushed? Has anyone examined the body? I'll do the autopsy myself if necessary."

"An autopsy?" Father Keller repeated.

"Maggie, he was old and frail."

"Exactly. So why would he be going down basement steps?"

"Actually, it's our wine cellar," Father Keller tried to explain.

Maggie stared at him, and Nick noticed her hands clenched into fists. It wouldn't have surprised him if she took a swing at the priest. Nick couldn't figure out her angle. If she was playing bad cop, good cop, he wished she'd let him know.

"What exactly are you implying, Father Keller?" she finally asked.

"Implying? I'm not implying anything."

"Maggie, maybe we should go," Nick said, taking her gently by the arm. Immediately, she wrenched it from his hold and shot him a look that made him take a step backward. She stared at Father Keller again, then suddenly pushed past both of them and headed for the door.

Nick glanced at the priest, who looked as embarrassed and confused as Nick felt. Without saying a word, he followed Maggie out the front door. He caught up with her on the sidewalk. He reached for her arm to slow her down, but thought better of it and simply increased his pace to stay alongside her.

"What the hell was that about?" he demanded.

"He's lying. I doubt that it was an accident."

"Father Francis was an old man, Maggie."

"He had something important to tell me. When we talked on the phone this morning, I could tell someone else was listening in. I'm guessing it was Keller. Don't you see, Nick?" She came to a halt and turned to look at him. "Whoever was listening decided to stop Father Francis before he had a chance to tell me whatever was so important. An autopsy may show whether or not he was pushed. I'll do it myself if—"

"Maggie, stop. There's not going to be an autopsy. Keller didn't push anybody, and I don't think he had anything to do with the murders. This is nuts. We need to start looking at some real suspects. We need to..."

She looked as though she would be sick. Her face went white, her shoulders slumped, and her eyes were watery.

"Maggie?"

She turned and hurried off the sidewalk into the snow, back behind the rectory and out of the bright streetlights. Shielded from the wind and clinging to a tree, she bent over and began retching. Nick grimaced and kept his distance. Now he understood the belligerence, the loud accusation, the uncharacteristic anger. Maggie O'Dell was drunk.

He waited until she finished, standing guard in the shadows, keeping his back to her in case she was now sober enough to be embarrassed.

"Nick."

When he turned, she was walking away from him, behind the rectory toward a grove of trees that separated the church property from Cutty's Hill.

"Nick, look." She stopped and pointed, and he wondered if she was delusional. Then he saw it, and immediately he, too, felt sick to his stomach. Tucked back in the trees was an old blue pickup with wooden side racks.

CHAPTER 57

"I'll get Judge Murphy to issue a search warrant first thing in the morning." Nick was still explaining when they got back to Maggie's hotel room. She wished that he would just shut up. Her head ached and her stomach hurt. Why in the world did she drink all that Scotch on an empty stomach?

She threw her laptop and jacket onto the bed and lay down next to them. She was lucky to get her room back with there being so many stranded motorists.

Nick stood in the doorway, looking uncomfortable, but making no effort to leave.

"I couldn't believe the way you were going at Keller. Jesus, I thought you were going to punch him."

She looked up at him without moving from her resting place. "I know you don't believe me, but Keller has something to do with all this. Either come in or leave, but don't stand in the open doorway. I have a reputation, after all."

He smiled and came in, closing the door. Once inside, he paced until he noticed her frowning at him. He pulled a chair to the edge of the bed where she could see him and not have to move.

"So what did you do, decide to have a little going-away party?"

"It seemed like a good idea at the time."

"Aren't you going to miss your flight?"

"I probably already have."

"What about your mother?"

"I'll call in the morning."

"So you came all the way back just for a piece of Keller?"

She pulled herself up on one elbow and dug through her jacket pockets. She handed him the small envelope and lay back down.

"What is it?"

"I was in the airport lounge when the bartender gave me that—said a guy at the bar asked him to deliver it to me. Only the guy was gone by the time I got it."

She watched him read it. There was confusion, and she remembered she hadn't told him about the first note.

"It's from the killer."

"How does he know where you live and your husband's name?"

"He's probing me, investigating me, digging into my background just like I'm doing to him."

"Jesus, Maggie."

"It comes with the territory. It's not that unusual." She closed her eyes and massaged the throbbing in her temples. "No one answered the phone at the rectory for hours. Plenty of time to make a trip to the airport and back."

When she opened her eyes, Nick was studying her. She sat up, suddenly feeling exposed under his concerned gaze. His chair was close to the bed. Their knees almost touched. The room started spinning, tipping to the right, setting everything off balance. She almost expected the furniture to start sliding.

"Maggie, are you okay?"

She looked into his blue eyes and felt the electrical current even before his fingers touched her face and his palm caressed her cheek. She leaned into it, closing her eyes again and allowing her body to absorb the spinning and the electricity. Suddenly, she vaulted from his touch, scrambling from the bed and from him. Her breathing was uneven, and she steadied herself with both hands, leaning against the dresser. She looked up and saw him in the mirror, behind her. Their eyes met in the reflection, and she held his gaze even though what she saw in his eyes made her stomach flutter. This time it wasn't because of the alcohol.

She watched as he came up behind her, so close she felt his breath on her neck even before he leaned down to kiss it. The Packers jersey had slipped off her shoulder, and she watched in the mirror as his soft, wet lips moved slowly, deliberately from her neck to her shoulder to her back. By the time they moved up her neck again, she had trouble breathing.

"Nick, what are you doing?" she gasped, surprised by her reaction and no longer able to control it.

"I've wanted to touch you for days."

His tongue flicked at her earlobe, and her knees went weak. She leaned back against him, afraid she'd fall.

"This isn't a good idea." It came out as a whisper, not the least bit convincing. And it certainly didn't stop his big, steady hands from coming around her waist, one palm flat against her stomach, sending a shiver down her back and the flutter from her stomach down between her legs.

"Nick." It was useless. She couldn't talk, couldn't breathe, and his gentle, urgent mouth was devouring her in soft, wet explorations while his hands made their way up her body. She noticed one had a bandage wrapped around the knuckles. She wanted to ask what had happened, but she couldn't concentrate on anything except her breathing.

She watched in the mirror as his hands moved over her breasts, swallowing them and beginning their circular caress, rendering her completely helpless. It was too much. It was sensory overload. She was already wet between her legs before one of his hands strayed and began to caress her there, the fingers gentle and expert. She was close to the edge when finally she found enough strength to twist herself around to face him, to push him away. But when her hands came up to his chest, they betrayed her, beginning their own exploration and unbuttoning his shirt, desperate to gain access to his skin.

He actually trembled when his mouth finally found hers. She hesitated, surprised by her own moans, her own urgency. His mouth urged her on with delicate but persistent nibbles until she couldn't stand it any longer and kissed him back with the same urgency. Again, her body seemed powerless, and she leaned against the dresser attempting to find relief from the magnetic force of his hot body. She was gasping for air when his mouth left hers and made its way to her neck and then down to her breasts, sucking at her nipples through the cotton of the jersey and sending a jolt so powerful she clung to the dresser top.

"Oh, God, Nick," she gasped. She needed to stop, couldn't stop. The room was spinning again. Her ears ringing. Her heart banging against her rib cage and her blood rushing from her head. That constant ringing. No, it wasn't her ears. It was the phone. The phone—reality—pulled her back from the edge.

"Nick...the phone," she managed.

He was kneeling in front of her. He stopped and looked up, his hands on her waist, his eyes filled with desire. How did she ever let it get this far? It was the Scotch. It was that damn fuzziness in her head. It was that delicious mouth and those strong hands. Damn it, she needed to gain control.

She pulled away from him and stumbled to the nightstand, knocking the phone and grabbing the receiver as the base crashed to the floor. She kept her back to Nick, avoiding his eyes, or she'd never be able to stop the trembling her body was experiencing.

"Yes," she said, trying her voice and disappointed that her breathing still came in gasps. "This is Maggie O'Dell."

"Maggie, oh, thank God, I got ahold of you. This is Christine Hamilton. I don't know what to do. I'm sorry I'm calling so late. I tried to get ahold of Nicky, but no one knows where he is."

"Calm down, Christine." She glanced back at Nick.

The mention of his sister's name brought him to attention. She watched his fingers fumble with his shirt buttons as though Christine had walked into the room and caught them. Maggie crossed her arms in an attempt to stop her breasts from tingling, the memory of his mouth on them still fresh, the front of her jersey still damp. She turned her back to Nick again, avoiding the distraction, and pushed her hair out of her face, tucking wild strands behind her ears.

"Christine, what's wrong?"

"It's Timmy. He wasn't here when I got home. I thought he just went home with one of his friends. But I've called. No one has seen him since this afternoon. They all went sledding on Cutty's Hill. The other kids said they saw him walking home, but he's not here. Oh, God, Maggie, he's not here. That was over five hours ago. I'm so scared. I don't know what to do."

Maggie cupped the mouthpiece and sat on the edge of the bed before her knees could give out.

"Timmy is missing," she said calmly, but felt the panic in the pit of her empty stomach. She watched Nick's eyes fill with his own panic.

"Jesus, no," he said, and they stared at each other, the electricity quickly replaced by the terrifying realization.

CHAPTER 58

Christine bit her nails, an old childhood habit absently resurrected as she watched her father pace her living room. At first, when she called Nick's and her father answered, she was surprised and relieved. But now there was no comfort in watching him stomp back and forth while he barked orders to the deputies who filled her house and yard. She felt even more helpless in his presence. Suddenly, she was that invisible little girl, incapable of doing anything.

"Why don't you go lie down, honey. Get some rest," her father said in one of his passes.

She only shook her head, unable to answer.

Not knowing what else to do, he simply ignored her.

When Nick and Maggie shoved their way into the crowded living room, Christine jumped up and almost ran to her brother. She stopped herself and teetered on weak knees, hovering close to the sofa. Even in her panic, throwing her arms around her brother seemed awkward. As if sensing all this, Nick made his way across the room. He hesitated in front of her, then gently pulled her to him and wrapped his strong arms around her without saying a word. Until now, she had held it together—her father's strong little soldier. Suddenly, the tears came in a choking rush that shook her entire body. She clung to Nick tightly, muffling her retching sobs into the stiff fabric of his jacket. Her entire body hurt, aching from her failed attempt at warding off the tremors.

Nick eased her back to the sofa, keeping an arm around her. When she finally looked up, Maggie was in front of them and handed her a glass of water. It was an effort to drink without spilling water all over herself. She looked to find her father, not surprised to see he had disappeared. Of course, he wouldn't want to witness such a sniveling display of weakness.

"Are you sure there isn't some place or someone you haven't checked?" Nick asked.

"I've called everyone." Her plugged nose distorted her voice. It was difficult to breathe. Maggie handed her several tissues. "They all said the same thing—that he was headed for home after sledding."

"Could he have stopped somewhere on the way?" Maggie asked.

"I don't know. Other than the church, there's only houses between Cutty's Hill and here. I tried calling the rectory, but never got an answer." She saw them exchange a glance. "What? What is it?"

"Nothing," Nick said, but she knew it was something. "Maggie and I were at the rectory earlier. I'm going to check what Dad has my men doing. I'll be right back."

Maggie took off her jacket and sat next to her. The impeccable Agent O'Dell wore a faded, stretched-out football jersey and blue jeans. Her hair was tousled and her skin flushed.

"Did I get you out of bed?" Christine asked. She was surprised to see her question embarrassed Maggie.

"No, not at all." She ran her fingers through her tangled hair. Then she looked down, as if only now noticing her inappropriate attire. "Actually, I was on my way home…home to Virginia. My flight was delayed. I checked all my luggage." She glanced at her watch. "It's probably somewhere over Chicago about now."

"You can borrow something of mine, if you like."

Maggie hesitated. Christine was sure she would decline, when Maggie said, "Are you sure you don't mind?"

"Not at all. Come on."

Christine led Maggie to her bedroom, surprised that her body had any energy left and suddenly relieved to have something to do. She closed the bedroom door behind them, though the sounds of voices and trampling couldn't be stifled. She opened her closet and several drawers. She was taller than Maggie, but otherwise about the same size, except for her flat chest next to Maggie's full breasts.

"Please, help yourself." Christine sat on the edge of the bed while Maggie very apprehensively pulled a red turtleneck sweater from one of the drawers.

"I don't suppose you have a bra I could borrow?"

"Top, left dresser drawer, though mine may be too small. You might try one of the sports bras. They, at least, have some extra stretch."

She sensed Maggie's discomfort. It had been a long time since Christine had had any girlfriends close enough to share a dressing room. She thought about leaving the room, but before she stood up, Maggie peeled off the football jersey and struggled into a gray sports bra. It stretched tightly across her full breasts, and she tugged at it as though it were a straitjacket. Before Christine looked away, she noticed a scar across Maggie's abdomen. In the mirror, Maggie caught her.

"I'm sorry," Christine said, but didn't look away. "Excuse me for asking, but that doesn't look like a surgical scar."

"No, it's not." It wasn't embarrassment in her voice. Christine detected something a bit more haunting. Maggie ran her fingertips carefully over the red puckered skin. There was a red gash on her shoulder blade, too. "This was a gift," she said quietly, almost reverently. "A reminder from a murderer I helped track down."

"I can't even imagine some of the horrible situations you must have experienced."

"It comes with the job. Do you have a camisole or tank top I could use instead?"

"Bottom left. How do you keep it from affecting you?"

"I never said it didn't affect me." Maggie squirmed out of the sports bra and pulled on a cream-colored camisole. Satisfied with the fit, she tucked it into the waistband of her jeans. "I try not to think about it."

The red turtleneck sweater was also tight, but the camisole helped smooth out the results. She left it untucked.

"Thanks," she said, turning back to Christine.

"Danny's and Matthew's bodies were cut badly, weren't they?"

Before, Christine had probed for all the grisly details to enhance her articles. Now she needed to know for herself.

The straightforward Maggie O'Dell looked uncomfortable, even a bit flustered. "We'll find Timmy. In fact, Nick has already called Judge Murphy. We're getting a search warrant, and we have a suspect."

The reporter in her should have been asking questions. Who was the suspect? What was the warrant for? But the mother in her couldn't shake the image of her small, fragile little boy cringing in a dark corner somewhere all alone. Could they really find him before his soft, white skin puckered with red gashes?

"He bruises so easily."

Christine felt the tears welling up in her eyes again, the intense panic gnawing at her insides. Maggie watched from the other side of the room, respecting the distance, for which Christine was grateful. She wouldn't break down, not now, not in front of this woman who had endured a madman slicing up her body. This woman who apparently had drained all emotion from her life and replaced it with strength. Yes, that's what Christine needed to do. Crying certainly wouldn't help Timmy.

She swiped at the few tears that escaped down her cheek and stood up feeling a new energy, despite the violent gnawing in her gut.

"Tell me what I can do to help," she said to Maggie, ignoring the tremor in her voice.

CHAPTER 59

Thursday, October 30

Sunlight streaked in through the rotted slats, waking Timmy up. At first, he didn't remember where he was, then he smelled the kerosene and the musty walls. The metal chain clanked as he sat up. His body ached from being curled up into the plastic sled. Panic filled his empty stomach. He needed to stop it this time, before it started the convulsions again.

"Think of good things," he said out loud.

In the sunlight he noticed the posters that covered the cracked and peeling walls. They looked like ones he had in his room back home. There were several Nebraska Cornhuskers, a *Batman* and two different *Star Wars*. He listened for sounds of traffic and heard none. Only the wind whistled in through the cracks, rattling the broken glass.

If he could just reach the window, he was sure he could pull the boards off. The window was small, but he could fit through and maybe call for help. He tried to shove the bed, but the heavy metal frame wouldn't budge. And he was weak and light-headed from not eating.

He stuffed a few of the French fries into his mouth. They were cold, but salty. Under the crate he found two Snickers bars, a bag of Cheetos and an orange. His stomach felt a little sick, but he devoured the orange and candy bars and started on the Cheetos while he examined the chain that connected him to the bedpost. The links were metal with a paper-thin slit in each, but it was impossible to pull any of them apart, not even to slip just one through the slit. It was useless. He wasn't strong enough and, again, he hated how small and helpless he was.

He heard footsteps outside the door. He scrambled up into the bed, crawling beneath the covers as the locks whined and the door screeched open.

The man came in slowly. He was bundled in a thick ski jacket, the black rubber boots and a stocking cap over the rubber mask that covered his entire head.

"Good morning," he mumbled. He set down a brown paper sack, but this time didn't remove his coat or boots to stay. "I brought you some things." His voice was soft and friendly.

Timmy came to the edge of the bed, showing his interest and pretending not to be frightened.

The man handed him several comic books, old ones, but in good condition. In fact, Timmy thought they were brand new until he saw the twelve-cent and fifteen-cent prices. He also handed him a stack of baseball cards, secured with a rubber band. Then he started unpacking some groceries and filling the crate where Timmy had found the candy bars. He watched as the man pulled out Cap'n Crunch cereal, more Snickers bars, corn chips and several cans of SpaghettiOs.

"I tried to get some of your favorite food," he said, looking back at Timmy, obviously wanting to please him.

"Thanks," Timmy found himself saying out of habit. The man nodded, the eyes sparkling again as though he was smiling. "How did you know I love Cap'n Crunch?"

"I just remember things," he said softly. "I can't stay. Is there anything else I can get you?"

Timmy watched him extinguish the kerosene lamp and felt a twinge of panic.

"Will you be back before dark? I hate being in the dark."

"I'll try to come back." He started for the door then glanced back at Timmy. He sighed and then dug in his pockets, finally pulling out something shiny.

"I'll leave my lighter, just case I don't get back. But be careful, Timmy. You don't want to start a fire." He tossed the shiny metal lighter next to Timmy on the bed. Then he left.

The panic stirred again in Timmy's stomach. Maybe it was all the junk food he had eaten. He hated being trapped, but at least if the man didn't come back he couldn't hurt him. He had the entire day to plan his escape. He picked up the lighter and ran his fingers over the smooth finish. Timmy noticed the logo stamped on the side of it. He recognized the dark brown crest. He had seen it many times on the jackets and uniforms his grandfather and Uncle Nick wore. It was the symbol for the sheriff's department.

CHAPTER 60

The smell of coffee nauseated Maggie, though it seemed to be the only thing to combat the effects of the Scotch. She picked at the scrambled eggs and toast while she watched the door of the diner. Nick said it would take only ten to fifteen minutes. That was an hour ago. The small diner was beginning to fill with its breakfast rush, farmers in feed caps next to business men and women in suits.

Maggie had hated leaving Christine this morning, though she knew she wasn't much of a comfort. She had never been good at offering words of reassurance or doing the hand-holding routine. After all, her only experience had been as a twelve year old, a small, gangly child struggling with and dragging a drunken mother up a flight of stairs to their run-down apartment. No words or courtesies had been necessary when dealing with someone who was half-conscious. Even as an FBI agent, etiquette skills were unnecessary. Most of the people she dealt with were corpses or psychos. Questioning the victims' families didn't require anything more than polite condolences, or so she had convinced herself long ago.

Last night she'd simply felt paralyzed. She hardly knew Christine. One dinner surely didn't enforce any obligation of friendship. Yet, Timmy's small, freckled face remained etched in her mind. In her eight years of tracking killers, no one she had known personally had ever been a victim. However, every corpse stayed with her, their ghosts a permanent part of her mental scrapbook. She couldn't imagine—didn't want to imagine—adding Timmy to that portfolio of tortured images.

Finally, Nick came into the diner. He spotted her immediately and waved, making his way to the booth but stopping several times to talk to customers. He was dressed in his usual uniform of jeans and cowboy boots, only this time under his unzipped jacket he wore a red Nebraska Cornhuskers sweatshirt. The swelling was gone from around his jaw, leaving a bruise. He looked exhausted. He hadn't bothered to comb his hair or shave after showering. He looked even more handsome than she remembered.

He slid into the booth opposite her and grabbed a menu from behind the napkin dispenser. "Judge Murphy is stalling on the search warrant for the rectory," he said quietly as he looked at the menu. "He didn't have a problem with the pickup, but he thinks—"

"Hi, Nick. What can I get for you?"

"Oh, hi, Angie."

Maggie watched the exchange between Nick and the pretty blond waitress and knew immediately the woman wasn't used to just taking his diner orders.

"How have you been?" she asked, trying to make it sound like casual conversation, though Maggie noticed she hadn't taken her eyes off Nick.

"Things have been pretty crazy. Could I just get some coffee and toast?" He avoided her eyes. His discomfort speeded up his speech.

"Wheat toast, right? And lots of cream with the coffee?"

"Yeah, thanks." He looked anxious for her to leave.

She smiled and left the table without even noticing Maggie, though before Nick's arrival she had been interested enough to fill Maggie's coffee cup three times.

"An old friend?" Maggie asked, knowing she had no right to, but enjoying his fidgeting.

"Who, Angie? Yeah, I guess you could say that." He dug Christine's cellular phone from his jacket pocket, set it on the table, then twisted out of the jacket. "I hate these things," he said, referring to the phone and desperately trying to change the subject.

"She seems very nice." Maggie wasn't ready to let him off the hook.

This time his eyes met hers, their intense blue looking deep inside her and reminding her once more of last night.

"She is nice, but she doesn't make my palms sweaty and my knees weak like you do," he said quietly, seriously, and managing to set that damn flutter going again in her stomach.

She looked away and concentrated on putting butter on her cold toast as though suddenly hungry.

"Look Nick, about last night…"

"I hope you don't think I was trying to take advantage of you. I mean, you did have a lot to drink."

She glanced at him. He leaned forward, his entire face serious. He was genuinely concerned. Had last night meant more to him than his ordinary trysts with women? Something made her want it to mean more, but she said, "I think it's best if we just forget last night ever happened."

He looked wounded, a slight grimace, then that same intensity.

"What if I don't want to forget? Maggie, I haven't felt like that in a long time. I can't—"

"Please, Nick, I'm not some naive waitress. You don't have to feed me some line or pretend—"

"It's not a line. Yesterday when I thought you were leaving and I'd never see you again, I felt as if someone had punched me in the gut. And then last night. Jesus, Maggie, you turn me inside out. I get all weak-kneed and tongue-tied. Believe me, that doesn't usually happen with me and women."

"We've been spending a lot of time together. We were both exhausted."

"I wasn't that exhausted. And neither were you."

She stared at him. Had it been that obvious how much she had wanted him? Or was it simply his ego?

"What did you expect to happen, Nick? Are you disappointed you're not able to add one more name to your list of conquests?" She glanced around them. No one seemed to notice her angry whispers.

"You know that's not what this is."

"Then maybe it's simply the thrill of being forbidden. I *am* married, Nick. It may not be the best marriage in the world, but it still means something. Please, let's just forget about last night." She stared at her coffee, feeling his eyes on her.

"Here's your toast and coffee," Angie interrupted, and Maggie found no relief in ending the subject. Maybe she didn't want to forget it, either.

Angie set the plate and cup in front of Nick, forcing him to sit back, though his eyes stayed on Maggie. She wondered if the pretty waitress could feel the tension.

"Can I get you anything else?" she asked only Nick.

"Maggie, do you need anything?" He purposely drew attention to Maggie, and Angie immediately looked embarrassed.

"No, thanks."

"Okay," Angie said, now anxious to make an exit.

There was an awkward moment of silence.

"You said Judge Murphy is hedging on the rectory warrant. Why?" Maggie tried to focus, still avoiding his eyes and pouring more sugar into her coffee. She waited out his silence, then finally she heard a sigh of resignation.

"Murphy and my dad come from a generation that believe you just don't mess with Catholic priests," he said, slathering his toast with quick, jerky swipes of butter.

"So is a warrant even possible?"

"I tried to convince him that it's Ray Howard we're after."

"You still think it is Howard."

"I don't know." He pushed the toast aside without taking a bite and scratched at his bristled jaw. She noticed the bandage again.

"What did you do to your hand?"

He stared at it for a moment as though he couldn't remember.

"It's no big deal. Look," he said, leaning toward her again, and she could smell the faint hint of his aftershave lotion though he obviously hadn't shaved. Behind the exhaustion in his eyes, Maggie could see the beginning panic he was so desperately trying to hide. Suddenly, she realized he was waiting for her attention.

"Sorry," she said, putting down the spoon, folding her arms and giving him her attention.

"Father Keller told me last night that Ray Howard left the seminary last year. While I was waiting on Murphy I did some checking. Howard was at a seminary in Silver Lake, New Hampshire. It's just across the border to Maine and less than five hundred miles from Wood River."

Now he did have her attention. She sat up and stared at him.

"How long was he there?"

"The last three years."

"Well, that rules him out on the Wood River murder."

"Maybe, but isn't that just a little too strange of a coincidence? Three years in the seminary, he should know a little about administering last rites."

"Was he here during the first murders?"

"I'm having Hal check it out. But I did talk to the head guy at the seminary. Father Vincent wouldn't give me the details, but he did say Howard was asked to leave due to improper conduct." He said it as if it were some sort of proof.

"Improper conduct at a seminary could be anything from breaking a vow of silence to spitting on the sidewalk. I don't know, Nick. Howard just doesn't seem sharp enough to pull this off."

"Maybe that's what he wants everyone to believe."

Maggie watched Nick fold his paper napkin over and over again, his fingers revealing his internal turmoil. Underneath the table, she heard his foot nervously tapping.

"Both Howard and Keller would have had the opportunity to get rid of Father Francis."

"Jesus, Maggie. I thought you believed that only because you were drunk last night. You really don't think it was an accident?"

"Father Francis told me yesterday morning that he had something very important to tell me. I know someone was listening in on our conversation. I could hear the click."

"So maybe it's a coincidence."

"I learned a long time ago that there are few coincidences. An autopsy might show whether he was pushed or whether he simply fell."

"Without any evidence, we can't just order an autopsy." Nick fidgeted with the cellular phone, and Maggie could feel his restlessness.

"Maybe I can talk to Father Francis' family. Or the archdiocese."

"Thing is, Maggie, we don't have time to wait for permission or for autopsies or even search warrants. I'd like to just scare the living crap out of Howard."

She couldn't believe he still thought it was Howard. Or was it simply his desperation, grabbing for easy answers. Instead of arguing, she said, "Whether it's Howard or Keller, we need to be very careful. If he panics..."

She stopped herself, remembering this was Timmy, Nick's nephew, they were talking about and not an anonymous victim. She hadn't shared with Nick her discovery of the killer's acceleration. She glanced at him and saw the realization there in his eyes. Somehow he already knew.

"We don't have much time," he said as though reading her mind. He was getting good at it. "He's speeding things up, isn't he?"

She nodded.

"Let's get out of here." He threw a wad of bills on the table without counting it out and wrestled back into his jacket, waiting while she did the same.

"Where are we going?"

"I need to impound a pickup, and you need to apologize to Father Keller for last night."

CHAPTER 61

Father Keller looked quite official this time when he answered the rectory door, still dressed from morning mass. However, Nick immediately noticed the white Nikes peeking out from under the black floor-length cassock.

"Sheriff Morrelli, Agent O'Dell. I'm sorry, but this is a surprise."

"Can we come in for a few minutes, Father?" Nick rubbed his hands together to ward off the cold. Although the sun had made its first appearance in days, the piles of snow and sharp wind kept the temperature well below freezing. Even for Nebraska, this was unusual Halloween weather.

Father Keller hesitated. At first, Nick thought he'd protest as he glanced at Maggie, checking to see if it was safe to let her in. Then he smiled and moved away from the door, leading them into the living room where a fire blazed in the grand fireplace. Only this morning there was a faint scent of something scorched—something not meant to burn. Immediately, Nick wondered if Keller was trying to hide something.

"I'm not sure how I can be of help to the two of you. Last night—"

"Actually, Father Keller," Maggie interrupted, this morning back to her cool, calm self. "I wanted to apologize for last night." She glanced up at Nick, and he saw a spark of indignation in her eyes. "I had a bit too much to drink, and I'm afraid I get somewhat antagonistic. It was certainly nothing personal. I hope you understand and accept my apology."

"Of course, I understand. And I'm relieved to know it wasn't anything I did. After all, we hadn't even met."

Nick watched the priest's face. Maggie's apology relaxed him. Even his hands dropped to his sides, no longer wringing behind his back.

"I was just about to make myself some hot tea. Can I get some for the two of you?"

"We are here on official business, Father Keller," Nick said.

"Official business?"

Nick watched the young priest stuff his hands into the deep pockets of the cassock, suddenly uncomfortable, though his voice appeared remarkably calm. Nick couldn't help wondering if this, too, was something Father Keller had learned in the seminary. He pulled the warrant from his jacket pocket and began unfolding it, while he said, "Last night we noticed the old pickup you have out back."

"Pickup?" Father Keller sounded surprised. Was it possible he didn't know or, again, was this only a part of his schooling?

"The one in the trees. It matches the description a witness gave of a pickup she saw Danny Alverez get into the day he disappeared." Nick waited and watched. Maggie stood silently by his side, but he knew she would memorize every twitch and shift Father Keller made.

"I don't know if that old thing even runs. I think Ray uses it when he goes to chop wood out by the river."

Nick handed Father Keller the warrant. The priest held it by its corner and stared at it as though it were a foreign object, secreting slime.

"Like I told you last night," Nick said calmly, "I'm just trying to follow up on as many leads as possible. You probably know that the sheriff's department has come under considerable fire lately. I just want to make sure no one can say we didn't check. Do you have the keys, Father?"

"The keys?"

"To the pickup?"

"I can't imagine that it's locked. Let me put on a coat and some boots, and I'll go back with you."

"Thanks, Father. I appreciate it." Nick watched the priest go to the side of the fireplace and slip on the pair of rubber boots he had noticed last night. So, they were Keller's boots. Last night, he had told Nick that he hadn't left the rectory. But then Nick reminded himself that snow-covered boots could mean that Keller had only stepped out to get more wood.

The three of them started for the door. Suddenly, Maggie grabbed on to a small table and doubled over.

"Oh, God. I think I'm going to be sick again," she mumbled.

"Maggie, are you okay?" He glanced at Father Keller and whispered, "She's been like this all morning." Then to Maggie, "What in the world did you drink last night?"

"Could I use your rest room?"

"Oh, sure." Father Keller's eyes darted across the floor, his obvious concern directed at the pearl-white carpeting. "Down the hall, second door on the right," he said quickly, as if to hurry her along.

"Thanks. I'll catch up with you guys." She disappeared around the corner, holding her side.

"Will she be okay?" Father Keller seemed concerned.

"She'll be fine. Believe me, you don't want to be too close. Earlier she made a mess all over my boots."

The priest grimaced and glanced at Nick's boots, then followed him outside to the back of the rectory.

Drifts encased the pickup, forcing them to shovel a path and dig out the old metal heap. The door stuck then creaked, metal grinding against metal, as Nick jerked and pulled it open. A musty, pent-up smell hit Nick's nostrils. The cab looked as though it had been closed up and unused for years. Disappointment stabbed at Nick. He was tired of coming up with empty leads. Still, he crawled into the cab with the flashlight and absolutely no clue as to what he was even looking for. Perhaps he should leave the search to the experts, but they were running out of time.

He lay on the cracked, vinyl seat then stretched and twisted his arm, allowing his hand to blindly search under the seats. The cramped quarters made it difficult to maneuver his body. The steering wheel cut into his side and the gearshift stabbed him in the chest. It reminded him of when he was sixteen and had used his dad's old Chevy for making out with his dates. Only his body ached more now and certainly wasn't as flexible as it used to be.

"I can't imagine there being anything but rats in this old heap," Father Keller said, standing outside the door.

"Rats?" He hated rats.

Nick snatched his hand back, hitting the raw knuckles on an exposed spring. He closed his eyes against the pain and bit down on his lower lip to contain the obscenities. He punched the glove compartment open and blasted the dark hole with the flashlight.

Carefully, he poked through the sparse contents: a yellowed owner's manual, a rusted can of WD-40, several McDonald's napkins, a matchbook from some place called the Pink Lady, a folded schedule with addresses and codes he didn't recognize and a small screwdriver. He palmed the matchbook, feeling Father Keller's eyes on him. Before he closed the compartment he ran his fingers back behind the contents in the deep groove. He felt something small, smooth and round, pinched it out of the groove and palmed it with the matchbook. He slipped both items into his coat pocket after checking to make sure he was out of Father Keller's line of vision. As he started to close the compartment, he noticed handwritten notes scrawled on the folded schedule. Unable to read the writing, he grabbed the paper and tucked it up his sleeve. Then he slammed the compartment shut.

"Nothing here," he said, scooting himself up and slipping the paper down into his pocket. He slid across the vinyl seat, taking one last look around. It occurred to him that, although the cab smelled musty and shut-up, everything—dash, seat, carpet—looked remarkably clean.

"Sorry you wasted your time," Father Keller said as he turned toward the rectory and started up the path.

"Actually, I still have the bed to search."

The priest stopped, hesitated, then turned back. The wind swirled the long cassock, snapping it violently, sounding like the crack of a whip. This time Nick noticed a hint of frustration in Father Keller's blue eyes—frustration, impatience. If he wasn't a priest, Nick would have said Father Keller simply looked pissed. Whatever it was, there was definitely something more. Something that made Nick anxious and apprehensive about what he might find in the pickup's bed.

CHAPTER 62

Maggie checked the window again. Nick and Father Keller were still at the pickup. She continued her search down the long hall, stopping in front of each closed door, listening and carefully peeking into every unlocked room. Several were offices, one a supply room. Finally, she came across a bedroom.

The room was plain and small with wooden floors and white walls. A simple crucifix hung above the twin bed. In the corner sat a small table with two chairs. Another stand sat in the opposite corner with an old toaster and teapot. An ornate lamp sat on the nightstand, looking out of place. Other than the lamp, there was nothing to draw attention. No clutter, no drawers or boxes.

She turned to leave, and immediately, three framed prints on the wall next to the door caught her eye. They hung side by side and were prints of Renaissance paintings. Though Maggie didn't recognize any of them, she recognized the style—the perfectly rendered bodies, the motion and color. Each one depicted the bloody torture of a man. Upon closer inspection she read the small print beneath each.

The Martyrdom of Saint Sebastian, 1475, Antonio Del Pollaivolo, showed a bound Saint Sebastian tied to a pedestal with arrows being shot into his body. *The Martyrdom of Saint Erasmus,* 1629, Nicolas Poussin, included winged cherubs hovering above a crowd of men who had one man stretched out and chained down while they pulled out his entrails.

Maggie wondered why anyone would want such artwork on their bedroom walls. She glanced at the last print. *The Martyrdom of Saint Hermione,*

1512, Matthias Anatello, showed a man tied to a tree while his accusers slashed at his body with knives and machetes. She started out the door when something made her look at the last print again. On the tortured man's chest were several bloody slashes, two perfect diagonals intersecting to create a jagged cross, or from Maggie's angle, a skewed X. Yes, of course. Now it made sense. The carving on each boy's chest wasn't an X at all. It was a cross. And the cross was part of his ritual, a mark, a symbol. Did he think he was making martyrs of the boys?

She heard footsteps. They were close and getting closer. She hurried into the hall just as Ray Howard turned the corner. She startled him, but he still noticed her hand on the doorknob.

"You're that FBI agent," he said in his accusatory tone.

"Yes, I'm here with Sheriff Morrelli."

"What were you doing in Father Keller's room?"

"Oh, is this Father Keller's room? Actually, I need to use the bathroom, and I can't seem to find it."

"That's because it's way down on the other end of the hall," he scolded, pointing and keeping his eyes on her as though he didn't trust her.

"Really? Thanks." She squeezed past him and made her way down the hall, stopping in front of the correct door and glancing back at him. "Is this it?"

"Yes."

"Thanks again." She went in and listened at the door for a few minutes. When she peeked out again, she saw Ray Howard disappear into Father Keller's bedroom.

CHAPTER 63

The bed of the pickup was filled with snow, but Nick crawled up over the tailgate.

"Could you hand me the shovel, Father?"

The priest stood paralyzed, staring at the drifts that swallowed Nick's legs. Keller's ungloved hands were at his chest, the long fingers intertwined as though he were in prayer. The wind whipped at his dark, wavy hair. His cheeks were red and his eyes watery blue.

"Father Keller, the shovel, please," Nick asked again, this time pointing when the priest finally looked up at him.

"Oh, sure." He made his way to the tree where they had left it. "I can't imagine there being anything of use to you."

"I guess we'll see."

Nick had to reach down to take the shovel, since Father Keller made no effort to lift it to him. The priest's behavior propelled Nick's adrenaline. There was something here. He could feel it. He started digging a bit frantically at first. He needed to slow down. How could he possibly find anything in all this snow? He scooped smaller shovelfuls for fear of tossing evidence over the side. The handmade wooden stockracks creaked and whined against the wind gusts. The cold sliced through Nick's jacket. It assaulted his eyes and pricked at his face, turning his ears into red pincushions. Yet, perspiration slid down his back. His palms were sweating inside the thick leather gloves he had found with the shovel in the storage shed.

Suddenly, the shovel struck something hard, encrusted beneath the snow.

The dull sound alerted Father Keller who approached the tailgate, close enough to look down into the hole Nick had created.

Carefully, Nick dug around the object with small scoops and delicate plunges. Unable to contain his curiosity, he tossed the shovel aside and dropped to his knees. With his gloved hands he brushed and wiped and scooped at the snow, feeling the edges of the object, but still not able to determine what it was. Snow crusted around it in chunks of ice. Whatever the object was, it had been warm when it was tossed into the pile of snow.

Finally, Nick could see what looked like skin. His heart raced. His hands frantically pulled and chipped at the ice. A huge chunk broke away, and Nick jerked backward in surprise.

"Jesus," he said, feeling his stomach lurch.

He glanced at Father Keller, who grimaced and stepped backward. Encased in the snow tomb was a dead dog, its black fur peeled away, its skin carved and shredded, and its throat slashed.

CHAPTER 64

Nick and Father Keller stomped their way up the steps just as Maggie came out the front door of the rectory. Immediately, Nick checked her eyes, anxious to see if she had found anything. Her quick glance and a smile for Father Keller left him without a clue.

"Are you feeling any better?" Father Keller sounded genuinely concerned.

"Much. Thank you."

"It's a good thing you didn't come with us," Nick said, still feeling sick to his stomach. Who could do something like that to a defenseless dog? Then he felt ridiculous. It was obvious who had done it.

"Why? What did you find?" Maggie wanted to know.

"I'll tell you about it later."

"Would the two of you like some tea now?" Father Keller offered.

"No, thanks. We need—"

"Yes, actually," Maggie interrupted Nick. "Perhaps that might settle my stomach. That is, if it's not an inconvenience?"

"Of course not. Come in. I'll see if we have some sweet rolls or perhaps doughnuts."

They followed the priest in, and again Nick tried to catch a glimpse of Maggie's face, unsure of her sudden enthusiasm to spend more time with the priest she despised.

"Nice to see you supporting the local merchants." Father Keller smiled as he took her jacket.

She smiled back without an explanation and went into the living room.

Nick brushed off his boots, staying on the welcome mat in the foyer. He glanced up to find Father Keller checking out Maggie's tight jeans. Keller's wasn't a simple glance, but a long, self-indulgent look. Suddenly, the priest looked back at Nick, and Nick bent over his jacket's zipper, pretending to struggle with it. Before the suspicion and anger crept into his mind, Nick reminded himself that even Father Keller was a man. And Maggie did look awfully good in jeans and that tight red sweater. Any man would have to be brain-dead not to notice.

Father Keller disappeared around the corner, and Nick joined Maggie in front of the fireplace.

"What's going on?" he whispered.

"Do you have Christine's cellular?"

"I think it's still in my jacket pocket."

"Could you please get it?"

He stared at her, waiting for some explanation, but instead she squatted in front of the fire to warm her hands. When he came back with the phone, she was poking through the ashes with an iron poker. He stood with his back to her, as though standing guard.

"What are you doing?" It was difficult to whisper through clenched teeth.

"I could smell something earlier. It smelled like burnt rubber."

"He'll be back any second."

"Whatever it was, it's ashes now."

"Cream, lemon, sugar?" Father Keller came around the corner with a full tray. By the time he set it on the bench in front of the window, Maggie was standing by Nick's side.

"Lemon, please," Maggie answered casually.

"Cream and sugar for me," Nick said, only now noticing that his foot was tapping nervously.

"If you two will excuse me, I need to make a phone call," Maggie said suddenly.

"There's a phone in the office down the hall." Father Keller pointed.

"Oh, no thanks. I'll just use Nick's cellular. May I?"

Nick handed her the phone, still looking for some sign as to what she was up to. She went back toward the foyer for privacy while Father Keller handed Nick a steaming cup of tea.

"Would you like a roll?" The priest offered a plate of assorted pastry.

"No, thanks." Nick tried to keep an eye on Maggie, but she was gone.

A phone began ringing, muffled but insistent. Father Keller looked puzzled, then headed quickly for the hallway.

"What on earth are you doing, Agent O'Dell?"

Nick slammed down his cup, spilling hot liquid on his hand and the polished table. He scrambled around the corner to see Maggie with the cellular phone to her ear as she walked down the hall, stopping and listening at each door. Father Keller followed close behind, questioning her and receiving no answers.

"What exactly are you doing, Agent O'Dell?" He tried to get in front of her, but she squeezed past.

Nick jogged down the hall, his nerves raw, the adrenaline pounding again.

"What's going on, Maggie?"

The muffled ringing of a phone continued, the sound getting closer and closer. Finally, Maggie pushed open the last door on the left, and the sound became crisp and clear.

"Whose room is this?" Maggie asked as she stood in the doorway.

Again, Father Keller seemed paralyzed. He looked confused, but also indignant.

"Father Keller, would you please get the phone," she asked politely, leaning against the doorjamb, careful not to enter. "It sounds as if it's in one of those drawers."

The priest still didn't move, staring into the room. The ringing grated on Nick's nerves. Then Nick realized that Maggie had called the number. He saw Christine's cellular phone in Maggie's hand, the buttons lit up and blinking with each ring of the hidden phone.

"Father Keller, please get the phone," she instructed again.

"This is Ray's room. I don't believe it's proper for me to go through his things."

"Just get the phone, please. It's a small, black flip-style."

He stared at her, then finally went into the room, slowly and hesitantly. Within seconds the ringing stopped. He came back out and handed her the small black cellular phone. She tossed it to Nick.

"Where is Mr. Howard, Father Keller? He needs to come down to the sheriff's department with us to answer some questions."

"He's probably cleaning the church. I'll go get him."

Nick waited until Father Keller was out of sight.

"What's going on, Maggie? Why are you suddenly convinced we need to question Howard? And what's with calling his cell phone? How the hell did you even know his number?"

"I didn't dial his number, Nick. I dialed *my* cellular phone number. That's not his phone. It's mine. It's the one I lost in the river."

CHAPTER 65

Christine squirmed to get comfortable in the swivel chair, drawing groans from the redheaded woman with the palette of makeup. As if out of punishment, the woman swabbed even more blush on Christine's cheeks.

"We're on in ten minutes," said the tall man with the headset strapped to his bald head.

Christine thought he was talking to her and nodded, then realized he was talking into the mouthpiece of the headset. He bent over her to snap a tiny microphone onto her collar, and she couldn't help noticing the reflection on his shiny head. The bright lights blinded her, their heat stifling and adding to the cockroaches in her stomach. Her palms were sweaty. Certainly it was only a matter of time before her face began to melt into pools of plum-glow blush, soft-beige foundation and lush-black mascara.

A woman sat in the chair opposite her. She ignored Christine while she riffled through the papers just handed to her. She swatted away the bald man's hand and grabbed the microphone to pin it on herself.

"I hope you got that fucking TelePrompTer fixed, because I'm not using these." She threw the handful of papers across the stage, and a frantic stagehand scrambled around the floor, scooping them up.

"It's fixed," the man patiently reassured her.

"I need water. There's no water on the side stand."

The same stagehand scurried over with a disposable cup.

"A real glass." She almost knocked it out of the girl's hand. "I need a real glass and a pitcher. For Christ's sake, how many times do I have to ask?"

Suddenly, Christine realized the woman was Darcy McManus, the evening anchor for the station. Perhaps she wasn't used to doing the morning news show. Perhaps she wasn't used to mornings. In the harsh lighting, McManus's skin looked weathered with crinkled lines at the eyes and mouth. Her usual shiny, black hair looked stiff and unnatural. The startling shade of red lipstick looked brash against her white skin until the redheaded makeup artist swabbed on a thick layer of artificial tan.

"One minute, people," the headset man called out.

McManus dismissed the makeup woman with a wave of her hand. She stood up, smoothed out her too-short skirt, straightened her jacket, checked her face in a pocket mirror, then sat back down. Just then, Christine realized she'd been staring at the woman the entire time. The countdown brought her back to reality, out of her trance. She wondered why in the world she had agreed to do this interview.

"Three, two, one..."

"Good morning," McManus said into the camera, her entire face transformed into a friendly smile. "We have a special guest with us today on *Good Morning Omaha*. Christine Hamilton is the reporter for the *Omaha Journal* who has been covering the Sarpy County serial killings. Good morning, Christine." McManus acknowledged Christine for the first time.

"Good morning." Suddenly, lights and cameras were real and all focused on her. Christine tried not to think about it. Ramsey had told her earlier that even ABC's network news would be broadcasting the segment live. That was, no doubt, why McManus was here instead of the show's regular host.

"I understand that this morning you're joining us not as a reporter, but now as a concerned mother. Can you tell us about that, Christine?"

She was intrigued by McManus, the convincing concern manufactured at a moment's notice. Christine remembered that McManus's career began as a Miss America, which spiraled her to broadcast news, skipping the field reporting and landing top anchor positions in medium-size markets like Omaha. Christine had to admit, the woman was good. Even as she appeared to be looking at Christine with that genuine, contrived concern, her eyes actually looked just over Christine's shoulder to the TelePrompTer. Suddenly, Christine realized McManus was waiting for her response, the impatience starting to reveal itself in the pursed lips.

"We think that my son, Timmy, may have been taken yesterday afternoon." Despite all the distractions, her lip quivered, and Christine resisted the urge to bite down and stop it.

"Oh, how awful." McManus leaned forward and patted Christine's folded hands, missing on the third pat and touching her knee instead. McManus snatched her hand back, and Christine wanted to turn to see if the Tele-PrompTer included gestures. "And the authorities think it's the same man who brutally murdered Danny Alverez and Matthew Tanner?"

"We don't know that for sure, but yes, there's a good possibility."

"You're divorced and raising Timmy all by yourself, aren't you, Christine?"

The question surprised her. "Yes, I am."

"Both Laura Alverez and Michelle Tanner were single mothers, as well, isn't that right?"

"Yes, I believe it is."

"Do you think perhaps the killer is trying to say something by choosing boys who are being raised by their mothers?"

Christine hesitated. "I have no idea."

"Is your husband involved in raising Timmy?"

"Not very much, no." She restricted the impatience to her hands wringing in her lap.

"Isn't it true that you and Timmy haven't seen your husband since he left you for another woman?"

"He didn't leave me. We got a divorce." The impatience bordered on anger. How would any of this help find Timmy?

"Is it possible your husband may have taken Timmy?"

"I don't think so."

"You don't think so, but there may be a possibility, isn't there?"

"It's unlikely." The lights seemed brighter, scorching hot. A trickle of perspiration ran down her back.

"Has the sheriff's department contacted your ex-husband?"

"Of course we would contact him if we knew how or where to... Look, don't you think I would much rather believe that Timmy is with his father than with some madman who carves up little boys?"

"You're upset. Perhaps we should take a few minutes." McManus leaned forward again, her brow creased with concern, but this time her hands reached over and poured a glass of water. "We all understand how difficult this must be for you, Christine." She handed her the glass.

"No, you don't." Christine ignored the offer, and McManus became flustered.

"Excuse me?"

"You can't possibly understand. Even I didn't understand. I just wanted the story, like you."

McManus looked around for the stage director, trying to appear casual while frustration clouded her cool exterior. The thin painted lips were pursed tightly over white, even teeth.

"I'm sure you're under a lot of stress, Christine. And this must also be stressful. Let's take a commercial break and give you a chance to pull yourself together."

McManus kept the smile until the camera lights dimmed and the stage director motioned to her. Then the anger erupted on her face with a scowl that cut new lines in her makeup. But the anger was directed at the tall, bald man and not Christine. In fact, Christine became invisible again.

"Where the hell are we going with this? I need something I can work with."

"Do I have time to go to the rest room?" Christine asked the stage director, and he nodded. She unsnapped the microphone and laid it next to the rejected glass of water.

McManus looked up at her and manufactured a curt smile.

"Don't take too long, honey. This isn't like your newspaper. We can't just stop the presses. We're live." She reached for the glass and drank in delicate sips so as not to mess up her lipstick.

Christine wondered if McManus even knew Timmy's name without the help of the TelePrompTer. The high-priced anchor didn't care about Timmy or Danny or Matthew. Dear God, how close had she come to being just like Darcy McManus?

Christine made her way backstage, carefully avoiding and stepping over all the cables and cords. As soon as she was out of the bright lights, her body felt a rush of cool air. She could breathe again. She marched down the narrow hallway, dodging stagehands and finding her way past the dressing rooms, past the rest rooms and, finally, escaping out the gray metal door marked Exit.

CHAPTER 66

"Am I under arrest?" Ray Howard wanted to know while fidgeting in the hard-backed chair.

Maggie stared at him. His pasty complexion made his eyes bulge out—eyes a dull, watery gray with red veins telegraphing his exhaustion. She rubbed her own exhaustion from the back of her neck. A tight knot pinched the muscles between her shoulders. She tried to remember when she had slept last.

The small conference room hummed with the percolating of fresh coffee, filling the room with its aroma. A stream of orange sunset seeped in through the dusted blinds. She and Nick had been here for hours, asking the same questions and getting the same answers. Even though she'd insisted they bring Howard in for questioning, she still believed he wasn't the killer. Nothing had changed, but she hoped he might know something, anything, and break under pressure. Nick, however, persisted, convinced Howard was their man.

"No, Ray. You're not under arrest," Nick finally answered.

"You can only hold me here for a certain number of hours."

"And how do you know that, Ray?"

"Hey, I watch *Homicide* and *NYPD Blue*. I know my rights. And I have a friend who's a cop."

"Really? You have a friend?"

"Nick," Maggie cautioned.

Nick rolled his eyes and pushed up the sleeves of his shirt. She noticed his clenched fists, his impatience boiling close to the surface.

"Ray, would you like some of this fresh coffee?" she asked politely. The well-dressed janitor hesitated, then nodded.

"I use cream and two teaspoons of sugar. Real cream. If you have it. And I prefer not using those little sugar cubes."

"How about something to eat. I know we kept you over lunch, and it's almost dinnertime. Nick, perhaps you could order all of us something from Wanda's."

Nick scowled at her from across the room, but Howard sat up, delighted.

"I love Wanda's chicken-fried steak."

"Great. Nick, would you please order Mr. Howard a chicken-fried steak?"

"With mashed potatoes and brown gravy, not the white. And I like creamy Italian dressing for my salad. But on the side."

"Anything else?" Nick didn't bother to hide his impatience or his sarcasm. Howard shrunk back into the chair.

"No, nothing else."

"And what for you, Agent O'Dell?" He shot her a look of contempt clouded with frustration.

"A ham and cheese sandwich. I believe you know how I like it." She smiled at him, pleased when his dark bristled jaw relaxed and his eyes softened.

"Yes, I do." It was obvious the memory immediately replaced the sarcasm and frustration. "I'll be right back."

She set a steaming mug of coffee in front of Howard, then paced the length of the room, waiting for him to relax. She flipped on the overhead lights. The fluorescents flooded the room, making him blink. He reminded her of a lizard with slow deliberate blinks while he tested the hot coffee with a long pointed tongue. He was listening to the noises of the sheriff's department. Though the walls muffled the activity, it was easy to hear footsteps scurrying, phones ringing and an occasional voice raised above the hum.

Just when she knew he had forgotten her presence, she stood behind him and said, "You know where Timmy Hamilton is, don't you, Ray?"

He stopped slurping. His back straightened, ready to defend himself again.

"No, I don't. And I don't know how that phone got in my drawer. I've never seen it before."

She came around the table and sat down directly across from him. The blinking lizard eyes tried to avoid hers and finally settled on her chin. There was a glance to her breasts. Quickly he looked back up, but not quick enough to stop the red from crawling up his otherwise white neck.

"Sheriff Morrelli thinks you killed Danny Alverez and Matthew Tanner."

"I didn't kill nobody," he blurted.

"See, I believe you, Ray."

He looked surprised and checked her eyes to see if it was a trick. "You do?"

"I don't think you killed those boys."

"Good, 'cause I didn't."

"But I think you know more than you're telling us. I think you know where Timmy is."

He didn't protest, but his eyes darted around the room—the lizard looking for an escape. He held the hot mug with both hands, and Maggie noticed the short, stubby fingers with chewed-off nails, some down to the quick. They certainly didn't look like the hands of a man obsessed with cleanliness.

"If you tell us, we can help you, Ray. But if we find out you knew and didn't tell us, well, you could end up going to jail for a long time, even if you didn't kill those boys."

His head cocked to one side. He was listening again to the activity on the other side of the door, perhaps listening for Nick's return or maybe for someone to rescue him.

"Where's Timmy, Ray?"

He brought a hand in front of his face, inspected the fingers then began biting and peeling what was left of his fingernails.

"Ray?"

"I don't know where any kid is!" he yelled, holding the anger behind clenched, yellow teeth. "And just because I drive the pickup sometimes to cut wood doesn't mean nothing."

Maggie dragged her fingers through her hair. The lack of sleep and food made her light-headed. Had they just wasted an afternoon? Keller could easily have hidden the cellular phone in Howard's room. Yet, Maggie couldn't imagine anything happening at the rectory without Howard making it his business to know.

"Where do you go to cut wood, Ray?"

He stared at her, still sucking on his fingertips. He was trying to figure out why she wanted to know.

"I've seen the fireplace in the rectory," she continued. "It looks like it would take a ton of wood over the winter, especially starting this early."

"Yeah, it does. And Father Francis likes…" He stopped and looked down at the floor. "God rest his soul," he muttered to his feet, then looked up again. "He liked it really warm in that room."

"So where do you go?"

"Out by the river. The church still owns a piece of property. Out where the old St. Margaret's is. It was a beautiful little church. It's falling apart now. I get lots of dried-out elm and walnut. Some oak. There's tons of river maples. The walnut burns the best." He stopped and stared out the window.

Maggie followed his empty gaze. The sun sank behind the snow-covered horizon, blood-red against the white. Cutting wood had reminded him of something, but what?

Yes, Ray Howard knew much more than he was letting on, and neither the threat of jail nor the promise of Wanda's chicken-fried steak would get him to talk. They were going to have to let him go.

CHAPTER 67

Nick hung up the phone and sat back in his office chair, rubbing the sting of anger from his eyes. He realized that Maggie must have seen how badly he wanted to hit something, maybe even Ray Howard. How could she remain so cool and calm?

He couldn't stop thinking about Timmy. He felt as though a time bomb had been planted inside his ribs, the ticking getting faster and faster, drumming against his chest. The ache was unbearable. It didn't help matters that he couldn't erase the image of Danny Alverez. That small body lying in the grass. Those vacant eyes staring up at the stars. He had looked so peaceful. That is if you didn't notice the red-raw slash under his chin and gouges in his small, white chest.

They were running out of time.

Aaron Harper and Eric Paltrow had been murdered less than two weeks apart. Matthew Tanner was taken exactly a week after Danny Alverez. It was only several days since Matthew, and now Timmy. The timetable grew shorter. Something was making the killer explode, sending him over the edge. And if they didn't catch him, would he simply disappear again for six years? Or worse, would he melt into the woodwork of the community just as he had before? If it wasn't Howard or Keller, who the hell was it?

Nick grabbed the crumpled paper from his desktop. The obscure schedule he had found in the pickup's glove compartment had a strange grocery list scrawled on the back. He scanned the items one more time, trying to make sense of them: wool blanket, kerosene, matches, oranges, Snickers bars, SpaghettiOs, rat poison. Perhaps it was a simple camping-trip list, yet something told Nick it was more.

There was a knock on the door, and Hal came in without waiting for an invitation. The big shoulders slumped from exhaustion. His normally well-groomed hair stuck to his head from too many hours stuffed in his hat. His shirt collar was unbuttoned and his coffee-stained tie was twisted loose and at an odd angle.

"What do you have, Hal?"

He sank into the chair opposite Nick on the other side of the desk. "The empty glass vial you found in the pickup contained ether."

"Ether? Where in the world did it come from?"

"More than likely the hospital. I checked with the director, and he said they have similar vials down in the morgue. They use it as some sort of solvent, but it could be used to knock someone out. All it takes is a couple whiffs."

"Who would have access to the morgue?"

"Anyone, really. They don't lock the door."

"You're kidding?"

"Think about it, Nick. The morgue's hardly ever used, and when it is, who's gonna want to mess around down there?"

"When there's a criminal investigation, it should be locked, with only authorized personnel allowed in." Nick grabbed a pen and started tapping out his anger. The desire to hit something still raged inside him.

Hal didn't respond, and when Nick glanced up at him he wondered if even Hal thought he was losing it. "Were you able to get any prints off the vial?"

"Just yours."

"What about the matchbook?"

"Well, it's not a strip joint. Get this—the Pink Lady is a small bar and grill in downtown Omaha, about a block from the police station. Evidently a lot of police officers hang out there. Eddie says they serve the best burgers in town."

"Eddie?"

"Yeah, Gillick was with the OPD before he moved here. I thought you knew that. 'Course, it's been a while...six or seven years now."

"I don't trust him," Nick blurted out, then regretted it as soon as he saw Hal's face.

"Eddie? Why in the world wouldn't you trust Eddie?"

"I don't know. Forget I said anything."

Hal shook his head and pushed himself out of the chair. He started for the door then turned back as if he had forgotten something.

"You know, Nick, I don't want you to take this the wrong way, but there's a lot of people in this department who feel the same way about you."

"What way is that?" Nick sat up. The tapping stopped.

"You have to admit, the only reason you got this job is because of your dad. What experience do you have in law enforcement? Look, Nick, I'm your friend, and I'm with you every step of the way. But I have to tell you, some of the guys aren't too sure. They think you're letting O'Dell run the show."

There it was—the slap he had been expecting for days. He wiped a hand across his jaw as if to erase the sting.

"I guess I figured as much, especially since my dad seems to be running his own investigation."

"That's another thing. Did you know he has Eddie and Lloyd tracking down this Mark Rydell guy?"

"Rydell? Who the hell's Rydell?"

"I think he was a friend or partner of Jeffreys'."

"Jesus. Doesn't anybody get it? Jeffreys didn't kill all three—" He stopped when he saw Christine standing in the doorway.

"Relax, Nick. I'm not here as a reporter." She hesitated, then came in. Her hair was a tangled mess, her eyes red, her face tear-stained, her trench coat unevenly buttoned. She looked like hell.

"I need to do something. You have to let me help."

"Can I get you some coffee, Christine?" Hal asked.

"Yes, thanks. That would be nice."

Hal glanced back at Nick as if looking to be excused, then left.

"Come, sit down," Nick said, resisting the urge to go to her and help her walk across the room. It unnerved him to see her this way. She was his big sister. He was the one always screwing up. She was the one who always held it together. Even when Bruce left. Now she reminded him of Laura Alverez—that unsettling quiet.

"Corby gave me a temporary leave of absence with pay from the newspaper. Of course, that was only after he made sure *The Journal* would have the exclusive on whatever happens."

She struggled out of her coat, tossing it carelessly onto a chair in the corner and only staring at it when it slid to the floor. Then she paced in front of his desk, though she didn't seem to have the energy to even stand.

"Any luck tracking down Bruce?" She avoided his eyes, but he already knew it was a touchy subject that his sister had no clue as to where her ex-husband was.

"Not yet, but maybe he'll hear about Timmy on the news and get in touch with us."

She grimaced. "I need to do something, Nick. I can't just sit at home and wait. What are you doing with that?" She pointed at the grocery list of items, which he'd turned over so that the strange schedule with its bizarre codes faced up.

"You know what this is?"

"Sure, it's a bundle label."

"A what?"

"A bundle label. The carriers get one each day with their newspapers. See, it shows the route number, the carrier's code number, how many papers there are to deliver, what inserts—if any—and the starts and stops."

Nick jumped out of his chair and came around to her side of the desk.

"Can you tell whose it is and what day it's for?"

"It looks like it was for Sunday, October 19. The carrier's code is ALV0436. From the addresses listed on the starts and stops, it looks like…" The realization swept over her face. She looked up at Nick with wide eyes. "This is Danny Alverez's route. It's for the Sunday he disappeared. Where did you find this, Nick?"

CHAPTER 68

When darkness came, it came quickly. Despite Timmy's efforts to remain calm, the inevitable prospect of the long, dark night ahead destroyed his defenses.

He had spent the day trying to come up with an escape plan or at least a way to send a distress signal. It certainly wasn't as easy as they made it look in the movies. Still, that helped him stay focused. He thought of Batman and Luke Skywalker. And Han Solo, who was his favorite.

The stranger had brought him *Flash Gordon* and *Superman* comic books. Yet, even equipped with the knowledge and secrets of all those superheroes, Timmy still couldn't escape. After all, he was a small, skinny ten year old. But on the soccer field, he had learned to use his smallness to his advantage, sneaking under and through other players. Maybe strength wasn't what he needed.

It was too hard to think with the dark swallowing up corners of the room. He could see that the lantern had very little kerosene left, so he needed to hold off lighting it for as long as possible. But already the panic crawled over him in shivers.

He considered the kerosene heater. Perhaps he could drain kerosene from it for the lantern. Gusts of wind still knocked at the boarded window, rattling slats and sneaking through the cracks. Without the heater he might freeze before morning. No, as much as he hated to admit it, he needed the heater more than he needed the light.

He replayed scenes from *Star Wars* in his mind, repeating dialogue out loud to keep himself occupied. He squeezed the lighter, reminding himself that he did have control over the darkness. Every once in a while he flicked it on and off, on and off. But the darkness wasn't the only enemy. The silence was almost as unsettling.

All day he forced himself to listen for voices, for barking dogs or car engines, for church bells or emergency sirens. Other than a distant train whistle and one jet overhead, he had heard nothing. Where in the world was he?

He had even tried yelling until his throat hurt, only to be answered by violent gusts of wind, scolding him. It was much too quiet. Wherever he was, he had the feeling it was far, far away from anyone who could help him.

Something skidded across the floor, a *click-click* of tiny nails on the wood. His heart pounded and the shivering took over. He flicked on the lighter, but couldn't see anything. Finally, he gave in. Without leaving the bed, he reached over to the crate and lit the lantern. Immediately its yellow glow filled the room. He should have felt relief. Instead, he curled up again into a tight ball, pulling the covers to his chin. And for the first time since his dad had left town, Timmy allowed himself to cry.

CHAPTER 69

She was smart, despite all the curves. Definitely a worthy adversary. But he wondered how much Special Agent Maggie O'Dell really knew and how much was just a game. It didn't matter. He enjoyed games. They took his mind off the throbbing.

No one noticed him as he walked down the sterile hallways. Those who did, nodded and scurried past. His presence was accepted here as easily as anywhere in the community. He fit in, though it was here—out in the open—that he wore another mask, one he couldn't just peel off like rubber.

He took the stairs. Today even the stairwells smelled of ammonia, immaculately scrubbed. It reminded him of his mother, down on her lovely hands and knees, quietly scrubbing the kitchen floor, often at two and three in the morning, while his stepfather had slept. Her delicate hands had turned red and raw from the pressure and harsh liquid. How many times had he silently watched without her knowing? Those stifled sobs and frantic swipes had been spent as though her secret early-morning ritual would somehow clean up the mess she had made of her life.

Now, here he was, so many years later, trying to clean up his own life, scrubbing out the visions of his past with his own secret rituals. How many more killings would be enough to wipe out the image of that sniveling, helpless boy from his childhood?

The door slammed shut behind him. He had been here before and found comfort in the familiar surroundings. Somewhere above, a fan wheezed. Otherwise there was silence, appropriate silence for this temporary tomb.

He snapped on the surgical gloves. Which will it be? Drawer number one, two or three? Perhaps four or five? He chose number three, pulling and wincing at the scrape of metal, but pleased to see he had been correct.

The black body bag looked so small on the long silver bed. He unzipped it carefully, reverently, tucking and folding it to the sides of the small gray body. The coroner's surgical wounds—precise slices and cuts—disgusted him, as did the puncture marks he, himself, had administered. Matthew's poor, little body resembled a road map. Matthew, however, was gone—to a much better place. Someplace free of pain and humiliation. Free of loneliness and abandonment. Yes, he had seen to it that Matthew's eternal rest would be peaceful. He could remain an innocent child forever.

He pulled on rubber gloves and unwrapped the fillet knife, setting it to the side. He needed to destroy the one piece of evidence that could link him to the murders. How careless he had been. How insanely stupid. Maybe it was even too late, but if that were true, Maggie O'Dell would now be reading him his rights.

He unzipped the body bag farther until he could examine Matthew's small legs. Yes, there it was on the thigh, the purple teeth marks. The result of the demon's rage inside him. Shame burned down into his stomach, liquid and hot. He moved the boy's leg and picked up the knife.

Somewhere outside the room and down the hall a door slammed. His hands stopped. He held his breath. He listened. Rubber-soled footsteps squeak-squawked, squeak-squawked—closer and closer, until they were right outside the door. They hesitated. He waited, the fillet knife clutched tightly in his gloved hand. How would he explain this? It could be awkward. It might be possible, but awkward.

Just as he was certain his lungs would burst, the squeak-squawk began again, passing the door. He waited for the footsteps to reach the end of the hall. He waited for the slam of the door, and then he drew in air, a generous gulp laced with enough ammonia to sting his nostrils. The powder inside the gloves caked to his sweaty palms, making them itch. A trickle of sweat slid down his back. He waited for it, anxious to feel it slither down into his underpants. Then ashamed when the thrill left him.

Yes, he was getting reckless. It was becoming harder and harder to clean up after himself, to stifle that hideous demon that sometimes got in the way of his mission. Even now, as he gripped the knife, he couldn't bring himself to cut. His hand shook. Sweat dripped from his forehead into his eyes. But soon it would be over.

Soon, Sheriff Nick Morrelli would have his prime suspect. He had already made sure of that, laying the groundwork and planting enough evidence, just enough clues. He was getting good at it. And it was so easy, exactly as it had been with Ronald Jeffreys. All it had taken with Jeffreys was an assortment of items in Jeffreys' trunk and an anonymous phone call to the super-sheriff, Antonio Morrelli. But he had been reckless even then, including Eric Paltrow's underpants in Jeffreys' treasure chest of incriminating items.

He had always taken each boy's underpants for his own souvenir, but with Eric, he had forgotten. It had been easy to retrieve them from the morgue. His mistake, however, had been including Eric's and not Aaron's underpants among the items he had planted in Jeffreys' trunk. Curiously, he had never known if his blunder had gone unnoticed or if the great and powerful Antonio Morrelli simply chose to ignore it. But he would not chance it this time. He would not be reckless. And soon, he would be able to put the throbbing to a stop, maybe for good. Just a few loose ends to tie up and one more lost boy to save. Then his demons could rest.

Yes, poor Timmy would finally be saved. So many bruises—he could only imagine what the boy had to endure at the hands of those who claimed to love him. And he did like the boy, but then, he had liked them all, chosen them carefully and saved each and every one of them. Delivered them from evil.

CHAPTER 70

Christine pushed the copier button and watched Timmy's toothy grin slide out into the tray. He'd hate that she was using last year's school photo. The one with his collar twisted and his cowlick sticking straight up. It was one of her favorites. Suddenly, it struck her how much younger he looked in the photo. Would anyone even recognize him? He had changed so much in one short year.

She set the counter and pushed the button again, watching a succession of the toothy grins slide one over another. Behind her, the sheriff's department rumbled and vibrated with mumbling voices, shuffling shoes and clicking machines. Despite her chore, she felt isolated, invisible. She wondered if the task simply kept her out of Nick's way. He insisted the more photos they got out to the news media and store owners, the better chance of triggering someone's memory. It was a far cry from the way he had treated the Danny Alverez case. But then, maybe they had all learned lessons, expensive lessons. Walking out of this morning's interview would cost her the high-priced TV job. But she didn't care. Right now, Christine couldn't care about anything but Timmy.

She felt him standing behind her. It came in a disturbing chill as if he had slipped an ice cube down her back. She turned slowly just as Eddie Gillick pressed in close against her, trapping her between the copy machine and his body. Sweat beads gathered on his lip above the thin mustache. He was breathing hard as though he had just come in running. The smell of his aftershave lotion assaulted her as his eyes traveled the length of her body.

"Excuse me, Christine. I just need to make a couple of copies of these photos." He flashed them at her. When she only glanced, he held them up to her, slowly shuffling them one after another. Glossy eight-by-tens, the brilliant color emphasized the red gashes. A close-up of skin peeled back. A throat slashed. And Matthew Tanner's pale face, his glassy eyes staring out at her.

Christine squeezed past, scraping her shin on the copy machine's stand in order to escape Eddie Gillick. He watched, smiling at her as she bumped into a state trooper, smashed a knee into a desk and finally made it across the room. Safe in the corner next to the watercooler, she leaned against the wall and stared out at the chaos. Were they all moving in slow motion or was it just her imagination? Even the voices sounded slow, all melting together into one low baritone. And that ringing, that constant high-pitched ringing. Was it a phone? Maybe a siren or a fire alarm? Shouldn't they be concerned? Couldn't someone stop the noise? Couldn't they hear it?

"Christine?"

She heard her name being called from another dimension, far away. She pressed her body against the wall, clinging to the smooth cool texture while the room moved. A slight tip to one side. No one else seemed to notice. Then a slight tip to the other side.

"Christine, are you okay?"

Lucy Burton's face appeared in front of her, the heart-shaped face oversize with wide eyes bulging like in one of those grocery-store mirrors. Only there were no mirrors. Lucy was saying something to her again. The brightly painted lips moved but emitted no sound. Where was the remote control? She needed to turn up Lucy Burton's volume.

The hands came at her from nowhere, clutching at her, grabbing for her. She batted them away, but they came again. She couldn't breathe. She needed water. The watercooler was next to her just to her left, several miles away, far in the distance. She slapped at the hands again.

"No, I can't hear you, Lucy," she said, and realized her words were confined to her thoughts.

She felt her body sliding down the wall. She couldn't catch it, had lost control of her own body as it, too, moved in slow motion. So many feet, scuffed shoes, red toenails, a pair of cowboy boots. Then someone shut off the lights.

CHAPTER 71

Nick came out of his office just in time to see a crowd gathered around the watercooler. He saw Christine slumped on the floor. Lucy fanned her with a file folder, while Hal held her up against his shoulder. Nick's father looked on with the rest, his hands deep in his pockets. Nick heard the irritation in his father's jingling pocket change. He recognized the taut jaw and rigid stance. Nick knew what he was thinking. How dare Christine show such weakness in front of his colleagues.

"What happened?" Nick asked Eddie Gillick at the copy machine.

"Don't know. Didn't see it happen," Eddie said as he pressed the copier's buttons, his back turned to the commotion.

It occurred to Nick that Eddie was the only one on this side of the room. He glanced down at the copies spitting out into the tray and watched pieces of Matthew Tanner cover Timmy's smiling face. Maybe asking Christine to make copies of her missing son's face was too much.

"You have the autopsy photos," he said, keeping his eyes on Christine.

"Yeah, just picked them up from the hospital morgue. I knew you'd be wanting copies."

"Great. Put the originals on my desk when you're finished."

At least Christine looked conscious now. Adam Preston handed her a paper cup, and she gulped water as if they had pulled her out of the desert. Nick watched from across the room, paralyzed, helpless. The ticking in his chest drummed harder than ever. He glanced at Eddie. Could he hear the ticking?

"Okay, everybody," his father announced. "Show's over. Let's get back to work."

Without hesitation they followed his orders. When he saw Nick, he waved him over. Nick stood firm, a last-ditch effort to gain back a shred of authority. His father signed something for Lloyd, then wandered over, completely oblivious to Nick's defiance.

"Lloyd's found Rydell. We're bringing him in for questioning."

"You have no authority to do that." Nick concentrated. He needed to sound calm, cool, in-charge.

His bushy eyebrows raised as he stared at Nick. "Excuse me?"

His father had heard perfectly well. It was part of his intimidation. It had always worked...in the past.

"You no longer have the authority to bring anyone in for questioning." He met his father's narrowed eyes.

"I'm trying to help you, boy, so you don't look like a fucking idiot to the whole goddamn community."

"Mark Rydell had nothing to do with any of this."

"Right. You're placing your money on some gimpy church janitor."

"I have evidence that implicates Ray Howard. What do you have on Rydell?"

By now the office had come to a standstill again. Only this time no one dared gather around them. Instead, they quietly watched from doorways and behind desks, pretending to go about their work.

"Rydell's a known fag. Has a rap sheet as long as my arm for beating up other fags. He was Jeffreys' fag for a while. I was never convinced that he wasn't in on the whole thing with Jeffreys. I'd bet the farm that he's your copycat killer. Only you can't see it 'cause you can't see beyond Agent Maggie's cute little ass."

The heat crawled up Nick's neck. His father turned away from him, finished, dismissing him in his usual manner. Nick glanced around at the eyes pretending to work. Then he saw Maggie in the doorway to the conference room. His eyes met hers. In an instant, he knew she had heard.

"This isn't a copycat killer," he said to his father's back.

"What the fuck are you talking about now?"

He only glanced at Nick over his shoulder. He took the set of autopsy photos from Eddie, who willingly handed over the originals without even looking in Nick's direction.

"Jeffreys was only responsible for Bobby Wilson's death." His father didn't look up from the photos. "He didn't kill all three boys. But then, you already knew that." Nick waited for the implication to sink in, for it to register as the accusation he meant it to be.

Finally, his father looked at him with the scowl usually powerful enough to transform him into a sniveling teenager. Nick stood straight, keeping his hands from hiding in his pockets. Instead, he crossed his arms over his chest. He was ready.

"What the fuck are you implying?"

"I've read Jeffreys' arrest file. I've seen all the autopsy reports. There's no way in hell Jeffrey committed all three murders. Even Jeffreys told you that, over and over again."

"Oh, so now you believe a goddamn murdering fag over your own father?"

"Your own reports prove Jeffreys didn't kill the other two boys. Only you were too blind. No, you wanted to be a hero. So you ignored the truth and let a killer get away. Or maybe you even helped plant the evidence. Now your own grandson's going to pay the price for your mistakes and your fucking pride."

The fist took Nick completely off guard. It slammed into his jaw and knocked him back into the copy machine. He caught his balance, but his vision was still blurred when the second fist slammed into his face. He looked up to see his father in the same place, same stance, photos still in his hands, a look of surprise on his face. Nick didn't even realize it wasn't his father's fists that had hit him until he saw Hal restraining Eddie Gillick.

CHAPTER 72

Maggie waited but wasn't surprised when Nick didn't come back to their makeshift interrogation room. Adam Preston delivered dinner from Wanda's. She told Ray Howard he was welcome to stay and eat his steak, then he was free to go. He eyed her suspiciously until Adam placed the steaming plate in front of him. Then all seemed to be forgotten.

She started to leave while Adam unpacked and laid out the rest of the food.

"Agent O'Dell, this is for you."

"I'm not very hungry." She turned to him, but it wasn't a sandwich he handed her. She stared at the small, white envelope from across the table. "Where did you get that?"

"It was in the order from Wanda's. It has your name on it." He held it out to her, his arm stretched over the table, but she made no attempt to take it. Even Howard looked up at her from his banquet.

"Agent O'Dell? What is it? Do you want me to open it?" Adam's green eyes were serious. His boyish face concerned.

"No, I'll take it." She slowly grabbed a corner, pretending—though it was too late—that it was no big deal. To prove it, she opened it without hesitation while Adam watched. Her fingers were amazingly steady though her stomach did acrobatic flips.

She read the note. It was simple, only one line: "I KNOW ABOUT STUCKY."

She glanced up at Adam.

"Is Nick around?" She needed to keep her breathing even and steady. She needed to contain the crawly things invading her insides.

"No one's seen him since..."

"Since Eddie decked him," Howard finished for Adam. He smiled up at them over a forkful of mashed potatoes. "Eddie's my man," he said, then stuffed his mouth.

"What do you mean by that?" Maggie snapped at him, and Howard's look told her it was too much, too shrill. She needed to be careful, but it was too late. She had set him on edge again.

"Nothin'. He's just a friend."

"Deputy Gillick is a friend of yours?" She looked at Adam who simply shrugged.

"Yeah, he's a friend. There ain't no crime in that, is there? We do stuff together. It's no big deal."

"What kind of stuff?"

Howard looked from her to Adam. His hands had stopped cutting and scooping. His back straightened. When he looked back at Maggie, she saw the cold defiance.

"Sometimes he comes over to the rectory and plays cards with Father Keller and me. Sometimes just him and me go out for burgers."

"You and Deputy Gillick?"

"Didn't you say I was free to go?"

She stared him down. She was right. Those clever, reptilian eyes did know more, much more. Deep down, she knew he wasn't the killer, despite Nick's hunches. Howard may have been unfortunate enough to be in possession of her cellular phone, but Ray Howard was not the killer. His limp would never allow him to maneuver the steep woods along the river, let alone carry a sixty-to seventy-pound boy. And despite his smart remarks, he simply wasn't smart enough to carry off a series of killings.

"Yes, I did say you were free to leave," she finally answered without breaking his gaze. She wanted him to see the suspicion. She wanted him to slip up, sweat a little. Instead, he ignored her and went back to scraping great globs of food onto his fork, anchoring it with his knife and stuffing his mouth full before he started to chew.

She gestured to Adam, and he followed her out. Safely down the hall, she stopped and leaned against the wall, holding herself up from the exhaustion. Adam waited patiently with quick glances in both directions, although making sure no one saw him alone with her. He was too young to be a leftover of Antonio Morrelli's regime, though he, too, seemed anxious to please, anxious to be a part of the group. Still, his respect for authority extended to Maggie, and his tall, thin frame slouched, ready to listen.

"You grew up in Platte City, right?"

The question surprised him. Of course, it would. He nodded, anyway.

"What can you tell me about the old church, the one in the country?"

"We checked it out, if that's what you mean. Lloyd and I went out there before the snow and then again after. The place is boarded up. Didn't look like anyone's been in there for years. No footprints, no tire tracks."

"It's close to the river?"

"Yeah, just off Old Church Road—guess that's probably where it gets its name. The church is listed as an historical landmark. That's why no one's torn it down."

"How do you know all of that?" She pretended to be interested, though its location was really all she needed to know. If Howard went there to cut wood, perhaps he had seen something close by. She rubbed the knot in her neck, squeezing and applying pressure. Exhaustion clouded her thoughts. Or maybe she just didn't want to think anymore.

"My dad owns land close by," Adam continued. "He wanted to buy the church property, tear down the building. It's prime farmland. Father Keller told him it couldn't be torn down on account of it's registered as an historical landmark. I guess it was used as part of John Brown's Underground Railroad in the 1860s. Supposedly there's a tunnel from the church to the graveyard."

Maggie stood up, suddenly interested.

Adam seemed pleased.

"They hid runaway slaves in the church. At night they used the tunnel to sneak them to the river where a boat would take them upstream to the next hideout. There's an old church down by Nebraska City that was used, too. They've made that one into quite the tourist trap. This one's too deteriorated. They say the tunnel's all caved in—too close to the river. They don't even use the graveyard anymore. A few years ago when the river flooded, it uprooted some graves. Even sent a few coffins floating down the river once. That was kind of a creepy sight."

Maggie imagined the deserted graveyard and the swift river current sucking corpses from their graves. Suddenly, it sounded like the perfect place for a killer obsessed with his victims' salvation.

CHAPTER 73

Maggie decided to leave Nick a note, though she had no clue what to say.

"Dear Nick, went off to find the killer in a graveyard." It sounded bizarre, but it would be more than what she had left before she ran off to find Albert Stucky. Except that night, she hadn't intended to really find Stucky. She had simply been checking a lead. Had hoped to find his hiding place. That he would be waiting for her, setting a trap for her, had never occurred to her until it was too late. Could that be what this killer was doing? Setting a trap and waiting for her to walk right into it?

"I think Nick's gone," Lucy announced from down the hall, catching Maggie with her hand on the knob of his office door.

"I know, I'm just leaving him a note."

Lucy didn't look satisfied, her hands planted firmly on her hips as if expecting more of an explanation. When Maggie didn't offer her one, she added, "There was a call for you earlier from the archdiocese's office."

"Any message?" Maggie had spoken to a Brother Jonathon, who assured her the church did not believe Father Francis' death to be anything criminal nor anything more than an unfortunate accident.

"Hold on." Lucy sighed and riffled through a stack of messages. "Here it is. Brother Jonathon said Father Francis has no living relatives. The church will be making all the burial arrangements."

"No mention of allowing us an autopsy?"

Lucy looked up at her, surprised. Maggie no longer cared.

"I took the message myself," Lucy said softly, now almost sympathetically, understanding what the need for an autopsy implied. "That's all he said."

"Okay, thanks." Maggie grabbed the doorknob to Nick's office again.

"I can take your message for Nick if you want."

The sympathy was gone, quickly replaced by mere curiosity.

"Thanks, but I'll just leave it on his desk."

Maggie went in, but she left the lights off, using the glow from the streetlights below to guide her. She bumped her shin into a chair leg.

"Damn it," she muttered, reaching down to catch the pain though it already shot up her thigh. While bent over and rubbing her leg, she noticed Nick sitting on the floor in the corner. In the dark, she saw him hugging his knees to his chest, staring out the window, apparently oblivious to her presence.

It would have been easy to pretend she hadn't seen him. She could write the note and be on her way. Without a word, she walked over to him and quietly, slowly took a place beside him on the floor. She followed his gaze out the window. From this angle only the black sky filled the frame. Out of the corner of her eye she saw the cracked lip, bruised and swollen. Dried blood stained that perfectly chiseled jaw. He still didn't move, still didn't acknowledge her presence.

"You know, Morrelli, for an ex-football player you fight like a girl."

She wanted to make him angry, to make him feel. She recognized that numbness, that emptiness, that could paralyze a person for a long, long time if not confronted. There was no response. She sat quietly by his side. Minutes passed. She should get up, leave. She couldn't afford to share his pain. She couldn't risk caring about him. Her own vulnerability was already a tremendous liability. She couldn't take on his.

Just as she stretched her legs to get up, he said, "My dad was wrong to say what he did about you."

She leaned back. "You mean I don't have a cute little ass?"

Finally, she caught a hint of a smile.

"Okay, only half-wrong."

"Don't worry about it, Morrelli. I've heard worse." Though the sting always surprised her.

"You know, when all this began, the only thing I cared about was how I'd look, whether people would think I was incompetent."

He kept his gaze out the window to avoid looking at her. Her eyes had adjusted to the dark now, and she studied him. Despite the disheveled look, he was remarkably handsome with all the classic features—strong, square jaw, dark hair against tanned skin, sensuous lips, even his earlobes were perfectly sculpted. Yet, those physical characteristics that she initially found so attractive now seemed minor. It was his smooth, steady voice she looked forward to. It was his warm, sky-blue eyes that made her weak in the knees. The way they held her, as if she was the most important person in the world. The way they searched deep inside her, as if hoping for a glimpse of her soul. Those eyes made her feel naked and alive. Now that he kept them from her, she felt robbed, removed from the intimate bond that had begun forming between them. At the same time, she knew it wasn't right to feel this close to a man she had met less than a week ago. She kept quiet and waited, half dreading that he would share some secret that would bring them even closer. At the same time, part of her hoped he would.

"I'm incompetent. I don't know the first thing about heading a murder investigation. Maybe if I had admitted that in the beginning...maybe Timmy wouldn't be missing."

His confession surprised her. This wasn't the same cocky, arrogant sheriff she had met several days ago. Yet, his admission wasn't self-pity. It wasn't even regret. Instead, Maggie sensed it was a relief for him to finally say it out loud.

"You've done everything possible, Nick. Believe me, if there was something I thought you should have done or should be doing differently, I certainly would have told you. If you haven't noticed yet, I'm not shy in that area."

Another smile. He leaned back against the wall and released his knees from his chest. He stretched those long, lean legs out in front of him. For a minute she thought it was over.

"Maggie, I am so...I keep imagining finding him. I keep seeing him... lying in the grass, that same vacant stare. I've never felt so..." The strong, steady voice hitched, caught on a lump in his throat. "I feel so fucking helpless." The knees came back to his chest, brushing his chin.

Her hand went up, then stopped in midair at the nape of his neck. She wanted to comfort him, caress him. She snapped back her hand, scooted farther away and leaned against the wall, trying to get comfortable, trying to dislodge the overpowering urge to touch him. Another glance. Moonlight crept into a corner of the window, framing his profile. What was it about Nick Morrelli that made her want to be whole again? That made her realize she wasn't whole?

"You know all my life I've done everything my dad told me...suggested I do." He kept his chin on his knees. "It wasn't even so much that I wanted to please him. It was just easier. His expectations always seemed to be lower than my own. Being sheriff of Platte City was supposed to be writing tickets and rescuing lost dogs, and breaking up a few bar fights now and then. Maybe an occasional traffic accident. But not murder. I'm not prepared for murder."

"I don't know if there's anything to prepare you for the murder of a child, no matter how many dead bodies you've seen."

"Timmy can't end up like Danny and Matthew. He can't. And yet...there's nothing I can do to stop it." The catch in his voice was back. She glanced over at him, and he turned his face away. "There's not a fucking thing I can do."

She heard the tears in his voice, though he tried his best to disguise them with anger. She reached out again, hesitated again, her hand hovering. Finally, she touched his shoulder. She expected him to bolt. Instead, he sat quietly. She stroked his shoulder blades and ran her hand over his back. When the comfort started turning too intimate for her, she pulled her hand away, but he reached up and caught it, gently trapping it in his large hand. He looked up at her and brought the palm of her hand to his face, rubbing it against his swollen jaw.

"I'm glad you're here." His eyes held hers. "Maggie...I think I—"

She snatched her hand back, suddenly uncomfortable with his attempted revelation. He was beyond flirting. She could see him testing, struggling with feelings she didn't want to know about.

"Whatever happens, it won't be your fault, Nick." She changed the subject while pretending to be on it. "You're doing everything possible. At some point you have to let yourself off the hook."

He looked at her with that deep gaze, the one that made her feel as if he was searching her soul. "Your nightmares," he said quietly. "You haven't let yourself off the hook for something. What is it, Maggie? Is it Stucky?"

CHAPTER 74

"How do you know about Stucky?" Maggie sat up, trying to ward off the tension brought on by just the mention of his name.

"That night at my house, you yelled out his name several times. I thought you'd tell me about him. When you didn't...well, I figured maybe it wasn't any of my business. Maybe it's still none of my business."

"By now it's a matter of public record."

"Public record?"

"Albert Stucky is a serial killer I helped capture a little over a month ago. We nicknamed him The Collector. He'd kidnap two, three, sometimes four women at a time, keeping them, collecting them in some condemned building or abandoned warehouse. When he got tired of them, he killed them, slicing their bodies, bashing in their skulls, chewing off pieces of them."

"Jesus, I thought this guy we're chasing was screwed up."

"Stucky is certainly one of a kind. It was my profile that identified him. Over the course of two years, we tracked him. Every time we got close, he moved to another part of the country. Somewhere along the line, Stucky discovered that I was the profiler. That's when the game began."

The moonlight flooded the office now. She glanced at him, uncomfortable under his penetrating blue eyes that were filled with as much concern as interest. He must have bitten down on his lip. It was bleeding again. She shifted, dug in her jacket pocket and pulled out a tissue, handing it to him. "You're still bleeding."

He ignored the tissue and wiped a sleeve across his mouth. "What else is new? I fight like a girl." Then his expression went serious again. "Tell me about the game."

"Stucky probed my background. Somehow he found out about my family, my father's death, my mother's alcoholism. He knew everything, or so it seemed. About a year ago I started receiving notes. Actually, it's not that unusual, but Stucky's were. He always included a piece of his victims—a finger, sometimes just a piece of skin with a birthmark or tattoo, once a nipple."

Nick shook his head but didn't say anything.

"He started a sort of scavenger hunt with me," she continued. "He'd send clues as to where he was keeping the women. If I guessed right, he rewarded me with a new clue. If I guessed wrong, he punished me with a dead body. I was wrong a lot. Every time we found one of his victims in a Dumpster, I felt like it was my fault."

She closed her eyes, allowing herself to see the faces. All of them with that same horrified stare. She could remember them all, could recite their names, addresses, personal characteristics. It sounded like a litany of saints. She opened her eyes, avoided Nick's and continued.

"He would quit for a while but only to move to another part of the country. We finally tracked him down in Miami. After a few clues I was almost certain I knew he was using an abandoned warehouse by the river. I dreaded being wrong. I didn't think I could handle another dead woman on my conscience. So I didn't tell anyone. I decided to check it out myself. That way, if I was wrong, no one ended up dead. Only, I was right, and Stucky was waiting for me. He ambushed me before I even saw it coming."

Her breathing was uneven. Her heart raced. Even her palms were sweaty. It was over. Why did it still have such an effect on her?

"He tied me to a steel post, and then he made me watch. I watched while he tortured and mutilated two women. Actually, the second one was punishment because I closed my eyes while he was bashing in the skull of the first woman. He had warned me that he would just keep bringing out another if I closed my eyes. He seemed so oblivious to their pain, to their screams."

God, it was hard to breathe. When would she stop seeing those pleading eyes, hearing those unbearable screams? "I watched him beat and slice and rip apart two women and I felt so…so goddamn helpless."

She stared out at the moon and stars. "I was so close…" She rubbed her shoulders. She could still feel it. "I was so close I could feel their blood splatter me, along with pieces of their brains, chips of their bones."

"But you did get him?"

"Yes. We got him. Only because an old fisherman heard the screams and called 911. We certainly didn't get him on my account."

"Maggie, you're not responsible for those women."

"Yes, I know that." Of course, she knew, but it didn't erase the guilt. She wiped at her eyes, disappointed to find her cheeks already wet. Then she stood, much too abruptly but gratefully closing the subject.

"That reminds me," she said, trying to resume normalcy. "I got another note." She dug out the crumpled envelope and handed it to Nick.

He pulled out the card, read it, and leaned back against the wall. "Jesus, Maggie. What do you suppose this means?"

"I don't know. Maybe nothing. Maybe he's just having some fun."

Nick untangled his legs and stood without assistance of the wall or desk. "So what do we do now?"

"How do you feel about raiding graveyards?"

CHAPTER 75

Timmy watched the lantern's flame dance. It was amazing how such a small slit of fire could light up the entire room. And it gave off heat, too. Not like the kerosene heater, but it did feel warm. It reminded him again of the camping trips he and his dad had taken. It seemed like such a long time ago now.

His dad hadn't been an experienced camper. It had taken them almost two hours to set up the tent. The only fish they had caught were tiny throwbacks they ended up keeping when they had gotten too hungry to wait for a bigger catch. Then his dad had melted his mom's favorite pot by leaving it in the fire too long. Still, Timmy hadn't minded the mistakes. It was an adventure he got to share with his dad.

He knew his mom and dad were mad at each other. But he didn't understand why his dad was mad at him. His mom had told him his dad still loved him. That he didn't want anybody to know where he was because he didn't want to pay them any money. That still didn't explain why his dad didn't want to see him.

Timmy stared at the flame and tried to remember what his dad looked like. His mom had put away all the pictures. She said she burned them, but Timmy had seen her looking through some of them a few weeks ago. It had been late at night, when she thought Timmy was asleep. She was up drinking wine, looking at pictures of the three of them and crying. If she missed him that bad, why didn't she just ask him to come home? Sometimes Timmy didn't understand grown-ups.

He brought his hands up to the lantern's glass to feel its glow. The chain attached to his ankle clinked against the metal bedpost. Suddenly, he stared at it, remembering the metal pot his dad had ruined on the campfire. The chain links weren't thick. How hot did metal need to get to bend? He didn't need to bend it that much—a quarter of an inch at the most.

His heart raced. He grabbed the glass, but snatched his hands back from the heat. He pulled off the pillowcase and wrapped his hands, then tried again, gently tugging the glass casing off without breaking it. The flame danced some more, reared up, then settled down. He put the pillowcase back on the pillow. Then he set the lantern on the floor in front of him and lifted his leg, grabbing a length of chain close to his ankle. He let several links swoop into the flame. He waited a few minutes, then started to pull. It wasn't working. It just took time. He needed to be patient. He needed to think of something else. He kept the links in the flame. What was that song his mom was singing the other morning in the bathroom? It was from a movie. Oh yeah, *The Little Mermaid.*

"Under the sea." He tried his voice. It shook a bit from the anticipation. Yeah, that was it, anticipation, not fear. He wouldn't think about being afraid. "Under the sea… Darling it's better, down where it's wetter." He pulled on the chain again. Still no movement. It surprised him how many of the words he remembered. He tried out his Jamaican accent. "Under the sea."

It moved. The metal was giving. Or was it his imagination? He strained, pulling as hard as he could. Yes, the slit between the two links grew little by little. Just a little more, and he could slip it through.

The footsteps outside the door sent his heart plunging. No, just a few more seconds. He pulled with all his might as the locks clanked and screeched open.

CHAPTER 76

Christine tried to remember the last time she had eaten. How long had Timmy been gone? Too long. Whatever it was, it was too long. She pulled herself up off the old couch where Lucy had left her, somewhere in a back office used to store files.

The couch smelled of stale cigarettes, though it looked clean. At least, there appeared to be no hideous stains. The rough-textured fabric left an imprint on her cheek. She could feel it tattooed into her skin.

Her eyes burned. Her hair was a tangled mess. She couldn't remember when she had combed it. Or brushed her teeth, though she was certain she had done all those things before her morning interview. God, that felt like days ago.

The door opened, its squeak startling her. Her father came in carrying more water. If she drank one more glass, she would vomit. She smiled and took it from him, taking only a sip.

"Feeling better?"

"Yes, thanks. I don't think I've eaten today. I'm sure that's why I got so light-headed."

"Yep. That'll do it."

Without the glass he seemed uncertain what to do with his hands and shoved them into his pockets, a trait Christine recognized in Nick.

"Why don't I order you up some soup," he said. "Maybe a sandwich."

"No, thanks. I really don't think I could eat."

"I called your mother. She's trying to catch a flight later this evening. Hopefully, she'll be here by morning."

"Thanks. It'll be nice to have her here," Christine lied. Her mother panicked at the mention of a crisis. How would she ever handle this? She wondered what her father had told her mother. How much had he watered down?

"Now, don't get upset, pumpkin, but I also called Bruce."

"Bruce?"

"He has a right to know. Timmy is his son."

"Yes, of course, and Nick and I have been trying to contact him. You know where he is?"

"No, but I have a phone number for emergencies."

"So you've known all along how to contact him?"

Her father looked stunned. How dare she direct such shrill anger toward him.

"And you knew that I've been trying to find him to make him pay child support for over eight months. Here, all this time, you've had his phone number?"

"For emergencies, Christine."

"Seeing that his son has food on the table isn't an emergency? How could you?"

"You're exaggerating, Christine. Your mom and I would never let you and Timmy struggle. Besides, Bruce said he left you with plenty in savings."

"That's what he said?" She laughed, and she didn't care that it sounded on the verge of hysteria.

"He left us with exactly 164.21 in our savings account and over five thousand dollars of credit card bills."

She knew her father hated confrontation. She had spent a lifetime tiptoeing around the great Tony Morrelli, letting his opinions be the only ones, his feelings more important than anyone else's. Her mother called it respect. Now Christine saw it for what it was—foolish.

He paced in front of her, his hands deep in his pockets, the change noisily keeping his fingers busy.

"That son of a bitch. That's not what he told me," he finally said. "But you threw the man out of his own house, Christine."

"He was fucking his receptionist."

His face grew scarlet with disapproval. A lady never used such language.

"Sometimes a man strays, Christine. A minor indiscretion. I'm not saying it's right, but it's not a reason to throw him out of his own house."

So there it was. She had suspected his disapproval, but until now neither of her parents had spoken it. Her father's world was fraught with double standards. She had always known that, had accepted it, kept quiet about it. But this was her life.

"I wonder, would you be this forgiving if I had been the one who had the affair?"

"What? Don't be ridiculous."

"No. I want to know. Would you have called it a minor indiscretion if I had fucked the UPS man?"

He winced again, and she wondered if it was her language or the image that disgusted him. After all, Tony Morrelli's little girl didn't fuck.

"Look, you're upset, Christine. Why don't I have one of the guys drive you home?"

She didn't answer, couldn't answer over the rage boiling inside. She only nodded, and he escaped.

After a few short minutes the door opened again, and Eddie Gillick came in.

"Your dad asked me to drive you home."

CHAPTER 77

What an idiot he was, Nick thought as he rammed the Jeep into gear, picking up speed and leaving Platte City behind. He glanced at Maggie sitting quietly next to him. He should have never allowed her to see the weakness, the absolute terror that had taken control of his insides. Despite her revelation about Stucky, she remained in control and composed, staring out at the dark countryside. How did she do it? How did she keep Albert Stucky and all the other horrors carefully tucked away? How did she keep herself from slamming a fist through a wall and shattering glass doors?

He couldn't think, could barely concentrate on the dark road. The drumming continued in his chest, a persistent pounding, a time bomb ticking off the seconds, each second maybe Timmy's last.

And through the panic, and maybe because of it, he had almost gone way over the line and told Maggie that he loved her. What an idiot—what a complete idiot he was. Maybe it wasn't just his virility and charm he was losing. Hell, maybe he was losing his mind, too.

Now sitting here in the quiet dark with Maggie beside him, he felt a sudden strength. He had to be strong for Timmy's sake, and maybe, just maybe, he could do that as long as he didn't have to do it alone. Jesus, that was a first—Nick Morrelli might actually need someone?

He could ignore the sick feeling in his gut. He would put the vision of Danny Alverez's vacant eyes out of his mind. Timmy had to be okay. It couldn't be too late. He stepped on the accelerator, zigzagging the Jeep over the black highway. Wisps of snow scampered across in spots, but the wind had died down considerably.

"Maybe you should fill me in," he said, managing to keep the panic from his voice. "Why are we going to a graveyard in the middle of the night?"

"I know your men checked the old church, but what about the tunnel?"

"The tunnel? I think that caved in years ago."

"Are you sure?"

"Well, no. Actually, I've never seen it. When I was a kid we thought it was just made up. You know, to scare us, to keep us from screwing around the church at night. There were stories about bodies rising from the dead, digging out of their graves and crawling through the tunnel. Finding their way back to the church to redeem their condemned souls."

"Sounds like the perfect place for a killer who believes in redemption."

"You think that's where he's keeping Timmy? In a hole in the ground?" He remembered Maggie's story about the father who buried his son in the backyard. Again, he slammed on the accelerator, drawing a concerned look from Maggie.

"It's only a hunch," she said, but her tone told him she thought it was more. "At this point, I don't think we have anything to lose by checking it out. Ray Howard mentioned going there to cut wood. He knows something. Maybe he's seen something."

"I can't believe you let him go."

"He's not the killer, Nick. But I think he might know who is."

"You still think it's Keller, don't you?" He shot her a look, but in the dark he saw only that her face was turned away from him, staring again into the black night.

"Keller could have easily planted my cell phone in Howard's room. He had access to the pickup. He keeps those strange paintings of tortured martyrs, martyrs with the sign of the cross sliced into their chests."

"The guy has bad taste in art, that doesn't make him a killer. Besides, anyone could have seen Keller's paintings and gotten the idea."

"Keller also knew all three boys."

"Actually, all five boys," Nick interrupted. "Lucy and Max were able to dig up lists and applications. Eric Paltrow and Aaron Harper did attend church camp the summer before they were murdered. But that means Ray Howard knew all the boys, too."

"It's more than that, Nick. Somehow, I think this killer believes he's making these boys martyrs, saving them from something. Most serial killers murder for pleasure, for sexual gratification or to fill some other egocentric need. It's like something clicks in this guy and sends him on a mission. Father Keller fits much of that profile. Who else would administer last rites to his victims but a priest? And who else would have the perfect opportunity to push Father Francis down a flight of stairs and get away with it?"

"Jesus, Maggie. You still won't let that go?"

"Looks like I may not have a choice. The archdiocese is in charge of Father Francis' remains, since there's no next of kin, and they see no reason for an autopsy."

There was silence between them. If Father Francis had been shoved down those stairs, Nick could imagine Howard being more than capable of doing it. But now he wondered what it was Father Francis wanted to share with Maggie.

"Maybe we've got this wrong," Nick said, unraveling the thought as he spoke. "Maybe Keller is involved, but maybe he's protecting someone."

"What do you mean?"

"Father Francis couldn't tell us about Jeffreys' confession. Suppose the killer confessed to Father Keller?"

Maggie sat quietly. She was obviously mulling over the idea. Perhaps it wasn't so far-fetched, Nick realized.

Suddenly, out of the darkness, Maggie said, "Did you know Ray Howard and Eddie Gillick are friends?"

CHAPTER 78

Christine knew it was the anger that had rendered her temporarily insane. Otherwise, why would she be climbing into Eddie Gillick's rusted Chevy? Even his apology about the state of the vehicle sounded half-sincere. Yet, here she was with her feet kicking empty McDonald's containers. A spring poked into her back, and crumb-filled stuffing grew out of the cushion next to her. It smelled of French fries, cigarettes and that annoying aftershave lotion. Something smelled like the back of her refrigerator.

Eddie slid into the driver's seat, tossing his hat into the back and stealing a long glance of himself in the rearview mirror. He stuck the key in the ignition, and the loose tailpipe sent the car vibrating.

Christine wished she had changed clothes after the interview. Despite her long trench coat, it felt as if something was crawling on her bare legs. She opened her coat to make sure there weren't black bugs skittering up her thighs. As she ran a hand over one leg, she noticed Eddie watching, smiling. She pulled her coat closed and decided bugs were better than Eddie's eyes.

He gunned the engine, slamming her back into the seat. She reached up for the seat belt and saw it had been cut out. He sped past the turn to her street and a fresh panic sent her hand to the door handle. It broke off with a snap, and Eddie frowned at her.

"Relax, Christine. Your dad said I should get you something to eat."

"I'm really not hungry," she blurted quickly, the panic slipping out. "Really, I'm just tired." That was better. She couldn't let it sound as if she didn't trust him.

"I can grill you up a steak that'll make your mouth water. Just happen to have a couple in my fridge."

Oh, God. Not his place.

"Maybe another time, Eddie." She made her voice as sweet as possible, despite the revulsion. "I really am tired. Could you please just take me home?"

She watched his face out of the corner of her eye. His mustache twitched, then a crooked smile. Another glance at himself in the rearview mirror.

"You came on to me pretty strong that evening out by the river," he said.

Big mistake. How could she be so stupid? Yet, other reporters did that sort of thing all the time, didn't they?"

"Look, I'm sorry about that, Eddie." Be sincere. Don't let him see you're scared. "It was my first big assignment. I guess I was nervous."

"It's okay, Christine. I know it's been over a year since your husband left. Hell, you don't have to play shy with me. I know women get horny, too."

Oh, dear God. This was not going well. She felt sick again as she watched houses pass by. A few more blocks and they'd leave streetlights behind. They were headed out of town. Her heart raced. She was beyond playing cool and calm. She shoved her weight against the door. It didn't move. Her shoulder throbbed. Eddie scowled at her, then the scowl grew into another twisted smile, telling her it didn't matter whether or not she played along.

His eyes were coal black to match his greased-back hair. She remembered he was about her height but muscular. After all, he had knocked Nick off his feet with two lousy punches. Of course, Nick hadn't seen it coming. Something told Christine that was how Eddie operated. Attacking when his victims least expected. Like a spider.

"Eddie, please." She was not above pleading. "My son's missing. I'm really in awful shape. Please just take me home."

"I know what you need, Christine. Take your mind off things for a while. Just relax."

Her eyes darted around the car. Anything...was there anything she could use as a weapon? Then in the glow of the panel lights she saw a long-necked beer bottle roll out from under the seat, as though answering her prayer.

He was driving awfully fast. She needed to wait. Wait until they stopped, or they'd end up in a snow-filled ditch, stranded in the middle of nowhere. Could she contain the panic until then? Could she keep the scream that clawed at her throat from escaping her lips?

"It wouldn't hurt you to be nice to me, Christine," he said slowly. "If you're nice, I might just tell you where Timmy is."

CHAPTER 79

Timmy hid his feet under the covers. He scooted into the corner while the stranger paced in front of the bed. Something was wrong. The stranger seemed upset. He hadn't said anything since he came into the room. Instead, he threw his ski jacket onto the bed and started pacing.

Timmy kept quiet and watched. Under the covers, he pulled and yanked the chain. The stranger forgot to close the door behind him, leaving it wide open. The smell of dirt and mold came in with a draft. It was black on the other side of the door.

"What happened to the lantern?" the stranger suddenly wanted to know. The glass casing still lay on the crate.

"I...I couldn't light it, so I had to take that thing off. Sorry, I forgot to put it back on."

The stranger took the glass and snapped it in place without looking at Timmy. When he bent over, Timmy saw black, curly hair sticking out from under his mask. Richard Nixon. That was the dead president the mask resembled. It had taken Timmy three attempts at naming the presidents before he remembered. But there was still something very familiar about Richard Nixon's blue eyes. Something in the way they stared at him, especially tonight. As if they were apologizing.

Suddenly, the stranger grabbed his jacket and wrestled into it.

"It's time to go."

"Where?" Timmy tried to control his excitement. Was it really possible that the stranger might take him home? Maybe he'd realized his mistake. Timmy crawled out of bed, keeping the chain behind his feet.

"Take off all your clothes, except your underpants."

Timmy's excitement shattered. "What?" he asked over the lump gathering in his throat. "It's awfully cold out."

"Don't ask questions."

"But I don't understand what—"

"Just do it, you little son of a bitch."

The unexpected anger felt like a slap in the face. Even Timmy's eyes stung, his vision suddenly blurred by the tears gathering. He shouldn't cry. He wasn't a baby anymore. But he was scared. So scared his fingers shook as he untied his shoes. He noticed the cracked sole on his tennis shoe as he kicked it off. It had leaked in snow when they were sledding, getting his feet cold and wet, but he couldn't imagine how cold it would be without shoes.

"I don't understand," he mumbled again. The lump obstructed his breathing now as well as his voice.

"You don't need to understand. Hurry up." The stranger paced, the huge rubber boots caked with snow and mud, a *thump-squash* sound with each step.

"I don't mind staying here," Timmy attempted again.

"Shut the fuck up, you little bastard, and hurry up."

Tears ran down Timmy's cheeks, and he didn't bother to wipe at them. His fingers were shaking something terrible as he undid his belt, remembered the chain on his ankle, then worked on his shirt buttons, instead. The stranger would need to unchain him. Would he notice the bent links? Would he get even more angry? Already Timmy felt a cold draft swirling around him. His stomach hurt. He wanted to throw up. Even his knees were shaking, and his vision blurred from the tears.

Suddenly, the stranger's pacing stopped. He stood perfectly still in the middle of the room, cocking his head to one side. At first Timmy thought the stranger was staring at him, but instead, he was listening. Timmy strained to hear over his thumping heart. He sniffed back tears and dragged a sleeve across his face. Then he heard it—a car engine in the distance, getting closer and slowing down.

"Fuck!" the stranger spat, grabbing the lantern and heading for the door.

"No, please don't take the light."

"Shut the fuck up, you little crybaby."

He wheeled back around, smashing the back of his hand across Timmy's face. Timmy scrambled into the bed, escaping into the corner. He hugged the pillow, but jerked away at the sight of the red blotch.

"You better be ready when I get back," the stranger hissed. "And stop bleeding all over the place."

The stranger ran out the door, slamming it and the locks back into place, leaving Timmy in a hole of solid black. He hurried out in such a rush that he didn't even notice Timmy's chain, broken and dangling over the edge of the bed.

CHAPTER 80

Christine didn't need to ask what Eddie was planning. She recognized the winding dirt road that climbed then plunged. It snaked through the towering maples and walnut trees that lined the riverbank. It was where all the kids went to make out, just off Old Church Road. It looked out over the river. It was deserted and quiet and black. This was where Jason Ashford and Amy Stykes were probably headed the night they were sidetracked. The night they stumbled over Danny Alverez's body.

Was it possible that Eddie knew where Timmy was? Christine remembered that a church janitor had been brought in for questioning. Could Eddie have overheard something? Yet, if Nick knew something, *anything,* wouldn't he have told her? No, of course not. He'd want to keep her out of the way, give her some menial task like photocopying pictures of her son.

Eddie disgusted her, but more importantly, he frightened her. He was reckless, a bit over the edge. She imagined him to be one of those cops who pulled you over for driving thirty-six in a thirty-five-mile-an-hour zone just because he could. But if he knew where Timmy was... Oh, God, if she could just have Timmy back, safe and sound. What price would she be willing to pay? What price would any mother—Laura Alverez, Michelle Tanner—what price would they pay to have their sons back? Christine had been willing to sell her soul for a lousy paycheck. What was she willing to do to save her son?

Nevertheless, when the car pulled off the road and slid into the clearing overlooking the river, the panic crawled through her, sending a shiver down her back. Her empty stomach churned. She felt light-headed again. No, she couldn't pass out. Something told her that if an unwilling woman couldn't stop Eddie, neither could an unconscious one.

Eddie cut the engine and extinguished the headlights. The dark engulfed them as though they hovered in it, looking down on black ruffled treetops, the glittering river below. Only the sliver of moon added a pathetic reassurance that the darkness couldn't swallow everything.

"Well, here we are," Eddie said, turning toward her expectantly, but staying behind the wheel.

Her foot found the beer bottle, and she kept it from sliding under the seat. Without the car's inside panel lights, it was too dark to see his face. She heard a wrapper crackle, followed by a slap. Then a match sizzled, the smell of sulfur attacking her nostrils as he lit a cigarette.

"Mind if I have one of those?"

In the light of his cigarette, she saw the twisted smile. He handed her one, lit another match and waited for her. The match burned down close to his fingers. By the time he lit hers, he ended up scorching his fingertips.

"Damn," he muttered and shook his hand. "I hate matches. Lost my lighter someplace."

"I didn't know you smoked." She inhaled, waiting, hoping the nicotine could calm her.

"I'm trying to quit."

"Me, too." She smiled at him. See, they did have something in common. She could do this, couldn't she? By now her eyes had adjusted to the dark, and she could see him. She wondered if it would have been easier if she hadn't been able to see him. He looked so cool and calm, his arm stretched out over the cracked seat. She needed to stay cool and calm, too. Maybe she could, at least, keep the situation from getting violent. "Do you really know where Timmy is?"

"Maybe," he answered in a puff of smoke. "What are you willing to do to find out?" He moved his arm across the seat until his stubby fingers brushed her hair, then wandered across her cheek, swooping down to her neck.

"How do I know this isn't just some trick?"

"You don't."

His fingers slid under her coat collar, unbuttoning and pulling the coat open until he could see her blouse and skirt. Her skin crawled under his touch. It was difficult not to grimace. Even the nicotine couldn't help.

"That's not really fair, Eddie. There has to be something in it for me."

He pretended to look hurt. "I would hope your incredible orgasm would be enough."

His fingertips brushed across her breasts. It was all she could do to stop from slamming her body against the side of the car, bolting from his reach. Instead, she sat perfectly still. Don't think, she told herself. Shut off. But she wanted to scream when his hand fondled her breast, squeezing her nipple, watching and smiling at it growing hard and erect under his touch.

He put out his cigarette and scooted closer so that his other hand could assault her thigh. The stubby fingers slithered up, and she watched as they disappeared under her skirt. She refused to part her thighs for him, and this time he laughed, his breath sour in her face.

"Come on, Christine, relax."

"I'm just nervous." Her voice quivered, and he seemed pleased. "Do you have protection?"

"Don't you use anything?" He shoved his hand between her thighs.

"I haven't..." It was hard to think with his rough gropes. She wanted to throw up. "I haven't been with anyone since Bruce."

"Really?" His fingers poked at her, pulling at her underwear to allow him access. "Well, I don't use condoms."

She couldn't breathe. "I'm afraid we can't do this if you don't."

He obviously mistook her breathlessness for excitement.

"That's okay," he said, running the fingertips of his other hand over her lips and pushing his thumb into her mouth. "There's other things we can do."

Her stomach lurched. Would she throw up? She couldn't...couldn't afford to make him angry. He reached down, unzipped his trousers and pulled out his erect penis. It snaked out of his pants, long and thick. He took her hand. She snatched it away. He smiled and took it again, wrapping her fingers around him and squeezing his hand over hers until she could feel the bulging vein throbbing alongside it. He groaned and leaned back.

She couldn't do this. There was no way she could put her mouth on him.

"Do you really know where Timmy is?" she asked one more time, trying to remind herself of her mission.

He closed his eyes and his breathing rasped. "Oh baby, squeeze and suck me real good, and I'll tell you anything you want to hear."

At least his hands were off her. Then she remembered the cigarette in her other hand, the long ash lingering at the end. She took another draw until the end glowed red-hot. She squeezed him, digging her nails into the hard thickness.

"What the fuck!"

His eyes flew open. He grabbed for her hand. She shoved the flaming cigarette into his face. He howled, reeling against the door and swatting at his scorched cheek. She reached around him, grabbing the door handle. His hands snapped around her wrists, immediately letting go when she slammed her knee up into his erect penis. He sucked in for air. She scooped up the beer bottle, and when he grabbed for her again, she cracked it across his head. Another howl, a high-pitched, inhuman screech. She scooted to her side of the seat, anchored her back against her impenetrable door. She brought her knees up, and with all the strength she could gather, slammed her high-heeled feet into his chest. Eddie flew out the door.

He sprawled in the snow and dirt, but was getting to his feet when she pulled his door shut, locking it and checking the other doors. He pounded on the glass as her fingers fumbled with the keys in the ignition. The Chevy sputtered to life with one try.

Eddie climbed onto the hood, screaming at her and kicking at the windshield. A small crack raced across, spreading into a spiderweb. She threw the car into reverse and slammed on the accelerator, sending the car careening backward, almost into the ditch. Eddie flew from the hood. He scrambled to his feet as she shifted into Drive and floored it, skidding recklessly from ditch to ditch, sending gravel spitting.

Then the car plunged down the winding road into a hole of black. The headlights. She grabbed at knobs, sending the wipers swishing and the radio blaring. She looked down for only a second, found the knob and lit up the road, just in time to see the sharp curve. Even with both hands twisting the steering wheel, it wasn't enough. Both her feet slammed on the brake, and the car screeched as it flew across the snow-filled ditch, through the barbed-wire fence and into a tree.

CHAPTER 81

Nick watched the dark church in the rearview mirror as the Jeep bounced over the deep tire tracks, the only things identifying the deserted road.

"You sure you didn't see a light?"

Maggie glanced over the back of the seat. "Maybe it was a reflection. There is a moon out tonight."

The wood-framed church looked dark and gray, disappearing from the rearview mirror as he took the sharp turn up into the graveyard. Now to his left, he stared at the church again. It was set in the middle of a snow-covered field with tall, brown grass stabbing through the white. The paint had peeled away years ago, leaving raw and rotting wood. All the stained-glass windows had been removed or broken and boarded up. Even the huge front door deteriorated behind thick boards that were haphazardly pounded in at odd diagonals.

"It looked like a light," Nick said. "In one of the basement windows."

"Why don't you check it out. I can wander around here for a while."

"I only have one flashlight." He leaned over, careful not to touch her, snapping open the glove compartment.

"That's okay, I have this." She shined the tiny penlight into his eyes.

"Oh, yeah. That should show you a lot."

She smiled, and suddenly he realized how close his hand was to her thigh. He grabbed the flashlight and made a hasty retreat.

"I can leave the headlights on." Though at this angle they shot into the trees, over the rows of headstones.

"No, that's okay. I'll be fine."

"I don't understand why they always build graveyards on hills," he said, switching off the headlights. They both sat still, neither making an effort to leave the Jeep. There was something more she was thinking about. He'd sensed it ever since they left his office. Was it Albert Stucky? Did this place—this dark—remind her of him?

"You okay?"

"I'm fine," she said too quickly, continuing to stare straight ahead. "Just waiting for my eyes to adjust to the dark."

A fence surrounded the graveyard, twisted wire held up by bent and leaning steel rods. The gate hung on one hinge, swinging and clicking back and forth though there was no wind. A chill slithered down Nick's back. He'd hated this place, ever since he was a kid and Jimmy Montgomery dared him to run up and touch the black angel.

It was impossible not to notice the angel, even in the black of night. At this angle, looking up the hill, the tall stone figure hovered above the other tombstones. Its chipped wings only made it more menacing. His memory was of Halloween, almost twenty-five years ago. Then suddenly, he remembered that tomorrow was Halloween. And, although it was silly, he swore he could hear the ghostly groans again. The pained, hollow moans rumored to seep from the tomb the angel guarded.

"Did you hear that?" His eyes darted over the rows. He flashed on the headlights, realized he was being ridiculous and snapped them off. "Sorry," he mumbled, avoiding Maggie's eyes, though he could feel them studying him now. Another bubbleheaded move like that and she'd be wondering why she'd invited him along. Thankfully, she said nothing.

As if reading each other's minds, they reached for the door handles at the same time. Again, hers clicked.

"Damn," he muttered. "I've got to get that fixed. Hold on."

He jumped out and hurried around to open the door for her. Then he stood silently by her side, mesmerized by the spot of moonlight caught on the angel's face, radiating a glow almost as if from within.

"Nick, are you okay?"

"Yeah, I'm fine." How could she not see that? He pulled his eyes away. "I'll just go… I'll check out the church."

"You're starting to spook me."

"Sorry. It's just…the angel." He waved a hand at it, streaking its surface with the light from his flashlight.

"It doesn't come to life at midnight, does it?"

She was making fun. He glanced at her. Her face was serious, only adding to the sarcasm. He started walking away, heading down the road to the church. Without looking over his shoulder, he said, "Just remember, tomorrow is Halloween."

"I thought we canceled that," she yelled back.

He didn't let her see his smile. Instead, he kept to his path, following the tunnel of light he created. Without the wind it was unbearably quiet. Somewhere in the distance a hoot owl tested its voice, receiving no reply.

Nick tried to stay focused, to ignore the blackness pressing against him, swallowing him with each step. It was ridiculous to let those old childhood fears creep into his gut. After all, he *had* crossed the dark cemetery that night. He had touched the angel while his friends watched, none of them attempting to follow. He had been reckless and stupid even back then, more afraid of what others would think than the consequences of his actions. Yet, if he remembered correctly, the earth hadn't opened up and swallowed him, though it had felt as if it would at the time. There had been that ghostly moan. And he wasn't the only one who had heard it.

On this side of the church, the side that faced the old pasture road, there were no footprints. Which meant Adam and Lloyd hadn't even bothered to get out of their vehicle. They simply had driven by, so they could honestly say they had checked. He wondered if they'd even stopped. He didn't blame Adam. The kid was young, wanted to make a good impression, be a part of the group. But Lloyd...damn it. Lloyd was just lazy.

Nick kicked at the snow and plodded through the unbroken drifts. He crouched at one of the basement windows and shined light through the rotted slats. There were crates stacked on crates. Movement in the corner. His light caught a huge rat escaping into a hole in the wall. Rats. Jesus, he hated rats.

He made his way to the next window and suddenly heard the crack of wood. It cut through the black silence. He shot light at the plugged windows ahead of him. He expected to see something or someone smashing through the rotted wood.

Another crack, then splintering of more wood and the tinkle of broken glass. It must be around the corner. He tried running. The snow slowed his feet. He extinguished the flashlight. His hand pulled at his gun—once, twice, three times—before he unsnapped the restraint. The noises continued. His heart drummed against his rib cage. He couldn't hear, couldn't see. He slowed as he approached the corner. Should he call out? He held his breath. Then he rushed the corner, pointing his gun into the blackness. Nothing. He snapped on the flashlight. Wood and glass lay scattered in the snow. The opening was no bigger than a foot wide and high.

Then he heard bursts of crunching snow. His light caught movement disappearing into the trees—a small, black figure and a flash of orange.

CHAPTER 82

Maggie concentrated on the ground, looking for any breaks in the snow or freshly dug holes. Timmy had disappeared after the snowfall. If he was here, the snow would be disturbed. If a tunnel existed, where in the world would the entrance be?

She glanced up at the black angel perched on what looked like an above-ground tomb. Weather had chipped at the facade, leaving white wounds. It stood high above everything else, four to five feet tall. The wings spread out, protecting the tomb beneath, an ominous creature exuding power simply with its presence.

Maggie's penlight searched the engraving: In memory of our beloved son, Nathan, 1906-1916. A child, of course, that was the reason for the guardian angel. Her fingers dug deep into her jeans pocket until she felt the chain and found the medallion at the end. Her own guardian angel, which she kept tucked out of sight. Did the same power exist for skeptics? Yet, how much of a skeptic was she if she still carried the thing?

A breeze swirled up out of the trees that lined the back of the graveyard. The huge maples were the beginnings of the thick woods that led down to the river. She tried to imagine frightened runaway slaves navigating the steep decline without the aid of flashlights or lanterns. Even with the sliver of moonlight and sprinkling of stars, the black overwhelmed.

A flapping sound came from behind her. Maggie spun around. Something moved. The tiny penlight picked out a black shadow sprawled on the ground at the end of the rows. Was it a body? She approached slowly. Her hand crawled inside her jacket and rested on the butt of her revolver. She recognized the black tarp, the kind used to cover freshly dug graves. She sighed, then remembered the graveyard hadn't been used in years. Wasn't that what Adam had told her? The adrenaline started pumping.

The tarp was down the hill, close to the tree line. Only a few headstones existed on this side. Here, she could no longer see the Jeep or the road, only a piece of the church roof in the distance.

The tarp looked new, no cracks or worn patches. Rocks and snow anchored the corners, but one corner flapped free, its rock set aside. Set aside, not blown aside, not by tonight's slight breeze.

She realized her hands were sweating, despite the cold. Her heartbeat pounded in her ears, too fast, too hard. She should wait for Nick, head back to the Jeep and wait. Instead, she pulled the loose corner and whipped the tarp aside. She didn't need extra light to see. Underneath was a door, narrow and long, thick wood rotting around the hinges and caving in slightly in the middle.

Again, she stopped and glanced up the hill. She should wait. Remember Stucky, she scolded herself. Then, suddenly, she remembered the note, "I know about Stucky." Was this another trap? No, the killer couldn't possibly know she'd come here.

She paced, staring at the door. Another quick glance. Her heart pounded too loudly for her to think. She needed to calm herself. She could do this.

She grabbed the edge of the door. There was no handle. She pulled and yanked until it gave way, but it was heavy, straining her muscles, splinters threatening her fingers. She dropped the door, got a better grip and tried again. This time she swung it open. The musty odor slapped her in the face. It was filled with decay, wet earth and mold.

She searched the black hole but couldn't see beyond the third step with her penlight. It would be ridiculous to go down with such poor lighting. The pounding of her heart continued. She pulled out her revolver and was annoyed by the tremor in her hand. She glanced back up the hill one more time. Silence. No sign of Nick. She descended slowly into the narrow, black hole.

CHAPTER 83

Timmy skidded down into a prickly bush. He had heard the stranger close behind, felt the flash of light on his back. He didn't dare stop or look back. He kept a hold of the sled, no matter how awkward. His breathing came in spastic gasps. Branches grabbed at him. Twigs slapped him in the face. He stumbled, did a little dance and kept from falling. He tried to keep quiet, but the snaps and cracks were explosions he couldn't prevent. He couldn't see his feet in the black. Even the sky had disappeared.

He stopped to catch his breath, leaned against a tree and realized in his rush he hadn't put on his coat. He couldn't breathe. His teeth chattered. His heart exploded against his chest. He wiped at his face and discovered more blood, as well as tears.

"Stop crying," he scolded himself. Han Solo never cried.

Then he heard it. In the black silence he heard branches snapping, snow crunching. The sounds came from behind him, close and getting closer. Could he hide, hope the stranger would pass right by? No, the stranger would surely hear the massive pounding of his heart.

He ran recklessly, tripping over stumps and smashing through the thicket. A twig swiped at his cheek and ripped at his ear. The sting brought fresh tears. Then suddenly he felt the ground slip out from under him. A steep decline forced him to grab on to a branch, a rock, anything to keep from sliding down. Below, he saw the glitter of water. He'd never make it. The woods were too thick, the ridge too steep. The cracking of branches was even closer now.

He noticed a clearing to his right. He climbed over the rocks that blocked his path, hanging on to tree roots with one hand while clutching his sled with the other.

It wasn't much of a clearing. Instead, it looked like an old horse trail, a path worn into the woods but now overgrown with spindly branches, alien arms with long, thin fingers waving to him. As far as Timmy could see, the path went all the way down to the river, with a few sharp turns. It looked like something from one of his video games, narrow and dangerous and clogged with heaps of snow. The snow made it impossible to climb without sliding. It was perfect. Of course, it was also reckless and crazy. His mom would have a fit.

A crack close behind made him jump. He crouched in the snow and grass. Even in the dark he saw the shadow crawling down, clinging to the ridge, his back to Timmy. He looked like a giant insect, tentacles outstretched gripping roots and jutted rocks.

Timmy laid his orange sled in the snow. He crawled in carefully, its angle steep—really steep. He allowed himself one more frantic glance over his shoulder. The shadow edged closer. Soon, the stranger would be at the rocks. Timmy pointed the sled into the horse trail and scooted his body down until he was almost lying. There was no other choice. This was it. He jerked, one quick shove, and the sled plunged downward.

CHAPTER 84

Nick stood at the edge of the woods, every nerve ending on alert. It was impossible to see with only a flashlight. Branches swayed in a fresh breeze. Night birds exchanged calls. The black figure was gone. Or hiding.

He remembered a road that snaked through the woods, not far from here. It went all the way to the river. He'd have a better chance with the Jeep. He hurried back toward the church. When he stuffed his gun into the shoulder holster, he realized the other bulge in his jacket was Christine's cellular phone. Great, he thought, pulling it out. At least he could avoid a flood of media hounds if he didn't use the Jeep's CB radio.

Lucy answered on the second ring.

"Lucy, it's Nick."

"Nick, where in the world are you? I've been so worried."

"I don't have time to explain. I'm going to need some men and searchlights. I think I just chased the killer into the woods, behind the old church. He's probably headed for the river again."

"Where do you want the guys to meet you?"

"Down by the river. There's an old gravel road that winds through the woods. It's just off Old Church Road past the state park, not far from where we found Matthew. You know the one?"

"Isn't that the one with Make-out Point?"

"Make-out Point?"

"Well, that's what the kids call it. There's a clearing overlooking the river. Kids go there to make out."

"Yeah, I'm sure that's the one. Lucy, tell Hal. Let him decide who to bring, okay?"

"Okay."

He slapped the phone shut. What if it was only a vagrant he'd seen, who had used the church to get in out of the cold? He'd look like a fool again. The hell with what he looked like. He didn't care, if they could just find Timmy.

He stopped at the window, kicked aside the wood and glass, then crouched to shine light into the hole. Sure enough, there was a bed, posters on the wall, a crate with food. Someone had been staying here. The light reflected off a glimpse of chain. Or someone had been imprisoned here. He saw the comic books, the scattered baseball cards and the small child's coat. Timmy's coat. The drumming started again, the rhythm an erratic war dance against his rib cage. He couldn't be sure it was Timmy's, he made a feeble attempt to convince himself. Yet, he knew this was it. This was where the boys had been kept. Maggie was right. Then he saw the bloody pillow.

CHAPTER 85

Maggie heard small creatures skitter across the ceiling above her. Dirt crumbled down into her hair, but she didn't dare look up. She swatted at cobwebs. Something ran across her foot. She didn't need light to tell her it was a rat. She could hear them in the corners, behind the dirt walls, escaping into their own little tunnels.

The space was small enough to take in with a few swipes of the penlight. She had counted eleven steps, carrying her deep into the ground where the damp air became heavier with each step. The hole resembled an old storm cellar, an odd comparison considering the graveyard's residents no longer needed shelter from any storm. Other than a thick wooden shelf and a large crate in the corner, the space was empty. Even the shelves were empty, coated with cobwebs and rat feces. Disappointingly, there were no signs of Timmy and no tunnel. How could she be so wrong? Had Stucky sabotaged her instincts, too?

Still, someone had cleared the snow from the door and attempted to hide it with the tarp. Was there something here, a clue, anything to help find Timmy? She surveyed the space again, stopping this time when the light hit the crate.

On closer inspection, the old wooden crate was actually in good shape with no signs of rot or beginning decay. It certainly had not spent much time in the wet dark hole. Very few crumbs of dirt covered its surface. Even the lid was attached with shiny new nails.

Maggie holstered her revolver. She pried at the lid, but her fingers weren't strong enough to loosen the nails. She found a broken steel rod in the corner and began using it to pry the lid. The nails screeched but held. Immediately, a rancid smell leaked out, quickly filling the small space. Maggie stopped and backed off just a few steps to examine the crate again. Was it big enough to hide a body? A child's body? She had seen body parts stuffed into smaller spaces. Like the pieces of Emma Jean Thomas, which Stucky had crammed into take-out containers and left in a Dumpster. Who would have guessed a pair of lungs could fit into a foam container the size of a sandwich?

She tried to lift the crate, hoping to drag it up into the fresh air. She could barely lift it a foot off the ground. She would never be able to drag it up eleven steps. She pried at the lid again. This time the smell made her gag. She spat out the penlight she had anchored between her teeth and let it lie on the ground. She held her breath and tried again.

Something scraped in the dirt. Maggie spun around. In the black there was movement. Something bigger than a rat. She dropped to her knees, grabbing for the penlight. She clutched the steel rod, holding it above her head, ready to strike. Then she held her breath again and listened. All sound, all movement had come to a halt. The narrow light whipped across the opposite wall. The wooden shelf leaned forward, shoved away from the wall. Maggie now saw a hole, large enough to be an entrance to the famed tunnel.

In the black silence, something stirred behind her. She was no longer alone. Someone stood behind her, blocking the steps. She felt his presence, heard the soft wisps of his breathing as though it was suctioned through a tube. The panic Stucky had left with her unleashed itself and raced through her veins, ice-cold and rapid. And just as her fingers snuck inside her jacket, a smooth knife blade slid under her chin.

CHAPTER 86

"Agent Maggie O'Dell, what a lovely surprise."

Maggie didn't recognize the muffled voice in her ear. The knife's razor-sharp point pressed into the softness of her neck. It pushed with a steady pressure, forcing her head back until her neck lay completely exposed, completely vulnerable. She felt a trickle of blood run down inside the collar of her jacket.

"Why a surprise? I thought you'd be expecting me. You seem to know so much about me." With every syllable she felt the knife dig deeper.

"Drop the steel rod." He pulled her against him, wrapping his free arm around the front of her, squeezing harder than necessary to emphasize his strength.

She dropped the rod while he dug inside her jacket. He carefully grabbed the butt of the gun, his hand jerking away when he accidentally grazed her breast. He tossed the gun into a dark corner where she heard it knock against the crate. Of course, she wasn't surprised he would be much more comfortable using the knife.

She tried to concentrate on his voice and the feel of him. He was strong and four to six inches taller than her. The rest of himself, he disguised. A brush of rubber against her ear and the muffled sound told her he wore a mask. Even his hands were camouflaged in plain black gloves. They were made of cheap-department store leather, sold by the hundreds.

"I wasn't expecting you. I thought perhaps you might have gone back home to your safe condo and your lawyer husband and your sick mother. How is your mother, by the way?"

"Why don't you tell me?"

The blade pushed up. Maggie sucked in air and resisted the urge to swallow while another trickle of blood found its way down her neck, traveling between her breasts.

"That wasn't very nice," he scolded.

"Sorry," she said carefully, not moving her mouth or chin. She could do this. She could play his game. She needed to stay calm, level the playing field somehow. "The smell is getting to me. Maybe we could discuss this outside."

"No, sorry. You see that's a bit of a problem. I'm afraid you won't be leaving here at all. What do you think of your new home?" He made her turn around to examine the area with her penlight while the knife scraped her flesh. "Or should I say your tomb?"

The ice shot through her veins again. Calm, she needed to remain calm. If only she could remove the image of Albert Stucky carving her abdomen. If only she could get this madman to ease the pressure. One small jerk and she'd be tasting the knife's metal in her mouth.

"It won't matter...getting rid of me." She talked slowly. "The entire sheriff's department knows who you are. About a dozen deputies will be here in a few minutes."

"Now, Agent O'Dell, you can't bluff me. I know you like to be on your own. That's what got you in trouble with Mr. Stucky, isn't it? And all you have on me is your little psychological profile. I bet I even know what it says. My mother abused me as a child, right? She turned me into a fag, so I murder little boys now." The attempt at laughter sounded like a manic cackle.

"Actually, I don't think your mother abused you." She tried frantically to remember what little family history she had found on Father Keller. Of course, his mother had been a single parent just like the victims' mothers. But she had died when Keller was young—a fatal accident. Why couldn't she remember the details? Why was it so hard to think? It was the smell, the pressure of the knife, the feel of her own blood.

"I think she loved you," Maggie continued when he remained silent. "And you loved her. But you *were* abused." A twitch told her she was right. "By a relative...perhaps a friend of your mother's...no, a stepfather," she remembered suddenly.

The knife slipped, only a quarter of an inch, but she could breathe again. He was quiet, waiting, listening. She had his attention. It was her move.

"No, you're not homosexual, but he made you doubt yourself, didn't he? He made you think that maybe you could be."

The arm around her waist loosened. She felt his breathing grow rapid, a steady movement against her back as his chest moved laboriously.

"You don't kill little boys for kicks. You try to save them because they remind you of that scared, vulnerable little boy from your past. They remind you of yourself. Do you think that by saving them, you might be able to save yourself?"

His silence continued. Had she gone too far? She tried to concentrate on his hand with the knife. If she jabbed her elbow into his chest, perhaps she could grab the knife before it cut her. She needed to keep him distracted.

She continued. "You deliver these poor boys from evil, is that it? By inflicting your own evil, you transform them into martyrs. You're quite a hero. You might even say yours is a perfect evil."

His arm squeezed tight and jerked her back against him. She had gone too far. The knife shot up to her throat, this time lengthwise so that the sharp blade pressed full against her skin. In one quick motion, he could slit her throat.

"That's a bunch of psychological bullshit. You don't know what you're talking about." The low guttural sound came from someplace deep inside him. "Albert Stucky should have gutted you when he had a chance. Now, I guess, I'll have to finish the job. We need more light." He dragged her to the tunnel's entrance and extracted a lantern. "Light it." He shoved her to her knees, keeping the knife at her throat and throwing a matchbook into the dirt. "Light it so that you can watch."

"I want you to watch," she heard Albert Stucky say, as if he stood in the dark corner, waiting. "I want you to see how I do it."

Her fingers felt as though they belonged to someone else. There was no feeling in them, but she lit the lantern on the first attempt. The yellow glow filled the small space. Her entire body felt numb. All the blood had drained from her veins. Her mind was paralyzed, preparing for the pain by disconnecting. She recognized all the familiar signs. It was Albert Stucky all over again. Her body responded to the overwhelming terror by simply shutting down.

It was hard to breathe the thick air, now filled with the smell of spoiled meat. Even her lungs refused to work. The knife blade continued to press against her throat. There was a slight tremble in his hand. Was it from anger or fear? Did it matter?

"Why aren't you crying or screaming?" It was anger.

She didn't answer, couldn't answer. Even her voice had abandoned her. She thought of her father, those warm brown eyes smiling at her while he put the chain with the medallion around her neck. "Wherever you go, it'll protect you. Don't ever take it off, okay, Mag-pie?" But it didn't protect you, Daddy, she wanted to tell him. And it didn't protect Danny Alverez.

The stranger grabbed her by the hair and yanked her back to her feet, the knife a permanent fixture at her throat. More blood trickled down between her breasts.

"Say something," he screamed at the back of her head. "Plead with me. Pray."

"Just do it," Maggie finally said, quietly and with much effort, having to coax her voice, her lips, her bruised and cut throat to cooperate just for those three simple words.

"What?" He sounded genuinely surprised.

"Just do it," she managed to repeat, this time louder, more forceful.

"Maggie?" Nick's voice sifted in from the top of the stairs.

The stranger spun around, startled and swinging Maggie along with him. As if watching from the corner, she saw her hand grab at the knife, snatching the stranger's wrist. She twisted out from his hold just as he jerked his hand away and slashed at her, the metal disappearing into her jacket, ripping fabric and flesh on the way out. He shoved her hard, sending her into the dirt wall with a loud thump.

Nick's stream of light came racing down the steps just as the black shadow grabbed the lantern and plunged into the hole. The wooden shelf teetered then crashed to the floor, almost hitting Nick.

"Maggie?" His light blinded her.

"In the tunnel." She pointed while struggling to her knees. A flash of pain set her back down again. "Don't let him get away."

Nick disappeared into the hole, leaving her in total darkness. She didn't need light to know she was bleeding. Her fingers easily found the sticky wound in her side. She dug deep in her pocket, pulled out the chain and medallion, rubbing her fingers over the smooth cross shape. In many ways the cool metal reminded her of the knife blade. Good and evil—was there really that fine a line between the two? Then she slipped the chain over her head and around her bleeding neck.

CHAPTER 87

Nick tried not to think. Especially now that the tunnel had started to curve and narrow, forcing him to crawl on his hands and knees. He could no longer see the masked shadow in front of him. The jerks of light from his flashlight revealed only more darkness ahead. Dirt and rock crumbled with every movement. Broken roots snaked out of the earth, sometimes dangling in front of him, sticking to his face like cobwebs. It was hard to breathe. The farther he went, the less air there was. What was left was stale and rancid, burning his lungs and adding to the ache already in his chest.

Fur brushed against his hand. He flung the flashlight, missing the rat and sending the batteries flying. The sudden darkness surprised him. Terror exploded inside him. Frantically, he groped for the flashlight, fistfuls of moldy dirt. One battery, two, finally three. Please let it work. He wasn't sure he could even turn around in the narrow, twisted space. Couldn't imagine backing all the way out.

He screwed the flashlight together. Nothing. He slapped it, tightened the clasp, slapped it again. Light, thank God. Only now he gasped for air. Had the darkness sucked out all the air?

He crawled faster. The tunnel narrowed even more, sending him to his stomach. He crawled using his elbows, propelling off his toes like a swimmer pushing against the current. He was an awful swimmer—a hot dog on the diving board, but lead in the water. And now he felt as if he was drowning, gulping for air and swallowing dirt from above.

How far had he come? How much farther could it possibly be? Other than the scratches of rat claws and the avalanche of dirt behind him, there was silence. Was he simply burying himself alive?

How could the shadow have disappeared so quickly? And if this was the killer, who had Nick seen disappear into the woods earlier?

This was nuts, absolutely crazy. He couldn't make it, couldn't breathe. Surely his lungs would explode any second. The dirt clung to him. Sandpaper scratched his eyes and throat. His mouth was dry with the taste of rot and death, gagging him. The walls narrowed still more, scraping against his body. He heard rips and tears—his clothing, sometimes his skin, catching on pieces of rock, wood, maybe even bones sticking out of the dirt walls.

How much farther? Was it a trap? Had he missed a turn somewhere back in the beginning where the tunnel seemed huge? Where he had walked crouched low, but still upright? Could he have missed another secret passage? That would explain why he couldn't see or hear the stranger up ahead. What if this tunnel led to a dead end, a wall of dirt?

Just as he felt certain he could go no farther, the flashlight caught a sliver of glittering white up ahead. Snow—it clogged the tunnel. In one last mad rush of panic, Nick clawed, pushed, tore and dug his way to the surface. Suddenly, he saw the black, starlit sky. And despite the miles he thought he had traveled, he realized he hadn't even left the cemetery. Instead, he rose from the ground like a corpse among the tombstones. Less than three feet away, the black angel hovered above him with a ghostly radiance that looked like a smile.

CHAPTER 88

Christine's neck ached like it usually did when she fell asleep on the sofa. She saw branches sticking through glass. Had the storm sent branches through her living-room window? She had heard a crash. And there was a hole in the ceiling. Yes, she could even see stars, thousands of them right there, sitting on top of her house.

Where was Grandma Morrelli's afghan? She needed something to stop the draft, to prevent the cold from swirling up around her. Timmy, turn up the furnace, please. Hot chocolate, maybe she could fix nice steaming mugs of hot chocolate for the two of them. If only she could push the furniture off her chest. And where were her arms when she needed them? She could see one of them lying next to her. Why couldn't she make it move? Had it fallen asleep like the rest of her?

Those annoying headlights made her eyes sting. If she could just find the plug, she could shut them off. They made the branches dance, a slow-motion rumba, bumping and grinding glass. It was too hard to keep her eyes open, anyway. Perhaps she could fall back to sleep if only that rasping sound would stop. It came from somewhere inside her coat, from somewhere inside her chest. Whatever it was, it was annoying and...and painful...yes, it was annoyingly painful.

What was President Nixon doing in the headlights? He waved at her. She tried to wave back, but her arm was still asleep. He came into her living room. He moved all the furniture off her chest. Then President Nixon carried her back to sleep.

CHAPTER 89

Timmy watched his sled drift downstream. The bright orange looked fluorescent in the moonlight. He crouched in the snow, hidden by the cattails along the river bank. All that catapulting practice on Cutty's Hill had paid off, though his mom would kill him if she ever found out.

He was feeling pretty confident. He only now realized he had lost a shoe in the jump. His ankle hurt. It looked funny, puffed up, almost twice the size of his other one. Then he saw the black shadow, spiderwebbing its way down the ridge, clinging to roots and vines, stretching and gripping rocks and branches. It moved quickly.

Timmy glanced back at the sled, now regretting that he hadn't stayed in it. The stranger came to the river's edge. He was watching the sled, too. It had drifted too far away for him to see inside. But maybe the stranger believed Timmy had stayed inside. He certainly didn't look as if he was in a rush anymore. In fact, the stranger just stood there, staring at the river. Maybe he was trying to decide whether to jump in after the sled.

Out here in the open the stranger looked smaller, and although it was too dark to see his face, Timmy could tell he wasn't wearing the dead president's mask anymore.

Timmy burrowed down farther into the snow. The breeze coming off the water brought a wet cold with it. His teeth started chattering and the shivers crawled over his body again. He hugged his knees to his chest and watched and waited. As soon as the stranger disappeared, Timmy decided he would follow the road. It looked all uphill, but it would be better than the woods again. Besides, it had to lead somewhere.

Finally, the stranger looked as if he was giving up. He fumbled through his pockets, found what he was looking for and lit a cigarette. Then he turned and started walking directly toward Timmy.

CHAPTER 90

Maggie clawed her way up the steps, annoyed that her knees wouldn't hold her. Her side burned, a fire blazing deeper and deeper, igniting her stomach and lungs. It felt as if the knife metal had broken off and was shooting through her insides. God, she should be getting good at this by now. Practice makes perfect. Yet, when she struggled up into the moonlight, the sight of her own blood made her light-headed and nauseated. It covered her side and soaked into her clothes, the red turtleneck black with dirt and blood.

She pushed her hair out of her face, away from her sweaty forehead, and realized her hand was filled with blood. She eased out of her jacket, pulled and ripped at the lining until she had a piece big enough to plug up her side. She wrapped chunks of snow inside the fabric, then applied it to the wound. Suddenly, the stars in the sky multiplied. She squeezed her eyes shut against the pain. When she opened them, a black shadow approached, staggering between the headstones like a drunkard. She reached for her gun, her fingers lingering at the empty holster. Of course, she remembered. Her gun lay somewhere below in a dark corner.

"Maggie?" the drunkard called out, and she recognized Nick's voice. Relief washed over her so completely she forgot about the pain for a second or two.

He was covered in mud and dirt, and when he knelt beside her, the smell of him made her gag. She leaned into him, anyway, and welcomed the feel of his arm around her.

"Jesus, Maggie. Are you okay?"

"I think it's just a flesh wound. Did you see him? Did you get him?"

She saw the answer in his eyes, only it wasn't just disappointment. There was something more.

"I think there must be a maze of tunnels down there," he said, out of breath. "And I took the wrong one."

"We need to stop him. He's probably at the church. Maybe that's where he has Timmy."

"Had."

"What?"

"I found the room where he kept them. Timmy's coat was left behind."

"Then we need to find him." She tried to get to her feet, but fell back into his arms.

"I think we're too late, Maggie." She heard the words struggle over a lump in his throat. "I also saw...there was a bloody pillow."

She leaned her head against his chest. Listened to the pounding, the uneven breathing. No, the uneven breathing belonged to her.

"Jesus, Maggie. You're bleeding awfully bad. I need to get you to the hospital. I sure as hell am not going to lose two people I love in the same night."

He propped her up while he crawled to his feet, still a bit wobbly. She held on to him and struggled to her knees. The pain came in fiery jabs, scorching and tearing, hot glass shards slicing farther and farther inside her. As she clung to his arm, she wondered if she had heard him correctly. Did he really just say that he loved her?

"Don't, Maggie. Let me carry you to the Jeep."

"I saw the way you were walking, Morrelli. I'll take my chances on my own two feet." She pulled herself up, gritting her teeth against the constant stab.

"Just hang on to me."

They were almost to the Jeep when she remembered the crate.

"Nick, wait. We have to go back."

CHAPTER 91

Christine stared up at the stars. She easily found the Big Dipper. It was the only thing she could ever find in the night sky. On the soft bed of snow and under the wonderfully warm and scratchy wool blanket, she hardly noticed that she was lying on the side of the road. And if only she could breathe without choking up chunks of blood, maybe she could sleep.

Reality came in short bursts of pain and memories. Eddie fondling her breast. Smashed metal against her legs, crushing her chest. And Timmy, oh, God, Timmy. She tasted tears and bit down on her lip to stop them. She tried to sit up, but her body refused to listen, couldn't comprehend the commands. It hurt to breathe. Couldn't she just stop breathing, at least for a few minutes?

The headlights came out of nowhere, rounding the corner and barreling down on her. She heard the brakes screech. Gravel pelted metal. Tires skidded. The light blinded her. When two stretched shadows emerged from the vehicle and came toward her, she imagined aliens with bulbous heads and bulging insect eyes. Then she realized it was the hats that made their heads look oversize.

"Christine. Oh, my good Lord, it's Christine."

She smiled and closed her eyes. She had never heard that kind of fear and panic in her father's voice. How totally inappropriate for her to be pleased by it.

When her father and Lloyd Benjamin knelt beside her, the only thing she could think to say was, "Eddie knows where Timmy is."

CHAPTER 92

Nick tried to convince Maggie to stay in the Jeep. They had stopped the bleeding for now, but there was no telling how much blood she had already lost. She could barely stand on her own, had completely lost all color in her face. Perhaps she was delusional, too.

"You don't understand, Nick," she continued to argue with him.

He was ready to pick her up and throw her into the Jeep. It was bad enough that she wouldn't let him drive her to the hospital.

"I'll go check what's in the stupid crate," he said finally. "You wait here."

"Nick, wait." She dug her fingers into his arm, wincing with pain. "It may be Timmy."

"What?"

"Inside the crate."

The realization struck him like a fist. He leaned against the Jeep's hood, suddenly weak in the knees.

"Why would he do that?" he managed to say, though his throat strangled the words. He didn't want to imagine Timmy stuffed into a crate. Timmy, dead. Yet, hadn't he already thought that? "That's not his style."

"Whatever is in the crate might be for my benefit."

"I don't understand."

"Remember the last note? If he knows about Stucky, he may have resorted to Stucky's habits. Nick, it could be Timmy inside that crate. And if it is, it isn't something you should see."

He stared at her. Blood and dirt streaked her face. More dirt and cobwebs filled her hair. Those beautiful full lips held tight against the pain. Those soft, smooth shoulders slouched from the effort to hold herself up. And still, she wanted to protect him.

He turned on his heel and stomped back up the hill.

"Nick, wait."

He ignored her calls. Surely she wouldn't—couldn't—follow without his assistance.

He hesitated at the steps Maggie had uncovered. Then forced himself back down into the earth. The entire space reeked with the stifling smell. He found a steel rod and Maggie's revolver, which he slid into his jacket pocket. Then he tucked the rod and flashlight under his arm and hoisted the crate, lugging it slowly up the steps. His muscles screamed at him to put it down. He ignored them until he was out of the hellhole, until he could breathe fresh air again.

Maggie was there, waiting, leaning against a headstone. She was even more pale.

"Let me," she insisted, reaching for the rod.

"I can do this, Maggie." He shoved the rod under the lid and started pumping up and down. The nails screeched and echoed in the silent darkness. Even with the breeze and in the cold the smell of death overpowered all other senses. Once the lid snapped free, he hesitated again. Maggie came beside him, reached around him and pulled open the lid.

Both of them took a step backward, but it wasn't because of the odor. Tucked carefully inside and wrapped in a white cloth was the small, delicate body of Matthew Tanner.

CHAPTER 93

There was no place for Timmy to run. Nowhere to hide. He slipped down the riverbank, close to the water. Could he swim across, float downstream? He examined the black, churning river racing past him. It was too strong, too fast and much too cold.

The stranger had stopped to finish his cigarette, but his direction hadn't changed. In the silence, Timmy heard the stranger mumbling to himself, but he couldn't make out the words. Every once in a while he kicked rocks and dirt into the water. The splashes were now close enough to spray Timmy.

He'd have to make a run for it, back into the woods. At least there he could hide. He'd never make it in the water. His shivers from the cold were already close to convulsions. The water would only make it worse.

Timmy peeked over the riverbank. The stranger was lighting another cigarette. Now. He needed to go now. He scrambled up the bank, kicking rocks and dirt into the water—explosive splashes giving him away. He barely made it to the road when his ankle buckled under him. He slammed down on knees and elbows. He struggled to his feet, then suddenly flew up off the ground. He kicked at air and clawed at the arm around his waist. Another arm squeezed around his neck.

"Settle down, you little shit."

Timmy started screaming and shouting. The arm squeezed harder, cutting off his air, choking him.

When the car came squealing down the winding road, the stranger still kept his vise grip on Timmy. The car skidded to a stop in front of them, and still the stranger made no attempt to move or flee. The headlights blinded Timmy, but he recognized Deputy Hal. Why didn't the stranger release him? Timmy's neck hurt bad. He clawed at the arm again. Why didn't the stranger make a run for it?

"What's going on here?" Deputy Hal demanded. He and another deputy got out of the car and approached slowly.

Timmy didn't understand why they didn't draw their guns. Couldn't they tell what was going on? Couldn't they tell the stranger was hurting him?

"I found the kid hiding in the woods," the stranger told them, only he sounded excited and proud. "You might say I rescued him."

"I see that," said Deputy Hal.

No, it was a lie. Timmy wanted to tell them it was all a lie, but he couldn't breathe, couldn't speak with the arm squeezing his neck. Why were they looking as if they believed the stranger? He was the killer. Couldn't they see that?

"Why don't the two of you get in with us. Come on, Timmy. You're safe now."

Slowly the arm released from around Timmy's neck. His feet touched the ground. Timmy pulled free and ran to Deputy Hal, tripping on his swollen ankle.

Hal grabbed Timmy by the shoulders and gently shoved him behind him. Then Deputy Hal pulled out his gun and said to the stranger, "Come on, now. You've got a lot of explaining to do, Eddie."

CHAPTER 94

Friday, October 31

Christine awoke to a room full of flowers. Had she died, after all? Through a blur, she saw her mother sitting next to the bed, and Christine knew immediately that she was, in fact, still alive. Certainly the blue and pink jogging suit her mother wore would never be acceptable attire for heaven—or hell.

"How are you feeling, Christine?" Her mother smiled and reached for Christine's hand.

Her mother was finally letting her hair go gray. It looked good. Christine decided to tell her later when a compliment would come in handy to combat the inquisition.

"Where am I?" It was a stupid question, but after the hours of delusions, hallucinations—whatever they were—she needed to know.

"You're in the hospital, dear. Don't you remember? You just got out of surgery a little while ago."

Surgery? Only now did Christine notice all the tubes going in and out of her. In a moment of panic, she ripped off the covers.

"Christine!"

Her legs were still there. Yes, thank God. She could move them. There were bandages on one, but she didn't care as long as the leg moved.

"You don't need to catch pneumonia." Her mother tucked the covers back in around her.

Christine raised both arms, flexed the fingers and watched the fluids drip into her veins. The pieces all seemed there and working. That her chest and stomach felt like chunks of beaten and sliced chopped liver didn't matter. At least she was all in one piece.

"Your father and Bruce went for coffee. They'll be so pleased to find you awake."

"Oh, God, Bruce is here?" Then Christine remembered Timmy, and the panic began to suck all the air from the room.

"Give him a second chance, Christine," her mother said, completely oblivious to the lack of air in the room. "This ordeal has really changed him."

Ordeal? Was that the newest term they had given to the disappearance of her son?

Just then, Nick peeked into the room and relief swept over Christine. There was a new cut on Nick's forehead, but the bruises and swelling around his jaw were hardly noticeable. He was dressed in a crisp blue shirt, navy tie, blue jeans and navy sports jacket. God, how long had she been asleep? If she didn't know better, she'd think he looked dressed for a funeral. She remembered Timmy again. What exactly had her mother meant by ordeal? A new wave of pain and terror came crashing down, adding its weight to her chest.

"Hi, honey," their mother said as Nick leaned down to kiss her cheek.

Christine studied the two of them, watching for signs. Did she dare ask? Would they only lie to protect her? Did they think she was too fragile?

"I want the truth, Nicky," she blurted in a voice so shrill she hardly recognized it as her own. They both stared at her, startled, concerned. But she could see in Nick's eyes that he knew exactly what she was talking about.

"Okay. If that's the way you want it." He headed back for the door, and she wanted to yell at him to stop, to stay, to talk to her.

"Nicky, please," she said, not caring how pathetic she sounded.

He opened the door, and Timmy stood there like an apparition. Christine rubbed her eyes. Was she hallucinating again? Timmy hobbled toward her, and she could see the scratches and bruises, a cut on one cheek and a purple swollen lip. However, his face and hair were scrubbed clean, his clothes crisp and fresh. He even wore new tennis shoes. Had it all been a horrible, horrible nightmare?

"Hi, Mom," he said as though it were any other morning. He crawled into the chair his grandmother held out for him, kneeling and making himself tall enough to look over the bed. She allowed the tears, had no choice, really. Was he real? She touched his shoulder, smoothed down his cowlick and caressed his cheek.

"Aw, Mom. Everybody's watching," he said, and she knew he was real.

CHAPTER 95

Nick escaped before it got mushy, before his own eyes got blurry. It was all still a little hard to believe. He turned the corner and almost ran into his father, who stepped back, as though worried the coffee he carried would spill.

"Careful there, son. You're gonna miss quite a bit being in such a hurry."

Nick checked his father's eyes and immediately saw the sarcastic criticism. He was in too good of a mood to let his father spoil it. So he smiled and started to walk around him.

"It's not Eddie, you know," his father called after him.

"Yeah?" Nick stopped and turned. "Well, this time that'll be up to a court of law to decide and not Antonio Morrelli."

"What the hell is that supposed to mean?"

Nick took a step closer until he was standing eye to eye with his father.

"Did you help plant evidence against Jeffreys?"

"Watch your mouth, boy. I never planted a thing."

"Then how did you explain the discrepancies?"

"As far as I was concerned, there were no discrepancies. I did what was necessary to convict that son of a bitch."

"You ignored evidence."

"I knew Jeffreys killed that little Wilson boy. You didn't *see* that boy. You didn't see what he made that boy go through. Jeffreys deserved to die."

"Don't you dare make your horrors superior to mine," Nick said, hands clenched into fists but quiet and steady at his sides. "I've seen enough this week to last me a lifetime. Maybe Jeffreys did deserve to die. But by pinning the other two murders on him, you let another murderer get away. You closed the investigation. You made a community feel safe again."

"I did what I thought was necessary."

"Don't tell me. Tell that to Laura Alverez and Michelle Tanner. Tell them how you did what was necessary."

Nick walked away, his knees feeling a bit spongy. There was little victory in telling Antonio Morrelli he had been wrong. Why had he expected there to be some feeling of celebration? But as his boot heels echoed down the quiet hall, he walked a bit taller.

He stopped by the nurses' station and was startled by the unit secretary dressed in a black cape and witch's hat. It took a minute before he noticed the orange and black crepe paper and pumpkin cutouts. Of course, today was Halloween. Even the sun had emerged, finally bright enough and warm enough to start melting some of the snow.

He waited patiently while the unit secretary recited ingredients of a recipe into the phone. Her eyes told him she'd only be a moment, but there was no urgency in her voice.

"Hi, Nick." Sandy Kennedy came up behind him, scooted back behind the secretary and grabbed a clipboard.

"Sandy, you finally made it to the day shift." He smiled at the shapely brunette, while thinking what a stupid thing to say. Why not "How are you" or "It's been a long time"? Then he wondered if there was anyplace in this city he could go without running into a former lover or one-night stand.

"Sounds like Christine is doing better," she said, ignoring his stupid comment.

He tried to remember why he had never pursued a relationship with Sandy. Just seeing her reminded him how bright and beautiful she was. But then, so were all the women he chose. However, not one of them could live up to Maggie O'Dell.

"Nick, are you okay? Can we do something for you?"

Both Sandy and the secretary stared at him.

"Can you tell me Agent O'Dell's room number?"

"It's 372," the secretary said without looking it up. "At the end of the hall and to the right. Although she may be gone."

"Gone? What do mean gone?"

"She checked out earlier and was just waiting for some clothes. Hers were pretty trashed when she came in last night," she explained, but Nick already was halfway down the hall.

He burst through the door without knocking, startling Maggie, who turned quickly from the window, then positioned her back—and the open hospital gown—to the wall.

"Jesus, Morrelli, don't you knock?"

"Sorry." His heart settled down, almost to its regular rhythm. She looked wonderful. The short, dark hair was smooth and shiny again. Her creamy skin had some color. And her eyes—those luscious brown eyes—actually sparkled. "They said you might be gone."

"I'm waiting for some clothes. One of the hospital volunteers offered to go shopping for me." She paced, carefully using the wall to shield her back. "That was about two hours ago. I just hope she doesn't come back with something pink."

"The doctor said it's okay for you to check out?" He tried to make it a simple question. Was there too much concern in his voice?

"He's leaving it to my discretion."

She caught him staring at her, and when their eyes met, he held her gaze. He didn't care if she saw the concern. In fact, he wanted her to see it.

"How's Christine?" she asked, breaking the trance.

"Surgery went well."

"What about her leg?"

"The doctor seems certain there won't be any permanent damage. I just took Timmy in to see her."

For a minute she stopped pacing. Her eyes softened, though there was a faraway look in them.

"If I didn't know better, I'd almost believe in happy endings," she said.

Her eyes met his again, this time accompanied by a faint smile, a slight tug at the corners of her lips. Jesus, she was beautiful when she smiled. He wanted to tell her that. Opened his mouth, in fact, to do just that, then thought better of it. Did she have any idea how scared he was when he thought she'd left without so much as a goodbye? Could she even tell what effect she had on him? The hell with her husband, her marriage. He needed to take the risk, let the chips fall where they may. He needed to tell her he loved her.

Instead, he said, "We arrested Eddie Gillick this morning."

She sat on the edge of the bed and waited for more.

"We brought in Ray Howard again for questioning. This time he admitted that sometimes he loaned the old blue pickup to Eddie."

"The day Danny disappeared?"

"Howard conveniently couldn't remember. But there's more—lots more. Eddie came to work for the sheriff's department the summer before the first killings. The Omaha Police Department had given him a letter of recommendation, but there were three separate reprimands in his file, all for unnecessary force while making arrests. Two of the cases were juveniles. He even broke one kid's arm."

"What about the last rites?"

"Eddie's mom—a single mom, by the way—worked two jobs just to send him to Catholic school, all the way through high school."

"I don't know, Nick."

She didn't look convinced. It didn't surprise him. He went on with the rest.

"He would have had access to the evidence in Jeffreys' case and could easily have framed him. He's also had access to the morgue. In fact, he was there yesterday afternoon picking up the autopsy photos. He could have easily snatched Matthew's body when he realized the teeth marks in the photos might ID him. Plus, it would have been easy for him to make a few phone calls, use his badge number and get information on Albert Stucky."

There was the twitch, the slight grimace at just the mention of the bastard's name. He wondered if she was conscious of it.

"The morgue is never locked," Maggie countered. "Anyone could have had access. And much of what happened with Stucky was publicized in the newspapers and tabloids."

"There's still more." He'd left this for last. The most incriminating evidence was the most questionable. "We found some stuff in the trunk of his car." He let her see his skepticism. Was it Ronald Jeffreys all over again? They were both thinking the same thing.

"What kind of stuff?" Now she was interested.

"The Halloween mask, a pair of black gloves and some rope."

"Why would he have all that in the trunk of his abandoned car if he knew we were hot on his trail? Especially if he was responsible for framing Jeffreys in the same manner? Also, how did he have time to do all this?"

It was exactly what Nick had wondered, but he wanted desperately for this to be all over.

"My dad just more or less admitted that he knew someone may have planted evidence."

"He admitted that?"

"Let's just say he admitted to ignoring the discrepancies."

"Does your father think Eddie could be the killer?"

"He said he's sure it's not Eddie."

"And that makes you even more convinced that it is?"

Jesus, she knew him well.

"Timmy has a lighter the guy gave him. It has the sheriff's department emblem on it. It's a reward type thing that my dad used. He never handed out that many of them. Eddie was one of about five."

"Lighters get lost," she said. She stood up and slowly made her way to the window.

This time her mind was clearly far away. She even forgot about the slit in the back of her hospital gown. Though from this angle he could only see a sliver of her back, part of her shoulder. The gown made her look small and vulnerable. He imagined wrapping his arms around her, wrapping his entire body around hers. Just lying with her for hours, touching her, running his hands along her smooth skin, his fingers through her hair. He simply wanted to get lost in her for a very long time.

Jesus, where in the world was this coming from? He dug his thumb and forefinger into his eyes, feigning exhaustion, when it was really that image he needed to dig out.

"You still think it's Keller?" he asked, but knew the answer.

"I don't know. Maybe it's just hard for me to realize I'm losing my touch."

Nick could certainly relate to that.

"Eddie doesn't fit your profile?"

"The man in that cellar wasn't some hothead who lost his temper and sliced up little boys. This was a mission for him, a well-thought-out and planned mission. Somehow, I really do think he believes he's saving these boys." She stared out the window and avoided looking at him.

He had never asked what had happened in the cellar before he got there. The notes, the game, the references to Albert Stucky—it all seemed so personal. Perhaps he could no longer count on Maggie to be objective.

"What does Timmy say?" She turned to him finally. "Can he identify Eddie?"

"He seemed certain last night, but that was after Eddie chased him down the ridge and grabbed him. Eddie claims he spotted Timmy in the woods and went after him to rescue him. This morning Timmy admitted he never saw the man's face. But, it can't all be just coincidence, can it?"

"No, it does sound like you have a case." She shrugged.

"But do I have a killer?"

CHAPTER 96

He stuffed his few belongings into the old suitcase. His fingers traced over the suitcase's fabric, a cheap vinyl that cracked easily. He had lost the combination years ago. Now he simply avoided locking it. Even the handle was a mass of black tape, sticky in summer, hard and scratchy in winter. It was the only thing he had of his mother's.

He had stolen it out from under his stepfather's bed the night he ran away from home. Home—that was certainly a misnomer. It had never felt like his home, even less after his mother was gone. Without her, the two-story brick house had become a prison, and he had taken his punishment nightly for almost three weeks before he left.

Even the night of his escape, he had waited until after his stepfather had finished and then collapsed from exhaustion. He had stolen his mother's suitcase and packed while blood trickled down the insides of his legs. Unlike his mother, he had refused to grow accustomed to his stepfather's deep, violent thrusts, the fresh tears and old ones not allowed to heal. That night, he had barely been able to walk, but still he had managed somehow to make it the six miles to Our Lady of Lourdes Catholic Church where Father Daniel had offered refuge.

A similar price had been paid for his room and board, but at least Father Daniel had been kind and gentle and small. There had been no more rips and tears, only the humiliation, which he had accepted as part of his punishment. He was, after all, a murderer. That horrible look still haunted his sleep. That look of utter surprise in his mother's dead eyes as she lay sprawled on the basement floor, her body twisted and broken.

He slammed the suitcase shut, hoping to slam out the image.

His second murder had been much easier, a stray tomcat Father Daniel had taken in. Unlike himself, the cat had received room and board with no price to pay. Perhaps that alone had been reason enough to kill it. He remembered its warm blood had splattered his hands and face when he slashed its throat.

From then on, each murder had become a spiritual revelation, a sacrificial slaughter. It wasn't until his second year of seminary that he murdered his first boy, an unsuspecting delivery boy with sad eyes and freckles. The boy had reminded him of himself. So, of course, he needed to kill him, to get the boy out of his misery, to save him, to save himself.

He checked his watch and knew he had plenty of time. He carefully placed the old suitcase by the door, next to the gray and black duffel bag he had packed earlier. Then he glanced at the newspaper folded neatly on his bed, the headline garnering yet another smile: Sheriff's Deputy Suspected in Boys' Murders.

How wonderfully easy it had been. He knew the minute he had found Eddie Gillick's lighter on the floor of the old blue pickup that the slick and arrogant bully would make the perfect patsy. Almost as perfect as Jeffreys had been.

All those evenings of excruciating small talk, playing cards with the egomaniac, had finally paid off. He had pretended to be interested in Gillick's latest sexual conquest, only to offer forgiveness and absolution when the good deputy finally sobered up. He had pretended to be Gillick's friend when, in fact, the conceited know-it-all turned his stomach. Gillick's bragging had also revealed a short temper, mostly targeted at "punk kids" and "cock-teasing sluts" who, according to Gillick, "had it coming." In many ways, Eddie Gillick reminded him of his stepfather, which would make Gillick's conviction even sweeter.

And why wouldn't Gillick be convicted, with his self-destructive behavior and all that damning evidence tucked neatly inside the trunk of the deputy's very own smashed Chevy? What luck, stumbling across it in the woods like that, making it so easy to stash the fatal evidence. Just like Jeffreys.

He remembered how Ronald Jeffreys had come to him, confessing to Bobby Wilson's murder. When Jeffreys asked for forgiveness there hadn't been a shred of remorse in his voice. Jeffreys deserved what had happened to him. And it had been so simple, too. One anonymous phone call to the sheriff's department and some incriminating evidence was all it had taken.

Yes, Ronald Jeffreys had been the perfect patsy just like Daryl Clemmons. The young seminarian had shared his homosexual fears with him, unknowingly setting himself up for the murder of that poor, defenseless paperboy. That poor boy whose body was found near the river that ran along the seminary. Then there was Randy Maiser, an unfortunate transient, who had come to St. Mary's Catholic Church seeking refuge. The people of Wood River had been quick to convict the ragged stranger when one of their little boys ended up dead.

Ronald Jeffreys, Daryl Clemmons and Randy Maiser—all of them such perfect patsies. And now, Eddie Gillick could be added to that list.

He glanced at the newspaper again, and his eyes rested on Timmy's photo. Disappointment clouded his good mood. Though Timmy's escape had brought a surprising amount of relief, it was that very escape that required his own sudden exodus. How could he continue his day-to-day routine knowing he had failed the boy? And, eventually, Timmy would recognize his eyes, his walk, his guilt. Guilt because he hadn't been able to save Timmy Hamilton. Unless...

He grabbed the newspaper and flipped to the inside story of Timmy's escape and his mother, Christine's, accident. He scanned the article using his index finger until he noticed the ragged fingernail, bitten to the quick. He tucked his fingers into a fist, ashamed of their appearance. Then he found the paragraph, almost at the end. Yes, Timmy's estranged father, Bruce, was back in town.

He glanced at his watch again. Poor Timmy and all those bruises. Perhaps somehow, some way, Timmy deserved a second chance at salvation. Surely he could make time for something that important.

CHAPTER 97

Maggie wanted to tell Nick it was over. That no more little boys would disappear. But even as they went over the case against Eddie Gillick, she couldn't dislodge that gnawing doubt. Was it possible she was just being stubborn, refusing to believe that she could be so wrong?

She wished the hospital volunteer would be as punctual as she had been perky. How could anyone carry on a serious conversation in these paper-thin gowns? And would it be so much trouble to provide a robe, a sash, anything to prevent a full view of her unprotected backside?

She could see Nick's eyes exercising extreme caution, but all it took was a few unintentional slips to remind her of how naked she was under the loose garment. Worse yet was that damn tingle that spread over her skin every time his eyes were on her. And that stupid fluttering sensation that teased between her thighs. It was like radar. Her entire body reacted beyond her control to its own nakedness and Nick's presence.

"Okay, so it does look as though Eddie Gillick could be guilty," she admitted, trying to keep her mind off her reactions to him. She crossed her arms over her chest and found her way back to the window, carefully keeping her back against the wall.

Today the sky was so blue and large it looked artificial, not even a hint of a cloud. Most of the snow had melted off the sidewalks and lawns. Soon only the piles of black ice chunks along the streets would be left. Trees that hadn't lost their leaves now shimmered with wet glossy gold, red and orange. It was as if a spell had been broken, a curse lifted, and everything was back to normal. Everything except the slight tug in Maggie's gut, not from the stitches, but from her own nagging doubt.

"What was Christine doing with Eddie last night?"

"I haven't talked to her about it this morning. Last night she said Eddie was supposed to take her home, but he took a detour. He told her if she had sex with him, he'd tell her where Timmy was."

"He said he knew where Timmy was?"

"That's what Christine said. Of course, I think she was delusional. She also told me President Nixon carried her to the side of the road."

"The mask, of course. He carried Christine out of the car then stuffed his disguise into the trunk."

"Then hurried along to chase Timmy through the woods," Nick added. "This, of course, is after he tried to rape Christine, then attack you in the graveyard cellar. Busy guy."

They stared at each other. The obvious left unsaid, settling between them and stirring up the same disappointment and panic that had driven them to this point.

"Did he try anything with you?" Nick finally asked.

"What do you mean?"

"You know... Did he..."

"No," she said, cutting him off, rescuing him. "No, he didn't."

Maggie remembered the killer fishing her gun out from inside her coat, accidentally grazing her breast. He had snapped his hand back instead of letting it linger. When he whispered into her ear, he never once touched her skin. He wasn't interested in sex, not with men and certainly not with women. His mother was a saint, after all. She remembered the images of tortured saints on Father Keller's bedroom wall. The priesthood and its vow of celibacy would have been an excellent escape, an excellent hiding place.

"We need to question Keller one last time," she said.

"We have absolutely nothing on him, Maggie."

"So humor me."

"Ms. O'Dell?" A nurse peeked around the door. "You have a visitor."

"It's about time," Maggie said, expecting the perky, blond volunteer.

The nurse held open the door and smiled flirtatiously at the handsome, golden-haired man in the black Armani suit. He carried a cheap overnight case, and a matching garment bag was slung over his arm.

"Hi, Maggie," he said, walking into the room as if he owned it, throwing a look at Nick before smiling his expensive-lawyer smile at Maggie.

"Greg? What in the world are you doing here?"

CHAPTER 98

Timmy listened for the vending machine to swallow his quarters before he made his selection. He almost chose a Snickers, but his gut remembered, and he punched the Reese button, instead.

He tried not to think about the stranger or the little room. He needed to stay focused on his mom and help her get better. It scared him to see her in that huge, white hospital bed, hooked up to all those machines that gurgled, wheezed and clicked. She seemed to be okay, even seemed happy to see his dad after, of course, she had yelled at him. But this time his dad didn't yell back. He just kept saying he was sorry. When Timmy left the room, his dad was holding his mom's hand, and she actually let him. That had to be a good sign, didn't it?

Timmy sat in the plastic waiting-room chair. He unwrapped his candy bar and separated out the two pieces. Grandpa Morrelli was supposed to bring him a sandwich from Subway after the two of them had inspected the cafeteria's meat loaf. The Subway was only across the street, but Timmy hadn't had breakfast. He popped one whole peanut butter cup into his mouth and let it melt before he started chewing.

"I thought you were a Snickers guy."

Timmy spun around in the chair, startled. He hadn't even heard footsteps.

"Hi, Father Keller," he mumbled over a mouthful.

"How are you, Timmy?" The priest patted Timmy's shoulder, his hand lingering on Timmy's back.

"I'm okay." He swallowed the rest of the candy bar, clearing his mouth. "My mom had surgery this morning."

"I heard." Father Keller slid a duffel bag into the seat next to Timmy's then knelt down in front of him.

Timmy liked that about Father Keller, how he made him feel special. He was genuinely interested. Timmy could see that in his eyes, those soft, blue eyes, that sometimes looked so sad. Father Keller really did care. Those eyes... Timmy looked again and suddenly a knot twisted in his stomach. Today, there was something different about Father Keller's eyes. Timmy didn't know what it was. He squirmed in his seat, and Father Keller looked concerned.

"You okay, Timmy?"

"Fine...I'm fine. It's probably just all the sugar. I didn't eat breakfast. You going someplace?" Timmy asked, swinging a thumb at the duffel bag.

"I'm taking Father Francis to his burial place. In fact, that's why I'm here, to make sure the body is ready."

"He's here?" Timmy didn't mean to whisper, but that's how it came out.

"Down in the morgue. Would you like to come with me?"

"I don't know. I'm waiting for my grandpa."

"It'll only take a few minutes, and I think you'll enjoy seeing it. It looks like something out of *The X-Files*."

"Really?" Timmy remembered watching Special Agent Scully doing autopsies. He wondered if dead people really did look all stiff and gray. "You sure it's okay if I come along? Won't the hospital people get mad?"

"Nah, there's never anyone down there."

Father Keller stood up and grabbed the duffel bag. He waited while Timmy shoved the rest of the Reese's into his mouth, accidentally dropping the wrapper. When he knelt to pick it up, Timmy noticed Father Keller's Nikes, crisp and white, as usual. Only today there was...there was a knot in one of the shoestrings. A knot holding it together. The knot in Timmy's stomach tightened.

He stood up slowly, a bit dizzy. A sugar rush—that was all it was. He glanced up at Father Keller's smiling face, the priest's hand outstretched to him, waiting. One last quick glance at the shoe. Why did Father Keller have a knot in his shoestring?

CHAPTER 99

"How did you find out I was in the hospital?" Maggie asked when she and Greg were alone. She spread out the suits she had carefully packed days ago, pleased with their appearance despite two trips halfway across the country.

"Actually, I didn't know until I arrived at the sheriff's department earlier this morning. Some bimbo in a leather skirt told me about it."

"She's not a bimbo." Maggie couldn't believe she was defending Lucy Burton.

"This just reiterates my point, Maggie."

"Your point?"

"That this job is much too dangerous."

She dug through the overnight case he'd brought her, keeping her back to him and vowing to ignore the mounting anger. She concentrated on how good it felt to have her own things back. Perhaps it was ridiculous, but fingering her own underwear gave her an odd sense of control and security.

"Why won't you just admit it?" Greg insisted.

"Admit what?"

"That this job is too dangerous."

"For who, Greg? You? Because I don't have a problem with it. I've always known there would be risks."

She stayed calm, glanced over her shoulder at him. He was pacing, hands on his hips as if waiting for a verdict. "When I asked you to pick up my bags from the airport, I didn't mean for you to deliver them." She tried a smile, but he looked determined not to let her off so easily.

"Next year I'll make partner. We're on our way, Maggie."

"On our way to what?" She pulled out a matching bra and panties.

"You shouldn't have to do all this dangerous fieldwork. For God's sake, Maggie, you've got eight stinking years with the Bureau. You finally have the clout to be...I don't know, a supervisor, an instructor...something, anything else."

"I enjoy what I do, Greg." She started to pull off the hideous gown, hesitated, then glanced over her shoulder. Greg threw his hands in the air and rolled his eyes.

"What? You want me to leave?" His voice was filled with sarcasm, a hint of anger. "Yes, maybe I should leave so you can invite your cowboy back."

"He's not my cowboy." Maggie felt the anger color her cheeks.

"Is that why you haven't returned my calls? Is there something going on with you and Sheriff Hardbody?"

"Don't be ridiculous, Greg." She yanked off the gown and struggled into the panties. It hurt to bend, to lift her arms. She was grateful a bandage covered the unsightly stitches.

"Oh my God, Maggie."

She spun around to find him staring at her wounded shoulder, a grimace contorting his handsome features. She couldn't help wondering whether it was disgust or concern. His eyes examined the rest of her body, finally resting on the scar below her breasts. Suddenly, she felt exposed and embarrassed, neither of which made sense. He was her husband, after all. Yet, she grabbed the gown and pressed it to her breasts.

"Not all of those are from last night," he said, the anger more prevalent than the concern. "Why didn't you tell me?"

"Why didn't you notice?"

"So this is my fault?" Again, the hands in the air. It was a gesture she recognized from when he practiced his summations. Perhaps it worked with jurors. To her, it was worthless melodrama, a simple technique to draw attention to himself. How dare he make her scars about him.

"It has nothing to do with you."

"You're my wife. Your job leaves your body carved up. Why shouldn't I be concerned?" His fair complexion turned crimson with anger, large raspberry splotches that looked like a rash.

"You're not concerned. You're angry because I didn't tell you."

"Damn right I'm angry. Why didn't you tell me?"

She threw the gown aside, giving him a good look at the scar.

"This is from over a month ago, Greg," she said, tracing the scar that Stucky had left. "Most husbands would have noticed. But we don't even have sex anymore, so how could you notice? You haven't even noticed that I don't sleep next to you. That I spend most nights pacing. You don't care about me, Greg."

"This is ridiculous. How can you say I don't care about you? That's exactly why I want you to leave the Bureau."

"If you really cared, you'd understand how important my job is to me. No, you're more concerned about how I make you look. That's why you don't want me in the field. You want to be able to tell your friends and associates that I have some big FBI title, a huge office, a secretary to put you on hold. You want me to be able to wear sexy black cocktail dresses to your fancy attorney parties so you can show me off, and my hideous scars don't fit into that scenario. Well, this is me, Greg," she said with her hands on her hips, trying to ignore the chill on her naked body. "This is who I am. Maybe I just don't fit into your country-club life-style anymore."

He shook his head at her, like a father impatient with his errant child. She grabbed the crumpled gown again and smashed it against her breasts, suddenly feeling vulnerable, having exposed much more than her nakedness.

"Thank you for bringing my things," she said quietly, calmly. "Now, I want you to leave."

"Fine." He swung his arms into his trench coat. "Why don't we get together for lunch after you've cooled off."

"No, I want you to go back home."

He stared at her, his gray eyes going cold, his pursed lips stifling the angry words. She waited for his next onslaught, but he turned on his expensive, leather heels and stomped out.

Maggie collapsed onto the bed, the pain in her side only a minor contributor to her exhaustion. She barely heard the tap on the door but braced herself for the rest of Greg's fury. Instead, Nick came in, took one look at her and spun around.

"Sorry, I didn't realize you weren't dressed."

She glanced down, only now realizing she just wore underpants and the thin gown carelessly pressed across her breasts, hardly covering anything. She looked up at him, checking to make sure his back was to her before she grabbed the bra and wrestled into it. The stabs in her side slowed her down.

"Actually, I should be the one to apologize," she said, adopting Greg's sarcasm. "It seems my scarred body repulses men."

She snatched a blouse from the pile and thrust her arms into it, then realized it was inside out. She whipped it off and tried again.

Nick glanced over his shoulder, but snapped back to his same position. "Jesus, Maggie, you should know by now that I'm the wrong one to say that to. I've been trying for days now to find one little thing about you that doesn't turn me on."

She heard the smile in his voice. Her fingers stopped at the buttons, a slight tremor making it difficult to continue as the heat crawled down her body. She stared at the back of him and wondered how in the world Nick Morrelli could make her feel so sensuous, so alive without even looking at her.

"Anyway, I didn't mean to barge in on you," he said, "but there's a slight problem with bringing in Father Keller for questioning."

"I know, I know. We don't have enough evidence."

"No, that's not it." Another glance to see if it was safe. Maggie had her trousers halfway up, but he turned again to the door. She smiled at his caution. After all, he had already seen her in much less. She remembered the football jersey and his soft, comfortable robe.

"If it's not evidence, what's the problem?" she asked.

"I just called the rectory and talked to the cook. Father Keller is gone and so is Ray Howard."

CHAPTER 100

As soon as they got off the elevator Timmy noticed the sign that read Restricted Area—Hospital Personnel Only. Father Keller didn't seem to notice the sign. He walked down the hallway without even hesitating, as if he had been down here many times before.

Timmy tried to keep up, although his ankle still hurt. It almost hurt more after the doctor wrapped it in all that elastic stuff, so tight Timmy was sure it was adding more bruises.

Father Keller glanced down at him, only now noticing the limp.

"What happened to your leg?"

"I guess I sprained my ankle last night in the woods."

Timmy didn't want to think about it, didn't want to remember. Every time he remembered, that terrible knot returned inside his stomach. Without much prompting, he knew the shivers would start again.

"You've been through quite a lot, huh?" The priest stopped, patted Timmy on the head. "You want to talk about it?"

"No, not really," Timmy said without looking up. Instead, he stared at his own brand-new Nikes. Air Nikes, the cool expensive kind. Uncle Nick had given them to him this morning.

Father Keller didn't insist, didn't ask more questions like the rest of the adults. Timmy was getting tired of all the questions. Everybody—Deputy Hal, the reporters, the doctor, Uncle Nick, Grandpa—everybody wanted to know about the little room, the stranger, his escape. He just didn't want to think about it anymore.

Father Keller pushed open a door and flipped a light switch. The huge room grew bright as the lights flickered on, one at a time.

"Wow, this does look like on *The X-Files,*" Timmy said, running his fingers over the spotless counters, stainless steel just like the table in the center of the room. His eyes jumped around the assortment of odd equipment and tools neatly placed on trays. Then he noticed the drawers, lined up side by side in the opposite wall. "Is that..." He pointed. "Is that where they keep the dead people?"

"Yes, it is," Father Keller said, but he seemed distracted. He carefully placed the duffel bag on the metal table.

"Is Father Francis in one of the drawers?" Timmy whispered, then felt stupid. After all, nobody could hear them.

"Yes, unless they have already picked up his body."

"Picked up?"

"The mortuary may have already picked up Father Francis and taken him to the airport."

"The airport?" Timmy was confused. He'd never heard of dead bodies traveling on planes.

"Yes, remember I told you I was taking Father Francis to his burial place?"

"Oh, okay." Timmy scanned the countertops again, this time paying more attention. He came in for a closer look, tempted to touch but keeping his hands at his sides. Some of the tools were sharp, some long and narrow with teeth. One of them looked like a miniature chain saw. He'd never seen such odd tools before. He tried to imagine what each one did.

"I heard your father is back in town," Father Keller said, standing stiff and still next to the table.

"Yeah, I'm hoping he'll stay," Timmy said with only half a glance at the priest. There were too many interesting vials, test tubes, even a microscope. Maybe he would ask for a microscope for his birthday.

"Really? You'd like your father to stay?"

"Yeah, I guess I would."

"Wasn't he mean to you?"

Timmy looked at Father Keller. The question surprised him, and he wondered what Father Keller meant, but the priest unzipped the duffel bag and was immediately preoccupied by its contents.

"How do you mean?" Timmy finally asked.

"Didn't he hurt you?" Father Keller said without looking up. "Didn't he do unpleasant things to you?"

Timmy wasn't sure what unpleasant things were. He knew he wore that scrunched look on his face that automatically happened when he was confused. He could hear his mom saying, "Don't look at me like that, or your face will stick that way." He tried to wipe it away before Father Keller noticed, but the priest was busy digging in the bag.

"My dad was mostly nice to me. Sometimes I guess he yelled."

"What about your bruises?"

Timmy felt his face grow warm with embarrassment. But, thankfully, Father Keller still didn't look up. "I guess I just bruise easily. Most of 'em are from soccer." Soccer and Chad Calloway.

"Then why did your mom make him go away?" Father Keller's voice surprised Timmy. Suddenly, it was low with a hint of anger while his eyes stayed focused inside the bag.

Timmy didn't want to make Father Keller mad. He heard the clink of metal and wondered what kind of tools Father Keller had in the bag.

"I don't know for sure why my mom made him leave. I think it had something to do with a slutty, big-breasted receptionist," Timmy said, trying to use the exact words he had overheard his mom use.

This time Father Keller did look up at him, only the piercing blue eyes sent a shiver through Timmy. Usually, Father Keller's eyes were kind and warm. But now...those eyes...no, it couldn't be. Timmy's stomach churned. He felt sick, tasted the sourness backing up into his mouth. He resisted the urge to throw up. The shivers started in his fingertips. One slid down his back. He felt dizzy.

"Timmy, are you okay?" Father Keller asked, and suddenly his cold eyes warmed with concern. "I'm sorry if I upset you."

The panic settled, sliding back down Timmy's throat and resting like a lump in his stomach. He never left Father Keller's eyes, mesmerized by the drastic change in them. Or had he imagined it all?

"Timmy," Father Keller said softly. "Do you think your mom and dad will get back together? Do you think you can be a real family again?"

Timmy swallowed hard, making sure the icky taste and feeling were gone for good. His stomach still ached. Maybe it was eating the candy bar on an empty stomach.

"I hope so," he answered. "I miss my dad. We used to go camping sometimes. Just the two of us. He'd let me bait my own hook. We'd talk and stuff. It was pretty cool. Except my dad's an awful cook."

Father Keller smiled at him now as he zipped up the duffel bag without ever taking anything out.

"Here you two are," Grandpa Morrelli said, swinging open the door to the morgue and startling both Timmy and Father Keller. "Nurse Richards thought she saw the elevator go down here. What are you two up to?"

His grandpa smiled at them while bracing the door open and staying in the doorway. His hands were filled with bags, all with the yellow Subway logo. Timmy could smell pastrami, vinegar and onion despite the overwhelming smell of cleaning solution in the room.

"Father Keller was just picking up Father Francis for their trip." Timmy checked the priest's face and was pleased to see the smile still there. Then to his grandpa, he said, "Doesn't this look like something from *The X-Files*?"

CHAPTER 101

Nick slowed his pace when he noticed the tight, pale look on Maggie's face. Of course, she was hurting and, of course, she wouldn't complain.

The Friday crowds had descended upon Eppley Airport. Business men and women hurried to get home. Fall vacationers and those getting away for the weekend moved more slowly, dragging too many pieces of home to really get away.

Mrs. O'Malley, St. Margaret's cook, had told Nick that Father Keller's flight left at two forty-five, and that he was escorting Father Francis' body to its final resting place. When Nick had asked to speak with Ray Howard, she said Ray was gone, too.

"I haven't seen that one since breakfast," she had told Nick. "He's always sneaking off somewhere, saying it's for Father Keller, but I never know when to believe him." Then she added in a whisper, "He's sneaky."

Nick had tried to ignore her extra comments. He had been in a hurry and not interested in the seventy-two year old's paranoia. Instead, he had tried to keep her focused and on the facts.

"Where is Father Francis being buried?"

"A place somewhere in Venezuela."

"Venezuela! Jesus." Mrs. O'Malley must have never heard the "Jesus," or Nick was certain she would have lectured him on using the Lord's name in vain.

"Father Francis absolutely loved it there," she had offered, glad to be the expert, to have and hold Nick's attention. "It was his first assignment out of seminary. A small, poor farming parish. I don't remember the name. Yes, Father Francis always talked about all those beautiful, brown-skinned children, and how some day he hoped to return. Too bad it couldn't have been under different circumstances."

"Do you remember what city it was close to?" Nick had interrupted.

"No, I can't say that I remember. All those places down there are so hard to remember, hard to pronounce. Father Keller will be back next week. Can't this wait until then?"

"No, I'm afraid it can't. What about the flight number or airline?"

"Oh my, I don't know if he said. Maybe TWA...no, United, I think. It leaves at two forty-five out of Eppley," she added, as if that should be all that was necessary.

Now Nick glanced at his watch. It was almost two-thirty. He and Maggie split up at the ticket counters, flashing credentials and badges to shove their way through the lines and hurry the desk clerks.

The tall woman at the TWA counter refused to be rushed by a county sheriff's badge. Nick wished he had Maggie's FBI influence. Instead, he used his smile and a little flattery. The woman's rigid expression slowly softened, though it was hard to see the change. Her hair was pulled back so tightly into a neat little bun that it made all her features look severe, stretched and pinned down. Perhaps that was also what made her lips so thin, barely moving when she talked.

"I'm sorry, Sheriff Morrelli. I cannot disclose our passenger list or information about any of our passengers. Please, you're holding up the line."

"Okay, okay. How about flights? Do you have a flight to anywhere in Venezuela, say in..." He glanced at his watch again. "In ten to fifteen minutes?"

She checked her computer screen, taking time despite the heavy sighs and shuffling coming from the line behind him.

"We have a flight to Miami that connects with an international flight to Caracas."

"Great! What gate?"

"Gate 11, but that flight left at two-fifteen."

"Are you sure?"

"Quite sure. The weather is excellent. All our flights are running on schedule." She looked around him at a short, gray-haired man, anxious to hand off his ticket.

"Can you check to see if a coffin was on that flight?" Nick asked, refusing to budge despite an elbow in his back.

"I beg your pardon?"

"A coffin, as in a dead body." He could feel the eyes around him, now staring, now interested. "It would be considered cargo. I'm sure I wouldn't be infringing on its rights." He tried another smile. From behind him, someone giggled.

The ticket clerk wasn't pleased. The thin lips drew even tighter. "I still cannot divulge that information. Now, if you'll step aside."

"You know I can get a court order and be back later this afternoon." No more Mr. Nice Guy. He was quickly losing his patience and time was slipping away.

"Perhaps that would be a good idea. Next, who was next, please?" she said, stepping aside when Nick wouldn't, so she could help the elderly man behind him in line. The man shoved his way to the counter, shooting Nick a look filled with anger and impatience.

Nick moved over to stand near where Maggie talked to another ticket agent.

"Thanks, anyway," she told the desk clerk at the United counter, then followed him to a corner out of the traffic.

She looked drained, even more pale, if that was possible. He wanted to ask if she was okay, but had already gotten three or four "I'm fine's" on the drive to the airport.

"TWA has a flight to Miami that connects to one that goes on to Caracas," Nick told her, watching her face.

"Let's go. What gate?" But she didn't move, leaning against the wall as if to catch her breath.

"It left about twenty minutes ago."

"We missed it? Was Keller on board?"

"The desk clerk wouldn't tell me. We may need a court order to find out. What do we do now? Is it worth going down there, trying to catch him before the connecting flight leaves? If he gets to South America we may never find him. Maggie?"

Was she even listening? It wasn't the pain that distracted her. Her eyes were focused over his shoulder.

"Maggie?" He tried again.

"I think I just found Ray Howard."

CHAPTER 102

Maggie recognized the confusion in Nick's face. She felt a bit of her own stuck somewhere down between her throat and chest. Confusion bordered on frustration, or perhaps frustration bordered on panic.

"Maybe he simply brought Father Keller to the airport," Nick said in a low, quiet voice, though Howard was clear across the ticket lobby, far from overhearing.

"I usually don't take along luggage when I drop people off at the airport," Maggie said.

The large gray and black duffel bag looked heavy, making Howard's limp more pronounced. He wore his usual uniform of well-pressed brown trousers, white shirt and tie. A navy blazer replaced the cardigan.

"Tell me again why he isn't a suspect?" Nick asked without taking his eyes off Howard.

Suddenly, Maggie couldn't remember any of her reasons. Finally, she said, "The limp. Remember the boys may have been carried into the woods. And Timmy was sure the guy didn't limp."

They watched Howard stop to examine the flight-schedule board, then head for the escalators.

"I don't know, Maggie. That duffel bag sure looks heavy."

"Yes, it does," she said, and hurried toward the escalators with Nick alongside.

Howard hesitated at the down escalator, waiting to get his footing right before stepping on.

"Mr. Howard," Maggie called out.

Howard looked over his shoulder, grabbed the railing and did a double take. This time a flash of panic appeared in his lizard eyes. He jumped onto the escalator and ran down the moving steps, clearing a path with the duffel bag, striking and pushing people out of the way.

"I'll take the stairs." Nick raced for the emergency exit.

Maggie followed Howard, ripping her revolver from its holster and holding it nose up.

"FBI!" she yelled, clearing her own path.

Howard's speed surprised her. He weaved through the crowd, zigzagging around luggage gurneys and leaping over an abandoned pet carrier. He shoved travelers aside, knocking down a small, blue-haired lady and smashing through a group of Japanese tourists. He kept looking back at Maggie, his mouth open to breathe, his forehead glistening with sweat.

She was closing in on him, though her own breathing disappointed her. The ragged gasps sounded as if they were coming from a ventilator, surely not her own chest. She ignored the flame in her side, burning her flesh once again.

Howard stopped suddenly, grabbed a luggage cart from a stunned flight attendant and shoved it at Maggie. The suitcases snapped free. One burst open, spewing cosmetics, shoes, clothes and assorted unmentionables across the floor. Maggie skidded on a pair of lace panties, lost her balance and fell into the mess, smashing a bottle of liquid makeup with her knee.

Howard headed for the parking garage, smiling over his shoulder. He was almost to the door, hugging the duffel bag, his gait finally staggered by the limp. He pushed open the door just as Nick grabbed his jacket collar and swung him around. Howard fell to his knees and covered his head with his arms as if expecting a blow. Nick's hands, however, never left Howard's collar.

Maggie struggled to her feet while the flight attendant scrambled for her belongings. Nick's eyes were filled with concern for Maggie, even as his hands clutched Howard's collar, rendering him immobile.

"I'm fine," Maggie said before he asked. But when she replaced her revolver, she felt the sticky wetness through her blouse. Her fingertips were smeared with blood when she brought her hand out from inside her jacket.

"Jesus, Maggie." Nick noticed immediately. Howard did, too, and he smiled. "What are you doing here, Ray?" Nick responded, tightening his grip and turning Howard's smile into a grimace.

"I brought Father Keller. He had a flight to catch. Why were you chasing me? I didn't do nothing wrong."

"Then why did you run?"

"Eddie told me to watch out for you two."

"Eddie did?"

"What's in the duffel bag?" Maggie interrupted the two of them.

"I don't know. Father Keller said he wouldn't be needing it anymore. He asked me to take it back for him."

"You mind if we take a peek?" She pried it out of his hands. His resisting arrest justified a search. The bag was heavy. She swung it up onto a nearby chair, stopped, then leaned against a pay phone until the faintness passed.

"You sure it's not your bag?" she said, grabbing the familiar brown cardigan and several well-pressed white shirts. Howard's face registered surprise.

A stack of art books accounted for the bag's weight. Maggie put them aside, more interested in the small, carved box tucked between several pairs of boxer shorts. The carved words on the lid were Latin, but she had no idea what they said. The contents didn't surprise her: a white linen cloth, a small crucifix, two candles and a small container of oil. She glanced up at Nick and watched his eyes examine the contents, his confusion replaced with frustration. Then Maggie reached underneath the pile of newspaper clippings to the bottom of the box. She pulled out a small pair of boy's underpants tightly wrapped around a shiny fillet knife.

CHAPTER 103

Sunday, November 2

Maggie punched another code into the computer and waited. Her laptop's modem was excruciatingly slow. She took another bite of her blueberry muffin, homemade, special delivery from—where else?—Wanda's. The computer screen still read "initializing modem." She sat down and looked around the hotel room, her foot tapping nervously, impatiently, but not making the computer work any faster.

Her bags were packed. She had showered and dressed hours ago, but her flight didn't leave until noon. She rubbed her stiff neck and still couldn't believe she had slept the entire night in the straight-backed chair. Even more surprised that she had slept through the night without visions of Albert Stucky dancing in her head.

Bored, she grabbed the huge Sunday edition of the *Omaha Journal*. The headlines only added to her frustration. However, she was glad to see Christine's byline back on the front page. Even from her hospital bed, Christine continued to crank out articles. At least she and Timmy were safe and sound.

Maggie scanned the article once again. Christine's writing now stuck to the facts, letting quotes from the experts draw the sensational conclusions. She found her own quote and read it for the third time.

> *Special Agent Maggie O'Dell, an FBI profiler assigned to the case, said it was "unlikely Gillick and Howard were partners. Serial killers," Agent O'Dell insisted, "are loners." However, the district attorney's office has filed murder charges against both former sheriff's deputy Eddie Gillick, and a church jani-*

tor, Raymond Howard, for the deaths of Aaron Harper, Eric Paltrow, Danny Alverez and Matthew Tanner. A separate charge has been entered for the kidnapping of Timmy Hamilton.

There was a tap at the door. Maggie tossed the paper aside and checked the computer screen again. "Redialing first number" flashed across the screen along with the low hum and a succession of beeps. It was Sunday morning. Why was it taking so long to make the connection?

On the way to the door, she checked her watch. He was early. They didn't need to leave for the airport for another thirty to forty minutes.

As soon as she opened the door, the uninvited flutter arrived. Nick stood smiling at her, the dimples in full force. Strands of hair fell across his forehead. His blue eyes sparkled at her as if there was a special secret his eyes shared with hers. He wore a red T-shirt and blue jeans, both tight enough to outline his athletic body, teasing her eyes and making her fingers ache to touch him. Why did he have this effect on her? she wondered as they exchanged hellos, and he came into the room. She caught herself checking out his backside, shook her head and silently chastised herself.

"It must be warm out," she heard herself say. Yes, resort to the weather. That seemed safe, considering the electrical current he had just brought into the room.

"It's hard to believe we had snow a few days ago. Nebraska weather." He shrugged. "Here, this is for you." He handed her a gift-wrapped box that had escaped her notice. "Sort of a thank-you, slash, goodbye present."

Her first inclination was to decline, to say it was inappropriate and leave it at that. But she took it and slowly unwrapped it, acutely aware of him watching her. She pulled out the red football jersey with a white number seventeen emblazoned on the back. She couldn't help but smile.

"It's perfect."

"I don't expect it to replace the Packers," he said with just a trace of embarrassment in his voice. "But I thought you should have a Nebraska Cornhuskers, too."

"Thanks. I love it."

"Seventeen was my number," he added.

Suddenly, the simple cotton jersey took on a greater significance. Her eyes met his, and without meaning it to, her smile disappeared as she combated the annoying flutter. However, he was the first to look away, and she saw a flicker of discomfort. It was times like this that he surprised her most, when the arrogant, self-assured bachelor showed just a hint of the irresistible, shy, sensitive man.

"Oh, and this is from Timmy."

She took the videotape, and as soon as she saw the cover, her smile returned. *"The X-Files."*

"He said that it has one of his favorite episodes—the one with the killer cockroaches, of course."

With no more gifts to keep his hands preoccupied, he shoved them into his pockets.

"I'll be sure to watch and...and I'll let Timmy know what I think," she said, surprised but pleased by the unfamiliar commitment to stay in touch.

They stood there staring at each other. Maggie didn't want to move, couldn't move. They had spent the last week together, almost around the clock, sharing pizza and brandy, exchanging opinions and views, wrestling madmen and holy men, dousing fears and expectations and grieving for small boys neither of whom they knew. She had allowed Nick Morrelli access to vulnerabilities she had shared with no one else, not even herself. Perhaps that was why she suddenly felt as if a major chunk of herself would be left behind. And, of all places, in a small Nebraska town she had never even heard of before. What had happened to the cool, aloof FBI agent who maintained her professionalism at whatever the cost?

"Maggie, I—"

"I'm sorry," she interrupted, not prepared for what might be a revelation of feelings. "I almost forgot. I'm trying to access some information." She escaped to the table in the corner. The computer connection had finally been made, and she punched several more keys, immediately annoyed by the unwarranted tremble in her fingers and the shortness of breath.

"You're still looking for him," he said without surprise or irritation, coming up behind her, too close to allow her normal breathing to resume.

"From Caracas, Father Francis' body was shipped by truck to a small community about a hundred miles to the south. Keller's airline ticket has him returning today. I'm trying to find out if he boarded the flight back to Miami or if he headed somewhere else."

"It amazes me the information you can access."

She felt him lean forward to examine the screen.

"At the airport," he continued, "I remember thinking how nice it would be to have FBI credentials instead of my measly sheriff's badge. I was way out of my jurisdiction."

"I certainly hope you aren't still worried about looking incompetent?"

"No. Actually, no, I'm not," he said, sounding like he definitely meant it.

Finally, the passenger list for TWA flight 1692 materialized on the screen. Maggie easily found Reverend Michael Keller's name, and it was on the list even after departure.

"Just because he's on the list doesn't mean he was on the plane."

"I know that." She scooted out from between the computer and Nick before turning to face him.

"So what happens if he doesn't come back?"

"I'll find him," she said simply. "What is that saying? He can run, but he can't hide."

"Even if you find him, we don't have a shred of evidence to implicate him."

"Do you honestly believe Eddie Gillick or Ray Howard killed those boys?"

He hesitated, glanced back at the computer, then around the room, stopping at her suitcases before returning to her.

"I'm not sure what part, if any, Eddie may have played in the murders. But you know I suspected Howard from the beginning. Come on, Maggie. We found him at the airport with what could be the murder weapon."

She frowned at him and shook her head. "He doesn't fit the profile."

"Maybe not, but you know what? I don't want to spend my last hour with you talking about Eddie Gillick or Ray Howard or Father Keller or anything to do with this case."

He approached slowly, cautiously. She nervously pushed her hair away from her face. Tucked a stubborn strand behind her ear. The look in his eyes made the tremble invade her fingers again, and the flutter raced from her stomach to between her thighs.

He touched her face gently, holding her eyes with an intensity that made her feel as though she was the only woman in the world—at least, for the moment. She could easily have stopped the kiss, had meant to when he first leaned down. But when his lips brushed hers, all her energy focused on keeping her knees from buckling. When she didn't protest, his mouth caught hers in a wet, soft kiss filled with so much urgency and emotion that she felt certain the room was spinning. Even after his mouth left hers, she kept her eyes closed, trying to steady her breathing, trying to stop the spinning.

"I love you, Maggie O'Dell."

Her eyes flew open. His face was still close to hers, his eyes serious. She saw a bit of boyish apprehension and knew how hard those words had been to say. She pulled away, only now realizing that, other than his fingers on her face and his mouth on hers, he hadn't touched her anywhere else. Which made her retreat disappointingly easy.

"Nick, we barely know each other." It was still hard to breathe. How could one simple kiss take her breath so completely away?

"I've never felt this way before, Maggie. And it's not just because you're unavailable. It's something I can't even explain."

"Nick..."

"Please, just let me finish."

She waited, braced herself and leaned against the dresser. The same dresser she had clung to the night they had come so dangerously close to making love.

"I know it's only been a week, but I can assure you, I'm not impulsive when it comes to...well, sex, yes, but not this...not love. I've never felt this way before. And I've certainly never told a woman I loved her before."

It sounded like a line, but she knew from his eyes that it was true. She opened her mouth to speak, but he raised a hand to stop her.

"I don't expect anything I say to compromise your marriage. But I didn't want you to leave without knowing, just in case it did make a difference. And I guess even if it doesn't, I still want you to know that I...that I am madly, deeply, hopelessly, head over heels in love with you, Maggie O'Dell."

It was his turn to wait. She couldn't speak. Her fingers clawed at the dresser top, keeping her from going to him and wrapping her arms around him.

"I don't know what to say."

"You don't have to say anything." His eyes told her he meant it.

"I obviously have feelings for you." She struggled with the words. She hated the thought of never seeing him again. But what did she know about being in love? Hadn't she been in love with Greg, once upon a time? Hadn't she vowed to love him forever?

"Things are really complicated right now," she heard herself say and wanted to kick herself. He had opened his heart to her, taken such a risk, and here she was being practical and rational.

"I know," he said. "But maybe they won't always be complicated."

"It does make a difference, Nick," she said, making a feeble attempt at correcting her ambiguity.

He seemed relieved by that simple revelation, as though it was more than he had ever hoped for.

"You know," he said, sounding more comfortable while her heart screamed at her to tell him how she felt. "You've helped me see a lot of things about myself, about life. I've been following in these huge, deep footsteps my father keeps leaving behind and...and I don't want to do that anymore."

"You're a good sheriff, Nick." She ignored the tug at her heart. Maybe it was better this way.

"Thanks, but it's not what I want," he continued. "I admire how much your job means to you. Your dedication—your stubborn dedication, I might add. I never realized before how much I want something like that, something to believe in."

"So what does Nick Morrelli want to be when he grows up?" she asked, smiling at him when she really wanted to touch him.

"When I was in law school I worked at the Suffolk County district attorney's office in Boston. They always said I was welcome to come back. It's been a long time, but I think I might give them a call."

Boston. So close, she couldn't help thinking.

"That sounds great," she said, already calculating the miles between Quantico and Boston.

"I'm going to miss you," he said simply.

His words caught her off guard, just when she thought she was safe. He must have seen the panic in her eyes, because he quickly checked his watch.

"I should get you to the airport."

"Right." Their eyes met again. One last tug, one last chance to tell him. Or would there be plenty of chances?

She brushed past him and closed down the computer, unplugging cords, snapping the lid shut and shoving the computer into its case. He grabbed her suitcase. She grabbed her garment bag. They were at the door when the phone rang. At first, she thought about ignoring it and leaving. Suddenly, she hurried back and grabbed the receiver.

"Maggie O'Dell."

"O'Dell, I'm glad I caught you."

It was Director Cunningham. She hadn't talked to him in days. "I was just on my way out."

"Good. Get back here as quickly as possible. I'm having Delaney and Turner meet you at the airport."

"What's going on?" She glanced at Nick, who came back into the room, his face filled with concern. "You make it sound like I need bodyguards," she joked, then tensed when his silence lasted too long.

"I wanted you to know before you hear it on the news."

"Hear what?"

"Albert Stucky has escaped. They were transferring him from Miami to a maximum-security facility in North Florida. Stucky ended up biting the ear off one guard and stabbing the other with—get this—a wooden crucifix. Then he blew both their heads off with their own service revolvers. Seems the day before, a Catholic priest visited Stucky in his cell. He had to be the one who left the crucifix. I don't want you to worry, Maggie. We got the bastard before, we'll get him again."

But the only thing Maggie heard was, "Albert Stucky has escaped."

EPILOGUE

One week later
Chíuchín, Chile

He couldn't believe how glorious the sun felt. His bare feet maneuvered the rocky shore. The minor cuts and scrapes were a small price to pay for the feel of the warm waves lapping at his feet. The Pacific Ocean stretched forever, its water rejuvenating, its power overwhelming.

Behind him, the mountains of Chile isolated this paradise, where poor, struggling farmers were as starved for attention as they were for salvation. The tiny parish included fewer than fifty families. It was perfect. Since he'd arrived, he hardly noticed the throbbing in his head. Perhaps it was gone for good this time.

A group of brown-skinned boys, clad only in shorts, chased a ball while they raced toward him. Two of them recognized him from the morning's mass. They waved and called out to him. He laughed at their mispronunciation of his name. When they gathered around him, he petted their black hair and smiled down at them. The one with the torn, blue shorts had such sad eyes, reminding him of himself.

"My name," he instructed, "is Father Keller. Not Father Killer."

* * * * *

Split Second

For Amy Moore-Benson, Dianne Moggy and Philip Spitzer,
an incredible team that makes dreams come true.
One book was a privilege; two, an honor.

PROLOGUE

North Dade County Detention Center
Miami, Florida
Halloween—Friday, October 31

Del Macomb wiped the sweat from his forehead with the sleeve of his shirt. The stiff cotton of his uniform stuck to his back, and it was only nine in the morning. How could it be this hot and humid in October?

He had grown up just north of Hope, Minnesota. Back home, ice would be forming at the edges of Silver Lake. His daddy would be writing his sermons while watching the last of the snow geese pass overhead. Del pushed wet strands off his brow. Thinking about his daddy reminded him that he needed a haircut. Crazy stuff to be thinking about. Even crazier that it was stuff that could still make him homesick.

"So who's the fucking asshole we're chaperoning today?"

Del's partner startled him. He winced at Benny Zeeks's language, then glanced over at the barrel-chested ex-marine to see if he had noticed. He certainly didn't need another lecture—not that he didn't have a lot to learn from Benny.

"Guys said his name is Stucky." He wondered if Benny had heard him. He seemed preoccupied.

At North Dade County Detention Center Benny Zeeks was somewhat of a legend, not only because he was a twenty-five-year veteran, but because he had spent most of that time working up in Starke on death row and even on X Wing. Del had seen his partner's scars from scuffles he'd won over X Wingers trying to avoid the coffinlike solitary confinement.

He watched Benny shove his shirtsleeves up over his veiny forearms, not bothering to fold or roll them, revealing one of those legendary scars. It intersected a tattoo, a Polynesian dancer who now had a jagged red line across her abdomen as if she had been sliced in half. Benny could still make the dancer dance, flexing his arm and sending the lower half of her into a slow, sexy sway while the other half—the top half—froze in place, disconnected. The tattoo fascinated Del, intriguing and repulsing him at the same time.

Now his partner climbed into the armored truck's passenger seat, concentrating on negotiating the narrow steps up into the cab. The man moved slower than usual this morning, and Del immediately knew his partner had another hangover. He swung up into the driver's seat, buckling himself in and pretending, once again, not to notice.

"Who'd you say this asshole is?" Benny asked, while he twisted his thermos lid, the short stubby fingers desperate to get at the coffee. Del wanted to tell him the caffeine would only compound his problem, but after four short weeks on the job, he knew better than to try to tell Benny Zeeks anything.

"We're taking Brice and Webber's run today."

"What the hell for?"

"Webber's got the flu and Brice broke his hand last night."

"How the fuck do you break a hand?"

"All I heard was that he broke it. I don't know how. Look, I thought you hated the monotony of our regular route. Plus, all the traffic just to get to the courthouse."

"Yeah, well, there better not be more paperwork," Benny shifted restlessly as if anticipating the dreaded change in his routine. "And if this is Brice and Webber's run, that means this asshole's headed up to Glades, right? Puttin' him in close custody until his fucking hearing. Means he's some big-time fuckup they don't want down here in our wussy detention lockup."

"Hector said the guy's name is Albert Stucky. Said he's not such a bad guy, pretty intelligent and friendly. Hector says he's even accepted Jesus Christ as his savior."

Del could feel Benny scowling at him. He turned the key in the ignition and let the truck vibrate, then rumble to a slow start while he braced himself for Benny's sarcasm. He turned the air-conditioning on, blasting them with hot air. Benny reached over and punched it off.

"Give the engine some time, first. We don't need that goddamn hot air in our faces."

Del felt his face grow red. He wondered if there would ever be anything he could do to win the respect of his partner. He ignored his simmering anger and rolled down the window. He pulled out the travel log and jotted down the truck's odometer and gas tank readings, letting the routine calm him.

"Wait a minute," Benny said. "Albert Stucky? I've been reading about this guy in the *Miami Herald*. Feebies nicknamed him The Collector."

"Feebies?"

"Yeah, FBI. Jesus, kid, don't you know anything?"

This time Del could feel the prickle of red at his ears. He turned his head and pretended to be checking the side mirror.

"This Stucky guy," Benny continued, "he carved up and slaughtered three or four women, and not just here in Florida. If he's the guy I'm thinking of, he's one badass motherfucker. And if he's claiming he's found Jesus Christ, you can bet it's because he wants to save his sorry ass from being fried by Old Sparky."

"People can change. Don't you believe people can change?" Del glanced at Benny. The older man's brow was beaded with sweat and the bloodshot eyes glared at him.

"Jesus, kid. I bet you still believe in Santa Claus, too." Benny shook his head. "They don't send guys to wait for their trial in close custody because they think he's found Jesus-fucking-Christ."

Benny turned to stare out the window and sip his coffee. In doing so, he missed Del wince again. He couldn't help it. Twenty-two years with a daddy for a preacher made it an instant reaction, like scratching an itch. Sometimes he did it without even knowing.

Del slipped the travel log into the side pocket and shifted the truck into gear. He watched the concrete prison in his side-view mirror. The sun beat down on the yard where several prisoners milled around, bumming cigarettes off each other and enduring the morning heat. How could they enjoy being outside if there was no shade? He added it to his mental list of unfair treatment. Back in Minnesota, he had been quite the activist for prison reform. Lately he'd been too busy with the move and starting his new job, but he kept a running list for when he had more time. Little by little he'd work his way up to battling causes like eliminating Starke's X Wing.

As they approached the final checkpoint he glanced at the rearview mirror. He almost jumped, startled to find their prisoner staring back at him. All Del could see through the thick slit of glass were the piercing black eyes, and they were looking directly at him in the mirror.

Del recognized something in the prisoner's eyes, and a knot tightened in his stomach. He had seen that look years ago as a boy, on one of his trips accompanying his father. They had visited a condemned prisoner, who Del's father had met at one of his prison fellowship meetings. During that visit, the prisoner had confessed all the horrible, unimaginable things he had done to his own family before he murdered them—a wife, five children and even the family dog.

As a boy, the details Del heard that day had been traumatizing, but even worse was the evil pleasure the prisoner seemed to get from retelling each detail and watching the impact on a ten-year-old boy. Now Del saw that same look in the eyes of the man in the back of the armored truck. For the first time in twelve years, he felt as if he was looking straight into the eyes of pure evil.

He made himself look away and avoided the temptation to glance back. He pulled out from the last checkpoint and onto the highway. Once they got on the open road, he could relax. He enjoyed driving. It gave him time to think. But when he took a quick left, Benny, who had appeared to be lost in his thoughts, suddenly became agitated.

"Where the hell you going? I-95's the other direction."

"I thought we'd take a shortcut. Highway 45 has less traffic, and it's a much nicer drive."

"You think I fucking care about nice?"

"It's shorter by about thirty minutes. We get the prisoner delivered, and then we'll have an extra half hour for lunch."

He knew his partner wouldn't argue with an extended lunch hour. In fact, he had hoped Benny would be impressed. Del was right. Benny leaned back in his seat and poured another cup of coffee. He reached over and punched the AC. This time, cool air began filling the cab, and Benny rewarded Del with a rare smile. Finally, he had done something right. Del sat back and relaxed.

They had left Miami's traffic and had been on the road only thirty minutes when a thump rattled the back of the truck. At first Del thought they had dropped a muffler, but the thumping continued. It came from the back of the truck but inside, not underneath.

Benny slammed his fist against the steel partition behind them. "Shut the fuck up."

He twisted around to look through the small rectangle of glass that separated the cab from the back. "Can't see a damned thing."

The noise grew louder, sending vibrations under the seat. It felt to Del as though a baseball bat were being swung against the truck's metal sides. Ridiculous, really. No chance the prisoner would have anything remotely like a baseball bat. Each blast sent Benny reeling, grabbing at his temples. Del glanced over and saw the Polynesian dancer swinging her hips with each slam of Benny's fist against the partition.

"Hey, cut it out," Del yelled, adding his voice to the noisy din that was beginning to make his head pound.

Obviously, the prisoner had not been completely restrained and was ramming himself against the walls of the truck. Even if it didn't drive them crazy during the rest of the trip, it could cause some serious damage to the prisoner. He certainly didn't want to be responsible for delivering a battered prisoner. He slowed down, pulled the truck to the side of the two-lane highway and stopped.

"What the hell you doing?" Benny demanded.

"We can't have this going on for the rest of the trip. The guys obviously didn't completely restrain him."

"Why would they? He's found Jesus Christ."

Del only shook his head. As he climbed out of the truck it occurred to him that he had no idea what to do with a prisoner who had gotten an arm or leg loose from one of the leather restraints.

"Now hold on, kid," Benny yelled after him, scrambling out from the passenger side. "I'll take care of this bastard."

It took Benny too long to come around the truck. When he did, Del noticed a stagger in his walk.

"You're still drunk!"

"The hell I am."

Del reached into the cab and pulled out the thermos, jerking it away when Benny grabbed for it. He twisted off the top and in one whiff could smell the alcohol-laced coffee.

"You son of a bitch." Del's words surprised him as much as they did Benny. Instead of apologizing, he threw the thermos and watched it explode against a nearby fence post.

"Shit! That was my only thermos, kid." Benny looked as though he might head into the overgrown ditch to retrieve the pieces. But he turned and stomped toward the back of the truck. "Let's make this fucker shut up."

The banging continued, louder, now rocking the truck.

"You think you're up for this?" Del asked, feeling angry and betrayed enough to allow the sarcasm.

"Hell, yes. I was shutting up assholes like this when you were still suckin' at your momma's tit." Benny grabbed at his service revolver, fumbling with the holster's snap before pulling the gun free.

Del wondered how much alcohol Benny Zeeks had in his system. Could he still aim his gun? Was the gun even loaded? Up until today, Brice and Webber transported the hard-core criminals, making the trips up to Glade and Charlotte, while he and Benny were assigned petty thieves and white-collar criminals, escorting them in the other direction to the county courthouse in Miami. Del unbuckled the strap on his holster, his hand shaking, the butt of his gun feeling awkward and unfamiliar.

The noise stopped as soon as Del started sliding the locks open on the heavy rear door. He looked to Benny who stood beside him with his revolver drawn. Immediately, Del noticed the slight tremor in Benny's hand. It sent a wave of nausea loose in Del's stomach. His back was soaked, his forehead dripping. Wet pools under his armpits soiled his once-crisp uniform. His heart pounded against his rib cage, and now in the silence, he wondered if Benny could hear it.

He took a deep breath and tightened his hold on the handle. Then he flung the door open, jumping aside and letting Benny have a full view of the dark inside. Benny stood, legs apart, arms extended in front of him, both hands gripping the gun as he tilted his head, ready to take aim.

Nothing happened. The door slammed back and forth, hitting against the side of the truck. The sound of metal clanking against metal was amplified by the peaceful surroundings and the deserted highway. Del and Benny stared into the darkness, squinting to see the corner bench where the prisoner usually sat, restrained by thick straps that snaked out of the wall and floor.

"What on earth?" Del could see the leather straps, cut and hanging from the wall of the truck.

"What the fuck?" Benny mumbled as he slowly approached the open truck.

Without warning, a tall, dark figure flew out at Benny, knocking him and the gun to the ground. Albert Stucky clamped his teeth onto Benny's ear like a rabid dog. Benny's scream dismantled Del. He stood paralyzed. His limbs refused to react. His heart knocked against his chest. He couldn't breathe. He couldn't think. By the time he pulled out his service revolver, the prisoner was on his feet. He ran straight at Del, colliding with him and shoving something sharp and smooth and hard into Del's stomach.

Pain exploded throughout his body. His hands were useless, and the gun slid from his fingers like water. He forced himself to look into Albert Stucky's eyes, and instantly he saw the evil staring back at him, cold and black, an entity of its own. Del felt the demon's hot breath on his face. When he glanced down, he saw the large hand still gripping the dagger. He looked up just in time to see Stucky's smile as he shoved the dagger deeper.

Del slipped to his knees. His eyes blurred as he watched the tall stranger split into several images. He could see the truck and a sprawling Benny. Everything began to spin and blur. Then he slammed hard against the pavement. The steaming concrete sizzled up through his wet back, but it wasn't as hot as his insides. A wildfire spread through his stomach, catching each of his organs on fire. Now, on his back, he saw nothing but the clouds swirling above him, brilliant white against solid blue. The morning sun blinded him. Yet, it was all so beautiful. Why hadn't he noticed before how beautiful the sky was?

Behind him a single gun shot blasted the silence. Del managed a weak smile. Finally. He couldn't see him but good ole' Benny, the legend, had come through, after all. The alcohol had just slowed him down a bit.

Del pulled himself up, just enough to look at the damage to his stomach. He was startled to find himself staring down at the bloody carved image of Jesus. The dagger causing his insides to spill onto the deserted highway was actually a mahogany crucifix. Suddenly, he couldn't feel the pain anymore. That had to be a good sign, didn't it? Maybe he'd be okay.

"Hey, Benny," he called out, laying his head on the pavement. He still wasn't able to see his partner behind him. "My daddy's gonna make a sermon out of this when I tell him I was stabbed with a crucifix."

A long, black shadow blocked the sky.

Once again Del found himself looking into those empty, dark eyes. Albert Stucky loomed above him, tall and straight, a lean, muscular man with sharp features. He reminded Del of a vulture, perched with black wings pressed patiently against its sides, cocking its head, staring, waiting for its prey to stop struggling, to give in to the inevitable. Then, Stucky smiled as though pleased with what he saw. He raised and pointed Benny's service revolver at Del's head.

"You won't be telling your daddy anything," Albert Stucky promised in a deep, calm voice. "Tell it to Saint Peter, instead."

The metal slammed into Del's skull. A blast of brilliant light swirled together with oceans of blue and yellow and white and then finally…black.

CHAPTER 1

Northeast Virginia
(just outside Washington, D.C.)
Five months later—Friday, March 27

Maggie O'Dell jerked and twisted, trying to make herself more comfortable, only now realizing she had fallen asleep in the recliner again. Her skin felt damp with perspiration and her ribs ached. The air in the room was stale and warm, making it difficult to breathe. She fumbled in the dark, reaching for the brass floor lamp, clicking the switch but getting no light. Damn! She hated waking to complete darkness. Usually she took precautions to prevent it.

Her eyes adjusted slowly, squinting and searching behind and around the stacks of boxes she had spent the day packing. Evidently Greg had not bothered to come home. She couldn't have slept through one of his noisy entrances. It was just as well he didn't come home. His temper tantrums would only annoy the movers.

She tried to get out of the recliner but stopped when a sharp pain raced along her abdomen. She grabbed at it, as if she could catch the pain and keep it from spreading. Her fingers felt something warm and sticky soaking through her T-shirt. Jesus! What the hell was going on? Carefully, she pulled up the hem and even in the dark she could see it. A chill slipped down her back and the nausea washed over her. A slit in her skin ran from below her left breast across her abdomen. It was bleeding, soaking into her T-shirt and dripping down into the fabric of the recliner.

Maggie bolted from the chair. She covered the wound and pressed her shirt against it, hoping to stop the bleeding. She needed to call 911. Where the hell was the phone? How could this have happened? The scar was over eight months old, and yet it was bleeding as profusely as the day Albert Stucky had cut her.

She knocked over boxes, searching. Lids popped open as cartons fell, scattering crime scene photos, toiletries, newspaper clippings, underwear and socks and sending pieces of her life bouncing off the floor and walls. Everything she had taken such care to pack suddenly flew, rolled, skidded and crashed around her.

Then, she heard a whimpering sound.

She stopped and listened, trying to hold her breath. Already her pulse beat too rapidly. Steady. She needed to stay calm. She turned slowly, cocking her head and straining to hear. She checked the desktop, the surface of the coffee table, the bookshelf. Oh dear God! Where the hell had she left her gun?

Finally, she saw the holster lying at the foot of the recliner. Of course, she would have kept it close by as she slept.

The whimpering grew louder, a high-pitched whine like a wounded animal's. Or was it a trick?

Maggie edged her way back to the recliner, eyes darting, watching all around her. The sound came from the kitchen. And now she could smell a foul odor seeping in from that direction, too. She picked up the holster and tiptoed toward the kitchen. The closer she got, the easier it was to recognize the smell. It was blood. The acrid scent stung her nostrils and burned her lungs. It was the kind of stench that came only from massive amounts of blood.

She crouched low and eased through the doorway. Despite the warning smell, Maggie gasped at the sight of it. In the moonlit kitchen, blood had sprayed the white walls and pooled on the ceramic tile. It was everywhere, splattered across the countertops and dripping down the appliances. In the far corner of the room stood Albert Stucky. His tall, sleek shadow hovered over a whimpering woman who was down on her knees.

Maggie felt the prickling start at the back of her neck. Dear God, how had he been able to get inside her house? And yet, she wasn't surprised to see him. Hadn't she expected him to come? Hadn't she been waiting for this?

Stucky yanked the woman's hair in one hand and in the other he held a butcher knife to the woman's throat. Maggie prevented another gasp. He hadn't seen her yet, and she pressed herself against the wall, into the shadows.

Steady. Calm. She repeated the mantra in her head. She had prepared herself for this very moment. Had dreaded and dreamed and anticipated it for months. Now was not a time to let fear and panic unravel her nerve. She leaned against the wall, strengthening her position, though her back ached and her squatting knees trembled. From this angle, she could get a clean shot. But she knew she'd be allowed only one. One was all she needed.

Maggie gripped the holster, reaching for her gun. The holster was empty. How could it be empty? She spun around, searching the floor. Had the gun dropped out? Why hadn't she noticed?

Then suddenly, she realized her startled reaction had just blown her cover. When she looked up, the woman was reaching out to her, pleading with her. But Maggie looked past the woman, her eyes meeting Albert Stucky's. He smiled. Then, in one swift motion, he slit the woman's throat.

"No!"

Maggie woke up with a violent jolt, nearly falling out of the recliner. Her fingers groped along the floor. Her heart pounded. She was drenched in sweat. She found her holster and this time ripped the gun out, jumping to her feet and swinging her outstretched arms back and forth, ready to spray the stacked cartons with bullets. Sunlight had only begun to seep into the room, but it was enough to show that she was alone.

She slumped down into the chair. The gun still clenched in her hand, she wiped the perspiration from her forehead and dug the sleep from her eyes with trembling fingers. Still not convinced it was a dream, she clawed at the hem of her T-shirt, pulling it up and twisting to see the bloody cut across her abdomen. Yes, the scar was there, a slight pucker of skin. But no, it was not bleeding.

She leaned back in the chair and raked her fingers through her tangled, short hair. Dear God! How much longer could she put up with the nightmares? It had been over eight months since Albert Stucky had trapped her in an abandoned Miami warehouse. She had chased him for almost two years, learning his patterns, studying his depraved habits, performing autopsies on the corpses he left behind and deciphering the bizarre messages for the game he, alone, had decided the two of them would play. But that hot, August evening, he had won, trapping her and making her watch. He had no intention of killing her. He simply wanted her to watch.

Maggie shook her head, willing the images to stay away. She knew she'd be successful as long as she remained awake. They had captured Albert Stucky that bloody night in August, only to have him escape from prison on Halloween. Her boss, FBI Assistant Director Kyle Cunningham, had immediately taken her out of the field. She was one of the Bureau's top criminal profilers, and yet Cunningham had stuck her behind a desk. He had exiled her to teaching at law enforcement conferences, as if complete boredom would be some sort of protection from the madman. Instead it felt like punishment. And she didn't deserve to be punished.

Maggie stood, immediately annoyed at her wobbly knees. She weaved through the maze of cartons to the cabinet in the corner. She checked the clock on the desktop and saw that she had almost two hours before the movers arrived. She laid her gun close by, sorted through the cabinet and brought out a bottle of Scotch. She poured herself a glass, noticing that already her hands were more steady, her heartbeat almost back to normal.

Just then she heard a high-pitched whine coming from the kitchen. Jesus! She dug her fingernails into her arm, feeling the sting and finding no comfort in the fact that she was, indeed, awake this time. She grabbed for her gun and tried to steady her pulse, already racing out of control. She slid against the wall, making her way to the kitchen, trying to listen and sniffing the air. The whining stopped as she got to the doorway.

She prepared herself, arms secure and close to her chest. Her finger pressed against the trigger. This time she was ready. She took a deep breath and swung into the kitchen, her gun pointed directly at Greg's back. He spun around, dropping the freshly opened can of coffee, jumping backward as it crashed to the floor.

"Damn it, Maggie!" He wore only silk boxers. His normally styled blond hair stuck up, and he looked as if he had just gotten out of bed.

"Sorry," Maggie said, desperately trying to keep the panic from her voice. "I didn't hear you come in last night." She tucked the Smith & Wesson .38 into the back waistband of her jeans in an easy, casual motion, as if this was a part of her regular morning routine.

"I didn't want to wake you," he snapped through gritted teeth. Already he had a broom and dustpan and was sweeping up the mess. Gently, he lifted the tipped can, rescuing as much of his precious gourmet coffee as possible. "One of these days, Maggie, you're gonna shoot me by mistake." Then he stopped and looked up at her. "Or maybe it wouldn't be a mistake."

She ignored his sarcasm and walked past him. At the sink, she splashed cold water on her face and the back of her neck, hoping he didn't notice that her hands were still shaking. Though she needn't worry. Greg saw only what he wanted to see.

"I'm sorry," she said again, keeping her back to him. "This would never happen if we had gotten a security system."

"And we would never need a security system if you'd quit your job."

She was so tired of this old argument. She found a dishcloth and wiped the coffee grounds from the counter. "I'd never ask you to quit being a lawyer, Greg."

"It's not the same thing."

"Being a lawyer means just as much to you as being an FBI agent means to me."

"But being a lawyer doesn't get me cut up and almost killed. It doesn't have me stalking around my own house with a loaded gun and almost shooting my spouse." He returned the broom, slamming it into the utility closet.

"Well, after today I guess it won't be an issue," she said quietly.

He stopped. His gray eyes met hers and for a brief moment he looked sad, almost apologetic. Then he looked away, snatching the dishcloth Maggie had set aside. He wiped the counter again in careful, deliberate swipes as though she had disappointed him even in this small task.

"So when are the guys from United getting here?" he wanted to know, as if it were a move they had planned together.

She glanced at the wall clock. "They'll be here at eight. But I didn't hire United."

"Maggie, you have to be careful about movers. They'll rip you off. You should know…" He stopped, as if reminding himself it was no longer any of his business. "Suit yourself." He started filling the coffeemaker with level, precise scoops, pursing his lips to confine the scolding he normally would have unleashed on her.

Maggie watched him, predicting his movements, knowing he'd fill the pot to the three-cup line and that he'd squat to eye level to make certain it was exact. She recognized the familiar routine and wondered when they had become strangers. After almost ten years of marriage, they couldn't even afford each other the courtesies of friendship. Instead, every conversation seemed to be through clenched teeth.

Maggie turned and went back to the spare room, waiting, but hoping he wouldn't follow her. Not this time. She wouldn't get through this day if he continued to scold and pout or worse, if he resorted to telling her he still loved her. Those words should have been a comfort; instead, they had come to feel like a sharp knife, especially when he followed them with, "And if you loved me you would quit your job."

She returned to the liquor cabinet where she had left the glass of Scotch. The sun had barely risen and already she needed her daily dose of liquid bravery to get her through the day. Her mother would be proud. The two of them finally had something in common.

She glanced around the room while she sipped. How could this stack of cartons be the sum of her life? She rubbed a hand over her face, feeling the exhaustion as though it had taken up permanent residence in her bones. How long had it been since she had slept through an entire night? When was the last time she had felt safe? She was so tired of feeling as though she was trapped on a ledge, coming closer and closer to falling.

Assistant Director Cunningham was fooling himself if he believed he could protect her. There was nothing he could do to stop her nightmares, and there was no place he could send her that would be out of Albert Stucky's reach. Eventually, she knew Stucky would come for her. Although it had been five months since Stucky's escape, she knew it with certainty. It could be another month or it could be another five months. It didn't matter how long it took. He would come.

CHAPTER 2

Tess McGowan wished she had worn different shoes. These pinched and the heels were too tall. Every nerve ending in her body concentrated on not tripping as she walked up the winding sidewalk, all the while pretending not to notice the eyes that followed her. The movers had stopped unloading the truck as soon as her black Miata pulled into the drive. Sofa ends stayed in midair. Hand-trucks remained tipped. Boxes were ignored while the men in sweaty, blue uniforms stopped to watch her.

She hated the attention and cringed at the possibility of a wolf whistle. Especially in this well-manicured neighborhood where the sanctuary-like silence would make the whistles even more obscene.

This was ridiculous; her silk blouse stuck to her, and her skin crawled. She wasn't close to being stunning or beautiful. At best, she had a decent figure, one for which she sweated hours at the gym, and she still needed to monitor her cravings for cheeseburgers. She was far from being *Playboy*-centerfold material, so why did she suddenly feel naked though dressed in a conservative suit?

It wasn't the men's fault. It wasn't even their primal instinct to watch that bothered her as much as what seemed to be her involuntary reflex to put on a show for them. The annoying habit clung to her from her past, like the scent of cigarette smoke and whiskey. Too easily she found herself reminded of Elvis tunes coming from a corner jukebox, always followed by cheap hotel rooms.

But that had been a lifetime ago, certainly too many years ago to trip her up now. After all, she was on her way to becoming a successful businesswoman. So why the hell did the past have such a hold on her? And how could something as harmless as a few indiscreet stares, from men she didn't know, dismantle her poise and make her question her hard-earned respectability? They made her feel like a fraud. As if, once again, she was masquerading as something she was not. By the time she reached the front entrance, she wanted to turn and run. Instead, she took a deep breath and knocked on the heavy oak door that had been left half-open.

"Come on in," a woman's voice called from behind the door.

Tess found Maggie O'Dell at the panel of buttons and blinking lights that made up the house's newly installed security system.

"Oh, hi, Ms. McGowan. Did we forget to sign some papers?" Maggie only glanced at Tess while she punched the small keyboard and continued to program the device.

"Please, you really must call me Tess." She hesitated in case Maggie wanted to say the same, but wasn't surprised when there was no such invitation. Tess knew it wasn't that Maggie was rude, just that she liked to keep her distance. It was something Tess could relate to, something she understood and respected. "No, there aren't any more papers. I promise. I knew today was the big move. Just wanted to see how things were going.

"Take a look around, I'm almost finished with this."

Tess walked from the foyer into the living room. The afternoon sunlight filled the room, but thankfully all the windows were open, a cool south breeze replacing the stale warm air. Tess wiped at her forehead, disappointed to find it damp. She examined her client out of the corner of her eyes.

Now, this was a woman who deserved to be ogled by men. Tess knew Maggie was close to her own age, somewhere in her early thirties. But without the usual power suit, Maggie could easily pass for a college student. Dressed in a ratty University of Virginia T-shirt and threadbare jeans, she failed to hide her shapely athletic figure. She had a natural beauty no one could manufacture. Her skin was smooth and creamy. Her short dark hair shone even though it was mussed and tangled. She possessed rich brown eyes and high cheekbones that Tess would kill for. Yet, Tess knew that the men who had stopped in their tracks just moments before to stare at her would not dare do the same to Maggie O'Dell, though they would definitely want to and it would take tremendous effort not to.

Yes, there was something about this woman. Something Tess had noticed the very first day they had met. She couldn't quite describe it. It was the way Maggie carried herself, the way she appeared, at times, to be oblivious to the outside world. The way she seemed totally unaware of her effect on people. It was something that invoked—no, demanded, respect. Despite her designer suits and expensive car, Tess would never capture that ability, that power. Yet for all their differences, Tess had felt an immediate kinship with Maggie O'Dell. They both seemed so alone.

"Sorry," Maggie said, finally joining Tess who had moved to the windows overlooking the backyard. "I'm staying here tonight," she explained, "and I want to make certain the alarm system is up and running."

"Of course," Tess nodded and smiled.

Maggie had been more concerned about the security system than the square footage or the seller's price of any of the houses Tess had shown her. In the beginning, Tess chalked it up to the nature of her client's profession. Of course FBI agents would be more sensitive to security matters than the average home buyer. But Tess had witnessed a look in Maggie's eyes, a glimpse of something that Tess recognized as vulnerability. She couldn't help wondering what the confident, independent agent hoped to lock herself away from. Even as they stood side by side, Maggie O'Dell seemed far away, her eyes examining her new backyard like a woman looking for and expecting an intruder, rather than a new home owner admiring the foliage.

Tess glanced around the room. There were plenty of stacked boxes, but very little furniture. Perhaps the movers had only begun to bring in the heavy stuff. She wondered how much Maggie was able to take from the condo she and her husband owned. Tess knew the divorce proceedings were growing messy. Not that her client had shared any of this with her.

Everything Tess knew of Maggie O'Dell, she had learned from a mutual friend, Maggie's attorney, who had recommended Tess. It was this mutual friend, Teresa Ramairez, who had told Tess about Maggie O'Dell's bitter lawyer husband, and how Maggie needed to invest in a substantial piece of real estate or risk sharing—maybe even losing—a large trust left in her name. In fact, Maggie O'Dell had confided nothing in Tess, other than those necessities required for the business transaction. She wondered if Maggie's secrecy and her aloof manner were an occupational hazard that carried over into her personal life.

It didn't matter—Tess was used to just the opposite. Usually clients confided in her as if she was Dear Abby. Being a real estate agent had proven to be a little like being a bartender. Perhaps part of her colorful past had been good preparation, after all. That Maggie O'Dell didn't wish to bare her soul was perfectly fine with Tess. She certainly didn't take it personally. Instead, she could relate. It was exactly the way she handled her own life, her own secrets. Yes, the less people knew, the better.

"So, have you met any of your new neighbors?"

"Not yet." Maggie answered while she stared out at the huge pine trees lining her property like a fortress. "Only the one you and I met last week."

"Oh sure, Rachel...um...I can't remember her last name. I'm usually very good with names."

"Endicott," Maggie supplied without effort.

"She seemed very nice," Tess added, though what little she had gleaned from the brief introduction made her wonder how Special Agent O'Dell would fit into this neighborhood of doctors, congressmen, Ph.D.'s and their stay-at-home society-conscious wives. She remembered seeing Rachel Endicott out for a jog with her pure white Labrador, while dressed in a designer jogging suit, expensive running shoes and not a blond hair out of place nor a single bead of sweat on her brow. And in contrast, here was Agent O'Dell in a stretched-out T-shirt, worn jeans and a pair of gray Nikes that should have been thrown out ages ago.

Two men grunted their way through the front entrance with a huge roll-top desk. Immediately, Maggie's attention transferred to the desk, which looked incredibly heavy and was quite possibly an antique.

"Where ya want this, ma'am?"

"Over against that wall."

"Sorta centered?"

"Yes, please."

Maggie O'Dell's eyes never left them until the piece was carefully set down.

"Dat good?"

"Perfect."

Both men seemed pleased. The older one smiled. The tall, thin one avoided looking at the women, slouching not from pain but as though he wasn't comfortable being tall. They unwrapped the tape and unlatched the plastic fasteners from the desk's many nooks. The tall man tested the drawers, then stopped suddenly, snapping his hand back as though he had been stung.

"Um...ma'am. Did you know you had this in here?"

Maggie crossed the room to look inside the drawer. She reached in and pulled out a black pistol encased in some kind of holster.

"Sorry. I forgot about this one."

This one? Tess wondered how many the agent had stashed. Maybe the obsession with security was a bit over the top, even for an FBI agent.

"We should be done in a bit," the older man told her, and he followed his partner out as though there was nothing unusual about hauling loaded guns.

"Do you have anyone coming to help you unpack?" Tess tried to disguise her mistrust, her distaste for guns. No, why kid herself? It was more than a simple distaste, it was a genuine fear.

"I really don't have much."

Tess glanced around the room, and when she looked back, Maggie was watching her. Tess's cheeks grew hot. She felt as though she had been caught, because that was exactly what she had been thinking—that Maggie O'Dell really didn't have much. How could she possibly fill the huge rooms that made up this two-story Tudor?

"It's just that...well, I remember you mentioning that your mother lives in Richmond," Tess tried to explain.

"Yes, she does," she said in a way that told Tess there would be no further conversation on the topic.

"Well, I'll let you get back to work." Tess suddenly felt awkward and anxious to leave. "I need to finish up the paperwork."

She extended her hand, and Maggie politely shook it with a strong, firm grip that again took Tess off guard. The woman exuded strength and confidence, but unless Tess was imagining things, Maggie's obsession with security sprung from some vulnerability, some deep-seated fear. Having dealt with her own vulnerabilities and fears for so many years, Tess could sense them in others.

"If you need anything, anything at all, please don't hesitate to call me, okay?"

"Thanks, Tess, I will."

But Tess knew she would not.

As Tess backed her car down the driveway, she wondered whether Special Agent Maggie O'Dell was simply cautious or paranoid, careful or obsessive. At the corner of the intersection, she noticed a van parked along the curb, an oddity in this neighborhood where the houses were set far back from the street and the long driveways afforded plenty of parking space for several cars or utility vehicles.

The man in dark glasses and a uniform sat behind the wheel, absorbed in a newspaper. Tess's first thought was how odd to be reading a newspaper with sunglasses on, especially with the sun setting behind him. As she drove by, she recognized the logo on the side of the van: Northeastern Bell Telephone. Immediately, she found herself suspicious. Why was the guy so far out of his territory? Then suddenly, she shrugged and laughed out loud. Perhaps her client's paranoia was contagious.

She shook her head, pulled out onto the highway and left the secluded neighborhood to return to her office. As she glanced back at the stately houses tucked away between huge oaks, dogwoods and armies of pine trees, Tess hoped Maggie O'Dell would finally feel safe.

CHAPTER 3

Maggie juggled the boxes that filled her arms. As usual she had taken on more than she should have. Her fingers searched the door, grasping for a knob she couldn't see, yet she refused to put anything down. Why in the world did she own so many CDs and books when she had no time to listen to music or read?

The movers had finally left, after a thorough search for one lost carton, or as they insisted—one misplaced carton. She hated to think of it still at the condo, and hated even more the thought of asking Greg to check. He would remind her that she should have listened to him and hired United Movers. And knowing Greg, if the carton was still at the condo, his anger and curiosity would not leave it alone. She imagined him ripping off the packing tape as though he had discovered some hidden treasure, which to him it would be. Because, of course, it would be the one container with items she'd rather have no one thumb through, items like her personal journal, appointment calendar and memorabilia from her childhood.

She had torn her car's trunk apart, looking through the few boxes she had loaded on her own. But these were the last. Perhaps the movers had honestly misplaced the carton. She hoped that was the case. She tried not to worry about it, tried not to think how exhausting it was to be on alert twenty-four hours a day, to be constantly looking over her shoulder.

She set the boxes on the handrail, balancing one with her hip, while she freed a hand to grab at the tightening knot in the back of her neck. At the same time, her eyes darted around her. Dear God, why couldn't she just relax and enjoy her first night in her new home? Why couldn't she concentrate on simple things, stupid everyday things, like her sudden and unfamiliar hunger?

As if on cue, her mouth began to water for pizza, and immediately she promised herself one as a reward. Her appetite had long been gone, making this craving a novelty, one she needed to relish. Yes, she would stuff herself with pizza garnished with spicy Italian sausage, green peppers and extra Romano cheese. That is, after she drank several gallons of water.

Maggie's T-shirt stuck to her skin. Before she ordered the pizza, she'd take a quick, cool shower. Ms. McGowan—Tess—had promised to call all the utility companies. Now Maggie wished she had double-checked with her to make certain she had done so. She hated depending on other people, having recently found herself with a full cast of them in her life, from movers and real estate agents, to lawyers and bankers. Hopefully the water would, indeed, be on. Tess's word had been good so far. In all fairness, there was no need to question it now. The woman had gone out of her way to make this accelerated sale go as smoothly as possible.

Maggie repositioned the boxes to her other hip. Her fingers found the knob. She pushed the door open, carefully maneuvering her way in, but still sending several loose CDs and books crashing onto the doorstep. She bent just enough to look down at Frank Sinatra smiling up at her through his cracked plastic window. Greg had given her the CD several birthdays ago, although he knew she hated Sinatra. Why did that gift suddenly feel like some prophetic microcosm of their entire marriage?

She shook her head and the thought out of her mind. The memory of their brief morning exchange stayed annoyingly fresh in her mind. Thankfully, he had left for work early, mumbling about all the construction on the interstate. But tonight he would be having his last laugh, sifting through her personal things. He would see it as his right. Legally she was still his wife, and she had given up long ago arguing with him when he shifted into lawyer mode.

Inside her new home, the wood floors' recent varnish glowed in the late-afternoon sunshine. Maggie had made certain there wasn't a stitch of carpet in the entire house. Footsteps were too easily muffled by floor coverings. Yet, the wall of windows had cinched the deal for Maggie, despite them being a security nightmare. Okay, so even FBI agents weren't always practical. But each individual window was set in a narrow frame that not even Houdini could squeeze through. The bedroom windows were another story, but reaching the second floor from outside would require a tall ladder. Besides, she had made certain that both security systems, inside and outside, rivaled those at Fort Knox.

The living room opened into a sunroom with more windows. These stretched from the ceiling almost to the floor, and though they were also thin and narrow, they made up three walls in the room. The sunroom extended into and looked out over the lush green backyard. It was a colorful, wooded fairyland with cherry and apple blossoms, sturdy dogwoods, a blanket of tulips, daffodils and crocus. It was a backyard she had fantasized about since she was twelve.

Back then, when she and her mother had moved to Richmond, they could afford only a tiny, suffocating third-floor apartment that reeked of stale air, cigarette smoke and the body odor of the strange men her mother invited overnight. This house was more like the one Maggie remembered of her real childhood, their house in Wisconsin, where they had lived before her father was killed, before Maggie was forced to grow up quickly and become her mother's caretaker. For years, she had longed for someplace like this with lots of fresh air and open spaces, but most importantly—plenty of seclusion.

The backyard sloped down only to be met by a dense wooded area that lined a steep ridge. Below, a shallow stream trickled over rocks. Though she couldn't see the stream from the house, Maggie had checked it out at great length. It made her feel safe, as if it were her own personal moat. It provided a natural boundary, a perfect barrier that was reinforced by a line of huge pine trees standing guard like sentries, tall and straight, shoulder to shoulder.

That same stream had been a nightmare for the previous owners who had two small children. Fences of any kind were against the development's covenant. Tess McGowan had told Maggie that the owners simply realized they couldn't keep two curious kids from being enticed or lured by such a dangerous adventure. Their problem became Maggie's safeguard, her potential trap. And their impulsive purchase became Maggie's bargain. Otherwise, she would never have been able to afford this neighborhood where her little red Toyota Corolla looked out of place next to BMWs and Mercedeses.

Of course, she still would never have been able to afford the house had she not used the money from her father's trust. Having received scholarships, grants, fellowships and then working her way through college and graduate school, Maggie had been able to leave most of the trust alone. When she and Greg got married, he was adamant about not touching the money.

In the beginning, she had wanted to use it to buy them a modest home. But Greg insisted he would never touch what he called her father's blood money.

The trust had been set up by fellow firefighters and the city of Green Bay to show appreciation for her father's heroism, and probably to assuage their guilt as well. Maybe that was part of the reason she had never been able to bring herself to use the money. In fact, she had almost forgotten about the trust until the divorce proceedings began and until her lawyer highly recommended she invest the money in something not so easily divided.

Maggie remembered laughing at Teresa Ramairez's suggestion. It was ridiculous, after all, knowing the way Greg had always felt about the money. Only it wasn't ridiculous when the trust showed up on an assets sheet, which Greg had shoved at her several weeks ago. What for years Greg had called "her father's blood money," he was now calling community property. The following day she asked Teresa Ramairez to recommend a real estate agent.

Maggie added the boxes to those already arranged and stacked in the corner. She glanced over the labels one last time, hoping the missing one would miraculously show itself. Then, with hands on her hips, she turned slowly around, admiring the spacious rooms decorated for the time being in Early American corrugated brown. She had brought very few pieces of furniture with her, but more than she had expected to extract from Greg's lawyerly clutches. She wondered if it was financial suicide for anyone to ask for a divorce from a lawyer spouse. Greg had handled all of their joint financial and legal affairs for almost ten years. When Teresa Ramairez had started showing Maggie documents and spreadsheets, Maggie hadn't even recognized some of the accounts.

She and Greg had married as college seniors. Every appliance, every piece of linen, everything they owned had been a joint purchase. When they moved from their small Richmond apartment to the expensive condominium in the Crest Ridge area, they had bought new furniture, and all of it went together. It seemed wrong to split up sets. Maggie smiled at that and wondered why she couldn't bring herself to split up furniture but could do so with their ten-year marriage?

She did manage to take with her the pieces of furniture which mattered most. Her father's antique rolltop desk had made the trip without a scratch. She patted the back of her comfortable La-Z-Boy recliner. It and the brass reading lamp had been exiled long ago to the condo's den, because Greg said it didn't match the leather sofa and chairs in the living room. Maggie couldn't recall much living having ever occurred on them.

She remembered when they had first bought the set. She had tried to break it in with some passionate memories. Instead of letting his body respond to her flirtatious suggestions, Greg had been horrified and angered by the idea.

"Do you know how easily leather stains?" He had scolded her as though she was a child spilling Kool-Aid instead of a grown woman initiating sex with her husband.

No, it was easy to leave those pieces behind. As long as the memory of their crumbling marriage stayed with them. She pulled out a small duffel bag from the pile in the corner and set it on the desk next to her laptop. Earlier she had opened all the windows to remove the stale, warm air. As the sun set behind the line of trees, a moist but cool breeze swirled into the room.

She unzipped the duffel bag and carefully removed her holstered Smith & Wesson .38 revolver. She liked the way the pistol fit in her hands. There was a familiarity and ease, like the touch of an old friend. While other agents had upgraded to more powerful and automatic weapons, Maggie drew comfort from the gun she knew best. The same gun with which she had learned.

She had depended on it numerous times, and though it had only six rounds compared to an automatic's sixteen, she knew she could count on all six without any jamming. As a newbie—as FBI recruits were called—she had watched an agent go down, helpless with a Sig-Sauer 9 mm and a magazine half-full, but jammed and useless.

She pulled out of the bag her FBI badge in its leather holder. She laid both it and the Smith & Wesson on the desk, almost reverently, alongside the Glock 40 caliber found earlier in the desk drawer. Also in the duffel bag was her forensic kit, a small black pouch that included an odd assortment of things she had learned over the years never to be without.

She left the forensic kit safely tucked in place, zipped the duffel bag and slid it under the desk. For some reason, having these things close by—her guns and badge—made her feel secure, complete. They had become symbols of who she was. They made this feel more like home than any of the possessions she and Greg had spent their adult lives collecting. Ironically, these things that meant so much to her were also the reasons she could no longer be married to her husband. Greg had made it quite clear that Maggie needed to choose either him or the FBI. How could he not realize that what he was asking her to do was like asking her to cut off her right arm?

She traced a finger over the leather case of her badge, waiting for some sign of regret. But when none came, it didn't necessarily make her feel any better. The impending divorce brought sadness, but no regret. She and Greg had become strangers. Why hadn't she seen that a year ago when she lost her wedding ring and hadn't felt compelled to replace it?

Maggie swiped at strands of hair that stuck to her forehead and the back of her neck. Its dampness reminded her that she needed a shower. The front of her T-shirt was dirty and stained. Her arms were marred with black and purple scuffs. She rubbed at one to discover a bruise instead of dirt. Just as she began to search for her newly installed phone, she noticed a police cruiser whiz by.

She found the phone under a stack of papers. She dialed from memory and waited patiently, knowing it would take more than five or six rings.

"Dr. Patterson."

"Gwen, it's Maggie."

"Hey, how the hell are you? Did you get moved in?"

"Let's just say my stuff is moved." She noticed the Stafford County Coroner's van drive past. She went to the window and watched the van curve to the left until it was out of sight. The street had no outlet. "I know you're swamped, Gwen, but I was wondering if you had a chance to check on what we talked about last week?"

"Maggie, I really wish you'd leave the Stucky case alone."

"Look, Gwen, if you don't have time, all you need to say is that you don't have time," she snapped, and immediately wished she could take her words back. But she was tired of everyone trying to protect her.

"You know that's not what I meant, Maggie. Why do you always make it so goddamn hard for people to care about you?"

She let the silence hang between them. She knew her friend was right. Suddenly in the distance, Maggie heard a fire engine's siren, and her stomach turned to knots. What was happening just around the corner? Her knees threatened to buckle at the thought of a possible fire. She sniffed the breeze coming in through the window. She couldn't smell or see smoke. Thank God. If it was a fire, she would be incredibly useless. The thought alone scared the hell out of her, reviving memories of her father's death.

"How about I stop over tonight?"

Gwen's voice startled Maggie. She had forgotten she was still on the phone.

"The place is a mess. I haven't even started to unpack."

"It doesn't bother me if it doesn't bother you. Why don't I pick up a pizza and some beer? We can picnic on the floor. Come on, it'll be fun. Sort of a housewarming party. A prelude to your new independence."

The fire engine's siren began to grow distant, and Maggie realized it was not on its way to her neighborhood. Her shoulders relaxed, and she sighed in relief.

"You can pick up some beer, but don't worry about the pizza. I'll have it delivered."

"Just remember, no Italian sausage on my side. Some of us need to watch our weight. I'll see you around seven."

"Fine. Sure. That'll work." But Maggie was already distracted as another police cruiser sped by. Without a second thought, she put down the phone and grabbed her badge. She quickly reset the security system. Then she tucked her revolver in her back waistband and headed out the front door. So much for seclusion.

CHAPTER 4

Maggie hurried past three of her new neighbors who politely stayed in the street, a safe distance from the house flanked with police cruisers. The coroner's van sat in the driveway, already empty. She ignored a police officer on his hands and knees who had gotten a roll of crime scene tape tangled in a rosebush. Instead of tearing it and starting over, he took on the thorns and kept snapping his hand back with each prick.

"Hey," he finally yelled when he realized Maggie was headed for the door. "You can't go in there."

When his voice didn't slow her down, he scrambled to his feet, dropping the roll of tape and sending it unraveling down the slope of the lawn. For a minute he looked as though he'd go for the tape instead of Maggie. She almost laughed, but kept her face serious as she held up her badge.

"I'm with the FBI."

"Yeah, right. And this is what the FBI is wearing these days." He snatched the leather case from her, but his eyes took their time making their way down her body.

Instinctively, Maggie stood up straight and crossed her arms over her sweat-drenched chest. Ordinarily, she paid close attention to her presentation and attire. She had always been self-conscious and aware that her hundred-and-fifteen-pounds, five-foot-five stature did not live up to the FBI's authoritarian image. In a navy blazer and trousers, her aloof, cold attitude could pull it off. In a T-shirt and faded jeans, she realized she might not be able to.

Finally, the officer took a closer look at her credentials. The smirk slid off his narrow face as he realized she was not a reporter or a curious neighbor playing around with him.

"Son of a bitch. You're on the level."

She held out her hand for the badge. Now a bit embarrassed, he quickly handed it back.

"I didn't realize this was something the FBI would be in on."

It probably was not. She failed to mention that she was just in the neighborhood. Instead, she asked, "Who's the lead detective?"

"Excuse me?"

She pointed to the house.

"Who's leading the investigation?"

"Oh, that would be Detective Manx."

She headed for the entrance, feeling his eyes follow her. Before she closed the door behind her, he hurried after the tangled ribbon of tape that now trailed over much of the front lawn.

No one greeted Maggie at the door. In fact, no one was in sight. The house's foyer was almost as large as Maggie's new living room. She took her time, peeking into each room, stepping carefully and touching nothing. The house looked impeccable, not a speck of dust, until she got to the kitchen. Scattered across the butcher-block island were all the makings for a sandwich, now dried up, wilted and crusty. A head of lettuce sat on a cutting board amongst the remnants of tomato seeds and bits and pieces of green pepper. Several candy bar wrappers, containers left on their sides and an open mayonnaise jar waited to be cleaned up and put away. In the middle of the table sat the sandwich, thick with its contents spilling over the wheat bread. Only one bite taken from it.

Maggie's eyes examined the rest of the kitchen, shiny countertops, sparkling appliances and a spotless ceramic floor, marred only by three more candy bar wrappers. Whoever made this mess didn't live here.

She could hear voices now, muffled and coming from above. She climbed the stairs while avoiding contact with the oak handrail. She wondered if the detectives had been as careful. On one of the steps she noticed a clump of mud, left perhaps by one of the officers. There was something unusual in it that glittered. She resisted the urge to pick it up. It wasn't as though she carried evidence bags in her back pocket. Though at one time it wouldn't have been odd to find a stray in one of her jacket pockets. These days the only evidence she came across was in books.

She followed the voices down the long, carpeted hall. There was no longer a need to scrounge for evidence. At the doorway to the master bedroom a puddle of blood greeted her, the imprint of a shoe stamped at one edge, while the other edge soaked into an expensive Persian rug. With little effort, Maggie could see a spatter pattern on the oak door. Oddly, the spatter reached only to about knee level.

Maggie was lost in thought and hadn't entered the room when the detective in a bright blue sports jacket and wrinkled chinos yelled at her.

"Hey, lady. How the hell did you get in here?"

The two other men stopped their work in opposite corners of the room and stared at her. Maggie's first impression of the detective was that he looked like a wrinkled advertisement for the Gap.

"My name's Maggie O'Dell. I'm with the FBI." She opened her badge to him, but her eyes were examining the rest of the room.

"The FBI?"

The men exchanged looks while Maggie took a careful step around the puddle and into the room. More blood speckled the white down comforter on the four-poster bed. Despite the spatter of blood, the bedcovers remained neatly spread with no indentations. Whatever struggle took place did not make it to the bed.

"What's the FBI's interest in this?" the man in the bright sports jacket demanded.

He scraped a hand over his head, and Maggie wondered if the buzz cut was recent. His dark eyes slid down her body, and again she was reminded of her inappropriate attire. She glanced at the other two men. One was in uniform. The other, an older gentleman—who Maggie guessed was the medical examiner—was dressed in a well-pressed suit and a silk tie held down by an expensive gold collar bar.

"Are you Detective Manx?" she asked the buzz cut.

His eyes shot up to hers, the look not only registering surprise but alarm that she knew his name. Was he worried that his superiors were checking up on him? He looked young, and Maggie guessed he was close to her age—somewhere in his early thirties. Perhaps this was his first lead in a homicide.

"Yeah, I'm Manx. Who the hell called you?"

It was time to confess.

"I live down the street. I thought I might be able to help."

"Christ!" The same hand swiped over his face as he glanced at the other two men. They quietly watched as though observing a standoff. "Just because you've got a fucking badge, you think you can barge in here?"

"I'm a forensic psychologist and a profiler. I'm used to examining scenes like this. I thought I could——"

"Well, we don't need any help. I've got everything under control."

"Hey, Detective." The yellow-tape officer from outside walked into the room and immediately all eyes watched him step into the puddle. He jerked his foot up and awkwardly stepped back into the hall, holding up the dripping toe of his shoe.

"Hell, I can't believe I did that again," he muttered.

Just then Maggie realized the intruder had been more careful. The toe print she had seen was worthless. When she looked back at Manx, his eyes darted away. He shook his head, disguising the embarrassment as disdain for the young officer.

"What is it, Officer Kramer?"

Kramer looked desperately for somewhere to place his foot. He glanced up apologetically as he rubbed the sole on the hall carpet. This time Manx avoided looking at Maggie. Instead, he shoved his large hands into his jacket pockets as if needing to restrain them from strangling the young rookie.

"What the hell do you need, Kramer?"

"It's just…there are a few neighbors out front asking questions. I wondered if maybe I should start questioning them. You know, see if anybody saw something."

"Get names and addresses. We'll talk to them later."

"Yes, sir." The officer seemed relieved to escape the new stain he had created.

Maggie waited. The other two men stared at Manx.

"So tell me, O'Donnell. What's your take of this mess?"

"O'Dell."

"Excuse me?"

"The name's O'Dell," she said, but she wouldn't wait for another invitation. "Is the body in the bathroom?"

"There's a whirlpool bath with more blood, but no body. In fact, we seem to be missing that small detail."

"The blood seems to be confined to this room," the medical examiner told her.

Maggie noticed he was the only one wearing latex gloves.

"If someone ran out, but was injured, you'd think there'd be some drips, some scuffs, something. But the house is fucking clean enough to eat off the floors." Manx swiped at his new hairdo again.

"The kitchen's not so clean," Maggie contradicted him.

He scowled at her. "How goddamn long have you been sneaking around here?"

She ignored him and kneeled down to get a closer look at the blood on the floor. Most of it was congealed, some dried. She guessed it had been here since morning.

"Maybe she didn't have time to clean up after lunch," Manx continued instead of waiting for her to answer his question.

"How do you know the victim is a woman?"

"A neighbor called us when she couldn't get her on the phone. Said they were supposed to go shopping. She saw the car in the garage, but no one answered the door. See, I'm thinking the guy—whoever he was—must have interrupted her lunch."

"What makes you think the sandwich was hers?"

The three of them stopped simultaneously. Again, they exchanged looks, then stared at Maggie, like foreign diplomats relying on each other for interpretation.

"What the hell are you saying, O'Donnell?"

"The name is O'Dell, Detective Manx." She let him hear her irritation this time. His blatant disregard was a small but familiar and annoying way to discredit her. "The victim's house is impeccable. She wouldn't have left a mess like that, let alone sit down to eat before she cleaned it up."

"Maybe she was interrupted."

"Perhaps. But there's no sign of a struggle in the kitchen. And the alarm system was off, right?"

Manx looked annoyed that she had guessed correctly. "Yeah, it was off, so maybe it was someone she knew."

"That's possible." Maggie stood and let her eyes take in the rest of the room. "If he did interrupt or surprise her, that didn't happen until they were up here. She may have been waiting for him, or perhaps she invited him up. That's probably why there's no signs of a struggle until we get into the bedroom. She may have changed her mind. Didn't want to go through with whatever they had agreed to. This spatter pattern here on the door is strange." She pointed to it, careful not to touch. "It's so far down, one of them would need to be on the floor when this wound was inflicted."

She walked to the window, feeling the men's eyes follow her. Suddenly she had their attention. Through the sheer curtains she could see the backyard, similar to her own, spacious and secluded by flowering dogwoods and huge pines. None of the neighbors' houses were even visible, all hidden by the foliage and trees. No one would see an intruder come or go back here. But how would he maneuver the steep ridge and the stream? Had she overestimated the strength of that natural barrier?

"There really is not much blood," she continued. "Unless there's a lot more in the bathroom. Perhaps there's not a body simply because the victim left on her own."

She heard Manx snort. "You think they had a nice little lunch, he beat the shit out of her because she decided not to fuck him, but then she left willingly with this guy? And in the meantime, the whole goddamn neighborhood didn't notice?" Manx laughed.

Maggie ignored his sarcasm. "I didn't say she left willingly. Also, this blood is much too congealed and dry to have happened a few hours ago during lunch. I'm guessing it happened early this morning. She glanced at the medical examiner for confirmation.

"She's right about that." He nodded in agreement.

"I don't think they had lunch together. He probably fixed the sandwich for himself. You should bag the sandwich. If you can't get a dental imprint, there may be some saliva for a DNA test."

When she finally turned to face him, Manx stared at her. Only now his frustration had turned to wonder and the crinkles at his eyes became more pronounced. Maggie realized he was older than her initial assessment. Which meant the clothes and the hair might be part of a midlife crisis rather than a youthful indiscretion. She recognized Manx's stunned look. It was the same look that often followed her on-the-spot, blunt profiles. At times, that look made her feel like a cheap fortune-teller or a psychic. But always beneath their skepticism lay just enough amazement and respect to vindicate that initial reaction.

"Mind if I check out the bathroom?" she asked.

"Be my guest." Manx shook his head and waved her through.

Before Maggie got to the bathroom door, she stopped. On the bureau was a photograph. She recognized the beautiful blond-haired woman who smiled out at her, one arm wrapped around a dark-haired man and the other around a panting white Labrador retriever. It was the same woman she and Tess McGowan had met the first day Maggie looked at her new house.

"What is it?" Manx asked, now standing directly behind her.

"I've met this woman before. Last week. Her name's Rachel Endicott. She was out jogging."

Just then, in the bureau mirror, she saw more blood. Only this was smeared on the bottom of the bed ruffle. She stopped and turned, hesitating. Was it possible that whoever had been bleeding was still under the bed?

CHAPTER 5

Maggie stared at the bloodied ruffle then slowly walked to the bed.

"Actually she was walking," she said, keeping the excitement from her voice. "She had a dog with her, a white Lab."

"We haven't found any fucking dog," Manx said. "Unless he's out in the backyard or the garage."

Carefully, Maggie got down on one knee. There was blood in the grooves of the hardwood floor, too. Here the intruder must have taken the time to mop it up. Why would he do that, unless some of it was his own?

The room grew silent as the men finally noticed the blood on the hem of the bed ruffle. Maggie felt them standing over her, waiting. Even Manx stood quietly, though out of the corner of her eye she could see the toe of his loafer tapping impatiently.

She lifted the ruffled material, avoiding the bloodied area. Before she could get a closer look underneath, a deep-throated growl caused her to jerk her hand away.

"Shit!" Manx spat, jumping back with such force he sent a nightstand scraping into the wall.

Maggie saw the glint of metal in his hand and realized he had drawn his service revolver.

"Move out of the way." He was next to her, shoving her shoulder and almost knocking her over.

She grabbed his arm as he recklessly took aim, ready to fire at anything that moved underneath the bed even though he couldn't see it.

"What the hell are you doing?" she yelled at him.

"What the fuck do you think I'm doing?"

"Calm down, Detective." The medical examiner took hold of Manx's other arm and gently pulled him back.

"This dog might be your only witness," Maggie said, getting down on her knees again but staying back a safe distance.

"Oh right. Like a dog's gonna tell us what happened."

"She's right," the M.E.'s voice was amazingly calm. "Dogs can tell us a lot. Let's see if we can get this one under control."

Then he looked to Maggie as if waiting for her instructions.

"Most likely, he's wounded," she said.

"And in shock," the M.E. added.

She stood and looked around the room. What the hell did she know about dogs, let alone how to subdue one?

"Check the closet and grab a couple of jackets," she told him. "Preferably thick, something like wool and something that's been worn and not laundered. Maybe there are some clothes on the floor."

She found a tennis racket leaning against the wall. She rummaged through the bureau's drawers then noticed a tie rack on the back of the closet door. She snatched a silk pinstripe and knotted one end of the tie to the handle of the racket. She made a slipknot at the other end.

The medical examiner came back with several jackets.

"Officer Hillguard," he instructed. "See if you can find some blankets. Detective Manx, get at the end of the bed. We'll have you lift up the bedspread when we're ready."

Maggie noticed Manx's impatience did not extend to the doctor. In fact, he seemed to regard the older man as an authority figure and willingly took his post at the end of the bed.

The medical examiner handed Maggie one of the jackets, an expensive wool tweed. She sniffed the sleeve. Excellent. There was still the faint scent of perfume. She pulled the jacket on backward, pushing the sleeves over her bare arms but keeping enough at the end to ball up in her fists. Then she grabbed the tennis racket and kneeled about two feet from the bed. The doctor kneeled next to her as Officer Hillguard set a quilt and two blankets on the floor beside them.

"Are we ready?" The medical examiner glanced at all of them. "Okay, Detective Manx. Lift the bedspread up, but slowly."

This time the dog was prepared, his eyes glazed, teeth bared, the growl deep and low. But he didn't lunge at them. He couldn't. Underneath the bloody mess of fur that was once white, Maggie spotted the main wound, a gash just above the shoulder and barely missing the throat. The matted fur must have temporarily stopped the bleeding.

"It's okay, boy," Maggie told the dog in a quiet, calm voice. "We're going to help you. Just relax."

She scooted closer, extending a part of the sleeve and letting it hang beyond her hand. He snapped at it, and Maggie jerked backward, almost losing her balance.

"Jesus!" she muttered. Had she completely lost her mind? She tried not to think of her aversion to needles, yet found herself wondering if the treatment for rabies was still six shots.

Maggie steadied herself. She needed to stay focused. She tried again, more slowly this time. The dog sniffed at the dangling sleeve, possibly recognizing the scent of his owner. His growl turned into a whine and then a whimper.

"It's okay," Maggie promised in a hushed tone, uncertain whether she was trying to convince the dog or herself. She inched closer with the tennis racket in her other hand, the tie's loop hanging down, moving in while the dog watched and continued to whimper. She let the dog sniff the tie. He didn't resist when she slipped it over his snout. Gently, she tightened the knot.

"How're we gonna get him out from under there?" Officer Hillguard was now on his knees on the other side of Maggie.

"Let's unfold one of those blankets and get it next to him."

But as soon as Officer Hillguard's hands got close, the dog snapped and snarled, growling and struggling against the makeshift muzzle. He jumped toward the officer, and Maggie used the opportunity to grab the dog's collar from behind. She yanked him forward onto the blanket, all the while holding the tennis racket and keeping the muzzle tight. The dog yipped, and immediately Maggie worried that she had opened one of the wounds.

"Holy shit," she heard Detective Manx say, but this time he kept his revolver in its holster.

"We got him." The medical examiner stood and waved Officer Hillguard over to his side. The two men tugged on the blanket corners and pulled the dog out from under the bed. "We can use my van to transport him to Riley's Clinic."

Maggie sat back on her feet, only now noticing that she was soaked with perspiration.

"Shit." Manx was back to his belligerent mood. "That means all the blood by the door and in the bathtub is probably the fucking dog's blood, and we don't have a damn thing."

"I wouldn't count on that," Maggie said. "Something violent happened here, and the dog's owner may have suffered the brunt of it." She watched the doctor and officer cover the trembling dog and secure their blanket stretcher, grateful they were too busy to notice how much effort it took for her to stand.

"I'm guessing this guy—" she pointed to the Lab "—tried to stop whatever happened. He may have gotten in a couple of good bites. There's a chance some of the blood, especially here by the bed, may be the intruder's. Your forensics people should be able to get a sampling even though it's been wiped up."

"You think you can allow me to do my own investigation?" Manx shot her a look of contempt.

Maggie wiped strands of hair off her forehead. Jesus! Couldn't this guy give her a break? Just then she realized she had blood on her hands and now had blood on her forehead and in her hair. When she glanced at the medical examiner, he was shaking his head at Manx and giving him a warning look as though he, too, was fed up with Manx's arrogance.

"Yes, of course, the investigation is all yours," Maggie finally said, and grabbed a corner of the blanket to help the men move the swaddled dog. "I'm sure the whole neighborhood will sleep soundly tonight, knowing you're on the case."

Manx seemed surprised by her sarcasm, then turned red when he noticed the two men would not be coming to his defense. Maggie caught the medical examiner smiling. She didn't turn to see if Manx had caught it, too.

"Just keep your big FBI badge and your pretty little butt out of my investigation," he said to her back, determined to get in the last word. "You got that, O'Donnell?"

She didn't bother to look at him or answer, the ungrateful son of a bitch. He wouldn't have even found the dog if it wasn't for her. Now she wondered if he would bother to take blood samples, simply because it had been her suggestion.

She held her corner of the blanket tight and followed Officer Hillguard and the medical examiner. As they reached the landing, Maggie turned to look at Manx, who had stayed in the bedroom's doorway.

"Oh, Detective Manx," she called to him. "One more thing. You might want to check out this mud here on the steps. Unless, of course, you're the one who tracked it in and contaminated your own crime scene."

Instinctively, Manx lifted his right foot, taking a look at the sole before he realized his defensive reaction. The M.E. laughed out loud. Officer Hillguard knew better and confined himself to a smile. Manx's face went red again. Maggie simply turned, concentrating on keeping their patient steady and calm while they hauled him down the stairs.

CHAPTER 6

Tess McGowan stuffed a copy of the closing papers into her leather briefcase, ignoring its worn sheen and cracked handle. A couple more sales and just maybe she could afford a new briefcase instead of the hand-me-down she had bought at the thrift store.

She jotted a note on her desk blotter, "Joyce and Bill Saunders: a dozen long-stemmed chocolate chip cookies." The Saunderses kids would get a kick out of them, and Joyce was a chocoholic. Then, she wrote, "Maggie O'Dell: a garden bouquet." Quickly, she scratched out the notation. No, it was too simple, and Tess liked to customize her thank-yous to her customers. They had become one of her trademarks and paid off big-time in referrals. But what would O'Dell like? Hey, even FBI agents liked flowers, and O'Dell seemed nuts about her huge backyard, but a bouquet didn't seem right. No, what seemed right for Agent O'Dell was a killer Doberman. Tess smiled and jotted down "a potted azalea" instead.

Pleased with herself, Tess switched off her computer and slipped on her jacket. The other offices had gone silent hours ago. She was the only one nuts enough to be working this late. Though it didn't matter. Daniel would be at his office until eight or nine and not ready to think about her for several more hours. But she wouldn't dwell on his inattentiveness. After all, she'd be running in the other direction if Daniel was constantly calling her, infringing on her independence or pushing for a commitment. No, she liked things just the way they were—safe and uncomplicated with very little emotional investment. It was the perfect relationship for a woman who couldn't handle any real commitments.

She passed by the copier room but stopped when she heard shuffling. Her eyes darted to the front door at the end of the hall, making certain nothing obstructed her path in case she needed to run. She leaned against the wall and peeked around the door to the room where a copy machine buzzed into action.

"Girl, I thought you went home hours ago." Delores Heston's voice startled Tess as the woman stood up from behind the machine and shoved a tray of paper into the mouth of the copier. Finally, she looked at Tess and her face registered concern. "Good Lord! I'm sorry, Tess. I didn't mean to scare you. You okay?"

Tess's heart pounded in her ears. Immediately she was embarrassed at being so jumpy. The paranoia was a leftover from her old life. She smiled at Delores while she leaned against the doorjamb and waited for her pulse to return to normal.

"I'm fine. I thought everyone else was gone. What are you still doing here? Aren't you supposed to be taking the Greeleys to dinner?"

Delores punched some buttons, and the machine whizzed to life with a soft, almost comforting, hum. Then she looked at Tess, hands on her ample hips.

"They had to reschedule, so I'm catching up on some paperwork. And please don't tell Verna. She'll scream at me for messing with her precious baby." The machine beeped as if on cue.

"Holy Toledo! What did I do now?" Delores turned and began punching buttons again.

Tess laughed. The truth was, Delores owned the machine just like she owned every last chair and paper clip. Delores Heston started Heston Realty nearly ten years ago and had made quite a name for herself in Newburgh Heights and the surrounding area. Quite an accomplishment for a black woman who had grown up poor. Tess admired her mentor who, at six o'clock in the evening after a full day of work, still looked impeccable in her deep purple custom-made suit. Delores's silky, black hair was swept up into a compact bun, not a strand out of place. The only indication that she was finished for the day were her stocking feet.

In contrast, Tess's suit was wrinkled from too many hours of sitting. Her thick, wavy hair frizzled from the humidity, strands breaking free from the clasp she used to tie it back. She was probably the only woman alive who dyed her naturally blond hair a nondescript brown in order to buy herself more credibility and to avoid sexual advances. Even the eyeglasses, which dangled from a designer cord around her neck, were a prop. Tess wore contact lenses, but didn't young, attractive women always look more intelligent when they wore glasses?

Finally, the machine stopped beeping and started spitting out copies. Delores turned to Tess and rolled her eyes.

"Verna's smart not to let me touch this thing."

"Looks like you've got it under control."

"So, girl, what are you doing here so late? Don't you have a handsome man you should be home snuggling with on a Friday evening?"

"Just wanted to finish all the paperwork on the Saunders' house."

"That's right. I forgot you closed this week. Excellent job, by the way. I know the Saunderses were in a hell of a hurry to sell. How much of a beating did we take?"

"Actually, it turned out quite well for everyone involved. Plus, we beat their two-week deadline, so on top of our commission we'll also be receiving the selling bonus they tacked on."

"Ooooh, I do so love to hear that. There's no better advertising than surpassing a customer's expectations. But that selling bonus is all yours, dearie."

Tess wasn't sure she heard her boss correctly.

"Excuse me?"

"You heard me. You're keeping that selling bonus for yourself. You deserve it."

For a minute Tess didn't know what to say. The bonus was almost ten thousand dollars. That was almost six months' pay back when she had been bartending. Her look of surprise sent Delores into gales of laughter.

"Girl, I wish you could see the look on your face."

Tess waited quietly. She managed a weak smile. She was embarrassed to ask if her boss was joking. It would be a cruel joke. But then, it wouldn't be the first time Tess had experienced such cruelty. In fact, she expected it, accepted it, almost more readily than kindness.

Delores was staring at her again, with a look of concern.

"Tess, I am serious. I want you to have the selling bonus. You worked your ass off to move that property in two weeks. I know it's a beautiful house and the asking price was a steal, but with all the paperwork and hedging and negotiating—selling anything right now that quickly, and especially in that price range, is nothing less than a miracle."

"It's...well, it's just an awful lot of money. Are you sure you want to—"

"Absolutely. I know what I'm doing, girlfriend. I'm investing in you, Tess. I want you to stick around. Don't need you going out on your own and becoming my competition. Besides, I'm making a nice piece of change off that property, as it is. Now go home and celebrate with that handsome man of yours."

On the way home Tess wondered if it was possible, the part about celebrating with her "handsome man." Daniel had been so angry with her last week when she'd refused to move in with him. She wasn't sure she blamed him. Why was it that every time a man wanted to get close to her, she pushed him away?

Jesus, she wasn't a kid anymore. In a couple of weeks she'd be thirty-five. She was becoming a successful and respected businesswoman. So why couldn't she get her personal life right? Was she destined to fail at every damn relationship she attempted? No matter what she did, the past seemed to follow her around, sucking her back into its old, comfortable, but destructive, cocoon.

The last five years had been a constant battle, but finally she was making progress. And this last sale had proven that she was actually good at this. She could make a living without conning anyone. Even Daniel had become a sort of trophy, with his refined handsome features, his educated and cultured background. He was sophisticated and ambitious and so completely unlike any man she had ever been with. So what if he was a little arrogant, or that they had so few things in common. He was good for her. She winced at the thought. It made Daniel sound like cod liver oil.

Tess found herself pulling her leased Miata into the back-alley parking lot of Louie's Bar and Grill. She decided to pick up a bottle of wine. Then she'd call Daniel, apologize for last week and invite him over for a late dinner to help her celebrate. Surely he would be excited for her. He had said he liked her independence and determination, and Daniel was stingy with compliments, even the halfhearted ones.

She sat back in the leather seat and tried to remember why she felt she needed to apologize to him again. Oh well. It didn't matter, as long as they put it behind them and moved forward. She was getting good at putting things in the past. Yet, if that were true, what was she doing back here at Louie's? Shep's Liquor Mart was only three blocks down the street and on her way home. What in the world did she need to prove to anyone? Or rather, what was it she still needed to prove to herself?

She reached for the key in the ignition and was just about to start the car and leave when the back door swung open, startling her. A stocky, middle-aged man came out, his hands filled with trash bags, his apron grimy and his balding head glistening with sweat. A cigarette hung from his lips. Without removing it, he heaved the bags into the Dumpster and wiped the sweat from his forehead with the sleeve of his shirt. As he turned to go back in, he saw her, and then it was too late.

He grabbed the cigarette—one last puff—and tossed it to the ground without stomping it out. He strolled up to the car, carrying his bulk with a swagger Tess knew he imitated from the professional wrestlers he idolized. He thought he looked cool. When, in fact, he simply looked like a pathetic, overweight, balding, middle-aged man. Despite all that, she found him endearing, the closest thing she had to an old friend.

"Tessy," he said, then waited as the window hummed opened. "What the hell you doin' here?"

She noticed the beginning of a smile before he wiped at it, pretending instead to scratch the five o'clock shadow.

"Hi, Louie." She got out of the car.

"Fuckin' nice ride ya got here, Tessy," he said, checking out the shiny black Miata.

She let him examine and admire it, neglecting to tell him it was a company car and not her own. One of Delores's mottoes was that to be successful you must first look successful.

Finally, Louie turned his sights on Tess. She felt his eyes slide down her designer suit and his whistle made her blush. She should have felt proud. Instead, his attention made her feel like a fraud for a second time in the same day.

"So whatcha doin' here? Slummin'?"

Immediately, her face grew hot.

"Of course not," she snapped.

"Hey, I'm just jokin' with ya, Tessy."

"I know that." She smiled, hoping she sounded convincing and not defensive. She turned to the car and pretended to lock the door, though the remote could do it from ten feet away. "I need to pick up a bottle of wine. Just thought I'd give you the business rather than Shep's."

"Oh really?" He stared at her, his eyebrow raised, but quickly gave in to a smile. "Well, I appreciate it. And you never need no excuse to come see us, Tessy. You know you're always welcome."

"Thanks, Louie."

Suddenly she felt like that restless, going-nowhere bartender she had left here five years ago. Would she ever be rid of her past?

"Come on," Louie said as he swung a muscular arm up around her shoulder.

Wearing heels, Tess was a couple inches taller, making the dragon tattooed on his arm stretch its neck. The smell of body odor and French fries made her stomach turn, only she was surprised to find it was homesickness she was feeling instead of nausea. Then she thought of Daniel. Later, he would smell the cigarette smoke and the greasy burgers. She realized that would be enough to ruin the celebration.

"You know what, Louie. I just remembered something I forgot back at the office." She turned and slipped out from under his arm.

"What? It can't wait a few minutes?"

"No, sorry. My boss will have my ass in a sling if I don't take care of it right now." She bleeped her car door open and climbed inside before Louie had a chance to do any more objecting. "I'll stop in later," she said through the half-opened window, knowing full well she would not. The window was already on its way up again when she said, "I promise."

She shifted the car into gear and carefully maneuvered the narrow alley, watching Louie in the rearview mirror. He looked more confused than pissed. That was good. She didn't want Louie pissed at her. Then immediately wondered why it mattered. She didn't want it to matter.

She turned the car onto the street, and when she knew she was safely out of sight, she gunned the engine. But it took several miles before she felt like she could breathe and before she could hear the car radio instead of the pounding of her heart. Then she remembered that she had passed Shep's Liquor Mart. She didn't care. She no longer felt as if she deserved a celebration, yet she tried to concentrate on her recent successes and not the past. In fact, she remained so focused, she hardly noticed the dark sedan following her.

CHAPTER 7

Before the pizza or Gwen arrived, Maggie poured a second Scotch. She had forgotten about the bottle until she discovered it staring up at her, safely stored in the box—a necessary antidote accompanying the contents of horror. The box was labeled #34666, the number that had been assigned to Albert Stucky. Perhaps it was no accident that his file number would end in 666.

Assistant Director Cunningham would be furious if he knew she had copied every last piece of paper from Stucky's official file. She would have felt guilty if each report, each document, each note had been recorded by someone other than herself. For almost two years Maggie had tracked Stucky. She had viewed every one of his scenes of torture and dissection, scanning his handiwork for fibers, hairs, missing organs, anything that would tell her how to catch him. She had a right to his file, considering it some strange documentation of a portion of her own life.

She had taken a quick shower after her unexpected trip to the vet. Her UVA T-shirt soaked in the bathroom sink. She might never be able to remove the bloodstains. The T-shirt was old, stretched and faded, but she had an odd attachment to it. Some people kept scrapbooks, Maggie kept T-shirts.

Her years at the University of Virginia had been good ones. It was there she discovered a life of her own outside of being her mother's caretaker. It was where she had met Greg. She glanced at her watch, then checked her cellular phone to make certain it was on. He still hadn't returned her call about the missing carton. He'd make her wait, but she wouldn't let herself get angry. Not tonight. She was simply too exhausted to take on one more emotion.

The doorbell chimed. Maggie glanced at her watch again. As usual, Gwen was ten minutes late. She tugged at her shirttail, making certain it hid the bulging Smith & Wesson tucked into her waistband. Lately, the gun had become as common an accessory as her wristwatch.

"I know I'm late," Gwen said before the door was fully open. "Traffic was a bitch. Friday night and everyone's trying to get the hell out of D.C. for the weekend."

"Good to see you, too."

She smiled and pulled Maggie in for a one-armed hug. For a brief moment Maggie was surprised by how soft and fragile the older woman felt. Despite Gwen's petite and feminine stature, Maggie thought of her as her own personal Rock of Gibraltor. She had leaned on Gwen and depended on her strength and character and words of wisdom many times during their friendship.

When Gwen pulled away, she cupped Maggie's cheek in the palm of her hand, attempting to get a good look at her.

"You look like hell," was her gentle assessment.

"Gee, thanks!"

She smiled again and handed Maggie the carton of long-necked Bud Light she carried in her other hand. The bottles were cold and dripping with condensation. Maggie took them and used the action as an excuse to keep her eyes away from Gwen's. It had been almost a month since the two women had seen each other, though they talked on the phone regularly. On the phone, however, Maggie could keep Gwen from seeing the panic and vulnerability that seemed to lie so close to the surface during these past several weeks.

"Pizza should be here any minute," Maggie told her as she reset the security system.

"No Italian sausage on my half."

"Extra mushrooms, instead."

"Oh, bless you." Gwen didn't wait for an invitation to come in. She took off to roam through the rooms.

"My God, Maggie, this house is wonderful."

"You like my designer?"

"Hmm...I'd say brown cardboard is you, simple and unpretentious. May I check out the second floor?" Gwen asked, already making her way up the stairs.

"Can I stop you?" Maggie laughed. How was it possible for this woman to sweep into a place and bring a trail of energy as well as such warmth and delight?

She and Gwen had met when Maggie had first arrived at Quantico for her forensic fellowship. Maggie had been a young, naive newbie who hadn't yet seen blood except in a test tube, and had never fired a gun except during training on the firing range.

Gwen had been one of the local psychologists brought in by Assistant Director Cunningham to act as a private consultant and to help profile several important cases. Even back then she had a successful practice in D.C. Many of her patients were some of the elite of Washington—bored wives of congressmen, suicidal generals and even one manic-depressed White House cabinet member.

However it was Gwen's research, the many articles she had written and her remarkable insight into the criminal mind that had attracted Assistant Director Cunningham when he first asked her to be an independent consultant for the FBI's Investigative Support Unit. Though Maggie learned quickly that the assistant director had been attracted to Dr. Gwen Patterson in other ways as well. A person would have to be blind not to see the ongoing chemistry between the two, though Maggie knew firsthand that neither had acted upon it, nor ever intended to.

"We respect our professional relationship," Gwen explained to Maggie once, making it clear she didn't want the subject brought up again, though this was long after Gwen's stint as a consultant had ended. Maggie knew that Assistant Director Cunningham's estranged marriage probably had more to do with their hands-off policy than any attempt to remain professional.

From the first time Maggie met Gwen, she had admired the woman's vibrancy, her keen intellect and her dry sense of humor. Gwen refused to think inside the box and didn't hesitate to break any of the rules while still appearing to be respectful of authority. Maggie had seen her win over diplomats as well as criminals with her sophisticated but charming manner. Gwen was fifteen years older than Maggie, but the woman had instantly become a best friend as well as a mentor.

The doorbell chimed again, and Maggie's hand reached back and grabbed her revolver before she could stop herself. She glanced up the stairs to see if Gwen had witnessed her knee-jerk reaction. She smoothed her shirttail over her jeans and checked the portico from the side window before she disarmed the alarm system. She stopped and looked out the peephole, examining the fish-eye view of the street, then she opened the door.

"Large pizza for O'Dell." The young girl handed Maggie the warm box. Already she could smell the Romano cheese and Italian sausage.

"It smells wonderful."

The girl grinned as though she had prepared it herself.

"It comes to $18.59, please."

Maggie handed her a twenty and a five. "Keep the change."

"Gee, thanks."

The girl bounced down the circular drive, her blond ponytail waving out the back of her blue baseball cap.

Maggie set the pizza down in the middle of the living room. She returned to the door to reset the security system just as Gwen came rushing down the steps.

"Maggie, what the hell happened?" she asked, holding up the dripping T-shirt, splattered with blood.

"What is this? Did you hurt yourself?" Gwen demanded.

"Oh, that."

"Yes, oh that. What the hell happened?"

Maggie quickly cupped a hand under the dripping T-shirt and grabbed it away, racing up the stairs to drop it back into the sink. She drained the red, murky water, tossed in more detergent and ran fresh water over the fabric. When she looked up in the mirror, Gwen was standing behind her, watching.

"If you're hurt, please don't try to take care of it yourself," Gwen said in a soft but stern voice.

Maggie met her friend's eyes in the mirror and knew that she was referring to the cut Albert Stucky had sliced into her abdomen. Maggie had slipped away into the night, after all the commotion had ended, and tried to discreetly dress her own wound. But an infection had landed her in the emergency room a few days later.

"It's nothing, Gwen. My neighbor's dog was injured. I helped take it to the vet. This is the dog's blood. Not mine."

"You're kidding." It took a minute for relief to wash over Gwen's face. "Jesus, Maggie, you just can't keep your nose out of anything that involves blood, can you?"

Maggie smiled. "I'll tell you about it later. We need to eat, because I am starving."

"That's new and different."

Maggie grabbed a towel, wiped her hands and led the way back downstairs.

"You know," Gwen said from behind her, "you need to put on some weight. Do you ever eat regular meals anymore?"

"I hope this isn't going to be a lecture on nutrition."

She heard Gwen sigh, but knew she wouldn't push it. They went into the kitchen, and Maggie pulled out paper plates and napkins from a carton on the counter. Each grabbed a cold bottle of beer and returned to the living-room floor. Already Gwen had kicked out of her expensive black pumps and thrown her suit jacket over the arm of the recliner. Maggie scooped up pizza as she noticed Gwen examining the open carton next to the rolltop desk.

"This is Stucky's, isn't it?"

"Are you going to rat me out to Cunningham?"

"Of course not. You know me better than that. But I am concerned about you obsessing over him."

"I'm not obsessing."

"Really? Then what would you call it?"

Maggie took a bite of pizza. She didn't want to think about Stucky, or her appetite would be ruined again. Yet that was one of the reasons Gwen was here.

"I simply want him caught," Maggie finally said. She could feel Gwen's eyes examining her, looking for signs, watching for underlying tones. Maggie hated it when her friend tried psychoanalyzing her, but she knew it was a simple instinct with Gwen.

"And only you can catch him? Is that it?"

"I know him best."

Gwen stared at her a few more moments then picked up her bottle by its neck and twisted off the cap. She took a sip and put the drink aside.

"I did some checking." She reached for a slice of pizza, and Maggie tried not to show her eagerness. She had asked Gwen to use her connections to find out where the Stucky case was stalled. When Assistant Director Cunningham exiled Maggie to the teaching circuit, he had also made it impossible for her to find out any information about the investigation.

Gwen took her time chewing. Another sip while Maggie waited. She wondered if Gwen had called Cunningham directly. No, that would have been too obvious. He knew the two of them were close friends.

"And?" She couldn't stand it any longer.

"Cunningham has brought in a new profiler, but the task force has been dismantled."

"Why the hell would he do that?"

"Because he has nothing, Maggie. It's been, what? Over five months? There's no sign of Albert Stucky. It's like he's fallen off the face of the earth."

"I know. I've been checking VICAP almost weekly." Initiated by the FBI, the Violent Criminal Apprehension Program recorded violent crimes across the country, categorizing them by distinguishing features. Nothing close to Stucky's M.O. had shown up. "What about in Europe? Stucky has enough money stashed. He could go anywhere."

"I checked my sources at Interpol." Gwen paused for another sip. "There's been nothing that looks like Stucky."

"Maybe he's changed his M.O."

"Maybe he's stopped, Maggie. Sometimes serial killers do that. They just stop. No one can explain it, but you know it happens."

"Not Stucky."

"Don't you think he'd be in touch with you? Try to start his sick game all over again? After all, you're the one who got him thrown in jail. If nothing else, he'd be mad as hell."

Maggie had been the one who had finally identified the madman the FBI had nicknamed The Collector. Her profile, and a lucky discovery of an almost indistinguishable set of fingerprints—arrogantly and recklessly left behind at a crime scene—were what led to the unveiling of The Collector as a man named Albert Stucky, a self-made millionaire from Massachusetts.

Like most serial killers, Stucky seemed pleased by the exposure, enjoying the attention and wanting to take the credit. When his obsession turned to Maggie, no one was really surprised. But the game that followed was anything but ordinary. A game that included clues to catch him, only the clues came as personal notes with a token finger, a dissected birthmark, and once, a severed nipple slipped into an envelope.

That was about eight or nine months ago. Almost a year had passed and Maggie still struggled to remember what her life had been like before the game. She couldn't remember sleep without nightmares. She couldn't remember not feeling the constant need to look over her shoulder. She had nearly lost her life capturing Albert Stucky, and he had escaped before she could remember what feeling safe felt like.

Gwen reached over and pulled a stack of crime scene photos from the box. She laid them out while she continued eating her pizza. She was one of the few people Maggie knew who wasn't a member of the FBI and who was able to eat and look at crime scene photos at the same time. Without looking up, she said, "You need to let this go, Maggie. He's chopping away pieces of you, and he isn't even around."

The images from the scattered photos stared out at Maggie, just as horrific in black and white as they had been in color. There were close-ups of slashed throats, chewed-off nipples, mutilated vaginas and an assortment of extracted organs. Earlier, with only a glance, she had discovered how many of the reports she still knew by heart. God, that was annoying.

Greg had recently accused her of remembering more details about entry wounds and killers' signatures than she remembered about the events and anniversaries in their life together. There had been no point in arguing with him. She knew he was right. Perhaps she didn't deserve a husband or a family or a life. How could any female FBI agent expect a man to understand her job, let alone something like this…this obsession? Was it an obsession? Was Gwen right?

She set the pizza aside and realized that her hands had a slight tremble. When she looked up, she saw that Gwen noticed the tremor, too.

"When was the last time you slept through the night?" Her friend's brow crinkled with concern.

She chose to ignore the question and avoided Gwen's green Irish eyes as well. "Just because there hasn't been a murder doesn't mean he hasn't started his collection again."

"And if he has, Kyle will be watching." Gwen rarely slipped, using Assistant Director Cunningham's first name, except times like now, when she seemed genuinely concerned and worried. "Let it go, Maggie. Let it go before it destroys you."

"It's not going to destroy me. I'm pretty damn tough, remember?" But she couldn't meet her friend's eyes for fear that Gwen would see the lie.

"Ah, tough," Gwen said, sitting back. "So that's why you're walking around your own home with a gun stashed in the back of your pants."

Maggie winced. Gwen caught it and smiled.

"Now, see, instead of tough," she told Maggie, "I think I would have called it stubborn."

CHAPTER 8

He couldn't remember pizza delivery girls being so cute back in his younger days when he had worked at the local pizza place. Hell, he couldn't remember there being delivery girls back then.

He watched her hurry up the sidewalk, strands of long blond hair trailing behind her. She had her hair in a cute ponytail—sticking out the back of her blue baseball cap, a Chicago Cubs cap. He wondered if she was a fan. Or maybe her boyfriend was. Surely she had a boyfriend somewhere.

It was too dark now to depend on the streetlights. His eyes were already stinging and a bit blurred. He slipped on the night goggles and adjusted the magnification. Yes, this was good.

He saw her check her watch as she waited on the front porch. This time another man answered the door. Of course, the guy would give her that dumb-ass look of astonishment. The man fished bills out of the pockets of his blue jeans, jeans that sagged at his bulging waist. He was a slob, grimy with sweat stains under the armpits of his T-shirt and a tuft of hair sticking up out the neckline. And yet...yep, there it was, another wiseass remark about how cute she was or what he wouldn't mind tipping her with. But again, she smiled politely, despite the color rising in her cheeks.

Just once he'd like to see her kick one of these idiots in the groin. Maybe that was a lesson he could teach her. If things worked out as he planned, he'd have plenty of time with her.

She hurried away along the winding sidewalk, and the cheap bastard who had tipped her only a dollar, watched her ass the whole trip back to her shiny little Dodge Dart. That sight alone was worth much more than a dollar. The cheap son of a bitch. How the hell was she supposed to put herself through college on dollar tips?

He decided that women were better tippers when it came to delivery services. Maybe they felt some odd sense of guilt for not having prepared the meal themselves. Who knew. Women were complicated, fascinating creatures, and he wouldn't change that if he could.

He replaced the goggles with dark sunglasses, simply out of habit now, and because the oncoming headlights burned his eyes. He waited for the Dodge Dart to reach the intersection before he turned around and followed. She was finished with this batch. He recognized the route back to the pizza place, Mama Mia's on Fifty-ninth and Archer Drive. The cozy joint took up the corner of a neighborhood strip mall. A Pump-N-Go occupied the other entrance. In between were a half-dozen smaller shops, including Mr. Magoo's Videos and Shep's Liquor Mart.

Newburgh Heights was such a friendly little suburb it gagged him. Not much of a challenge. Nor much challenge in the cute pizza delivery girl either. But this wasn't about challenge, it was simply for show.

The girl parked behind the building, near the door, and gathered up the stack of red insulators. She'd be back in a few minutes with another load ready to deliver.

The neon sign for Mama Mia's included a delivery number. He flipped open the cellular phone and dialed the number while he unfolded a real estate flyer. The description promised a four-bedroom colonial with a whirlpool bath and skylight in the master bedroom. How romantic, he mused, just as a woman barked in his ear.

"Mama Mia's."

"I'd like two large pepperoni pizzas delivered."

"Phone number."

"555-4545," he read off the flyer.

"Name and address."

"Heston," he continued reading, "at 5349 Archer Drive."

"Would you like some breadsticks and soda with that?"

"No, just the pizza."

"It'll be about twenty minutes, Mr. Heston."

"Fine." He snapped the phone shut. Twenty minutes would be plenty of time. He pulled on his black leather driving gloves, and then he wiped the phone with a corner of his shirt. As he drove by the Dumpster, he tossed the phone.

He headed south on Archer Drive, thinking about pizza, a moonlit bath and that cute delivery girl with the polite smile and the tight ass.

CHAPTER 9

Maggie's eyes begged to close. Her shoulders slouched from exhaustion. It was almost midnight by the time Gwen left. Maggie knew she'd never be able to sleep. She had already checked every window latch twice, leaving only a choice few open to keep the wonderful chilly breeze flowing through the main floor. Likewise, she had double-checked the security system several times after Gwen's departure. Now she paced, dreading the night hours, hating the dark and vowing to put up drapes and blinds tomorrow.

Finally she sat back down cross-legged in the middle of the pile created from the contents of Stucky's personal box of horror. She pulled out the folder with newspaper clippings and articles she had downloaded. Ever since Stucky's escape five months ago, she had watched newspaper headlines across the country by using the Internet.

She still couldn't believe how easily Albert Stucky had escaped. On his way to a maximum-security facility—a simple trip that should have taken a couple of hours—Stucky killed two transport guards. Then he disappeared into the Florida Everglades, never to be seen again.

Anyone else may not have been able to survive, having become a nifty snack for some alligator. But knowing Stucky, Maggie imagined him emerging from the Everglades in a three-piece suit and a briefcase made of alligator skin. Yes, Albert Stucky was intelligent and crafty and savvy enough to charm an alligator out of its own skin, and then reward it by slicing it up and feeding it to the other alligators.

She sorted through the most recent articles. Last week, the *Philadelphia*

Journal had an article about a woman's torso found in the river, her head and feet found in a Dumpster. It was the closest thing she had seen in months to Stucky's M.O., yet it still didn't feel like him. It was too much. It was overkill. Stucky's handiwork, though inconceivably horrible, had never included chopping away a victim's identity. No, Stucky enjoyed doing that with subtle psychological and mental tricks. Even his extraction of an organ from the victim was not a statement about the victim but rather his attempt to continue the game. Maggie imagined him watching and laughing as some unsuspecting diner found Stucky's appalling surprise, often tucked into an ordinary take-out container and abandoned on an outside café table. It was all a game to Stucky, a morbid, twisted game.

The articles that frightened Maggie more than the ones with missing body parts were the ones of women who had disappeared. Women like her missing neighbor, Rachel Endicott. Intelligent, successful women, some with families, all attractive, and all described as women who would not suddenly leave their lives without telling a soul. Maggie couldn't help wondering if any of them had become part of Stucky's collection. By now he had surely found somewhere isolated, somewhere to start all over again. He had the money and the means. All he needed was time.

She knew Cunningham and his defunct task force, and now his new profiler, were waiting for a body. But if, and when, the bodies did start showing up, they were the ones Stucky killed only for fun. No, the ones they should be looking for were the women he collected. These were the women he tortured—who ended up in remote graves deep in the woods, only after he was completely finished playing his sick games with them. Games that would drag on for days, maybe weeks. The women Stucky chose were never young or naive. No, Stucky enjoyed a challenge. He carefully chose intelligent, mature women. Women who would fight back, not those easily broken. Women he could torture psychologically as well as physically.

Maggie rubbed her eyes. She wanted another Scotch. The two earlier, added to the beer, were already making her head buzz and her vision blur. Though she had brewed a pot of coffee earlier for Gwen, she hated the stuff and stayed away from it. Now she wished she had something to help her stay alert. Something like the Scotch, which she knew was becoming a dangerous anesthetic.

She lifted another file folder and a page fell out. Seeing his handwriting still sent chills down her spine. She picked it up by its corner as though its evil would contaminate her. It had been the first of many notes in the sick game Albert Stucky had played with her. He had written in careful script:

> What challenge is there in breaking a horse without spirit? The challenge is to replace that spirit with fear, raw animal fear that makes one feel alive. Are you ready to feel alive, Margaret O'Dell?

It had been their first insight into the intellect of Albert Stucky, a man whose father had been a prominent doctor. A man who had been afforded all the best schools, all the privileges money could buy. Yet he was thrown out of Yale for almost burning down a women's dormitory. There were other offenses: attempted rape, assault, petty theft. All charges had been either dropped or were never pressed, due to lack of evidence. Stucky had been questioned in the accidental death of his father, a freak boating accident though the man had supposedly been an expert yachtsman.

Then, about six or seven years ago, Albert Stucky took up a business partner, and the two of them succeeded in creating one of the Internet's first stock-market trading sites. Stucky became a respectable businessman, and a multimillionaire.

Despite all of Maggie's research, she never felt certain about what had set Stucky off in the first place. What had been the event, the precursor? Usually with serial killers, their crimes were precipitated by some stressor. An event, a death, a rejection, an abuse that one day made them decide to kill. She didn't know what that had been for Stucky. Perhaps evil simply couldn't be harnessed. And Stucky's evil was especially terrifying.

Most serial killers murdered because it gave them pleasure, some form of gratification. It was a choice, not necessarily a sickness of the mind. But for Albert Stucky, the kill was not enough. His pleasure came from psychologically breaking down his victims, turning them into sniveling, pleading wretches—owning them body, mind and soul. He enjoyed breaking their spirit, turning it into fear. Then he rewarded his victims with a slow, torturous death. Ironically, those he killed immediately, those whose throats he slashed and whose bodies he discarded in Dumpsters—only after extracting a token organ—those were the lucky ones.

The phone startled her. She grabbed the Smith & Wesson .38 that sat by her side. Again, it was a simple reflex. It was late, and few people had her new number. She had refused to give it to the pizza place. She had even insisted Greg use her cell phone number. Maybe Gwen had forgotten something. From the floor, she reached up to the desktop and pulled the phone down.

"Yes?" she said, her muscles tense. She wondered when she had stopped answering hello.

"Agent O'Dell?"

She recognized Assistant Director Cunningham's matter-of-fact tone, but the tension did not leave her.

"Yes, sir."

"I couldn't remember if you were already using the new number."

"I just moved in today."

She glanced at her wristwatch. It was now after midnight. They spoke infrequently these days, ever since he had taken her out of the field and assigned her to training duty. Was it possible he had some information on Stucky? She sat up with an unexpected flutter of hope.

"Is there something wrong?"

"I'm sorry, Agent O'Dell. I just realized how late it is."

She imagined him still at this desk at Quantico, never mind that it was Friday night.

"That's quite all right, sir. You didn't wake me."

"I thought you might be leaving for Kansas City tomorrow, and I didn't want to miss you."

"I leave on Sunday." She kept the question, the anticipation from her voice as best she could. If he needed her to stay, she knew Stewart was able to fill in for her at the law enforcement conference. "Does there need to be a change to my schedule?"

"No, not at all. I just wanted to make sure. I did, however, receive a phone call earlier this evening that gave me great concern."

Maggie imagined a body, sliced and left for some unsuspecting person to find beneath the trash. She waited for him to give her the details.

"A Detective Manx from the Newburgh Heights Police Department called me."

Maggie's anticipation quickly dissipated.

"He told me that you interfered with a crime scene investigation this afternoon. Is that true?"

Maggie reached to rub her eyes again, only now realizing she still gripped the revolver. She put it aside and sat back, feeling defeated. Damn that prick, Manx.

"Agent O'Dell? Is that true?"

"I just moved into the neighborhood this afternoon. I noticed police cruisers at the end of the block. I thought perhaps I could help."

"So you did barge in uninvited on a crime scene."

"I did not barge in. I offered my help."

"That's not the way Detective Manx described it."

"No, I don't imagine it is."

"I want you to stay out of the field, Agent O'Dell."

"But I was able to—"

"Out of the field means you don't go using your credentials to walk onto crime scenes. Even if they are in your own neighborhood. Is that understood?"

She ran her fingers through her tangled hair. How dare Manx. He wouldn't have discovered the dog, had it not been for her.

"Agent O'Dell, is that clear?"

"Yes. Yes, it's perfectly clear," she said, almost expecting an additional reprimand for the sarcasm in her voice.

"Have a safe trip," he said in his usual abrupt manner and then hung up.

She threw the phone onto the desktop and began rifling through the files. The tension tightened in her back, her neck and shoulders. She stood up and stretched, noticing the anger still slamming in her chest. Damn Manx! Damn Cunningham! How long did he think he could keep her out of the field? How long did he intend to punish her for being vulnerable? And how could he ever expect to catch Stucky without her help?

Maggie reset the security system a third time, double-checking the red On light, even though the mechanical voice told her each time, "Alarm system has been activated." The hell with the buzz in her head. She poured another Scotch and convinced herself that one more would surely relieve the tension.

The mess stayed scattered on the living-room floor. It seemed appropriate that her new home be initiated with a pile of blood and horror. She retreated to the sunroom, grabbing her revolver and snatching an afghan from a box in the corner, wrapping it around her shoulders. She shut off all the lights, except the one on the desk. Then she curled into the recliner that now faced the wall of windows.

She cradled and sipped the Scotch as she watched the moon slip in and out of the clouds, making shadows dance in her new backyard. In her other hand she gripped the revolver resting in her lap, tucked under the cover.

Despite the progressive blur behind her eyes, she would be ready. Perhaps Assistant Director Cunningham couldn't stop Albert Stucky from coming for her, but she sure as hell would. And this time, it would be Stucky's turn for a surprise.

CHAPTER 10

Reston, Virginia
Saturday evening
March 28

R. J. Tully peeled off another ten-dollar bill and slid it under the ticket window. When had movie tickets started costing $8.50 each? He tried to remember the last time he had been to a movie theater on a Saturday night. He tried to remember when he had last been to a movie theater, period. Surely he and Caroline had gone some time during their thirteen-year marriage. Though it would have been early on—before she began preferring her co-workers to him.

He glanced around to find Emma dawdling far behind him, off to the side and at least three moviegoers back. Sometimes he wondered who the hell this person was. This beautiful, tall fourteen-year-old with silky blond hair and the beginnings of a shapely body she blatantly emphasized with tight jeans and a tight knit sweater. She looked more and more like her mother every day. God, he missed the days when this same girl held his hand and jumped into his arms, anxious to go anywhere with him. But just like her mother, that too had changed.

He waited for her at the ticket taker and wondered how she'd be able to sit next to him for two hours. He saw her eyes dart around the crowded lobby. Immediately, his heart sank. She didn't want any of her new friends to see her on a Saturday night, going to a movie with her dad. Was she really that embarrassed by him? He couldn't remember ever feeling that way about either of his parents. No wonder he spent so many hours at work. At the moment, understanding serial killers seemed much easier than understanding fourteen-year-old girls.

"How 'bout some popcorn?" he offered.

"Popcorn has, like, tons of fat."

"I don't think you have a thing to worry about, Sweet Pea."

"Oh my God, Dad!"

He stopped abruptly, checking to see if he had stepped on her toes. She sounded so pained.

"Don't call me that," she whispered.

He smiled down at her, which seemed to embarrass her more.

"Okay, so no popcorn for you. How about a Pepsi?"

"Diet Pepsi," she corrected him.

Surprisingly, she waited next to him in line at the concession stand, but her eyes still roamed the crowded lobby. It had been almost two months since Emma had come to live with him full-time. The truth was, he saw even less of her than when they were all back in Cleveland, and he was only a weekend dad. At least then they did things together, trying to make up for lost time.

When they first moved to Virginia he had tried to make sure they had dinner together every night, but he was the first to break that routine. His new job at Quantico had swallowed up much more of his time than he realized. So in addition to he and Emma settling into a new home, a new job, a new school and a new city, she also had to get used to not having her mother.

He still couldn't believe that Caroline had agreed to the arrangement. Maybe when she got tired of playing CEO by day, and the dating game by night, she would want her daughter back in her life full-time.

He watched Emma's quick, nervous swipes at the misbehaving strands of her long hair. Her eyes were still casing the theater. He wondered if fighting for full custody had been a mistake. He knew she missed her mother, even if her mother had been less available to her than he was. Damn it! Why did this parenting thing have to be so damn hard?

He almost ordered buttered popcorn, but stopped himself and ordered plain, hoping Emma might change her mind and snitch some.

"And two medium Diet Pepsis."

He looked to see if she was impressed by her influence on him. Instead, her light complexion paled, as discomfort converted to panic.

"Oh my God! It's Josh Reynolds."

Now she stood so close, Tully had to take a step back to collect their sodas and popcorn.

"Oh God! I hope he didn't see me."

"Who's Josh Reynolds?"

"Just one of the coolest kids in the junior class."

"Let's say hi."

"Dad! Oh God, maybe he didn't see me."

She stood facing Tully, her back to the young, dark-haired boy who was making his way toward them, his destination definitely Emma. And why shouldn't it be? His daughter was a knockout. Tully wondered if Emma was really panicked or if this was part of the game. He honestly had no clue. He didn't understand women, so how could he possibly expect to understand their predecessors?

"Emma? Emma Tully?"

The boy was closing in. Tully watched in amazement as his daughter manufactured a nervous but glowing smile from the twisted panic that had existed just seconds before. She turned just as Josh Reynolds squeezed through the concession line.

"Hi, Josh."

Tully glanced down to check if some impostor had replaced his obstinate daughter. Because this girl's voice was much too cheerful.

"What movie you seeing?"

"Ace of Hearts," she admitted reluctantly though it had been her choice.

"Me too. My mom wants to see it," he added much too quickly.

Tully found himself sympathizing with the boy, who shoved his hands into his pockets. What Emma called cool visibly took effort. Or was Tully the only one who could see the boy nervously tapping his foot and fidgeting? After an awkward silence and them ignoring his presence, Tully said, "Hi, Josh, I'm R. J. Tully, Emma's father."

"Hi, Mr. Tully."

"I'd offer you a hand, but they're both filled."

Out of the corner of his eye he could see Emma roll her eyes. How could that possibly embarrass her? He was being polite. Just then his pager began shrieking. Josh offered to take the sodas before it even occurred to Emma. Tully snapped the noise off, but not before getting several irritated stares. Emma turned a lovely shade of red. At a glance, he recognized the phone number. Of all nights, why tonight?

"I need to make a phone call."

"Are you a doctor or something, Mr. Tully?"

"No, Josh. I'm an FBI agent."

"You're kidding? That is so cool."

The boy's face brightened, and Tully saw that Emma noticed. Instead of heading directly for the phone bank, Tully stalled.

"I work at Quantico, in the Investigative Support Unit. I'm what you'd call a criminal profiler."

"Wow! That is so cool," Josh repeated.

Without looking at her, Tully saw Emma's face change as she watched Josh's reaction.

"So do you track serial killers just like in the movies?"

"I'm afraid the movies make it look more glamorous than it is."

"Geez! I bet you've seen some pretty weird stuff, though, huh?"

"Unfortunately, yes, I have. I really need to make a phone call. Josh, would you mind keeping Emma company for a few minutes?"

"Oh sure. No, problem, Mr. Tully."

He didn't look at Emma again until he was safely at the pay phone. Suddenly, his belligerent daughter was full of smiles, genuine this time. He watched the two teenagers talk and laugh while he dialed the number. For the first time in a long time, he felt happy and glad that Emma was with him. For a few minutes, he had almost forgotten that the world could be cruel and violent, then he heard Assistant Director Cunningham's voice.

"It's Tully, sir. You paged me?"

"Looks like we may have one of Stucky's."

Tully felt instant nausea. He had been anticipating and dreading this call for the last couple of months.

"Where at, sir?"

"Right under our noses. About thirty to forty-five minutes from here. Can you pick me up in about an hour? We can go to the site together."

Without asking, Tully knew Cunningham meant picking him up at Quantico. He wondered if the man ever went home.

"Sure. I'll be there."

"I'll see you in an hour."

This was it. After years of sitting behind a desk in Cleveland and profiling killers from afar, this was his chance to prove himself and join the real hunters. So why did he feel sick to his stomach?

Tully made his way back to his daughter and her friend, anticipating her disappointment.

"I'm sorry, Emma, I've got to leave."

Immediately, her eyes grew dark, her smile slid off her face.

"Josh, did you say you were here with your mom?"

"Yeah, she's getting us popcorn." He pointed to an attractive redhead in the line. When she noticed Josh pointing, she smiled at him and shrugged at the stagnant line in front of her.

"Josh, Emma, would you mind if I ask Josh's mom if Emma could join you for the movie?" Tully steeled himself for his daughter's panic and horror.

"No, that would be cool," Josh said without hesitating, and Emma immediately seemed pleased.

"Sure, Dad," she said.

Tully wondered if she knew how cool she was pretending to be right now.

When he introduced himself to Jennifer Reynolds, she also seemed pleased to help him out. He offered to repay her another night by treating all of them to another movie. Then he kicked himself when he noticed her wedding band. But Jennifer Reynolds accepted his offer without hesitation, and with a flirtatious look that even an out-of-practice, newly single guy didn't need to decipher. Despite his curiosity, he couldn't help feeling a bit excited.

He smiled all the way to his car, greeting people in the parking lot and jingling his car keys. The evening was still warm and the moon promised to be brilliant despite wisps of clouds. He slid behind the steering wheel and checked his reflection in the rearview mirror, as though he had forgotten the configuration of his face when it was happy. What an unusual feeling, happiness and excitement, and all in the same evening. Two things he hadn't felt in years, though he knew both would be short-lived. He drove out of the theater's parking lot feeling he could take on anything and anyone. Maybe even Albert Stucky.

CHAPTER 11

Tully followed Cunningham's directions and turned at the intersection. Immediately, he saw spotlights in the back alley of a small strip mall. Police cruisers blocked the street, and Tully pulled up beside one, flashed his badge and drove through the maze. He tried to take a lesson from his daughter's new friend Josh by pretending to be cool. Fact was, his stomach felt hollow and perspiration slid down his back.

Tully had seen plenty of crime scenes, severed limbs, bloodied walls, mutilated bodies and sick, disgusting killer signatures that ranged from a single long-stemmed rose to a decapitated corpse. But all those scenes, up until now, had been only in photographs, digital scans and illustrations sent to him at the FBI Cleveland Field Office. He had become one of the Midwest's experts in developing precise criminal profiles from the bits and pieces law enforcement officers sent him. It was his accuracy that had prompted Assistant Director Kyle Cunningham to offer Tully a position at Quantico in the Investigative Support Unit. In one phone call and without ever having met him, Cunningham had offered Tully a chance to work out in the field, starting with the hunt for one of the FBI's most infamous fugitives—Albert Stucky.

Tully knew Cunningham had been forced to dismantle the task force after months of nothing to show for their time and expense. He also knew he owed his good fortune to the agent he had replaced, an agent who had been temporarily assigned to teaching at law enforcement conferences. Without much digging, he discovered the agent was Margaret O'Dell, whom he had never met but knew by reputation. She was one of the youngest and one of the best profilers in the country.

The unofficial word was that O'Dell had burned out and needed a break. Rumors suggested that she had lost her edge, that she was combative and reckless, that she had become paranoid and obsessed with recapturing Albert Stucky. Of course, there were also rumors that Assistant Director Cunningham had sidelined Margaret O'Dell to protect her from Stucky. The two had played a dangerous game of cat and mouse about eight months ago that had eventually led to Stucky's capture, but only after he had tortured and almost killed O'Dell. Now after months of studying, searching and waiting, Tully would finally meet the man nicknamed The Collector, if only through his handiwork.

Tully pulled the car as close to the barricades as he could. Cunningham jumped out before Tully had it in park. He almost forgot to turn off the lights. He noticed his palms were sweaty when he pulled the key from the ignition. His legs seemed stiff, his knee suddenly reminding him of an old injury as he hurried to catch up with his boss. Tully stood four inches taller than the assistant director, and his strides were long, yet it took an effort to keep up. He guessed Cunningham to be at least ten years his senior, but the man had a lean, athletic body, and Tully had witnessed him bench-pressing twice the weight the academy recruits started at.

"Where is she?" Cunningham wasted no time asking a police detective who looked to be in charge.

"She's still in the Dumpster. We haven't moved a thing, except the pizza box."

The detective had a neck as thick as a linebacker's and the seams of his sports jacket bulged. He was treating this like an everyday traffic check. Tully wondered which big city the detective had come from, because he definitely had developed his no-nonsense manner somewhere other than Newburgh Heights. He and the assistant director seemed to know one another and took no time for introductions.

"Where is the pizza box?" Cunningham wanted to know.

"Officer McClusky gave it to the doc. The kid who found it sorta dropped it, and the stuff got all jostled."

Suddenly the smell of stale pizza and the sounds of police radios made Tully's head hurt. During the drive, the adrenaline had pumped him into action. Now the reality was a bit overwhelming. He ran unsteady fingers through his hair. Okay, this couldn't be that much different than looking at photos. He could do this, and he ignored the recurring nausea as he followed his boss to the Dumpster where three uniformed officers stood guard. Even the officers stood a good ten feet away to avoid the stench.

The first thing Tully noticed was the young woman's long blond hair. Immediately, he thought of Emma. He could see over the Dumpster's edge easily, but waited as Cunningham pulled up a crate. His boss's face remained emotionless.

Though covered in garbage, Tully could tell the woman had been young, not much older than Emma. And she had been beautiful. Discarded lettuce and spoiled tomatoes clung to her naked breasts. The rest of her was buried in garbage, but Tully saw glimpses of thigh, and then realized she wore only a blue baseball cap. He could also see that her throat had been slashed from ear to ear, and there was an open wound in her side, almost at her lower back. But that was all. There were no severed limbs, no bloody mutilation. He wasn't sure what he had expected.

"She looks like she's in one piece," Cunningham said as though reading Tully's thoughts. He stepped off the crate and then addressed the detective again. "What was in the box?"

"Not sure. Looked like a bloody glob to me. Doc can probably tell you. He's over in the van."

He pointed to a dusty silver van marked with the Stafford County emblem on the side. The doors were open and a distinguished gray-haired man in a well-pressed suit sat in the back with a clipboard.

"Doc, these gentlemen from the FBI need to see that special delivery."

The detective turned and started to leave just as a media van pulled into an adjacent parking lot.

"Excuse me, gentlemen. Looks like the zoo visitors have arrived."

Cunningham stepped up into the van, and Tully followed, though it seemed crowded with the three of them. Or was Tully the only one having problems breathing? Already he could smell the contents of the box, which sat in the middle of the floor. He sat on one of the benches before his stomach started to churn.

"Hello, Frank." Assistant Director Cunningham knew the medical examiner, too. "This is Special Agent R. J. Tully. Agent Tully, Dr. Frank Holmes, deputy chief medical examiner for Stafford County."

"I don't know if this is your man, Kyle, but when Detective Rosen called me, he seemed to think you might be interested."

"Rosen worked in Boston when Stucky kidnapped Councilwoman Brenda Carson."

"I remember that. What was that two, three years ago?"

"Not quite two."

"Thankfully, I was on vacation. Fishing up in Canada." The doctor cocked his head as though trying to remember some sporting event. Tully found everyone's ease, all the casualness, a bit unnerving. He sat still, hoping no one could hear his heart pounding. The doctor continued. "But now if I remember right, Carson's body was buried in a shallow grave in some woods. Outside Richmond, wasn't it? Certainly not in some Dumpster."

"This guy's complicated, Frank. The ones he collects are the ones we rarely find. These women...these are his rejects. They're simply for sport—for show-and-tell." Cunningham sat forward, leaning his elbows on his knees, the balls of his feet rocking as though ready to jump into action at any moment. Everything about Cunningham telescoped his constant energy, his immediacy. Yet, his face, his voice remained calm, almost soothing.

Tully stared at the pizza box on the floor of the van. Despite the scent of pizza dough and pepperoni, he recognized the acrid scent as blood. So much for eating pizza ever again.

"Nothing happens in this quiet little suburb," Dr. Holmes said while continuing to jot details on the forms he had clipped to his board. "Then two homicides in one day."

"Two?" Cunningham's patience seemed to wear thin with the doctor's slow, deliberate manner. He stared at the pizza box, and Tully knew his boss wouldn't touch it without first being invited to do so by Dr. Holmes. Tully had discovered early on that despite the director's authority, he showed great respect for those he worked with, as well as for rules, policy and protocol.

"I'm not aware of another homicide, Frank," he said when the doctor took too long to offer an explanation.

"Well, I'm not sure the other one is a homicide, yet. We never did find a body." Dr. Holmes finally put the clipboard aside. "We had an agent on the scene. Maybe one of yours?"

"Excuse me?"

"Yesterday afternoon. Not far from here in the nice quiet neighborhood of Newburgh Heights. Said she was a forensic psychologist. Just moved into the victim's neighborhood. Very impressive young woman."

Tully watched Cunningham's face and saw the transformation from calm to agitated.

"Yes, I did hear about that. I had forgotten her new neighborhood was in Newburgh Heights. I apologize if she got in the way."

"Oh, no apology necessary, Kyle. On the contrary, she proved very helpful. I think the arrogant bastard who was supposed to be investigating the scene may have even learned a thing or two."

Tully caught the assistant director with a smile at the corner of his lips, before he realized he was being watched. He turned to Tully and explained, "Agent O'Dell, your predecessor, just bought a new home in this area."

"Agent Margaret O'Dell?" Tully held his boss's eyes until he saw that Cunningham had now made the same connection Tully had just made. Both of them stared at Dr. Holmes as he slid the pizza box closer. Suddenly, Tully knew it didn't matter what they found in the box. Whatever had been discarded, neither of them needed to see the bloody mess to confirm that this was most likely the work of Albert Stucky. And Tully knew it was no coincidence that he had chosen to start again, close to Agent Margaret O'Dell's new home.

CHAPTER 12

Exhaustion seeped into his bones and threatened to incapacitate him by the time he returned to the safety of his room. He shed his clothes with minimal movement, letting the fabric slide off his lean body, though what he really wanted to do was rip and tear. His body disgusted him. It had taken almost twice as long for him to come this time. Of all the fucking things he had to deal with, that one was the most annoying.

His fingers fumbled through his duffel bag, searching frantically, tossing items haphazardly to the floor. Suddenly, he stopped when he felt the smooth cylinder. Relief washed over him, chilling his sweat-drenched body.

The fatigue had moved to his fingers. It took three attempts to snap off the plastic cap and poke the needle into the orange rubber top of the vial. He hated not having complete control. The anger and the irritability only added to his nausea. He steadied his hands as best he could and watched the syringe suck the liquid from the vial.

He sat on the edge of the bed, his knees weak and perspiration sliding down his naked back. In one quick motion he stuck the needle into his thigh, forcing the colorless liquid into his bloodstream. Then he lay back and waited, closing his eyes against the red lines that jetted across his field of vision. In his mind he could hear the blood vessels popping—pop, pop, pop! The thought might drive him completely mad before it drove him completely blind.

Through closed eyelids he was aware of the flickers of lightning that invaded his dimly lit room. A rumble of thunder vibrated the window. Then the rain began again, soft and gentle, tapping out a lullaby.

Yes, his body disgusted him. He had pushed it to be strong and lean, using weights, steel machines and gut-wrenching wind sprints. He ate nutritious meals high in protein and vitamins. He had freed himself of all toxins including caffeine, alcohol and nicotine. Yet, his body still failed him, screaming out its limitations and reminding him of its imperfections.

It had only been three short months since he had noticed any of the symptoms. The first ones were simply annoying, the eternal thirst and the constant urge to piss. Who knew how long this damn thing had been lying dormant inside him, ready to strike at just the right moment.

Of course, it would be this one abnormality that would eventually do him in, a gift from his greedy mother whom he had never even known. The bitch would have to give him something that could destroy him.

He sat up, ignoring the slight dizziness in his head, his vision still blurred. The lapses came more often and were getting harder and harder to predict. Whatever the limitations, he refused to let them interfere with the game.

The rain tapped more persistently now. The lightning came in constant flickers. It made the room crawl with movement. Dusty objects sprang to life, jerky miniature robots. The whole frickin' room jumped and jerked.

He grabbed the lamp on the bedstand and twisted it on, making the movement halt in the yellow glow. In the light, he could see the heap from his spilled duffel bag. Socks, shaving kit, T-shirts, several knives, a scalpel and a Glock 9 mm lay scattered on the plush carpet. He ignored the familiar buzz that had begun to invade his head, and rifled through the mess, stopping when he found the pink panties. He rubbed the soft silk against his bristled jaw, then breathed in their scent, a lovely combination of talcum powder, come and pizza.

He noticed the real estate flyer crumpled under the pile and pulled it out, unfolding it and smoothing its wrinkles. The eight-and-half-by-eleven sheet of paper included a color photo of the beautiful colonial house, a detailed description of its amenities and the shiny blue logo of Heston Realty. The house had definitely lived up to its promises, and he was sure it would continue to do so.

At the bottom corner of the flyer was a small photo of an attractive woman, trying to look professional despite something...what was it in her eyes? There was an insecurity, something that made her look uncomfortable in her cute conservative white blouse and navy blue suit. His thumb rubbed over her face, smudging the ink and dragging a trail of black and blue over her skin. That looked better. Yes, already he could feel her vulnerability. Perhaps he could see and feel it only because he had spent so much time watching her, had taken time to study and examine her. He wondered what it was that Tess McGowan was trying so hard to hide.

He walked across the room, taking slow, deliberate steps deciding not to get angry because his knees were still weak. He tacked the flyer to the bulletin board. Then, as if the memory of Tess and those shapely legs of hers had reminded him, he slid a box out from under the table. Unfortunately, movers were so negligent these days. Going off and taking breaks without tending to the precious possessions left in their care. He smiled as he broke the packaging tape and then flipped off the lid that was marked "M. O'Dell."

He took out the yellowed newspaper clippings: Firefighter Sacrifices Life, Trust Fund Established for Hero. What a horrible way for her to lose her father, in a hellish fire.

"Do you dream about him, Maggie O'Dell?" he whispered. "Do you imagine the flames licking off his skin?"

He wondered if he had finally found an Achilles' heel to the brave, unflinching Special Agent O'Dell.

He set the articles aside. Underneath, he discovered a bigger treasure—a leather appointment book. He flipped to the upcoming week, immediately disappointed. The anger returned as he double-checked the penciled notation. She would be in Kansas City at a law enforcement conference. Then he calmed himself and smiled again. Maybe it was better this way. Still, what a shame Agent O'Dell would miss his debut in Newburgh Heights.

CHAPTER 13

Sunday, March 29

Maggie unpacked the last of the boxes labeled Kitchen, carefully washing, drying and placing the crystal goblets on the top cupboard shelf. It still surprised her that Greg had allowed her the set of eight. He claimed they had been a wedding gift from one of her relatives, though Maggie didn't know anyone remotely related to her who could afford such an expensive gift or have such elegant taste. Her own mother had given them a toaster oven, a practical gift void of sentiment, which more likely reflected the characteristics of the O'Dells she knew.

The goblets reminded her that she needed to call her mother and give her the new phone number. Immediately, she felt the familiar tightness in her chest. Of course, there would be no need for the new address. Her mother rarely left Richmond and wouldn't be visiting any time soon. Maggie cringed at the mere thought of her mother invading this new sanctuary. Even the obligatory phone call felt obtrusive to her quiet Sunday. But she should call before leaving for the airport. After years, flying still unhinged her, so why not take her mind off being out of control at thirty thousand feet with a conversation that was sure to clench her teeth?

Her fingers moved reluctantly over the numbers. How could this woman still make her feel like a twelve-year-old caretaker, vulnerable and anxious? Yet, Maggie had been more mature and competent at twelve than her mother ever was.

The phone rang six, seven times, and Maggie was ready to hang up when a low, raspy voice muttered something incomprehensible.

"Mom? It's Maggie," she said in place of a greeting.

"Mag-pie, I was just going to call you."

Maggie grimaced, hearing her mother use the nickname her father had given her. The only time her mother called her Mag-pie was when she was drunk. Now Maggie wished she could just hang up. Her mother couldn't call her without the new number. Maybe she wouldn't even remember this call.

"You wouldn't have gotten me, Mom. I just moved."

"Mag-pie, I want you to tell your father to stop calling me."

Maggie's knees buckled. She leaned against the counter.

"What are you talking about, Mom?"

"Your father keeps calling me, saying stuff and then just hanging up."

The counter wasn't good enough. Maggie made it to the step stool and sat down. The sudden nausea and chill surprised and annoyed her. She placed her palm against her stomach as if that would calm it.

"Mom, Dad's gone. He's been dead for over twenty years." She gripped a kitchen towel, the nearest thing she could lay her hands on. My God, could this be some new dementia brought on by the drinking?

"Oh, I know that, sweetie." Her mother giggled.

Maggie couldn't ever remember her mother giggling. Was this a sick joke? She closed her eyes and waited, not sure there would be an explanation, but certain she had no idea how to continue this conversation.

"Reverend Everett says it's because your father still has something he needs to tell me. But hell, he keeps hanging up. Oh, I shouldn't swear," and she giggled, again.

"Mom, who's Reverend Everett?"

"Reverend Joseph Everett. I told you about him, Mag-pie."

"No, you haven't told me anything about him."

"I'm sure I have. Oh, Emily and Steven are here. I've got to go."

"Mom, wait. Mom..." But it was too late. Her mother had already hung up.

Maggie dragged her fingers through her short hair, resisting the urge to yank. It had only been a week...okay, maybe two weeks, since she had talked to her last. How could she be making so little sense? She thought about calling her back. She hadn't even given her the new phone number. But then her mother wasn't in any condition to remember it. Maybe Emily and Steven or Reverend Everett—whoever the hell these people were—maybe they could take care of her. Maggie had been taking care of her mother for far too long. Maybe it was finally someone else's turn.

The fact her mother was drinking again didn't surprise Maggie. Years ago, she had accepted the compromise. At least when her mother was drinking she wasn't attempting suicide. But that her mother thought she was talking to her dead husband disturbed Maggie. Plus, she hated the reminder that the one person who had truly loved her, loved her unconditionally, had been dead for more than twenty years.

Maggie tugged the chain around her neck and brought out the medallion from under her shirt collar. Her father had given her the silver cross for her First Holy Communion, claiming it would protect her from evil. Yet, Maggie couldn't help remembering that his own identical cross had not saved him when he ran into that burning building. She often wondered if he had honestly believed it would protect him.

Since then Maggie had witnessed enough evil to know that a body armor of silver crosses would never be enough to protect her. Instead, she wore the medallion out of remembrance for her brave father. The medal against her chest dangled between her breasts and often felt as cool and hard as a knife blade. She let it remind her that there was a fine line between good and evil.

In the last nine years she had learned plenty about evil, its power to destroy completely, to leave behind empty shells that once were warm, breathing individuals. All those lessons were meant to train her to fight it, to control it, to eventually annihilate it. But in doing so, it was necessary to follow evil, to live as evil lives, to think as evil thinks. Was it possible that somewhere along the way evil had invaded her without her realizing it? Was that why she felt so much hatred, so much need for vengeance? Was that why she felt so hollow?

The doorbell rang, and again Maggie had her Smith & Wesson in her hand before she realized it. She tucked the revolver into what was becoming its regular spot, the back waistband of her jeans. Absentmindedly, she pulled down her T-shirt to conceal it.

She didn't recognize the petite brunette standing on her front portico. Maggie's eyes searched the street, the expanse between houses, the shadows created by trees and bushes before she moved to disarm the security system. She wasn't sure what she expected. Did she honestly believe Albert Stucky would have followed her to her new house?

"Yes?" she asked, opening the door only wide enough to place her body in the space.

"Hi!" the woman said with a false cheerfulness.

Dressed in a black-and-white knit cardigan and matching skirt, she looked ready for an evening out. Her dark shoulder-length hair didn't dare move in the breeze. Her makeup enhanced thin lips and concealed laugh lines. The diamond necklace, earrings and wedding ring were modest and tasteful, but Maggie recognized how expensive they were. Okay, so at least the woman wasn't trying to sell anything. Still, Maggie waited while the woman's eyes darted around her, hoping for a glimpse beyond the front door.

"I'm Susan Lyndell. I live next door." She pointed to the split-timber house, only a corner of its front roof visible from Maggie's portico.

"Hello, Ms. Lyndell."

"Oh, please call me Susan."

"I'm Maggie O'Dell."

Maggie opened the door a few inches more and offered her hand, but stayed solidly in the doorway. Surely the woman didn't expect an invitation inside. Then she caught her new neighbor glance toward her own house and back at the street. It was a nervous, anxious look, as though she was afraid of being seen.

"I saw you on Friday." She sounded uncomfortable, and it was obvious she wasn't here to welcome Maggie to the neighborhood. There was something else on her mind.

"Yes, I moved in on Friday."

"Actually I didn't see you move in," she said, quick to make the distinction. "I mean at Rachel's. I saw you at Rachel Endicott's house." The woman stepped closer and kept her voice soft and calm even though her hands were now gripping the hem of her cardigan.

"Oh."

"I'm a friend of Rachel's. I know that the police..." She stopped and glanced this time in both directions. "I know they're saying Rachel may have just left on her own, but I don't think she would do that."

"Did you tell Detective Manx that?"

"Detective Manx?"

"He's in charge of the investigation, Ms. Lyndell. I was simply there trying to lend a hand as a concerned neighbor."

"But you're with the FBI, right? I thought I heard someone say that."

"Yes, but I wasn't there in an official capacity. If you have any information, I suggest you talk to Detective Manx."

All Maggie needed was to step on Manx's toes again. Cunningham had already questioned her competency, her judgment. She wouldn't let some prick like Manx make matters worse. However, Susan Lyndell didn't seem pleased with Maggie's advice. Instead, she stalled, fidgeting, her eyes darting around while she seemed to become more and more agitated.

"I know this is an awkward introduction, and I certainly apologize, but if I could just talk to you for a few minutes. May I come in?"

Her gut told her to send Susan Lyndell home, to insist she call the police and talk to Manx. Yet, for some reason she found herself letting the woman into her foyer, but no farther.

"I have a flight to catch later this afternoon," Maggie allowed impatience to show in her voice. "As you can see I haven't had time to unpack, let alone pack for a business trip."

"Yes, I understand. It's quite possible I'm simply being paranoid."

"You don't believe Ms. Endicott just left town for a couple of days? Maybe to get away?"

Susan Lyndell's eyes met Maggie's and held her.

"I know there was something...something in the house that suggests Rachel didn't do that."

"Ms. Lyndell, I don't know what you've heard—"

"It's okay." She stopped Maggie with a wave of a small hand, long slender fingers that reminded Maggie of a bird's wing. "I know you can't divulge anything you may have seen." She fidgeted again, shifting her weight from one foot to another as though her high-heeled pumps were the cause of her discomfort. "Look, I don't have to be a rocket scientist to know that it's not routine for three police cruisers and the county medical examiner to come rescue an injured dog. Even if it belongs to the wife of Sidney Endicott."

Maggie didn't recognize the man's name nor did she care. The less she knew about the Endicotts, the easier it would be to keep out of this case. She crossed her arms over her chest and waited. Susan Lyndell seemed to interpret it as having Maggie's full attention.

"I think Rachel was meeting someone. I think this someone may have taken her against her will."

"Why do you say that?"

"Rachel met a man last week."

"What do you mean she met a man?"

"I don't want you to get the wrong impression. It's not something she's in the habit of doing." She said this quickly, as if needing to justify her friend's actions. "It just sort of happened. You know how that is." She waited for some sign of agreement from Maggie. When there was none, she hurried on. "Rachel said there was this...well, she described the guy as wild and exciting. It was strictly a physical attraction. I'm sure she had no intention of ever leaving Sidney," she added as though needing to convince herself.

"Ms. Endicott was having an affair?"

"Oh God, no, but I think she was tempted. As far as I know, it was just some heavy-duty flirting."

"How do you know all this?"

Susan avoided Maggie's eyes, pretending to watch outside the window.

"Rachel and I were friends."

Maggie didn't point out that Susan had suddenly switched to past tense. "How did she meet him?" she asked, instead.

"He's been working in the area for the last week or so. On the phone lines. Something to do with new cable that's going to be laid. I haven't heard much about it. It seems like they're constantly putting in something new and different in this area."

"Why do think this man may have taken Rachel against her will?"

"It sounded like he was getting serious, trying to escalate their flirting. You know how guys like that can be. They really just want one thing. And for some reason they always seem to think us lonely, rich wives are more than ready to let them—" She stopped herself, realizing she may have revealed more than she intended. Immediately, she looked away, her face a bit flushed, and Maggie knew Susan Lyndell was no longer talking about her friend, but speaking from experience. "Well, let's just say," she continued, "that I have a hunch this guy wanted more from Rachel than she meant to give him."

The image of the bedroom came to Maggie. Had Rachel Endicott invited a telephone repairman to her bedroom and then changed her mind?

"So you think she may have invited him in and that things got carried away?"

"Isn't there something in the house that makes it look that way?"

Maggie hesitated. Were Susan Lyndell and Rachel Endicott really friends, or was Susan simply looking for some juicy gossip to share with the other neighbors?

Finally Maggie said, "Yes, there is something that makes it look like Rachel was taken from the house. That's all I can tell you."

Susan paled beneath the carefully applied makeup and leaned against the wall as though needing the support. This time, her response seemed genuine.

"I think you need to tell the police," Maggie told her again.

"No," she said quickly, and immediately her face grew scarlet. "I mean,

I…I'm not even sure she met him. I wouldn't want Rachel to get in trouble with Sid."

"Then you need to at least tell them about the telephone repairman so they can question him. Have you seen him in the area?"

"Actually, I've never seen him. Just his van once—Northeastern Bell Telephone Company. I'd hate to have him lose his job because of my hunch."

Maggie studied the woman who clutched and wrung the hem of her cardigan. Susan Lyndell didn't care about some nameless repairman's job.

"Then why are you telling me all this, Ms. Lyndell? What do you expect me to do?"

"I just thought…well…" She leaned against the wall again, and seemed flustered that she had no clue what she expected. Yet, she made a weak effort to continue. "You're with the FBI. I thought maybe you could find out or do a check…you know, discreetly without…well, I guess I don't know."

Maggie let the silence hang between them as she examined the woman's discomfort, her embarrassment.

"Rachel's not the only one who's flirted with a repairman, is she, Ms. Lyndell? Are you afraid of your husband finding out? Is that it?"

She didn't need to answer. The anguished look in Susan Lyndell's eyes told Maggie she was right. And she wondered if Ms. Lyndell would even call Detective Manx, though she promised to as she turned and left, hurrying away, her head pivoting with worried glances.

CHAPTER 14

Tess McGowan smiled at the wine steward who waited patiently. Daniel had rambled on into the cellular phone the whole time the tall young man had uncorked the bottle and poured the obligatory amount for the taste test. At first, when he noticed Daniel on the phone, he had offered the glass to Tess. She quickly shook her head. Without a word, she directed the steward to Daniel with her eyes, so as not to embarrass the inexperienced man, whose smooth, boyish face still blushed.

Now they both waited. She hated all the interruptions. It was bad enough they were having an unusually late Sunday dinner because of Daniel's business dealings. Why couldn't he, at least, take Sundays off? She fingered the long-stemmed rose he had brought her, and found herself wishing that just once he could be more creative. Why not some violets or a clump of daisies?

Finally, Daniel firmly, but calmly, called the person on the other end of the line "an incompetent asshole." Fortunately for Tess and the wine steward, that was his closing.

He snapped the cellular phone in half and slipped it into his breast pocket. Without looking up, he grabbed the glass, sipped then spit the wine back without giving it a swirl in his mouth.

"This is sewer water. I asked for a 1984 Bordeaux. What the hell is this crap?"

Tess felt her nerves tense in anticipation. Not again. Why couldn't they ever go out without Daniel making a scene. She watched the poor wine steward twist the bottle around, desperate to read the label.

"It *is* a 1984 Bordeaux, sir."

Daniel snatched the bottle from the young man's hands and took a look. Immediately, he snorted under his breath and handed it back.

"I don't want a goddamn California wine."

"But you said domestic, sir."

"Yes, and as far as I remember, New York is still in the United States."

"Yes, of course, sir. I'll bring another bottle."

"So," Daniel said, letting her know he was ready to talk to her though his hands rearranged his silverware and folded the napkin in his lap. "You said we had something to celebrate?"

She pushed up her dress strap, wondering why she had spent two hundred and fifty dollars on a dress that wouldn't stay up on her. A sexy, black dress that Daniel hadn't noticed. Even when he looked up at her, he raised an eyebrow at her fumbling instead of at the dress, and instantly he frowned at her. Dear God, she didn't need another lecture about fidgeting in public. The man spent more time rearranging his dinnerware than he did eating, and yet, he felt he could lecture her about fidgeting. She pretended not to notice his frown and launched into her good news. If she kept enthusiastic, he couldn't possibly ruin this night for her. Could he?

"I sold the Saunders' house last week."

His brow furrowed, reminding her that he didn't have time to remember where the hell each of her clients lived.

"It's the huge Tudor on the north side. But the best part is that Delores is letting me keep the entire selling bonus."

"Well, that *is* good news, Tess. We should be having champagne and not wine." He turned in his chair, going into what looked like a search-and-destroy mode. "Where the hell is that incompetent imbecile?"

"No, Daniel, don't."

He scowled at her for squelching his noble gesture, and she hurried to correct it.

"You know I enjoy wine much more than champagne. Please, let's have wine."

He raised his hands in mock defeat. "Whatever pleases you. Tonight is your night."

He began to sip from his water glass but stopped, grabbed his napkin and wiped at the water spots. Tess braced herself for another scene, but Daniel managed to get the glass in satisfactory condition on his own. He replaced his napkin and the glass without taking a sip.

"So, how much is this selling bonus? I hope you didn't spend it all on that overpriced frock that won't stay on your shoulders."

She felt the heat crawl up her neck before she had a chance to contain it.

"Of course not." She kept her voice strong and managed a quick smile, pretending to enjoy his savage attempt at what he called dry humor.

"So? How much?" he wanted to know.

"Almost ten thousand dollars," she said, holding up her chin proudly.

"Well, that is a nice little chunk of change for you, isn't it?"

This time he sipped his water without cleaning the glass. Already his eyes darted around the room, looking for familiar faces. She knew it was a sort of professional habit and not meant to be rude, but each time, she felt as though he was hoping to be rescued from a mundane conversation with her.

"Do you think I should invest it?" she asked, hoping to bring his attention back to her with the one topic he loved to discuss.

"What's that, sweetie?" His eyes only glanced at her. He had spotted a couple he seemed to know at the reservation stand, waiting for their table.

"The bonus. Do you think I should invest it in the stock market?"

This time he looked back at her with that smile she immediately recognized as the beginning of another lesson.

"Tess, ten thousand dollars really isn't enough for you to be getting into the market. Maybe a nice little CD or less risky mutual fund. You really don't want to mess with something you don't understand."

Before she could protest, his cellular phone started ringing. Daniel quickly flipped it out of his pocket as though it were the most important thing in the room. Tess pushed up her strap. Why kid herself. The damn phone *was* the most important thing in the room.

The wine steward returned, glanced at Daniel on the phone again, and Tess wanted to laugh at the young man's pained expression.

"Why the hell is it so hard to fucking get this right?" Daniel barked into the phone loud enough for other diners to look over. "No, no, forget it. I'll do it myself."

He slapped the phone shut and was on his feet before he had it tucked back into his pocket.

"Tess, sweetie, I need to go take care of something. These idiots can't seem to get one fucking thing right." He pulled out a credit card and slipped out two hundred-dollar bills from his money clip. "Please have a shamefully expensive dinner to celebrate your bonus. And you don't mind taking a cab home, do you?"

He handed her the credit card and the folded bills. He pecked her on the cheek and then left before she could object. But she noticed he had enough time to stop at the door and talk to the couple he had seen earlier.

Suddenly, she realized the wine steward was still at the table and now staring at her, stunned and waiting for her instructions.

"I think I'd like the bill, please."

He continued to stare, then held up the uncorked bottle. "I didn't even pour one glass."

"Enjoy it later with the other waiters."

"Are you serious?"

"I'm serious. On me. Really. Oh, and before you bring the bill, would you add two of the most expensive entrées you have on the menu."

"You want them as takeout?"

"Oh no. I don't want them at all. I just want to pay for them." She smiled and held up the credit card. Finally, he seemed to get the message, smiled back and hurried off to take care of it.

If Daniel insisted on treating her like a hooker, she could certainly accommodate him. Maybe her silly little mind couldn't possibly comprehend something as complex as the stock market, but there were plenty of other things she knew about that Daniel didn't have a clue about.

She signed the bill for the wine steward, making sure to add a hefty tip for him. Then she took her two hundred dollars and hailed a cab, hoping the anger would burn off by the time she got home. How could he ruin this for her? She had been looking forward to a celebration. Maybe ten thousand dollars was a drop in the bucket for Daniel, but for her it was a tremendous accomplishment in a long journey uphill. She deserved a pat on the back. She deserved a celebration. Instead, she had a long, lonely cab ride home from D.C.

"Excuse me," she said, leaning forward in the stale-smelling cab. "When we get to Newburgh Heights, forget the address I gave you. Take me to Louie's Bar and Grill on Fifty-fifth and Laurel."

CHAPTER 15

Kansas City, Missouri
Sunday evening

It was almost midnight when Agents Preston Turner and Richard Delaney knocked on Maggie's hotel-room door.

"How 'bout a nightcap, O'Dell?"

Turner wore blue jeans and a purple golf shirt that enhanced the rich brown of his skin. Delaney, on the other hand, still wore a suit, his lopsided tie and open collar the only indications that he was no longer on duty.

"I don't know, guys. It's late." Not that sleep mattered. She knew she wouldn't be going to bed for hours.

"It's not even midnight." Turner grinned at her. "Party's just gettin' started. Besides, I'm starved." He glanced back at Delaney for reassurance. Delaney only shrugged. Five years older than both Turner and Maggie, Delaney had a wife and two kids. Maggie imagined Delaney had been a conservative Southern gentleman even when he was ten years old, but somehow Turner managed to bring out a reckless competitive side.

Both men noticed that Maggie had answered the door with her Smith & Wesson gripped firmly in her right hand, dropped at her side. However, neither mentioned it. Suddenly it felt extra heavy. She wondered why they put up with her, though she knew Cunningham purposely assigned the three of them to the same conferences. They had been her shadows since Stucky had escaped last October. When she complained to Cunningham, he had been insulted by her accusation that he was providing watchdogs to make certain she didn't go after Stucky on her own. Only later did it occur to her that her boss might do so in an attempt to protect her. Which was ridiculous. If Albert Stucky wanted to hurt her, no show of force would stop him.

"You know you guys don't need to baby-sit me."

Turner pretended to be wounded and said, "Come on, Maggie, you know us better than that."

Yes, she did. Despite their mission, Turner and Delaney had never singled her out as some damsel in distress. Maggie had spent years working to be treated like one of the guys. Perhaps that's why Cunningham's motive, however honorable or well intentioned, still angered her.

"Ah, come on, Maggie," Delaney finally joined in. "Knowing you, your presentation is all ready for tomorrow."

Delaney politely stayed in the hallway while Turner leaned against the door frame as though taking up permanent residence until she agreed.

"Let me get my jacket."

She closed the door enough to make Turner retreat into the hall and give her some privacy. She strapped on her holster, looping the leather contraption over her shoulder and buckling it tight against her side. Then she slid her revolver in and put on a navy blazer to hide the bulge.

Turner was right. The nearby bar and grill in what was called Westport buzzed with late-night conventioneers. Turner explained that the midtown Bohemian district, which still showed quaint signs of its early days as a trading post, was "KC's nightlife hub." How Turner always knew these details Maggie had never bothered to find out. It did seem as if Turner quickly became the expert at finding the hot spots in every city they visited.

Delaney led the way, squeezing through the crowd along the bar and finding a table in a dark corner. Only when he and Maggie sat down did they realize they had lost Turner, who had stopped to talk to a couple of young women perched on bar stools. From their tight knit dresses and shiny dangling earrings, Maggie took a wild guess that they weren't law enforcement officers, but rather a couple of single women looking to meet a man with a badge.

"How does he do that so easily?" Delaney asked, watching and admiring.

Maggie glanced around while she scooted her chair against the wall so she could see the entire room. She hated having her back to a crowd. Actually, she hated crowds. Clouds of cigarette smoke hung over the room like fog settled in for the evening. The din of voices and laughter blended together, making it necessary to speak louder than comfortable. And though she would be with Turner and Delaney, she hated the looks thrown her way, some of which reminded her of vultures waiting for their prey to be left alone and vulnerable.

"You know, even when I was single, I hated dating," Delaney confessed, still watching his buddy. "But Turner makes it all look so easy." He twisted his chair closer to the table and leaned in as though ready to give Maggie his full attention. "So what about you? Are you thinking about getting back into the game?"

"The game?" She had no idea what he was talking about.

"The dating game. What's it been? Three, four months?"

"The divorce isn't final yet. I just moved out of the condo on Friday."

"I didn't realize the two of you were still living together. I thought you broke up months ago."

"We did. It was more practical for both of us to live there until things were settled. Neither one of us is hardly ever there."

"Shoot! For a minute there I thought maybe the two of you were thinking about giving it another shot." He looked hopeful. She knew Delaney was a firm believer in marriage. Despite admiring his partner's finesse at dating, Delaney seemed to love being married.

"I don't think reconciliation is possible."

"You sure?"

"What would you do if Karen made you choose between her and being in the FBI?"

He shook his head, and before he answered she was sorry she'd asked. He pulled his chair closer and his face got serious. "Part of the reason I became an instructor was because I know Karen gets nervous about me being in the middle of hostage negotiations. That last one in Philly, she had to watch most of it on TV. Some sacrifices are worth making."

She didn't want to have this conversation. Discussing her failed marriage accomplished nothing these days except to remind her of the hollowness in her gut.

"So I'm the bad guy because I'm not willing to sacrifice my career to make my husband feel better?" The anger in her voice surprised her. "I would never ask Greg to stop being a lawyer."

"Relax, Maggie. You're not the bad guy." Delaney remained calm and sympathetic. "There's a big difference between asking and expecting. Karen would never have asked. *I* made the decision. Besides, Greg's got some major screws loose if he would let you get away, period."

Her eyes met his, and he smiled, then quickly looked back around to see that Turner was still with his new friends. Though Delaney, Turner and Maggie spent hours together, week after week, there were usually no emotional revelations or personal discussions.

"Do you miss it?"

He glanced back at her and laughed. "What's to miss? Standing in freezing-cold or stinking-hot weather for hours, trying to talk some asshole out of blowing away innocent people?" He rested his elbows on the table and scratched his jaw, his eyes serious again. "Yeah, I do miss it. But I get called in on a case every now and then."

"What can I get you two?" a waitress asked as she squeezed between two diners to get to their table.

Immediately, Maggie felt a wave of relief, welcoming the interruption. She saw Delaney's face relax, too.

"Just Diet Coke for me." He smiled up at the pretty redhead.

Maggie was impressed with his unconscious flirting. Had it simply become a habit from hanging around Turner so long?

"Scotch, neat," she said when the waitress looked her way.

"Oh, and that guy over at the end of the bar—" Delaney pointed "—it doesn't look like it now, but he will eventually be joining us. Is your grill still on?"

The waitress checked her watch. A small beauty mark above her upper lip twitched as she scrunched her eyes to make out the time. In the dim light, Maggie could see the lines of exhaustion in the woman's attractive face.

"They're supposed to close down at midnight." She kept her voice friendly though Maggie could tell it was an effort. "There are still a few minutes if I get it in now." Her offer was genuine. "Any idea what he wants?"

"A burger and fries," Delaney said without hesitation.

"Medium rare," Maggie added.

"With pickles and onion."

"And a bottle of A.1 sauce, if you have it."

"Oh, and cheddar cheese on the burger, too."

The waitress smiled at them. Maggie glanced at Delaney, and they burst out laughing.

"God, I wonder if Turner realizes how predictable he is?" Maggie said while wondering if there was anyone who paid as much attention to her habits and quirks.

"It sounds like the three of you are very good friends." The waitress had relaxed, looking a little less fatigued. "I don't suppose you know what he'll be drinking?"

"Do you have Boulevard Wheat?" Delaney asked.

"Of course. Actually, it's a Kansas City brew."

"Okay. Well, that's what he'll want."

"I'll get his order in and bring back your drinks. Sure I can't get either of you something to eat?"

"Maggie?" Delaney waited for her to shake her head. "Maybe some fries for me."

"You got it."

"Thanks, Rita," Delaney added as though they were old friends.

As soon as she left their table, Maggie gave Delaney's shoulder a shove. "I thought you said you weren't good at this stuff?"

"What stuff?"

"This flirting stuff. Usually Turner's doing it, so I don't get to see the real master at work."

"I don't have any idea what you're talking about." But it was obvious from his grin that he was enjoying the attention.

"'Thanks, Rita'?"

"That's her name, Maggie. That's why they wear those name tags, so we can all share a friendly meal."

"Oh, right, only she never gets to know our names or sit down and eat with us. How friendly is that?"

"Hey, guys." Turner slid into the last chair. "Lots of attorneys here this time."

"Those two women are attorneys?" Delaney craned his neck to get a better look.

"You betcha." He waved a piece of paper with their phone numbers before tucking it into his pocket. "And I never know when I might need an attorney."

"Yeah, right. Like the three of you were talking legal matters."

Maggie ignored their banter and simply asked, "What conference is this anyway?"

Both men stopped and stared at her as if waiting for the punch line.

"You're serious?" Turner finally asked.

"Hey, I make the same presentation every time, whether I'm in Kansas City or Chicago or L.A."

"You really don't get into these things, do you?"

"It's definitely not why I joined the FBI." Suddenly she felt uncomfortable with both of them studying her as if she had slipped and said something wrong. "Besides, Cunningham keeps my name off the program roster, so it's not like anyone is coming specifically to hear me and my words of wisdom."

She had interrupted their jovial moods, reminding them why she was really here. Not because she longed to teach profiling to a bunch of cops, but to keep her out of the field, away from Albert Stucky. Rita returned, relieving Maggie once again, this time with a tray of drinks. Turner immediately raised his eyebrows at her when she placed the bottle of beer and a glass in front of him.

"Rita, you're a mind reader." He wasted no time using her name just as Delaney had, as if they, too, were old friends.

The pretty waitress blushed, and Maggie watched Delaney, searching for signs of rivalry. Instead, he seemed pleased to leave the flirting to his single friend.

"Your burger and fries should be ready in about ten minutes."

"Oh my God! Rita, will you marry me?"

"Actually, you should thank your friends. They got the order in just before Carl closed the grill." She smiled at Maggie and Delaney this time. "I'll bring out the rest of the order as soon as it's ready." Then she hurried away.

Maggie couldn't help thinking that Rita was a seasoned waitress who already knew which of her customers were the big tippers. Turner rewarded his waiters and waitresses with attention and familiarity, but it was Maggie or Delaney who remembered to leave a substantial tip.

"So, Turner," Delaney said. "Why are there attorneys at this conference?"

"Mostly prosecutors. Sounds like they're all here for that computer workshop. You know, the database thing the Bureau's been setting up. Lots of D.A. offices are finally getting connected. At least in the bigger cities. And since they're all *sooooo* very busy, and can never spare an experienced attorney, it looks like they've sent their fresh young things." He sat back and surveyed the room.

Maggie and Delaney shook their heads at each other. Just as Maggie tipped back her glass, she saw a familiar figure in the long mirror that stretched behind the bar. She slammed her glass down and stood, sending the table rocking and her chair screeching. She looked over in the direction from where she thought the mirror had reflected the image.

"Maggie, what is it?"

Turner and Delaney stared at her as she stretched to see over the bar patrons. Was it her imagination?

"Maggie?"

She checked the mirror again. The figure in the black leather jacket was gone.

"What's going on, Maggie?"

"Nothing," she said quickly. "I'm fine." Of course she was fine. Yet her eyes searched for and found the door. There was no man in a long, black leather jacket coming or going.

She sat down, pulling her chair in and avoiding her friends' eyes. They were getting used to her jumpy, erratic behavior. Soon, she'd be like the little boy who cried wolf, and no one would pay any attention. Maybe that was exactly what he wanted.

She grabbed her glass and watched the amber liquid swirl. Had it only been her imagination? Had she really seen Albert Stucky or was she simply losing her mind?

CHAPTER 16

He waited for her at the rear exit, knowing this was the door she would use when she was finally ready to leave. The alley was dark. The brick buildings stood tall enough to block out any moonlight. A few bare lightbulbs glowed above some of the back doors. The bulbs were dull, covered with bug shit and swarmed by moths, but still his eyes stung when he looked at them directly. He tucked his sunglasses into his jacket pocket and checked his watch.

Only three cars remained in the small parking lot. One was his, and he knew neither of the other two belonged to her. He knew she wouldn't be driving this night. He had decided to offer her a ride, but would she accept?

He knew how to be charming. That was simply a part of the game, a part of his disguise. If he was to take on this new identity, he would need to play the role that came with it. And out of the two of them, women always preferred him to Albert.

Yes, he knew what women liked to hear, and he didn't mind telling them. In fact, he enjoyed it. It was part of the manipulation, an integral piece of the puzzle to gaining complete control. He had discovered that even strong, independent women didn't mind giving up control to a man they found charming. What silly, wonderful creatures. Maybe he would give her his sad story about his failing eyesight. Women loved being caretakers. They loved to play roles of their own.

The challenge excited him, and he could feel his erection swelling. He would have no trouble tonight. Now, if he could just wait. He must be patient—patient and charming. Could he be charming enough to get her to invite him home with her? Already, he tried to imagine what her bedroom looked like.

A door screeched open halfway down the alley, and he stepped into the shadows. A short, burly guy in a stained apron came out to toss several trash bags into the Dumpster. He lingered, lighting a cigarette and sucking in several quick drags before stomping it out and going back in.

Most of the other places had closed. He didn't worry about being seen. If anyone noticed him, he could tell them almost anything, and they would believe it. People heard what they wanted to hear. Sometimes it was too easy. Though if he had guessed right, she would be a bit of a challenge. She was much older, much more street savvy than the cute little pizza girl. He would need to do some serious talking to get her to trust him. He would need to pour on the charm, compliment her and make her laugh. Again, he could feel his erection as he thought of winning her over, wondering how far he could go.

Perhaps he would start with a gentle touch, a simple caress of her face. He'd pretend he was getting a strand of her lovely hair out of her eyes or tell her she had an eyelash on her cheek. She would think him concerned, attentive and sensitive to her needs. Women loved that crap.

Suddenly the door opened, and there she was. She hesitated, looking around first. She checked the sky. A light mist had begun about fifteen minutes ago. She popped open a bright red umbrella and started walking quickly toward the street. Red was definitely her color.

He waited, giving her a head start, while he reached down and checked the scalpel, safe in its custom-made, leather sheath, and tucked inside his boot. He caressed its handle, his fingers lingering, but he left it there. Then he followed her down the alley.

CHAPTER 17

Monday, March 30

Tess McGowan awoke with a splitting headache. Sunlight streamed through her bedroom blinds like lasers. Damn it! She had gone to bed again without removing her contact lenses. She threw her arm over her eyes. Why hadn't she gotten the type she could leave in forever? She hated this recent reminder of her age. Thirty-five was not old. Okay, so she had squandered her twenties. She wasn't doing the same with her thirties.

Suddenly she realized she was naked beneath the covers. And then she felt the sticky mess beside her. Alarmed, she pushed herself up, keeping the bedsheets to her breasts, searching the room through blurred vision for clues.

Why couldn't she remember Daniel being here? He never stayed over at her house. He said it was too quaint. She noticed her clothes in a tangled mess on the chair across the room. Heaped on the floor next to the chair were what looked like men's trousers, the tips of shoes peeking out from underneath. A black leather bomber jacket hung from the doorknob. She didn't recognize it as anything Daniel would wear. That's when she heard the shower, aware of its sound only as the water stopped. Her pulse quickened as she tried to remember something, anything, from last night.

She checked the bedside stand. It was eight forty-five. Somehow she remembered it was Monday morning. She knew she didn't have any appointments on Mondays, but Daniel would. Why couldn't she remember him coming over? Why couldn't she remember herself coming home?

Think, Tess! She rubbed her temples.

Daniel had left the restaurant and she had taken a cab home, but of course she hadn't gone straight home. The last thing she did remember was doing tequila shooters at Louie's. Had she called Daniel to pick her up? Why couldn't she remember? And would he be furious if she asked him to fill in the blanks? Obviously he hadn't been angry with her last night, and she shifted away from the damp spot.

She laid her head back on the pillows, squeezing her eyes shut and wishing the throbbing would stop threatening to split her head open.

"Good morning, Tess," a rich, deep voice came into the room.

Before she could open her eyes, she knew the voice didn't belong to Daniel. In a panic she sat up again and pushed her back against the headboard. The tall, lean stranger with only a blue towel wrapped around his waist looked startled and concerned.

"Tess?" he said softly. "You okay?"

Then she remembered, as if a dam broke loose in her brain, releasing the memories in a flood. He had been at Louie's, watching her from the corner table, handsome and quiet, so very unlike anyone who frequented Louie's. How could she have brought him into her home?

"Tess, you're starting to scare me."

His concern seemed genuine. At least she hadn't brought home a mass murderer. But then, how in the world did she think she'd know the difference? With his hair still wet, he looked harmless, wrapped in only a towel. Immediately she noticed his hard, firm body and realized he would be strong enough to overpower her without much effort. How could she have been so foolish?

"I'm sorry. I...you startled me." She tried to keep the alarm from her voice.

He grabbed his trousers from the floor but stopped suddenly before putting them on as if something had just occurred to him.

"Oh Christ! You don't remember, do you?"

Beneath the morning bristles, his boyish face looked embarrassed. He fumbled into his trousers, stumbling once and accidentally dropping the towel before the trousers were all the way up. Tess watched, flustered and annoyed that his muscular body was turning her on, despite her confusion. She should be worried he could hurt her, instead she found herself wondering how young he was. And dear God, why couldn't she remember his name?

"I should have known you had too much to drink," he apologized as he frantically searched for his shirt, going through her things and carefully folding them as he put them back on the chair. He stopped at her bra, and his embarrassment only grew. His distraught politeness made her smile. When he glanced over at her, he did a double take, startled by her expression. He sank into the chair, now ignoring her clothes and absently wringing his hands and her bra without realizing it.

"I'm a complete idiot, aren't I?"

"No, not at all." She smiled again, and his obvious discomfort relaxed her. She sat up, keeping the sheet carefully pressed against her as she drew her knees up to her chest and placed her arms on top to rest her chin.

"It's just that I don't do this sort of thing," she tried to explain. "At least, not anymore."

"I don't usually do this sort of thing at all." He noticed her bra in his hands, folded it and set it on the nearby bookcase. "So you really don't remember any of last night?"

"I remember you watching me. I remember being very attracted to you." Her revelation surprised her almost as much as it surprised him.

"That's it?" He looked wounded.

"Sorry."

Finally, he grinned and shrugged. She couldn't believe how comfortable she felt with him. There was no more panic, no more alarm. The only tension seemed to be the obvious sexual attraction, which she tried to ignore. He didn't look as if he was even thirty. And he was a stranger, for heaven's sake. She wanted to kick herself. Dear God! How could she have been so reckless? Had she not changed at all after all this time?

"If I ever find my shirt, could I maybe take you to lunch?"

Then she remembered Daniel. How would she explain any of this to Daniel? She felt the sapphire ring he had given her stabbing into the soft underside of her chin, like some painful reminder. What was wrong with her? Daniel was a mature, respectable businessman. Sure, he was arrogant and self-absorbed sometimes, but at least he wasn't some kid she had picked up in a bar.

Still, she watched the handsome young stranger put on socks and shoes while he waited for her answer. He glanced around the room in search of the missing shirt. Her toes felt a wad at the end of the bed. She reached beneath the covers, unearthing a pale blue, wrinkled oxford shirt. She held it up to him and instantly remembered having worn the shirt. The memory of him taking it off her made her cheeks flush.

"Is it salvageable?" he asked, stretching to take it from her while keeping a safe distance.

He was being a gentleman, pretending he hadn't had access to every inch of her body only hours ago. The thought should have repulsed or terrified her. It didn't. Instead, she continued to watch him, enjoying his nervous but fluid motions, yet at the same time annoyed with herself. She should not be noticing that the color in his shirt brought out the blue flecks in his otherwise green eyes. How had she been so certain he wouldn't hurt her? One of these days a stranger's eyes might not be a safe way to judge his character.

"So what about lunch?" he asked, looking as though he was steeling himself for further rejection. He had trouble buttoning the shirt, had it almost finished when he realized he was off a button and started all over again.

"I don't even remember your name," Tess finally admitted.

"It's Will. William Finley." There was a glance and a hesitant smile. "I'm twenty-six, never been married. I'm a lawyer. Just moved to Boston, but I'm visiting a friend here in Newburgh Heights. His name's Bennet Cartland. His father has a law practice here. Pretty high-profile one, actually. You can check it out if you want." He hesitated. "Probably more than you wanted to know, right?" When she rewarded him with a smile, he continued. "What else? I have no diseases, except I did have the mumps when I was, like, eleven, but then so did my buddy, Billy Watts, and he has three kids. Oh, but don't worry, I used protection last night."

"Um...there's a damp spot," she said quietly.

When he met her eyes, the embarrassment seemed to be replaced by a flicker of desire that his memory must have triggered.

"I had only two condoms, but the third time I...well, I pulled out before, well, you know."

Suddenly she remembered the intensity, could feel it fill her body. The unfamiliar rush surprised her, frightened her. She couldn't allow herself to slip back into her old habits. She wouldn't. Not now when she had worked so hard.

"I think maybe you better leave, Will."

He opened his mouth to say something, maybe to try to change her mind. He hesitated, staring at his feet. She wondered if he wanted to touch her. Did he have the urge to kiss her goodbye or to convince her to let him stay? Maybe she even wanted him to. Instead, Will Finley found his jacket on the doorknob and left.

She lay back into the pillows, now noticing remnants of his aftershave, a subtle scent, not like Daniel's overpowering musk. Dear God, twenty-six fucking years old! Almost ten years her junior. How could she be such an idiot? Yet, this time when she closed her eyes, their night together started coming back to her in clear, crisp sights and sounds and sensations. She could feel his body rubbing against hers, his tongue and hands playing her like some delicate instrument, knowing just where and when to touch her and how to send her to places she hadn't been in a long time.

The memories that embarrassed her more were those of her own urgency, her own hunger, her own fingers and mouth devouring him. They had taken turns ravishing each other as if they had been starving. The passion, the urgency, the desires were nothing new. She had experienced plenty in her sordid past. What was new, what was different had been Will's gentle caresses, what seemed to be a genuine concern that she feel the same pleasure, the same sensations he was experiencing. What was new and different was that she and Will Finley hadn't just had sex last night, but that Will Finley had actually made love to her. Perhaps she should have taken some comfort in that realization. Instead, it stirred up an unsettling restlessness within her.

Tess rolled onto her side, twisting her pillow and hugging it to her. She couldn't let someone like Will Finley sidetrack her. Not now. Not when she had worked so hard for what she had. She needed to remain focused. She needed to think of Daniel. Despite their differences, Daniel gave her credibility in a community where credibility was everything. He was good for her in all the ways that were necessary for her to become a respected, successful businesswoman. So why did she feel as though she had let something valuable slip from her fingers when she asked Will Finley to leave?

CHAPTER 18

Will slammed the front door, rattling its beveled glass. For a brief moment, his anger gave way to concern while he checked to make sure he hadn't cracked or broken anything. The door looked old but solid. The glass looked custom-made, maybe antique. Not that he would know such things. But he had noticed that Tess McGowan had a taste for antiques. Her small cottage was decorated with an eclectic mix, creating a soothing, comfortable environment. He had felt incredibly warm and cozy waking up and being surrounded by lavender sheets and wallpaper with tiny little violets.

Last night when she invited him in, he had initially been surprised. He would never have guessed that the wild, passionate woman who had shamelessly hustled him at pool while throwing back tequila shooters would surround herself with old lace, hand-carved mahogany and what looked like original watercolors. But after only one night, he knew Tess McGowan's home was a reflection of a woman who was as passionate and independent as she was sensitive and vulnerable.

It was that unexpected vulnerability that had made it difficult to leave. It had surprised him last night—or was it already early this morning—when he held her in his arms. She had curled into his body as though finding some long-sought-after shelter.

He scraped a sleeve over his face in an attempt to wake up to reality. Christ! Where did he come up with this crap? Vulnerability and finding shelter. He sounded like something out of a fucking chick flick.

He got into his car and immediately glanced up at what he knew to be the bedroom window. Hell, maybe he expected her to be standing there, watching him. But it was easy to see no one was standing behind the sheer curtain.

He felt angry again, used. It was ridiculous. He was the one who had picked her up. His friends had dared him, goaded him into one last fling before his impending wedding. A wedding that at one time seemed far into the future was now suddenly less than a month away.

At first he did it simply to shock his friends. They'd never expect good ole' Will, the eternal choirboy, to flirt with any woman, let alone a woman like Tess. Geez, maybe he needed some new friends, ones whose maturity levels weren't stuck back in college. But he couldn't blame them for his stupidity last night, nor for his going as far as he had. Nor could he say he'd had too much to drink, because unlike Tess, he had known exactly what he was doing from start to finish.

He had never met anyone like Tess McGowan. Even before she shed her conservative black shawl and started shooting pool with the bar's owner, Will thought she was the sexiest woman he had seen. It wasn't like she was a knockout or centerfold-sexy. She was definitely attractive, with thick, wavy hair she wore loose and down to her shoulders. And she had a good body, not like some bulimic model, but with plenty of curves and amazing shapely legs. God, he got hot just thinking about her. Just thinking about running his hands over the curve of her hips and the swell of her breasts.

Back at Louie's, long before he had up-close-and-personal access, it wasn't those curves so much as it was the way she moved—it was the way she carried herself that had gotten his attention. His and everyone else's. And it was like she enjoyed the attention, enjoyed putting on a show, hiking her dress's skirt up to her thighs to take a shot while straddling the corner of the table. Every time she leaned over her pool cue, the strap of her dress slipped off her shoulder, the silky fabric allowing just a peek at her voluptuous breasts captured behind black lace.

Will shook his head and jammed the key into the ignition. It had been a hell of a night, one of the most passionate, erotic, exciting nights of his life. Instead of being angry, he should be patting himself on the back that Tess McGowan was letting him off with no strings attached. He was a lucky bastard. Hell, he hadn't been with another woman since he and Melissa had started seeing each other. And four years of sex with Melissa couldn't come close to one night with Tess.

He glanced up at the bedroom window again, and caught himself hoping Tess would be there. What was it about this woman that made him not want to leave? Was he simply imagining that there had been some connection, some special bond? Or had it just been sex?

He checked his wristwatch. He had a long trip back to Boston. He'd be pushing it to get there in time for dinner with Melissa and her visiting parents. It had been the only reason he had taken off a precious Monday from his brand-new job. And here he was, miles away from Boston and miles away from even thinking about Melissa.

Christ! How would Melissa not see the betrayal in his eyes? How fucking stupid was he to risk throwing away the last four years for one night of passion? So if it was such a mistake, why hadn't he left already? Why couldn't he get Tess's fragrance, the taste of her skin, the sounds of her passion... why couldn't he erase it all? Why did he want to go back up and do it all over again? That certainly didn't sound like a remorseful guy. What the hell was wrong with him?

He shifted the car into gear and peeled out of her driveway, letting his frustration squeal the tires. He swerved into the street and almost sideswiped a car parked at the opposite curb. Briefly the man behind the wheel glanced up at him. He wore sunglasses and had a map spread over the dash as though he was looking for directions. Tess's neighborhood was blocks away from any major thoroughfare. Immediately, Will wondered if the guy had been watching the house. Was it possible this was the owner of the expensive sapphire ring Tess wore on the wrong hand?

Will checked the rearview mirror and took one last look at the car. Then he noticed it had District of Columbia license plates instead of Virginia. Maybe because it was a little odd, maybe because he was a new assistant D.A.—hell, maybe it was just out of curiosity about the type of man who thought he owned Tess McGowan. Whatever the reason, Will committed the license number to memory, then headed back to Boston.

CHAPTER 19

The conference room went silent as soon as Maggie walked through the door. Without hesitating she continued to the front, disappointed to find the room arranged for a lecture. Chairs were set side by side, all facing the front of the room instead of at long, narrow tables as she had requested. She preferred more of a business setting where she could scatter crime scene photos in front of the participants. Where they felt more comfortable discussing rather than simply listening. However, the only table in the room was filled with coffee, juice, soft drinks and an assortment of pastries.

She felt her audience's stares as she pulled up a chair for her briefcase. Then, she began digging through the contents, pretending to search for something she had to have before she could start. Instead, she was waiting for her stomach to settle. She had eaten breakfast hours ago, and never got nauseated anymore before presentations. But her lack of sleep and several additional Scotches in her room last night, long after Turner and Delaney had left her, now punished her with a fuzzy head and a dry mouth. It was definitely not a good way to start a Monday.

"Good morning," she finally said, buttoning her double-breasted jacket. "I'm Special Agent Margaret O'Dell with the FBI. I'm a criminal profiler with the Investigative Support Unit at Quantico, which some of you may still refer to as the Behavioral Science Unit. This workshop focuses—"

"Wait a minute, ma'am," a man in the second row interrupted, shuffling uncomfortably in a chair that was too small to accommodate his considerable size. He wore tight trousers, a crisp, short-sleeved button-down shirt that stretched across his swollen belly, and scuffed shoes that refused to look new despite a fresh polish.

"Yes?"

"No disrespect intended, but what happened to the guy who was supposed to give this workshop?"

"Excuse me?"

"The program..." He looked around the room until he seemed to find encouragement from some of his comrades. "It said the guy wasn't just an FBI profiler, but an expert in tracking serial killers, a forensic psychologist with, like, nine or ten years' experience."

"Did the program actually say this person was a man?"

Now he looked puzzled. Someone beside him handed over a copy of the conference's program.

"Sorry to disappoint you," Maggie said, "but I'm him."

Most of the men simply stared at her. One woman in the group rolled her eyes in empathy when Maggie looked her way. Maggie recognized two men in the back. She had briefly met the Kansas City detectives Ford and Milhaven last night at the Westport bar and grill. Both men smiled as though they were in on her secret.

"Maybe they should say that in the program," the man persisted, trying to justify his objection. "They don't even use your name."

"Would it matter?"

"Yeah, to me it would've. I came here to learn some serious stuff, not listen to some desk jockey."

Her evening dosage of Scotch must have desensitized her emotions. Instead of feeling angry, his chauvinism simply made her feel more exhausted.

"Look, Officer—"

"Wait a minute. What makes you think I'm an officer? Maybe I'm a detective." He shot a smug grin to his buddies, giving himself away and reinforcing Maggie's initial assessment.

"Let me take a shot here," she said, walking to the center of the room, standing in front of him and crossing her arms. "You're a street cop in a metropolitan area, but not here in Kansas City. You're used to wearing a uniform and not business attire, not even business casual. Your wife packed your bag and picked out what you're wearing now, but you've gained some weight since she last bought anything for you. Except the shoes. You insisted on wearing your beat shoes."

Everyone including the officer shuffled in their chairs to get a look at his shoes. She failed to point out the subtle but permanent indentations in his close-cropped hair from too many hours spent wearing a hat.

"You're not able to carry your weapon at the conference, but you feel lost without your badge. It's inside your jacket pocket." She motioned to the tan jacket hidden by his hefty bulk and draped over the back of the chair. "Your wife also insisted on the jacket, but again you're not used to wearing one. Not like perhaps a detective might be used to wearing a jacket and tie."

Everyone waited as if watching a magic act, so the officer reluctantly twisted around, tugged at the jacket and brought out his badge to show them.

"All lucky guesses," he said to Maggie. "Whatcha expect from a roomful of cops?"

"You're right. You're absolutely right." Maggie nodded as eyes came back to her face, still waiting, still testing. "Most of what I said might be seen as obvious. There's a certain profile that goes along with being a cop. Just like there's a certain profile that goes along with being a serial killer. If you can pinpoint what those characteristics are and which ones apply—though some of them may seem obvious—you can use that information, that knowledge, as the beginning foundation for a profile."

Finally she had their attention, and with their minds diverted from what she looked like to what she was saying, her entire body began to relax, to access some auxiliary energy and override her initial fatigue.

"However, the tricky part is looking beyond the obvious, picking apart and examining small tidbits that might seem insignificant. Like, for instance, in this case—I'm sorry, Officer, would you mind telling me your name?"

"What? You mean you can't guess that?" He smirked, proud of what he considered a quick comeback and drawing a few laughs from the others.

Maggie smiled.

"No, I'm afraid my crystal ball leaves out names."

"It's Danzig, Norm Danzig."

"If I were to examine your profile, Officer Danzig, I'd try to break down everything I did know."

"Hey, you can examine me all you like." He continued to play with her, enjoying the attention, while looking at his buddies instead of Maggie.

"I'd wonder," she continued, ignoring his comment, "why your wife had bought clothes for you that were the wrong size."

Suddenly Officer Danzig sat still and quiet.

"I'd ask myself if there was a reason." From the rising color in his face, Maggie knew the reason was one he didn't care to expose. Her guess was that he and his wife had not shared a bed for some time. Perhaps there had even been a temporary separation, one that included Officer Danzig eating a few more fast-food meals. That could account for the extra pounds his wife hadn't expected when she purchased his clothes for the conference. Instead of embarrassing him with her theory, she simply said, "I'd guess your wife finally got fed up with you wearing the same outdated navy blue suit that you keep in the back of your closet."

The others laughed, and Officer Danzig looked around at them, smiling with relief. But when his eyes met Maggie's, she saw a hint of humbled awareness. His subtle show of appreciation was the slightest shift in his chair, crossing his arms, facing the front of the room as if finally ready to give her his full attention.

"It's also important not to get bogged down by the stereotypes." She began her ritual pacing. "There are a handful of stereotypes that seem to be perpetuated with serial killers. We should start by laying some of those to rest. Anyone care to guess what some of those stereotypes are?"

She waited out their silence. They were still summing her up. Finally, a young Hispanic man decided to take a shot.

"How about the idea that they're all crazy. They're total mental cases. That's not necessarily true, right?"

"Right. In fact, many serial killers are intelligent, well educated and as sane as you and I."

"Excuse me," a graying detective from the back of the room interrupted. "Son of Sam claiming a Rottweiler made him do it, that's not mental?"

"Actually it was a black Labrador named Harvey. But even Berkowitz later owned up to the hoax when profiler John Douglas interviewed him.

"I'm not saying some of these killers are not crazy, what I am saying is that it's a mistake to believe they have to be insane to do the things they do. When, in fact, killing for them is a conscious choice. They are masters of manipulation. Their crimes are all about dominating and controlling their victims. It's not usually because they hear orders to kill from a three-thousand-year-old demon living inside a black Lab.

"If they were simply nuts, it wouldn't be possible for them to carry out their elaborate murders over and over again—to perfect their methods and still avoid getting caught for months, sometimes years. It's important to recognize them not as deranged crazies, but for what they are. What they are is evil."

She needed to change the subject before she got carried away with a sermon on the effects of evil. How there was a shadow side to everyone's human nature; a shadow side that was capable of evil. But to discuss it always led to the question of what made some step over the line, while others dared not. After years of examining evil, Maggie hadn't a clue what that answer was.

"What about motive?" she asked instead. "What are some of the stereotypical motives?"

"Sex," a young man in the back said loudly, enjoying the sudden attention and laughs that the single word drew. "Don't most serial killers get some sexual gratification from killing, just like rapists?"

"Hold on," the one woman challenged. "Rape isn't about sex."

"Actually, that's not a true statement," Maggie said. "Rape is very much about sex."

Immediately there were a few sighs, some disgruntled shakes of heads as though they expected this from a woman.

"Rape is very much about sex," she repeated, ignoring their skepticism. "It's the one variable that distinguishes rape from any other violent crime. No, that's not to say that rapists rape simply for sexual gratification, but yes, they do use sex as one of their weapons to achieve their goals. So it's wrong to say rape isn't about sex when sex is definitely one of the weapons they use.

"In fact, rapists and serial killers use sex and violence in much the same way. Both are powerful weapons used to degrade the victim and gain control. Some serial killers even start out as serial rapists. But somewhere along the line they decide to take it a step further to achieve their gratification. They might begin by experimenting to reach different levels, starting with torture, working up to strangulation or stabbing. Sometimes that's not enough, so they begin different rituals with the dead body. That's when you see cases like the Pied Piper who sliced up his victims, made stew and fed it to his other captives.

She caught several of them grimacing. Skepticism seemed to be replaced by morbid curiosity.

"Or in Albert Stucky's case," she continued, "he began to experiment with different rituals of torture, slicing off victims' clitorises or nipples, just to hear them scream and plead with him."

She said these things calmly and casually, yet she could feel the tension in her muscles, an involuntary reflex as her body seemed to prepare for flight or fight anytime she thought of Stucky.

"Or you find more solemn rituals," she said, trying to expel Stucky from her mind. "Last fall in Nebraska, we tracked a killer who gave his young victims their last rites after he strangled and stabbed them to death."

"Hold on," Detective Ford interrupted. "Nebraska? You're the profiler who worked on that case with the dead little boys?"

Maggie cringed at the simplicity of his description.

"Yes, that was me."

"Morrelli was just telling us about that case last night."

"Sheriff Nick Morrelli?" An unexpected but pleasant flutter invaded her already tense body.

"Yeah, we all went out for ribs last night. But he's not Sheriff Morrelli anymore. Turned in his badge for a suit and tie. He's with the D.A.'s office in Boston."

Maggie retreated to the front of the room, hoping the distance would shield her and prevent them from witnessing her sudden discomfort. Five months ago, the cocky, small-town sheriff had been a thorn in her side from the day she arrived in Platte City, Nebraska. They had spent exactly one week chasing a killer and sharing an intimacy so palpable, just the thought of it was able to generate heat. Her class was staring at her, waiting. How was it possible for Nick Morrelli to dismantle her entire thought process by simply being in the same city?

CHAPTER 20

Tully reached under his glasses and tried to rub out the exhaustion. As though blaming them for lack of relief, he pulled the glasses off, tossing them onto one of the many piles on his desk. The glasses used to be for reading only. Now he found himself wearing them more often.

Ever since he'd hit forty three years ago, his body parts seemed to be failing him, one by one. Last year it was surgery on his knee, just a torn ligament, but it had put him out of commission for two weeks. Of course, it didn't help matters having a fourteen-year-old daughter telling him how "out of sync" he was. It seemed as if he couldn't do anything right as far as Emma was concerned.

Earlier she had been furious with him for having to spend another evening next door with Mrs. Lopez. Maybe that was part of the reason he was still here working, stalling, avoiding going home to his own daughter and the silence she wielded as punishment. Ironically, this was the same daughter he had fought so hard to keep near him.

Though it wasn't much of a fight once Caroline realized what kind of freedom she might have without the responsibility of a teenage daughter. This was the same woman who couldn't bear to be separated from her daughter and husband six or seven short years ago, when she took an account executive job at a national advertising firm. But as the high-profile clients rolled in and the promotions took her all the way to the top, somehow those expensive trips to New York City and London and Tokyo seemed to get a lot easier. By the final years of their marriage, she had become a stranger to him. A beautiful, sophisticated, ambitious woman, but a complete stranger.

Tully stretched back in his chair, lacing his fingers together behind his head. God, how he hated change! He glanced around the small fluorescent-lit room. He missed having an office with windows. In fact, if he even thought about being sixty feet under ground, he knew his claustrophobia would easily kick in. He had seriously considered turning down the position at Quantico, knowing the Investigative Support Unit was still located in what he considered the bowels of the training facility.

He was rubbing his eyes again when he heard the tap on his open door.

"Agent Tully, you're here late."

Assistant Director Cunningham wore shirtsleeves, but still carefully buttoned at the wrists and collar, whereas Tully's sleeves were rolled up in uneven folds and shoved above his elbows. Cunningham's tie was cinched tight at his neck, making Tully self-conscious about his own, now wrinkled and tossed aside somewhere on a file cabinet, leaving his collar unbuttoned and open.

"I was waiting for a phone call from the medical examiner," Tully explained. "From Dr. Holmes."

"And?"

The assistant director leaned against the door, and Tully wondered if he should clear off one of the chairs. Unlike his boss's immaculately neat office, Tully's looked like a storage closet, with piles of papers, scattered files and overflowing bookcases. He sorted through the stack of notes from his phone call, not wanting to depend on his memory, which at this time of night had shut down like a computer hard drive.

"The girl...the young woman had an incision in her left side that extended to the small of her back about four inches long. Dr. Holmes said it was very precise, almost as if he had performed surgery on her."

"Sounds like our boy."

"He removed her spleen."

"A spleen isn't very big, is it? It looked like there was much more in that pizza box."

Tully reached for the copy of *Gray's Anatomy* that he had borrowed from the library. He quickly thumbed to the place where he had used a gum wrapper as a bookmark. He grabbed his glasses.

"The spleen is about five inches in length, three inches in breadth and an inch or an inch and a half in thickness," he read out loud, then closed the book and set it aside. "The book says the spleen weighs about seven ounces, but that depends on what stage of digestion it's in. It can get much bigger. Our victim hadn't eaten much that day, so her spleen was fairly small. Dr. Holmes said that some of the pancreas was also attached."

"Were there fingerprints found anywhere at the scene?"

"Yes, we got two pretty good ones—a thumb and an index finger. But they're not matching Stucky's. It's possible they may have been made accidentally by someone on the scene, but it sure seems as though they were left behind on purpose. The entire rim of the Dumpster was wiped down, and then there are these two fingerprints right smack in the middle."

Cunningham frowned, his weathered brow creasing as if he remembered something. "Double-check Stucky's early file. Make sure the prints haven't been switched or altered or that there were any computer mistakes. If I remember correctly, Agent O'Dell was finally able to identify him because of a fingerprint Stucky left behind. He blatantly left it behind, too. But it took us a while to identify it at the time. Someone hacked into the county computer system and switched the prints on file."

"I'll double-check, sir, but we're not dealing with a county sheriff department's computer system here. We're checking these against the ones AFIS has on Stucky, prints they've taken directly off Stucky. And with all due respect, I don't think anyone can easily hack into the Bureau's system." AFIS (Automated Fingerprint Identification System) was the FBI's master database. Though it networked with local, state and federal agencies, dozens of precautions were in place against computer hackers.

Cunningham sighed and scratched his jaw. "You're probably right," he conceded with a fatigue Tully hadn't witnessed before.

"It may end up being a rookie cop's," he told his boss, as if hoping to relieve some of Cunningham's exhaustion. "If it is, we'll know in the next twenty-four hours. If they don't make a match to any law enforcement officers, then I'll have someone do a cold search."

Tully kept his glasses in place, feeling more alert with them on and needing to appear in control. "Sir, I haven't found anything that would suggest Stucky is trying to send some sort of message by which organ he extracts. I wonder if I'm missing something."

"No, you're not missing anything. Stucky does this for shock value and simply because he can," Cunningham said as he came farther into Tully's office, but remained standing.

"Did he study to be a surgeon at some point in his life?" Tully flipped through a file Agent O'Dell had put together on Stucky's past. In many ways it read like a résumé for a Fortune 500 executive.

"His father was a doctor." Cunningham wiped a hand over his jaw. Tully recognized the gesture as something his boss did when exhausted and trying to retrieve information from his vast memory bank. He took the opportunity to study his boss's face, which seemed thinner, the hollows in his cheeks and eyes darker in the fluorescent light. Even exhausted, his posture remained straight, no hunched shoulders as he now leaned against the bookcase. Everything about the man spoke of a quiet dignity.

Finally he continued, "If I remember correctly, Stucky and his partner started one of the first Internet, online stock-trading companies. Made millions and has it stashed in foreign banks."

"If we could track some of those accounts, maybe we could track him."

"The problem is we've never been able to find out how many different accounts he has or what names he uses. Stucky's sharp, Agent Tully. He's cunning, very intelligent and almost always in control. He's not quite like any of the others. He doesn't kill because he needs to, or because it's a mission or some urgency. Or even because he hears some inner voices. He kills for one major reason—because he enjoys it. It's a game for him to manipulate, to break down the human spirit, to shock people with what he's capable of doing, and also to thumb his nose at those of us who are trying to catch him."

"Certainly even Albert Stucky makes mistakes."

"Let's hope so. Have you found anything on where the victim may have been taken?"

Again, Tully dug out his notes from a variety of stacks, not wanting to depend on his fatigued memory. Immediately he found himself self-conscious and a bit embarrassed. His notes were scrawled on everything from a deli napkin to a brown paper towel from the men's rest room.

"We know she was taken before she finished her route. There were some customers who called complaining they hadn't received their pizzas. The manager is working on getting me a list of the addresses she was to deliver to."

"Why is that taking so long?"

"They write down the addresses in one place as the orders are phoned in. The delivery person takes the only copy."

"You're kidding," Cunningham sighed, and for the first time Tully thought he saw that it was an effort for him to confine his frustration. "Doesn't seem very efficient."

"It's probably never been a problem until now. The lab is trying to raise the addresses from the indentations on the notepad page underneath. Of course, our best bet is if we find the victim's car. Maybe the lists will have been left behind."

"Any luck finding the car?"

"Not yet. I got the make, model and plate number from DMV. Detective Rosen put out an APB. Nothing's shown up so far."

"Have Reagan National and Dulles airport security check their long-term parking lots."

"Good idea." Tully jotted another note to himself, this time using the cash-register receipt from his lunch. Why the hell didn't he have notepads like the rest of the world?

"He had to take her someplace," Cunningham said, staring over Tully's head, lost in thought. "Somewhere he could have plenty of uninterrupted time with her. I'm guessing he didn't go far from where he apprehended her. If we could get that list, we might be able to narrow down some possible locations."

"The thing is, sir, I've driven around within a ten-mile radius of where the body was found. The whole area is this picture-book community. We're not going to find any abandoned warehouses or condemned buildings."

"It's also easy to miss the most obvious place, Agent Tully. You can bet Stucky will be gambling on us doing just that. What else do you have?" he asked more brusquely now as he stood away from the bookcase, suddenly in a rush.

"There was a cellular phone recovered from the Dumpster. It was reported stolen a few days ago from a local shopping mall. I'm hoping once I get the phone record, maybe it'll lead us someplace, depending on what calls were placed."

"Good. Sounds like you've got everything under control." Cunningham started to leave. "Let me know what help you need. Unfortunately, I can't promise a whole task force again, but maybe I can pull a few people from other cases. Now, you need to go home, Agent Tully. Spend some time with your daughter."

He pointed to the photo Tully kept on the edge of his desk. It was the only one he had. It included the three of them, arms wrapped around each other and smiling for the camera. It couldn't have been taken that long ago, and yet he couldn't remember them being that happy. It was the first time

Cunningham had referred to Tully's personal life. He was surprised his aloof boss remembered that his wife hadn't made the move with him.

"Sir?"

Cunningham stopped halfway into the hall.

Tully wasn't sure how to ask. "Should I give Agent O'Dell a call?"

"No." The answer was brisk and firm.

"You want to wait until we're sure it's Stucky?"

"I'm ninety-nine percent certain it is Stucky."

"Then shouldn't we at least tell Agent O'Dell?"

"No."

"But, sir, she might—"

"What part of my answer did you not understand, Agent Tully?" Again, his manner was firm without raising his voice. Then he turned and left.

CHAPTER 21

Once again, Turner and Delaney dragged Maggie from her hotel room to join them for dinner. This time their new Kansas City friends, Detectives Ford and Milhaven, treated them to what they claimed was the best barbecue place in the city, located not far from the bar and grill they had visited the night before.

Maggie had never seen two men put away more ribs than her FBI buddies. Their compulsion to compete with each other was ridiculous and getting old. Although Maggie recognized it was no longer for her benefit, but was now extended to their new friends. Ford and Milhaven encouraged Turner and Delaney's heartburn fest like spectators at a major sporting event. Ford had even placed a five-dollar bill on the table for the first man who would clean the current stack of ribs off his plate.

Maggie sat back, sipped her Scotch and tried to find something more interesting to watch through the dimly lit, smoke-filled restaurant. She found her eyes wandering to the entrance. She half expected to see Nick Morrelli walk in, and then realized she had no idea what she would do if he were to show up. Ford had told Maggie after class that he and Nick had gone to college together at the University of Nebraska. He said he had left a message at the hotel's front desk for Nick to join them at dinner. Now hours later, Nick obviously hadn't gotten the message or had other plans for the evening. Yet, Maggie found herself watching for him. It was ridiculous, but just knowing that he was at the conference had stirred up all those feelings she thought she had safely tucked away since the last time she had seen him.

That was over five months ago. To be more precise, it had been the Sunday after Halloween when she left Platte City, Nebraska, to go home to Virginia. She and Nick, who had been the county sheriff at the time, had spent exactly one week together, hunting a religious psychopath who had murdered four little boys. Two men had been captured and were awaiting trial, neither of whom Maggie was convinced was the real killer. Despite all the circumstantial evidence, Maggie still believed the real killer was a charismatic Catholic priest named Father Michael Keller. Only, Keller had disappeared somewhere in South America, and no one, not even the Catholic Church, seemed to know what had happened to him.

For the last five months, all Maggie had come up with were rumors of a handsome young priest who traveled from one small farming community to another, serving as their parish priest, though no assignment had officially been made. By the time Maggie tracked down the location, the elusive priest was gone, disappearing into the night with no explanation. Months later, the rumors would find him at another small parish, miles away. But again, by the time the location was narrowed down, Keller was gone. It was as though the communities protected him, keeping him safe like some fugitive unjustly accused. Or perhaps like some martyr.

The thought made Maggie sick to her stomach. That was what Maggie believed to be Keller's motive for murdering boys he thought were abused. He had hoped to make martyrs of them, as though he could administer a perfectly evil salvation. It seemed unfair that Keller would now be protected like a martyr, instead of executed for the evil monster he was. She wondered how long it would take before these poor farmers would start to find their little boys dead along some riverbank, strangled and stabbed to death but washed clean and given their last rites.

Would they be willing to see Keller punished then? There seemed to be a problem with punishing evil these days, an evil that gained strength by conspiring with other evil. Maggie knew Keller had been the one who had visited Albert Stucky in a Florida prison. Several guards had later identified Keller from a photograph. And though she had no proof, she also knew it had been Keller who had given Stucky the wooden crucifix. It was that dagger-like crucifix Stucky had used to cut himself free of his restraints and stab a transport guard.

She shook the thought from her mind and gulped the remainder of her Scotch. Turner and Delaney looked as though they were finally at a standstill. Delaney looked miserable. Turner's brown face had a greasy sheen to it, despite his efforts at wiping it clean. She was about to order another Scotch when Ford waved down the waitress for the check. Neither detective had allowed any of the FBI agents to pay. Maggie insisted on at least leaving the tip, which Ford did allow. Maybe he realized his detective's salary would never be able to keep up with Turner and Delaney's appetites.

Milhaven had driven them, but Maggie wished she could walk rather than be squashed once again into the Grand Am's back seat between her two bodyguards. The night was clear but crisp enough to provoke a shiver. Before they got to the parking lot, they noticed a gathering in the alley. One uniformed cop stood in front of a metal Dumpster and attempted to keep a small crowd of well-dressed onlookers at a distance.

Without a word, the detectives and FBI agents made their way to the scene.

"What's the problem here, Cooper?" Ford knew the frustrated officer.

"Let's move out of the way," Milhaven said to the onlookers as he and Delaney pushed them back into the parking lot that ran parallel to the alley.

The officer glanced at Maggie and Turner.

"It's okay," Ford reassured him. "They're FBI. Here for the conference. So what's going on?"

Officer Cooper pointed to the Dumpster behind him with a tilt of his head.

"Dishwasher at the Bistro took out the trash about a half hour ago. Noticed a hand sticking up out of the pile. Freaked. Called it in, but not before he announced it to the whole goddamn world."

Maggie felt the familiar knot in her stomach. Turner was already at the Dumpster, his six-foot-three frame allowing him to look over the edge without assistance. Maggie dragged an empty milk crate and joined him. Now she wished she hadn't drunk so much. She paused and waited for the brief spell of light-headedness to pass.

The first thing Maggie noticed was a red umbrella, its handle looped over the edge of the Dumpster as if the owner hadn't meant for it to be mistaken for trash. Or had it purposely been left as evidence?

"Officer Cooper." She waited for his attention. "You might mention to the detectives when they arrive that there's an umbrella here. It probably should be bagged and taken in for fingerprints."

"Will do."

Without disturbing anything, Maggie could see the woman was naked and lying on her back. The patch of red pubic hair was a stark contrast to the white skin. Immediately, Maggie knew the scene had been tampered with. Officer Cooper said the dishwasher had noticed only a hand sticking up out of the pile, yet the woman's entire torso was exposed. What looked like vegetable peels had been tossed onto her face. Her head was turned to the side, her brilliant red hair littered with pieces of leftovers.

Maggie could see the woman's mouth, partially opened as though something may have been shoved inside. Then she noticed a dot, a beauty mark above the upper lip. The knot in her stomach tightened. She leaned forward, stretched on tiptoe, sending the crate wobbling while she reached in.

"O'Dell, what the hell are you doing?" Turner scolded her as he watched.

Gently, she swiped at a potato peel and a clump of angel-hair pasta that was stuck to the side of the woman's face.

"It's Rita," she said, wishing she had been wrong.

"Rita? Rita who?"

Maggie waited, glanced at Turner and watched the recognition register on his face.

"Shit! You're right."

"You guys know her?" Ford asked as he looked over the top.

"She's a waitress from the bar and grill down the street," Maggie explained as her eyes continued to examine what she could of Rita's body.

Her throat had been slashed, so deep it had nearly decapitated her. The rest of her body had few bruises and no punctures except for her wrists, which showed ligature marks. Whatever the method of capture, the struggle had been minimal, suggesting that hopefully death had come quickly. Maggie found herself relieved and at the same time disparaged to be relieved by such a thing.

Then she saw the bloody incision in Rita's side underneath a mass of spaghetti. She shoved herself away from the Dumpster, half jumping, half falling off the crate. The light-headedness was quickly replaced by a dizzy buzz. She rushed a safe distance away before she wrapped her arms around herself to stop the wave of panic. Damn it! She never got sick at crime scenes anymore. But this was different. This was a mixture of dread and fear, not nausea.

"O'Dell, you okay?"

Turner was at her side. His large hand touched her shoulder, startling her. She avoided his eyes.

"Stucky did this," she said, keeping her voice steady and free of the quiver invading her lower lip.

"O'Dell, come on now."

"I thought I saw him when we were in the bar and grill last night."

"As I remember, we all had plenty to drink."

"No, Turner, you don't understand. Stucky must have seen her. He must have noticed us talking, joking with her. He chose her because of me."

"O'Dell, we're in Kansas City. You're not even on the conference roster. Stucky couldn't possibly know you're here."

"I know you and Delaney think I'm losing it. But this is exactly Stucky's M.O. We should start looking for a container, a take-out container, before someone else finds it."

"Look, O'Dell. You're just on edge."

"It's him, Turner. I know it. And whatever he sliced out of her is going to show up at some outdoor café table. Maybe even in front of this restaurant. We need to—"

"O'Dell, slow down," he whispered, looking around as if to make sure he was the only one witnessing her hysteria. "I know you're feeling like you need to be checking over your shoulder, thinking—"

"Damn it, Turner. This isn't my imagination."

He went to touch her shoulder again, and this time she jerked back just as she noticed a dark figure across the alley.

"O'Dell, relax."

The man stood at the edge of the crowd, a crowd that had doubled in only a few minutes. He was too far away, and it was too dark for her to be certain, but he wore a black leather jacket, like the man she had seen last night.

"I think he's here," she whispered, and positioned herself behind Turner so she could look without being obvious. Her pulse quickened.

"O'Dell." By the tone of his voice, she knew Turner was growing impatient.

"There's a man in the crowd," she explained, keeping her voice low, "tall, thin, dark, sharp features. From what I can see of his profile, it could be Stucky. My God, he's even carrying what looks like a take-out container."

"As are a whole bunch of others. Come on, O'Dell, this is a restaurant district."

"It could be Stucky, Turner."

"And it could be the mayor of Kansas City."

"Fine—" she let him hear her anger "—I'll just go talk to him myself."

She started around him, but Turner grabbed her arm.

"Stay put and stay cool," he said with an exaggerated sigh.

"What are you going to do?"

"I'm gonna talk to the man. Ask a few questions."

"If it's Stucky—"

"If it's Stucky, I'll recognize the bastard. If it's not, you're picking up the dinner tab tomorrow night. I'm thinking you better get your credit card ready for prime rib."

She watched Turner while trying not to be obvious about it. She positioned herself behind Delaney and Milhaven, who were deep in discussion about baseball. Neither man seemed to notice her. Through the space between them, Maggie could see Turner walk with his casual yet authoritarian gait toward the crowd. She knew he wasn't taking her seriously, and he wouldn't be prepared if it was, indeed, Stucky.

She reached inside her jacket and unsnapped the restraint on her holster, then kept her hand on the butt of the gun. Already her heart was pounding against her rib cage. All other motion, all other conversation stood still as she concentrated on the man in the black leather jacket. Could it really be Stucky? Could the bastard be so arrogant to kill in a city crawling with law enforcement officers from across the country, then stand back and watch? Yes, Stucky would love the challenge. He'd love to be able to thumb his nose at them all. A shiver slid down her back as a night breeze swirled around her, wet and cold.

Turner didn't reach the crowd before the man turned to leave.

"Hey, wait a minute." Turner yelled at the man loud enough for even Delaney and Milhaven to look. "I want to talk to you."

The man bolted and so did Turner. Delaney started to ask Maggie something, but she didn't wait to hear. She raced across the parking lot, gun drawn, its nose to the ground. The crowd scattered out of her way with gasps and one scream.

All Maggie could think was this time Albert Stucky would not escape.

CHAPTER 22

Maggie's heart slammed against her chest. Turner had disappeared around a corner and into another alley. She followed without slowing down and without hesitation. Halfway down, she made herself stop. The alley was unusually narrow, barely wide enough to accommodate a small vehicle. The tall brick buildings blocked out any streetlights. The moon was only a sliver, leaving dim bulbs to light the way, some cracked but most bare, hanging above rickety back doors.

She squinted, examining the shadows and trying to listen over the pounding in her ears. By now she was breathing much too hard from such a short run. Her skin felt clammy. Every nerve ending in her body seemed to be on alert. Her muscles tensed. Where the hell had they gone? She had been minutes, no, seconds, behind them.

Something rattled behind her. She spun around, her Smith & Wesson kept close to her body, but aimed and ready to blow to pieces the empty Burger King cup. She watched the breeze lift and push it down the alley as she tried to steady her nerves. Calm. She needed to stay calm, keep focused.

She turned, keeping her grip firm on the revolver. Again she strained to hear over the thunder in her ears. The cool night air sent a shiver down her back. She needed to breathe, to control the gasps. They were gasps caused by fear, not exhaustion. Damn it! She wouldn't let him do this to her. She needed to slow down. She needed to concentrate.

She took careful steps as she proceeded. The cobblestone street was old, with uneven and chipped bricks, some oddly spaced. It would be easy to twist an ankle, to stumble or trip, to become vulnerable. Still, she didn't look down. She kept her eyes moving, watching though it was difficult to see beyond fifty to a hundred feet. Was it getting darker, or was it simply her imagination? Her eyes darted over everything, checking stacks of boxes, black doorways, rusty fire escapes, anyplace Albert Stucky could hide behind or sneak into. He wouldn't trick her this time.

Where the hell was Turner? She wanted to call out, but couldn't risk it. Was it possible they had run another way? No, she was certain they had disappeared around this corner and into this alley.

Ahead she could see an open space where two cars were parked. A Dumpster blocked her view of the entire area. Behind her in the distance footsteps ran past, missing this narrow alley. From the open space she heard muffled voices. She pushed her body against the grimy brick wall and inched her way along. Her chest ached. Her knees felt mushy. Her palms were sweaty, but she gripped the gun's handle, keeping her finger on the trigger and the gun's nose down.

She came to the edge of the building and had nowhere else to go. She crouched and snuck behind the Dumpster. Where the hell were Delaney and Milhaven? By now they should have backtracked. Her eyes strained to see beyond the darkness to the end of the alley. Nothing. Now the voices ahead of her were more clear.

"Hold on a minute." She recognized Turner's voice. "What the hell do you have there?"

She waited, but there was no answer to his question. If Stucky had a knife, she'd never hear the damage until it was too late. She peeked out just enough to see the back of the leather jacket. Good. He was facing the opposite direction. He wouldn't see her. But how close was he to Turner?

She heard footsteps behind her, making their way noisily toward her over the cobblestone. From her hiding spot, she couldn't see them, couldn't wave them off, couldn't warn them. Damn it! In seconds Stucky would hear them, too, if he hadn't already. She needed to move now, take her chances.

In one quick motion, she jumped out from behind the Dumpster, scrambling to take a firm stance, legs apart, arms in front, aim focused on the back of the bastard's head. It wasn't until she cocked the gun's hammer that she saw Stucky flinch.

"Don't move an inch, or I'll blow your goddamn head off."

"O'Dell," she heard Turner say.

She could finally see him. He was standing close to the building, a shadow covering most of his face. With Stucky between them, Maggie couldn't see if Turner had his gun drawn. Instead, she concentrated on her target, not ten feet in front of her.

"O'Dell, it's okay," Turner told her, yet he still didn't move.

Did Stucky have a gun pointed at him?

"Drop whatever you're holding and put your hands up behind your head. Do it. Now!" she yelled, surprised at her own voice, amplified and bouncing off of the brick buildings.

The footsteps behind her had slowed, their echo making what Maggie knew to be only several men sound instead like a whole troop. She didn't turn. Her eyes never left the back of Stucky's head. He hadn't moved, but hadn't obeyed her command either.

"I said hands up. Now, goddamn it!"

"O'Dell, it's okay," Turner said again.

But there was still no movement, not from Stucky, not from Turner, not from the men keeping their distance behind her. Maggie inched closer. Perspiration trickled down her back. A breeze swept strands of damp hair off her forehead but whipped others into her face. Still, she didn't move, didn't flinch. Her finger remained firmly on the trigger, pressing, ready to squeeze. Her entire body had gone rigid, freezing much too stiffly, threatening to lock her muscles into position.

"Last time. Drop what you're holding and put your hands up behind your head, or I'll blow your skull wide open." This time the ultimatum came through clenched teeth. Maggie's head throbbed. Her hand began to ache from the effort it took not to squeeze the trigger.

Finally, his hands went up while something slapped and crunched against the cobblestone. She could feel it splatter her feet, and knew it was the plastic take-out container he had been carrying. But she refused to look down. She didn't want to see what part of Rita had been spread all over the ground. Instead, she kept her sights on where the nose of her gun pointed, in the middle of the tuft of black hair at the base of his skull. At this close range and at this angle, the bullet would drive through the skull and into the brain, shredding the cerebellum and ripping through the frontal lobe before it exited the top of his forehead. He'd be dead by the time his body hit the ground.

"Ease up, Maggie," she heard Delaney say, and suddenly he was beside her.

The others stayed behind them. Turner stepped out so she could see that he hadn't been injured. Silence filled the alley so completely, she wondered if they were all holding their breaths. Yet, she hadn't dropped her stance or lowered her weapon.

"Turn around," she ordered the back of Stucky's head.

"O'Dell, you can put away your gun," Turner said, but she didn't look at him. She wouldn't slip this time. She wouldn't let her guard down.

"I said turn around, damn it." Her stomach twisted into a series of knots. Would she be able to look him in the eyes?

He turned slowly. Her finger pressed tighter. All it would take was a minor adjustment, a split second for her to refocus between his eyes. Then one more second to squeeze the trigger. But she wanted him to see it coming. She wanted him to look at her. She wanted him to know what it felt like to know another person had total control over his life. She wanted him to feel fear, and yes, she wanted to see that fear in his eyes.

The man stared down at her with wide, frightened eyes, a thin, drawn face and shaking bony hands. He looked as if he'd faint from fear. It was the exact reaction Maggie had dreamed about. It was the exact revenge she had hoped for. Only the man was not Albert Stucky.

Chapter 23

Early Tuesday morning
March 31

Maggie opened her hotel-room door to Delaney. Without a word or an invitation, she turned and walked back into the room, leaving him there while she continued the pacing he had interrupted. Out of the corner of her eyes, she saw him hesitate. Even after coming in, he held on to the doorknob, looking as though he wished he could escape. She wondered how he and Turner had decided which of them would talk to her. Had Delaney lost the coin toss?

She ignored him as he walked across the room, careful to stay out of her path. He sat down at a small table that wobbled when he leaned his elbows on it. He picked up her empty plastic glass and fingered the miniature bottle of Scotch, giving both a sniff before replacing them. His shirtsleeves were rolled up. His collar button opened. His tie removed. He looked wrinkled and tired. During one of her turns, she saw him rub his hands over his bristled face and up through his thinning hair. She'd make him speak first. She was in no mood to talk. And certainly in no mood for a lecture. Why couldn't they just leave her alone?

"We're worried about you, Maggie."

So there it was. He'd have to start with a low blow, all that worrying-and-caring stuff. Plus, he was using her first name. This was serious stuff. She almost wished Turner had come instead. At least he would yell a little.

"There's no need to worry," she said calmly.

"Look at you. You're wound so tight you can't even sit still."

She shoved her hands into the pockets of her trousers, briefly alarmed, noticing for the first time how baggy the pants felt. When had she lost weight? She continued to pace, keeping her hands hidden in her pockets. No sense in showing Delaney how badly her hands had been shaking since she'd returned to her room.

"It was an honest mistake," she defended herself before he had a chance to make the obvious accusation.

"Of course it was."

"From the back he looked exactly like Stucky. And why the hell did he ignore my instructions three times?"

"Because he doesn't understand English."

She stopped and stared at him. The thought had never occurred to her. Of course it hadn't. She had been convinced it was Stucky. There had been no doubt in her mind.

"Then why did he run from Turner?"

"Who knows." Delaney dug his fingers into his eyes. "Maybe he's an illegal alien. Point is, Maggie, you not only made him splatter his veal capellini all over the pavement, you almost blew his frickin' head off."

"I did not almost blow his head off. I followed protocol. I couldn't see Turner. I couldn't see what this fucking idiot had in his hands, and he wasn't responding. What the hell would you have done, Delaney?"

His eyes met hers for the first time, and she held him there, despite his discomfort.

"I probably would have done the same thing." But his admission made him look away.

Maggie thought she saw a hint of embarrassment. There was more to this little visit than concern or a lecture. She braced herself and leaned against the chest of drawers, the only solid piece of furniture in the room.

"What's going on, Delaney?"

"I called Assistant Director Cunningham," he said, glancing up at her but avoiding her eyes. "I had to tell him what happened."

"Goddamn you, Delaney," she said under her breath, and began pacing once more to steady the brewing anger.

"We're worried about you, Maggie."

"Right."

"I saw the look in your eyes, Maggie, and it scared the hell out of me. I saw how much you wanted to pull the trigger."

"But I didn't, did I? Doesn't that count for anything? I didn't pull the goddamn trigger."

"No, not this time."

She stopped at the window and stared down at the lights of the plaza below. She bit her lower lip. The lights were beginning to blur. She would not cry. She closed her eyes tight against the urge. Behind her, Delaney remained still and quiet. She refused to give him anything other than her back.

"Cunningham wants you to return to Quantico," he said in a low, apologetic voice. "He's sending Stewart to finish your workshop. He'll be here in a couple of hours, so you don't need to worry about the morning session."

She watched several cars below as they glided through intersections. At this height, they reminded her of a slow-motion video game. Streetlights flickered, confused whether to stay on or shut off as the sky lightened in anticipation of sunrise. In less than an hour, Kansas City would be waking up, and she hadn't even been to bed yet.

"Did you, at least, tell Cunningham about Rita?"

"Yes."

When he offered nothing more, she turned to him, suddenly hopeful. She watched his face when she asked, "Does he believe it was Stucky?"

"I don't know. He didn't say, and I didn't ask."

"So maybe he wants me to return to finally help on the case?"

Again, Delaney looked away, staring at the tabletop. She knew without any response that she was wrong.

"Jesus! Cunningham thinks I'm losing it, too," she said quietly, and turned back to the window. She leaned her forehead against the cool glass, hoping it would steady her nerves. Why couldn't she just feel numb, instead of all this anger and now this sudden feeling of defeat?

After a long silence, she heard Delaney get up and start for the door.

"I already made arrangements for you. Your flight leaves a little before one this afternoon. I don't have any sessions today, so I can drive you to the airport."

"Don't bother. I'll take a cab," she said without moving.

She heard him waiting, fidgeting. She refused to give him her eyes. And she certainly would not give him the absolution she knew Delaney would feel guilty without. Down below, cars began to fill the video-game slots, black and red and white, stopping and going.

"Maggie, we're all just worried about you," he said again, as if it should be enough.

"Right." She didn't bother to disguise the hurt and anger.

She waited for the soft slap of the door to close behind him. Then she crossed the room and turned the dead bolt. She stood with her back leaning against the door, listening to her heart pound, waiting for the anger and disappointment to leave. Why couldn't she replace it with acceptance or, at least, complacency? She needed to go home to her new, huge Tudor house with her belongings stacked in cardboard boxes and her shiny new state-of-the-art security system. She needed to let this go, before she did slip so far over the edge there would be no return.

She waited, pressed against the door, staring at the ceiling and listening, if not for her heart to stop banging then at least for her common sense to return. Then making up her mind, she stomped to the middle of the room. She began stripping out of the clothes she had worn since yesterday morning. In minutes she was dressed in blue jeans, a sweatshirt and an old pair of Nikes. She slipped on her shoulder holster, shoved her badge into the back pocket of her jeans and wrestled into a navy FBI windbreaker.

Her forensic kit hadn't been used in months, but she still didn't leave home without it. She pulled out several pairs of latex gloves, some evidence bags and a surgical face mask, transferring the items to the pockets of her jacket.

It was almost 6:00 a.m. She had only six hours, but she wasn't leaving this city until she connected Albert Stucky to Rita's murder. And she didn't care if that meant checking every last Dumpster and every last discarded take-out container in Westport's market district. Suddenly feeling energized, she grabbed her room's key card and left.

CHAPTER 24

"Hey lady. What the hell you looking for?"

Maggie looked over her shoulder but didn't stop digging through the rubble. She was up to her knees in garbage. Her Nikes were stained with barbecue sauce, her gloved hands sticky. Her eyes stung from a smelly concoction of garlic, mothballs, spoiled food and general human crap.

"FBI," she finally shouted through the paper face mask, and turned just enough for him to see the yellow letters on the jacket's back.

"Shit! No kidding? Maybe I can help"

She glanced at him again, resisting the urge to swipe at the strands of hair in her face, instead waving at the flies who regarded her as an invader of their territory. The man was young, probably in his early twenties. A scar, still pink and swollen, ran along his jaw and a purple bend in his nose indicated a recent break. Maggie's eyes darted around the alley, wondering if the rest of his gang was close by.

"Actually, I have more help than I need. The KC cops are a couple of Dumpsters down" she lied, pleased when the kid immediately began a nervous dance. His head jerked in both directions. He shifted his weight from one foot to the other as if preparing to run.

"Yeah, well. Good luck then." Rather than decide which direction to risk, he found an unlocked door and disappeared into the back of a warehouse.

She tossed a bulging garbage bag to the side without opening it. Stucky would never leave it hidden inside a bag. In the past, his surprises had been left in plain sight, where they were easily discovered, often by unsuspecting citizens. Maybe she was wasting her time going through Dumpsters.

Just then she saw the corner of a white cardboard take-out container. Slowly, she stepped closer, lifting each leg high as if wading through water, ignoring the squish-squash sounds beneath her feet. The last two containers had yielded one green meatball sandwich and some moldy ribs. Yet, each time she spotted a new one her pulse quickened. She felt a surge of adrenaline as she swatted at flies and brushed off wilted lettuce, cigarette butts and wadded pieces of tinfoil.

She lifted the container carefully, keeping it level and setting it on the edge of the Dumpster. The box was about the size of a small cake or pie. It'd provide ample room for a kidney or a lung. Neither organ required much space. She had once found a lung from one of Stucky's victims stuffed inside a container no bigger than a sandwich.

Sweat trickled down her back, despite the morning being damp and chilly. By now, she imagined she reeked as bad as the garbage she stood in. She steadied her fingers and sucked in her breath. The surgical mask clung to her mouth and nose. She slipped off the container's tab and pulled open the lid. The smell made her turn her head and hold her breath. After a few seconds, she was able to look again. Who'd ever guess spoiled fettuccine Alfredo would curdle and stink like rotten eggs? At least that's what Maggie thought the contents had once been. It was difficult to tell without lifting the thin film of fuzzy green and gray scum off the top. She closed and secured the lid.

"Find anything interesting?"

The deep voice startled her. Had the young gangster changed his mind? She grasped the Dumpster's edge so she wouldn't slip and fall backward into the trash. When she turned, she found Detective Ford staring up at her. Only this morning she hardly recognized him. Like her, he was dressed in street clothes, blue jeans, a gray hooded sweatshirt and a blue Kansas City Royals baseball cap. He looked much younger without the suit and tie and without his older partner.

She tugged off the surgical mask and let it dangle at her neck.

"I'm finding that we waste entirely too much food in this country," she said, dropping the container and wading to the opposite side of the Dumpster where she had left a milk crate on the cobblestone to aid in her climb.

"I didn't realize the FBI was trying to police that sort of thing."

She checked to see if there would be a lecture. He smiled.

"So are you undercover or off duty?" she asked, pointing to the baseball cap as she peeled off the latex gloves.

"I should ask you the same thing."

"I had some free time this morning," she said, as if that should be explanation enough for her to be knee-deep, sifting through garbage.

"Hey, Ford, where the hell did you disappear?" a familiar voice called from around the corner.

"Over here," Detective Ford answered.

Even before he came into view, Maggie felt the annoying flutter in her stomach. Nick Morrelli looked just as handsome as she had remembered, tall and lean with a confident stride. He, too, wore blue jeans with a red Nebraska Cornhuskers sweatshirt. He was at Ford's side before he recognized her, and when he did, his smile revealed dimples in an otherwise strong, square jaw.

"Maggie?"

She tossed the sticky gloves and yanked off the surgical mask from around her neck, adding it to the garbage.

"Hi, Nick." She pretended to sound casual while wading the rest of the way out, suddenly acutely aware of flies now attracted and interested in her. She swatted at them and tucked wild strands of hair behind her ears and away from her face.

"That's right. I keep forgetting you two know each other." Ford was smiling, too. "Maggie had some free time this morning," he said to Nick.

"Jesus, it's good to see you, Maggie."

Immediately, she felt her face flush.

"It might not be so good to smell me," she said, needing to stop any sentimental reunion.

She gripped the edge of the Dumpster and swung a leg over the side. Her foot dangled, searching for the milk crate. Before she could find it, Nick's hands were on her waist to help. Her hip brushed against his chest on the way down. Despite being bombarded with smells all morning, she recognized the subtle scent of his cologne.

Once both her feet were on the ground, his hands lingered, but she avoided looking up at him. She avoided looking at either of them, needing the extra time to compose herself while waiting for the unexpected flutter to leave. Damn it! She wasn't some schoolgirl. Why the hell did her body respond like this?

She occupied herself wiping the sticking garbage from her pant legs and shoes. Unfortunately, when she did look up, both men were watching her. She continued to avoid Nick's eyes, remembering how they could look deep inside her and uncover vulnerabilities she had hidden even from herself.

"So," Ford finally said, glancing back into the Dumpster, "did you find anything interesting?"

She wondered how much Turner and Delaney had shared with Ford about her obsession with Stucky. Had Detective Ford seen how close to the edge she had come last night? And what had he discussed with Nick? She didn't think for a minute he had forgotten they knew each other. After all, Ford had invited Nick to have dinner with them last night, though there had never been an explanation as to why Nick hadn't joined them. Suddenly she was curious if Nick had simply wanted to avoid seeing her again. After all, if he was now living in Boston, why hadn't he called? She could feel his eyes taking her in, watching her, smiling at her, but thankfully not making a big deal of their reunion.

"No, I didn't find anything," she finally answered. She needed to change the subject before Detective Ford discovered it was body parts she had been rummaging for and not simply overlooked evidence. "Is this your case now?"

"Not officially. More than likely Milhaven and I will be putting in some hours on it. Today's supposed to be my day off. Nick and I were just about to get an early lunch."

"And you always take the alleys?"

Ford grinned and glanced at Nick.

"She doesn't let anybody get away with anything, does she?"

"No, she certainly doesn't." Nick's eyes caught hers, and she knew his simple statement had much deeper meaning, reminding her of the intimacies they had shared and those they had almost shared.

"So come on, Detective Ford." She needed to keep things light, capitalize on their jovial mood. She needed to keep Ford from realizing she had no business snooping around in his jurisdiction. She was already in enough trouble with Cunningham. "You're down here taking another look, too, right?"

"Okay, you caught me." He held up both hands as if in surrender. "I was telling Nick about last night."

Maggie cringed, and again she wondered what exactly had been discussed. Nick knew the whole story, all the gory details about her and Stucky. He had experienced firsthand her nightmares. Still, she kept her face impassive, pretending last night had been just another routine chase for her. Truth was, she didn't care if Ford thought she was losing it. But maybe she did care if Nick thought it. She waited and Ford continued.

"You sorta got my curiosity up last night, O'Dell."

Oh God, she thought, but instead said, "How is that?"

"All that talk about Albert Stucky sorta spooked me."

She glanced from Detective Ford to Nick, looking for some indication of whether or not they were taking her seriously. If this was Ford's way of patting her on the head and reassuring her how mistaken she was, she didn't need to waste her breath responding.

"You think I'm being paranoid?" She couldn't help it. The beginning anger slipped out. Nick noticed immediately and looked concerned. Ford looked genuinely confused.

"No, that's not at all what I meant.... Well, that's not exactly true. I guess I was thinking that last night."

"Albert Stucky has the financial wherewithal and the intelligence to go anywhere he wants, anytime he chooses. Don't think for a second Kansas City is safe, simply because he hasn't struck in the Midwest before." There it was. She hadn't meant to let the anger out. She hated how Stucky had such power over her emotions, triggering them with the mere mention of his name. Again she avoided Nick's eyes, and again she could feel them.

Ford stared at her, but there was no accusation on his face. Instead, he looked as though he was only waiting for her to finish her tirade.

"Can I talk now?"

"Be my guest." Maggie crossed her arms over her chest, bracing herself and yet doing her best to look defiant. It was a newly acquired talent.

"That was my way of thinking last night. Like, why in the world would this Stucky guy just happen to pick Kansas City instead of the East Coast? I know enough about serial killers to know they keep to familiar territory. But before I met Nick this morning, I sat in on the autopsy of your friend, Rita."

Detective Ford glanced at Nick, and it was obvious this was what the two of them had already discussed. He looked back at Maggie, waited until he had her full attention then said, "Seems our victim is missing her right kidney."

CHAPTER 25

Tully checked his watch. It wasn't like Assistant Director Cunningham to be late for a meeting. He sat back and waited. Maybe his watch was running fast again. According to Emma, it was ancient and uncool.

Tully stared at the huge map spread on the wall behind his boss's desk. It was Cunningham's personal log for his twenty years as head of the Investigative Support Unit. Each pushpin indicated a spot where a serial killer had struck. Each pushpin color designated a particular serial killer. Tully wondered how soon the assistant director would run out of colors. Already there were repeats: purple, light purple and translucent purple.

Tully knew his boss had worked on some of the most shocking cases, including John Wayne Gacy and the Green River Killer. By comparison, Tully was a rookie, with only six years' experience in profiling and most of that on paper, not in the field. He wondered how anyone lived day in, day out for decades examining such brutality without becoming jaded or cynical.

He glanced around the office again. Everything on the desk—a leather appointment book, two Bic pens with the caps intact (a talent Tully had not yet perfected), a plain memo pad with no doodles in the corners and a brass nameplate—all of it was organized in straight lines, perpendicular to one another, almost as if Cunningham used a T square every morning. It occurred to Tully that the tidy but stark office contained not one single personal item. There were no sweatshirts wadded in the corner, no miniature basketballs, not a single photo. In fact, Tully knew very little of who his boss was outside the office.

He had noticed a wedding band, yet Assistant Director Cunningham seemed to live at Quantico. There was never any rearranging of appointments for Little League games or school plays or visits to kids in college. Before this morning, he had never even been late for an appointment. No, Tully knew absolutely nothing about the quiet, soft-spoken man who had become one of the most respected men in the FBI. But at what cost? Tully wondered.

"Sorry to keep you waiting," Cunningham said as he breezed in, shedding his suit jacket and swinging it carefully over the back of his chair before sitting down. "What have you found out?"

In the beginning, that brisk, straight-to-the-point attitude had flustered Tully, who was accustomed to the courtesies of the Midwest. Now he appreciated getting down to business with no obligatory exchanges of chitchat or greetings. Though it also prevented the two men from knowing a single thing about each other's personal lives.

"I just received the files faxed over from the Kansas City police."

He pulled out the summary sheet from a group of folders he had brought along. He made certain it was the correct one and handed it across the desk. Cunningham pushed up his glasses.

Tully continued, "Early autopsy reports indicate a slashed throat as cause of death. No other defense wounds or injuries. There was one incision in the victim's right side through which the right kidney was extracted."

"Any sign of the organ?"

"No, not yet. But then the Kansas City cops weren't looking for it right away. It's quite possible someone found it, had no clue what it was and tossed it."

Tully waited patiently, watching his boss as he finished reading. He laid the report on the desk, sat back and rubbed a hand over his jaw.

"What's your perspective on this, Agent Tully?"

"The timing is off. It's much too soon after the delivery girl. And it's much too far away, entirely out of his territory. There was another latent fingerprint, a thumb. Again, it looks like it was deliberately left behind on an umbrella that belonged to the victim. Didn't even have the victim's fingerprints on it. It was definitely wiped down with the print left later. And again, it doesn't match Albert Stucky."

Cunningham frowned, squinting at the report and tapping his index finger to his lip. Tully thought the lines in his face seemed more pronounced this morning, his short hair peppered with more gray.

"So is it Stucky, or isn't it?"

"The M.O. definitely matches Stucky's," Tully said. "And there hasn't been enough in the news or even enough time for a copycat to get motivated. The print may belong to someone who came across the scene. A waiter found her. There's some speculation the scene had been contaminated. KC's faxing a copy of the print to the guys at CJIS in Clarksburg. We'll see if it matches the unidentified one left in Newburgh Heights. There's a good chance these belong to civilians coming across the scene after everything's been wiped clean."

"Okay, let's say that's the case. So what if it is Stucky?"

Tully knew exactly what Cunningham was thinking, but he evidently wanted or needed to hear it, to confirm what seemed to be the obvious.

"If it is Stucky, it's more than likely he followed O'Dell to Kansas City. He may be looking for a way to drag her into this again."

Cunningham glanced at his wristwatch. "She should be headed back right now."

"Actually, I checked, sir. I thought I'd meet her at the airport. She changed to a flight later tonight."

Cunningham shook his head and let out a sigh of frustration as he grabbed his phone and punched several buttons.

"Anita, do you have Special Agent Margaret O'Dell's hotel phone number in Kansas City?" He sat back while he waited.

Tully imagined the methodical Anita quickly accessing her records. Assistant Director Cunningham had kept the same secretary, inheriting her from his predecessor and yielding to her experience and expertise on important matters he couldn't saddle himself with. If such a thing was possible, Anita was even more meticulous than her boss.

"Good," Cunningham said into the phone. "Would you please get in touch with her even if it's through a message. Track her down if she's already checked out. I want to see her in my office tomorrow morning at eight."

He hesitated and listened as he rubbed the bridge of his nose under his glasses. "Oh yes, I forgot about that. Tell O'Dell nine o'clock then. Thanks, Anita."

He replaced the receiver and looked up at Tully, waiting.

"How long do you intend to keep her off this case?" Tully finally asked what he thought was the obvious question.

"For as long as is necessary."

Tully studied his boss's face, but had no clue how to read the composed and reserved expression. He respected the man tremendously, but he didn't know him well enough to know how far he could push him. He decided to take a chance anyway.

"You realize she's checking this one out on her own? That's more than likely why she's taking a later flight."

"All the more reason to get her back here." Cunningham held Tully's eyes, warning him to step carefully. "What else is happening in Newburgh Heights?"

"We found the pizza delivery girl's car. It was left in long-term parking at the airport, right next to a telephone company van that was reported stolen a couple of weeks ago."

"I knew it," Cunningham sat back and began drumming his fingers on the desk. "Stucky's done it before. He'll steal a vehicle, or sometimes only the license plates, from the airport's long-term parking. Chances are he has the plates or even the vehicle returned before the owner is back home. Has forensics impounded the van?"

Tully nodded, sorting through the information he had on both vehicles. "Not likely they'll find anything. It's pretty clean. However, we did find two delivery slips in the girl's car."

He dug in the folder, pulling out one torn piece of paper and another creased with fold lines. Both had been recovered from the floor of the girl's car. A red stain on one corner had tested as pizza sauce, not blood. Tully handed both over the desk. "The torn one is from her first route. Number four on the list is Agent O'Dell's new home address."

Cunningham sat forward, resting elbows on his desk. For the first time in Tully's three months of working at Quantico, he saw anger on his boss's face. The assistant director's dark eyes narrowed and his hands clenched the paper.

"So the damn bastard not only knows where she lives, but he's watching her."

"It looks that way. When I talked to Agent Delaney, he said the waitress in Kansas City had joked and talked with the three of them Sunday evening while she served them. He may be choosing women O'Dell comes in contact with in hopes of making her feel responsible."

"It's another of his goddamn games. He's still obsessed with O'Dell. I knew it. I knew he wouldn't let it go."

"It appears that way. May I say one more thing, sir?"

"Of course."

"You've offered me another agent to help on this case. You've also offered a forensic psychologist, which O'Dell is. You even suggested we have someone on hand to answer medical-related questions. If I'm not mistaken, Agent O'Dell has a premed background."

Tully hesitated, giving Cunningham a chance to cut him off. Instead, he only stared at Tully, his face back to its stoic expression as he simply waited.

"Rather than three or four people," Tully continued, "I'm officially requesting Agent O'Dell. If Stucky is targeting her, she may be the only one who can help us catch him."

Tully expected a flicker of anger or at least impatience. But Cunningham's face remained unchanged.

"I'll give your request careful consideration," he said. "Let me know what else you find out from Kansas City."

"Yes, sir," Tully said as he stood to leave, recognizing the signs of dismissal. Before he reached the door, Cunningham was on the phone again, and Tully couldn't help wondering if his request had also been dismissed.

CHAPTER 26

Maggie couldn't wait to peel off her damp, smelly clothes. Everyone in the hotel lobby had confirmed her suspicions—she reeked. Two people insisted on getting off the elevator, and the brave souls who continued the ride up with her looked as though they had held their breath for all twenty-three floors.

Detective Ford had dropped her and Nick at the front door then drove home to explain to his wife why he smelled like garbage on his day off. Nick's room was in the south tower of the huge hotel complex, explaining why they hadn't run into each other before. Which meant both banks of elevators would need disinfecting.

The three of them had spent several hours digging through Dumpsters, sifting through trash cans and looking for discarded containers on outdoor tables, window ledges, fire escapes and flower boxes. Maggie hadn't even noticed the thick, gray thunderheads that had rolled in until the rain came in sheets, forcing them to end their search and take shelter. She would have continued if she had been alone. The rain had felt good, slashing at her and perhaps peeling away the tension along with the rancid smells from her skin. But the cracks of thunder and flashes of lightning only made her more anxious and jumpy.

Detective Ford had assured her that Albert Stucky would, indeed, be considered a suspect in Rita's murder, despite their not finding the missing kidney. Maggie couldn't understand why Stucky would deviate from his game, or had some unsuspecting customer taken the container home? Was it possible someone could have placed it in his refrigerator without looking, without knowing what was inside? That seemed ridiculous, and Maggie didn't even want to think about it. The fact was, there wasn't anything more she could do.

As soon as she came into her room, she noticed the phone's red message light flashing. She grabbed the receiver and punched in the necessary numbers to retrieve her voice messages. She was used to getting emergency messages about her mother who attempted suicide as often as other women her age treated themselves to a manicure. But weren't her mother's new friends supposed to be taking care of her? Who could be calling? There was only one message, and it was, indeed, marked urgent.

"Agent O'Dell. This is Anita Glasco calling for Assistant Director Cunningham. He needs to see you in his office tomorrow morning at nine. Please call me back if you won't be able to make it. Thank you and have a safe trip home, Maggie."

Maggie smiled at Anita's soothing voice, though the message itself set her on edge. She listened to her options, punched the number to erase and hung up. She began pacing, trying to contain the anger before it grabbed hold of her. It was Cunningham's way of seeing to it that she returned immediately. He knew she would never blow off a request to meet with him. She wondered what he already knew about Rita's murder, or if he had even considered looking into it. After all, Delaney had probably made it sound as though she was losing her mind, simply imagining things.

She checked her wristwatch and scraped something dry and crusty from its face. She still had about six hours before her rescheduled evening flight. It was the last one to D.C. tonight. If she was to make the appointment with Cunningham in the morning, she couldn't afford another delay. But how the hell could she leave Kansas City knowing Albert Stucky was here, lurking somewhere in the city? Maybe looking for his next victim right this very minute.

She double-checked the door, making sure it was locked. She added the chain and rammed the back of the wooden desk chair up under the knob, kicking the legs until she was satisfied it was secure. Then she stripped down to her underwear and bra and tossed her smelly clothes and shoes into one of the plastic dry-cleaning bags in the closet. Still smelling them, she triple-bagged them, until the scent seemed to be contained.

She brought her Smith & Wesson with her to the bathroom, leaving it close by on the counter. She left the bathroom door open, slipped out of her bra and panties, then crawled into the shower.

The water beat and massaged her skin. She turned the temperature as hot as she could stand it. She wanted to be rid not only of the smells, but of that crawly feeling just under her skin. That infestation of maggots that invaded her system every time she knew Albert Stucky was nearby. She scrubbed at her skin until it was red and raw. She wanted her mind to be swept clean, and her body to forget the scars.

When she stepped out of the shower, she wiped at the foggy mirror. The brown eyes stared back at her with that damn vulnerability so close to the surface. And the scars were still there, too. Her body was becoming a scrapbook.

The scar began just beneath her breast. With the tip of her index finger, she forced herself to touch it. To trace its puckered line down across her abdomen.

"I could gut you in seconds," she remembered him telling her—no, promising, not telling. By then, she had resigned herself to death. He had already trapped her. He had already forced her to watch while he bludgeoned and gutted two women to death. He had threatened that if Maggie closed her eyes he would simply bring out another woman and start all over. And he had been true to his word.

There was still no escaping those images and sounds: bloodied breasts, the crack of bones, the hollow thud of a baseball bat against a skull. There had been so much blood from severed arteries and from knives sinking into flesh, into abdomens and vaginas—places where knives should never be allowed. No place was out of limits for Stucky. Nothing on a woman's body was sacred. He carved and sliced, pleased and encouraged by the screams.

After feeling the splatters of blood, the pieces of bone and brain, after hearing the mind-shattering cries for help and smacks of bloodied flesh, what more could he have done to her? Death would have been a relief. So instead, he left her with a constant reminder of himself, a scar.

Maggie snatched a T-shirt and wrestled into it, anxious to cover herself despite her skin being damp. She marched to the dresser and pulled out clean underwear and khakis. Her hair was still dripping as she rummaged through the service butler, relieved to find two new miniature bottles of Scotch. Thank God for the hotel staff's efficiency.

A soft tap on the door startled her. She stopped at the bathroom, retrieving her revolver. Before pulling the chair away, she checked the peephole.

Nick's hair was damp and tousled. He wore clean blue jeans and a crisp oxford shirt with the sleeves rolled up.

She returned the chair to the desk and slipped the revolver into the back of her waistband. It wasn't until she opened the door and his eyes slid down her body that she realized she had nothing on underneath the thin T-shirt that now clung to her damp body.

"That was fast," she said, ignoring the flutter this man seemed to activate on sight.

"I was anxious to crawl out of those clothes." He returned to her face, a hint of embarrassment coloring his own. "I think I might need to throw out my shoes. There's gunk on them that I don't even want to know about."

They stared at each other. His presence, his scent seemed to dismantle her thought process. She felt hot and damp. She told herself it was from her shower and the extra-hot water she had used.

"I thought maybe we could get something to eat or drink," he finally said. "You do still have time before your flight?"

"I should...um...put something else on."

His eyes wouldn't let her go. Suddenly it unnerved her how much she wanted to touch him. She needed to close the door, get control of her senses, pull herself together. Instead, she heard herself saying, "Why don't you come in."

He hesitated, enough so that she could have taken back the invitation. Instead, she moved away from the door. She retreated to the dresser again, pulling things out at random, pretending to be searching while giving herself any excuse not to look up at him.

He came in and closed the door behind him.

"We seem to spend a lot of time in hotel rooms."

She glanced at him, immediately annoyed that the reminder brought a flush to her cheeks. In a small hotel room in Platte City, Nebraska, they had come dangerously close to making love. Five months later, she could still feel the same rush of heat. With all the emotions assaulting her over the past few days, how was it possible for Nick Morrelli to walk in and assault her with a whole new set?

She pulled out a white crew-neck sweater, the cotton knit cool but bulky and comfortable. She snatched a bra from the drawer as well.

"I'll just be a minute," she said as she disappeared into the steamy bathroom.

She changed quickly, avoiding any extra touches. She toweled the wetness out of her hair and brushed it back, grabbing the blow dryer, then deciding against it. She reached to remove her Smith & Wesson, hesitated, and left it in her waistband, pulling the loose sweater down and checking in the mirror to make sure it couldn't be seen. She knew she'd have to grab her badge on the way out.

Nick was at the window and watched as she tugged on socks and slipped on shoes. She noticed he had both miniature bottles of Scotch in his hand.

"Still having nightmares?" His eyes searched hers as he returned the bottles to the small table.

"Yes," she said quite simply, and gave him her back as she found her badge and some cash. She didn't need Nick Morrelli barging into her life and thinking he had any right to share or expose her vulnerabilities.

"Ready?" she asked as she headed for the door and opened it before looking back at him. She almost tripped over the room-service tray that sat on the floor outside her door. She stared down at the single dinner plate covered by a silver insulator. The two empty glasses and accompanying silverware sparkled on a crisp, white linen napkin.

"Did you order something from room service?" she turned to ask, but Nick was already by her side.

"No. And I didn't hear a knock, either."

He stepped over the tray and out into the hallway to look in both directions. Maggie listened. There were no slamming doors, no footsteps, no wisping elevators.

"Probably just a mistake," Nick said, but she could hear his tension.

Maggie kneeled next to the tray. Her pulse quickened. Carefully, she slipped the linen napkin out from under the silverware, using thumb and index finger. She unfolded it, then used it to grab the handle of the metal insulator. She lifted it slowly and immediately the smell filled the hall.

"Jesus," Nick said, jerking back a step.

In the middle of the shiny dinner plate lay a bloody glob Maggie knew was Rita's missing kidney.

CHAPTER 27

Within minutes, the hotel's lobby was filled with law enforcement officers from across the Midwest. All entrances and exits were guarded. Elevators were checked and watched. Stairwells were examined at all twenty-five levels. The hotel's room-service kitchen had been invaded and the staff questioned. Despite the overwhelming brigade of manpower, Maggie knew they would never find him.

Most criminals would consider it suicide to show up in a hotel where hundreds of cops, sheriffs, detectives and FBI agents were staying. For Albert Stucky it would simply be another challenge to his game. Maggie imagined him sitting somewhere, watching and amused by the commotion, the blunders, the unsuccessful attempts at catching him. That's why she was checking the most obvious places.

The second floor included an atrium overlooking the lobby. She stayed at the brass railing while her eyes searched down below—the line at the reservations counter, the man at the grand piano, the few diners at bistro tables in the glass-encased café the man behind the concierge desk, the cabdriver hauling out luggage. Stucky would blend in. He'd look as though he belonged. Even the room-service staff would not have noticed him had he walked into their kitchen in a white jacket and black tie.

"Any luck?"

Maggie jumped but managed to restrain herself from automatically reaching for her gun.

"Sorry." Nick looked genuinely concerned. "He'd be nuts to stick around. I'm guessing he's long gone."

"Stucky likes to watch. It isn't much fun if he doesn't get to see people's reactions. Half of these officers don't know what he looks like. If he plays it cool, they might never spot him. He has the uncanny ability to blend in."

Maggie continued searching, standing quietly and still. She could feel Nick examining her. She was tired of everyone watching for signs of some kind of mental meltdown, though she knew Nick was sincere.

"I'm fine," she said without looking at him, answering his unspoken question.

"I know you are. I still get to be concerned." He leaned over the railing, conducting his own search. His shoulder brushed against hers.

"Assistant Director Cunningham thinks he's protecting me by keeping me off the investigation."

"I wondered why you were teaching. John said there were rumors that you were burned out, losing your touch."

She had guessed as much, yet it felt like a slap in the face to hear it out loud. She avoided looking at him. She pushed strands of damp hair out of her eyes, tucking them behind her ears. She probably looked the part of the crazed FBI agent, with her tangled hair and baggy clothes.

"Is that what you think?" she asked, not certain she wanted to hear his answer.

They stood side by side, leaning against the railing, shoulders brushing while their eyes stayed safely ahead and away from each other. His silence lasted too long.

"I told John that the Maggie O'Dell I know is tough as nails. I saw you take a knife to the gut and still not give up."

Another of her scars. The mad child killer she and Nick had chased in Nebraska had stabbed her and left her for dead in a graveyard tunnel.

"Getting stabbed seems so much easier than what Stucky's doing to me."

"I know this isn't what you want to hear, Maggie, but I think Cunningham may be smart in keeping you out of this."

This time she turned to stare at him.

"How can you say that? It's obvious Stucky is playing with me again."

"Exactly. He wants to drag you into his little games. Why give him exactly what he wants?"

"But you don't understand, Nick." The anger bubbled too close to the surface. She tried to keep her voice calm and level. Talking about Stucky could bring her to the edge of sounding hysterical. "Stucky will continue to goad me whether I'm on the case or not. Cunningham can't protect me. Instead, he's keeping me from the one way I have to fight back."

"I'm guessing he must have told you he wants you on that flight back to D.C. tonight?"

"Agent Turner is escorting me." Why bother hiding her anger. "It's ridiculous, Nick. Albert Stucky is right here in Kansas City. I should stay here."

More silence. They were back to searching the crowd below, standing side by side, again leaning their elbows on the railing and again keeping their hands and eyes carefully away from each other. Nick moved closer as though purposely bringing their bodies in to contact. His shoulder no longer accidentally brushed hers. Now it stayed against her. She found a weird sense of comfort in this subtle touch, this slight contact, feeling perhaps that she wasn't in this alone.

"I still care about you, Maggie," he said quietly, without moving and still not looking at her. "I thought I didn't care anymore. I tried to stop. But when I saw you this morning, I realized I hadn't stopped caring at all."

"I don't want to have this conversation, Nick. I really can't. Not now." Her stomach churned with anticipation, with panic, with fear. She didn't need to feel anything more.

"I called you when I first moved to Boston," he continued as if he hadn't heard her.

She glanced at him. Was this some line? That boyish charm, that flirtatious reputation of his surely couldn't have disappeared so easily.

"I didn't get any message," she said, now curious and anxious to call him on his bluff if, in fact, that was what it turned out to be.

"Quantico wouldn't give me any information as to where you were, or when you'd be back. I even told them I was with the Suffolk County D.A.'s office." He glanced at her and smiled. "They weren't impressed."

It was a safe story. She wouldn't be able to confirm it or deny it. She concentrated on the lobby. Below, three men toted luggage behind a well-dressed woman with silver hair and a London Fog raincoat that didn't have a raindrop on it.

"I ended up calling Greg's law firm."

"You did what?"

She pushed herself away from the railing and waited until he did the same, giving her his attention and his eyes.

"Neither of you are listed in the Virginia telephone directory," he defended himself. "I figured the law office of Brackman, Harvey and Lowe might be more understanding. They might actually care about someone from a D.A.'s office getting in touch with one of their attorneys. Even if it was after hours."

"You talked to Greg?"

"I didn't mean to. I was hoping to catch you at home. I thought if Greg answered, I could tell him I needed to talk to you about unfinished business in Nebraska. After all, I knew you were still looking for Father Keller."

"But Greg didn't buy it."

"No." Nick looked embarrassed. He continued anyway. "He told me the two of you were working on your marriage. He asked me as a gentleman to respect that and stay away."

"Greg said that? About being a gentleman? As if he knew." She shook her head and returned to her perch, pretending to be distracted by the activity below. Greg had become so good at lying, Maggie wondered if he actually believed his own bullshit. "How long ago was this?"

"Couple months ago." He joined her again, but this time kept some distance.

"Months ago?" She couldn't believe Greg hadn't mentioned it, or that he hadn't let it slip out during one of their arguments.

"It was right after I moved, so it had to be around the last week of January. I got the impression the two of you were still living together."

"Greg and I both decided to stay at the condo, since neither of us were there that often. But I asked Greg for a divorce on New Year's Eve. That probably sounds heartless—I meant to wait." She watched as a maintenance crew pushed huge floor waxers into the lobby. "We were at his law firm's holiday party. He wanted us to masquerade as the happy couple."

The supervisor of the maintenance crew had a clipboard and wore shiny leather dress shoes. Maggie craned over the railing to get a glimpse of his face. Too young and too tall to be Stucky.

"People at the party kept congratulating me and welcoming me to the firm. They spoiled Greg's surprise. He had managed to get me a job as the head of their investigations department without even talking to me about it. Then he couldn't understand why I wouldn't jump at the chance to be digging through corporate files, looking for misappropriation of funds instead of digging through Dumpsters, looking for body parts."

"Right. Jesus, how silly of him."

She turned and rewarded his sarcasm with a smile.

"I am a pain in the ass, aren't I?" she said.

"An awfully beautiful pain in the ass."

She felt a blush and looked away, annoyed that he could make her feel sensual and alive while the world was going nuts around them.

"I finally moved into a house of my own last week. In a few weeks the divorce should be final."

"Maybe it would have been safer to stay at the condo. I mean as far as this thing with Stucky is concerned."

"Newburgh Heights is just outside D.C. It's probably one of the safest neighborhoods in Virginia."

"Yeah, but I hate thinking about you being all alone."

"I'd rather be alone when he comes for me. That way no one else gets hurt. Not this time."

"Jesus, Maggie! You *want* him to come after you?"

She avoided looking at him. She didn't need to see his concern. She couldn't take on the weight of it, the responsibility of it. So instead, she concentrated on the men in blue overalls wrestling with cords and mops. When she didn't answer, Nick reached for her hand, gently taking it. He intertwined her arm with his, bringing her hand to his chest and keeping it there, warm and tight against the pounding of his heart. Then they stood there while they watched the hotel lobby get its floors waxed.

CHAPTER 28

Washington, D.C.
Wednesday, April 1

He could feel Dr. Gwen Patterson staring at him while he stabbed at her furniture with his white cane, fumbling for a place to sit down. Nice stuff. The office even smelled expensive, fine leather and polished wood. But why would he expect anything less? She was a classy woman; sophisticated, cultured, wise and talented. Finally, a challenge to up the ante, so to speak.

He swiped his hand across her desktop, but there wasn't much to disturb—a phone, a Roledex, several legal pads and a daily calendar, flipped open to Wednesday, April 1. Only now did it occur to him that it was April Fools' Day. How ironically appropriate. He resisted the urge to smile, instead turning again and bumping into a credenza, barely missing an antique vase. The window above the credenza looked out over the Potomac River. In its reflection, he watched her grimace at his bold and reckless fumblings.

"The sofa is just to your left," she finally instructed, but stayed seated behind her desk. Though her voice sounded tight, restraining her impatience, she wouldn't embarrass him by coming to his rescue. Excellent. She had passed his first test.

He put his hand out and patted down the soft leather, feeling for the arm, and carefully sitting himself down.

"Would you like something to drink before we get started?"

"No," he snapped, being unnecessarily rude. Invalids could get away with shit like that. It was one of the few advantages he could look forward to. Then, to let her know he wasn't such a bad guy, he politely added, "I'd rather we just get started."

He set the cane by his side where he could find it easily. He bunched up his leather jacket and laid it in his lap. The room was dark, the blinds half-closed, and he wondered why she had bothered. He adjusted his sunglasses on the bridge of his nose. The lenses were extra dark so that no one could see his eyes. So that no one could catch him watching. It was a lovely twist to voyeurism. Everyone thought they were being the voyeurs, safe in staring at him, watching him, pitying him. No one seemed to question whether or not a blind guy could actually see. After all, why in the world would someone fake something like that?

Except that, ironically, the lie might be coming true. The drugs weren't working, and he couldn't deny that his eyesight was getting worse. He had lucked out so many times before, was his number finally up? No, he didn't believe in such a stupid thing as fate. So what if he needed a little extra help these days, a prop or two, or some assistance from an old friend to bring a little excitement into his life. Wasn't that what friends were for?

He cocked his head to one side, waiting, pretending to need to hear her before he could turn in her direction. In the meantime, he watched her. Through the dark lenses in the dark room, he found himself squinting. She was still staring at him, sitting back in her chair, looking comfortable and in control.

She stood and reached for her suit jacket on the back of her chair, but stopped, glanced over at him and left the jacket there. Then she came around to the front of the desk, leaning against the pristine top and standing directly in front of him. She looked soft and fragile, curves in all the right places, tight skin and few wrinkles for a woman in her late forties. She wore her strawberry-blond hair loose, letting it brush her jawline in delicate wisps. He wondered if it was her natural color, and he caught himself smiling. Maybe he would need to find out for himself.

He leaned back into the sofa, waiting, sniffing in her fragrance. God, she smelled good, though he couldn't name the fragrance. Usually he could narrow it down, but this scent was new. Her red silk blouse was thin enough to reveal small, round breasts and the slight pucker of nipples. He was glad she thought she didn't need the jacket. He tucked his hands into his lap, making sure his folded jacket covered the swelling bulge, pleased that his new diet of porn movies seemed to be helping his temporary lapses.

"As with all my patients, Mr. Harding," she said finally, "I'd like to know what your goals are. What you hope to accomplish in our sessions?"

He held back a smile. She was already accomplishing one of his goals.

He tilted his head toward her and continued to stare at her breasts. Even if she could see his eyes, people accepted, they expected his eyes to be looking anywhere but in their own eyes.

"I'm not sure I understand the question." He had learned it was good to make women explain. It allowed them to feel in control, and he wanted her to believe she was in control.

"You told me on the phone," she began carefully as though measuring her words, "that you had some sexual issues you wanted to work on." She neither emphasized nor hesitated over the phrase "sexual issues." That was good, very good. "In order for me to help you, I need to know, more specifically, what you expect from me. What you'd like to see come out of these sessions."

It was time to see how easily she could be shocked.

"It really is quite simple. I want to be able to enjoy fucking a woman again."

She blinked and her light complexion flushed slightly, but she didn't move. It was a bit of a letdown. Maybe he should go ahead and add that he wanted to enjoy fucking a woman without wanting to fuck her to death. His new habit really wasn't much different than many of those in the animal and insect world. Perhaps he should compare his sexual habits to those of the female praying mantis who bites off her mate's head just as he is beginning to copulate.

Would she understand that the orgasm, the erotic surge was incredibly powerful when it included pain? Should he confess that seeing his women smeared in blood and screaming for mercy made him come in an orgasmic explosion like none he could achieve otherwise? Could she understand that this hideous thing inside threatened to take away the foundation of his being, his last primal instinct?

But no, he wouldn't share any of this with her—that would probably be a bit much. That was something Albert Stucky would do or say, and he needed to resist the urge to stoop to his old friend's level.

"Can you do that, Doc?" he asked, sticking his chin out and up as though he was listening for her movement, for her reaction.

"I can certainly try."

He looked over her shoulder, his body slightly turned to the side, despite her standing in front of him.

"You're blushing," he said, and allowed a curt smile.

The color in her cheeks deepened. Her hand went to her neck in the useless attempt to stop the blush.

"What makes you say that?"

Would she deny it? Would she disappoint him this soon and lie?

"I'm guessing," he said, letting his voice be soft and soothing, encouraging her to confide in him, hoping to gain access to her own vulnerabilities. If he was to accomplish his ultimate goal, he would need Dr. Gwen Patterson not to feel threatened. The good doctor had a reputation for delving into some of the most famous and devious of criminal minds. He wondered what she would think if she knew she was to be the guinea pig this time.

"Let me just say, I've been a psychologist quite a while." She tried to explain her reaction away casually, but he noticed the color remained in her cheeks. "I've heard many shocking things, much more so than your problem. You needn't worry about embarrassing me, Mr. Harding."

Okay, so she chose to play it safe and cool, refusing him access to her inner self. The idea of this excited him nevertheless. He did so enjoy a challenge.

"Perhaps," she continued, "we should start by you telling me why you no longer enjoy sex."

"Isn't that obvious?" He used the tone he had perfected. The one that sounded angry, offended, yet sad enough to invoke the right amount of pity. It usually worked.

"Of course it's not obvious."

He let one of his hands stray under the pile of leather. She was making this so easy. Playing right into his hands, so to speak. He cupped a palm over his erection.

"If you're thinking your—" she hesitated "—your handicap—"

"It's okay. You can call it what it is. I'm blind. I don't mind anyone saying the word."

"Okay, but your blindness certainly should not mean a loss of libido."

He liked the way she said "libido." Though her lips were thin and her mouth small, he liked the shape. He enjoyed watching the upper lip curl a bit at the corner. He detected a slight accent, but he couldn't place it—maybe upper New York? It made him anxious to hear her say "penis" and "fellatio," and he wondered how her lips would curl around those words.

"Is that what you're saying, Mr. Harding?" she interrupted his thoughts. "That somehow your loss of sight has rendered you incapable of performing?"

"Men are highly visual creatures, especially when it comes to being sexually aroused."

"Very true," she said as she reached behind her and grabbed a file folder, his folder, his case history. "When did you begin losing your eyesight?"

"About four years ago. Do we have to talk about that?"

She looked up at him over the open file. She had shifted to the other end of the desk, but he kept his gaze on the spot where she had been.

"If it will help us deal with your current problem, then yes, I do think we should talk about it."

He liked her decisive manner, her direct tone. She wouldn't be pussyfooting around him. What a wonderful word—pussyfooting. He rubbed his hidden hand against his bulge.

"Do you have an objection to that, Mr. Harding? You certainly don't appear to be a man who runs away from a challenge."

He hesitated only because he didn't want to interrupt the sensation. It was okay. She'd think he simply needed a moment to think about it.

"I have no objection," he said, having some difficulty containing a smile. No, anyone who knew Walker Harding would never accuse him of running away from anything. But if he was to accept his new challenge, he'd need to depend on the master criminal mind that Dr. Patterson yet had the pleasure of examining. Yes, despite playing this new role, he would still need to depend on the genius of his old friend, Albert Stucky.

CHAPTER 29

Tully ripped off the latest fax that had just come in from the Kansas City Police Department. He scanned its contents while he gathered folders and notes and crime scene photos. In ten minutes he was meeting with Assistant Director Cunningham, and yet his mind was still preoccupied with the argument he'd had with his daughter less than an hour ago. Emma had waited until he was dropping her off at school to drop her bomb. Damn she was good. But then what did he expect? She had been schooled in the fine art of surprise attack by none other than the master, her own mother.

"Oh, by the way," she had announced in a matter-of-fact voice. "Josh Reynolds asked me to the junior/senior prom. It's a week from Friday, so I'll need to buy a new dress. Probably new shoes, too."

Immediately he had gotten angry. She was only a freshman. When had they decided she could date?

"Did I miss that conversation?" he had asked with enough sarcasm that he was now embarrassed in retrospect.

She had given him her best insulted, wounded look. How could he not trust her? She was "almost fifteen." Practically an old maid compared to her friends who, she assured him, had been dating for two or three years already. He passed on the opportunity to counter with the old argument that just because your friends jump off a bridge... Besides, the real problem was not that he didn't trust her. At forty-three, he could still remember how horny fifteen- and sixteen-year-old boys could get. He wished he could discuss it with Caroline, but he knew she'd side with Emma. Was he really just being an overprotective father?

He jammed the fax sheets into a file folder, adding it to the pile in his arms and headed down the hall. After talking to Kansas City Detective John Ford late last night, Tully was prepared for Cunningham to be in a foul mood. The waitress's murder looked more and more like the work of Albert Stucky. No one else would deliver the woman's kidney to Agent O'Dell's hotel room. Actually, Tully couldn't figure out why he wasn't on a plane to Kansas City to join O'Dell.

"Good morning, Anita," he greeted the gray-haired secretary who looked alert and impeccable at any hour of the day.

"Coffee, Agent Tully?"

"Yes, please. Cream but—"

"No sugar. I remember. I'll bring it in to you." She waved him by. Everyone knew not to set foot into the assistant director's office until Anita gave the signal.

Cunningham was on the phone, but nodded to Tully and pointed to one of the chairs in front of his desk.

"Yes, I understand," Cunningham said into the phone. "Of course I will." He hung up, as was his usual manner, without a goodbye. He adjusted his glasses, sipped coffee, then looked at Tully. Despite the crisp white shirt and perfectly knotted tie, his eyes betrayed him. Swollen from too little sleep, the red lines were magnified by the bifocal half of his glasses.

"Before we get started," he said, glancing at his watch, "do you have any information on Walker Harding?"

"Harding?" Tully had to think past horny high-school boys and pink prom dresses. "I'm sorry, sir, I don't recognize the name Walker Harding."

"He was Albert Stucky's business partner," a woman's voice answered from the open doorway.

Tully twisted in his chair to look at the young, dark-haired woman. She was attractive and wore a navy blue suit jacket with matching trousers.

"Agent O'Dell, please come in." Cunningham stood and pointed to the chair next to Tully.

Tully stared up at her, shuffling his files, awkwardly shoving them aside.

"Special Agent Margaret O'Dell, this is Special Agent R. J. Tully."

The chair wobbled as Tully stood and shook Agent O'Dell's outstretched hand. Immediately he was impressed with her firm grip and the way she looked directly into his eyes.

"I'm pleased to meet you, Agent Tully."

She was genuine. She was professional. There was no trace of what she must have gone through last night. This certainly didn't look like an agent who was on the verge of mental collapse.

"The pleasure is mine, Agent O'Dell. I've heard a great deal about you."

Tully could see Cunningham already growing impatient with all these pleasantries.

"Why were you asking about Walker Harding?" O'Dell asked as she sat down.

Tully picked up his files again. Okay, so she was used to the assistant director's style of getting right down to business. Now Tully wished he had spent some time preparing instead of agonizing over Emma's virginity. He honestly hadn't thought O'Dell would show up.

"For Agent Tully's benefit," Cunningham began explaining, "Walker Harding and Albert Stucky started an Internet stock-trading business, one of the first of its kind, in the early 1990s. They ended up making millions."

"I'm sorry, but I don't think I have any information on him," Tully said as he riffled through his files, double-checking.

"You probably don't." Cunningham sounded apologetic. "Harding was out of the picture long before Stucky took up his new hobby. He and Stucky sold their company, split their millions and went their separate ways. There was no reason for any of us to know about Walker Harding."

"I'm not sure I follow," Tully said, glancing at Agent O'Dell to see if he was the only one missing something. "Is there some reason why we should now?"

Anita interrupted, floating into the room and handing Tully a steaming mug.

"Thanks, Anita."

"Anything for you, Agent O'Dell? Coffee? Or perhaps your usual early-morning Diet Pepsi?"

Tully watched Agent O'Dell smile in a way that said the two women were quite familiar with each other.

"Thank you, Anita, but no, I'm fine."

The secretary squeezed the agent's shoulder in a gesture that looked more motherly than professional, and then she left, closing the door behind her.

Cunningham sat back and made a tent with his fingertips, picking up the conversation exactly where they had left off, as if there had been no interruption. "Walker Harding became a recluse after he and Stucky sold their business. Practically disappeared off the face of the earth. There seems to be virtually no records, no transactions, no sign of the man."

"Then what does this have to do with Albert Stucky?" Tully was puzzled.

"I checked the airline schedules within the last week for flights going from Dulles or Reagan National to Kansas City. Not that I expected to find Albert Stucky's name on any of the manifests." He looked from Tully to O'Dell. "I was looking for any of the aliases Stucky has used in the past. That's when I noticed that there was a ticket sold for a KC flight, Sunday afternoon out of Dulles, to a Walker Harding."

Cunningham waited, looking for some reaction. Tully watched, tapping his foot nervously but not impressed with the information.

"Excuse me, sir, for saying so, but that may not mean much. It may not even be the same man."

"Perhaps not. However, Agent Tully, I suggest you find out whatever you can about Walker Harding."

"Assistant Director Cunningham, why am I here?" Agent O'Dell asked politely but with enough candor to indicate she wasn't willing to continue without an answer.

Tully wanted to smile. Instead, he kept his eyes and his attention on Cunningham. It was hard not to like O'Dell. Out of the corner of his eye, he could see her shift in her chair, uncomfortable and restless but holding her tongue. She had been kept off this investigation since the beginning. Tully wondered if she was angry with having to sit and listen to these details if she couldn't be involved. Or had Cunningham changed his mind? Tully studied his face, but saw no clue as to what his boss was thinking.

When he didn't answer immediately, O'Dell must have seen it as an opportunity to proceed.

"I mean no disrespect, but the three of us are sitting here talking about a ticket that may or may not have been issued to a man who Albert Stucky may or may not have talked to for years. Yet, there is one thing that we can be certain of—Albert Stucky murdered a woman in Kansas City, and most likely he is still there."

Tully crossed his arms and waited, all the while wanting to applaud this woman he had heard was burned out and slipping over the edge. She certainly soared at the top of her game this morning.

Cunningham caved in his finger tent and sat forward, leaning elbows on his desk and looking as though he had been ambushed in a chess match. But now he was ready for his move, his turn.

"Saturday night about twenty miles from here, a young woman was found murdered, her body tossed into a Dumpster, her spleen surgically removed and placed inside a discarded pizza box."

"Saturday?" Agent O'Dell fidgeted while she calculated the unusually short time line. "Kansas City is not a copycat. He left the goddamn kidney at my door."

Tully winced. Forget chess. This would be more like a showdown at the OK Corral. Cunningham, however, didn't blink.

"The young woman was a pizza delivery person. She was taken while delivering her route."

Agent O'Dell became agitated, crossing her legs, then uncrossing them as if restraining her words. Tully knew she had to be exhausted.

Cunningham continued, "She had to have been taken somewhere close by. Perhaps in the neighborhood. He raped and sodomized her, slit her throat and removed her spleen."

"By sodomized are you saying he raped her himself from behind or with another item?"

Tully couldn't see a difference. Wasn't either hideous enough? Cunningham looked to him for the answer. This, unfortunately, he could answer without digging through a single file. The young girl had looked too much like Emma for him not to remember every detail. Whether he wanted them to be or not, they were stamped in his memory.

"There was no semen left behind, but the medical examiner seemed convinced it was penile stimulation. There were no traces or remnants that a foreign object might leave behind."

"Stucky's never done that before." O'Dell sat at the edge of her chair, suddenly animated. "He wouldn't do that. There would be no point. He likes to watch their faces. He enjoys seeing their fear. He wouldn't be able to see that from behind."

Cunningham tapped his fingertips on the desktop as if waiting for O'Dell to finish.

"The young woman delivered a pizza to your new home the night she was murdered."

The silence seemed amplified when the drumming of the fingertips stopped. Cunningham and Tully watched O'Dell. She sat back, looking from one to the other. Tully saw the realization in her eyes. He expected to see fear, maybe anger. It surprised him to find what looked like resignation. She rubbed a hand over her face and tucked strands of hair behind her ears. Otherwise, she sat quietly.

"That's why, Agent O'Dell, I'm guessing it didn't matter that you stayed in Kansas City. He'll follow you." Cunningham loosened his tie and rolled up his sleeves as though he was suddenly too warm. Both gestures seemed foreign. "Albert Stucky is pulling you into this, no matter what I do to keep you out of it."

"And by keeping me out of it, sir, you're taking away my only defense." O'Dell's voice had an undeniable quiver to it. Tully saw her bite down on her lower lip. Was it to restrain her words or control the quiver?

Cunningham glanced over at Tully, sat back and released his own sigh of resignation. "Agent Tully has requested that you assist him on the case."

O'Dell stared at Tully with surprise. He found himself a bit embarrassed and not sure why. It wasn't as if he had made the request to do her any favors. It could be putting her in even more danger. But the fact was, he needed her.

"I've decided to grant Agent Tully's request on two conditions, neither of which I'm willing to negotiate or compromise." Cunningham leaned forward again, elbows on his desktop, hands fisted together. "Number one, Agent Tully is to remain the lead on this investigation. I expect you to share all information and knowledge as soon as it becomes available to you. You will not—and I repeat, Agent O'Dell—you will not go off on a wild-goose chase or check on hunches without Agent Tully accompanying you. Is that understood?"

"Of course," she answered, her voice now strong and firm again.

"Number two. I want you to see the Bureau's psychologist."

"Sir, I really don't think—"

"Agent O'Dell, I said there will be no negotiating, no compromise. I'll leave it up to Dr. Kernan as to how many times he wants to see you each week."

"Dr. James Kernan?" O'Dell seemed appalled.

"That's right. I had Anita set up your first appointment. Check with her on your way out for the time. She's also setting up an office for you. Agent Tully occupies your old one. I saw no reason in moving both of you. Now, if the two of you will excuse me." He sat back, dismissing them. "I have another appointment."

Tully gathered his mess and waited for O'Dell at the door. For a woman who had just been given what she had wanted for the last five months, she looked more agitated than relieved.

CHAPTER 30

Tess looked forward to her morning appointment, although while she drove down the empty streets, the guilt crept over her for tiptoeing out of Daniel's house without waking him to say goodbye. She simply didn't have the energy for another battle. He would grumble about her leaving so early to run home and shower and change clothes, when she could do all that just as easily at his house. What he really wanted was for her to stay, because he was more easily aroused in the mornings, and he wanted to have sex.

Yet he would say ridiculous things like, "We have so little time for each other, we need those few extra minutes in the morning."

Each time she stayed over, it was the same thing, the same old argument—"How will we ever know if we're compatible, Tess, if we don't read the *New York Times* together or share breakfast in bed?"

He had actually given those examples. How could he believe any of that when he barely spoke to her over their dinners together? The mornings when he wanted her to stay for a quick fuck seemed to be the only time he was concerned about their compatibility. Ninety-nine percent of the time, he could care less what was good for their relationship. Not that Tess had any clues about what made a successful relationship. Maybe it did include sharing the *New York Times* and breakfasts in bed. How would she know? She had never been in a relationship she could call a success, and she had never been in one with someone like Daniel Kassenbaum.

Daniel was sophisticated, intelligent, refined and cultured. My God, the man completed the *New York Times* crossword puzzle in ink. But unlike Daniel, she didn't kid herself about their relationship. She knew they had little in common. He certainly didn't consider her his equal, and often pointed out her deficiencies as if she were his Eliza Doolittle. Even the other night when she had asked him about investing her bonus money, she had felt as if he had patted her on the head with his "don't get into something you don't understand" comment.

However, the one area where Tess excelled, above and beyond Daniel, was sex. What Daniel lacked, Tess made up for. He had told her many times—though only in the heat of passion—that she was "phenomenally the best fuck" he had ever had. For some twisted reason, it pleased her to have this power over him, though it left her cold and hollow inside. Having sex with Daniel, despite being phenomenal for him, was neither enjoyable nor satisfying for Tess.

In fact, she had begun to wonder whether she was capable of feeling genuinely aroused—if she would ever feel the sort of passion she continuously faked with Daniel. Having Will Finley, a complete stranger, resurrect those feelings proved more unsettling and annoying than reassuring. And having those memories, still so fresh in her mind, of Will's hands and mouth knowing exactly how to touch her, made Daniel's inadequacies more pronounced. She almost wished that she had never been able to remember her night with Will, that the tequila could have erased her memory. Instead, she seemed able to think of nothing else. And those memories reeled over and over in her mind.

At one time she had been so good at blocking out memories. That was usually the purpose of the tequila. In the past, she used to drink too much. She danced and flirted and had sex with as many men as she wanted. She played and hustled pool, putting on wild, sexy shows for anyone interested in encouraging her. She used to believe that if her life ran constantly in fast-forward, she could forget the horrors of her childhood. After all, nothing she could do would be more shocking, more destructive, more frightening than what she had lived through as a child, right?

But in the process, all Tess had managed to do was create a life empty and hollow. Ironically, it had taken a fifth of vodka and a bottle of sleeping pills to wake her up. That was almost seven years ago. The last five years she had worked her ass off to re-create herself and leave not only her childhood behind, but those dark years spent covering it up and running away from it.

In order to do that, she had left the mad rush of D.C. and all its temptations of drugs, all-night clubs and congressmen's beds. Louie's had been a sort of halfway house for Tess. She took a job tending bar and found a tiny apartment by the river. When she finally felt ready, she went back to Blackwood, Virginia, and sold the family farm—the living hell—where she had lived with her aunt and uncle. They had died years before, her only notice coming by way of certified letter from an attorney. Somehow she had expected to automatically know when they died, as if the earth would sigh a relief. There had been no sigh, no relief.

Tess glanced up at herself in the rearview mirror, annoyed that the memories could still wrinkle her brow and clench her teeth. After her aunt's and uncle's deaths, she had let the farm sit empty, refusing to set foot on the property. Finally she had the courage to sell the place, but first destroying the house and all the dilapidated buildings. She had made certain that the storm cellar—her personal punishment chamber—had been bulldozed and filled in. Then, and only then, was she able to sell the place.

It had brought a decent price, supplying her with enough money to start a new life, which only seemed fair since it had taken away half her life in the first place. It was enough money for Tess to go back to school and get her real estate license, and to buy and furnish her brick cottage, in a nice neighborhood, in a quiet city, where no one knew her.

After getting the job at Heston Realty, she joined several business associations. Delores signed her on as a member at the Skyview Country Club. She had insisted it would be essential, allowing Tess to meet potential clients. Although Tess still had a problem seeing herself as a member of a country club. It was there she had met Daniel Kassenbaum. It had been a tremendous victory, proof of her successful new lifestyle. She would be able to do anything, go anywhere, if she was able to win someone as sophisticated, arrogant, well-bred and cultured as Daniel.

She reminded herself that Daniel was good for her. He was stable, ambitious, practical and most importantly, he was taken seriously. All things she wanted—no, needed in her life. That he didn't know or care how to touch her mattered very little in the larger scope of things. Besides, it wasn't as if she was in love with him. She preferred having no emotional investment. Love and emotions had never been key ingredients to a successful relationship. If anything, they had been ingredients for disaster.

Tess pulled the Miata in front of 5349 Archer Drive. Her eyes checked up and down the cul-de-sac, confirming that she had arrived too early. There was no sign of her 10:00 a.m. appointment. Actually, there were no signs of life. The neighborhood's residents had already left for their long commute, and those who were able to stay behind were probably still in bed. She decided to use the extra time to make certain the two-story colonial was in show condition.

She checked her reflection one more time. When had the lines around her mouth and eyes become so pronounced? For the first time in her life she was actually beginning to look her age. It had taken her years to get to where she was. Daniel was an important piece of the puzzle for her new professional persona. He lent credibility to her. She couldn't ruin it now. So why did she keep remembering Will Finley in that blue towel, looking so lean and handsome, and arousing senses she had buried long ago?

She shook her head and grabbed her briefcase, slamming her car door too hard and sending the echo throughout the quiet neighborhood. To make up for the noise, she walked slowly up the sidewalk, preventing her heels from clacking.

The house had been on the market for over eight months with little activity in the last three months. However, the sellers continued to stand firm on their selling price. Like so many of the houses on the outskirts of Newburgh Heights, money seemed to be no problem for the owners, which certainly made negotiations a problem.

Tess went to unlock the steel security door, but the key turned too easily. The dead bolt didn't click. The door wasn't locked, and now standing in the foyer, she could see the security system had also been disarmed.

CHAPTER 31

"Damn it!" Tess muttered, and flipped the light switch. Yes, the electricity was on, so there was no excuse for the alarm system not to be working.

She made a mental note to check on the last agent who had shown the house. Without even looking, she could guess it had been one of the imbeciles from Peterson Brothers. They were constantly forgetting things like this, and they had the professional ethics of pimps. There had been recent rumors about one of the Peterson brothers using empty client houses for sleazy sex parties.

Suddenly Tess remembered that this house had an extra-large master bedroom and bath with a skylight.

"There better not be a mess."

She checked her wristwatch. Only fifteen minutes left. She tossed her briefcase into a corner of the living room, pushed up the sleeves of her suit jacket, and started up the stairs, stopping to kick off her heels. She didn't need this crap, not this morning. Not when her patience and nerves had already been frayed and tested by her disappearing act from Daniel's bed. He'd be getting to his office right about now. Thankfully, she had left her cellular phone in the car, because knowing Daniel, he'd be calling to scold her.

She stomped up the stairs when halfway up she heard the front door open. He was early. Why did he have to be early? She shoved her sleeves back in place and searched for her leather pumps, slipping them on one by one as she found them. By the time she reached the bottom of the staircase, a tall, dark-haired man was wandering through the spacious living room.

Without window treatments, sunlight cascaded in sheets of blinding light, surrounding him.

"Hello?"

"I know I'm a bit early."

"That's fine." Tess kept the annoyance from her voice, wishing she had been able to check the damn master bedroom first.

He turned, and only then did she notice the white cane. Immediately, she wondered how he had gotten here. She glanced out the window but saw no signs of another vehicle in the winding circular driveway.

She guessed he was around her age, middle to late thirties, though she found it hard to determine anyone's age when she couldn't see his eyes. His Ray-Ban sunglasses contained particularly dark lenses. She took notice of his designer silk shirt with the open collar, his expensive leather jacket and well-pressed chinos. She caught herself checking to see if everything matched. His features were handsome but sharp, with a chiseled jaw that was much too taut, thin but nicely curved lips and pronounced cheekbones. He had a bit of a widow's peak, but his dark hair was thick and close cropped.

"I'm Walker Harding," he said. "Are you the agent I spoke to on the phone?"

"Yes, I'm Tess McGowan." She offered her hand, then snatched it back quickly, embarrassed, when she realized he couldn't see it.

He hesitated and slowly removed his hand from his pocket. She noticed how strong and muscular it was as he held it out to her. He was a little off target, his fingers pointed to the side of her. She stepped in closer and shook it. Immediately she felt his large hand swallow hers. The long fingers wrapped all the way around her wrist, surprising her in what felt more like a caress than a handshake. She dismissed the thought and ignored her unexpected discomfort.

"I just arrived," she said, extracting her hand. "I didn't get a chance to make a quick run-through," she explained, wondering how in the world he would know the difference. How was she supposed to show him a house when he couldn't see a damn thing?

He left her and wandered without a word across the living room, tapping his cane in front of him and walking confidently. He stopped at the bay window that looked out over the backyard. He fumbled for the latch and opened it. Then he stood quietly, staring out as if transfixed by something in the yard.

"The sun feels wonderful," he finally said, tilting his head back and letting his face be warmed by the brilliant light. "I know it might seem silly, but I like lots of windows."

"No, it's not silly at all." She caught herself talking louder and immediately chastised herself. He was blind not deaf.

Tess studied his profile. The straight nose had a slight bend, and from this angle she could see a scar just below his jawline. She couldn't help wondering if his blindness had been caused by an accident of some kind. Despite his disability, he seemed to possess confidence. There was a self-assurance in his manner, the way he walked, the way he handled himself. However, his gestures seemed stiff, his hands constantly retreated to his pockets. Was he nervous, anxious?

"How big are the evergreens?" he asked, his voice startling her as though she had forgotten what they were here for.

"Excuse me?"

"I can smell evergreens. Are there a lot and are they big or small?"

She walked up beside him, keeping a safe distance without seeming rude and still being able to look out the window. The property lots here were huge, and the evergreens, mostly cedar and pine, created a natural border at the far edge. She couldn't smell them. But of course his other senses had probably become more refined.

"They're very large. Some cedar, some pine. There's a line of them that separates the properties."

"Good. I do like my privacy." He turned to her and smiled. "I hope you're not uncomfortable having to describe things to me."

"No, of course not," Tess said, hoping that she sounded convincing. "Where would you like to start your tour?"

"I was told there is a fabulous master bedroom. Could we start there?"

"Good choice," she told him. Damn it! She wished she had come earlier. That Peterson asshole better not have left a mess. "Do you prefer walking alone or would you like me to take your arm?"

"You smell quite lovely."

She stared at him, taken off guard.

"It's Chanel No. 5, right?"

"Yes, it is." Was he flirting with her?

"I'll follow your lovely scent. Just lead the way."

"Oh, yes. Okay."

She walked slowly, almost too slowly, causing his outstretched hand to bump into her once on the landing. He let it linger on her hip as though needing to get his bearings. Or at least that was what Tess told herself. She had experienced more outrageous come-ons and intentional gropes than this.

The master bedroom smelled of cleaning formula, and Tess's eyes darted around. Whoever had been here last had indeed cleaned up. Thankfully, the room looked in order. In fact, it smelled and looked freshly scrubbed. Tess found it odd that Mr. Harding, whose senses had been so keen downstairs, made no comment about these new overpowering scents.

"This room is about thirty by twenty," she proceeded casually. "There's another bay window on the south wall that looks out over the backyard. The floor is an oak parquet. There's a—"

"Excuse me, Ms. McGowan."

"Please, call me Tess."

"Tess, of course." He stopped and smiled. "I hope you won't find this offensive, but I like to have an idea of what the person I'm talking to looks like. May I touch your face?"

At first she thought she must have heard him wrong. She didn't know what to say. She remembered his touching her on the landing and now wondered if indeed it had been a grope and not a harmless miscalculation.

"I'm sorry. You're offended," he said apologetically, his voice low and soothing.

"No, of course not," she answered quickly. If she wasn't careful, her paranoia could lose her the sale. "I'm afraid I'm just not as prepared as I should be to help you."

"It's really quite painless," he told her as though he were explaining a surgical procedure. "I use only my fingertips. I assure you, I won't be pawing you." His lips curved into another smile, and Tess felt ridiculous making a fuss.

"Please, go ahead." She stepped closer, despite her apprehension.

He set the cane aside and started slowly, gently at her hair, using both hands, but only the tips of his fingers. She avoided looking up at him, staring off over his shoulder. His hands smelled faintly of ammonia, or was it simply the overpowering scent of the freshly scrubbed wooden floor? His fingers stroked her forehead and moved over her eyelids.

She tried to ignore their dampness, but glanced at his face for any indication that he was as uncomfortable as she was. No, he seemed calm and composed and his fingers began their descent on either side of her face, sliding down her cheeks. She dismissed what felt like a caress. But then his fingertips moved to her lips. His index finger lingered too long, rubbing back and forth. For a second it felt as though he might press it into her mouth. Startled by the sensation and the thought, Tess looked at his eyes. She tried to see beyond the dark lenses, and when she was successful, getting a glimpse of his black eyes, she saw that he was staring directly at her. Was that possible? No, of course not. She was simply being paranoid, an annoying tendency left over from her past life.

By now his fingers had wandered to her chin, tracing their way down to her neck. They briefly wisped beneath the neckline of her blouse, brushing her collarbone, hesitating as if he was testing her, as if asking how far she would let him go. She began to step back just when he wrapped his fingers around her throat.

"What are you doing?" Tess gasped and grabbed at his large hands.

Now he squeezed, choking her, his eyes definitely staring into hers, a twisted smile at his lips. She clawed at the fingers, steel vise grips clamped like the jaws of a pit bull. She struggled and twisted, but he shoved her back. Her head knocked into the wall with such a force she closed her eyes against the pain. She couldn't breathe. She couldn't think. God, he was so strong.

When she opened her eyes, she saw that he had released one of his hands. She was able to suck in air, her lungs aching and greedy. Before she could gather her strength, he shoved his arm up against her to hold her in place, stabbing his elbow into her throat and cutting off her air once again. That's when she saw the syringe in his free hand.

The terror spread through her quickly, her arms and legs flaying in defense. It was useless. He was much too strong. The needle poked through her jacket and sunk deep into the skin of her arm. She felt her entire body jerk. In seconds the room began to spin. Her hands, her knees, her muscles became limp, and then the room went black.

CHAPTER 32

The minute Maggie walked into Dr. James Kernan's office she felt like a nineteen-year-old college student again. The feelings of confusion, wonder and intimidation all came back to her in a rush of sights and smells. His office, set in the Wilmington Towers in Washington, D.C., and no longer on the University of Virginia's campus, still looked and smelled the same.

Immediately, her nostrils were accosted by stale cigar smoke, old leather and Ben-Gay rubbing ointment. The tiny space was littered with the same strange paraphernalia. A human brain's dissected frontal lobe bulged in a mason jar filled with formaldehyde. The jar acted as a makeshift bookend, ironically holding up such texts as *Explaining Hitler: The Search for the Origins of Evil,* Freud's *Interpretation of Dreams* and what Maggie knew to be a rare first edition of *Alice In Wonderland.* Of the three, the last seemed most appropriate for the professor of psychology who easily conjured up images of the Mad Hatter.

On the mahogany credenza across the room were antique instruments, their shapes and points intriguing until they were recognized as surgical instruments once used to perform lobotomies. On the wall behind the matching mahogany desk were black-and-white photographs of the procedure. Another equally disturbing photograph included a young woman undergoing shock treatment. The woman's empty eyes and resigned posture beneath the ominous iron equipment had always reminded Maggie more of an execution than a medical treatment. Sometimes she questioned how she could be involved in a profession that, at one time, could be so brutal while pretending to cure the ailments of the psyche.

Kernan, however, embraced the eccentricities of their profession. His office was simply an extension of the strange little man. A man as notorious for his crude jokes about "nutcases" as he was for his own version of shock treatment, which he had perfected on his students.

The man loved mind games and could lure and trick a person into them without warning. One moment he would drill an unprepared freshman with rapid-fire questions, not allowing the poor student to even answer. The next minute he'd be in a corner of the classroom, standing silently with his face to the wall. Then still later, he'd climb atop a desk and lecture while teetering from one desk to another, his small, stocky but aging body threatening to send him falling while he lectured and did a balancing act at the same time. Even the seniors in his classes had no idea what to expect of their odd professor. And this was the man the FBI trusted to determine her sanity?

Maggie heard the familiar clomp-squeak of his footsteps outside the office. Instinctively, she sat up straight and stopped her browsing. Even the man's footsteps transformed her into an incompetent college kid.

Dr. Kernan entered his office unceremoniously and shuffled to his desk without recognizing or acknowledging Maggie. He plopped down into the leather chair, sending it into a series of creaks. Maggie couldn't be sure that all the creaks came from the chair and not the old man's joints.

He began rummaging through stacks of papers. She watched quietly, her hands folded in her lap. Kernan looked as though he had shrunk since the last time she had seen him, over ten years ago. Back then he had seemed ancient, but now his shoulders were hunched, his hands trembled and were speckled with brown spots. His hair, just as white as she remembered, was thin and feathery, revealing more brown spots on his forehead and the top of his head. Tufts of white hair protruded from his ears.

Finally he appeared to find what he had been so desperately in search of. He struggled to open the tin box of breath mints, took two without offering any to Maggie and snapped the container shut.

"O'Dell, Margaret," he said to himself, still not acknowledging her presence.

He sorted through the rubble again. "Class of 1990." He stopped and thumbed through a folder. Maggie glanced at the cover to see if he was reading her file, only to discover a label that read, Twenty-five Best Internet Porn Sites.

"I remember a Margaret O'Dell," he said without looking up at her, and in a voice that sounded like a senile old man talking to himself. "O'Dell, O'Dell, the farmer and the dell."

Maggie shifted in her chair, forcing herself to be patient, to be polite. Nothing had changed. Why was she surprised to find him treating patients the same way he had treated his students, playing silly word games, reducing names and identities to nursery rhymes? It was all part of his intimidation.

"Premed," he continued while riffling through the list of porn sites. Several times he stopped, smacking his lips together or hissing out a "tis, tis." "Sat in the back left corner of my classroom, taking very few notes. B student. Asked questions only about criminal behavior and hereditary traits."

Maggie hid her surprise. These could easily be odd little facts he may have noted and kept in a student file. And of course, he would have reviewed her file before she arrived, so as to have an advantage. Not that he needed an advantage. She waited, forcing her hands to keep still when they wanted to grip the arms of her chair. She wanted to dig her fingernails into the leather to steady herself and prevent her from storming out of this ridiculous inquisition.

"Got a master's in behavioral psychology," he went on in his droll tone. "Managed to land a forensic fellowship at Quantico." Finally he looked up at her, his pale blue eyes magnified and swimming behind the thick square glasses. Bushy white eyebrows stuck out in every direction. He rubbed his jaw and said, "Wonder what the hell you would have done if you'd been an A student." Then he stared at her, waiting.

As usual, he caught her off guard. She didn't know what to say. He had a talent for disarming people by making them feel invisible. Then suddenly he expected a response to what was never a question. Maggie remained silent and returned his steady gaze, vowing not to flinch. She hated that he could reduce her to an unsure, speechless teenager with only a few words and that goddamn look of his. This was certainly not her idea of therapy. Assistant Director Cunningham was way off base on this one. Sending her to see anyone was a waste of time. Sending her to see Kernan would only challenge her sanity further and would certainly not be a remedy.

"So, Margaret O'Dell, the quiet little bird in the corner, the B student who was so interested in criminals but didn't think she belonged in my classroom, is now Special Agent Margaret O'Dell, who wears a gun and a shiny badge and now doesn't think she belongs in my office."

He stared at her again, waiting for a response, still not asking a question. His elbows leaned on the wobbly stacks of paper as he laced his fingers together.

"That's true, isn't it? You don't think you should be here?"

"No, I don't," she answered, her voice strong and defiant despite the man's ability to intimidate the hell out of her.

"So your superiors are wrong? All those years of training. All that experience, and they're flat out wrong. Is that right?"

"I didn't say that."

"Really? That wasn't what you said?"

Word games, mind games, confusion—Kernan was a master. Maggie needed to concentrate. She couldn't let him twist her words. She wouldn't let him trap her.

"You asked me if I thought I should be here," she explained calmly. "I simply said no, I don't think that I should be here."

"Awwww," he said, drawing it out into a sigh as he sank back in his chair. He rested his hands on his thick chest, letting his wrinkled jacket fall open. "I'm so glad you clarified that for me, Margaret O'Dell."

She remembered that her one-on-one encounters with the man had always felt like an interrogation. It was disconcerting that this befuddled, little old man who looked as if he slept in his clothes, still possessed that same power. She refused to let him unnerve her. Instead, she stared at him and waited.

"So, tell me, Margaret O'Dell, who doesn't think she belongs in my office, do you enjoy this obsession you have with Albert Stucky?"

Suddenly she felt a knot in her stomach. Damn it! Leave it to Kernan to cut to the chase, to strike without warning.

"Of course I don't enjoy it." She kept her voice steady, her eyes level with his. She mustn't blink too many times. He would be counting the blinks. Despite those Coke-bottle glasses, Kernan wouldn't miss a twitch or a grimace.

"Then why do you continue to obsess?"

"Because I want him caught."

"And you're the only one who can catch him?"

"I know him better than anyone else."

"Oh yes, of course. Because he shared his little hobby with you. That's right. He left you with a little tattoo, a sort of brand to remember him by."

She had forgotten how cruel Kernan could be. Yet she forced herself to stay calm. She couldn't let him see the anger. That was exactly what he wanted.

"I spent two years tracking him. That's why I know him better than anyone else."

"I see," he said, tilting his head as if necessary to do so. "Then your obsession will end after you catch him?"

"Yes."

"And after he's punished?"

"Yes."

"Because he must be punished, right?"

"There is no punishment great enough for someone like Albert Stucky."

"Really? Putting him to death won't be punishment enough?"

She hesitated, well aware of his biting sarcasm and anticipating his trap. She proceeded anyway.

"No matter how many victims, no matter how many women Stucky kills, he can die only once."

"Ah yes, I see. And that wouldn't be a fitting punishment. What would be?"

She didn't answer. She wouldn't take his bait.

"You'd like to see him suffer, wouldn't you, Margaret O'Dell?"

She held his gaze. Don't flinch, she told herself. He was waiting for her to slip. He was setting her up, pushing her, forcing her to expose her anger.

"How would you choose to make him suffer? Pain? Excruciating, drawn-out pain?" He stared at her, waiting. She stared back, refusing to give him what he wanted.

"No, not pain," he said finally, as if her eyes had answered for her. "No. You prefer fear, don't you? You want him to suffer by feeling fear," he continued in a casual voice with neither accusation nor confrontation, inviting her to confide in him.

Her hands stayed in her lap. She continued to sit up straight, eyes never leaving his while the anger began churning in her stomach.

"You want him to experience the same fear, that same sense of helplessness that each of his victims felt." He sat forward in his chair, the creak amplified in the silence. "The same fear that you felt when he had you trapped. When he was cutting you. When his knife was slicing into your skin."

He paused, and she felt him examining her. The room had become hot, with very little air. Yet she kept her hands from wiping the strands of hair that had become damp on her forehead. She resisted the urge to bite down on her lower lip. Instead, she simply returned his stare.

"Is that it, Margaret O'Dell? You want to see Mr. Albert Stucky squirm, just like he made you squirm."

She hated that he referred to Stucky with the respect of using mister. How dare he?

"Seeing him squirm in the electric chair isn't enough for you, is it?" he continued to push.

Maggie's fingers started wringing in her lap. Her palms were sweaty. Why was it so damn hot in the room? Her cheeks were flushed. Her head began to throb.

"No, the electric chair isn't a punishment appropriate for his crimes, is it? You have a better punishment in mind, don't you? And how do you propose to administer this punishment, Margaret O'Dell?"

"By making him look directly at me when I shoot the goddamn bastard between his eyes," she blasted, no longer caring that she had just allowed herself to be swallowed whole into Dr. James Kernan's psychological trap.

CHAPTER 33

Tess McGowan tried to open her eyes, but her eyelids were too heavy. She managed a flutter, seeing a flash of light, then darkness. She was sitting up, but the earth was moving beneath her in a low rumble and steady vibration. Somewhere a soft, deep voice with a country twang was singing about hurting the ones you love.

Why couldn't she move? Her arms were limp, her legs like concrete. But the only restraint was across her shoulder, across her lap. A car. Yes, she was buckled into a car. That explained the movement, the vibration, the muffled sounds. It didn't explain why she couldn't open her eyes.

She tried again. Another flutter. Headlights flickered before her heavy eyelids fell closed. It was night. How could it be night? It had just been morning. Hadn't it?

She leaned against the headrest. She smelled jasmine, just a hint, soft and subtle. Yes, she remembered a few days ago she had bought a new sachet and stuck it under the passenger seat. So she was in her own car. The scent, the notion calmed her until she realized that if she wasn't driving, someone else was here with her. Was it Daniel? Why couldn't she remember? Why did her mind feel as though it was filled with cobwebs? Had she gone out drinking again? Oh dear God! Had she picked up another stranger?

She turned her head slightly to the side without removing it from the headrest. It took such effort to move, each inch as if in slow motion. One more time she attempted to open her eyes. Too dark, but there was movement. The eyelids dropped shut again.

She listened. She could hear someone breathing. She opened her mouth to speak. She would ask where they were going. It was a simple question, but nothing came out. There was a slight groan but even that hadn't come from her. Then the car began to slow, followed by a faint electric buzz. Tess felt a draft, smelled fresh tar and knew the window had opened. The car stopped, but the engine continued to hum. Gas fumes told her they were stalled in traffic. She tried once again to open her eyes.

"Good evening, Officer," a deep voice said from the seat next to her.

Was it Daniel? The voice sounded familiar.

"Good evening," another voice bellowed. "Oh, sorry," came a whisper. "Didn't see your wife sleeping."

"What seems to be the problem?"

Yes, Tess wanted to know, too. What was the problem? Why couldn't she move? Why couldn't she open her eyes? What wife was sleeping? Did the officer mean her?

"We've got an accident we're cleaning up on the other side of the toll bridge. A leftover from the rush-hour traffic. Be just a minute or two. Then we'll let you through."

"No hurry." the voice said much too calmly.

No. It wasn't Daniel. Daniel was always in a hurry. He'd be making the officer understand how important he was. He'd be causing a scene. Oh, how she hated when he did that. But it if wasn't Daniel beside her, then who?

A flutter of panic crawled over her. "No hurry?" Yes, the voice was familiar.

She began to remember.

"You smell quite lovely," that same voice had told her. It came to her in pieces. The house on Archer Drive. He wanted to see the master bedroom. "I hope you're not offended."

He wanted to see her face. "It's really quite painless." No, he wanted to feel her face. His hands, his fingers on her hair, her cheeks, her neck. Then wrapping those hands around her throat, tight and hard, the muscles squeezing. She couldn't breathe. She couldn't move. Dark eyes. And a smile. Yes, he had smiled while his fingers squeezed and wrung her neck. It hurt. Stop it. It hurt so bad. Her head hurt, and she could hear the smack of it hitting against the wall. She fought with fists and fingernails. God, he was strong.

Then she had felt it. A prick of the needle as it sunk deep into her arm. She remembered the rush of heat that flowed through her veins. She remembered the room spinning.

Now she tried to raise that same arm. It wouldn't move, but it ached. What had he given her? Who the hell was he? Where was he taking her? Even the fear felt trapped, a lump caught deep inside her throat, straining to be set free. She couldn't wave or swing her arms. She couldn't kick or run. My God, she couldn't even scream.

CHAPTER 34

Maggie had passed the exit for Quantico without a glance and had gone straight home after her meeting with Kernan. Meeting? That was a joke. She shook her head and now continued to pace in her living room. The hourlong drive from D.C. hadn't even begun to cool off her anger. What kind of psychologist left his patients wanting to slam fists through walls?

She noticed her bags at the bottom of the staircase, still packed from her Kansas City trip. Boxes remained stacked in the corners. Her nerves felt as if they had been rubbed raw. A knot tightened at the base of her neck and her head throbbed. She couldn't remember when she had last eaten. It had probably been on the flight last night.

She considered changing and going for a run. It was getting dark but that had never stopped her before. No, what did stop her was knowing Stucky could be watching. Had he returned from Kansas City? Was he out there somewhere hiding, waiting, watching? She paced from window to window, examining the street and then the woods behind her house, squinting to study the twilight shadows dancing behind the trees. She searched for anything out of the ordinary, anything that moved, but in the light breeze every rustle of a bush, every sway of a branch made her uneasy. She could already feel her muscles tightening, her nerves unraveling.

Earlier she had noticed a construction worker at the end of her street inspecting sewage grates and setting up pylons. His coveralls had been too clean, his shoes too polished. Maggie knew immediately that he had to be one of Cunningham's surveillance crew. How the hell did Cunningham expect to catch Stucky with such amateurish strategies? If Maggie had been able to see through the impostor, certainly Stucky, a professional chameleon, would find it laughable. Stucky took on identities and roles with such ease that surely he would spot someone doing the same thing, only doing it poorly.

She hated feeling like a caged animal in her own home. To make matters worse, the house was deathly quiet. Other than the clicking of her heels on the polished wood floor, Maggie heard nothing. No lawn mowers, no car engines, no children playing. But wasn't the peace and quiet, a piece of seclusion, exactly what she longed for when she bought this house? Hadn't that been her intention? What was that old saying—be careful what you wish for?

She unearthed her CD player, an inexpensive oversize boom box. She dug through the overflowing box of CDs. Some were in sealed wrappers, gifts from friends she hadn't taken time to open, let alone enjoy. Finally she decided on an early Jim Brickman, hoping the piano solos would soothe her agitated insides. The music barely began when Maggie noticed Susan Lyndell making her way up the circular drive. It looked as though there would be no stress relief.

She opened the door before Susan made it up the steps to the portico. Her eyes darted everywhere but at Susan, checking, double-checking.

"How was your trip?" Susan asked as though they were old friends.

"It was fine." Maggie grabbed the woman's elbow gently and quickly urged her into the foyer.

Susan stared at her, surprised. On her first visit Maggie had barely let the woman through the door, and now she was pulling her in.

"I got back late last night," Maggie continued, closing the door. All she could think about was Stucky watching. Stucky choosing his next victim.

"I tried to call but you're not listed yet."

"No, I'm not," she said with finality in case Susan expected she might tell her. "Did you speak with Detective Manx?"

"Actually, that's what I wanted to tell you. I think I was mistaken about what we discussed the other day."

"Why do think you were mistaken?" Maggie waited while her neighbor glanced around at her stacked cartons, taking in Maggie's living room and probably wondering how Maggie could ever afford such a house.

"I spoke with Sid," Susan told her, finally looking at Maggie, though she still seemed distracted by Maggie's things, or rather her lack of things.

"Mr. Endicott? What exactly did you speak to him about?"

"Sid's a good man. I hate to see him going through this all alone. I felt he had a right to know. Well, you know...about Rachel and that man."

"The telephone repairman?"

"Yes." Now Susan wouldn't meet Maggie's eyes, but it had nothing to do with the surroundings.

"What did you tell him?"

"Just that quite possibly she may have left with him."

"I see." She wondered why Susan Lyndell could so easily betray her friend. And why was it suddenly so easy to believe Rachel had left with some stranger who, only days ago, Susan thought might hurt her friend? "And what did Mr. Endicott say?"

"Oh, maybe you haven't heard. Rachel's car was not in the garage. The police initially saw Sid's Mercedes and didn't realize that Rachel's was gone. See, she usually drives Sid to the airport when he goes out of town so he won't need to leave the car in airport parking. Sid's always worried about his car. Anyway, I think Rachel must have taken off with this guy. She was certainly infatuated by him."

"What about the dog?"

"The dog?"

"We found her dog stabbed...injured under the bed."

Susan shrugged. "I have no idea about that," she said as if she couldn't be expected to figure out everything.

Maggie's cellular phone started ringing from inside her jacket pocket. She hesitated. Susan waved a birdlike hand at her to go ahead and get it as she backed away. "I won't keep you. Just wanted to fill you in." Before Maggie could protest, her neighbor was out the door and walking down the driveway in what Maggie thought looked almost like a skip. She definitely didn't seem like the same nervous, anxious woman she had met a few days ago.

Maggie quickly closed the door and took time to activate the alarm system while the phone continued to ring. Finished, she twisted the contraption out of her pocket.

"Maggie O'Dell."

"Jesus, finally. You need a better cell phone, Maggie. I think your battery must be low again."

Immediately, Maggie felt the tension return to her neck and shoulders. Greg's greetings always sounded like scoldings.

"My phone's been off. I've been out of town. You got my message." She went directly to the point, not wanting to encourage his attempt to chastise her for being unreachable.

"You should have some sort of messaging service," he persisted. "Your mother called me a couple of days ago. She didn't even know you moved. For Christ's sake, Maggie, you could at least call your mother and give her your new number."

"I did call her. Is she okay?"

"She sounded great. Said she was in Las Vegas."

"Las Vegas?" Her mother never left Richmond. And what a choice. Yes, Las Vegas was the perfect place for a suicidal alcoholic.

"She said she was with a Reverend Everett. You need to keep better tabs on her, Maggie. She is your mother."

Maggie leaned against the wall and took a deep breath. Greg had never understood the dynamics between Maggie and her mother. How could he? He came from a family that looked as if it had been special-ordered from a 1950s family catalog.

"Greg, did I leave a carton at the condo?"

"No, there's nothing here. You do realize that none of this would have happened if you had used United?"

Maggie ignored his I-told-you-so. "Are you sure? Look, I don't care if you've opened it or if you've gone through it."

"Listen to you. You don't trust or believe anybody anymore. Can't you see what this goddamn job is doing to you?"

She rubbed her neck and squeezed at the knot. Why did he have to make this so difficult?

"Did you check in the basement?" she asked, knowing there was no way it had ended up there, but giving him one last chance for a way out if he had, indeed, opened the box.

"No, there's nothing. What was in it? One of your precious guns? Are you not able to sleep at night without all three or four or however many of those things you have?"

"I have two, Greg. It's not unusual for an agent to have a backup."

"Right. Well, that's one too many for me."

"Would you just call me if the carton shows up?"

"It's not here."

"Okay, fine. Goodbye."

"Call your mom sometime soon," he said in place of a closing and hung up.

She leaned her head against the wall and shut her eyes. She tried to calm the throbbing in her head and neck and shoulders. The doorbell chimed, and she was grabbing for her revolver before she even realized it. Jesus! Maybe Greg was right. She did live in a crazy paranoid world.

Beside a lamppost in her driveway, she could see a van with Riley's Veterinary Clinic imprinted on the side. A man in white overalls and a baseball cap stood on the portico. Sitting patiently beside him with a blue collar and leash was a white Labrador retriever. Despite there being no massive bandage around the dog's chest and shoulder, Maggie recognized it as the dog she had helped rescue from the Endicotts' house. Nevertheless, she examined the man, making certain this wasn't a disguise. Finally she decided he was too short to be Stucky.

"The Endicotts live farther down the street," she said as soon as she opened the door.

"I know that," the man snapped. His jaw was taut, his face red, his forehead glistening with sweat as though he had run here instead of driving. "Mr. Endicott refuses to take the dog."

"He what?"

"He won't take the dog."

"Is that what he said?" Maggie thought the idea incredible after what the dog had been through.

"Well, his exact words were, it's his wife's frickin' dog—excuse my language, I'm just repeating what he said, but let me tell you, he didn't use 'frickin',' okay? Anyway, he said it's his wife's frickin' dog and if she took off and left the stupid dog, then he doesn't want him either."

Maggie glanced at the dog who cowered close to the ground, either from the man's raised voice or because he knew they were talking about him.

"I'm not sure what you expect me to do. I don't think my talking to Mr. Endicott will change his mind. I don't even know the man."

"Your name and address is on the release form you signed when you brought in the dog. Detective Manx told us to leave the dog with you."

"He did, did he?" Of all the nerve. It was Manx's one last dig. "And what if I refuse to take him? What will you do with him?"

"I have orders from Mr. Endicott to take him to the pound."

Maggie looked at the dog again, and as if on cue he stared up at her with sad, pathetic brown eyes. Damn it! What did she know about taking care of a dog? She wasn't home enough to take care of a dog. She couldn't have a dog. Her mother had never allowed her to have one while she was growing up. Greg was allergic to dogs and cats, or so he had said once when she had brought home a stray she had found while out running. Allergic or not, she knew he would never have been able to tolerate anything with four paws climbing on his precious leather furniture. Suddenly Maggie realized that seemed like a good enough reason.

"What's his name," she asked as she took the dog's leash from the man's hand.

"It's Harvey."

CHAPTER 35

Boston, Massachusetts
Thursday, April 2

Will Finley couldn't sit still. He had been jumpy all morning. Now he roamed the halls of the county courthouse. He swiped a jerky hand over his face. Too much caffeine. That was his problem. That and very little sleep. It also didn't help matters that Tess McGowan hadn't returned any of his phone calls. Today was already Thursday. Since Monday, he had left messages on her answering machine and at her office. Or, at least, what he thought was her office. He had taken one of her business cards from the antique desk in her bedroom. Otherwise, he wouldn't have had her home phone number or known her last name. Hell, he had even tried leaving her messages at Louie's until the burly owner told him to "leave Tess alone and fuck off."

So why couldn't he leave her alone? Why did she consume his thoughts? He had never been obsessed with a woman before. Why this one? Even Melissa had noticed his preoccupation, but she had accepted his explanation of being overloaded at his new job and stressed out about all the last-minute wedding preparations.

It didn't help matters that he had avoided having sex with her since his night with Tess. Hell, it had only been three nights and yet he'd been afraid Melissa would notice, especially last night when she had hinted about spending the night at his place. He had practically shoved her out the door, using the lame excuse that he had to get some sleep for a big trial in the morning. What was his problem? Was he really afraid that Melissa would discover his betrayal somehow if he touched her differently? Or did he simply not want to erase the memories of having sex with Tess? Because he had played back that night over and over in his head so many times he could conjure it up at will.

Shit, he was fucked up!

As he turned the corner, heading to Records he ran into Nick Morrelli. The contents of Will's folder spilled across the floor, and he was on his knees before Nick had a chance to know what hit him.

"Hey, what's the hurry?" Nick said, joining Will on the floor.

Others stepped around them, not paying any attention as their heels smashed and crumpled the scattered papers.

Nick handed him the papers he had gathered while they stood up. But Will's eyes darted across the floor, making sure he had everything. That was all he needed—to lose some piece of paper that would give the defense an edge in whatever this trial was.

"So what's the rush?" Nick asked again, hands in his pockets, waiting.

"No rush." Will straightened the stack and raked his fingers through his hair. He wondered if Nick could see the slight tremor in his hand. Although the two men were new to the D.A.'s office, Nick had been one of Will's professors in law school back at the University of Nebraska. He still looked up to Nick as a mentor instead of a colleague. And he knew Nick had sort of taken him under his wing, helping a fellow Midwesterner adjust to the rush of big-city life in Boston.

"You look like shit." Nick looked concerned. "You feeling okay?"

"Yeah. Sure. I'm fine."

Nick didn't look convinced. He glanced at his watch. "It's almost lunchtime. How 'bout we get burgers down the street? I'm buying."

"Okay. Yeah, sure. If you're buying." Geez! Even his speech was jerky. "Let me drop this stuff at Records."

It was warm enough for shirtsleeves, but both men wore their jackets. Will realized he'd need to wear his jacket for the rest of the day if the pools under his arms were as obvious as they felt. Maybe all these physical reactions were simply cold feet. After all, the wedding was, what, three or four weeks away? Holy crap! How could it be that close?

Will filled the conversation with boring stuff about the trials Nick had missed while in Kansas City. It was the only way to ignore the concerned look in his ex-professor's eyes. Nick politely listened, then seemed to wait until Will's mouth was full of fries before he asked.

"So you ready to tell me what the hell's bugging you?"

Will wiped away the ketchup on the corner of his mouth and swallowed. He grabbed his Pepsi and washed down what threatened to stick in his throat.

"What makes you think something's wrong?"

"I didn't say wrong. I said what's bugging you?"

"Oh." He wiped his mouth again, buying time. Leave it to a lawyer to fuss over the wording.

"So what's wrong?"

Will shoved his plate aside. He had managed to wolf down half his burger and almost all his fries before Nick had taken a second bite of his burger. He could feel the heartburn tightening into a fist and settling in the middle of his chest. As if he needed one more physical discomfort.

"I think I fucked up big time."

Nick continued eating, waiting, examining him over the burger that he held with both hands. Finally he said, "It wasn't the Prucello case, was it?"

"No. No, it wasn't anything to do with work."

Nick looked relieved. Then his brow furrowed again. "You getting cold feet about the wedding?"

Will gulped his Pepsi. He waved at the waiter and pointed to his glass for another, wishing he could trade it for something stronger.

"Maybe. I don't know." Then he pulled in his chair and leaned across the table so he could keep his voice down despite the noisy lunch-hour crowd. Two of the tables next to them were filled with people he knew from the courthouse.

"Sunday night I met this woman. Christ, Nick! She was...incredible. I haven't been able to stop thinking about her."

Nick chewed and watched him as if contemplating what to say. If anyone would understand, surely it would be Nick Morrelli. Will knew that years ago, all the talk around campus about Nick and some of his own students, as well as several female professors, had not been idle rumor. Nick Morrelli had had his share of one-night stands. Even after he had left the university to take the position as sheriff of Platte City, the reputation and the activity had followed him.

"This woman," Nick said slowly, carefully, "was she a hooker?"

Will almost choked.

"No, hell no," he said, glancing around the small diner to make certain no one noticed he was agitated. "The guys—Mickey, Rob, Bennet—they sort of dared me into picking up this woman who was at the bar. She was incredible, sexy and so...I don't know, uninhibited. But no, she's no goddamn hooker." He stopped and lowered his voice, noticing two women at the next table staring at him. "She's older, probably about your age. Very attractive with this amazing...sensuality. But in a sophisticated sort of way, not, you know, cheap or anything like that. In fact, I think she's a real estate agent or something."

The waiter brought Will's refill. He slid back in his chair, grabbed the glass and gulped half of it. Nick continued eating, as if it was no big deal. Will started feeling anxious and a bit angry. Hell, he had just spilled his guts, and Nick seemed more interested in finishing his goddamn burger.

"So what you're really saying is that she's a pretty incredible fuck?"

"Jesus Christ, Nick!"

"Well? Isn't that what this is all about?"

"You know, man, I thought you of all people would understand this. But forget it. Forget I mentioned it." Will pulled his plate closer and started shoving French fries into his mouth, avoiding looking at Nick. One of the women at the next table smiled at him. Evidently she didn't know that he was an idiot.

"Come on, Will. Be sensible for one minute." Nick waited until he had Will's attention. "Are you willing to piss away three or four years with Melissa for one incredible fuck?"

"No. Of course not." Will slumped in his chair and wrestled with the knot in his tie. He looked up and met Nick's eyes. "I don't know what to think."

"Look, Will. I've been with a lot of women, incredible women. But you can't let one incredible fuck rule your life's decisions."

They sat in silence as Nick finished eating. Will sat up, leaned across the table again, only now noticing the sleeve of his jacket dripping with ketchup. Shit! These days he seemed to spend more money on dry cleaning than he did on food.

"It wasn't just the sex, Nick." He felt he needed to explain, but wasn't sure he understood it himself. "There was something else. I don't know what. Something about her. I can't get her out of my mind. I mean, here's this strong, passionate, sexy, independent woman, who could also be...oh, hell I don't know...vulnerable and sweet and funny and...and real. I know we both had too much to drink, and we know very little about each other, but...I can't stop thinking about her."

He watched Nick take out crisp bills and lay them on the plastic tray with the tab. Had it been a mistake to say any of this out loud? Should he have kept it to himself?

"Okay, so what do you want to do about it?"

"I don't know," Will said, giving in and fidgeting with the ketchup on his sleeve. "I guess maybe I want to see her again, just to talk, to see...hell, I don't know, Nick."

"So call her. What's stopping you?"

"I tried. She won't return my messages."

"Then stop by and see her, buy her lunch. Women like a guy taking action, not just talking."

"It's not that easy. It's a five-hour drive. She lives in this little town outside D.C.—Newton, Newberry, Newburgh. Yeah, Newburgh, I think."

"Wait a minute. Outside D.C.? Newburgh Heights? In Virginia?"

"Yeah. You know it?"

"I think a friend of mine bought a house there."

"Small world." Will watched Nick, whose mind suddenly seemed preoccupied. "You think they know each other?"

"I doubt it. Maggie's an FBI profiler."

"Hold on. Is this the same FBI Maggie who helped you on that case last fall?"

Nick nodded, but he didn't need to answer at all. Will could see it was the same woman. Will had noticed months ago that this woman couldn't be mentioned in general conversation without Nick getting all weirded out. Maybe this woman was Nick's obsession.

"So how come you've never called this Maggie or stopped by to see her?"

"Well, for one thing I didn't realize until a few days ago that she was getting a divorce."

"A few days ago? Wait a minute. Was she at the Kansas City thing?"

"Yes, she was at the Kansas City thing. She was one of the presenters."

"And?"

"And nothing."

Will noticed Nick's demeanor had changed to frustration with a hint of irritation. Yep, he was all weirded out again.

"But you saw her, right? You talked to her?"

"Yeah. We spent an afternoon digging through garbage together."

"Excuse me? Is that some new code for foreplay?"

"No, it isn't," Nick snapped, suddenly not in the mood for Will's attempt at humor. "Come on. Let's get back to work."

Nick stood, straightening his lopsided tie and buttoning his jacket, indicating that was the end of this conversation. Will decided to ignore it and press on.

"It sounds like this Maggie is your Tess."

"Jesus, kid. What the hell is that supposed to mean?" Nick shot him a look, and Will knew he was right.

"This Maggie drives you as crazy as Tess drives me. Maybe we both need to make a trip down to Newburgh Heights."

CHAPTER 36

Maggie was surprised to find that Agent Tully had managed to make her old office look smaller than it was. Books that didn't fit in the narrow floor-to-ceiling bookcase formed leaning towers in the corner. A chair intended for visitors was hidden under stacks of newspapers. On his desk, the in-tray was crushed under a pile of lopsided documents and file folders. Strings of paper clips were left in odd places, a nervous habit of a man who needed to keep his fingers occupied. One lone mug teetered on a stack of legal pads and computer manuals. Peeking from behind the door, Maggie glimpsed gray running gear where normal people hung a trench coat or rain slicker.

The only thing in the office that held some prominence was a photo in a cheap wooden frame that sat on the right-hand corner of the desk. The entire corner had been cleared for its place of honor. Maggie immediately recognized Agent Tully, though the photo appeared to be several years old. The little blond girl had his dark eyes, but otherwise looked exactly like a younger version of her mother. The three of them looked so genuinely happy.

Maggie resisted the urge to take a closer look, as if doing so might expose their secret. What was it like to feel that completely happy? Had she ever felt that way, even for a brief period? Something about Agent Tully told her that happiness no longer existed for him. Not that she wanted to know. It had been years since she had worked with a partner, and the fact that Cunningham had made it one of the conditions of her return to the Stucky investigation was annoying. She felt as if he was still punishing her for the one stupid mistake of her career—going to that Miami warehouse alone. The warehouse where Stucky had been waiting for her. Where he had trapped her and made her watch.

Okay, so partly she knew Cunningham was doing it to protect her. Agents usually worked together to protect each other's backs, but profilers often worked alone and Maggie had grown accustomed to the solitude. Having Turner and Delaney hanging around had been stifling enough. Of course, she would abide by Cunningham's rules, but sometimes the best agents, the closest partners forgot to share every detail.

Agent Tully came in carrying two cartons, stacked so that he peered around the sides of them. Maggie helped him find a clear spot and unload his arms.

"I think these are the last of the old case files."

She wanted to tell him that every last copy she had made for herself had fit nicely into one box. But instead of pointing out what a little organization could do, she was anxious to see what had been added to the case in the last five months. She stood back and allowed Agent Tully to sort through the mess.

"May I see the most recent file?"

"I have the delivery girl on my desk." He jumped up from his squatting position next to the cartons and quickly riffled through several piles on his desk. "The Kansas City case is here, too. They've been faxing us stuff."

Maggie resisted the urge to help. She wanted to grab all his piles and make order of them. How the hell did this guy get anything done?

"Here's the file on the delivery girl."

He handed her a bulging folder with corners of papers and photos sticking out at odd angles. Immediately, Maggie opened it and started straightening and rearranging its contents before examining any of them.

"Is it okay if we use her name?"

"Excuse me?" Agent Tully continued to rummage over his messy desktop. Finally he found his wire-rimmed glasses, put them on and looked at her.

"The pizza delivery girl. Is it okay if we use her name when we refer to her?"

"Of course," he said, grabbing another file folder and shuffling through it.

Now he was a bit flustered, and Maggie knew he didn't know the girl's name without looking. It wasn't a matter of disrespect. It helped to disconnect. Profilers often referred to a body simply as "the victim" or "Jane Doe." Their first introduction to the victims came when they were bloody, tangled messes, often sharing little or no resemblance to their former selves. Maggie used to be the same, using general terms to disassociate, to disconnect. But then several months ago she met a little boy named Timmy Hamilton who took time to show her his bedroom and his baseball card collection just before he was abducted. Now it suddenly seemed important to Maggie to know this girl's name. This beautiful, young, blond woman who she remembered being so cheerful when she had delivered Maggie's pizza less than a week ago. And who was now dead simply because she had done so.

"Jessica," Agent Tully finally blurted out. "Her name was Jessica Beckwith."

Maggie realized she could have found the girl's name just as easily. The top document was the medical examiner's autopsy report, and the girl had already been identified at that point. She tried not to think of the parents. Some disconnection was necessary.

"Any trace recovered at the scene that could be used for DNA testing?"

"Nothing substantial. Some fingerprints, but they aren't matching Stucky's. Weird thing is, everything looked wiped clean except for this set of fingerprints—one index, one thumb. Chances are they belong to a rookie cop who touched stuff he wasn't supposed to touch and now he's afraid to admit it. AFIS hasn't come up with anything yet."

He sat on the edge of the desk, laying his folder open on a pile, leaving his fingers free to string more paper clips together.

"The weapon was not retrieved. Is that right?"

"Correct. Looks to be very thin, razor sharp and single edged. I'm thinking maybe even a scalpel, from the way he's able to slice and dice so easily."

Maggie winced at his choice of description, and he caught her.

"Sorry," he said. "That's the first thing that came to mind."

"Any saliva on the body? Any semen in the mouth?"

"No, which I know is different from Stucky's usual M.O."

"If it is Stucky."

She felt him staring at her but avoided his eyes and examined the autopsy report. Why would Stucky hold back or pull out early now? He certainly wouldn't go through the trouble of using a condom. After they had revealed his identity as being Albert Stucky, he had blatantly gone on to do whatever he wanted. And that usually meant showing off his sexual prowess by raping his victims several times, and often forcing them to perform oral sex on him. She wished she could take a second look at the girl's body. By now she knew what kinds of things to look for, otherwise insignificant physical evidence that telegraphed Stucky's patterns. Unfortunately, she saw at the bottom of the form that Jessica's body had already been released to her family. Even if she stopped the transfer, all the PE would be gone, washed away by a well-intentioned funeral director.

"We did find a stolen cellular phone in the Dumpster," Agent Tully said.

"But it was wiped clean?"

"Right. But the phone records show a call to the pizza place earlier that evening."

Maggie stopped and looked up at Agent Tully. My God, could it have been that easy? "That's how he abducted her? He simply ordered a pizza?"

"Initially that's what we were thinking," he explained. "We just found the delivery lists in her abandoned car. We've been running down the list, checking addresses and phone numbers. When Cunningham recognized Newburgh Heights as your new neighborhood, we checked for your address. Found it right away. Likewise, all the addresses are residential. But most of the people I've talked to so far were actually home and did receive their pizza. I have only a few left that I can't reach by phone, but I plan to drive to Newburgh Heights and check them out."

He handed her two photocopies of what looked like pieces of paper torn from a spiral notebook. The copier had even picked up the frayed edges. There were almost a dozen addresses on both lists. Hers was close to the top of the list labeled "#1." She leaned against the wall. The exhaustion from the night before was catching up with her. Of course, she had spent most of last night pacing from window to window, watching and waiting. The only sleep she had gotten had been on the flight back from Kansas City, and how could anyone get any rest while bobbing thirty-eight thousand feet above control? Now she couldn't even remember how long ago that was.

"Where did you find her car?"

"The airport's long-term parking lot. Also found a telephone company van parked alongside it that was reported stolen a couple of weeks ago."

"Any trace inside Jessica's car?" she asked as she glanced over the list of addresses.

"There was some mud on the accelerator. Not much else. Her blood and some blond hair—also hers—were recovered from the trunk. He must have used her own car to dump her body. No signs of a struggle inside the car, though, if that's what you're thinking. He had to have taken her someplace where he could take his time with her. Problem is, there aren't many abandoned warehouses or condemned properties in Newburgh Heights. I was thinking he might have given a business address, knowing the offices would be empty at night. But nothing commercial shows up on either list."

Suddenly Maggie recognized an address on one of the lists. She stood up straight and away from the wall. No, it couldn't be this easy. She reread the address.

"Actually, he may have had someplace much more luxurious in mind."

"Did you find something?" Agent Tully was at her side, staring at the list that he must have examined over and over himself. But of course, he wouldn't have seen it. How could he?

"This address," Maggie pointed halfway down the page. "The house is for sale. It's empty."

"You're kidding? Are you sure? If I remember correctly, the phone is still connected to a voice messaging service."

"The owners may be forwarding their phone calls. Yes, I'm sure it's for sale. My real estate agent showed it to me about two weeks ago."

She no longer cared about the rest of the file, which she had tucked under her arm. She was almost out the door before Agent Tully stopped her.

"Hold on," he said, grabbing his wrinkled jacket from the chair behind his desk. As he did so, he stumbled over a worn pair of sneakers Maggie hadn't noticed. Agent Tully reached for the corner of his desk to catch his balance and one of the piles gave way, scattering papers and photos across the floor. When he waved off her help, Maggie leaned against the doorjamb and waited. It was bad enough Cunningham was making her see Dr. James Kernan, but saddling her with her Dudley DoRight seemed almost laughable.

CHAPTER 37

Maggie tried to wait patiently while Delores Heston of Heston Realty attempted to find the right key. The sun was sinking behind the ridge of trees. She couldn't believe how much time they had wasted trying to track down Tess McGowan. And although Ms. Heston had been more than accommodating, Maggie felt agitated, on edge and overly anxious. She knew this was where Albert Stucky had killed Jessica Beckwith. She could feel it. She could sense it. It was so easy, so simple, so very much like Stucky.

Ms. Heston dug out another bundle of keys and Maggie fidgeted, shifting her weight from one foot to the other. Ms. Heston noticed.

"I don't know where Tess is. I'm sure she probably just decided to take a couple of days off."

It was the same explanation the woman had given Maggie over the phone, but again Maggie could hear the concern.

"One of these has to work."

"I would think you'd have them labeled." Maggie tried to contain her irritation. She knew Ms. Heston was doing them a favor by letting them take a look after their bogus explanation about investigating possible break-ins. Since when did the FBI get involved in local burglaries? Luckily, Ms. Heston didn't question them.

"Actually, these are the spare keys. We do keep a labeled set, but Tess must have forgotten to return it after she showed the house yesterday."

"Yesterday? She showed the house to someone yesterday?"

Ms. Heston stopped and gave Maggie a nervous glance over her shoulder. Maggie realized her voice must have sounded too shrill, too alarmed.

"Yes, I'm sure it was yesterday. I checked the show schedule before I left the office tonight—Wednesday, April 1. Is there a problem? Do you think the house may have been broken into before that?"

"I really can't say," Maggie said, trying to sound indifferent when she wanted to kick in the door. "Do you know who she showed the house to?"

"No, we keep the names off the schedule for confidentiality reasons."

"You don't have the name of the person written down anywhere?"

Ms. Heston shot her another concerned look over her shoulder. The woman's flawless deep brown skin now had worry lines in her forehead and around her mouth. "Tess would have it written down somewhere. I trust my agents. No need for them to have me standing over their shoulder." Concern was quickly turning to frustration.

Maggie hadn't meant to make the woman defensive. She simply wanted the goddamn door opened.

She glanced around and saw Agent Tully finally emerge from the house across the street. He had been inside a long time, and Maggie wondered if the blonde in spandex who had answered the door simply found him charming, or if she really had some information to share. Judging by the woman's smile and wave, Maggie guessed it to be the former. She watched the tall, lanky agent hurry across the street. Out here, he moved with a confident, long-legged gait. In his dark suit, sunglasses and closely cropped hair, he looked like standard government-issue FBI, except that Agent Tully was too polite, too friendly and much too accommodating. If he hadn't told her he was from Cleveland, she would have guessed the Midwest. Maybe it was something in Ohio's water.

"This house has a security system." Ms. Heston was still trying to find the right key. "Oh, here we go. Finally."

The lock clicked as Agent Tully bounded up the steps. Ms. Heston turned, startled by his sudden appearance.

Ms. Heston, this is Special Agent R. J. Tully.

"Oh my. This must be important."

"Just routine, ma'am. We tend to travel in pairs these days," Tully said with a smile that relaxed the woman and immediately reminded Maggie of Sergeant Joe Friday.

She wanted to ask him if he had learned anything from the neighbor, but knew she'd have to wait for a more appropriate time. She hated waiting.

As soon as they entered the foyer, Maggie noticed the security system had been disarmed. None of the regular lights flashed or blinked.

"Are you certain the service has been continued?" Maggie asked as she pointed out the silent box. By now it should have been buzzing incessantly, screeching for the correct code to be entered.

"Yes, I'm quite certain. It's in our contract with the owners." Heston punched several buttons and the box came alive. "I don't understand this. Surely Tess wouldn't have forgotten to set it."

Maggie remembered Tess McGowan being very careful about deactivating and reactivating the alarm systems of the houses she had shown Maggie, this one included. Security systems had been one of Maggie's priorities, and she knew this one had not been anything out of the ordinary. She remembered it as being sufficient for the regular home owner. Most people didn't need to barricade themselves in at night away from serial killers.

"Mind if we look around?" Agent Tully asked, but Maggie was already halfway up the open staircase. She reached the first landing when she heard Ms. Heston's panicked voice.

"Oh, good Lord!"

Maggie leaned over the oak railing to see Ms. Heston pointing to a briefcase she had discovered in the corner of the living room.

"This belongs to Tess." Up until now, the woman had been incredibly professional. Now her sudden panic was unnerving.

By the time Maggie came down the steps, Agent Tully had taken the briefcase and started carefully extracting its contents with a white handkerchief.

"No way that girl's gonna leave this and not come back for it." The panic rushed her words, reducing her previous crisp dialect to a slang version she obviously found more comfortable. "There's her appointment book, her pocketbook...good Lord, something's just not right here."

Maggie watched as Agent Tully brought out the last item—a labeled set of keys. Without getting a closer look, Maggie knew they were the keys for this house. Suddenly she felt nauseated. Tess McGowan may have shown this house yesterday, but she certainly didn't leave of her own free will.

CHAPTER 38

"We don't know that Stucky had anything to do with this." Tully tried to sound convincing, but he wasn't sure he believed his own words.

It was obvious he needed to be the objective one. Ever since Ms. Heston left them, Agent O'Dell seemed to be coming apart at the seams. The calm, controlled professional now paced, quick long steps, back and forth. She ran her fingers through her short dark hair too many times, tucking strands behind her ears, tousling it with her fingers and tucking it in again. Her voice was clipped, and possessed an edge that hadn't existed before. Tully thought he heard it quiver several times.

He felt as if he was watching from the sidelines as she passed by him. She didn't seem to know what to do with her hands. They ducked into her trouser pockets, then a quick swipe through her hair again. Several times they slipped into her jacket, and he knew she was checking her revolver. Tully wasn't sure what to do with her. This was so unlike the woman he had spent most of the day with.

It had gotten dark, and Agent O'Dell had gone through the entire two-story house, turning on lights and pulling closed what few draperies there were, but only after staring out into the night at each window. Was she expecting him to be there?

She was doing a second check downstairs now. Tully decided they needed to leave. The house was spotless. Though the master bedroom smelled strongly of a recent dousing of ammonia, there was no trace that anything had occurred in the house. Least of all, a brutal murder and a violent kidnapping.

"There's no evidence that anything suspicious happened here," he tried again. "I think it's time we leave." He glanced at his watch and cringed when he saw that it was after nine. Emma would be furious with him for having to spend the entire evening with Mrs. Lopez.

"Tess McGowan was the real estate agent who sold me my house," O'Dell repeated. It was the most she had said to him in the last several hours. "Don't you see? Don't you get it?"

He knew exactly what she was thinking. It was the same thing he was thinking. Albert Stucky would have known too, especially since he must be spending a good deal of time watching Agent O'Dell. He would have seen the two of them together, just the way he saw the pizza girl and the Kansas City waitress. But the truth was, they had absolutely no evidence that McGowan was even missing, other than a forgotten briefcase, and that was hardly proof. He refused to fuel O'Dell's panic.

"Right now there's nothing substantial to prove Ms. McGowan was abducted. And there's nothing more we can do here. We need to call it a night. Maybe we can track down Ms. McGowan tomorrow."

"We won't track her down. He's taken her." The quiver was there though she did her best to hide it. "He's added her to his collection. She may be dead already." Her hands reached for her holster then disappeared into her pockets. "Or if she's not dead, she may be wishing she was," she added in almost a whisper.

Tully rubbed his eyes. He had removed his glasses hours ago. O'Dell was starting to spook him. He didn't want to think about the fact that Albert Stucky may have added to his collection. Back on his desk, buried under manuals and documents, he had a bulging file of missing women from across the country. Women who had disappeared without a trace in the last five months since Stucky's escape.

The volume wasn't that unusual. It happened all the time. Some of the women left and didn't want to be found. Others had been abused by husbands and lovers and chose to disappear. But too many were gone without any explanation, and Tully knew enough about Stucky's games to pray that none of them in his file folder were actually in Stucky's new collection.

"Look, there's nothing more we can do tonight."

"We need to do a luminol test. We can have Keith Ganza bring it and the Lumi-Light, so we can go over the master bedroom."

"There's nothing here. There's absolutely no reason to believe anything happened in this house, Agent O'Dell."

"The Lumi-Light might show any latent prints. And the luminol will show any blood left in the cracks, any stains we can't see. He obviously tried to clean things up, but you can't clean enough to get rid of blood." It was almost as if she didn't hear him. As though he wasn't there and she was talking to herself.

"We can't do anything more tonight. I'm exhausted. You must be exhausted." When she started for the stairs again, he gently grabbed her arm. "Agent O'Dell."

She wrenched her arm away, turning on him with eyes flashing anger. She stood solidly, firmly in place, staring at him as though challenging him to a dual. Then without warning she turned on her heel and marched to the door, snapping off lights in her path.

Tully followed her cue before she changed her mind. He ran upstairs and shut off those lights, and when he returned, O'Dell was in the foyer, activating the security system. It wasn't until he locked the front door and walked alongside her to his car that he saw her revolver in her hand, dropped at her side but in a tight grip.

Suddenly Tully realized that the hysteria, the frustration, the anger he had witnessed was actually fear. How stupid of him not to have seen it before now. Special Agent Maggie O'Dell was scared to death, not just for Tess McGowan, but for herself, too.

CHAPTER 39

Tess jerked awake. Her throat felt like sandpaper, so dry it hurt to swallow. Her eyelids felt like lead shutters. Her chest ached as though some massive weight had pressed against her. There was nothing on top of her now. She lay on what appeared to be a narrow, lumpy cot. The room was dimly lit, forcing her to squint. The smell of mildew surrounded her. A draft made her pull the scratchy blanket up under her chin.

She remembered feeling paralyzed. In a mad panic, she lifted both her arms, grateful to find no restraints but quickly disappointed to find her limbs heavy, movement awkward. They felt detached and unresponsive. But at least she could move and at least she was not tied down.

She started to sit up, and immediately her muscles protested. The room began to spin. Her head throbbed and nausea washed over her so sudden and so strong, she lay back. She was used to hangovers, but this was much worse. Something had been injected into her bloodstream. Then she remembered the dark-haired man and the needle. Dear God, where the hell had he taken her? And where was he?

Her eyes darted around the small space. The nausea forced her to keep her head on the pillow as she twisted and turned her neck to examine her accommodations. She was inside some sort of wooden shack. Rotted wood allowed faint light to seep in between the slats. That was the only light. From what Tess could tell, it was cloudy or else too early or late for sunshine. Either way, she'd only be able to guess. There were no windows, or at least not anymore. One wall had boards nailed over a small area that may have been a window at one time. Other than the cot, there was nothing else except a tall plastic bucket in the corner.

Tess's eyes searched and found what looked like a door. It was difficult to tell. The wood blended in with the rest of the shack. Only a couple of rusted hinges and a keyhole gave it away. Of course, it would be locked, maybe even bolted from the outside, but she needed to make an attempt.

She sat up slowly and waited. Again, the nausea sent her head to the pillow.

"Damn it!" she shouted, and immediately regretted it. What if he was watching, listening?

She needed to concentrate. She could do this. After all, how many hangovers had she survived? But her surroundings only added to her vulnerability. Why was he doing this? What did he want from her? Had he mistaken her for someone else? A fresh panic began to crawl in her stomach. She couldn't think about his intentions now or about him. She couldn't think about how she got here. She wouldn't think about any of it or it would immobilize her exactly like the contents of that syringe.

She rolled onto her side to assuage the nausea. A sharp pain pierced her side, and for a brief moment she thought she had rolled onto a spike. But there was nothing there, only the hard, lumpy mattress. She moved her fingers up under her blouse, noticing the hem had already been pulled out from her trouser's waistband. A button was missing and the rest were off a buttonhole.

"No, stop it," she scolded herself in a whispered rush.

She had to focus. She couldn't think about what he may have done while she had been unconscious. She needed to check and see if she was okay.

Her fingers found no open wound, no sticky blood, but she was almost certain one of her ribs had been broken or badly bruised. Unfortunately, her past afforded her the knowledge of what broken ribs felt like. Carefully, her fingers probed the area under her breasts while she bit down on her lower lip. Despite the stabbing pain, she guessed bruised, not broken. That was good. She could function just fine with bruised ribs. Broken could sometimes puncture a lung. Another piece of trivia she wished she didn't know firsthand.

She slipped a foot out from under the covers and dangled it close to the floor. She was barefoot. What had he done with her shoes and stockings? Again, she glanced around the room. Her eyes had adjusted to the dim light, though her vision remained a bit off focus and her contact lenses felt gritty. It didn't matter. There was nothing more to see in the shack.

She let her toes and the ball of her foot touch the floor. It was colder than she expected, but she kept the foot there, forcing her body to grow accustomed to the change in temperature before she tried to stand up. The air in the shack felt damp and chilly.

Then she heard the beginning tap-tap-tap, soft against the roof. The sound of rain had usually been a comfort to her. Now she frantically wondered how badly the rotted roof leaked and felt a new chill. She knew the bucket in the corner hadn't been placed there for leaks. Instead, it was meant to accommodate her. He obviously intended to keep her here for a while. The thought reawakened the fear.

She pushed herself out of the cot and stood with both feet flat on the cold floorboards while she bent at the waist and held on to the bed. Again, she bit her lip, ignoring the taste of blood, fighting the urge to vomit and waiting for the room to stop spinning.

Her pulse quickened. The sound inside her head hummed like wind in a tunnel. She tried to concentrate on the tap-tap-tapping of the rain. Maybe she could find some level of comfort, some level of sanity, in the rain's natural and familiar rhythm. A sudden rumble of thunder startled her like a gunshot, and she spun around to the door as though expecting to see him there. When her heart settled back in her chest, she almost burst out laughing. It was only thunder. A little bit of thunder. That's all.

Slowly she tested her feet, coaxing her stomach to behave, trying to ignore the pain in her side and the panic from strangling her. Only now did she realize that her breathing came in gasps. A lump obstructed her throat, and it threatened to come out screaming. It took a conscious effort to prevent it from doing so.

Her body began shivering. She grabbed the wool blanket, wrapped it around her shoulders and tied two ends together in a knot at her neck, keeping her hands free. She checked under the cot, hoping to find something, anything to aid in her escape, or at least her shoes. There was nothing, not even furballs or dust. Which meant he had prepared this place for her, and recently. If only he hadn't taken her shoes and stockings. Then she remembered she had worn panty hose under her trousers.

Oh God! He had undressed her, after all. She mustn't think about it. She had to concentrate on other things. Stop remembering. Stop feeling aches and bruises in places that might remind her of what he had done. No, she couldn't, she wouldn't remember. Not now. She needed to focus all her energies on getting out of here.

Again she listened to the rain. Again she waited for its rhythm to calm her, to regulate her raspy breathing.

When she could walk without the threat of nausea crippling her, she carefully made her way to the door. The handle was nothing more than a rusted latch. One more time, she looked around to see if she had missed anything that could be used to help pry open the door. Even the corners had been swept clean. Then she saw a rusted nail swept into a groove in the floor. She pried it out with her fingernails and began examining the keyhole. The door was indeed locked, but was it bolted as well?

She steadied her fingers and inserted the nail into the keyhole, slipping it in and out, jingling and twisting it expertly. Another talent acquired in her not so illustrious past. But it had been years, and she was out of practice. The lock groaned in rusted protest. Oh, dear God, if only—something gave way with a metallic click.

Tess grabbed the latch and gave it a yank. The door swung open freely, almost knocking her over in her surprise. No force had been necessary. It hadn't been bolted. She waited, staring at the open doorway. This was too easy. Was it a blessing or another trap?

CHAPTER 40

Friday, April 3

Tully drove with one hand on the steering wheel and the other fumbling with the plastic lid of his coffee container. Why did fast-food places have to make the contraptions like child-protective caps? His finger punched at the uncooperative triangular perforation, cracking the plastic and splashing hot coffee onto his lap.

"Damn it!" he yelled as he swerved to the side of the road and screeched on the brakes, splattering more coffee onto the fabric of his car seat. He grabbed napkins to sop it up, but already the brown stain spread deep into the cream color. As an afterthought, he checked the rearview mirror, relieved no one was behind him.

He shoved the car's gearshift into park and released his foot from the brake pedal, only now realizing how tense and rigid his body had become in response to the stress. He sat back and rubbed a hand over his jaw, immediately feeling the nicks he had inflicted earlier with his razor. It had been one day and already Agent O'Dell had him feeling as if he was on the rim of her personal cliff, and he was straddling the ledge while pieces of rock crumbled at his feet.

Maybe it had been a mistake asking Assistant Director Cunningham to let O'Dell help on the Stucky case. Last night may have been proof that she simply couldn't handle the pressure. But then her phone message this morning telling him to meet her back at the Archer Drive house made Tully realize that he was in for an even more difficult task.

They had found nothing at the house to warrant a further search. Yet

O'Dell had told him she had written permission from Ms. Heston and the owners to do so. Now he wondered if she had gotten them out of bed. How else had she been able to obtain written permission between last night and early this morning? And how the hell would he make her see that she was being irrational and paranoid and possibly wasting precious time?

After last night, Tully knew O'Dell was wound so tight, that controlling her could be impossible, and trying to restrain her could make matters worse. But he wouldn't talk to Cunningham. He couldn't. Not yet. He needed to handle this. He needed to settle O'Dell down so they could move forward.

He sipped what coffee was left and glanced at his watch. Today the damn thing was slow, according to the car's digital clock. It wasn't even seven o'clock. O'Dell had left the message on his machine at about six while he was in the shower. He wondered if she had gone to bed at all last night.

He put the coffee container safely into a cup holder, massaged the tension in his neck and then shifted into drive. He had only three blocks to go. When he turned onto the street, his tension turned to anger. Parked in the driveway were O'Dell's red Toyota and a navy blue panel van, the kind the forensic lab used. She hadn't wasted any time nor bothered to wait for his okay. What was the use of being lead in an investigation if no one paid any goddamn attention? He needed to put a stop to this now.

As he walked toward the front door, lampposts along the driveway blinked, trying to decide whether to stay on or shut off. They needed rain. Each time it looked like spring showers, the rains dumped on the shoreline or just offshore before rolling inland. But this morning thick clouds smudged out the sunrise. A low rumble could be heard in the distance. It suited Tully's mood, and he caught himself making fists as he got closer to the door. He hated confrontation. If he couldn't get his own daughter to obey him, then how the hell did he expect to get Agent O'Dell to?

The front door was unlocked, the security system silent. He followed the voices upstairs to the master bedroom. Keith Ganza wore a short white lab coat, and Tully wondered if the man even owned an ordinary sports jacket.

"Agent Tully," O'Dell said, coming from the master bathroom, wearing latex gloves and carrying jugs of liquid. "We're almost ready. We just finished mixing the luminol."

She set the jugs on the floor in the corner where Ganza had set up shop.

"You two know each other, right?" O'Dell asked as though she thought that was the reason for Tully's frown.

"Yes," he answered, trying to restrain his anger and maintain his professionalism.

Ganza simply nodded at Tully and continued loading and preparing a video camera. A Will comm camera on a tripod stood in the center of the room, already assembled. Several duffel bags, more jugs and four or five spray bottles were carefully set on the floor. A black case leaned against the wall. Tully recognized it as the Lumi-Light. Each of the windows were covered with some kind of black film taped to the frames so that light couldn't filter in from the outside. Even now the room required the ceiling light. The bathroom lights were on too, and Tully wondered what, if anything, they had used to block out the skylight. This was ridiculous.

Agent O'Dell began filling spray bottles with the luminol, using a funnel and steady hands. There seemed to be no sign of the jumpy, nervous, frazzled woman he had seen last night.

"Agent O'Dell. We need to talk."

"Of course, go ahead." Except she didn't look up at him and continued to pour.

Ganza appeared oblivious to Tully's anger, and he wanted to keep it that way.

"We need to talk in private."

Both O'Dell and Ganza looked up at him. Yet neither stopped what they were doing. O'Dell screwed the spray top onto the bottle she had filled. Tully expected her to see his anger. He expected her to be concerned or at least somewhat apologetic.

"Once we have the luminol mixed, we need to use it immediately," she explained, and began filling another spray bottle.

"I realize that," Tully said through clenched teeth.

"I have written permission," she continued without interrupting her pouring. "The luminol is odorless, and it leaves little residue. Nothing more than a sprinkle of white power when it dries. Hardly noticeable."

"I know that, too," Tully snapped at her, though her tone was not at all condescending. This time O'Dell and Ganza stopped and stared at him. How had he suddenly become the hysterical one, the irrational one?

"Then what seems to be the problem, Agent Tully?" She stood to face him, but again there was nothing challenging in her manner, which only made it worse.

Even the expression on Ganza's lined and haggard face was one of impatience. They continued to stare at him, waiting as though he was holding up the process unreasonably.

"I thought we decided last night that there was nothing here."

"No, we decided there was nothing more we could do last night. Although it would have been much better to do this last night. Hopefully, it'll be dark enough. We lucked out with it being so cloudy."

Ganza nodded. They both waited. Suddenly all of Tully's objections—which seemed completely logical minutes ago—now sounded immature and arrogant. There was nothing here. It was a ridiculous waste of time and effort. But rather than telling O'Dell that, perhaps it was better for her to see for herself. Maybe only then would she be satisfied.

"Let's get this over with," he finally said. "What do you want me to do?"

"Close the door and stay there next to the light switch." Ganza motioned to him while he picked up the video camera. "I'll let you know when to flip it off and on again. Maggie, grab a couple of spray bottles. You spritz. I'll be right beside you filming."

Tully got into position, no longer bothering to hide his reluctance or his impatience. However, he could see that anything he did would be wasted on O'Dell and Ganza. They were so involved in the task at hand, they barely noticed him except as a utility.

He watched O'Dell load both her hands with spray bottles, holding them like revolvers, her index fingers ready on the triggers.

"Let's start at the wall closest to the door and move toward the bathroom," Ganza instructed in his monotone. He reminded Tully of Icabod Crane. The man's voice never showed emotion—a perfect match for his tall, slumped appearance and deliberate and precise movements.

"Maggie, you remember the drill. Start on the walls, top to bottom. Then the floor, wall to center," Ganza went on. "Let's keep a steady spray going all the way to the bathroom. We'll stop at the bathroom door. You'll probably need to reload with luminol by then."

"Gotcha."

Tully just then realized that O'Dell and Ganza had done this as a team before. They seemed comfortable with each other, knowing each other's roles. And O'Dell had managed to get Ganza here at the break of dawn, despite the man's overloaded schedule.

Tully manned his post, waiting with arms crossed over his chest and his shoulder leaning against the closed door. He caught himself tapping his foot, an unconscious nervous habit that Emma accused him of when he was being "close-minded." Where the hell did she come up with stuff like that? Nevertheless, he stopped his foot from tapping.

"We're ready, Agent Tully. Go ahead and hit the lights," Ganza told him.

Tully flipped the switch and immediately felt swallowed by the pitch black. Not a hint of light squeezed in past the film on the windows. In fact, Tully could no longer tell where the windows were.

"This is excellent," he heard Ganza say.

Then Tully heard a faint electronic whine and a tiny red dot appeared where he imagined the video camera was in Ganza's hands.

"Ready when you are, Maggie," Ganza said as the red dot bobbed up.

Tully heard the spritz of liquid, steady and insistent. It sounded as if she was dousing the entire wall. Tully wondered how many bottles, how many jugs of luminol it would take for her to realize that there was nothing here. Suddenly the wall began to glow. Tully stood up straight, and so did the hairs on the back of his neck and arms.

"Jesus Christ," he gasped, staring in disbelief at the streaks, the smudges and handprints that smeared the entire wall and now glowed like fluorescent paint.

CHAPTER 41

Maggie stepped back, giving Keith room. It was worse than she expected. The smears stretched, reached, clawed and swiped with the undeniable motion of someone desperate and terrified. The handprints were small, almost child-size. She remembered Jessica Beckwith's delicate hands holding out the pizza box for her.

"Jesus, I can't believe this."

She heard Tully's voice again come out of the black. She knew he had believed they wouldn't find a thing, that nothing had taken place here. There was no victory in proving him wrong. Instead, she found herself light-headed and nauseated. Suddenly it was too hot in the room. What the hell was the matter with her? She hadn't been sick at crime scenes since the early days, those first years of initiation. Now for a second time in less than a week, her stomach attempted to revolt against her.

"Keith, what are the chances of this being a cleaning solution? The house is for sale. It still smells like someone has given it a recent scrubbing."

"Oh, it's been scrubbed all right. Someone was trying to get rid of this."

"But luminol can be sensitive to bleach," she continued. "Maybe a residential-cleaning company scrubbed down everything including the walls." After a fitful, sleepless night of anticipating, of knowing what they'd discover, why did she not want to believe it? Why did she find herself wanting to believe the streaks and swipes in front of her were simply an overzealous maid?

"In the linen closet there's a bunch of cleaning supplies. Mop, bucket, sponges and liquid cleaners. Smells like the same stuff that was used. None of it contains bleach," Ganza countered. "I checked. Besides, no one cleans and leaves handprints like that."

She forced herself to stare at the prints before they faded. The small fingers were elongated as they had grabbed and clawed and slid. She closed her eyes against the images her mind was trained to concoct. With little coaxing, she knew she could see it all in slow motion as if visualizing a scene from a movie, a horror movie.

"Ready, Maggie?" Keith's voice made her jump. He was right beside her again as the room started to return to darkness. "Let's get the floor from here to the bathroom."

She felt her fingers shaking as she repositioned them on the spray bottles. Gratefully, neither Keith nor Tully could see them. She steadied herself and tried to remember exactly what direction and how far it was to the bathroom. Once she felt back in control, she began spritzing, keeping the mist away from her feet as she slowly walked sideways. Maggie hadn't reached the bathroom door when the floor began lighting up like a runway, long skid marks following her.

"Oh my God!" She heard Tully mutter from his dark perch, and she wanted to tell him to shut up. His shock unnerved her and worse, reminded her of her own.

Ganza pointed the red dot to the floor, following the trail that had once been bloody feet dragged across the parquet floor. Maggie pushed back strands of hair and swiped at the perspiration on her forehead. Was Jessica unconscious by the time he got her to the bathroom? The girl would have lost a lot of blood putting up a fight like the one smeared on the wall. Maggie wondered if she was conscious when Stucky lifted her into the whirlpool bath. When he told her all the horrible things he would do to her. Was she dead or alive when he started cutting?

"Let's take a break here," Keith said. "Agent Tully, go ahead and switch the lights back on."

Maggie blinked against the burst of light, relieved at the interruption of her mind's descent into the depths of hell. If she tried, she would be able to hear Jessica's screams, her pleas for help. Maggie's memory bank seemed filled with audio clips of what sheer terror sounded like. It was something she'd never forget, no matter how many years went by.

"Agent O'Dell?"

Tully startled her, suddenly standing in front of her. She looked around to see Keith busy in the corner, and only now did she notice that he had taken the spray bottles from her hands and was filling them.

"Agent O'Dell, I owe you an apology," Agent Tully was saying. At some point he had removed his jacket and rolled up his shirtsleeves in haphazard and uneven folds. He unbuttoned his collar and twisted the knot of his tie loose. "I really thought there was nothing here. I feel like such an asshole."

Maggie stared at him and tried to remember the last time anyone, especially in law enforcement, had apologized to her, let alone admitted to making a mistake. Was this guy for real? Instead of looking embarrassed, he genuinely looked sorry.

"I have to admit, Agent Tully, I was simply acting on gut instinct."

"Maggie, we should remember to pull the drain from the whirlpool bath," Ganza interrupted without looking up. "I'm betting that's where he cut her open. We may find some leftovers."

Agent Tully's face grew paler, and she saw him wince.

"One thing we didn't check last night, Agent Tully, was the garbage cans outside," she told him, offering to save him. "Since the house is for sale and empty, the garbage collectors may have skipped it."

He seemed grateful for the chance to escape. "I'll go check."

As he left, Maggie realized he could possibly find something equally shocking in the garbage. Perhaps she wasn't saving him at all. She pulled out a fresh pair of latex gloves from her forensic kit and tossed out the ones she had contaminated with luminol. Keith unpacked a wrench, screwdriver and several evidence bags.

"You're being awfully nice to the new guy," he said.

She glanced at him. Though he kept his eyes on the items he was unearthing from his bag, she could see the corner of his mouth caught in a smile.

"I can be nice. It's not like it's an impossibility."

"Didn't say that it was." He dug out Q-Tips, several brushes, forceps and small brown bottles, lining everything up as if taking inventory. "Don't worry, Maggie, I won't tell anyone. Wouldn't want to ruin your reputation." This time he gave her his eyes, light blue behind hooded, heavy lids that Maggie knew in the last thirty years had seen more horror and evil than any one person should ever be allowed to see. Yet now they were smiling at her.

"Keith, what do you know about Agent Tully?"

"I've heard nothing but good things."

"Of course there are nothing but good things. He looks like a cross between Mr. Rogers and Fox Mulder."

"Fox Mulder?" He raised his eyebrows at her.

"You know, from the TV show *The X-Files?*"

"Oh, I know who he is. I'm just surprised you know who he is."

She found herself blushing as though he'd discovered some secret.

"I've caught a couple of episodes. What things have you heard? About Tully?" She quickly returned to the subject.

"He's here from Cleveland at Cunningham's request, so the guy has to be good, right? Someone said he's able to look at crime scene photos alone and come up with a profile that nine times out of ten is on target."

"Crime scene photos. That explains why he's so squeamish with the real thing."

"I don't think he's been with the Bureau long—five, six years. Probably slipped in right at the age limit."

"What did he do before? Please don't tell me he's a lawyer."

"Something wrong with lawyers?" Agent Tully interrupted from the doorway.

Maggie checked his eyes to see if he was angry with them. Keith went back to his task, leaving Maggie feeling as though she was the one who needed to explain.

"I was just curious," she said without apology.

"You could just ask me."

Yes, he was angry, but she saw him pretending not to be. Did he always make certain his emotions were so carefully kept in check?

"Okay. So what did you do before you joined the Bureau?"

He held up a black garbage bag in one hand.

"I was an insurance fraud investigator." In his other latex-gloved hand he held up a wad of what looked like candy bar wrappers. "And I'd say our boy has a serious sweet tooth."

CHAPTER 42

Maggie gripped the revolver and aimed at the dark figure in front of her. Her right hand shook. She could feel her jaw clench and her muscles tense.

"Goddamn it!" she yelled though no one could hear her in the empty firearms target alley. She had come in just as Agent Ballato, the firearms instructor, had ended his class. This late on a Friday, she would have the place to herself.

She relaxed her stance once again, dropping her arms and rolling her shoulders, flexing her neck. Why the hell couldn't she relax? Why did she feel wound so tight? Like something would explode inside her at any minute?

She pushed her goggles up on top of her head and leaned against the half wall of her galley. After she and Agent Tully had left the house on Archer Drive she had called Detective Ford in Kansas City. She had listened to him describe the details of Rita's murder, of her blood-soaked apartment, the semen-stained sheets and the remnants of skin and tissue the KC forensic team had found in Rita's bathtub. It wasn't that different from what they had found in the whirlpool bath at Archer Drive. Only, Stucky didn't bother to clean up after himself in Rita's apartment. Why did he clean up at Archer Drive after killing Jessica? Was it because he needed to use the house again? Did he lure Tess McGowan there and take her for later? And if he did take her, where the hell was he keeping her?

Maggie closed her eyes and wished the tightness in her chest would let up. She needed to focus. She needed to relax. It was too easy to conjure up the images. It was what she had been trained to do, but this time she wished she could shove them away. Her mind wouldn't listen. Despite her effort to stop the images, they came anyway. She could see Jessica Beckwith's small hands passing her the pizza box. Then she could see those same hands clawing and grabbing at the walls of the empty bedroom. Why hadn't anyone heard her screams when they seemed so loud and vivid in Maggie's head?

She set the gun aside and rubbed her eyes with both hands. It didn't help. She could remember Rita's face, the waitress's fatigued but friendly smile as she had served the three of them Sunday evening in the smoke-filled bar and grill. And then, without effort or warning, came the images of Rita's garbage-riddled body, her slashed throat and the glob that once was her kidney lying on a shiny dinner plate. Both women were dead only because they had had the misfortune of meeting her. And now Maggie was certain that two more women had been taken for the same reason; they had met her.

She wanted to yell and scream. She wanted the throbbing to go away. She wanted her goddamn hand to stop shaking. Ever since Tully found that handful of candy bar wrappers, Maggie kept wondering about Rachel Endicott. Was it possible she was simply jumping to conclusions, trying too hard to connect Rachel's disappearance with Tess's?

There had been mud on the steps in Rachel's house. Mud with some odd metallic substance. Tully had said that a sparkling dirt had been found on Jessica's car accelerator. Could it be the same? There was something else that Tully had told her. She couldn't remember what it was. It nagged at Maggie, but she couldn't remember. Maybe something in the police report?

"Goddamn it!" Why couldn't she remember?

Lately she felt as if her mind was unraveling, pieces shredding and peeling away. Her nerves felt raw, her muscles exhausted from constantly being on alert. And the worst part, the most infuriating part, was that she seemed to have absolutely no control over any of it.

Albert Stucky had her right where he wanted her, clinging to some imaginary mental ledge. He had made her an accomplice to his evil. He had made her his partner by letting her choose who his next victim would be. He wanted her to share the responsibility. He wanted her to understand the power of evil. By doing so, did he also expect to unleash some evil beast from inside her?

She picked up the Smith & Wesson, letting her hands stroke the cool metal, wrapping her fingers around the handle with care, almost reverence. She ignored the earplugs dangling around her neck and left the goggles perched on top of her head. She raised her right arm, keeping the elbow bent, just a little. Her left hand crisscrossed her right, adding strength and reinforcement. She stared down the front sight, willing it, commanding it not to move, not to quiver. Then without further hesitation, she squeezed the trigger, firing in rapid succession until all six bullets were spent and the scent of the discharge filled her nostrils.

Her ears were ringing when she allowed her arm to relax and drop to her side. Her heart pounded as she punched the button on the wall, flinching at the screech of the pulley as it wheeled the target toward her. The dark figure, the silhouette of her pretend assailant stopped in front of her with a rustle of paper and a clank of metal. Maggie saw that her aim had been right on target. She took a deep breath and sighed. She should have been relieved at her precision. Instead, she felt that ledge getting closer and crumbling beneath her. Because the six bullets she had just fired had expertly and intentionally been placed right between the eyes of her target.

CHAPTER 43

Tess skidded to a stop. Her bare feet were caked with mud. She could smell it and looked to find mud stuck to her hands, her trousers, her skinned elbows. She didn't remember ripping her blouse, yet both elbows showed through, the flesh scraped and bloody, and now dirty with rancid mud. The rain had stopped without her noticing, but she knew it would be temporary because the clouds had darkened and the fog became a thicker gray, wisping around her like unsettled spirits rising from the ground. Dear God, she couldn't think of such things. She shouldn't think at all, just run.

Instead, she leaned against a tree, trying to catch her breath. She had followed the only path she could find in the dense woods, hoping it would lead to freedom. Her nerves were frayed. The terror raced inside her, completely beyond her control. She expected him to step out and grab her at any second.

Dry burrs and broken twigs poked through her blanket cape. It had been caught many times, yanking her backward like hands gripping her neck. It was a constant reminder of the painful bruises his fingers had left. Yet she refused to let it go, as if it was a flimsy shield, a makeshift security blanket. She was soaked from the rain and her own perspiration, wet strands of hair plastered against her face. Her silk blouse clung to her like a second skin.

The thick fog added to the dampness. In less than an hour darkness would enshroud these endless woods. The thought brought fresh panic. She could hardly see through the damp haze. Twice she had slid down a ridge, almost tumbling into the body of water that had seemed like a gray mist when seen from above. The dark would make further movement impossible.

He had taken her wristwatch, for obvious reasons, though he had left the sapphire ring and earrings. She'd gladly trade the three-thousand-dollar ring for her Timex. She hated not knowing the time. Did she know what day it was? Could it still be Wednesday? No. She remembered it being dark when she was in the car. Yes, there had been oncoming headlights. Which meant she had slept most of Thursday. Suddenly it occurred to her that she really had no idea how long she had been unconscious. It may have been days.

Her breathing became labored again as the fear crawled through her insides. Calm. She needed to stay calm. She needed to figure out what to do for the night. She would take this moment by moment. Despite the instinct to continue running, it was more important that she find someplace to wait out the night. Now she wondered if she should have stayed in the shack. Had she really accomplished anything by leaving it? At least it had been dry, and that lumpy cot now sounded wonderful. Instead, she had no idea where she was. It certainly didn't feel as if she had gotten any closer to escaping this endless wooded prison, though she must have covered several miles.

She crouched down, her back pressed against the rough bark. Her legs begged to sit, but she needed to stay alert and ready to run. Black crows screeched down at her. They startled her, but she remained still and quiet, too tired, too weak to move out of their way. The crows were settling in the treetops for the night. Hundreds of them flapped overhead, coming from all directions, their rude caws a warning as they claimed their evening roost.

Suddenly it occurred to Tess that these birds wouldn't settle here if they didn't perceive it to be somewhat safe. And if there was danger sometime during the night, they would probably react better than an alarm system.

Her eyes began searching the area for a safe resting place. There were plenty of fallen leaves and pine needles, bits and pieces left over from last fall. However, everything was damp from the rain and fog. She shivered just thinking about lying on the cold ground.

The crows' squawks continued. She looked up and began examining branches. She hadn't climbed a tree since she was a kid. Back then it had been a survival tactic, one more way to hide from her aunt and uncle. Her aching muscles reminded her how foolish the thought of climbing anything was right now. Foolish or not, it would be the safest place to be. He'd never look for her up above, not to mention other nightly predators. Dear God, she hadn't even thought of other animals.

The tree beside her had a perfect Y to accommodate her. Immediately, she pushed herself into action and began dragging logs and branches. She stacked them, crisscrossing the larger ones to construct a crude stepladder. If she could reach the lower branches, she might be able to swing her feet up into the Y.

She tried to ignore her fatigue, tried to pretend her feet weren't already cut and stinging. With every load of branches or lift of a log, her muscles screamed out for her to stop. But she could feel a new surge of energy. Her heart pounded in her ears, only this time with excitement.

Overhead the crows had gone silent, as if watching and interested in her frantic work. Or did they hear something else? She stopped. Her arms were full. Her breathing rasped. She couldn't hear over the pounding of her heart. She held her breath as best she could and listened. It was as if the entire woods had gone silent, as if the impending dark had swallowed every sound, every movement.

Then she heard it.

At first it sounded like a wounded animal, a muffled cry, a high-pitched hum. Tess turned slowly, her eyes squinting against the fog and into the dark. A sudden breeze created night shadows. Swaying branches became waving arms. Rustling leaves sounded like footsteps.

Tess unloaded her arms while her eyes continued to dart around her. Could she get into the tree without building her makeshift ladder? Her fingers clawed into the bark. Her feet tested the pile's strength and structure. She pulled herself up and grabbed onto the closest branch. It creaked under her weight, but didn't break. Her fingers clung to the branch despite loose bark falling into her eyes. She was ready to swing her feet up into the Y when the muffled cry transformed into words.

"Help me. Please, help me."

The words, drifting with the breeze, were crisp and clear. Tess froze. She hung from the branch, her toes barely reaching the pile. Maybe she was hearing things. Maybe it was simply exhaustion playing tricks on her.

Her arms ached. Her fingers felt numb. If she was going to make it up into the tree, she needed to use this last surge of energy.

The words came again, floating over her as if a part of the fog.

"Please, someone help me."

It was a woman's voice, and it was close by.

Tess dropped to the ground. By now she could see only a foot or two into the thickening darkness. She walked slowly, following the path, silently counting her steps with arms stretched out in front of her. Twigs grabbed at her hair and unseen branches reached for her. She moved in the direction of the voice, still afraid to call, afraid to give away her presence. She stepped carefully, continuing her count so she could turn around and hopefully find her tree sanctuary.

Twenty-two, twenty-three. Then suddenly the ground opened beneath her. Tess fell and the earth swallowed her.

CHAPTER 44

Tess lay at the bottom of the pit. Her head roared. Her side burned as if on fire. Her breathing came in gasps and quick bursts as the terror swept through her veins. Mud oozed up around her, sucking at her arms and legs like quicksand. Her right ankle twisted under her. Even without attempting to move it, she knew she would have trouble doing so.

The smell of mud and decay gagged her. The black dark squeezed around her. She couldn't see in any direction. Above her she could barely make out a few shadows of branches, but the fog and the night had already begun devouring the twilight. What shadows she could see were only enough to reveal how deep her earthly tomb was. It had to be at least fifteen feet to the top. Dear God, she'd never be able to climb out.

She struggled to stand, falling when the ankle refused to hold her up. A fresh wave of panic sent her to her feet again. This time she clawed and scratched at the dirt to hold herself up. She ripped at the wall with fingers digging and searching for a ledge that didn't exist. Chunks of damp earth came off in her hands. She could feel the worms slithering through her fingers. She flung them off. They reminded her of snakes. And dear God, how she hated snakes. The thought alone unleashed a new terror.

Suddenly her bare feet and hands slashed and pounded, climbed and slid. The wind tunnel in her head continued to roar. Her heart slammed against her rib cage. She couldn't breathe. That's when she realized she was screaming. It wasn't the sound that alarmed her as much as her raw throat and her aching lungs. When she stopped, the screaming continued. Surely she was losing her mind. The scream transformed into a whine, then a low moan that emanated from the black corner of the hole.

A shiver slid down Tess's mud and sweat-drenched back. She remembered the voice. The voice that had led her to this hellhole. Had it all been a trap?

"Who are you?" she whispered into the dark.

The moans became muffled sobs.

Tess waited. She slid along the wall, ignoring her throbbing ankle and refusing to sit back down. She needed to be alert. She needed to be ready. She glanced up, expecting her captor to be smiling down at her. Instead, there was a flicker of light she recognized as lightning. A low rumble in the distance confirmed it.

"Who are you?" she shouted this time, giving in to the raw emotion that squeezed her chest and made it difficult to breathe. "And what the hell are you doing here?" She wasn't sure she wanted or needed an answer to her second question.

"He...did this." The voice came with effort, high-pitched and quaking. "Awful things..." she continued. "He did...this. I tried to stop him. I couldn't. I wasn't strong enough." She started moaning again.

The woman's fear was palpable. It grabbed Tess by the throat and crawled under her skin. She couldn't afford to take on this woman's terror, too.

"He had a knife," the woman said between sobs. "He...he cut me."

"Are you hurt? Are you bleeding?" But Tess stayed against the wall, unable to move. Her eyes tried to adjust to the dark, but she could see nothing but a huddled shadow only six or seven feet away from her.

"He said...he told me he'd kill me."

"When did he put you down here? Do you remember?"

"He tied my wrists."

"I can help you untie—"

"He tied my ankles. I couldn't move."

"I can—"

"He ripped my clothes, then he took off my blindfold. He said...he told me he wanted me to watch. He...wanted me to see. Then he...then he raped me."

Tess wiped at her face, replacing tears with mud. She remembered her own clothes, the misbuttoned blouse, the missing panty hose. She felt nauseated. She couldn't think about it. She didn't want to remember. Not now.

"He cut me when I screamed." The woman was still confessing, her voice rambling now out of control. "He wanted me to scream. I couldn't fight him.

He was so strong. He got on top of me. So heavy. My chest…he crushed my chest, sitting there on top of me. He was so heavy. My arms were pinned under his legs. He sat on top of me so he could stick…so that he could… he shoved himself down my throat. I gagged. He shoved farther. I couldn't breathe. I couldn't move. He kept—"

"Shut up!" Tess yelled, surprising herself. She didn't recognize her own voice, frightened by the shrillness of it. "Please just shut up!"

Immediately there was silence. No moans. No sobs. Tess listened over the pounding of her heart. Her body shook beyond her control. A liquid cold invaded her veins. Air continued to leak out, replaced by more of the rancid smell of death.

Thunder grew closer, vibrating the earth against her back. The flashes of lightning lit up the world above, but didn't make it down into the black pit. Tess leaned her head against the dirt wall and stared up at the branches, eerie skeletal arms waving down at her in the flickering light. Her entire body hurt from trying to control the convulsions threatening to take over.

She wrapped her arms around herself, determined to ward off those childhood memories, those childhood fears she had worked so hard to destroy. She could feel them crashing through her carefully constructed barriers. She could feel them seeping into her veins, a poison infecting her entire body. She couldn't…she wouldn't allow them to return and render her helpless. Oh dear God! It had taken years to lock them away. And several more years to erase them. No, she couldn't let them back in. Please, dear Lord, not now. Not when she was already feeling so vulnerable, so completely helpless.

The rain began, and Tess let her body slide down against the wall until she felt the mud sucking at her again. Her body began rocking back and forth. She hugged herself tight against the cold and against the memories, but both broke through anyway. As though it had been only yesterday, she remembered what it felt like. She remembered being six years old and being buried alive.

CHAPTER 45

"I think Stucky may have taken my neighbor, too."

"Come on, Maggie. Now you're just sounding paranoid." Gwen sat in Maggie's recliner, sipping wine and petting Harvey's huge head, which filled her lap. The two had become instant pals. "By the way, this wine is very nice. You're getting good at this. See, there are things other than Scotch."

However, Maggie's glass of wine remained full to the rim. She rummaged through the files Tully had given her on Jessica's and Rita's murders. Besides, she hadn't waited for Gwen to arrive before she drank just enough Scotch to settle the restlessness that seemed to have taken up permanent residence inside her. She had hoped target practice would have helped dislodge it. But even the Scotch had not done its usual job of anesthetizing it. Still she was having trouble reading her own handwriting through the blur. She was pleased, though, that she had finally been able to choose a wine that Gwen liked.

A gourmet cook, Gwen enjoyed fine food and wine. When she had called earlier, offering to bring over dinner, Maggie had rushed out to Shep's Liquor Mart to search the aisles. The clerk, an attractive but overly enthusiastic brunette named Hannah, had told Maggie that the Bolla Sauve was "a delicious semi-dry white wine with touches of floral spiciness and apricot." Hannah assured her that it would complement the chicken and asparagus en papillote that Gwen had promised.

Wine was much too complex. With Scotch she didn't need to choose from merlot, chardonnay, chablis, blush, red or white. All she needed to remember was Scotch, neat. Simple. And it certainly did the job. Though not this evening. The tension strangled her muscles and tightened her rib cage, squeezing and causing her chest to ache.

"What do the police say about Rachel's disappearance?"

"I'm not sure." Maggie flipped through a file folder with newspaper clippings, but still couldn't find what she was looking for. "The lead detective called Cunningham and complained about me barging in on his territory, so it's not like I can just call him up and say, 'Hey, I think I know what happened with that case you want me to keep my nose out of.' But my other neighbor gave me the impression everyone, including the husband, is treating it as though Rachel just decided to leave."

"That seems odd. Has she done this sort of thing before?"

"I have no clue. But doesn't it seem odder that the husband wouldn't want the dog?"

"Not if he thinks she ran off with someone. It's one of the few ways he has left to punish her."

"It doesn't explain why we found the dog in the condition we did. There was a lot of blood, and I'm still not convinced it was all Harvey's." Maggie noticed Gwen stroking Harvey's head as though administering therapy. "Who names a dog Harvey?"

He looked up at Maggie's mention of his name, but didn't budge.

"It's a perfectly good name," Gwen declared as she continued her generous strokes.

"It was the name of the black Lab that David Berkowitz believed was possessed."

Gwen rolled her eyes. "Now, why is it that you think of that immediately? Maybe Rachel is a Jimmy Stewart fan or a classic-movie buff, and named him after Harvey the six-foot invisible rabbit."

"Oh, right. Why didn't I think of that?" It was Maggie's turn for sarcasm. The truth was, she didn't want to think of Harvey's owner and what she believed may have happened to her, or was still happening to her. She returned her attention to the folders. She wished she could remember exactly what it was that Agent Tully had said. There was something nagging at her. Something that connected Rachel's disappearance to Jessica's murder. Not just the mud. Yet she couldn't remember what it was that made her think that. She was hoping one of the police reports would trigger her memory.

"Why the hell isn't the husband the prime suspect?" Gwen suddenly sounded irritated. "That would be a logical explanation to me."

"You'd need to meet Detective Manx to understand. He doesn't seem to be approaching any of this logically."

"I'm not so sure he's the only one. The husband does seem to be the logical suspect, and yet here you are jumping to the conclusion that Stucky kidnapped her because...let me get this straight. You think Stucky kidnapped Rachel Endicott because you're sure he killed this pizza delivery girl and you found candy bar wrappers at both scenes."

"And mud. Don't forget the mud." Maggie checked the lab's report on Jessica's car. The mud recovered from the accelerator contained some sort of metallic residue that Keith was now going to break down. Again she remembered the mud with sparkling flecks on Rachel Endicott's stairs. But what if Manx hadn't bothered to collect it? And even if he had, how would she be able to compare the two? It wasn't like Manx would easily hand over a sample.

"Okay," Gwen said. "The mud I can understand, if you can make a match. But finding candy bar wrappers at both houses? I'm sorry, Maggie, that's a bit of a stretch."

"Stucky leaves body parts in take-out containers just for fun, to toy with people. Why wouldn't he leave candy bar wrappers, sort of his way of thumbing his nose at us? Like he was able to commit this inconceivably horrible murder and then have a snack afterward."

"So the wrappers are part of the game?"

"Yes." She glanced up. Gwen didn't buy it. "Why is that so hard to believe?"

"Did you ever consider they could be a necessity? Maybe the killer or even the victims have an insulin deficiency. Sometimes people with diabetes keep candy bars to prevent fluctuations in their insulin intake. Fluctuations possibly caused by stress or an injection of too much insulin."

"Stucky's not diabetic."

"You know that for sure?"

"Yes," Maggie said, quite certain, then realized their lab analysis of Stucky's blood and DNA had never been tested for the disease.

"How can you be so certain?" Gwen persisted. "About a third of people with Type 2 diabetes don't even know they have it. It's not something that's routinely checked unless there are symptoms or some family history. And I have to tell you, the symptoms, especially the early ones, are very subtle."

She knew Gwen was right. But she would know if Stucky had diabetes. They had his blood and DNA on file. Unless this was some recent development. No, she couldn't imagine Albert Stucky being susceptible to anything other than silver bullets or maybe a wooden stake through his heart.

"How about the victims?" Gwen suggested. "Maybe the candy bars belonged to the victims. Any chance they're diabetic?"

"Too much of a coincidence. I don't believe in coincidences."

"No, you'd much rather believe that Albert Stucky has kidnapped your neighbor, who by the way wasn't your neighbor yet, *and* took a real estate agent simply because you bought a house from her. I have to tell you, Maggie, it all sounds a bit ridiculous. You have absolutely no proof that either of these women are even missing, let alone that Stucky has them."

"Gwen, it's no coincidence that the waitress in Kansas City and the pizza delivery girl had both come in contact with me only hours before they were murdered in the same manner. I'm the only link. Don't you think I want to believe that neither Rachel nor Tess were taken by Stucky? Don't you think I'd rather believe they are both on some secluded beach sipping piña coladas with their lovers?"

She hated that her voice could get so shrill, that her hands could shake and her heart pound in her ears. She went back to the pile, shuffling through the folders and trying to make sense of Tully's attempt at order, or rather his disorder. She could feel Gwen's eyes examining her. Maybe Gwen was right. Perhaps the paranoia skewed her rationality. What if she was blowing all this out of proportion? What if she was slipping over some mental edge? It certainly felt like that.

"If that's true, then it would mean Stucky is watching you, following you."

"Yes," Maggie said, trying to sound as matter-of-fact as possible.

"If he's choosing women he sees you with, then why hasn't he chosen me?"

Maggie looked up at her friend, startled by the flicker of fear she thought she saw in the otherwise strong and confident eyes. "He only targets women I come in contact with, not women I know. It makes his next move less predictable. He wants me to feel like an accomplice. I don't think he wants to destroy me. And hurting you would destroy me."

She went back to her search, wanting to close the subject and dismiss the possibility. Fact was, she had thought about Stucky moving on to those who were close to her. Nothing would stop him from doing so if he wanted to up the ante.

"Have you talked to Agent Tully about any of this?"

"You're my friend, and you think I'm nuts. Why in the world would I share any of it with him?"

"Because he's your partner, and the two of you should be working through this mess together, no matter how crazy every tidbit appears to be. Promise me you won't be checking out stuff on your own."

Maggie found a new set of documents and began flipping through the pages. Was it possible she was only imagining that there was something else that linked Rachel Endicott to Stucky?

"Maggie, did you hear me?"

She glanced up to find Gwen's normally smooth forehead wrinkled with concern, her warm green eyes filled with worry.

"Promise me you won't go off on your own again," Gwen demanded.

"I won't go off on my own again." She dug out a brown manila envelope and started extracting its contents.

"Maggie, I mean it."

She stopped and looked up at her friend. Even Harvey stared at her with sad, brown eyes. This from the same dog who had spent the last two nights going back and forth, checking the front door and each of the windows, looking for and waiting for his master to pick him up as though he couldn't stand to spend one more moment with Maggie.

"Please, don't worry, Gwen. I promise I won't do anything stupid." She unfolded several copies and immediately found what she had been searching for. It was the report from the airport authority and a police impound notice for a white Ford van. "Here it is. This is it. This is what's been nagging at me."

"What is it?"

Maggie stood and began pacing.

"Susan Lyndell told me that the man Rachel Endicott may have run off with was a telephone repairman."

"So what's your proof? Her phone bill?" Gwen sounded impatient.

"This is an impound notice. When the police found Jessica Beckwith's car at the airport, they found a van parked alongside it. The van had been stolen about two weeks ago."

"I'm sorry, Maggie, but I'm lost. So Stucky stole a van and abandoned it when he was finished with it. What does that have to do with your missing neighbor?"

"The van that was recovered belonged to Northeastern Bell Telephone

Company." Maggie waited for Gwen's reaction, and when it was less than satisfactory, she continued, "Okay, it's a long shot, but you have to admit, it's too much of a coincidence and—"

"I know, I know." Gwen raised her hand to stop her. "And you don't believe in coincidences."

CHAPTER 46

Tess couldn't remember a night so long and dark and brutal, despite having a repertoire of many in her childhood. She sat curled in a corner, hugging her knees and trying not to think about her bare, swollen feet buried in the rancid mud. The rain had finally stopped although she heard thunder in the distance, a low rumble like a boulder rolling overhead. Was it the clouds that were preventing the sun from rising or had the madman made a deal with the devil?

At times she could hear the woman moaning quietly to herself. Her breaths, her gasps were so close. Thankfully, the sobs and the high-pitched whine had stopped. As the sky lightened, the huddled form began to take shape.

Tess closed her eyes against the gritty, burning sensation. Why had she been so stubborn and refused the ever-wear contact lenses? She wanted to rub and dig at her eyes. Soon she'd need to make a choice about taking the contacts out or leaving them in. When she opened her eyes again, she blinked several times. She couldn't believe what she was seeing. In the dim light she saw the woman across from her was completely naked. She had twisted herself into a fetal position, her skin slathered in mud and what looked and smelled like blood and feces.

"Oh dear God," Tess mumbled. "Why didn't you tell me you had nothing on?"

Tess struggled to her feet. Her ankle rebelled, sending her to her knees. Now her pain seemed minor. She forced herself up again, putting all the weight on her other foot. Her fingers frantically pulled at the knot keeping her blanket cape around her shoulders. The woman's body shivered. No, she wasn't just shivering. Her muscles looked to be in some sort of convulsions. Her teeth chattered and her lower lip was bleeding where she must have bitten herself repeatedly.

"Are you in pain?" Tess asked, realizing how stupid the question sounded. Of course she was in pain.

She ripped the blanket off and draped it carefully around the woman. It was damp but the wool had somehow kept her own body heat from escaping all night long. Hopefully it wouldn't make matters worse. How could it possibly make things worse?

Tess kept a safe distance as she examined the horrible bruises, the raw cuts and torn flesh left from what looked like bites—human bites.

"Dear God. We need to get you to a hospital." Another ridiculous thing to say. If she couldn't get out of this pit, how could she get her to a hospital?

The woman didn't seem to hear Tess. Though her eyes were wide and open, they stared at the mud wall in front of her. Her tangled hair stuck to her face. Tess reached down and wiped a clump away from her cheek. The woman didn't even blink. She was in shock, and Tess wondered if her mind had retreated inside herself, into a deep, unreachable cavern. It was exactly what Tess had done so many times as a child. It had been her only defense in combating the long stays of punishment that had exiled her to the dark storm cellar, sometimes for days at a time.

She caressed the woman's cheek, wiping mud and hair from her face and neck. Her stomach lurched when she saw the bruises and bite marks that covered her neck and breast. A raw gash also circled her neck. It looked like an indentation left from a rope or cord pulled so tight it had dug into the flesh.

"Are you able to move?" Tess asked, but got no response.

She looked up to survey the depths of their hell now that light seeped down to them. It was not as deep as she had initially thought—twelve, maybe fifteen feet at the most, about five feet wide and ten feet long. It looked to be an old trench, partially caved in with uneven sides. Tree roots snaked out and rocks jutted out in places. But there were fresh spade marks that told her he intended for this to be a trap.

What kind of monster did this to a woman and then threw her into a pit? She couldn't think about him. She couldn't wonder or imagine, or it would completely paralyze her. Instead, she needed to concentrate on getting them out of here. But how the hell could she do that?

She kneeled next to the woman. The blanket seemed to reduce the convulsions. She'd need to examine her for broken bones. There were enough gashes in the walls and jutting rocks that they could climb their way out, but she'd never be able to pull or carry the woman.

Just as Tess reached to touch the woman's shoulder, she saw what it was that the woman's eyes were focused on so intently. Startled, she jumped back. Slowly she forced herself closer for a better look, despite her amazement, despite her revulsion. Directly in front of her, buried in the dirt wall and partially unearthed by the rain was a human skull, the empty eye sockets staring out at them. And then, Tess realized. This wasn't a trap, at all. It was a grave. It was their grave.

CHAPTER 47

Saturday, April 4

She wore another red silk blouse. She looked good in red. It emphasized her strawberry-blond hair. It had become a habit for her to leave off her jacket and stand in front of her desk, half sitting on the corner. Today, she didn't bother to pull down the skirt hem that hiked up just enough to reveal shapely smooth thighs. Lovely, tender thighs that made him wonder what it would feel like to sink his teeth into them.

She waited for him to talk while she scribbled in her notepad, probably not even taking notes on him. If the notes were about him, he wasn't the least bit curious about what they said. He was more interested in what her moans would sound like when he finally stuck himself inside her, thrusting deep and hard until she was screaming. He so enjoyed it when they screamed, especially when he was inside them. The vibration felt like shock waves, like he was causing a fucking earthquake.

It was one of many things he had in common with his old friend, his old partner. At least it was one thing he didn't need to fake. He pushed the sunglasses up on the bridge of his nose and realized she was waiting.

"Mr. Harding," she interrupted his thoughts. "You never answered my question."

He couldn't remember what the fucking question had been. He cocked his head to the side and jutted out his chin in that pathetic gesture that said, "Forgive me, I'm blind."

"I asked if any of the exercises I suggested have helped."

Sure enough. If he waited, people always made it easy, supplying the answer, repeating themselves or getting up and doing whatever it was they had wanted him to do. He was getting good at this. Probably a good thing, in case it became permanent.

"Mr. Harding?"

She didn't have much patience today. He wanted to ask how long it had been since she had been fucked. That was, no doubt, the problem. Or perhaps she needed a few porn movies from his new private collection.

He knew from his personal research that she was divorced, for almost twenty-five years now. It had been a short, two-year marriage, a youthful indiscretion. Certainly there must have been several lovers since, though, of course, those details weren't easily accessible on the Internet.

Now he could see her impatience growing in the way she crossed her arms. Finally, he said politely, "The exercises worked quite well, but that doesn't prove or help anything."

"Why do you say that?"

"What good does it do to get myself...well, excuse the expression...to get my little general all hot, hard and bothered when I'm alone?"

She smiled, the first she had surrendered since they had met.

"We need to start somewhere."

"Okay, but I'm afraid I must object if you suggest I move on to blow-up dolls."

Another smile. He was on a roll. Should he tell her he'd like her to be his blow-up doll? He wondered how good a blow job she could give with that sweet, sexy little mouth of hers. He was certain he could fill it quite nicely.

"No, I won't make any more suggestions for the time being," she said, detecting none of what went through his mind. "However, I would encourage you to continue with the exercises. The idea is to have a—excuse the expression—surefire method of arousal to fall back on should you find yourself wanting to perform with a woman but not able to."

She was idly swinging her left foot as she sat on the corner of the desk. Her black leather pump teetered at the end of her toes as she played with it. He wished the shoe would fall off. He wanted to see if she had painted her toenails. He loved red painted toenails.

"Whether we want to believe it or not, many of our preconceived notions about sex," she continued, though he paid little attention, "come from our parents. Boys especially find themselves imitating their fathers' behaviors. What was your father like, Mr. Harding?"

"He certainly had no problems when it came to women," he snapped, and immediately regretted letting her see that the subject was a touchy one. Now she wouldn't leave it alone. She'd insist they poke and probe through it until she found a way to bring his mother into it as well. Unless...unless he turned it around somehow and embarrassed her away from the subject entirely.

"My father brought women home quite frequently. He even let me watch. Sometimes the women let me join in. What other thirteen-year-old boy can say he got his cock sucked by a woman while his dad fucked the shit out of her from behind?"

There it was—that look of utter shock. Soon it would be followed by the pity look. Funny how the truth possessed such remarkable power. A knock at the door made her jump. He stared off into oblivion like a good little blind fucker.

"Sorry to interrupt," her secretary called from the door. "That phone call you've been waiting for is on line three."

"I need to take this call, Mr. Harding."

"That's fine." He stood and fumbled for his cane. "Perhaps we can end early today."

"Are you sure? This really will take but a minute or two."

"No, I'm exhausted. Besides, I think you more than earned your money today." He rewarded her with a smile so that she wouldn't continue to object. He found the door before she could offer to call his make-believe driver. As he waited for the elevator, the anger began to churn inside his guts. He hated thinking about his parents. She had no right bringing them into this. She had overstepped her bounds. Yes, today, Dr. Gwen Patterson had gone too far.

CHAPTER 48

Assistant Director Cunningham had commandeered a small conference room for them on the first level. Tully was so excited about having windows—two that looked into the woods at the edge of the training field—he didn't care that he had to walk up and down stairs, clear to the other end of the building to bring stuff from his cramped office.

He spread out everything they had gathered in the last five months, while O'Dell followed behind him, insisting on putting it all in neat little stacks, lining it up on the long conference table so that it flowed from left to right in chronological order. Instead of being irritated by her anal-retentive process, he found himself amused. So they approached puzzles differently. She liked to start by finding all the corner pieces and lining them up, while he liked to scatter all the pieces in the center, picking and choosing random sections to piece together. Neither way was right or wrong. It was simply a matter of preference, although he doubted that O'Dell would agree with that assessment.

They had tacked up a map of the United States, marking the recent murders in Newburgh Heights and Kansas City with red pushpins. Blue pins marked each of the other seventeen areas where Stucky had left victims before his capture last August. At least those were the ones they knew about. The women Stucky kept for his collection were often buried in remote wooded areas. It was believed there could be as many as a dozen more, hidden and waiting to be discovered by hikers or fishermen or hunters. All this, Stucky had accomplished in less than three years. Tully hated to think what the madman may have done in the last five months.

Tully continued to examine the map and left O'Dell to her housekeeping. For the most part, Stucky had stayed on the eastern edge of the United States from as far north as Boston to as far south as Miami. The Virginia shoreline seemed to be a fertile ground for him. Kansas City appeared to be the only anomaly. If Tess McGowan was, in fact, missing, that meant Stucky really was playing with O'Dell again, bringing her in, making her a part of his crimes. And by choosing only women who she came in contact with, rather than friends or family members, he made it virtually impossible for them to know who might be next. After all, what could they do? Lock O'Dell up until they caught Stucky? Cunningham already had several agents watching her house and following her. Tully was surprised O'Dell hadn't objected.

Saturday morning and she was already digging in as if it were any other weekday. After the week she had, anyone else would still be at home in bed. Although this morning he did notice that she hadn't bothered to use makeup to conceal the dark, puffy lines under her eyes. She wore an old pair of Nike running shoes, a chambray shirt with the sleeves rolled up to the elbows and the tails neatly tucked into the waistband of faded jeans. Though they were in a secured facility, she kept her shoulder harness on, her Smith & Wesson .38 ready at her side. Compared to O'Dell, he felt overdressed, except when Assistant Director Cunningham stopped by, looking as crisp, spotless and wrinkle-free as usual. That was when Tully noticed the coffee stains on his own white shirt and his loosened and lopsided tie.

Tully checked his watch. He had promised Emma lunch and a total discussion of this prom thing. He had already decided to stand firm on the matter. Emma could call it being close-minded if she wanted to, but he simply didn't want to start thinking about her as being old enough to date. At least not yet. Maybe next year.

He glanced over at O'Dell who stood over the reports they had received earlier from Keith Ganza. Without looking up at him, she asked, "Any luck with airport security?"

"No, but now that Delores Heston has filed a missing-person's report, we can get an APB out on the car. A black Miata can't be that hard to miss. I don't know, though. What if McGowan just decided to take off for a couple of days?"

"Then we ruin her vacation. What about the boyfriend?"

"The guy has a house and business in D.C., and another house and office in Newburgh Heights. I finally tracked down Mr. Daniel Kassenbaum last night at his country club. He didn't sound very concerned. In fact, he told me he suspected McGowan might be cheating on him. Then he quickly added that their relationship was a no-strings sort of thing. That's what he called it. So, I guess if his suspicions are true, maybe she simply took off with some secret lover."

O'Dell looked up at him. "If the boyfriend thought she was cheating on him, can we be certain he didn't have something to do with her disappearance?"

"I honestly don't think the guy cares, not as long as he was getting what he wanted." O'Dell looked puzzled. Tully felt a surge of emotion and knew this was a touchy subject with him. Kassenbaum reminded him too much of the asshole Caroline had left him for. Still, he continued, "He told me the last time he saw her was when she stayed over at his house in Newburgh Heights Tuesday night. Now, if the guy thinks she's cheating on him, why is he still having her stay overnight at his house?"

O'Dell shrugged. "I give up. Why?"

He wasn't sure if she was serious or being sarcastic. "Why? Because he's an arrogant asshole who doesn't care about anyone other than himself. So as long as he's getting his jollies serviced, what does he care?" She was staring at him. He should have known when to quit. "What do women see in guys like that?"

"Getting his jollies serviced? Is that what you call it in Ohio?"

Tully felt his face grow red, and O'Dell smiled. She went back to the reports, letting him off the hook, and evidently not realizing how hot the subject made him. Last night, Daniel Kassenbaum had treated him like some servant he didn't have time for, scolding Tully for interrupting his dinner. Like the guy didn't think maybe Tully was interrupting his own dinner by looking for his girlfriend? Maybe Tess McGowan really did take off with some secret lover. Good for her.

He stood facing the map again. They had circled possible sites, mostly remote wooded areas. There were way too many to check. The only clue they had was the sparkling dirt found in Jessica Beckwith's car and in Rachel Endicott's house. Keith Ganza had narrowed down the chemical concoction that made up the metallic substance, but even that didn't narrow down the sites. In fact, it made Tully wonder if they were looking in the wrong places. Maybe they should be checking out deserted industrial sites instead of wooded areas. After all, Stucky had used a condemned warehouse in Miami to hide his collection until O'Dell found him.

"What about an industrial site?" He decided to try out his theory on O'Dell.

She stopped what she was doing and came beside him, studying the map.

"You're thinking of the chemicals Keith found in the mud?"

"I know it doesn't follow his pattern, but neither did the warehouse down in Miami." As soon as he said it, he glanced at O'Dell, realizing the subject may still be a touchy one. If it was, she made no indication.

"Wherever he's hiding, it can't be far. I'm guessing an hour, maybe an hour and a half at most." She traced the area with her index finger, a fifty-to-seventy-mile radius, with her home in Newburgh Heights at the center. "He couldn't drive too far and still keep watch over me."

Tully watched her out of the corner of his eyes, again looking for any signs of the frenzy, the terror he had witnessed the other night. He wasn't surprised to find it masked. O'Dell wouldn't be the first FBI agent he knew who could compartmentalize her emotions. With O'Dell, however, he could see it was an effort. He wondered just how long she could contain them without cracking at the seams again.

"The map may not show old industrial sites that have been closed. I'll check with the State Department and see if they have anything."

"Don't forget Maryland and D.C."

Tully jotted notes on the McDonald's brown paper sack that had held his breakfast; a sausage biscuit and hash browns. For a brief moment he tried to remember the last meal he had eaten that hadn't come from a bag. Maybe he'd take Emma somewhere nice for lunch. No fast food. Somewhere with tablecloths.

When he turned back, O'Dell was back at the table. He looked over her shoulder at the crime scene photos she had sorted. Without looking at him, she said in almost a whisper, "We need to find them, Agent Tully. We need to find them very soon or it'll be too late."

He didn't need to ask who she meant. She was talking about the McGowan woman, and also her neighbor, Rachel Endicott. Tully still wasn't convinced either woman was missing, let alone taken by Stucky. He didn't share his doubts with O'Dell, nor did he share with her that he had talked to Detective Manx in Newburgh Heights. With any luck Manx would find it in his stubborn, isolationist pig head to share whatever evidence he recovered from the Endicott house. Though Tully didn't expect much. Detective Manx had told him the case was nothing more than a bored housewife running off with a telephone repairman.

He hated to think Manx might be right. Tully shook his head. What was it with married women these days? He didn't like being reminded of Caroline for the second time that morning.

"If you are right about Tess McGowan and the Endicott woman," Tully said, careful to keep his own doubts aside, "that means Stucky has killed two women and taken two others in a span of only one week. Are you sure Stucky could pull that off?"

"It would be tough but not impossible. He would have had to take Rachel Endicott early last Friday. Then come back to Newburgh Heights, watch Jessica deliver my pizza, lure her to the house on Archer Drive and kill her late Friday evening or early Saturday morning."

"Doesn't that seem like a bit much?"

"Yes," she admitted, "but not for Stucky."

"Then somehow he finds out that you'd be in KC. Even finds out where you're staying. Again, he watches you, Delaney and Turner with the waitress—"

"Rita."

"Right, Rita. That was what, Sunday night?"

"Around midnight...actually early Monday morning. If Delores Heston is correct, Tess showed the house on Archer Drive Wednesday." She avoided Tully's eyes. "I know it sounds like a lot, but keep in mind what he's done in the past."

She started sorting through the photos again. "It's never been easy to track. Some of the bodies were found much later, long after they were reported missing. Most of them were so badly decomposed we could only guess at the time of deaths. But the spring before we caught him, we estimated that he killed two women, leaving them in Dumpsters, and that he had taken five others for his collection. That was all in the span of two or three weeks. At least that's the time frame that the women were first discovered missing. We didn't find those five bodies until months later, and they were all in one mass grave. The women had been tortured and killed at different intervals. There were signs that he may have even hunted down a couple of them. We found evidence that he may have used a crossbow and arrows."

Tully recognized the photos. O'Dell had laid out a series of Poloraids that chronicled one victim's wounds. If the photos hadn't been marked, it would be difficult to tell that they were all the same woman. This was one of those five victims who had been found in that mass grave. The corpse was one of the rare ones found before decomposition or before animals had ravaged it. It was one of the few that was intact and whole.

"This was Helen Kreski," O'Dell said without looking up the name. "She was one of the five. Stucky choked and stabbed her repeatedly. Her left nipple had been bitten off. Her right arm and wrist were broken. There was a puncture through her left calf with a broken arrow still intact." O'Dell's voice was calm, too calm, as though she had resolved herself to something beyond her control. "We found dirt in her lungs. She was still alive when he buried her."

"Christ, this is one sick son of a bitch."

"We need to stop him, Agent Tully. We need to do it before he crawls back into a hole someplace. Before he runs off and hides and starts playing with his new collection."

"And we'll do that. We just need to find out where the hell he's hiding." He didn't want to notice that she had used the word *stop* instead of *catch*.

He left her side and checked his watch again.

"I need to leave around eleven. I promised my daughter we'd have lunch together." O'Dell had moved back to the reports they had received from Ganza. She had the fingerprint analysis and was reading it over for the third time. He wondered if she had even heard him. "Hey, why don't you join us?"

She glanced up, surprised by his invitation.

"I still think the print was left by someone who looked at the house earlier," he said, referring to the fingerprint report and taking her off the hook if she really didn't want to accept his invitation.

"He wiped down everything in the bathroom," she said, "but he missed two clean and whole fingerprints. No, he wanted us to find these. He's done it before. It was how we finally confirmed who he was."

He watched her rub her eyes as if the memory brought on a whole new fatigue.

"At that time, we had no name, no idea who The Collector was," she continued. "Stucky evidently thought we were taking too long to figure it out. I think he left us a print on purpose. It was so blatant, so careless, it had to be on purpose."

"Well, if this one was on purpose, why bother to clean up the place at all? He never seemed to care before."

"Maybe he cleaned up because he wanted to use the house again."

"For McGowan?"

"Yes."

"Okay. But why bother to leave us a print that doesn't even belong to him? Just like on the Dumpster behind the pizza place and on the umbrella in Kansas City."

O'Dell hesitated, stopping her hands from shuffling papers and looking at him as if wondering whether or not to tell him something. "Keith hasn't been able to find a match for those prints in AFIS. But he says he's almost certain all three sets of prints belong to the same person."

"You're kidding. He knows that for sure? If that's the case, maybe these murders aren't Stucky, after all."

He stared at her, waiting for some kind of reaction. Her face remained impassive, just like her voice when she said, "Jessica's murder and Rita's in Kansas City are awfully close together. I know I just said that Stucky could pull it off, but the anal penetration with Jessica is not Stucky's M.O. Also, she's much younger than any of his other victims."

"So what are you saying, O'Dell. You think this one was a copycat?"

"Or an accomplice."

"What? That's crazy!"

She buried her eyes in the files again. He could see she was having a difficult time with the theory herself. O'Dell was used to working and brainstorming alone. Suddenly he realized that it probably took a good deal of trust for her to share this idea with him.

"Look, I know you're serious, but why would Stucky take on an accomplice? You have to admit, that's out of character for any serial killer."

In reply, O'Dell pulled out several photocopied pages that looked like magazine and newspaper articles and handed them to Tully.

"Remember Cunningham said he found the name Walker Harding, Stucky's old business partner, on an airline manifest?"

Tully nodded and began sorting through the articles.

"Some of those go back several years," she told him.

They were articles from *Forbes*, the *Wall Street Journal*, *PC World* and several other business and trade periodicals. The *Forbes* article included a picture. Though the grainy black-and-white copy had obliterated most of the men's features, the two of them could have passed for brothers. Both had dark hair, narrow faces and sharp features. Tully recognized Albert Stucky's piercing black eyes, which he knew to be void of color despite the poor reproduction. The younger man smiled while Stucky's face remained stoic and serious.

"I'm guessing this must be the partner?"

"Yes. A couple of the articles mention how much the two men had in common and how competitive they were with each other. However, they seemed to have ended their partnership amicably. I wonder if they might still be in contact with each other. Maybe still in competition with each other, only with a new game."

"But why now after all these years? If they were to do something like this, why not when Stucky first started his game?"

O'Dell sat down and tucked strands of hair behind her ears. She looked exhausted. As if reading his thoughts, she sipped her Diet Pepsi, which he had noticed was her coffee substitute. This was her third one of the morning.

"Stucky has always been a loner," she explained. "I haven't done any research on Harding except for these articles, but for Stucky to have chosen anyone as a business partner is remarkable. I've never thought about it before, but perhaps the two men had, and still have, some strong connection, a connection Stucky didn't realize until recently. Or perhaps there's some other reason he decided he needed his old friend."

Tully shook his head. "I think you're grasping at straws, O'Dell. You know as well as I do that statistically, serial killers don't take on partners or accomplices."

"But Stucky is far from fitting any of the statistics. I'm having Keith run a check to see if Harding has ever been fingerprinted. Then we can see if we have a match to the fingerprints being left at the crime scenes."

Tully looked over the articles, scanning the text until something caught his eye.

"Looks like there's a slight problem with your theory, O'Dell."

"What's that?"

"There's a footnote to this *Wall Street Journal* article. Stucky and Harding ended their partnership after Harding was diagnosed with some medical problem."

"Right. I saw that."

"But did you finish reading it? This part is blurred at the bottom from the copier. Unless Walker Harding found some miracle cure, he can't be Stucky's accomplice. It says here he was going blind."

CHAPTER 49

Maggie waited until Tully left to meet his daughter. Then she began unearthing every scrap of information she could find on Walker Harding. She pounded the computer's keys, searching the FBI's files and other Internet sites and directories. The man had virtually disappeared after announcing his ambiguous medical problem almost four years ago. Now she realized Keith Ganza might never find a fingerprint record, either. Perhaps it was simply a gut instinct, but she felt certain Harding was still connected to Stucky, helping him somehow, continuing to work with him.

From what little she had read, she knew Harding had been the brains of their business, a whiz with computers. But Stucky had been the one who had taken all the financial risk, investing a hundred thousand dollars of his own money; money he had joked about winning one weekend in Atlantic City. Maggie couldn't help noticing that the investment capital and the start-up of the business happened the same year Stucky's father died in a freak boating accident. Stucky had never been charged though he had been questioned in what looked like a routine investigation, and only because Stucky had been the sole beneficiary of his father's estate, an estate that made that hundred thousand dollars look like pocket change.

Harding appeared to have been reclusive long before his business venture with Stucky. Maggie could find nothing about his childhood, except that he—like Stucky—had been raised by a single, overbearing father. One directory listed him as a 1985 graduate of MIT, which made him about three years younger than Stucky. The state of Virginia listed no marriage license, driver's license or property owned by a Walker Harding. She had begun a search of Maryland's records when Thea Johnson from down the hall knocked on the open conference-room door.

"Agent O'Dell, there's a phone call for Agent Tully. I know he left for a while, but this sounds important. Do you want to take the call?"

"Sure." Maggie didn't hesitate and reached behind her for the phone. "What line?"

"Line five. It's a detective from Newburgh Heights. I believe he said his name was Manx."

Immediately, Maggie's stomach took a dive. She sucked in a deep breath and punched line five.

"Detective Manx, Agent Tully is at lunch. This is his partner, Agent Margaret O'Dell."

She waited for the name to register. Even after a sigh, there was a pause.

"Agent O'Dell. Barge in on any crime scenes lately?"

"Funny thing, Detective Manx, but here at the FBI we usually don't wait for engraved invitations." She didn't care if he heard the irritation in her voice. If he was calling Tully, he wanted something from them. Besides, what was he going to do? Go tell Cunningham she was mean to him again?

"When's Tully gonna be back?"

So that was the way he wanted to play.

"Gee, you know, I don't remember if he told me. He might not be back until Monday."

She waited out his silence and imagined the scowl on his face. He was probably swiping a frustrated hand over that new buzz hairdo of his.

"Look, Tully talked to me last night about this McGowan woman down here in Newburgh Heights that's supposedly missing."

"She is missing, Detective Manx. Seems you have a problem with women disappearing in your jurisdiction. What's up with that?" She was enjoying this too much. She needed to back off.

"I thought he should know that we checked out her house this morning and found a guy snooping around."

"What?" Maggie sat up and gripped the phone.

"This guy said he was a friend and was worried about her. He had a screen off a back window and looked like he was getting ready to break in. We brought him in for questioning. Just thought Tully might like to know."

"You haven't released him yet, have you?"

"No, the boys are still chatting with him. I think we got him pretty damn scared. First thing, he insisted on calling his fucking lawyer. Makes me think he's guilty of something."

"Don't release him until Agent Tully and I have a chance to talk to him. We'll be there in about a half hour."

"Sure, no problem. Lookin' forward to seeing you again, O'Dell."

She hung up, grabbed her jacket and was almost out the door before she realized she should probably call Tully. She patted her jacket down until she felt the cellular phone in the pocket. She'd call him from the road. No, of course, this wasn't a matter of her running off on her own. It wasn't breaking any of Cunningham's new rules. She simply didn't want to ruin Agent Tully's lunch with his daughter.

That was what she told herself. The fact was, she wanted to check this out on her own. If Manx had Albert Stucky or even Walker Harding, Maggie wanted him all to herself.

CHAPTER 50

As the sun moved overhead and more light seeped down, Tess could see the hellhole for what it was. The skull that stared out from the earth wall was not the only human remains that surrounded them. Other bones glistened, washed white by the rains, protruding at odd angles from the uneven walls and the muddy floor.

At first Tess told herself it was some ancient burial ground, maybe a mass grave from a Civil War battle. Then she found a black underwire bra and a woman's leather pump with a broken heel sticking out of the ground. Neither looked old enough or deteriorated enough to have been there much longer than weeks, maybe months.

Dirt had been recently thrown into one of the corners. The mound looked fresh despite the rain packing it down. She stared at it, but didn't dare go near it, staying away as if the pile would crumble and reveal some new horror. If that was at all possible.

The rays of sunshine felt wonderful, though they wouldn't last long. She managed to gently drag the woman to the center, so she could be warmed directly. Even the wool blanket had begun to dry. Tess stretched it out across some rocks, leaving the woman naked but bathed in sunlight.

Tess was getting used to the rancid smell of the woman. She could stay close without the urge to vomit. The woman had defecated in her corner several times and had accidentally rolled in it. Tess wished she had some water to clean her. The thought reminded her how dry and raw her mouth and throat were. Surely the woman was already in a state of dehydration.

Her convulsions had calmed to a mild shiver and her teeth had stopped chattering. Even her breathing seemed to return to normal. Now with the sunlight on her skin, Tess noticed she had closed her eyes, as though finally able to rest. Or had she finally decided to die?

Tess sat on a broken branch and examined the pit again. She knew she could climb out. She had tried twice, reaching the top both times. Each time she peered over the edge, the relief and satisfaction overwhelming her to tears. But each time, she lowered herself back down, carefully easing the pressure on her swollen ankle.

Though she didn't want to think about the madman, she realized there could be safety in this pit. He must have dumped the woman here, expecting her to die from her wounds and exposure. Eventually, he would return to throw some dirt over her and create yet another mound. When he discovered Tess was gone from the shack, he might not think to look for her down here.

That didn't mean she wanted to stay. She hated feeling trapped. And this hellhole reminded her too much of the dark storm cellar her aunt and uncle had used as punishment for her. As a child, being buried beneath the ground for an hour was terrifying. One or two days, unimaginable. Even as an adult, she could never remember what she had done to deserve such punishment. Instead, she had readily believed her aunt when she called her an evil child and dragged her down to the damp torture chamber. Each time, Tess had screamed how sorry she was and pleaded for forgiveness.

"No apologies accepted," her uncle would always say, laughing.

In the dark, Tess would pray over and over for her mother to come and rescue her, remembering her mother's last words, "I'll be right back, Tessy." But she never came back to rescue Tess. She never returned at all. How could her mother leave her with such evil people?

As Tess grew older and stronger, her aunt was no longer a match for her. That's when her uncle took over. Only, her uncle's form of punishment came late at night when he let himself into her bedroom. When she tried to lock him out, he removed the door to her room. At first she screamed, knowing her aunt could now hear without the door to muffle the sounds. It didn't take long for her to realize that her aunt had always heard, had always known. She just didn't care.

Tess ran away to D.C. when she was fifteen. Quickly, she had learned that she could make quite a bit of money doing what her uncle had taught her for free. Fifteen years old, and she was fucking congressmen and four-star generals. That was almost twenty years ago, and yet she had only recently found her escape from that life. She had finally begun a life that was her own. And she sure as hell would not end it here. Not now. Not in this remote grave where no one would ever notice.

She got to her feet and approached the woman. She squatted next to her and put a gentle hand on her shoulder.

"I don't know if you can hear me. My name is Tess. I want you to know I'm going to get us out of here. I'm not going to leave you here to die."

Tess pulled a branch closer so she could sit next to the woman in the sunlight. She needed to rest her ankle. She buried her toes into the mud. Despite the slimy earthworms against her skin, the mud did soothe the cracks and cuts and bruises on her feet.

She surveyed the jutting rocks and tree roots, trying to come up with a plan. Just when she began to think it would be impossible, the woman moved slightly to her side. Without opening her eyes, she said, "My name's Rachel."

CHAPTER 51

Maggie wasn't sure what she expected. Could Albert Stucky or Walker Harding be stupid enough to get caught by the Newburgh Heights Police Department? Yet, when Manx showed her into the interrogation room, her heart sank. The handsome young man looked more like a college student than the hardened criminal Manx had described when he had insisted the man was guilty of something.

The kid even stood up when she entered the room, not able to stifle his good manners despite the situation.

"There's been a huge misunderstanding," he told her as if she was the new face of reason.

He wore khakis and a crew-neck sweater. Maybe this was what Manx expected burglars to wear in Newburgh Heights.

"Sit the hell down, kid," Manx snapped at him as though he was jumping up to attack her.

Maggie walked around Manx and sat down at the table opposite the young man. He slid back into his chair, wringing his hands in front of him on the table, his eyes darting from Manx to the other two uniformed officers already in the room.

"I'm Special Agent Margaret O'Dell with the FBI." She waited for his eyes to settle on hers.

"FBI?" He looked worried and fidgeted in his chair. "Something's happened to Tess, hasn't it?"

"I know you may have already explained all this, but how do you know Ms. McGowan, Mr.—"

"Finley. My name's Will Finley. I met Tess last weekend."

"Last weekend? So you haven't been friends for very long. Did she show you a piece of real estate?"

"Excuse me?"

"Ms. McGowan is a real estate agent. Did she show you a house last weekend?"

"No. We met at a bar. We...we spent the night together."

Maggie wondered if it was a lie. Tess McGowan hadn't looked like the barfly type. Plus, she guessed Tess to be close to her own age. She couldn't imagine Tess giving this college kid a second glance. Unless she had been trying to get back at her big-shot, country-club boyfriend. Of course, she also couldn't imagine Tess McGowan with the guy who Agent Tully called an arrogant asshole. But then she realized she really hadn't taken time to get to know anything about Tess McGowan. Nevertheless, she was certain Will Finley had nothing to do with Tess's disappearance. Now she was glad she hadn't dragged Tully away from lunch with his daughter for this.

"What's happened to Tess?" Will Finley wanted to know. He looked genuinely concerned.

"Maybe you ought to be tellin' us," Manx said from behind Maggie.

"How many times do I have to tell you? I didn't do anything to her. I haven't seen her since Monday morning. She hasn't returned any of my phone calls. I was worried about her." He scraped a shaking hand over his face.

Maggie wondered how long they had kept him here. He looked exhausted, his nerves frayed. She knew after enough hours of the same questions, in the same room, sitting in the same position, that the most innocent of men could break down.

"Will." She waited again for his eyes. "We're not sure what happened to Tess, but she is missing. I'm hoping you might be able to help us find her."

He stared at her as though he wasn't sure whether to believe her or if this was a trick.

"Is there anything you can remember?" she continued, keeping her voice calm and steady, unlike Manx's. "Anything you might be able to tell us that could help us find her?"

"I'm not sure. I mean, I really don't know her very well."

"Well enough to fuck her, though, right?" Manx said, insisting on playing out his role as the bad cop.

Maggie ignored him, though Will Finley stared at him and fidg-eted with the appropriate amount of guilt. Manx was right about the kid hiding something. It was the illicitness of the affair, not that he had hurt Tess.

"Where did you spend the night together?"

"Look, I know my rights, and I know I don't have to answer these questions." He sounded defensive now. Maggie didn't blame him, especially since Manx treated him like a suspect.

"No, you don't need to answer any of my questions. I just thought you might want to help us find her." Maggie gently tried to persuade him.

"I don't see how knowing where or when or how or what we did that night is going to help."

"Hey, kid, you banged an older woman. You should be jumping at the chance to share the details."

Maggie stood and faced Manx, trying to maintain her calm and bridle her impatience.

"Detective Manx, do you mind if I have a word with Mr. Finley alone?"

"I don't think that's a good idea."

"And why is that?"

"Well…" Manx hesitated while he manufactured a reason. She could practically hear his rusty gears grinding. "Might not be safe to leave you alone with him."

"I'm an experienced FBI agent, Detective Manx."

"You sure don't dress like one, Agent O'Dell," he said as he purposely let his eyes slide slowly over her body.

"Tell you what. I'll take my chances with Mr. Finley." She glanced over at the officers. "You gentleman can verify that I said that."

Manx stalled, then finally waved the two officers out of the room. He followed but not before shooting a warning look in Finley's direction.

"I'd apologize for Detective Manx, but that would mean I was trying to excuse his behavior, and quite honestly, there is no excuse for his behavior."

She sat back down with a sigh and an absent rub at her eyes. When she looked up at Will Finley, he was smiling.

"I just realized who you are."

"Excuse me?" Maggie asked.

"You and I have a mutual friend."

The door opened again, and Maggie jumped to her feet, ready to snap at Manx. It was, instead, one of the other officers. His entire face seemed to be apologetic.

"Sorry, but the kid's lawyer just got here. He's insisting on seeing him before any more questioning is—"

"You shouldn't be questioning him at all," a voice from the hall interrupted. "At least not without his attorney present." Nick Morrelli pushed past the officer and into the room. Immediately, his eyes found Maggie's and his anger gave in to a smile. "Jesus, Maggie. We have to stop meeting like this."

Chapter 52

Harvey greeted Nick at the door with an impressive growl, teeth bared and his upper lip curled back. Maggie smiled at Nick's surprise even though she had warned him.

"I told you I have my own private bodyguard. Down, Harvey. Actually, we're temporary roommates." She petted the dog's head, and his entire hind end started wagging. "Harvey, this is Nick. He's one of the good guys."

Nick extended an apprehensive hand for the dog to sniff. In seconds, Harvey decided Nick deserved the royal treatment, and the dog stuck his snout in Nick's crotch. Maggie laughed and pulled back on Harvey's collar. Nick seemed more amused than embarrassed.

"So I see you have him checking out other things for you as well."

His comment caught her off guard. She led Harvey into the living room, hoping Nick didn't notice.

"I just moved in last week. I don't have a lot of furniture yet. I barely got some of the blinds up late last night."

"It's an incredible house, Maggie," he said, wandering into the sunroom and looking out at the backyard. "Pretty secluded. How safe is it?"

She looked up from the alarm system she was resetting. "About as safe as I would be anywhere. Cunningham has me under twenty-four-hour surveillance. Didn't you notice the cable TV van down the street? He says it's so we can catch Stucky, but I know he thinks it'll protect me."

"You don't sound convinced."

She opened her jacket to show him her revolver in her shoulder harness.

"This is the only thing that I find convincing these days."

He smiled. "Geez, I get so turned on when you show me your gun."

She found herself blushing from his innocent flirting. Immediately, she looked away. Damn it! She hated that he could get her pulse racing by his simple presence. Had it been a mistake to invite him here? Maybe she should have sent him back home to Boston with Will.

"I'm going to check if dinner is possible. I only have the very basics." She retreated to the kitchen, wondering what she would do if he went beyond flirting. Would she remember to act sensibly? "Would you mind taking Harvey out in the backyard?"

"No, not at all."

"His leash is by the back door. Press the green flashing button on the security system."

"It's a little like living in a fort." He motioned to the sensors and the alarm boxes. "Are you okay with all this?"

"I don't have much of a choice, do I?"

He shrugged and met her eyes. She realized he was feeling helpless, as though there must be something he should be able to do.

"It's part of the job, Nick. A lot of profilers live in gated communities or houses with elaborate alarm systems. After a while you get used to having an unpublished phone number and making certain your address isn't listed in any directory. It's all a part of my life, the part Greg didn't want to deal with. Maybe he shouldn't have had to deal with it. Maybe no one should."

"Well, Greg was a fool," he said as he snapped the leash onto Harvey's collar. Harvey licked Nick's hand in advanced appreciation. "But then, I sorta see Greg's loss as my gain." He smiled at her, then pushed the green button and let Harvey pull him into the backyard.

Maggie watched them, wondering what was it about this man and that lean body and those charming dimples that could so easily stir up feeling and emotions she hadn't accessed in years? Was it just a physical attraction? Did he simply set off her hormones? Nothing more?

When she met Nick last fall in Platte City he was a cocky, arrogant sheriff with a playboy reputation. Immediately, she had been annoyed with herself for being attracted to his charm and classic good looks. But over the course of that terrifying, exhausting week, she had the opportunity to see a sensitive, caring man who truly wanted to do the right thing.

Before she left Nebraska, he had told her that he loved her. She wrote it off with all the other confusing emotions people think they feel after being thrown together during a crisis. In Kansas City, he said he still cared about her. Now that he knew she was divorcing Greg, she wondered what Nick's intentions were. Did he really care about her, or was she only one more notch he wanted to carve in his bedpost?

It didn't matter. She didn't have the energy to entertain such thoughts. She needed to remain focused. She needed to start listening to her head and her gut, not her heart. And more importantly, she didn't want to care about someone who Stucky could take away from her in a split second.

What Gwen had said last night about Stucky coming after her stayed with Maggie, gnawing at her. Although she honestly didn't believe Gwen needed to worry. They all believed Stucky had chosen women who were mere acquaintances of hers, in order to make it impossible to predict who his next target might be. But the fact of the matter was, Maggie had few people she allowed into her life. Gwen claimed it was because she wasn't over the loss of her father. What a bunch of psychobabble that was. Gwen believed that Maggie purposely made herself off-limits, emotionally, to her friends and co-workers. What Maggie called professional distancing, Gwen called fear of intimacy.

"If you don't let people in, they can't hurt you," Gwen had lectured in her motherly tone. "But if you don't let people in, they can't love you either."

Nick and Harvey were coming back, Harvey carrying the bone Maggie had bought him. She thought he had taken it out and buried it because he didn't want it. Instead, the fresh hole under the dogwood was merely for safe storage. She certainly had a lot to learn about her new roommate.

As soon as Nick unleashed Harvey, he bounded up the stairs.

"He looks like a guy with a mission." Nick watched.

"He'll plop down in the corner of my bedroom and gnaw on that thing for hours."

"The two of you seem to be getting attached to each other."

"No way. The smelly brute goes home as soon as they find his mom." Or at least, that's what she kept telling herself. Fact was, she would feel horribly betrayed when Rachel Endicott showed up and Harvey ran to her without so much as a glance in Maggie's direction. The thought alone felt like a stab. Okay, maybe not a stab—a poke or a pinch.

The point was, Gwen was full of crap. Letting anyone in, including a goddamn dog, usually ended up hurting like hell. So she protected herself. It was one of the few things in her twisted life she could protect herself from. One of the last things she could have control over.

She realized Nick was leaning against the kitchen counter, watching her, concern clouding his crystal blue eyes.

"Maggie, are you okay?"

"I'm fine," she answered, and his smile told her she had hesitated much too long to convince him.

"You know what?" he said as he walked slowly across the kitchen toward her, stopping directly in front of her, his eyes holding hers. "Why don't you let me take care of you for one evening?"

His fingertips stroked her cheek. The familiar current of electricity raced through her, and she knew exactly what he meant by saying he wanted to take care of her.

"Nick, I can't."

She felt his breath in her hair. His lips didn't pay attention to her words as they traced where his fingers had been. Her breathing was already uneven by the time his lips brushed hers. But instead of kissing her, he moved to her other cheek. His lips moved over her eyelids and nose and forehead and hair.

"Nick," she tried again, only she wondered if the word was audible. Her own heart beat so noisily in her ears, she couldn't hear herself think. Not that her thought process was in any kind of working condition. Instead of concentrating on what his hands and lips were doing, she kept thinking about the edge of countertop that was cutting into the small of her back as if that would allow her to hang on to reality and not be swept away.

Finally, Nick stopped, his eyes meeting hers, his face still so close. God, she could easily get lost in his eyes, the warm blue oceans. His hands caressed and massaged her shoulders. His fingers strayed inside her collar to gently touch her throat and then the nape of her neck.

"I just want to make you feel good, Maggie."

"Nick, I really can't do this," she heard herself say while the flutter in her stomach disagreed with her words, screaming at her to take them back.

Nick smiled, and his fingers caressed her cheek again.

"I know," he said, taking a deep breath. There was no disappointment or hurt, only resignation, almost as if her response had been a foregone conclusion. "I know you're not ready. It's too soon after Greg."

It was great that he understood, because Maggie wasn't sure she did. How could she explain it to him?

"With Greg, it was so comfortable." It was the wrong thing to say. She saw the wounded look in his eyes.

"And it's not comfortable with me?"

"With you, it's..." His fingers were distracting her, still exploring, making her breathing uneven. Was he trying to change her mind? Did he realize how easy it could be to change her mind? "With you," she tried to continue, "it's so intense, it scares me." There, she said it. She had admitted it out loud.

"And it scares you because you might lose control." He looked into her eyes.

"God, you know me well, Morrelli."

"Tell you what. When you're ready, and I'm emphasizing when. No ifs," he said, his eyes not letting her go, his fingers still touching her. "I'll let you have all the control you want. But tonight, Maggie, I just want to make you feel good."

The flutter reawakened, immediately kicking into overdrive.

"Nick—"

"Actually, I was thinking maybe I could fix you dinner."

Her shoulders relaxed immediately, and she sighed with a smile. "I didn't realize you knew how to cook."

"There are a lot of things I know how to do that I haven't shown you... yet." And this time, he smiled.

CHAPTER 53

Maggie couldn't believe such delicious aromas were coming from her kitchen. Even Harvey had come down for a look and a closer sniff.

"Where did you learn to cook like this?"

"Hey, I'm Italian." Nick faked an accent that sounded nothing like Italian as he stirred the tomato sauce. "Don't tell Christine, okay?"

"Afraid you might ruin your reputation?"

"No, I don't want her free dinner invitations to stop."

"Is this enough garlic?" She stopped chopping and mincing long enough for him to examine her progress.

"One more clove."

"How are Christine and Timmy?" Maggie had grown attached to Nick's sister and his nephew in the short time she had spent in Nebraska.

"They're good. Really good. Bruce has taken an apartment in Platte City. Christine's making him earn his way back into their lives. I think she wants to make sure his philandering days are completely over. Here, taste this." He held the wooden spoon out to her, keeping an open palm underneath to catch any drips.

She took a careful lick. "A little more salt and definitely more garlic."

"So can you tell me anything about this Tess who Will is so crazy about? Any idea what happened to her?"

Maggie wasn't sure where to begin, or how much she wanted to share. All of it was still speculation. She watched him take salt in the palm of his hand, make a fist and sprinkle it into the simmering pot. She liked the way he moved around her kitchen, as though he had been fixing her dinners for years. Already Harvey followed him, anointing Nick the new master of the house.

"Tess was my real estate agent. She sold me this house, then less than a week later, she disappeared."

She waited, wondering if it would sink in, if he would make the connection on his own. Or was she the only one who could see that connection so clearly? He came over to the island where she sat on a bar stool and minced garlic. He poured more wine into both their glasses and took a sip. Finally, he looked at her.

"You think Stucky's murdered her?" He said it calmly and frankly.

"Yes. Or if he hasn't murdered her, she may be wishing he had."

She avoided his eyes and pretended to concentrate on the pieces of garlic. She didn't want to think about Stucky carving up Tess McGowan or playing his little torture games with her mind and body. Now Maggie's mincing had turned into vicious chops and hacks. She stopped herself and waited for the beginning fury to settle back down. She handed the cutting board to Nick.

Thankfully, he took it without commenting on the slight tremor in her hands. He scraped the garlic bits into the steaming sauce and immediately the new aroma filled the kitchen.

"Will told me there was a car parked outside Tess's house that morning he left."

"Manx ran the license-plate number through the DMV." It was one of the few things Manx had grudgingly shared with her. "The number belongs to Daniel Kassenbaum, Tess's boyfriend."

Nick glanced over his shoulder. "The boyfriend? Did anyone question him?"

"My partner did, briefly. Manx promised he would question him in more detail."

"If he saw Will leaving her house, then he should be pissed. Maybe Stucky doesn't have anything to do with her disappearing."

"I don't think it's that simple, Nick. Apparently, the boyfriend doesn't much care that Tess is missing or that she may have been cheating on him. My gut tells me Stucky has everything to do with this."

Maggie's cellular phone rang, startling both of them. She grabbed her jacket and searched until she found it in the breast pocket.

"Maggie O'Dell."

"Agent O'Dell, it's Tully."

Damn it! She had forgotten all about Tully. She hadn't called him, hadn't even left him a message.

"Agent Tully." She probably owed him an apology or at least an explanation.

Before she had a chance to say anything he said, "We've got another body."

CHAPTER 54

At first, Tully had been relieved when he heard the body wasn't in Newburgh Heights. The call came from the Virginia State Patrol. The state patrolman told Tully that a trucker had grabbed a take-out container from the counter of a small café. On the phone, he explained with a quaking voice how the truck driver hadn't made it back to his truck before he discovered the container was leaking. What he thought was his leftover chicken-fried steak was suddenly dripping blood.

Tully remembered the truck stop, just north of Stafford, off Interstate 95 but it wasn't until he pulled into the café's parking lot that he realized this was probably Agent O'Dell's route home from Quantico. His relief quickly dissipated. If this wasn't Tess McGowan, chances were, O'Dell would still recognize the body.

Tully cursed when he saw the media vans and strobe lights already set up for the TV cameras. They had been lucky up to this point. Only local media had taken the time to be interested. Now he could see the national players were here. A group was crowded around a large, bearded man who Tully guessed was the truck driver.

Thank God, the State Patrol had had enough sense to confiscate the take-out container, and restrict the area behind the café. That's where a battered gray, metal trash bin rested against a chain-link fence. The trash bin was one of the extra-large commercial ones. Tully estimated it to be at least six feet tall. How the hell did Stucky dump the body? Never mind that, how had he gone undetected, with the gas pumps and the café open twenty-four hours a day, seven days a week?

He flashed his badge at a couple of uniforms keeping the media behind the sawhorses and yellow crime scene tape. His long legs allowed him to step over the ribbon without much effort. The Stafford County detective Tully had previously met behind the pizza place was already on the scene, directing the commotion. Tully couldn't remember his name, but as soon as the detective saw him, he waved him over.

"She's still in the Dumpster," he said, wasting no time. "Doc Holmes is on his way. We're trying to figure out how the hell to get her out of there."

"How did you find her?"

The detective took out a pack of gum. He unwrapped a piece and popped it into his mouth. The pack was in his pocket before he thought to offer Tully a piece. He started grabbing for it again, but Tully shook his head. He couldn't imagine having an appetite for anything, even gum.

"Probably wouldn't have found her," the detective finally said, "if not for that snack pack he left behind."

Tully grimaced. He wondered how many years it would take before he could refer to body parts in such a nonchalant way.

The detective didn't notice and continued, "Least not until the trash truck dumped this sucker. But you know, these big ones hold a lot. We might never've found her. Not like anyone would complain about the smell. This stuff always smells. So it looks like this guy's on a roll again."

"It appears so."

"I was working in Boston the last time."

Tully would have guessed the accent had the detective not told him. He was keeping an eye on the reporters near the ribbon, constantly looking over Tully's shoulder. Tully had the impression not much got past this guy. Without knowing anything more, he decided he liked him. But whether Tully liked him or not probably would matter little to the detective. And Tully liked that about him, too.

"Yeah, I remember the last time when they found that councilwoman's body in the woods. Bite marks, skin ripped off, cuts in places you don't need to see cuts."

"Stucky's one sick bastard, that's for sure." Tully remembered the photos of Stucky's collection that O'Dell had laid out on the conference-room table. Side by side they looked like a savage pack of wolves had ripped up the bodies and left them for the vultures.

"Wasn't he playing games with one of your agents back then? I remember reading something. That he was messin' with her head, sending her notes and stuff?"

"Yes, yes he was."

"Whatever happened to that agent?"

"If I'm not mistaken, that's her red car pulling into the parking lot."

"Fuck, no kidding? She's still working on this case?"

"She doesn't have much choice."

"She's got some balls."

"I guess you could say that," Tully said, now distracted. "More than likely, Agent O'Dell will be able to identify the victim for us."

He watched O'Dell. Her badge was getting her across the barriers but not without a lot of glances and long looks. He had worked with other attractive women in law enforcement and in the Bureau, but none quite like O'Dell. There was no discomfort and certainly no preening. Instead, she seemed oblivious to the stares, almost as if she had no clue they were aimed at her.

Tully didn't see it until O'Dell was closer to them. She carried a small black bag, not a purse but a case. They couldn't touch the body until the medical examiner got to the scene. He hoped O'Dell didn't have other plans.

Her eyes met his as her only greeting. He could see the exhaustion, the nervous anticipation.

"Detective—" Tully again realized he didn't know the man's name "—this is Special Agent Maggie O'Dell."

She offered him her hand, and immediately Tully could see the detective's tough exterior softening.

"Sam Rosen," he said, more than willing to fill in the blank for Tully.

"Detective Rosen." O'Dell gave him her polite and professional greeting.

"Call me Sam."

Tully resisted the urge to roll his eyes.

"Sam here—" Tully tried to keep the sarcasm to a minimum "—is with the Stafford County Sheriff's Department. He was at the first crime scene with the pizza delivery...with Jessica Beckwith."

"Is the victim still in the Dumpster?" O'Dell appeared anxious and unwilling, or unable, to hide her anticipation.

"We're waiting for Doc Holmes," Sam told her.

"Is there any way I can take a look without disturbing the scene?" She was already taking out a pair of latex gloves from her black case.

"Probably not a good idea," Tully said, knowing that O'Dell wanted to see if she recognized the victim. He saw her eyeing the trash bin. The thing was almost a foot taller than her. She brushed past them for a closer look.

"How were your men able to look inside?"

"We pulled a cruiser alongside. Davis crawled up on the roof. He took a couple of Polaroids. Want me to get them for you?" Sam looked as if he'd do just about anything she asked. Tully couldn't help being amazed. And even more amazing was how oblivious O'Dell seemed to it all.

"Actually, Sam, would you mind pulling the cruiser alongside it again?"

Or maybe she wasn't entirely oblivious. Without hesitation, Detective Rosen shouted at one of the uniforms holding back the reporters. He left them to meet the officer halfway and started telling him what he wanted, with hands gesturing as quickly as he talked.

"There's a chance it might not be her," Tully said while Detective Rosen was still busy giving directions. He knew she was expecting this to be the missing real estate agent.

"I want to assist with the autopsy. Do you think we can convince Dr. Holmes to do it tonight?" She avoided looking at him and kept her eyes on Rosen.

It was the first time she had asked anything of him, and he could tell it was not an easy thing for her to do.

"We'll insist he do it tonight," he promised.

She nodded, still keeping her eyes from him. They stood quietly, side by side, watching the police cruiser drive up as close as possible to the metal trash bin. He heard her take a deep breath as she set down the black case and threw the pair of gloves she had extracted on top. Detective Rosen met her at the bumper, offering her a hand, but she waved it off. She kicked out of her shoes and crawled up on the trunk with bare feet and little effort.

She paused, almost as if preparing herself mentally. Then she carefully stepped up on top of the roof and stood upright, able to stare down into the trash bin.

"Does anyone have a flashlight?" she called out.

One of the officers from the group who had gathered around to watch hurried to the cruiser to hand her a long-handled flashlight. O'Dell shone a stream of light into the bin, and Tully watched her face. She took her time, sweeping the inside, back and forth. He knew she was trying to examine as much of the scene as she could with her eyes since she couldn't use her hands. Her face remained composed, indifferent, and he couldn't tell whether she recognized the victim as the McGowan woman or not.

Finally she crawled down. She handed back the flashlight, tapped the cruiser's window to thank the driver and then found her shoes.

"Well?" Tully asked, still watching her closely.

"It's not Tess McGowan."

"That's a relief," he sighed.

"Not really a relief at all."

Now under a lamppost, he could see she looked agitated, her face tight with tension, the exhaustion clouding her eyes.

"It's not Tess, but I do recognize her."

Tully felt the knot winding around his stomach. He couldn't begin to imagine what O'Dell was feeling.

"Who is she?"

"Her name's Hannah. She's a clerk at Shep's Liquor Mart. She helped me pick out a bottle of wine last night."

She rubbed a hand over her face, and Tully saw the slight tremor in the fingers.

"We need to stop this goddamn son of a bitch," she said, and Tully heard that the tremor had also invaded her normally calm voice.

CHAPTER 55

Tess felt the panic seeping into her system as the last bit of light turned everything into shadows. She tried to ignore the little voice in the back of her mind that kept telling her to crawl out of this tomb, to run as far away as possible. It didn't matter what direction or where she ended up, at least she would be out of this hell pit, this grave of mutilated bones and lost souls.

She sat next to the woman named Rachel, close enough to hear her ragged breathing. Soon she wouldn't be able to see, but she had made certain the blanket covered her. The woman would not spend another cold night exposed to the elements.

Tess wasn't sure why she had returned. Why hadn't she just left for good? She knew it would be best for Rachel if she went for help. But after an afternoon of roaming the endless woods, she knew help was not close by. She had barely found her way back, trying to leave herself a trail of pinecones. Now she wondered if it had been a mistake to come back. If by doing so, she might be guaranteeing her own death. But for some reason, she couldn't bring herself to leave this woman. She wasn't certain whether she was being gallant or just selfish, because she couldn't bear to spend an entire night out here alone.

Tess had managed to bring back a shoeful of water, using the broken-heeled leather pump she had unearthed. Rachel had to be incredibly thirsty, yet she drank little, most of it dribbling out of her cut and swollen lips and trickling down her bruised chin.

She had said little since uttering her name. Sometimes she answered

Tess's questions with a simple yes or no. Most of the time she remained silent as though breathing took all her effort. And Tess had noticed that the woman's breathing had become more raspy, more labored. She had a fever and her muscles went into spasms for long periods racking her entire body, no matter what Tess tried to do to help her.

After hours of analyzing the area, and examining every possible rock step, dirt ledge and sturdy root, Tess had resigned herself to the fact that she could not pull or carry or drag Rachel out. And no amount of rest would cure or repair the damage already done to her body.

Tess leaned her head against the dirt wall, no longer caring that pieces crumbled inside her collar and down her back. She closed her eyes and tried to think of something or somewhere pleasant. A difficult task, considering her empty reservoir of pleasant experiences. Without much effort, Will Finley came to mind. His face, his body, his hands, his voice were all so easily retrieved from her memory bank. He had touched her so gently, so lovingly, despite his urgency and his insatiable passion. It was as though he genuinely felt something deeper than pleasure. And he seemed so intent on pleasing her, as though it truly mattered that she feel what he was feeling.

In all her many experiences with men and sex, she had never thought to associate sex with love. Oh sure, she knew that was the way it was supposed to be, but it had certainly never been a part of her experiences. Even with Daniel, she felt nothing remotely close to love. But she had never expected to—she had never promised or lied to herself that it would ever happen.

She didn't know Will Finley, so how was it possible to feel something remotely close to love? He was a stranger, a one-night stand. How could that be any different than any of the many johns she had serviced? Yet, even here—especially here—she couldn't lie to herself. Will Finley and their one night together had been different. She wouldn't turn it into something cheap and dirty. Not when it could be the closest she may ever get to feeling real love. And not now, when she needed it most. So she tried to remember. She remembered his soft lips, his gentle exploring hands, his hard body, his whispers, his energy, his warmth.

It worked for a short while, carrying her away from the smell of decay and the feel of mud. She thought perhaps she might even sleep. Then suddenly Tess noticed how quiet it was. She held her breath and listened. When the realization came, it swept over her like ice water being injected into her veins. The panic rushed through her, squeezing her heart. Her breathing resumed in quick bursts, frantic gasps. Her body began shaking uncontrollably, and she wrapped her arms tightly around herself, rocking back and forth.

"Oh dear God. Oh God, no," she mumbled over and over like a madwoman. When she could get her body to keep still for a moment, she listened again, straining over the pounding of her heart, straining to hear, willing the truth to be untrue. It was no use. The silence couldn't lie. She knew Rachel was dead.

Tess curled into the damp corner and then allowed herself to do something she hadn't done since she was a child. She cried out loud, releasing years of welled-up sobs and letting them rack her entire body in hysterical convulsions over which she had absolutely no control. The sound pierced the silent darkness. At first she didn't recognize it as something coming out of her, coming up from some deep well inside herself. But there was no stopping, no confining it. And so, she surrendered herself to it.

CHAPTER 56

Maggie watched from across the metal table as Dr. Holmes sliced into the woman's chest, making a precise Y incision that curved under the woman's breasts. Though she had gowned up, her gloved hands ready, she restrained herself from taking part. Instead, she waited for his permission, participating only when asked, trying to confine her impatience when things took too long. She reminded herself that she should be grateful the medical examiner had agreed to do the autopsy on a Saturday night rather than waiting for Monday morning.

He had allowed her to do the busywork; helping insert the body block, scraping behind the woman's nails, taking the external measurements and then the samples of hair, saliva and body fluids. Maggie couldn't stop thinking that Hannah had put up the fight of her life. Bruises covered her body, the one to her hip and thigh suggesting she had fallen down some stairs in the process.

Now, as Maggie watched Dr. Holmes, she found herself going through the woman's brutal murder, step by step, from the telltale signs her body telegraphed. Hannah had scratched and clawed as Jessica had, only Hannah managed to get pieces of Stucky under her nails. Why had her death not been simple and swift? Why wasn't he able to tie her up, rape her and slit her throat as he had with Jessica and Rita? Had Stucky not been prepared for this challenge?

Maggie wanted to shove her sleeves up. The plastic apron was making her sweat. God, it was hot. Why wasn't there better ventilation?

The county morgue was larger than she had expected, with dingy gray walls and the overpowering scent of Lysol. The counters were a dull yellow Formica rather than stainless steel. The overhead fluorescent lighting unit hung low over the table, almost brushing the tops of their heads when they stood up straight. Dr. Holmes was not much taller than Maggie, but she noticed he had grown accustomed to the light fixture, ducking automatically each time he came underneath it.

Her forensic and premed background had allowed her to perform many autopsies on her own and assist in plenty of others. Maybe it was her exhaustion or perhaps it was simply the stress of this case, but for some reason she was having difficulty disconnecting from the body on the metal table in front of her. Her face felt hot from the hovering light. The windowless room was threatening to suffocate her, though a hidden fan circulated the stale air in the room. She resisted the urge to swipe at the strands of hair that stuck to her damp forehead. The tension in her neck had spread to her shoulders, and was now knotting its way down to take control of her lower back.

Ever since she had recognized the woman, Maggie couldn't help feeling responsible for her death. Had she simply not asked for help in choosing a bottle of wine, the woman would still be alive. Maggie knew the thoughts were counterproductive. They were exactly what Stucky wanted her to be thinking, to be feeling. But she couldn't shut them off. She couldn't stop the growing hysteria that gnawed at her insides, the exploding anger that whispered promises of revenge. She couldn't control the brewing desire of wanting to put a bullet between Albert Stucky's eyes. This anger, this need for revenge was beginning to scare her more than anything Albert Stucky could do to her.

"She hasn't been dead for very long," Dr. Holmes said, his voice bringing her mind back to where it needed to be. "Internal temperature indicates less than twenty-four hours."

Maggie knew this already, but also realized he was saying this for the tape recorder on the stand next to them, and not for her benefit.

"There appears to be no signs of livor mortis, so she was definitely murdered somewhere else and moved within the span of two or three hours." Again, he said this in a matter-of-fact tone for the recorder.

Maggie appreciated his casual manner, his conversational style. She had worked with other M.E.'s whose hushed reverence or clinically cold methods acted as a constant reminder of the brutality and violence that had brought them to their task. Maggie preferred to view an autopsy only as a fact-finding mission, the soul or spirit long gone by the time the body lay on the cold metal table. The best thing for the victim at this stage was a search for evidence that could help catch whoever had committed such an act. Although this time, she knew there would be little Hannah could tell them that would bring them any closer to finding Albert Stucky.

"I heard you ended up with the dog."

It took Maggie a minute to realize Dr. Holmes was talking to her and not speaking for the recorder. When she didn't answer immediately, he looked up and smiled.

"He seemed like a good dog. Tough son of a bitch to survive whoever stabbed him."

"Yes, he is."

How could she have forgotten about Harvey? Already she wasn't a very good dog owner. Greg had been right about her. She had no room for anything or anyone else in her life.

"That reminds me. May I use your phone?"

"Over in the corner, on the wall."

She had to stop and try to remember what her new phone number was. Before she dialed, she took off her latex gloves and wiped her forehead with the sleeve of the borrowed gown. Even the telephone receiver smelled of Lysol. She punched in the numbers and listened to it ring, feeling guilty that she had completely forgotten. She certainly wouldn't blame Nick if he had been angry enough to leave. She checked her wristwatch. It was a quarter past ten.

"Hello?"

"Nick? It's Maggie."

"Hey, are you all right?"

He sounded concerned, not a hint of anger. Maybe she shouldn't expect his reactions and responses to be similar to Greg's.

"I'm okay. It wasn't Tess."

"Good. I was kinda worried that Will would flip out if it was."

"I'm at the county morgue, assisting with the autopsy." She paused, waiting to hear some sign of anger. "Nick, I'm really sorry."

"It's okay, Maggie."

"I might be a couple more hours." Again, she paused. "I know I ruined our plans...your dinner."

"Maggie, it's not your fault. This is what you do. Harvey and I went ahead and ate. We saved you some. It'll warm up fine in your microwave whenever you're ready for it."

He was being so understanding. Why was he being so understanding? She didn't know how to respond to this.

"Maggie? Are you sure you're okay?"

She'd left too much of a pause.

"Just very tired. And I am sorry I missed having dinner with you."

"Me too. Do you want me to stay with Harvey until you get back?"

"I can't ask you to do that, Nick. I don't even know for sure how late I'll be."

"I carry around an old sleeping bag in my trunk. Would you mind if I crashed here for the night?"

For some reason the thought of Nick Morrelli sleeping in her huge and empty house brought an incredible feeling of comfort.

"Maybe it's not such a good idea," he added quickly, misreading her hesitation.

"No, it's a good idea. Harvey would really like that." She had done it again, disguising her true emotions—careful not to reveal a thing. It had become habit. "I'd really like it, too," she said, surprising herself.

"Be careful driving home."

"I will. Oh, and Nick."

"Yeah?"

"Don't forget to always reset the alarm system after you've taken Harvey out. And there's a Glock 40 caliber in the bottom desk drawer. Remember to shut the blinds. If you need—"

"Maggie. I'll be just fine. You concentrate on taking care of you, okay?"

"Okay."

"I'll see you when you get back."

She hung up the phone and leaned back against the wall, closing her eyes and feeling the exhaustion and a chill seep into her bones. She needed to ignore the strong urge to leave now. To go home and curl up with Nick in front of a warm, crackling fire. She could still remember what it had felt like to fall asleep in his arms, though it had happened only once and that was over five months ago. He had comforted her and tried to shield her from her nightmares. And for a few hours, it had worked. But there was nothing Nick Morrelli could do to help her escape Stucky. These days Albert Stucky seemed to be in everything she touched and everyplace she went.

She looked back at the metal table with the woman's gray body splayed open. Dr. Holmes was now removing organs, one by one, weighing and measuring them like a butcher preparing different cuts of meat. She tucked her hair behind her ears, pulled on a fresh pair of gloves and joined him.

"Not easy having a life of your own in this business, is it?" He didn't look up as he continued to cut.

"It's certainly not a life for a dog. I'm never home. Poor Harvey."

"Well, he's still better off with you. From what I understand, Sidney Endicott is an idiot. It wouldn't surprise me if he had murdered his wife and stashed her body somewhere so we'll never find it."

"Is that the direction Manx is going?"

"I have no idea. Take a look at the muscle tissue here and here." He pointed to the layers he had cut through.

Maggie only glanced at the area. She was wondering if the medical examiner realized that what he said regarding Mr. Endicott would be caught on tape. But what if he was right? Maybe Stucky hadn't taken Rachel Endicott. Perhaps her husband did have something to do with her disappearance, although it seemed much too easy. Suddenly she realized Dr. Holmes was staring at her over the bifocals that had slipped down to the tip of his nose.

"I'm sorry, what was it you were looking at?"

He pointed again, and immediately she could see that there was hemorrhage in the muscle tissue. She leaned against the counter behind her and felt the anger swelling up inside her again.

"If there's this much hemorrhage in the muscle tissue it has to mean—"

"Yes, I know," she stopped him. "It means she was still alive when he started cutting her."

He nodded and returned to his task, quickly and expertly tying string to each of the arteries as he cut, leaving generous lengths for the local mortician who would later use these same arteries when he or she injected the embalming fluids. Then with both hands, Dr. Holmes carefully scooped out the woman's heart and set it on the scale. "Heart looks to be in good condition," he said for the recorder. "Weight is 8.3 ounces."

While he dunked the organ in a container of formaldehyde, Maggie forced herself to take a closer look at the incision Stucky had made. Now that she could look into the body cavity, she could follow the path. His precision continued to amaze her. He had extracted the woman's uterus and ovaries as though it had been a surgical procedure. On the counter at the other end of the room lay his handiwork, still enclosed in the plastic take-out container that the truck driver had had the misfortune of picking up.

Dr. Holmes looked at what had drawn her attention. On his way back from the sink, he brought the container with him and set it on the table with their instruments. He flipped open the lid and began examining the contents.

The intercom on the wall buzzed, and Maggie jumped.

"It's probably Detective Rosen. He said he'd stop by if they found anything." He headed for the door, removing his gloves.

"Wait, are you sure?" She couldn't believe he'd open the door without checking first. "It's pretty late, isn't it?"

"Yep, it sure is," he said, stopping and looking at her over his shoulder. "But in case you didn't notice earlier, I think Rosen has developed a crush on you."

"Excuse me?"

"No, I didn't think you noticed." He smiled but didn't wait to explain, instead turning the dead bolt without hesitation or caution.

Maggie's fingers dug into her gown, groping to get at her holster and her gun, but Dr. Holmes was already opening the door.

"Evening, Sam."

"Hey, Doc." Detective Rosen's eyes found Maggie without even noticing the corpse. He held up a couple of evidence bags with what looked like dirt in them. "Agent O'Dell, I think we found something kinda interesting."

After Dr. Holmes's comment, she wondered if Sam had really discovered something at the scene or if he would try to pass off dirt as evidence in order to justify his stop. She was being ridiculous. Maybe Greg had been right about that, too. She didn't trust anyone.

He handed her one of the Ziploc bags over the table. This time he glanced down at the body. It didn't seem to bother him. She guessed that Detective Rosen had seen his share of autopsies, which meant he hadn't always belonged to the Stafford County Sheriff's Department.

She took and inspected the bag of dirt and immediately recognized it. She held the bag up to the light. Yes, there were bits of silver and yellow that sparkled under the bright fluorescent.

"Where did you find this?"

"On the side of the trash bin closest to the chain-link fence. There's actually some metal rails, sorta like steps. We found muddy prints from shoes or boots. That's probably how he was able to climb up and toss in her body. It faces away from the parking lot. No one would see him there."

Rosen seemed excited with the discovery, and she wondered why. "Did you show this to Agent Tully?"

"Nope, not yet. But I figure this has gotta be a big break. It should lead us to where this guy has been hiding out."

Maggie waited for the detective to explain. Now he seemed to be distracted by Dr. Holmes, or rather the bloody glob in the take-out container that Dr. Holmes was examining.

"Detective Rosen," Maggie waited for his attention. "Why do think this will lead us anywhere?"

"For one thing, it's mud." He stated the obvious as though he had uncovered a secret. When he realized she didn't see the significance, he continued, "Well, it hasn't rained for quite a while. It's looked like it several times, but nothing. Not around here anyway. Always offshore."

She drummed her fingers on the counter, waiting for something more than this weather report. He noticed her impatience, quickly opened one of the bags and pinched some of the dirt between his fingers, bringing it out and showing her.

"It's a thick, sticky clay. Even smells a bit moldy. Again, nothing like we have around here."

She could put an end to all of this by simply admitting she had seen the stuff before, that they had actually analyzed and broken it down. Instead, she let him go on.

"A couple of the guys who've lived here all their lives said they haven't seen anything like this stuff before. Take a close look. It's unusual, with bits of reddish rock, and that yellow and silvery crap is pretty weird…maybe even man-made."

Finally, she confessed, "We have found similar dirt at two other crime scenes, Detective Rosen, but—"

"Sam."

"Excuse me?"

"Call me Sam."

Maggie brushed annoying, damp strands off her forehead. Had Dr. Holmes been right about Detective…Sam? Was he really only here to flirt and try to impress her?

"Sam, we have analyzed this stuff. It may be from a closed-down industrial site. We do have several people trying to find a possible location."

"Well, I think I can save you some time."

She stared at him, growing more impatient with his cocky smile. He was wasting their time with this grandstanding.

"I think I know where this came from," he said, pleased with himself despite Maggie's look of skepticism. "I went fishing a couple of weekends ago. A little spot about fifty miles from here on the other side of the toll bridge. I was supposed to meet a buddy, but I still don't know this area very well. I ended up getting lost in this isolated wooded area. When I got home I noticed this sticky mud covering my boots. Took me almost two hours to clean them. The mud looked just like this crap. Couldn't figure out what the hell that silver dust was."

Now he had Maggie's full attention. She could feel her pulse begin to race. The area sounded exactly like someplace Stucky would hole up. Detective Rosen was right. This could be their big break.

"Well, I hope this pans out," Dr. Holmes interrupted, only now looking up from the contents of the plastic container. "This guy is one sick bastard. I think this woman may have confessed to him, tried appealing to him, hoping he had one ounce of human dignity in him."

"What are you talking about?" Maggie watched the medical examiner wipe his forehead, suddenly not caring that he smeared blood from his gloves to his face. The calm, experienced professional seemed visibly shaken by his discovery.

"What is it?" she tried again.

"Might not be a coincidence that he chose to extract her uterus." He stepped back from the table and shook his head. "This woman was pregnant."

CHAPTER 57

Detective Rosen had called and filled in the Newburgh Heights Police Department when they realized Hannah Messinger may have been taken from the downtown liquor store. O'Dell had anxiously accompanied Dr. Holmes, and Rosen had stayed behind at the truck stop, gathering evidence, so Tully decided to accompany Manx and his men. After talking to Detective Manx earlier in the week and not being impressed with his foot-dragging tactics on the Tess McGowan case, Tully knew he should be here if any evidence showed up.

As he waited for one of Manx's officers to jimmy the lock on the back door, he found himself wondering if Detective Manx had been called away from some nightclub. He was dressed in chinos and a bright orange jacket with a blue tie. Okay, maybe the jacket could pass for brown. It was difficult to tell under the street lamps. But he was certain the tie had little dolphins on it. He took a sidelong look at Manx. He looked to be about his age. His buzz cut emphasized his square features, but Tully supposed women probably found Manx attractive in a brutish sort of way. Actually, he had no clue what women found attractive anymore.

From this position in the alley, Tully recognized the back of Mama Mia's Pizza Place on the corner. A shiny new Dumpster replaced the one they had found Jessica Beckwith in. Perhaps it was the owner's way of getting rid of any and all memories. What would they think when they found out that another woman had been taken and murdered only several stores away?

He pulled up the collar of his jacket against the sudden chill of the night. Or perhaps the chill came simply from the memory of that beautiful young woman tangled unceremoniously in a web of garbage. Thinking of young Jessica Beckwith reminded Tully of Emma. How could he ever make Emma understand he only wanted to protect her? That he wasn't simply being mean. Not that she wanted any explanation. And of course, now she wasn't even talking to him since he had prevented her from going to the prom with Josh Reynolds.

"We tried to get hold of the owner," Manx interrupted Tully's thoughts. "He's out of town, won't be able to get back until late tomorrow. His wife said Messinger was taking care of things."

Tully reached for his eyeglasses and noticed the officer was making a mess of the door's lock. Finally something clicked just as the door handle came loose and fell off.

Manx found a light switch and not only did the back storeroom brighten, but the entire shop lit up, aisle by aisle. It didn't take much time to inspect the small shop and realize nothing seemed to be out of place. The cash register had been shut down and locked up. Even the Closed sign had been turned on. There was no indication of forced entrance.

"He may have grabbed her while she was walking to her car," Manx said, scratching his head, reminding Tully of one of the Three Stooges.

An officer took off out the door to check the alley, while the other started rummaging through the storeroom.

"Rosen filled me in, told me about O'Dell."

Tully stopped and glanced over at Manx from behind the counter. The detective's bulldog features softened. He actually looked sympathetic, if that was possible. Tully decided the jacket was definitely orange. In the bright light of the store there was no doubt.

"Now maybe you'll understand," Tully said, "why she's been overly anxious about your investigation of the McGowan woman's disappearance."

"Well, I figure there might be a reason to rethink the Endicott case, too." Manx hesitated as though making a major concession. "I've got copies of the case file for you in my car."

"Detective," the officer from the storeroom called out. He appeared at the door, his face pale and his eyes wide. "There's a wine cellar below the storeroom. I think you better take a look."

Tully followed Manx. They started down the narrow steps, only a bare lightbulb above to guide the way. But Tully didn't need to see anything to know they had found the murder site. No farther than the third or fourth step, he could smell the blood, and he knew his stomach was not ready for what was below.

CHAPTER 58

He couldn't believe that she had escaped. How had she been able to unlock the door so easily? He should have felt disappointment rather than exhilaration. But even his fatigue would not deprive him of the thrill and challenge of a good hunt.

The night goggles seemed to make little difference. Sure they helped him see, but there was nothing to see. Where could that little cunt have wandered off to? He shouldn't have left her unattended for so long, but he had been distracted with the cute brunette. She had been so thoughtful, just as she had been with Agent Maggie. She had taken her time, helping him pick out a nice bottle of wine, not minding that it was closing time. In fact, she had already shut off the Open sign and was locking the front door, when he hurried in. Yes, she had been most helpful, insisting he try the crisp, white Italian for his special occasion, all the while not realizing that she herself would be the denouement of his special occasion.

But his little detour had taken its toll on him. He should have simply taken his prize and left her body in the cellar of the liquor store. At least then his muscles wouldn't be aching. His eyes were having problems focusing. The red lines were appearing more frequently, or were the night goggles malfunctioning? He hated to think that his eyesight had gotten worse in less than a week. He hated the idea of depending on someone else. But he would do whatever was necessary to accomplish his goal, to finish this game.

He wandered through the dark woods, annoyed that his feet kept tripping over tree roots and slipping on the mud. He had fallen once, but not again. He bet she hadn't wandered far from the shed. They never did. Sometimes they even came back, afraid of the dark or wanting to get out of the cold or the rain. Stupid bitches, so gullible, so naive. Usually they followed the same path, hoping the worn trail would lead them to freedom. Never thinking it might lead them, instead, to another trap.

He had to hand it to Tess McGowan. She had managed to hide herself quite nicely. But it wouldn't last. He knew these woods like the back of his hand. There was no way for her to escape unless she was willing to swim. Funny, he thought as he adjusted the goggles to a different setting, none of them ever attempted that. But then, not many of them had had the opportunity. Tess was lucky he had been held up—even luckier that she had found a way to escape from the shack. He should have been angry with her, but her talents excited him. He did so love a challenge. It would make it all the sweeter to finally take her down, to possess her—mind, body and soul.

As he climbed the ridge he hoped he wouldn't find her with a broken neck at the bottom of some ravine. That would be a total waste. He was hoping she would make up for his disappointment in Rachel. She hadn't lived up to his expectations at all. She had been such a flirt as long as she thought he was a lowly utility worker she could tease and control. She seemed to have so much energy and vibrancy, yet she had whimpered like a helpless child when he was fucking her, the fight driven out of her so easily it was pathetic. To make matters worse, she lasted less than a half hour when he released her into the woods. What a shame.

He grabbed onto the vines and pulled himself up to the top of the ridge. Here he'd be able to look down and see for quite a distance. Nothing registered. There was no mass of heat that lit up his goggles. Where the hell had she gone?

He reached under the contraption to rub his eyes. Maybe he needed sleep more than he needed to punish Tess McGowan with a good fuck. With the familiar lethargy taking over his body, he didn't need the added disappointment if he did find her and wasn't able to...fuck her. He didn't even want to think about that. No, he'd start again in the morning, when he had the energy and could enjoy a good hunt. Yes, he'd start bright and early. He looped the rope over his shoulder, picked up the crossbow and headed back. Maybe he'd open that nice bottle of Italian wine that Hannah had promised would delight him.

CHAPTER 59

Maggie felt numb. It took all her effort to keep her eyes open. She didn't realize until she pulled into her driveway that she had been functioning on autopilot. She couldn't remember leaving the interstate nor winding along Highway 6 with its sharp curves and steep ditches. It was a wonder she had found her way in the dark of night and through the fog of her mind.

Nick had left the light on in the portico for her. His Jeep remained where he had parked it earlier. She pulled up next to it, surprised to find the sight of its dusty sides and huge rugged tires supplied her with a wave of comfort. Now she was glad Detective Rosen had convinced her to wait until morning. How could she have thought to go hunting for Stucky in strange, dark woods in the middle of the night? Yet it had made plenty of sense only an hour ago. She had been prepared to stage a sneak attack, forgetting so quickly that she had lost the last one to Stucky. Why was it so easy for Albert Stucky to destroy all her common sense with a sweep of a hand, or rather a cut of his knife?

She knew Dr. Holmes was right, despite the probability that they would never be able to confirm it. She knew the liquor store clerk must have pleaded with Stucky. Maggie could hear it in her head—it came without warning and she couldn't seem to turn it off.

She could hear Hannah pleading, and when she realized Stucky didn't care, she must have begged for her unborn baby's life. He would have laughed at her. It would not have made any difference to him. But she would have continued to beg and cry. Was that why he started cutting while she was still alive? Had he attempted to show her the unborn fetus? It would have been a new challenge to add to his repertoire of horror. It seemed grotesquely inconceivable, but, for Stucky, she knew it was not.

Maggie tried to shut out the images. She unlocked the door, and she tried to be as quiet as possible. It had been a long time since she had come home to anyone or anything other than a dark, empty house. Even before she and Greg had begun avoiding each other, their schedules conflicted more often than not. In the last several years they had become nothing more than roommates who left behind notes for each other. Or at least there had been notes in the beginning. Gradually, the only signs of double occupancy had been the empty milk cartons in the frig and unrecognizable socks and underwear in the laundry room.

The alarm system beeped only once before Maggie punched in the correct code. Immediately, she felt Harvey's cold nose sniffing her from behind. She reached out a hand in the dark, and his tongue found it.

Though the foyer was dark, the living room was bathed in moonlight. Nick hadn't closed any of the blinds, and she was glad he hadn't. She liked the blue glow that made the room seem magical. She saw him stretched out on the floor, his long body only halfway encased in the sleeping bag. He was bare-chested and the sight of his skin, his knotted arms, his tight stomach brought a flutter to her stomach. And just when she thought she was too tired to feel anything more.

She set down her forensic kit, took off her jacket and began peeling off her shoulder holster, when she heard the sleeping bag rustle. Harvey had returned to Nick's side, laying his head on the bundle of legs.

"Don't get too comfortable here," she told Harvey.

"Too late," Nick said, rubbing a hand over his face and lifting himself up onto one elbow.

"I meant Harvey." She smiled.

"Ah. Good."

He ran his fingers through his short hair, causing it to stick up in places. Suddenly Maggie had an incredible urge to smooth it down for him, to run her own fingers through his hair and along that strong, square jawline.

"How are you holding up?" Even in the blue light, she could see the concern in his eyes.

"I honestly don't know, Nick. Maybe not so good." She leaned against the wall and rubbed her eyes. She didn't want to remember the dead clerk's eyes. She didn't want to see the shriveled-up fetus still clinging to the wall of its mother's uterus.

"Hey," Nick said quietly, "why don't you join Harvey and me." He pulled back the top of the sleeping bag, inviting her inside. In doing so, he also revealed tight jockey shorts and muscular thighs.

Again, the stirrings of arousal surprised her. Her face felt hot, and she was a bit embarrassed by her reaction, because she knew Nick didn't mean the invitation as anything more than to curl up next to him. But now, however, he seemed to be reading her thoughts.

"I promise I'll let you have as much control as you want." His eyes were serious, and she knew he had managed to zoom in on her feelings. Was she that transparent?

All she wanted was to feel something other than the frayed nerves, the exhaustion, the emotions that had rubbed her mentally raw. She could no longer remember what it felt like to feel warm and safe. Earlier, in her kitchen, Nick's presence had reminded her just how few times in the past several years she had felt any stirrings of passion and desire. Ironically, the only times she could remember were when she and Nick had been together back in Nebraska.

Without a word, she slipped off her shoes and started undoing her jeans. She met his eyes and saw a bit of surprise mixed with anticipation. He looked as though he wasn't sure what to expect. She had no idea herself.

She left on her chambray shirt. Her underpants were already damp before she climbed in next to him. Harvey stood up, turned around three times and flopped down with his back up against Nick. They both laughed, and Maggie was grateful for the release of tension.

They lay facing each other, each braced up on an elbow. His eyes held her, but he kept his hands away. She realized he was serious about letting her have control. He looked anxious to see what she might do with him. She touched his face with her fingertips, stroking his cheek, his bristled jaw and lingering at his lips. He kissed the tips of her fingers, his mouth warm and wet and inviting.

She moved down to the scar, the slight pucker of white on his chin. Then, to his throat, watching him swallow hard as though trying to contain his emotions. Her eyes stayed with his as her fingers caressed the muscles of his chest and traced a path over his hard, flat stomach. His breathing was already uneven by the time her fingers made it to the bulge in his jockey shorts. As soon as she touched him, he sucked in air like a man no longer able to stifle himself.

"Jesus, Maggie," he managed breathlessly. "If I'd known this was what it would be like to give you control—"

She didn't let him finish. She kissed him lightly on the lips while her hand slipped into his waistband. His entire body quivered. Then his mouth urged her on. Each of her nerve endings seemed to come alive, though he still touched her nowhere except her lips. She knew she had him close to the edge, but he was holding back. She brought the length of her body against his. The kisses had become deep and urgent, but she left his mouth and moved her lips to his ear. She let her tongue run along his outer ear and then slip inside, rewarded immediately by a groan. She whispered, "Don't hold back, Nick."

It didn't take long and his breathing came in gasps through clenched teeth. Moments later, her hand was wet and sticky. Nick collapsed onto his back, his eyes closed, waiting to gain control over his body again. Maggie's own body was still a live wire, tingling without any stimulation other than in reaction to Nick. How was it possible for this man to make her feel so alive, so whole and full of electricity without even touching her? As she watched him, she realized she had never before felt so sensual or so completely satisfied.

He put his hands behind his neck. Sweat glistened on his forehead. His breathing had almost returned to normal. He was looking up at her now, as if trying to read her thoughts, maybe even wondering what was next. He glanced over at Harvey who had moved to the sunroom.

"Is he giving us some privacy, or is he tired of us waking him up?"

She smiled but didn't answer. She braced herself up on her elbow again, lying on her side and watching him. Why was she suddenly not exhausted anymore?

Nick reached up and touched her hair, pushing back a strand and letting his fingers caress her cheek. She closed her eyes and absorbed the lovely sensation being sent through her body. When she opened her eyes again, he was on his side, leaning so close she could feel his breath. Yet he kept their bodies from touching while his hand gently made its way down her neck and into the collar of her shirt. He unbuttoned her shirt, hesitating at each button to give her time to protest. Instead, she lay back, inviting his touch. He was going slowly, cautiously, as if that would give her control. As if that would reduce the intensity. It only made her ache.

He sensed her urgency and let his mouth replace his fingers, gently kissing her. He tugged open the rest of her shirt and his mouth wandered, taking his time moving down her body. Suddenly he stopped. She was breathing too hard to notice at first. Then she felt his fingertips on her stomach, lightly tracing the scar that ran across her abdomen. The hideous scar that Albert Stucky had left. How could she have forgotten it?

She sat up abruptly and disentangled herself from the sleeping bag, escaping before Nick could react. In her rush, she almost tripped over poor Harvey. Now, she stood looking out over the backyard, the front of her shirt gathered into a fist. She heard him come up behind her. She realized she was shivering though she wasn't cold. Nick wrapped his arms around her, and she leaned into his warm body, resting her head back against his chest.

"You gotta know by now, Maggie," he whispered into her hair, "there isn't anything you can say or show me that's gonna scare me away."

"You sure about that?"

"Positive."

"It's just that he's with me all the time, Nick." Her voice was hushed, and there was an annoying catch in it. "I can't seem to get away from him. I should have known that there would be some way for him to ruin even this."

He tightened his hug and nuzzled her neck. But he didn't say anything. He didn't try to persuade her that she was wrong. He didn't try to contradict her just to make her feel better. Instead, he just held her.

CHAPTER 60

Maggie got up before dawn. She left Nick a scrawled note, apologizing for last night and giving him brief instructions for setting the alarm. He had said that he needed to get back to Boston to prepare for a trial, but she knew as he was telling her that he was trying to figure a way out of it. She told him she didn't want him to jeopardize his new job. What she left out was that she didn't want him close by for Albert Stucky to hurt.

She called Agent Tully from the road, but when he answered his door he didn't look as if he expected her. He wore jeans and a white T-shirt and was barefoot. He hadn't shaved yet, and his short hair stuck up. He let her in without much of a greeting and gathered up a scattered edition of the *Washington Post*. He grabbed a coffee mug from the top of the TV.

"I'm brewing coffee. Would you like a cup?"

"No, thanks." She wanted to tell him there was no time for coffee. Why did he not feel the same urgency she was feeling?

He disappeared into what she thought must be the kitchen. Instead of following, she sat down on a stiff sofa that looked and smelled brand-new. The house was small with very little furniture, and most of it looked like hand-me-downs. It reminded her of the apartment she and Greg had right out of college—with milk crates for a TV stand, and concrete blocks and stained two-by-sixes for bookshelves. The only thing missing was a lime green beanbag chair. The sofa and a black halogen floor lamp were the only two new pieces.

A girl wandered into the room rubbing her eyes and not bothering to acknowledge Maggie. She wore only a short nightshirt. Her long blond hair was tangled and her steps were those of a sleepwalker. Maggie recognized the teenager as the little girl in the photo Tully paid homage to on his office desk. The girl plopped into an oversize chair facing the TV, found a remote between the cushions and turned the TV on, flipping through the channels but not paying much attention. Maggie hated feeling that she had gotten the entire household out of bed as if it was the middle of the night instead of morning.

The girl stopped her channel surfing in the middle of a local news report. With the volume muted, Maggie still recognized the truck stop behind the handsome, young reporter who gestured to the gray trash bin cordoned off with yellow crime scene tape.

"Emma, shut the TV off, please," Tully instructed after only a glance at the screen. His coffee mug was filled to the brim and the aroma filtered in with him. He handed Maggie a cold can of Diet Pepsi.

"What's this?" she asked, taken by surprise.

"I remembered Pepsi is sorta your version of morning coffee."

She stared at him, amazed that he would have noticed. No one except Anita ever remembered.

"Did I get it wrong? Is it regular and not diet?"

"No, it's diet," she said, finally taking the can. "Thanks."

"Emma, this is Special Agent Maggie O'Dell. Agent O'Dell, this is my ill-mannered daughter, Emma."

"Hi, Emma."

The girl looked up and manufactured a smile that looked neither genuine nor comfortable.

"Emma, if you're up for the morning, please put on some regular clothes."

"Yeah, sure. Whatever." She pulled herself out of the chair and wandered out of the room.

"Sorry about that," he said while he skidded the chair Emma had vacated around to face Maggie and the sofa rather than the TV. "Sometimes I feel like aliens abducted my real daughter and transplanted this impostor."

Maggie smiled and popped open the Diet Pepsi.

"You have any kids, Agent O'Dell?"

"No." The answer seemed simple enough, but she noticed Tully still staring at her as though an explanation should follow. "Having a family is a little bit tougher to accomplish when you're a woman in the FBI than when you're a man in the FBI."

He nodded as though it was some new revelation, as though he had never considered it before.

"I hope I didn't wake your wife, too."

"You'd have to be pretty noisy to do that."

"Excuse me?"

"My wife lives in Cleveland...my ex-wife, that is."

It was still a touchy subject. Maggie could see it in the way he suddenly avoided making eye contact. He sipped his coffee, wrapping both hands around the mug and taking his time. Then, as though he remembered why they were here in his living room on a Sunday morning, he stood up abruptly, set down the mug on the overflowing coffee table and started digging through the piles. Maggie couldn't help wondering if there was any part of Agent Tully's life that he kept organized.

He pulled out a map and started unfolding and spreading it out over the surface of uneven piles.

"From what you told me on the phone, I'm figuring this is the area we're talking about."

She took a close look at the spot he had highlighted on the map in fluorescent yellow. Here she had thought he wasn't even listening to her when she had called and woken him.

He continued, "If Rosen was lost, it's hard telling exactly where he was, but if you cross the Potomac using this toll bridge, there is this piece of land about five miles wide and fifteen miles long that hangs out into the river sort of like a peninsula. The toll bridge passes over the top half. The map shows no roads, not even unpaved ones down in the peninsula part. In fact, it looks like it's all woods, rocks, probably ravines. Pretty tough terrain. In other words, a great place to hide out."

"And a difficult place to escape from." Maggie sat forward, hardly able to contain her excitement. This was it. This was where Stucky was hiding out and keeping his collection. "So when do we leave?"

"Hold on," Tully sat down and reached for his coffee. "We're doing this by the book, O'Dell."

"Stucky strikes hard and fast and then disappears." She let him hear her anger and urgency. "He's already killed three women and possibly kidnapped two others in a week. And those are just the ones we know about."

"I know," he said much too calmly.

Was she the only one who seemed to understand this madman?

"He could pick up and leave any day, any minute. We can't wait for court orders and county police cooperation or whatever the hell you think we need to wait for."

He sipped his coffee, watching her over the rim. "Are you finished?"

She crossed her arms over her chest and sat back. She should never have called Tully. She knew she could talk Rosen into assembling a search team, though the area in question was across the river, which meant not only a different jurisdiction but also a different state.

"First of all, Assistant Director Cunningham is getting in touch with the Maryland officials."

"Cunningham? You called Cunningham? Oh wonderful."

"I've been trying to find out who owns the property." He ignored her and went on. "It used to be owned by the government, which may account for that weird chemical concoction in the dirt. Probably something they were testing. It was purchased by a private corporation about four years ago, something called WH Enterprises. I can't seem to find out anything about it, no managing CEO, no trustees, nothing."

"Since when does the FBI need permission to hunt down a serial killer?"

"We're operating on hunches, Agent O'Dell. We can't send in a SWAT team when we don't know what's there. Even the mud simply means that Stucky may have been in this area. Doesn't prove he's still there."

"Goddamn it, Tully!" She stood up and paced his living room. "This is the only lead we have as to where he might be, and you need to analyze it to death when we could just go find out!"

"Don't you want to know what you might be walking into this time, Agent O'Dell?" He emphasized "this time," and she knew he was referring to last August when she went running off to find Albert Stucky in an abandoned Miami warehouse. She hadn't told anyone else. She had been following up on a hunch then, too. Only Stucky had been expecting her, waiting for her with a trap. Was it possible he'd be waiting for her again?

"So what do you suggest?"

"We wait," Tully said as though waiting was no big deal. "We find out what's there. The Maryland authorities and their resource people can fill us in. We find out who owns the property. Who knows? We certainly don't want to go onto private property if there's some white supremacist group holed up with an arsenal that could blow us off the planet."

"How long are we talking?"

"It's tough getting in touch with everyone we need on a Sunday."

"How long, Agent Tully?"

"A day. Two at the most."

She stared at him, the anger clawing to reveal itself.

"By now you should know what Albert Stucky can do in a day or two." She calmly walked to the door and left, allowing the slamming door to enunciate what she thought about waiting.

CHAPTER 61

Tully sank into the chair and laid his head back against the cushion. He listened to O'Dell slam her car door and then gun the engine, squealing the tires—taking out her anger on his driveway. He could understand her frustration. Hell, he was frustrated, too. He wanted Stucky caught just as badly as O'Dell. But he knew this was personal for O'Dell. He couldn't imagine what she must be feeling. Three women, all of them acquaintances of hers, all of them brutally murdered simply because they had the misfortune of meeting Maggie O'Dell.

When he looked up, Emma stood in the door to the hallway, leaning against the wall and watching him. She hadn't changed or combed her hair. He was suddenly too tired to remind her. She continued to stare at him, and he remembered that she still wasn't talking to him. Well, fine. He wasn't talking to her either. He laid his head back again.

"Was that your new partner?"

He glanced at her without moving from his comfortable position, trying to keep the surprise of her sudden armistice to himself in case she had temporarily forgotten.

"Yeah, O'Dell's my new partner."

"She sounded really pissed at you."

"Yeah, I think she is. I guess I really have a way with women, don't I?"

Surprisingly, Emma smiled. He smiled back and then she laughed. In two steps she came to him and crawled into his lap the way she used to do when she was a little girl. He wrapped his arms around her and held her tight against him before she could change her mind. She tucked her head under his chin and settled in.

"Do you like her?"

"Who?" Tully forgot what they were talking about. It felt so good to hold his little girl again.

"O'Dell, your new partner."

"Yeah, I guess I like her. She's a smart, tough lady."

"She's really pretty."

He hesitated, wondering if Emma was concerned he would run off with one of his co-workers just as her mother had done.

"Maggie O'Dell and I are only partners at work, Emma. There isn't anything else going on between us."

She sat quietly, and he wished she'd talk to him about any fears she might have.

"She did seem really pissed at you," she finally said with a bit of a giggle.

"She'll get over it. I'm more concerned about you."

"Me?" She twisted around to look at him.

"Yeah. You seemed really pissed at me, too."

"Oh, that," she said, settling in against him again. "I'm over that."

"Really?"

"I was thinking if we don't spend all that money it'd cost me to go to the prom, I thought maybe I could get a really cool CD Walkman, instead?"

"Oh, really?" Tully smiled. Yes, he was quite certain he'd never understand women.

"Don't have a cow. I have enough of my own money saved." She wiggled out of his arms and out of his lap. Now she stood in front of him, arms crossed, waiting for his response and looking more like the teenager he remembered. "Can we go pick one out today?"

Was this any way to raise a teenage daughter, teaching her that she would receive some material thing for good behavior? Instead of analyzing it, he simply said, "Sure. Let's go this afternoon."

"All right!"

He watched her practically skip back to her room while he got up and wandered over to the coffee table. He found the file folder and slid it out from under one of the piles. He flipped it open and started going through the file: a police report, a copy from a DNA lab, a plastic bag with a pinch of metallic-flecked dirt stapled to an evidence document, a medical release form from Riley's Veterinary Clinic.

Last night Detective Manx had given him the file marked Rachel Endicott, the missing neighbor O'Dell suspected Stucky had taken. Now, from the looks of the evidence and a recent DNA lab report, even the arrogant, stubborn Manx had been able to figure out that Ms. Endicott may have indeed been kidnapped. After seeing how close to the edge O'Dell was this morning, Tully wondered whether or not he should show her the file. Because according to the lab's DNA test, Albert Stucky had not only been in Rachel Endicott's house, but he'd helped himself to a sandwich and several candy bars. And now there was no doubt in Tully's mind that Stucky had also helped himself to Ms. Endicott.

CHAPTER 62

Maggie drove without a destination, hoping only to burn off the mounting anger. After an hour, she pulled into the busy parking lot of a pancake house, thinking some food might settle her nerves and her stomach. She was at the door of the restaurant, her hand on the door handle when she spun around, almost bumping into two customers before hurrying back to the car. She didn't dare have breakfast. How could she possibly risk another waitress's life?

Back on the road, Maggie's eyes darted all around her, checking the rearview mirror and every car alongside her. She pulled off the interstate, drove several miles down a deserted two-lane highway, then returned to the interstate. Several miles later, she exited at a rest stop, circled around, parked, waited, then headed back onto the interstate.

"Come on, Stucky," she said to the rearview mirror. "Where the hell are you? Are you out there? Are you following me?"

She used her cellular phone and tried to call Nick, but he must have already left for Boston. Desperate for a distraction, any distraction, she dialed her mother's phone number. Maybe she could drive down to Richmond. That would certainly take her mind off Stucky. Her mother's answering machine picked up on the fourth ring.

"I can't come to the phone right now," a cheerful voice answered, and Maggie immediately thought she had dialed the wrong number. "Please call back another time, and remember, God watches out for those who can't watch out for themselves."

Maggie snapped the phone shut. Oh God, she thought, wishing the voice had not been her mother's, and that she indeed had the wrong number. However, she recognized the raspy, cigarette-smoking tone despite the false cheerfulness. Then she remembered what Greg had said about her mother being out of town. Of course, she was with Reverend Everett—whoever the hell he was. They were in Las Vegas. Where else would manic-depressed alcoholics go to find God?

She noticed the gas tank getting low so she pulled off the interstate and found an Amoco station. She had the gas cap off when she realized the pumps were not set up for credit cards and a pay-at-the-pumps. She glanced over at the station's shop. As soon as Maggie saw the female clerk's blond curls, she replaced the gas cap and got back into the car.

It took two more attempts and about twenty more miles before she found a pay-at-the-pumps station. By now her nerves were rubbed raw. Her head hurt and the nausea had left her feeling hollow and sick to her stomach. There was nowhere she could go. Running away would not solve anything. Nor could she coax Stucky into coming after her. Unless he was already waiting for her. She decided to take her chances and return home.

CHAPTER 63

Tess ran, her ankle throbbing. Her feet ached and were now bleeding despite her attempt to wrap them with what once were the sleeves of her blouse. She had no idea where she was headed. The sky had clouded up again, bulging gray and ready to burst. Twice she had come to a ledge that overlooked water. If only she had learned to swim, she wouldn't have cared how far away the other side appeared to be. Why couldn't she escape this eternal prison of trees and vines and steep ridges?

She had spent the morning eating wild strawberries or, at least, that's what she thought they were. Then she drank from the muddy bank of the river, not caring what algae also slipped into her cupped hands. Her reflection had frightened her at first. The tangled hair, the shredded clothes, the scratches and cuts made her look like a madwoman. But wasn't that exactly what she had been reduced to? In fact, she couldn't think of Rachel without feeling something raw and primitive ripping at her insides.

She couldn't be sure how much time had gone by while she cringed in a corner of the hole. She had cried and rocked, hugging herself with her forehead pressed against the wall of dirt. At times she had felt herself slipping into some other dimension, hearing her aunt shouting down at her from the top of the hole. She could swear she had seen her aunt's pinched face scowling at her and waving a bony finger, cursing her. She had no clue whether she had spent one night or two or three. Time had lost all meaning.

She did remember what had brought her out of her stupor. She had felt a presence, someone or something rustling above at the ledge of the hole.

She had expected to look up and see him like a raptor, perched and ready to jump down on her. She didn't care. She wanted it to end. But it wasn't the madman, or a predator. Instead, it was a deer looking into the hole. A young, beautiful doe curiously staring down at her. And Tess found herself wondering how something so lovely and innocent could exist on this devil's island.

That's when she pulled herself together, when she decided once again that she would not die, not here, not in this hellhole. She had covered her temporary companion as best she could with branches from a pine tree, the soft needles like a blanket on the battered, gray skin. And then she crawled out into the open. However, there had been no sense of relief in leaving the earthly tomb that, ironically, had become a sanctuary of sorts. Now after running and walking for miles, she felt farther away from safety than she had felt inside that musty grave.

Suddenly she saw something white up on the ridge and through the trees. She climbed with new energy, pulling herself up with tree roots, ignoring the cuts in her palms that she hadn't noticed before. Finally on level ground again, she was gasping for air, but she had a better view. Hidden by huge pine trees was a huge white, wooden frame house.

Tess's pulse quickened. She blinked, hoping the mirage would not disappear. An incredible wave of relief swept over her as she noticed a wisp of smoke coming from the chimney. She could even smell the wood from the fireplace. She heard a wind chime and immediately saw it hanging from the porch. Along the house, daffodils and tulips were in full bloom. She felt like Little Red Riding Hood finding her way through the woods to her grandmother's warm and inviting house. Then she realized the analogy might prove more real than fantasy. An alarm seemed to go off in her head. The panic raced through her veins. She turned to run and slammed right into him. He gripped both her wrists and smiled down at her, looking exactly like a wolf.

"I was looking for you, Tess," he said calmly while she pulled and twisted against his strength. "I'm so glad you found your way."

CHAPTER 64

Washington, D.C.
Monday, April 6

Maggie couldn't believe Cunningham had insisted she keep her Monday-morning appointment with Dr. Kernan. It was bad enough that they had to wait for some kind of unofficial permission from the Maryland authorities. How could they be sure Stucky wouldn't find out? If any of the information leaked, they wouldn't need to worry about Stucky setting another trap. No, this time he'd be long gone. It would be another five or six months before they heard from him again.

She had made the trip, angry and on edge—an hour's drive in D.C.'s early-morning rush. And now she had to wait some more. Once again Kernan was late. He shuffled in, smelling of cigar smoke and looking as though he had just crawled out of bed. His cheap brown suit was wrinkled, his shoes scuffed, with one shoestring untied and dragging behind him. He had plastered down his thin white hair with some foul-smelling gel. Or maybe it was the Ben-Gay assaulting her nostrils. The man looked like a poster model for homeless mental patients.

Again, he didn't acknowledge her as he shifted and creaked in his chair, back and forth, until he decided he was comfortable. This time Maggie felt too restless and angry to be intimidated. She didn't care what strange insights he might probe from her psyche. Nothing Kernan could do or say would reduce or heal the chaotic storm ticking away inside her chest like some time bomb ready to explode without warning.

She tapped her foot and drummed her fingertips on the arm of the chair.

She watched him sift through his mess. God, she was sick of everyone's messes. First Tully's, now Kernan's. How did these people function?

She sighed, and he scowled at her over his thick glasses. He smacked his lips together in a "tis, tis," as if to scold her. She continued to stare at him, letting him see her contempt, her anger, her impatience. Letting him see it all, and not giving a damn what he thought.

"Are we in a hurry, Special Agent Margaret O'Dell?" he asked as he thumbed through a magazine.

She glanced at his fingers and caught a glimpse of the magazine's cover. It was a copy of *Vogue*, for God's sake.

"Yes, I am in a hurry, Dr. Kernan. There's an important investigation I'd like to get back to."

"So you think you've found him?"

She looked up, surprised, checking to see if he knew. But he appeared engrossed in the magazine's pages. Was it possible Cunningham had told him? How else would he know?

"We may have," she said, careful not to reveal anything more.

"But everyone is making you wait, is that it? Your partner, your supervisor, me. And we all know how much Margaret O'Dell hates to wait."

She didn't have time for his stupid games.

"Could we please just get on with this?"

He looked up at her again over his glasses, this time surprised. "What would you like to get on with? Would you like some special absolution, perhaps? Some sort of permission to go racing after him?"

He put the magazine aside, sat back and brought his hands together over his chest. He stared at her as if waiting for an answer, an explanation. She refused to give him any of what he wanted. Instead, she simply stared back.

"You'd like us all to get out of your way," he continued. "Is that it, Special Agent Margaret O'Dell?" He paused. She pursed her lips, denying him a response, and so he continued, "You want to go after him all by yourself again, because you're the only one who can capture him. Oh no, excuse me. You're the only one who can stop him. Perhaps you think stopping him this time will absolve *you* of his crimes?"

"If I was looking for absolution, Dr. Kernan, I'd be in a church and certainly not sitting here in your office."

He smiled, a thin-lipped smile. Maggie realized it was the first time she had ever seen the man smile.

"Will you be looking for absolution after you shoot Albert Stucky between the eyes?"

She winced, remembering their last session and how out of control she had been. It reminded her that she still felt out of control, only now the anger gave her a false sense of how close the ledge really was. If she remained angry, perhaps she wouldn't see the ledge at all. Would she even feel herself slipping or would the fall be abrupt and sudden when it happened?

"Maybe I've been around evil too long to care about what I need to do to destroy it." She was no longer concerned with what she told him. He couldn't use any of it to hurt her. No one could hurt her more than Stucky already had. "Maybe," she continued, letting the anger drive her, "maybe I need to be as evil as Albert Stucky in order to stop him."

He stared at her, but this time it was different. He was contemplating what she had said. Would he have some smart-ass response? Would he try his reverse psychology on her? She wasn't one of his naive students anymore. She could play at his game. After all, she had played with someone ten times as twisted as him. If she could play at Albert Stucky's game, then Dr. James Kernan's would be nothing more than child's play.

She stared him down, without flinching, without fidgeting. Had she rendered the old man speechless?

Finally he sat forward, elbows on his messy desk, fingers constructing a tent of bent and misshapen digits.

"So that's what concerns you, Margaret O'Dell?"

She had no idea what he was talking about, but she kept the question from her face.

"You're concerned," he said slowly, as if approaching a delicate subject. It was an unfamiliar gesture, one that immediately made Maggie suspicious. Was it another of Kernan's famous tricks or was he genuinely concerned? She hoped for a trick. That, she could handle. The concern, she wasn't too sure about.

"You're worried," he began again, "that you may be capable of the same sort of evil Albert Stucky is capable of."

"Aren't we all, Dr. Kernan?" She paused for his reaction. "Isn't that what Jung meant when he said we all have a shadow side?" She watched him closely, wanting to see how it felt to have one of his students contradict him with his own teachings. "Evil men do what good men only dream of doing. Isn't that true, Dr. Kernan?"

He shifted in his chair. She should have counted the succession of eye blinks. She wanted to smile, because she had him on the ropes, so to speak. But there was no victory in this truth.

"I believe—" he hesitated to clear his throat "—I believe Jung said that evil is as essential a component of human behavior as good. That we must learn to acknowledge and accept that it exists within all of us. But no, that doesn't mean we're all capable of the same kind of evil as someone like Albert Stucky. There's a difference, my dear Agent O'Dell, between stepping into evil and getting your shoes muddy, and choosing to dive in and wallow in it."

"But how do you stop from falling in headfirst?" She felt an annoying catch in her throat as the inner frenzy threatened to reveal itself. Her thoughts of revenge were black and evil and very real. Had she already dived in?

"I'm going to tell you something, Maggie O'Dell, and I want you to listen very closely." He leaned forward, his face serious, his magnified eyes pinning her to the chair with their unfamiliar concern. "I don't give a rat's ass about Jung or Freud when it comes to this evil crap. Remember this and only this, Margaret O'Dell. The decisions we make in a split second will always reveal our true nature, our true self. Whether we like it or not. When that split second comes, don't think, don't analyze, don't feel and never second-guess—just react. Trust. Trust in yourself. You do that—just that—and I'm willing to bet you end up with nothing more than a little mud on your shoes."

CHAPTER 65

Tully punched at the laptop's keyboard. He knew the computer down in his office was much faster, but he couldn't leave the conference room. Not now that he had had all the calls forwarded, and every last file on the case was spread out over the tabletop. Agent O'Dell would be furious about the mess. Though he doubted she could get much angrier. He hadn't seen or talked to her since she had stormed out of his house yesterday.

Assistant Director Cunningham had informed him that O'Dell would be spending the morning in D.C. at a previously scheduled appointment. He didn't elaborate, but Tully knew the appointment was with the Bureau psychologist. Maybe it would help calm her down. She needed to keep things in perspective. She needed to realize that everything that could be done, was being done, and as quickly as possible. She needed to get past her own fear. She couldn't keep seeing the bogeyman in every corner and expect to handle it by running after him with guns blazing.

Although Tully had to admit, he was also having a tough time waiting. The Maryland authorities were hesitant to go storming onto private property without just cause. And no government department seemed willing to admit or confirm that the metallic mud could have come from the recently closed and sold government property. All they had was Detective Rosen's fishing story, and now that Tully had repeated it over and over to top government officials it was beginning to sound more and more just like a fish story.

It might be different if the property in question wasn't miles and miles of trees and rocks. They could drive down the road and check things out.

But from what he understood, this property had no road, at least not a public one. The only dirt road available included an electronic gate, a leftover from when the government owned the property and had allowed no unauthorized access. So Tully searched for the new property owners, hoping to find something that would tell him who or what WH Enterprises was.

He decided to use a new search engine and keyed in "WH Enterprises" again. Then he sat, elbows on the desk, his chin resting on his hand as he watched the line crawl along the bottom of the screen...3% of document transferred...4%...5%... This would take forever.

The phone rescued him. He wheeled his chair around and grabbed the receiver.

"Tully."

"Agent Tully, this is Keith Ganza—over in forensics. They told me Agent O'Dell was out this morning."

"That's right."

"Any chance I could get hold of her? Maybe her cell phone? I was wondering if you had the number."

"Sounds important."

"Don't really know for sure, but I figure that's up to Maggie to determine."

Tully sat up straight. Ganza's voice was a constant monotone, but the fact that he didn't want to talk to him alarmed Tully. Had O'Dell and Ganza been on to something that she wasn't letting him in on?

"Does this have anything to do with the luminol tests you did? You know Agent O'Dell and I are working on the Stucky case together, Keith."

There was a pause. So he was right. There was something.

"Actually, it's a couple of things," he finally said. "I spent so much time analyzing the chemicals in the dirt and then the fingerprints that, well, I'm just getting to that bag of trash you found."

"It didn't look too unusual except for all the candy bar wrappers."

"I might have an explanation for those."

"The candy wrappers?" He couldn't believe Ganza would waste his time with those.

"I discovered a small vial and a syringe at the bottom of the trash bag. It was insulin. Now, it could be that one of the previous owners of the house has diabetes, but then we should have found more. Also, most diabetics I know are fairly conscientious about properly disposing of their used syringes."

"So what exactly are you saying, Keith?"

"Just telling you what I found. That's what I meant about Maggie determining whether or not it was important."

"You said there were a couple of things?"

"Oh yeah..." Ganza hesitated again. "Maggie asked me to do a search of prints for a Walker Harding, but it's been taking me a while. The guy has no criminal record, never registered a handgun."

Tully was surprised Maggie hadn't stopped Ganza after they had read the article and discovered that Harding was going blind. He couldn't possibly be a suspect. "Save yourself the time," he told Ganza. "Looks like we don't need to check."

"I didn't say I wasn't able to find anything. The cold search just took a bit longer. The guy had a civil servant job about ten years ago, so his prints are on file after all."

"Keith, I'm sorry you went through all that trouble." Tully only half listened to Ganza as he watched the computer screen. The search engine must be accessing something on WH Enterprises if it was taking this long. He started tapping his fingers.

"Hopefully, it was worth the trouble," Ganza went on. "The prints I lifted from the whirlpool bath were an exact match."

Tully's fingers stopped. His other hand gripped the phone's receiver. "What the hell did you just say?"

"The fingerprints I lifted off the bathtub at the house on Archer Drive... they matched this Walker Harding guy. It's an exact match. No doubt about it."

The pieces of the puzzle were falling into place, but Tully didn't like the picture they were forming. On an obscure Web site designed to look like some clearinghouse run by the Confederacy, he found computer video games for sale. All were wholesale priced, and the search could be completed by clicking on the tiny Confederate-flag icons. The games were available though a company called WH Enterprises. Most of them guaranteed graphic violence and others promised to be of pornographic nature. These were not the types of games kids could pick up at Best Buys or Kids "R" Us.

The sample that could be viewed with a simple click of the mouse included a naked woman being gang-raped, with the player being able to gun down all the assailants, only to be rewarded by raping the woman himself. Despite the animation, the video clip was all too real. Tully found himself sick to his stomach. He wondered if any of Emma's friends were into this sort of garbage.

One of the Web site's features was the "Lil' General's Top Ten List," including a note from the CEO of WH Enterprises. Tully knew what he'd find before he scrolled down to see the message ending with, "Happy hunting, General Walker Harding."

Tully paced the conference room, walking from window to window. Walker Harding may have been going blind, but he sure as hell could see now. How else could he run a computer business like this one? How else could he be at each crime scene, helping his old pal, Albert Stucky?

"Son of a bitch," Tully said out loud. O'Dell had been right. The two men were working together. Maybe they were still competing in some new game of horror. Whatever it was, there was no denying the evidence. Walker Harding's fingerprints matched those found on the Dumpster with Jessica Beckwith's body. They matched the umbrella in Kansas City, and they matched the prints left on the whirlpool bath at the house on Archer Drive.

Earlier, the Maryland authorities had finally confirmed that there was a large two-story house and several wooden shacks on the property. All government buildings had been bulldozed before the sale. The rest of the property, Tully was informed, was surrounded on three sides by water and covered with trees and rock. There were no roads except a dirt path that led to the house. No electrical lines or telephone cables had been brought in from the outside. The new owner used a large generator system left behind by the government. The place sounded like a recluse's dream come true and a madman's paradise. Why hadn't he realized sooner that, of course, WH Enterprises would belong to Walker Harding?

Tully checked his wristwatch. He needed to make some phone calls. He needed to concentrate. He took several deep breaths, dug the exhaustion out from under his glasses and picked up the phone. The waiting was over, but he dreaded telling Agent O'Dell. Would this be the final thread to unravel her already frayed mental state?

CHAPTER 66

Tess woke slowly, painfully. Her body ached. Her head throbbed. Something held her down. She couldn't move. Couldn't open her eyes again, the lids were too heavy. Her mouth felt dry, her throat was raw on the inside as well as the outside. She was thirsty and ran her tongue over her lips, alarmed when she tasted blood.

She forced her eyes open and strained against the shackles that clamped her wrists and ankles to the small cot. She recognized the inside of the shack, could feel its dampness and smell its musty odor. She twisted, trying to free herself. She felt a scratchy blanket beneath her and that's when she realized she was naked. Panic rushed through her insides, shoving against the walls of her body. A scream stuck in her throat, but nothing came out except a gasp of air. That was enough, however, to send a scrape of pain down her throat as though she were swallowing razor blades.

She settled down, trying to calm herself, trying to think before terror took control of her mind. She no longer had control over her body, but no one would control her mind. It was a painful lesson she had learned from her aunt and uncle. No matter what they did to her body, no matter how many times her aunt had banished her to the dark cellar or how many times her uncle had shoved himself inside her, she had retained control over her mind. It was the ultimate defense. It was her only defense.

Yet, when she heard the locks to the door clicking open, Tess felt the terror clawing at the flimsy barricades to her mind.

CHAPTER 67

Maggie swerved around slower-moving traffic, trying to keep her foot from pushing the accelerator to the floor. Her heart hadn't stopped ramming against her chest since Tully's phone call. All the anger she had accessed in Kernan's office had been converted to sheer panic. It no longer ticked quietly like a time bomb. Instead, it pressed against her rib cage like some heavy weight being lowered, little by little, threatening to crush her.

She knew Walker Harding was involved. It made sense that Stucky would call on his old pal. Though she still had a difficult time believing Stucky would allow anyone to help, even his ex-partner—unless the two men were competing at some bizarre game. And from Tully's description of Harding's new entrepreneurial venture, it seemed more than possible that he was capable of the same sort of twisted, perverted evil as Stucky was.

She tucked her hair behind her ears and rolled down the window. The breeze whipped through the car's interior, bringing with it the fumes of exhaust and the scent of pine trees.

Dr. Kernan had said she shouldn't think so much—just trust. All her life she had felt as if she was the only person she could trust. There was no one else. Did he understand how incredibly frustrating, how…hell, why not admit it?—how frightening it was to think she could no longer trust the one person she had trusted her whole life? That she could no longer trust herself?

She had a B.A. in criminal psychology, and a master's in behavioral psychology. She knew all about the shadow side, and she knew it existed in everyone. There were plenty of experts who debated the fine line between good and evil and they all hoped to explain why some people choose evil, while others choose good. What was the determining factor? Did anyone really know?

"Trust in yourself," Kernan had told her. And that the decisions she made in a split second would somehow reveal her true self.

What kind of psychobabble was that? What if her true self really was her shadow side? What if her true self was capable of Stucky's blend of evil? She couldn't help thinking that all it would take was a split second for her to aim and fire one bullet right between those black eyes. She no longer wanted to capture him, to stop Albert Stucky. She wanted him to pay. She wanted— no, she needed—to see fear in those evil eyes. The same kind of fear she felt in that Miami warehouse when he cut her abdomen. The same fear she felt every night when darkness came and sleep would not.

Stucky had made this a personal war between the two of them. He had made her an accomplice to his murders, making her feel as though she had handpicked each woman for his disposal. If he had somehow managed to coerce Walker Harding into his game of horror, then there were now two of them who needed to be destroyed.

She glanced at the map spread out on the passenger seat. The toll bridge was about fifty miles from Quantico. Tully was still making arrangements. It would take several hours before he had everything ready according to his careful, by-the-book standards. There would be more waiting. They'd be lucky to make it to Harding's property by nightfall. Tully was expecting her back at Quantico in the next ten to fifteen minutes. Up ahead a sign indicated that her exit was just ten miles away.

She pulled out her cell phone and slowed the car to the speed limit, allowing her to maneuver more easily with one hand on the steering wheel. She punched in the number and waited.

"Dr. Gwen Patterson."

"Gwen, it's Maggie."

"You sound like you're on the road."

"Yes, I am. Just coming back from D.C. Can you hear me okay?"

"Little bit of static, but not bad. You were in D.C.? You should have stopped in. We could have done lunch."

"Sorry, no time. Look, Gwen, you know how you're always saying I never ask anything of my friends? Well, I need a favor."

"Wait a minute. Who did you say this was?"

"Very funny." Maggie smiled, surprised she was able to amidst all the internal tension. "I know it's out of your way, but could you check on Harvey this evening—let him out, feed him...all those dog things that a real dog owner normally does?"

"You're off fighting serial killers, and you're still worried about Harvey. I'd say you already sound like a dog owner. Yes, I will stop and spend some quality time with Harvey. Actually, that's the best offer I've had in a long time as far as spending an evening with a male companion goes."

"Thanks. I really appreciate it."

"Does this mean you're simply working late or have you found him?"

Maggie wondered how long it had been since her friends and co-workers could simply ask her about "him" and automatically mean Albert Stucky.

"I don't know yet, but it's the best lead we've had so far. You may have been right about the candy bar wrappers."

"Wonderful. Only I don't remember what it was I said."

"We dismissed Stucky's old business partner as an accomplice because the guy was supposedly going blind due to some medical condition. Now the evidence suggests that the condition could be diabetes. Which means the blindness may not have been sudden or complete. In fact, he could be hoping to control it with insulin injections."

"Why would Stucky be working with an accomplice? Are you sure that makes sense, Maggie?"

"No, I'm not sure it makes sense. But we keep finding fingerprints at the scenes that don't belong to Stucky. This morning we found out the prints are a perfect match with Stucky's old business partner, Walker Harding. The two sold their business about four years ago and supposedly went their separate ways, but they might be working together again. We also discovered a remote piece of land just across the river registered to Harding. This place sounds like the perfect hideout."

Maggie glanced down at the map again. The exit to Quantico was getting closer. Soon she'd need to make a decision. She knew a shortcut to the toll bridge. She could be there in less than an hour. Suddenly she realized that Gwen's pause had lasted too long. Had she lost the call?

"Gwen, are you still there?"

"Did you say the partner's name is Walker Harding?"

"Yes, that's right."

"Maggie, last week I started seeing a new patient who is blind. His name is Walker Harding."

CHAPTER 68

Tully ripped off the fax and began piecing the four sheets together. The Maryland Parks Commission had faxed an aerial view of Harding's property. In black and white not much could be seen through the acres of treetops. The first thing Tully noticed was that, from above, the area looked like an island except for a sliver that connected it to the mainland. The property jutted out into the water with the Potomac River on two sides and a tributary river on the third.

"The SWAT team is assembled and ready to go," Cunningham said as he entered the conference room. "Maryland State Patrol will meet you on the other side of the toll bridge. Are those any help?" He came around the table and looked at the map Tully had just finished taping together.

"Can't see any buildings. Too many trees."

Cunningham pushed his glasses up the bridge of his nose and bent down to examine the map. "From what I understand, the facility housing the generator is in the upper northwest corner." He ran his index finger over the spot that resembled a black-and-gray mass. "I would think the house would need to be close by. Any idea how long Harding has lived here?"

"At least four years. Which means he's settled and knows the area. It wouldn't surprise me if he had a bunker somewhere on the property."

"That seems a bit paranoid, doesn't it?" Cunningham raised his eyebrows.

"The guy was a recluse long before he and Stucky started their business. Some of the computer video games he sells are his own creations. The guy may be a computer genius, but he's weirder than hell. A lot of the games are antigovernment, white supremacist garbage. He even has one called 'Waco's Revenge.' Lots of Armageddon-type stuff, too. Probably sold truckloads of it in 1999, so it wouldn't surprise me if he's well prepared."

"What are you saying, Agent Tully? You mean we might have more problems on our hands than busting a couple of serial killers? You think Harding may have an arsenal in there, or worse, have the property booby-trapped?"

"I don't have any proof, sir. I just think we should be prepared."

"But be prepared for what? A stand-off?"

"Anything. I'm just saying if Harding is as extreme as his games would suggest, he could freak out with the FBI showing up on his doorstep."

"Wonderful." Cunningham stretched his back and walked over to the bulletin board where Tully had tacked up printouts of Harding's Web site next to photos of the crime scenes.

"When is Agent O'Dell scheduled to be here?"

Tully glanced at his watch. She was already a half hour late. He knew what Cunningham was thinking.

"She should be here any minute now, sir," Tully said without indicating he thought that she might not show up. "I think we have everything we need. Is there anything I'm forgetting?"

"I want to brief the SWAT team. We should let them in on your suspicions," Cunningham said, looking at his own watch now. "What time did Agent O'Dell leave D.C.?"

"I'm not really sure. Will they need any extra preparations?" He avoided his boss's eyes, just in case he could see that Tully was stalling and changing the subject.

"No extra preparations. But it is important they know what they're in for."

When Tully looked up, Cunningham was staring at him with his brow furrowed.

"You're sure Agent O'Dell is on her way here?"

"Of course, sir. Where else would she be headed?"

"Sorry, I'm late," O'Dell came in as if on cue.

Tully restrained the deep sigh of relief he felt.

"You're just in time," he told her.

"I need a few minutes with the SWAT team, and then you're on your way." Cunningham headed out the room.

As soon as it was safe, Tully asked, "So how close to the toll bridge did you get before you turned back?"

O'Dell stared at him in surprise.

"How did you know?"

"Lucky guess."

"Does Cunningham know?" Suddenly she seemed more angry than concerned.

"Why would I tell Cunningham?" He pretended to look wounded. "There are some secrets only partners should share." He grabbed a bundle from the corner, handed her a bulletproof vest and waited for her at the door. "Coming?"

CHAPTER 69

"We have to stay back and let them attempt to serve the search warrant," Tully instructed. He wasn't sure that O'Dell was even listening. He could hear her heart pounding. Or was that his own heart? The thumping seemed indistinguishable from the rumble of thunder in the distance.

They had left their vehicles far back on the other side of the electronic gate that blocked the road. Not much of a road, really. Tully had seen cow paths that were more easily accessible. Now as he and O'Dell crouched in the brush and mud, he regretted wearing his good shoes. A crazy thing to be thinking about when they were this close to capturing Stucky and Harding.

The Maryland State Patrol had supplied them with a half-dozen officers—officially for the sole purpose of serving the search warrant to the owner or occupants of the house. If no one responded, the FBI SWAT team would secure the area and accompany Tully and O'Dell in a search of the house and grounds. Tully was quick to notice that all the members of the SWAT team wore sturdy boots. At least O'Dell had remembered the FBI windbreakers. He was sweating under the weight of the bulletproof vest, but that didn't protect him from the wind. Out here in the woods the wind swirled around the trees, crisp and cold. If the thunder was any indication, they would also be wet before the night was over. Night would come quickly in these woods, and with the thick cloud cover they would soon be in the pitch black. Already the twilight was providing eerie shadows that grew darker by the minute.

"There's smoke coming out of the chimney," O'Dell whispered. "Someone must be here."

A faint light appeared in one of the windows, but it could easily be set to a timer. The smoke, however, was a little more difficult to manufacture without someone stoking a fire in the fireplace.

Two of the state patrol officers approached the front door as several of the SWAT team members moved in behind the bushes along the cobblestone path that led to the door. Tully watched, hoping he was wrong about Harding's paranoia and hoping that the patrolmen would not simply be easy targets. He pulled out his own revolver and started scanning the windows of the house, looking for gun barrels peeking through. The house sat nestled in the woods like something out of a fairy tale. There was a porch swing and Tully could hear a wind chime. He couldn't help noticing that there were way too many windows for a man who was going blind.

No one was answering the patrolman's knock. He tried again while everyone else waited quietly. Tully wiped his forehead and suddenly realized that all the chirping birds and rustling forest creatures had also gone silent. Maybe they knew something their human counterparts did not. Even the wind had settled down. The thunder rumbled closer and flashes of lightning streaked across the horizon beyond the wall of trees.

"Perfect," Tully whispered to no one in particular. "Isn't it bad enough that this place already looks like something out of *Dark Shadows?*"

"*Dark Shadows?*" O'Dell whispered back.

"Yeah, the old TV show." He glanced at her, only now she had a blank look on her face. "You know, with Barnabus Collins and The Hand?" There was still no glint of recognition. "Forget it. You're too young."

"Doesn't sound like I missed much."

"Hey, watch it. *Dark Shadows* was a classic."

The two patrolmen looked over their shoulders and into the bushes. Not very discreet. One shrugged. The other put an ear to the door. Then he knocked one last time. For some reason he tried the doorknob, then again looked over to the bushes, pointing and indicating that the door was unlocked. Of course, Tully found himself thinking, why the hell would anyone lock the door out here?

Agent Alvando, who was heading the SWAT team, hurried over to Tully and O'Dell.

"We're ready to go in. Give us a few minutes. I'll come back out and give an all-clear sign."

"Okay," Tully said, but O'Dell was up, looking as if she was ready to go in with the SWAT team.

"Come on, Agent Alvando," O'Dell began to argue, and Tully wanted to pull her back down into the brush. "We're trained agents, too. It's not like you're here to protect us."

She looked to Tully as if for reassurance. He wanted to disagree, but she was right. The SWAT team was here for backup, here to help with the search-and-arrest mission, not to protect them.

"We'll go on in with you, Victor," he reluctantly told Agent Alvando.

There was barely enough light to see inside the house. The entry included a hallway down the middle with a great room to the left and an open staircase over to the right. The second-floor landing was visible, separated only by a balcony railing. The team split up with half of them going upstairs, and the other half covering the main floor. Tully followed Agent O'Dell up the stairs. Before they got to the landing, they noticed the SWAT team members had stopped at the end of the hall. Tully could hear what sounded like a voice on the other side of the door where the three men hesitated. They motioned to each other, getting into position. Tully followed O'Dell's lead and pressed himself against the wall. One of the men kicked the door open, and they stormed the room without a word to each other.

O'Dell looked disappointed when they got to the door and discovered the voice came from one of the half-dozen computers lined up along the wall.

"Click twice for confirmation," the electronic voice said. "Speak into the microphone when ready."

From another computer, an electronic voice gave different instructions. "That order has been shipped. Please check the status in twenty-four hours."

"What the fuck is this?" one of the SWAT team asked.

O'Dell was taking a closer look while the rest of them stayed next to the door watching their backs.

"It's a whole computer system set up to be voice activated." She walked from one computer to the next, examining the screens without touching anything. "Looks like it reports the status of his video-game business."

"Why would anyone want a voice-activated system?" Agent Alvando was at the door.

O'Dell looked back at Tully, and he knew what she was thinking. Why, indeed, unless that person was blind—not just partially, but totally blind.

CHAPTER 70

Tess squeezed her eyes shut. She could do this. She could pretend she was somewhere else. After all, she had done it many times before. There wasn't much difference really. She needed to convince herself of that. What did it matter whether a paying john fucked her or some madman?

She needed to relax or it would only hurt more. She needed to stop feeling his thrusts, stop thinking about his hands fondling her breasts, stop hearing his groans. She could do this. She could survive this.

"Open your eyes," he grunted between clenched teeth.

She squeezed them tighter.

"Open your goddamn eyes. I want you to watch."

She refused. He hit her across the mouth, whipping her head so violently to the side that she heard her neck crack. Immediately, she tasted blood. She kept her eyes closed.

"Goddamn you, bitch. Open your fucking eyes."

He was gasping, rocking back and forth with such force she thought he'd crack her insides open as well. She felt his hot breath on her neck and suddenly his teeth sank into her skin. His hands clamped down on her breasts, and he was hanging on to her, riding her, every part of him scraping, rubbing and thrusting at her, devouring her like a rabid dog.

She bit down on her lower lip. She forced her eyes to remain shut. Not much longer. She could do this. He would come, and then it would be over. Why the hell didn't he come already? It wouldn't be much longer. It couldn't be. She twisted her head as far away as possible and kept her eyelids closed tight.

Finally, his body jerked, his teeth let go, his hands gave a final squeeze and he relaxed. He crawled off her, jamming his knee into her stomach and slamming his elbow against her head. Finally, it was over. She lay still, swallowing blood and pretending not to feel the sticky mess between her legs. Instead, she reminded herself that she had survived.

He was so quiet, she wondered if he had gone. She opened her eyes to find him standing over her. The yellow glow of the lantern he had brought with him created a halo behind him. When she met his eyes, he twisted his lips into a smile. He looked as calm and composed as he had when he entered the shack. How was it possible? She had hoped that he would be exhausted, spent and ready to leave. But he showed no signs of fatigue.

"This part you will watch," he promised. "Even if I need to cut your fucking eyelids off." He held up a shiny scalpel for her to see.

Her weak, muffled scream made it past the raw pain in her throat.

"Scream all you want." He laughed. "No one can hear you. And quite frankly, I like it."

Oh dear God. The terror rushed through her veins and exploded in her head. She pulled and shoved against the restraints. Then suddenly she noticed him backing away, his head cocked to the side, as though he was listening to something outside the shack.

Tess strained to hear over the pounding in her head and chest. She lay still, watching him, and then she heard it. Unless she had gone mad, it sounded like voices.

CHAPTER 71

Maggie wondered if they were too late. Had Stucky and Harding escaped into the woods? She looked out the window and watched as Agent Alvando and his men combed the area, disappearing into the woods. Soon they wouldn't be able to see anything without flashlights and strobes, things they hated to use, because the lights made them easy targets for snipers. As much as she wanted to be out there looking with them, she knew Alvando was right. She and Tully weren't equipped or trained to participate in a SWAT team sweep of the woods.

The rain had started softly with a pitter-patter on the metal gutters. The sound was almost comforting, except that the approaching roar of thunder promised a storm. Maggie was grateful the house depended on a generator and not electricity that could easily be knocked out.

"Could we have been wrong about this place?" Agent Tully asked from the other side of the room. He had pulled out some of the cartons from under the computer desks, and with latex gloves on he sifted through what looked like ledgers, mail orders and other business documents.

"All of this could simply be preparation for him losing his sight entirely. I'm not sure what to think." Perhaps it was the impending storm and the electrical current thick in the air. Whatever it was, she couldn't shake the feeling of dread and restlessness. "Maybe we should go check and see if they got that room opened in the basement."

"Alvando told us to stay put." Tully shot her a warning look.

"It could be a torture chamber, not some bunker."

"I'm only guessing it's a bunker. We won't know for sure until Alvando's men can get it opened."

She glanced around the room. It looked like a typical home office except for the talking computers. What a disappointment. What a letdown. She had psyched herself up for a showdown with Albert Stucky, and he was nowhere to be found.

"O'Dell?" Tully was hunched over another of the cartons he had unearthed. "Take a look at this."

She looked over his shoulder expecting to see more X-rated computer software and videos. Instead, she found herself staring at newspaper clippings about her father's death.

"Where the hell do you suppose he got this?" Tully asked.

She was wondering the same thing until she saw her appointment book and childhood photo album. It was her missing carton from the move. She had completely forgotten about it. So Greg had been telling the truth. The carton hadn't been left at the condo. Somehow Stucky had been watching and had managed to take it from the movers. A shiver slid down her back as she thought about him handling her personal possessions.

"Maggie?" Tully stared up at her, concern in his eyes. "Do you think he broke into your house without you knowing?"

"No, I've been missing it since the day I moved in. He must have stolen the box before it made it into the house."

The rage began in the pit of her stomach. She left Tully to dig through the other cartons while she paced the room from window to window.

"That means Stucky has been here," Tully said without looking up.

She kept her eyes on the windows as she walked back and forth. The lightning struck closer, igniting the sky and making the trees look like skeleton soldiers standing at attention. Suddenly she saw a reflection of someone in the hallway walking past the door. She spun around, her revolver gripped firmly, outstretched in front of her. Tully jumped to his feet and had his gun out in seconds.

"What is it, O'Dell?" He kept his eyes ahead watching the doorway. She moved slowly across the room, gun aimed, hammer cocked.

"I saw someone walk by," she finally explained.

"Are any of the SWAT team still in the house?"

"They were finished up here," she whispered. Her heart slammed against her chest. Her breathing was already coming too quickly. "They wouldn't come back up and not announce themselves, right?"

"Do you smell something?" Tully was sniffing the air.

She smelled it, too, and the terror that had begun to crawl up from her stomach started to explode.

"It smells like gasoline," Tully said.

All Maggie could think was that it smelled like gasoline and smoke. It smelled like fire. The thought grabbed hold of her, and suddenly she couldn't breathe. She couldn't think. She couldn't walk the rest of the distance to the door—her knees had locked. Her throat plugged up, threatening to strangle her.

Tully ran to the door and carefully peeked out, his gun ready.

"Holy crap," he yelled, looking out into the hallway in both directions without stepping out. "We've got flames on both sides. There's no way we're getting out the way we came in."

He returned his gun to his holster and hurried to the windows, trying to open one while Maggie stood paralyzed in the middle of the room. Her hands shook so badly she could barely grip her revolver. She stared at her hands as though they belonged to someone else. Her breathing was out of control, and she worried she might start to hyperventilate.

The smell alone sparked images from her childhood nightmares: flames engulfing her father and scorching her fingers every time she reached for him. She could never save him, because her fear immobilized her.

"Damn it!" She heard Tully struggling behind her.

She turned toward him, but her feet wouldn't move. He seemed so far away, and she knew she was losing visual perception. The room began to tilt. She could feel the motion, though she knew it couldn't possibly be real. Then she saw him again, a reflection in the window. She twisted around, but it felt as if she was moving in slow motion. Albert Stucky stood tall and dark in the doorway, dressed in a black leather jacket and pointing a gun directly at her.

She tried to raise her own gun, but it was too heavy. Her hand wouldn't obey the command. The room had tilted to the other side, and she felt herself slipping. He was smiling at her and seemed to be oblivious to the flames shooting up behind him. Was he real? Had her panic, her terror, brought on hallucinations?

"This damn thing is stuck," she heard Tully yell somewhere far off in the distance.

She opened her mouth to warn Tully, but nothing came out. She expected the bullet to hit her squarely in the heart. That's where he was aiming. Everything in slow motion. Was it a dream? A nightmare? He was pulling back the hammer. She could hear wood creaking, giving way in crashes outside the room. She pulled at her arm one more time as she saw Stucky begin to squeeze the trigger.

"Tully," she managed to yell, and just then Stucky slid his aim to the right of her and pulled the trigger. The explosion jolted her like an electrical shock. But she wasn't hit. He hadn't shot her. She looked down. She wasn't bleeding anywhere. It was an effort to move her arm, but she raised it, ready to fire at the now-empty doorway. Stucky was gone. Had it all been her imagination? There was a groan behind her, and before she turned to look, she remembered Tully.

He gripped his bloody thigh with both hands and stared at it as though he couldn't believe what he was seeing. The smoke had entered the room and burned their eyes. She ripped off her windbreaker. She could do this. She had to be able to do this. She ran to the door, forcing herself not to think of the heat and the flames. She slammed the door shut, wadded up her jacket and shoved it into the crack under the door.

She came back to Tully and kneeled next to him. His eyes were wide and beginning to glaze over. He was going into shock.

"You're gonna be okay, Tully. Breathe but not too deeply." Already the smoke was seeping in between the cracks.

She pulled at his necktie, undoing the knot and removing it. Gently she moved his hands away from the wound. She tied the necktie around his thigh, just above the bullet hole, tightening it and wincing when he shouted out in pain.

Smoke was filling the room. The crashing of beams sounded closer. She could hear a commotion of voices outside. Tully hadn't managed to make either window budge. Maggie crawled to her feet, trying to focus only on Tully and getting them out of the room, out of the house. She would not think of the flames on the other side of the door. She would not imagine the hellish heat licking at the floorboards beneath them.

She grabbed one of the computer monitors, yanking the cords and cables until they became unplugged.

"Tully, cover your face."

He only stared at her.

"Goddamn it, Tully, cover your face and head. Now!"

He pulled up his windbreaker and turned to face the wall. Maggie felt her arms weakening under the weight of the monitor. Her eyes burned, and her lungs screamed. She hurled the monitor through the window, and then quickly kicked out the chunks of glass. She grabbed Tully under the arms.

"Come on, Tully. You're going to have to help me."

Somehow she managed to drag him out the window and onto the roof of the porch. Agent Alvando and two other men were down below. It wasn't a great distance to the ground, but with a bullet in his thigh, she couldn't expect Agent Tully to jump. She held on to his arms as he lowered his body over the edge and waited for the men below to grab him. The entire time, his eyes held hers. But there wasn't shock now. There wasn't fear. Instead, what she saw in Agent Tully's eyes surprised her even more. The only thing she saw was trust.

CHAPTER 72

Tully's leg hurt like hell. Most of the flames were out. He sat a safe distance away, but the heat actually felt good. Someone had thrown a blanket around his shoulders. He didn't remember it happening. He also didn't remember that it was raining until he discovered his clothing wet and his hair plastered to his forehead. Somehow Agent Alvando had managed to get the ambulance past the electronic gate and all the way to the burning house.

"Your ride is here." Agent O'Dell appeared from behind him.

"Let them take the McGowan woman first. I can wait."

She studied him as if she would be the judge of whether he waited or not.

"Are you sure? They might be able to fit both of you."

He looked past O'Dell to examine Tess McGowan himself. She was sitting in one of the SWAT team's trucks. From what he could see of her, she looked to be in bad shape. Her hair was tangled and wild like Medusa. Her body, now wrapped in a blanket, had been covered with bloody cuts and bruises. She could barely stand. Alvando's men had found her locked in a wooden shack not far from the house. She had been shackled to a cot, gagged and naked. She had told them that the madman had left only seconds before they found her.

"I'm not bleeding anymore," Tully said. "She's been through God knows what. Get her out of here and into a nice warm bed somewhere."

O'Dell turned and caught one of the men's attention, then waved to him. He seemed to know exactly what she meant and went directly to the truck to escort Ms. McGowan to the ambulance.

"Besides," Tully said, "I want to be here when they bring them out."

The men had found a fire hydrant in back, probably a leftover from when the property had been occupied by the government. They were dousing the entire house with thick streams of water that were much more efficient than the light rainfall. Firefighters from some neighboring community had stomped their way to the scene about an hour ago, but only after their truck had gotten stuck in the mud about a mile from the entrance. Now they ventured into the burned-out hull of the house as though on a mission. They had discovered two dead and burned bodies in the basement bunker.

Tully rubbed the soot from his face and eyes. O'Dell sat down on the ground next to him. She pulled her knees up to her chest, wrapping her arms around her legs and resting her chin on the tops of her knees.

"We don't know for sure that it's them," she said without looking at him.

"No, but who else would it be?"

"Stucky doesn't seem like the suicidal type."

"He may have thought the bunker was fireproof."

She glanced over at him, not moving from her position. "I never thought of that." She looked almost convinced. Almost.

The firefighters came out of the wreckage, hauling a body on a gurney. It was draped with a black canvas. Two more followed with another gurney. O'Dell sat up straight. Tully heard her suck in air, and he thought she was holding her breath as she watched. The second gurney approached the FBI's truck, when suddenly the dead man's arm slipped out from under the canvas. The arm slipped off the gurney, hanging down, clothed in what looked like a leather jacket. He felt O'Dell stiffen. Then finally, he heard her breathe a deep sigh of relief.

CHAPTER 73

If it hadn't been so late, Maggie would have offered to take Gwen out for dinner. However, she had spent too much time at the hospital making sure Tess was comfortable and that Agent Tully had no permanent damage to his leg.

Though she should have been completely exhausted, for the first time in a very long time she felt like celebrating. So she searched and discovered a Chinese place that was still open on the north side of Newburgh Heights. She could finally stop by a restaurant again without worrying the waitress would end up in a Dumpster the next day. She picked up kung pao chicken, sweet-and-sour pork and plenty of fried rice. She asked for extra fortune cookies and wondered whether Harvey liked egg rolls.

Maggie arrived home to find the two of them curled up in the recliner watching Jay Leno on the portable TV. The cartons reminded her once again of the carton Stucky had stolen, now gone forever, literally up in flames. The photo album had contained the only pictures she had possessed of her father. She didn't want to think about it right now. Not now when she was enjoying what felt like some sort of liberation.

Gwen saw the bags of takeout and smiled. "Thank God! I'm starved."

She had called Gwen from the road, filling her in on most of the details. Her friend had sounded relieved not only for Maggie but for herself as well. At least she wouldn't have to worry about Walker Harding ever again.

"Why don't you spend the night here?" Maggie suggested over a forkful of chicken.

"I have an early-morning appointment. I'd rather drive tonight. I'm worthless in the morning." She was examining Maggie while she scooped out more rice. "How are you? Honestly?"

"Honestly? I'm fine."

Gwen frowned at her as though that was too easy an answer.

"I came close to getting Tully and myself killed," she said, now serious. "I panicked with the fire. I couldn't move. I couldn't breathe. But you know what?" She smiled. "I survived. And I got us out of there."

"Very good. Sounds like you passed some major personal test, Maggie."

Harvey shoved his nose under Maggie's arm, insisting on another egg roll. She gave him a half-eaten roll and patted his back.

"I don't think you're supposed to feed dogs egg rolls, Maggie."

"And how would I know that? Is there a book with all these rules?"

"I'm sure there are several. I'll pick one up for you."

"Might not be a bad idea since it looks like Harvey and I are going to be permanent roommates."

"Does that mean you were right about his owner?"

"Tess told us there was another woman. A woman named Rachel who's dead in a pit somewhere on the property. Of course we don't know yet, but I feel certain it's Rachel Endicott." She noticed Gwen's grimace. "They'll continue to search for her tomorrow. Tess said there were other bodies, bones, skulls. Stucky and Harding may have been using this property for years."

"What do you suppose Harding had planned for me?"

"Don't, Gwen," Maggie snapped at her, and immediately she apologized. "I'm sorry, I just don't want to think about it, okay?"

"I suppose it makes sense that the two of them would have eventually moved on to women you knew more intimately. Friends, relatives...oh, speaking of intimately—" she smiled "—that reminds me. You had a phone call earlier. That hunky ex-quarterback from Nebraska."

"Nick?"

"What, you know more than one hunky ex-quarterback?" Gwen looked as if she was enjoying Maggie's annoying blush.

"Did he want me to call him back tonight?"

"Actually, he said he was headed for the airport. I took a message." Gwen pulled herself up off the floor. "You need to shop for a table, Maggie. I'm getting too old to be eating on the floor." She found the note she had left on the desk. She read the message, squinting as though someone else had written it. "He said his dad had a heart attack."

"Oh Jesus." Now Maggie wished she had talked to him. Nick and his father had a complex relationship, one in which Nick had only recently been able to get away from. "Is he going to be okay? He's not dead, is he?"

"No, but I think Nick said they were talking about surgery as soon as possible." Gwen scrunched up her face as she continued to decipher her notes.

"This is something that I didn't understand. He said his dad had received a letter, and that's what they think may have caused the heart attack. But unless I'm mistaken, I could swear Nick said the letter was from South America."

Maggie felt sick to her stomach. Had Father Michael Keller sent Antonio Morrelli some sort of confession? Maggie seemed to be the only one who believed the charismatic young priest was the one who had killed four boys in Platte City, Nebraska. But he had left the country before she had been able to prove it. The last she knew, he was still in South America.

"That's it," Gwen said. "Does any of that makes sense to you?"

The phone startled both of them.

"Maybe this is Nick." Maggie untangled herself out of the cross-legged position on the floor and grabbed the phone. "Maggie O'Dell."

"Agent O'Dell. It's Assistant Director Cunningham."

She checked her watch. It was late, and she had just seen him at the hospital a couple of hours ago.

"Is Tully okay?" It was the first thing that came to mind.

"He's fine. I'm with Dr. Holmes. He was good enough to do the autopsies tonight."

"Dr. Holmes has had his share of autopsies in the past two weeks."

"There's a problem, Agent O'Dell." Cunningham didn't waste any time.

"What kind of problem?" Maggie prepared herself, leaning against the desk and gripping the phone. Gwen watched from her perch on the recliner.

"Walker Harding died of a gunshot wound to the back of his head. He was shot with a .22, execution style. Not only that, but his organs are in an extremely advanced state of decomposition. Dr. Holmes is guessing he's been dead for several weeks."

"Several weeks? That's impossible, sir. We found his fingerprints at three of the crime scenes."

"I think we might have an explanation for that. Several of his fingers are missing, cut off, including his thumb. I'm guessing Stucky did it. Took the fingers with him. Preserved them and used them at the crime scenes to throw us off."

"But Gwen has had two sessions with Harding." She glanced at Gwen and her friend's face showed concern and alarm. Even Harvey started pacing in the sunroom, tilting his head, listening.

"Dr. Patterson has never seen Albert Stucky," Cunningham said, keeping his cool professional tone and ignoring the frantic edge to Maggie's. "If we ask her to describe the man she had the sessions with, I'm guessing she'll describe Stucky. I've only seen one or two photos of Harding, but if I remember correctly, there was an uncanny resemblance between the two men. Stucky must have been using Harding's identity for some time now, pretending to be him. That probably also explains the airline ticket in Harding's name."

"Jesus." Maggie couldn't believe it. Though it all made sense. She wasn't sure she had completely believed Stucky would allow anyone, even Harding, in on his game. "So he had the perfect disguise and the perfect hiding place."

"There's more, Agent O'Dell. The other body has been dead for several weeks, too, and it's not Albert Stucky."

Maggie sat down before her knees gave out from under her. "No, this can't be happening. He can *not* have escaped again."

"We're not sure who it is. Maybe a friend or caretaker of Harding's. Harding was definitely blind. Dr. Holmes says both his retinas were detached, and there were no signs of diabetes."

Maggie was barely listening anymore. She could hardly hear him over the pounding of her heart as she glanced frantically around the room. She noticed Harvey sniffing at the back door, now agitated. Where the hell had she left her Smith & Wesson? She opened the desk drawer. The Glock was gone.

"I've sent several agents back to watch your house," Cunningham said as if that would be enough. "I suggest you not leave tonight. Stay put. If he comes after you, we'll be ready."

If he comes after me, I'll be a sitting duck, but she kept the thought to herself.

She met Gwen's questioning eyes. The fear began invading Maggie's system like cold liquid injected into her veins. Still, she held herself up and pushed away from the solid security of her father's rolltop desk.

"Stucky wouldn't dare come after me again."

CHAPTER 74

He crawled through the bushes, staying low to the ground. The damn bushes had prickly branches that kept grabbing his sweatshirt. This sort of thing would never happen with his leather jacket. He missed it already, though it had been a worthy sacrifice to see Special Agent Maggie O'Dell's look of relief and know it to be false. He had fooled them all, slipping in and out of hiding places he had specifically prepared for just such an occasion.

He rubbed at his eyes. Fuck, it was dark! He wished the red lines would go away. Pop, pop—no, he wouldn't think of the fucking blood vessels rupturing in his eyes. The insulin stabilized his body, but there seemed to be nothing to stop the exploding blood vessels in his eyes.

He could still hear Walker's tinny laugh, telling him, "You'll be a blind fucker just like me, Al." Walker was still laughing when he put the .22 at the base of his head and pulled the trigger—pop, pop.

The lights were completely out now. He had seen her moving back and forth in what he knew to be the bedroom. He wished he could see her face, relaxed and unsuspecting, but the curtains were drawn and not sheer enough.

He had already intercepted and dismantled the security system with a handheld gadget that Walker had invented for him a few months ago. Blind as a bat, but the man had been an electronics genius. He didn't even know how the thing worked. But he had tested it on the house on Archer Drive, and it did, indeed, work.

He started up the trellis that was hidden by vines and more bushes. He hoped it was sturdier than it looked. Actually, all of this seemed too easy, not much of a challenge. But then, she would be the challenge. He knew she wouldn't disappoint him.

He thought of the scalpel in its thin sheath, tucked safely inside his boot. He'd take his time with her. The anticipation aroused his senses so intensely he needed to stifle what sounded like panting. Yes, this would be well worth the effort.

CHAPTER 75

Maggie sat in the dark corner. Her back pressed against the wall of the bedroom, her outstretched arms leaning on her knees. Her hands gripped her Smith & Wesson, her finger on the trigger. She was ready for him this time. She knew he had been watching. She knew he would come. Yet, when she heard him at the foot of the trellis, her pulse began to race. Her heart slammed against her chest. Sweat trickled down her back.

In a matter of minutes, he was at the window. She saw his shadow hovering, a black vulture. Then his face was at the glass, startling her and almost making her jump. Don't move. Don't flinch. Stay calm. Steady. Yet the terror hammered away at her, raw and unyielding to any of her mental commands. A slight tremor threatened her aim. She knew she was safe in the dark corner. Besides, he would be looking at the curled-up bundle of pillows he would mistake for his sleeping victim.

Would he be surprised that she had gotten so good at his game? Would he be disappointed that she could predict his moves? Certainly he wouldn't expect that they had already discovered the second body to not be his. He must have realized they would and soon, because he was wasting no time coming after his ultimate victim, his ultimate blow to his nemesis. This would be his grand finale, his final scar to leave Maggie with before the diabetes left him completely blind.

She tightened her grip. Instead of the terror, she concentrated on the faces of his victims, the litany of names, now adding Jessica, Rita and Rachel to the list. How dare he make her an accomplice to his evil. She let the anger seep into her veins, hoping it would replace the crawly feeling that invaded her insides.

He eased the window up, gently, quietly, and before he stepped into the room, she could smell him, the scent of smoke and sweat. She waited until he got to the edge of the bed. She waited for him to draw the scalpel from his boot.

"You won't be needing that," she said calmly, not moving a muscle.

He spun around, holding the scalpel. With his free hand he stripped off the bedcovers, then grabbed for the lamp on the nightstand. The yellow glow filled the room, and when he turned toward her, she thought she saw a flash of surprise in his colorless eyes. He quickly composed himself, standing straight and tall, replacing the surprise with one of his twisted smiles.

"Why, Maggie O'Dell. I wasn't expecting you."

"Gwen isn't here. In fact, she's back at my house. I hope you don't mind me taking her place?" Stucky hadn't dared come for her. That would have been too easy. Just like in that Miami warehouse eight months ago. It would have been easier to kill her. Instead, he left her with a scar, a constant reminder of him. So this time, why wouldn't he do it again? No, Stucky didn't intend to kill her. He simply wanted to destroy her. It would be his ultimate blow, to hurt a woman Maggie knew, one she cared about and loved.

"You're good at our little game." He seemed pleased.

Without warning, she squeezed the trigger, and his hand flew back, the scalpel clinking to the floor. He stared at his bloodied hand. His eyes met hers. This time she saw more than alarm. Was that the beginning of fear?

"How does it feel?" she asked, trying to keep the quiver out of her voice. "How does it feel to have me beating you at your own game?"

There was that smile again, a cocky smirk that she wanted to shoot off his face.

"No, I should be asking you, Maggie. How does it feel to play at my game?"

She felt the hairs on the back of her neck stand up. She could do this. She would not let him win. Not this time.

"It's over," she managed to say. Could he see her hand tremble?

"You like seeing me bleeding. Admit it." He raised his hand to show her the blood dripping down his sleeve. "It's a powerful feeling, isn't it, Maggie?"

"Is it a powerful feeling to kill your best friend, Stucky? Is that why you did it?"

She thought she saw him grimace. Maybe she had finally found his Achilles' heel.

"Why did you do it? Why did you kill the one man, the only person who could stomach being your friend?"

"He had something I needed. Something I couldn't get anywhere else," he said, holding up his chin and looking away from the light.

"What could a blind Walker Harding possibly have that was worth killing him for?"

"You're a smart lady. You already know the answer to that. His identity. I needed to become him." Now he laughed and squinted.

Maggie watched his eyes. The light was bothering him. Yes, she was right. Whether it was diabetes or something else, Stucky was losing his eyesight.

"Not like Walker was doing much with his identity anyway," Stucky continued. "Sitting in that house in the boonies with his cyberlife. Jacking off to porn videos instead of enjoying the real thing." His lips curled into a snarl as he added, "He was pathetic. Never would I become what he was, at least, not without a fight."

He reached for the lamp again to turn it off. Maggie pulled the trigger. This time the bullet shattered his wrist. He grabbed at his hand, the anger and pain distorting his face while he tried to keep it composed.

"Are your eyes giving you a little trouble?" she taunted him, despite the panic sliding down into her legs and paralyzing her. She couldn't run. She needed to stay put. She couldn't let him see her fear.

He managed another smile, his face void of the pain that had to be shooting up his arm. He started walking toward her. Maggie pulled back the hammer and squeezed the trigger again. This time the bullet ripped into his left kneecap, knocking him to the floor. He stared at his knee in disbelief, but he didn't wince or cry out in pain.

"You like this, don't you? Have you ever felt such power before, Maggie?"

His voice began to unnerve her. What was he doing? If she wasn't mistaken, he was the one taunting her. He wanted her to continue.

"It's over, Stucky. This is where it ends." But she heard the quiver in her voice. Then a new fear rushed through her when she realized that he had heard it, too. Damn it! This wasn't working.

He crawled back to his feet. Suddenly her previous plan seemed ridiculous. How could she incapacitate him enough to bring him down, let alone bring him in? Was it possible to harness someone as evil as Stucky? As he started toward her again, she wondered if it was possible to even destroy him. He barely limped from his shattered kneecap, and now she could see that he had retrieved the scalpel while he had been down on the floor. How many bullets did she have left in the chamber? Had she fired twice or three times? Why the hell could she suddenly not remember?

He held up the scalpel for her to see, flipping it around and getting a better grip on it in his good hand.

"I was hoping to leave your good friend Gwen's heart on your doorstep. Seemed kind of poetic, don't you think? But now I guess I'll have to settle for taking out yours instead."

"Put it down, Stucky. It's over," but even she wasn't convinced by her words. How could she be with her hands shaking like this?

"The game ends only when I say it ends," he hissed at her.

She took aim, trying to steady her hands, concentrating on her target—that space between his eyes. Her finger twitched as she kept it pressed against the trigger. He wouldn't win this time. She forced herself to stare into his black eyes, the evil holding her there, pinning her against the wall. She couldn't let it dismantle her. But as he continued slowly toward her, she felt the wall of fear blocking her, the raw hysteria strangling her and blurring her vision. Before she could squeeze the trigger, the door to the room flew open.

"Agent O'Dell," Cunningham yelled, rushing in with his revolver drawn.

He stopped when he saw the two of them, stunned, hesitating. Maggie was startled, looking away for a split second. Just long enough for Stucky to dive at her, the scalpel plunging down. Gunfire exploded in the small bedroom, in rapid succession—the echoes bouncing off the walls.

Finally, the sound stopped as suddenly as it had started.

Albert Stucky lay slumped over Maggie's knees, his body jerking, blood spraying her. She wasn't sure whether or not some of it was hers. The scalpel stuck into the wall, so close she felt it against her side, so close it had ripped the side of her shirt open. She couldn't move. Was he dead? Her heart and lungs slammed against each other, making it difficult to breathe. Her hand shook uncontrollably as she still gripped the warm revolver. She knew without checking that its cylinder was empty.

Cunningham shoved Stucky's body off her, a thud with no sound of life. Suddenly Maggie grabbed Stucky's shoulder, desperate to see his face. She rolled him over. Bullets riddled his body. His lifeless eyes stared up at her, but she wanted to cry out in relief. With all the holes in his body, there was *not* a single one between his eyes.

CHAPTER 76

Tess leaned against the glass. Now she realized she should have taken the wheelchair that the Nurse Ratched look-alike had recommended. Her feet burned and the stitches pinched and pulled with little provocation. Her chest ached, and it was still difficult to breathe. She had been wrong about the ribs, two cracked, two bruised. The other cuts and bruises would heal. In time she would forget about the madman they called Albert Stucky. She would forget his cold, black eyes pinning her to the table like the leather shackles that had held her wrists and ankles. She would forget his hot breath on her face, his hands and body violating her in ways she thought were not possible.

She gathered the front of the thin robe in her fist, warding off the shiver, the icy fingers that could still strangle her whenever she thought about him. Why fool herself? She knew she would never forget. It was one more chapter to try to erase. She was so very tired of rewriting her past in order to survive her future. Now she struggled to find a reason why she should even bother. Perhaps that was what had brought her here.

She looked past her battered reflection in the window and watched the wrinkled red faces. Little chunky fists batted at the air. She listened to the newborns' persistent cries and coos. Tess smiled. What a cliché to come here looking for the answers.

"Girlfriend, what are you doing out of bed?"

Tess glanced over her shoulder to find Delores Heston in a bright red suit, lighting up the sterile white corridor as she marched toward her. She wrapped her arms around Tess, carefully and gently hugging her. When she pulled away, the hard-nosed business owner had tears in her eyes.

"Oh mercy, I promised myself I wouldn't do this." Delores swiped at her eyes and the running mascara. "How are you feeling, Tess?"

"I'm fine," she lied, and tried to smile. Her jaw hurt where he had punched her. She found herself checking over her teeth again with the tip of her tongue. It amazed her that none of them had been chipped or broken.

She realized Delores was studying her, examining for herself whether Tess was fine. She lifted Tess's chin with her soft hand, taking a closer look at the bite marks on her neck. She didn't want to see the horror and pity in Delores's face so she looked away. Without a word, Delores wrapped her arms around her again, this time holding her, stroking her hair and rubbing her back.

"I'm making it my job to take care of you, Tess," she said emphatically as she pulled away. "And I don't want a single argument, you hear me?"

Tess had never had anyone make her such an offer. She wasn't sure what the correct response was. But of all her choices, tears did not seem appropriate. Not now. Delores took out a tissue and dabbed at Tess's cheeks, smiling at her like a mother preparing her child for school.

"You have a handsome visitor waiting for you in your room."

Tess's insides clenched. Oh God, she couldn't handle facing Daniel. Not like this.

"Could you tell him I'll call later and thank him for the roses?"

"Roses?" Delores looked confused. "Looked like a bunch of purple violets he was clutching. He's squeezing those flowers so tight, they're probably potpourri by now."

"Violets?"

She looked over Delores's shoulder, and Tess could see Will Finley, watching, hesitating at the end of the corridor. He looked incredibly handsome in dark trousers, a blue shirt and, if her blurred vision served her correctly, a bunch of violets in his left hand.

Maybe there were a few new chapters in her life that needed writing, after all.

EPILOGUE

One week later

Maggie wasn't sure why she had come. Perhaps she simply needed to see him lowered into the ground. Maybe she needed to be certain that this time Albert Stucky would not escape.

She stood back, close to the trees, looking at the few mourners and recognizing most of them as reporters. The religious entourage from St. Patrick's outnumbered the mourners. There were several priests and just as many altar boys carrying incense and candles. How could they justify sending off someone like Stucky with all the same ceremony given an ordinary sinner? It didn't make sense. It certainly didn't seem fair.

But it didn't matter. She was finally free. And in more ways than one. Stucky had not won. And neither had her own shadow side. In a split second, she had chosen to defend herself, but had not given in to true evil.

Harvey nudged her hand, suddenly impatient and probably wondering what use it was to be out in the open if they were not going to walk and enjoy it. She watched the procession make its way from the grave down the hill.

Albert Stucky was finally gone, soon to be buried six feet under like his victims.

Maggie petted Harvey's soft fur and felt an incredible sense of relief. They could go home. She could feel safe again. The first thing she wanted to do was sleep.

* * * * *

talk about it

Let's talk about books.

Join the conversation:

 on facebook.com/harlequinaustralia

 on Twitter @harlequinaus

www.harlequinbooks.com.au

If you love reading and want to know about our authors and titles, then let's talk about it.